Emma Blair was b
Devon. She is the
including *Scarlet Rib*
which were shortlisted for the Romantic Novelist of the
Year.

EMMA BLAIR OMNIBUS

Three Bites of the Cherry

Twilight Time

sphere

SPHERE

This omnibus edition first published in Great Britain by
Sphere in 2009
Emma Blair Omnibus copyright © Emma Blair 2009

Previously published separately:
Three Bites of the Cherry first published in Great Britain by
Time Warner Books in 2006
Copyright © Emma Blair 2006

Twilight Time first published in Great Britain by
Time Warner Paperbacks in 2004
Copyright © Emma Blair 2004

A CIP catalogue record for this book is available from the British Library.

ISBN 978-0-7515-4146-5

Typeset in Adobe Garamond by Palimpsest Book Production Limited,
Polmont, Stirlingshire
Printed and bound in Great Britain by Clays Ltd, St Ives plc

Sphere
An imprint of
Little, Brown Book Group
100 Victoria Embankment
London EC4Y 0DY

An Hachette UK Company
www.hachette.co.uk

www.littlebrown.co.uk

Three Bites of the Cherry

Part 1

John

1924–1926

Chapter 1

John Mair came bolt upright as his wife's scream brought him abruptly awake. He stared at her in the darkness of their bedroom. She too was sitting up.

'Dear God, Georgie, what's wrong?' he asked, reaching out and placing a hand on her arm.

The screaming stopped as she shuddered into consciousness.

'Georgie?' he queried softly, feeling her trembling under his touch.

Georgie took a deep breath, followed by another, then seemed to collapse forward on to herself. 'Awful. Terrible,' she muttered in a strangulated voice.

Squirming closer, John put his arm round her shoulders. 'Did you have a nightmare?'

She nodded confirmation.

'Bad, eh?'

Georgie turned to face him, gazing at him out of huge, frightened eyes. 'It was about you.'

'Me?'

'I . . . I . . .' She trailed off, and gulped in more air.

'I'm here, darling. There's no need to be afraid.'

Tears appeared and spilled down her cheeks. Then she was hugging him tightly, clutching at him, as though afraid he might somehow disappear. Vanish in a puff of smoke like some will-o'-the-wisp. John could feel her heart thumping in her chest.

'Tell me, Georgie. Tell me what it was all about.'

'It was terrible,' she said hoarsely.

'You've already said that.'

'I was in a room. A very gloomy room lit only by a couple of candles. And . . .'

'And what?' he prompted when her voice again trailed off.

'Oh, Jesus, John. It was so real. I was convinced it was actually happening. That I was there. With you.'

He frowned. Whatever the dream had been, it had really shaken her. He couldn't remember ever having seen her this upset before. The love he felt for her welled inside him in sympathy. 'What was I doing, then?'

'Nothing. You were dead.'

That rattled him. 'Dead?'

'And in your coffin. Your eyes were closed, your complexion a sort of milky colour. You were wearing your suit, best white shirt and red tie, and your hands were folded in front of you.'

'Bloody hell,' he whispered. She was right. It was horrible.

'I started to scream . . .'

'You did that all right,' he interjected. 'It's what woke me up.'

4

'You mean I actually did?'

'Oh yes. I can assure you of that.'

A new thought came to her. 'I hope I didn't wake Ian as well. You know how light a sleeper he can be at times.'

Ian was their five-year-old son, and only child so far, sleeping in the kitchen. They both listened, but heard nothing.

'I'd better check,' Georgie said.

John knew there was no point in arguing. She'd never settle down again unless she went to look. He nodded. 'On you go.'

Georgie swung her legs out from under the covers and shrugged into her dark-green candlewick dressing gown. Silently she padded from the room.

John lit his bedside candle and reached for his cigarettes. A few moments later he was re-joined by his wife, who slipped back into bed again. 'He's fine,' she announced. 'Sleeping sound as can be.'

'Good.'

'It would be a bad night to disturb him, with his starting school in the morning.'

'Aye,' John agreed.

'Can I have a puff of that fag?'

'Help yourself,' he replied, handing it over.

Georgie took several deep drags, then returned it. 'I needed that. Though you know I don't agree with smoking in bed.'

John smiled wryly. It was an old bone of contention between them. 'Feeling better now?'

'A bit.'

She wiped her face, where the tears had now dried. A glance at the clock on the bedside table informed her it was a little past midnight.

'Dead and in my coffin, eh?' he joked, trying to cheer her up.

She nodded.

'And all dolled up like a dish of fish?'

That annoyed her. 'Stop it, John. It was anything but funny. As I said, it was ever so real.'

'I'm sorry.'

She stared at him. 'No, you're not. I can see it in your face.'

John ground out the remains of his cigarette in the ashtray, thinking how beautiful his wife looked, even distraught as she was. A wave of warmth and tenderness swept through him. Not for the first time he told himself how lucky he was to have met and married Georgina McKeand. If ever a couple were right for one another, they were, in his opinion.

'I wonder why you dreamt what you did,' he said.

She shook her head, not having an answer.

'Well, you know what they say.'

'What?'

'That dreams never come true.'

'Do they really say that?'

'You mean you've never heard it before?'

'No.'

'Well, they do. So there. Anyway,' he tapped his chest, 'just look at me. You'll go a long way to find a healthier specimen. Isn't that so?'

She had to admit it was true. Why, she couldn't even

recall the last time he had had a cold, let alone anything worse. 'You're right,' she admitted.

'There then. It was probably that cheese you ate earlier gave you the nightmare. You shouldn't have had it so late on.'

It might well have been the cheese, she reflected. But why that particular nightmare? There was absolutely no reason for it. At least, none she could think of.

Reaching over, he ran the tips of his fingers down her cheek. 'Ready for sleep again?'

'Just about.'

'Would a cuddle help?'

Despite herself, she smiled. 'It always does.'

'Then that's what you shall have.'

They switched off their lights and he snuggled down beside her, his front against her back.

'You said a cuddle, not a grope,' she admonished almost instantly.

He laughed in the darkness. 'A grope's far more interesting.'

'No, it's not. Now behave yourself.'

'Do I have to?'

'Yes, you do.'

He pretended to groan. 'Spoilsport.'

She didn't reply to that, but merely smiled. Closing her eyes, she prayed that the nightmare wouldn't recur. Thankfully, it didn't.

'Aren't you hungry?'

Young Ian, washed and scrubbed and staring dully at his breakfast, shook his head.

Georgie sighed, knowing full well what the trouble was. 'Is it the thought of school?'

He nodded.

'There's nothing to be scared of, you know. Why, I enjoyed myself there. Honestly I did.'

He glanced up at her in disbelief. He'd heard stories from other boys – stories he hadn't liked one little bit. The strap, for example. If you were naughty, you were sent to the headmaster and told to hold your hands out in front of you while he gave you 'six of the best' on alternate palms.

'Well, you'll have to eat something,' Georgie went on. 'You can't start your first day without anything in your stomach. So get on with it.'

Reluctantly, Ian spooned some of the boiled egg in front of him into his mouth. The egg was supposed to be a special treat to mark the occasion. Normally they only ever had eggs at the weekends, and then only sometimes.

Georgie glanced at the clock. Almost time to go. God, she was hating this, despite the brave face she was trying to put on. Her wee son starting school! It didn't bear thinking about. She was going to miss him dreadfully during the day.

'Right,' she declared some minutes later. 'Put your coat on.'

Ian felt sick inside as he dragged himself away from his chair. It seemed to his overactive imagination that he was going to his execution. The world as he knew it was about to change for ever. And not for the better, either.

'Mum?'

'What?'

He opened his mouth to plead to be allowed to stay at home, then shut it again, knowing she'd never agree. Not in a trillion zillion years would she do that.

Outside, Georgie took his hand as they walked along the grey but friendly Glasgow streets to the local school, where Ian's fate awaited him.

Ian turned a strained, anxious face up to his mum. The dreaded moment had finally arrived. They were in the playground together and the bell to call him inside had just been rung.

Georgie took a deep breath. 'I'll have to leave you now, son, as there's the janny about to lock the gates. Now, don't worry. You'll be fine. I promise. And I'll be waiting for you at dinnertime.'

Ian's narrow chest began to heave. All he wanted was to stay with his mum, be with her as he always had except when out playing in the street.

'Your pals will be here, so you'll have friends about you,' Georgie declared, attempting a cheerful tone which didn't quite come off. She was as upset as he was. 'Off you go, then.'

Turning, she strode purposefully towards the gate where the janny, the same Mr Green who'd been janitor when she'd been a pupil here, was patiently waiting. They exchanged a friendly word, and then she was outside the gates. She mustn't look back, she told herself. That would only make matters worse. But despite herself, she did.

Ian stood rooted where she'd left him, his gaze fastened on hers. Suddenly he was running towards the fence that

9

surrounded the school until he came up against it, his face awash with tears.

'Mummy, please don't leave me. Please don't leave me,' he screamed hysterically, one arm extended beseechingly through the bars.

'Oh, Christ,' Georgie muttered. This was turning out even worse than she'd expected. She remained where she was. 'Go inside now, Ian,' she said sternly, feeling anything but stern.

'Mummy, please, please!'

There was nothing else for it. Turning away from him, she went on her way with his hysterical screams ringing in her ears.

Ashen-faced, Georgie sank gratefully into a chair, her hands still shaking from the ordeal she'd been through.

'I'll put the kettle on,' her mother Chrissie announced.

'He screamed and screamed, Ma. Even halfway back down the road I could still hear him.'

Chrissie clucked her sympathy. 'Aye, that sort of thing was never easy. Your sister Lena was the worst I had to deal with. Though I have to admit, she wasn't as bad as that.'

Georgie pulled out her cigarettes and lit up. 'Poor wee soul. It was heart-wrenching, Ma.'

Chrissie, who'd been filling the kettle at the sink, now put it on the stove and lit the gas. 'Children can put you through it, right enough. And I should know, having had five.' She paused for a moment, thinking of the boy who'd died directly after birth. That had been a bitter blow, one it had taken her quite a time to recover from. If, indeed, she ever had. Kenneth, they'd called him, though there hadn't been enough time to have him christened. Even now she occasionally went to visit his grave.

Georgie glanced out of the window. 'Looks like it's going to rain.'

Chrissie followed her gaze. 'I wouldn't be surprised. At least it isn't wash day. That's something.'

Georgie nodded her agreement.

'That's the trouble when you only have the one,' Chrissie went on. 'They're never as tough, to begin with anyway, until others come along.' She regarded Georgie hopefully. 'Any news in that department?'

Georgie shook her head.

Chrissie frowned. 'Five years is a long time. You should have been expecting again by now.'

'Well, it's certainly not for the lack of trying, Ma, before you ask. I can guarantee that.'

Chrissie grunted her approval. 'I wish I could give you a biscuit, but I've none in, I'm afraid.' She patted her ample stomach. 'It won't harm me to do without, and that's a fact.' After five children her figure was not what it had been, although once she'd been as slim as Georgie. Still, her husband, Big Tam, always protested he preferred her with a bit of meat on her bones. A lie, of course, or so she believed, but kind of him. That was the sort of man he was.

Georgie watched Chrissie clatter out some cups and saucers. 'I had a horrible nightmare last night,' she said quietly. 'Woke up screaming, according to John.'

'Oh aye?'

'Fair put the wind up me. Worst nightmare I've ever had.'

Chrissie paused to stare at her daughter. 'Ian screaming, you screaming? Dearie me. What was the nightmare about?'

Georgie told her.

'Sounds terrible, right enough. No wonder it gave you the willies.'

Georgie shook her head at the memory. 'The most frightening thing was that I felt I was actually there. It was ever so real.'

'It would have scared me half to . . .' Chrissie hesitated, then went on, 'I was about to say to death. But that's hardly an appropriate way of putting it.'

Georgie had to smile at that, for it was true enough. 'The one good thing, according to John, is that dreams never come true. Have you heard that?'

'Oh aye.' Chrissie nodded. 'That's what they say. Thank God.'

Something about the way Chrissie said it prompted Georgie to ask, 'Why thank God?'

Chrissie looked embarrassed. 'I was thinking of a dream I had myself some while back. I suppose you could've called that a nightmare too.'

'And?'

'And what?'

'Tell me about it.'

'Och no. I'm sorry I mentioned it now.'

Georgie was intrigued. 'Come on, Ma. Spill the beans.'

'You'll laugh.'

'No, I won't.'

'Oh yes you will. I guarantee it. So I'm not telling.'

Georgie took a deep draw on her cigarette, even more intrigued. 'Suit yourself,' she declared in an off-hand manner, as if it was of no further interest to her. 'Though it's hardly fair.'

'What isn't fair?'

'I told you my nightmare, so it seems only fair you tell me yours. But no matter.'

Chrissie busied herself with the teapot while Georgie, pretending she'd taken the huff, remained silent. Knowing Chrissie as she did, she was sure her mother would eventually crack.

'Aye, all right then,' Chrissie said at last. 'But you must promise me not to laugh.'

Georgie kept a straight face. 'I promise.'

'Mind you keep it then.'

Georgie waited expectantly while Chrissie took a deep breath. 'Daft, really,' she declared. 'But in my dream I was standing stark naked in the middle of Sauchiehall Street on a Saturday afternoon, when the place was teeming.'

Georgie stared at her mother in amazement. 'Stark naked?' she repeated incredulously.

'Not a stitch on and everyone gaping and pointing at me.'

It was one of the funniest things Georgie had ever heard. Her mother naked in Sauchiehall Street, one of Glasgow's main thoroughfares. Now what on earth had made Chrissie dream that?

Despite her promise, Georgie threw back her head and roared with laughter at the very thought of it.

Chrissie scowled. 'See, I said you'd laugh. But just remember, that didn't come true either.'

Georgie couldn't reply. She was completely convulsed.

*   *   *

13

'You're home then,' Georgie said when John appeared in the kitchen that evening.

He went to her and kissed her on the cheek. 'What's for tea? I'm starved.'

'Toad in the hole.'

'Fair enough. That'll do.'

'How was work?' she enquired, as she did every time he got back.

'All right. Nothing untoward happened. Ardrossan and return. Slick as you like.'

John was a fireman with the recently formed London, Midland and Scottish Railway. His job was to stoke the engine boiler: back-breaking graft but a job he enjoyed none the less. It was his great ambition to be a driver one day.

'Good.' Georgie nodded, aware that some shifts could be worse than others, especially if they had trouble with the engine, or, as could happen, it broke down altogether. Fortunately, such occurrences were rare.

From his seat at the table, Ian watched his father cross to the sink and give himself a quick wash.

'So, how was school then?' John asked with a smile when he had finished.

Ian glanced at his mother, who was sworn not to tell his father about the scene in the playground that morning. He muttered something unintelligible.

John raised an eyebrow. 'That good, eh?' he said ironically.

'He met up with a few pals, which made things easier,' Georgie chipped in.

John came and sat at the table facing Ian. 'What's your teacher called?'

14

'Miss Hamilton.'

'Is she nice?'

'I suppose so.' Reluctantly.

'Just suppose so? Don't you know?'

Ian shrugged.

'I see. Is she young or old?'

'It's hard to say.'

'And why's that?'

Another shrug.

'What did you do at playtime?'

'Someone had a ball and we had a game of footie. I enjoyed that.'

John smiled. 'So school wasn't too awful then?'

'I got a sore bum sitting at my desk. Wood isn't very comfortable.'

'I remember.' John nodded. 'My bum used to get sore as well.'

Ian blushed to hear John use that word. It just didn't seem right coming from his father.

'And who are these pals you've met up with?' John went on.

'Just other boys.'

John sighed. He wasn't getting very far here. 'From the street?'

'And round about.'

'Good pals?'

Yet another shrug.

'Was it their first day too?'

'For one of them. The others are already there.'

'They'll be able to show you the ropes, then.'

Ian frowned. 'I don't understand that.'

'Where to go and what to do,' John explained.

'Oh aye.'

'That'll make it easier for you.'

Ian took a deep breath. 'School's useless anyway.'

John glanced at Georgie, then back again at his son. 'Why useless?'

'I spent the whole day there and at the end of it I picked up a book and still couldn't read.'

'You still . . .'

'Useless,' Ian repeated doggedly.

For the second time that day Georgie burst out laughing. So did John. What a thing to come out with! Absolutely priceless. It had the pair of them in stitches.

Chapter 2

'I see you've started on the whisky already.'

Big Tam McKeand glanced over at his wife from where he was sitting beside the fire. 'Are you complaining, woman?'

'No,' she replied drily. 'Just commenting.'

It was early Saturday evening and, as always on a Saturday after his one o'clock finish at McNair's, where he was a foreman moulder in the manufacture of marine pumps, Tam had returned home with a bottle of whisky and eighty cigarettes to last him through the weekend.

'That's all right then,' Tam muttered, and busied himself again with his newspaper.

'Where are you off to tonight, Lena?' Chrissie asked her second oldest, who was applying make-up in front of the mirror that hung above the mantelpiece.

'Don't know, Mum. I'm meeting up with Pet and we'll take it from there.' Pet McQueen was Lena's best friend.

No one in the family ever mentioned the fact, but Lena

was as ugly as sin. Not just plain, but downright ugly. She had the sort of face that would have made a good model for a gargoyle. On top of that she had a thin, bony figure with hardly any bust to speak of. It was not surprising, Chrissie thought regretfully, that she had never been very successful with men.

'Probably the pictures,' Lena added as an afterthought.

'What's on?' Chrissie asked.

'No idea. Pet will probably know.'

'Where are you meeting her?'

Lena mentioned a local spot.

'So you're not going into town, then?'

'We haven't planned to.'

Tam swallowed a mouthful of whisky, then placed his glass back on the floor, just as his son Tom came into the room. At eighteen, Tom was still serving his apprenticeship at McNair's, where he worked under his father, and, with his greased-back hair and slightly olive complexion, was the apple of his mother's eye. None of them knew where the olive skin came from, but it certainly didn't run in the family. Not that there was any question of his paternity: the similarity in looks between him and Tam was striking. He had been christened Thomas after his father, but Tam preferred the Scottish version.

'As you're wearing a collar and tie I suppose it's the jigging for you the night.' Chrissie smiled. Tom was dancing mad.

'That's right, Mum. I met a wee lassie last week and am kind of hoping she'll turn up again. She was a smashing dancer. A real twinkletoes.'

'Twinkletoes!' Tam snorted, lighting a cigarette. 'Whoever heard the like?'

Tom smiled, well used to his father's disparaging remarks, and knowing there was no malice in them. It was simply Tam's way. 'Twinkle twinkle,' he said teasingly, doing a fancy shuffle with his feet.

'The lad's an idiot,' Tam muttered.

'He's nothing of the sort,' Chrissie rebuked her husband. 'And you shouldn't say such things. You'll dent his confidence.'

'It'll take a lot more than me to do that,' Tam declared. 'He's got so much bloody confidence the stuff almost oozes out of him. Far too much of it in my opinion.'

'You do talk rot at times, Tam McKeand,' Chrissie admonished him. 'For an intelligent man, that is.'

That pleased Tam. He liked the idea of being thought of as intelligent, having left school at the age of nine. He'd gone to the Ragged School, he always said. No shoes, and your bare arse hanging out of your pants. He'd been brought up in hard times when a boy went to work at the first opportunity to help bring money into the house. A proper education for their sons was something the likes of his parents hadn't been able to afford.

With a most unladylike grunt Lena finished her make-up and returned her bits and pieces to the small bag she kept for that purpose. 'I'll be off then,' she announced.

'Mind how you go,' Chrissie said.

'I always do, Mum. Ta-ra then!' And with that she swept from the kitchen.

Tam stared after his daughter, wondering if she'd ever find a man. He doubted it. Which probably meant she'd never move out and would be with them for the rest of their days: a prospect he wasn't entirely sure he relished.

Tom also left the room to come back a few minutes later wearing his overcoat. 'Don't wait up for me,' he said with a smile. 'I might be late.'

'Don't worry, we won't,' Tam growled, and drank more whisky, enjoying the warmth and bite of it coursing down his throat.

'Are you thinking you might be lumbering this wee lassie you mentioned?' Chrissie enquired, wanting to know whether Tom intended to take the girl home with the possibility of arranging a further meeting.

'Possibly,' Tom reluctantly admitted. 'I've no idea where she lives. There's no point if it's too far away. I don't mind a walk but I've no intention of hiking miles and miles.'

Chrissie could see the sense in that. 'Well, enjoy yourself anyway. See you in the morning.'

'Night, Papa.'

Tam glanced up from his paper. 'Night, son. And good luck.'

'Thanks, Papa.'

'Twinkletoes,' Tam muttered to himself when Tom had gone, and chuckled.

Chrissie waited till Tam had had a few whiskies and was in a mellow mood before coming over to sit facing him.

'There's something I want to talk to you about,' she declared. 'And now's a good time as we're on our own.'

'What's that about then?'

'Mary.'

Tam's face clouded over with displeasure at the mention of their oldest child. 'I'm not in the mood to discuss her and her nonsense,' he growled.

'Things can't go on as they are,' Chrissie persisted. 'We haven't seen her in over a year now. Eighteen months, more like.'

'That's not my fault.'

'It was you started the barney the pair of you had last time she was here.'

'I did nothing of the sort!' he protested.

'Yes, you did. And you know it.'

Tam sat further up in his chair, drained his glass and poured himself another. 'She began spouting religion to me yet again, and I wasn't having it. She's become a complete nutter on the subject.'

'She's still our daughter.'

'Look, woman, she's welcome here whenever she likes, but when she comes in this house I insist she leaves all her preaching and holier-than-thou business at the door. I don't want to hear any of that guff.' He shook his head. 'Always going on about this sect she's joined, and their meetings she's forever going to. Christ, she's done so much praying I'm amazed her bloody knees haven't worn out.'

Chrissie couldn't help but smile. It was true enough. Mary was always mentioning this meeting she'd attended, or that one, or another. She'd become something of a one-woman crusade, though not for the Church of Scotland, to which the rest of the family belonged.

'I don't know how James puts up with it,' Tam went on. James was Mary's husband, and father of her two children. 'I'd have given her a good skite long before now.'

'That's because he's weak and lets Mary walk all over him.'

Tam nodded his agreement. 'Nice enough chap. But, as you say, weak as sugarallywater.'

'But brave. You can't deny that, now.'

There had been a bad fire some years previously at the tannery where James worked. When he was told that his brother was trapped in the burning building he had wrestled clear of those who were trying to stop him and dashed back inside to rescue him. James had received a special citation for bravery.

'No, I can't,' Tam admitted. 'He was a hero when it counted and no one can ever take that away from him.'

Tam drank more whisky and then lit another cigarette. He'd aye liked James Davidson but despised the way he kowtowed to his wife. It upset Tam that he was estranged from Mary whom he'd doted on as a child, she being their firstborn. He wished things could go back to how they'd been before she'd fallen in with those holy rollers and absorbed their weird notions. According to them the world was going to end in twenty-something years' time, and everyone would go to hell who didn't hold to their beliefs and practices. Hence Mary's anxiety to get the rest of the family to join, and therefore be 'saved'. As he'd pointed out to her, it didn't seem very likely that God would destroy the vast majority of mankind and save only those souls who believed the teachings – rantings, more

22

like – of the sect. That wasn't very logical to his way of thinking. Or, or as he'd once put it more succinctly, in his opinion the whole thing was nothing more than a load of old shite.

Chrissie sighed, deciding to drop the subject. For now, anyway. But just for now.

Miss Hamilton stopped to peer over Ian's shoulder. Suddenly acutely aware of her presence, he blushed bright red.

'What a lovely house you've painted, Ian,' she said. 'I'm impressed.'

He thought Miss Hamilton was smashing, and she always smelt wonderful. 'Thank you, miss,' he managed to croak.

She pointed a finger. 'And this little chap here. Is that you?'

'Yes, miss.'

'And the lady?'

'My mum.'

'I see. And what about your dad?' John was noticeably absent.

'He's at work.'

The originality of the reply amused her. 'Is he away at work a lot, then?'

'Yes, miss.'

'What does he do?'

'He's an engine fireman on the railway, miss.'

'How interesting. And such a responsible job.'

'He wants to be a driver one day, miss.'

'Well, I'm sure he will be. Well done, Ian.' She produced a little booklet from which she peeled a gold star, and Ian was fit to burst with pride when the star was stuck to the top of his picture.

He stared after Miss Hamilton in adoration as she continued on down the line of desks.

'Now you're sure you know the way and won't get lost?' Georgie asked anxiously. It was Ian's first day of being allowed to go to school by himself, Georgie having been taking him there and back for the past fortnight.

'I won't get lost,' Ian assured her.

She stooped and straightened his tie, which was already askew. 'Off you go then. And make certain you're careful crossing the roads.'

'I will, Mum, I promise.'

She wasn't too worried about his crossing the roads involved as there was hardly any traffic to speak of. Trams, of course, and the occasional delivery cart and van, but it was rare to encounter a private car. Cars were the preserve of rich people, doctors and the occasional commercial traveller. Nevertheless, Georgie's heart was in her mouth as she kissed Ian on the cheek and ushered him off down the stairs, where he quickly vanished from sight.

How fast they grow up, she reflected, back in the kitchen once more. How very, very fast. She was about to start washing the breakfast dishes when it suddenly came to her what she must do for peace of mind. If she didn't she'd fret every single minute till dinnertime when he was due to come home again. Hurriedly, she snatched up her coat from the hall peg where it lived, and dashed out of the door, locking it behind her.

Down the street she went, following in his footsteps, anxiously scanning the road ahead. He finally came in sight just as he, and lots of others, was entering the school gates.

Safe, she thought with relief. He'd made it safe and sound. It was as though a huge burden had been lifted from her shoulders.

Safe and sound, she thought again, as she began returning the way she'd come. It had been daft of her to chase after him like that. Quite unnecessary.

But he was her son, after all. And she loved him dearly. She'd only done what any mother in her position might.

'I was thinking,' John declared during tea a few weeks later. 'As we seem to be having something of an Indian summer this year what about going to the seaside on Saturday?'

'Aren't you working?' Georgie asked in surprise.

He shook his head. 'Got the weekend off. Not due in again till Tuesday night.'

That explained it. 'You're back on night duty, then?'

'For a while, I'm afraid. No idea how long.'

Georgie hated his being on nights. But it came with the job and had to be done. There was no getting out of it.

Ian was almost squirming with excitement. The seaside! 'Can we take a picnic?' he asked, eyes glowing with eagerness.

'That depends on your mum, son.'

'Mum?'

Georgie smiled at him, noting his enthusiasm. How could she possibly refuse? 'I don't see why not.'

'Yippee!' Ian yelled.

'Providing the weather stays good, that is,' she added, thinking that a picnic would be cheaper than having to buy something there. She began mentally planning what they might take.

'Thanks, Mum.' Ian was beaming.

'Now where shall we go?' John asked. Wherever it was, they'd travel by rail as he had a free pass for himself and family.

They fell to discussing destinations.

Ian sat staring out of the carriage window at the country-side flashing past. The good weather had continued, as he'd desperately hoped it would, and now they were on their way to Helensburgh on the Firth of Clyde.

Georgie glanced at John, who'd dropped off to sleep, which took years off him. What a good man he was, she reflected. She'd been lucky. She only hoped she was as good a wife to him as he was husband to her. And father to Ian.

She smiled as he snorted, changed position and started to snore. Thank goodness they were the only ones in the carriage. She'd have been obliged to wake him if they hadn't been.

'Enjoying yourself so far?' she asked Ian.

'Oh, yes, Mum. But I can't wait to get to the seaside. That's going to be even better.

Georgie couldn't remember when she'd last been so content.

Chrissie was halfway down Buchanan Street when she spotted Mary coming towards her. She pulled up short, wondering what to do.

Mary went white when she saw her mother, hesitated, then carried on walking, only stopping when she reached Chrissie.

'Hello, Ma.'

'Mary. How are you?'

'Fine. Yourself?'

'Not too bad.'

There was a strained silence between them for a few seconds, then Chrissie asked, 'Still going to your meetings?'

Mary immediately bridled. 'Of course,' she snapped. 'Why shouldn't I be?'

Oh dear, Chrissie thought. She'd said the wrong thing. Trust her. 'No reason,' she murmured. 'I was just asking, that's all.'

Mary's expression softened slightly. 'Aye, well, there we are.'

Suddenly Chrissie wanted away from her daughter, who'd quite unnerved her. 'I'd better be getting along,' she declared. 'I've got a lot yet to do.'

'Me too.'

''Bye then, Mary.'

''Bye, Mother.'

A few moments later Chrissie turned to watch Mary's retreating back.

She could have wept.

'Oh, this is glorious,' Georgie sighed, lying prostrate with the sun beating down on her. John was alongside her, Ian happily playing at the water's edge. They didn't have trunks for the boy who was stripped down to his underpants. There were about a dozen other people scattered along the beach, plus an old fisherman sitting outside a hut nearby mending some nets by hand.

'Those egg sandwiches were really tasty,' John muttered, eyes closed, as were Georgie's. 'I don't know what you did to them but they were truly delicious.'

'Good.'

'The fish paste ones weren't bad either. Certainly hit the spot.'

Georgie opened her eyes and rolled over on to her side to stare at him. She'd always thought him a beautiful man, and never more so than at that moment. 'A penny for them?' She smiled.

He was smiling too. 'They're not worth a penny.'

'Oh, come on,' she teased him. 'I'm sure they are.'

'You'd be wrong.'

'Tell me anyway.'

He opened his eyes to gaze at her. 'I was thinking about going back on nights . . .' He stopped when she groaned. 'Told you they weren't worth a penny.'

'How can you think about work on a day like this?' she said accusingly.

'Quite easily actually. It just sort of drifted into my mind.'

Suddenly they both became aware of some sort of commotion. Looking round they saw that the old fisherman was now on his feet and wildly gesticulating.

'The boy, the boy!' the old man shouted. 'He's gone under.'

'Gone under?' John frowned, glancing down at the water's edge.

'Someone do something!' The old man was waddling as quickly as he could in the direction he was pointing.

'Oh, my God!' Georgie breathed, realising there was no sign of Ian. 'It's Ian he's on about.'

The colour drained from John's face as he leapt up. Vaguely, he heard Georgie screaming behind him as he ran to where he'd last seen Ian. Georgie sat petrified with fright, unable to move a muscle. It was as though she'd been turned to stone.

Tiny waves lapped at John's feet and legs as he went rushing into the water, almost instantly spotting his son, lying submerged a yard or two further on. He grabbed him and hauled him out of the water. Ian was limp in his hands, and did not appear to be breathing.

Fearing the worst, John quickly returned to the beach, and laid Ian out face down on the sand.

'Let me,' said the old fisherman, kneeling down beside them. Rough, callused hands immediately began working on Ian's back.

A distraught Georgie joined them, having somehow overcome her paralysis. 'Is he . . . is he . . . ?'

With a gasp, Ian convulsed. Water shot out of his mouth, and he sucked in breath after breath.

The old fisherman gave a sigh of relief and sat back on his haunches. 'He'll be all right now,' he declared to Georgie and John. 'But it was a close thing.'

Georgie sank to her knees and pulled Ian into her embrace. 'Oh, my darling. My darling,' she crooned.

'I slipped, Mum. I slipped and fell in,' Ian explained, shaking all over. 'I'm sorry.'

'We can't thank you enough,' John told the old fisherman. 'We could easily have lost him. I blame myself for not keeping an eye out.'

Georgie turned her head away from Ian, and was violently sick.

Chapter 3

'This is a day I'll never forget for the rest of my life,' Georgie said quietly. It was later that night, and Ian was fast asleep in his recessed bed, having, it seemed, recovered completely from his earlier ordeal.

'Me neither,' John agreed, and had a swallow of whisky from the bottle he'd bought on their way home. An extravagance perhaps, but one he'd declared they were entitled to.

'If that old man hadn't . . .' Georgie broke off, and shuddered. 'It doesn't bear thinking about.'

'No, it doesn't.' John nodded.

Georgie lit a cigarette with a hand that hadn't stopped shaking since the incident.

'Are you still feeling cold?' John queried.

'As ice inside.'

'Shall I put the fire on?'

She thought about that. 'We'll be going to bed soon so it would be a waste. Anyway, it's only me that's cold. The weather's warm enough.'

- 'I can still light it.'

She smiled at him, the smile disappearing as she thought for the umpteenth time how differently things might have turned out. 'I don't think I'll sleep much tonight.'

John leant across and refilled her glass. 'Try more of that. It might do the trick.'

Georgie doubted it. Despite having already had four large ones she was sober as a judge. Even the whisky hadn't helped warm her insides.

'It was my fault,' John said yet again. 'I should have known better than not to keep watching him.'

'I was just as much to blame as you. More so, as I'm his mother.'

They both glanced over to where Ian lay sleeping soundly, trying not to imagine what it would have been like if he'd drowned. Their wee son. Their only child. Georgie began to cry silently, which she'd been doing on and off since the accident. John rose, went to her and put an arm round her shoulders. He felt like crying himself. 'There there, lassie. There there. That won't help any.'

'I know,' she said huskily. 'But I can't stop myself.'

He gently rocked her back and forth for a few minutes while she continued to cry, gripped by the emotions that were rampaging through them both. Strongest of all was guilt.

'Are you asleep?'

'No.'

'I didn't think you were.' John reached out and took Georgie by the hand, giving it a slight squeeze.

They lay like that for a little while, then she turned and snuggled up to him. 'I'm so empty inside, John,' she whispered. 'So terribly empty.'

'Still cold as well?'

'Yes.' Despite the sheet, four blankets and quilt which covered them. But her coldness had nothing to do with the lack of that kind of comforter.

'John?'

'What, darling?'

'I need . . . Well, you know?'

It surprised him. 'Do you?'

'I appreciate it's late. But please, John. I just need that.'

He was only too willing to comply, and found as much solace in the act as she did.

Finally they both drifted off to sleep.

Chrissie gasped. 'That's too tight, Lena. Far too tight.' She was putting on her new corset for the first time at home, her old one having finally given up the ghost.

Lena relaxed the laces a little. 'How's that?'

'Better.'

'Right then.' Lena tied the laces off and stepped back to admire her handiwork. 'It seems to fit all right.'

'It's far stiffer than I'm used to. But it would be, being new, I suppose.'

Lena grunted her agreement. She thought corsets horrible, constricting things, but, according to fashion, they were almost obligatory once you got older.

Chrissie moved her arms about, to see if they were restricted in any way. They weren't.

'Was it expensive?' Lena asked.

Chrissie told her how much it had cost.

'Enough for what's only a bit of material and a few pieces of whalebone, when all is said and done,' Lena commented.

'Don't forget the labour that goes into the making of it. That has to be paid for as well.'

True enough, Lena thought. She hadn't considered that. She watched as Chrissie slipped into her dress, a green one with large white polka dots that was a long-standing favourite of her mother's. And which, she had to admit, suited Chrissie.

'I haven't told you – or anyone else in the family, come to that – but I bumped into Mary last Saturday while in town shopping.'

'Oh aye? And how's my big sister?'

'Same as always.'

'Still spouting religion all over the place?'

Chrissie nodded miserably. 'I asked her if she was still going to the meetings and she nearly bit my nose off. Well, you know what she's like.'

'Only too well.' Lena sighed. 'A pain in the backside.'

Chrissie couldn't have agreed more. 'I just wish things were different. I know it upsets your papa enormously that we're estranged.'

'I'm not surprised. Mary was always his favourite,' Lena said bitterly.

'Now, you know that's not so.'

'It damn well is. Oh, give him his due, he tried to hide it. But the rest of us could see right through that. She was his favourite by a long shot.'

'Well, she certainly isn't now. He's terribly disappointed in her, though he rarely says.'

'A thaw in relations will come sooner or later. Has to. You'll see.'

'I'm not so sure,' Chrissie replied, her face filled with sadness. 'One thing I'm certain about, any thawing, as you put it, won't come from your father. You know how stubborn he is—'

'As is Mary,' Lena cut in. 'They're so alike, those two. They stick to their guns and won't budge.'

Chrissie sighed. 'If only she'd see some sense. Believe in her religion, if she has to, but shut up about it in front of the rest of us. Stop trying to ram it down our throats.'

'Some hope,' Lena sniffed.

Chrissie eyed her daughter speculatively, finally getting round to why she'd started this conversation in the first place. 'You and she aye got on well in the past.'

'Not too bad,' Lena grudgingly admitted. 'For sisters, that is.'

'You got on far better with her than you ever did with Georgie and Tom. Not that you didn't get on with those two, but you know what I mean.'

'As I recall it was always Georgie and Tom against Mary and me. That pair have always been as thick as thieves.'

'It's an age thing, I suppose.' Chrissie smiled. 'The two youngest ganging up against the two oldest.'

'Huh!' Lena snorted. 'Probably.'

'So I was wondering . . .' She trailed off, looking at Lena in a strange way.

'Wondering what?' Lena queried, slightly alarmed at the expression on her mother's face. It spelt trouble.

'If you'd go and see Mary. Have a word with her. Try to build a few bridges.'

'Me!' Lena exclaimed.

'You're the obvious choice. If she'll listen to anyone she'll listen to you.'

Lena didn't fancy the idea at all. She was as fed up with Mary's religious claptrap as the rest of the family.

'Come on,' Chrissie urged. 'Say you'll go. For my sake if nothing else.'

Lena was still reluctant. 'I don't think it would do any good, Mum. Honestly I don't.'

'You can at least try. Where's the harm?'

'Plenty if my visit ends up in a shouting match.'

'There's no need for that if you keep your temper and don't let rip.'

'And what if she starts?'

'Don't react. Be all sweetness and light itself. Try to make her see reason.' Chrissie hesitated, then added, 'Please, Lena? It would mean so much to me and your papa if we were all reconciled.'

Lena caved in, though visiting her sister was the last thing she wanted to do.

'All right then,' she sighed eventually. 'I'll go.'

Chrissie beamed at her. 'Thank you.'

God, Lena thought. What had she let herself in for? She dreaded to think.

Tam came out of his office at the end of the day's work to find Tom waiting for him, as his son always did. As usual, they would walk home together.

Tom waited till they were clear of McNair's before asking the question he had in mind. 'There was a pile of scrap metal tucked away in a corner out back of the foundry that I noticed has disappeared. Do you know about that, Papa?'

Tam's eyes slid to his son, and then away again. 'You're observant.'

'Not really. Not particularly so. I just happened to notice it's gone.'

'Have you mentioned this to anyone else?'

Tom shook his head. 'No.'

'Then don't.'

Tom was intrigued. 'Can I ask why?'

'Just don't mention it, that's all.'

'If you wish.'

'I do. Now let's drop the subject.'

Tom couldn't help but be puzzled. Why on earth was his father taking that attitude? What if it was theft? There was money to be made in scrap metal. Particularly lead and copper. Good money, too.

And then the penny dropped. His father was at it. He was the one responsible. He was selling the damn stuff on the fly. That had to be the answer, for Tam would have been down like a ton of bricks on anyone else who tried it.

Well well well, Tom mused. This was a new side to his father whom he'd always considered to be above anything untoward.

He just hoped and prayed that Tam never got caught. There again, in Tam's position as gaffer, that was highly unlikely.

The subject was never broached between them again.

'Have you ever contemplated living abroad?' Pet McQueen asked Lena. The two of them were in a café having coffee. Pet had enormous breasts, brassily dyed blonde hair, and lips that she was forever coating in the brightest of bright-red lipstick. Together, albeit they were the best of pals, she and Lena made an incongruous pair.

Lena stared at her friend in surprise, then shook her head. 'Whereabouts abroad?'

'Oh, I don't know. Canada maybe. Or America. America certainly appeals. If it's anything like the movies, that is.'

'America,' Lena mused. 'Do you mean Hollywood?'

'Why not? I've read that's a helluva place to be. Especially if you can break into films.'

'Not much chance of that in my case.' Lena laughed. 'I may be many things but a beauty I'll never be.'

Pet clucked in sympathy. That was true enough. Whereas she, on the other hand, was – at least so she believed. 'You don't have to be a beauty to be in films,' she pointed out. 'There are all sorts of people employed by the studios. Make-up ladies, for example. And many others who never go in front of the cameras, most of whom get paid extremely well.'

Lena thought about her own job. It wouldn't take much to be paid better than she was.

'Just imagine.' Pet sighed dreamily. 'All that sunshine, day after day. And they say fruit just falls off the trees there. You can pick yourself a fresh orange or peach any time you like. That must be absolutely fantastic.'

Lena thought so too. And what a contrast to cold and rainy old Glasgow – not to mention snow. No comparison whatever. 'Are you really thinking of going there?' she demanded with a frown that completely furrowed her forehead.

Pet shrugged. 'I might be.'

'It's awfully far away.'

'So?'

'It would be difficult getting back again.'

'Once there who'd want to come back? I doubt I would. Another thing to consider, there are lots and lots of rich blokes in Hollywood with more dosh than they know what to do with. Driving big flashy cars, living in houses like palaces. All with swimming pools too.' Pet shook her head in wonder. 'It would be the life of Riley right enough.'

Lena had to agree.

Georgie was still finding it strange not having Ian around for most of the day, although he had now settled in at school and was doing well. Why, he was actually keen to get there in the morning because he was enjoying it so much. But it left a large hole in her life.

And then there was John working nights. Home during the day, but asleep in bed which meant she had to pad around quietly so as not to disturb him. Everything had gone topsy-turvy in her world.

A glance at the clock told her it was time to put the dinner on as Ian would be back for it in a wee while. Several hours after that she'd have to feed John when he got up. It was a pain they couldn't eat together.

Crossing to the sink she began peeling potatoes, relishing the sunlight streaming through the window above the sink. The Indian summer was still continuing. It seemed as if it would go on for ever.

She smiled lovingly when she heard the sound of snoring coming from the bedroom. Within minutes John was giving it big licks.

Mary opened the door to find Lena standing there. She frowned. 'This is a surprise.'

'Am I welcome?'

'Of course. Come in and I'll put the kettle on.'

Lena stepped nervously into the hallway which was immaculate as usual, as would be the rest of the house. Even the tiniest speck of dust was never allowed to settle, Mary being obsessive about cleaning and polishing.

'So who sent you?' Mary challenged her as she filled the kettle. 'Mum or Papa?'

Lena blinked, having been caught off guard. 'No one,' she stuttered. 'I came of my own accord.'

Mary flashed her a look which plainly showed she didn't believe her, just as three-year-old Cora waddled into the room. She was a fat child, though Mary had always sworn in the past that she didn't overfeed her.

Lena smiled. 'You've grown since I saw you last.' Cora's response was to go and hide behind her mother's skirt.

'You just caught me,' Mary said. 'Another half an hour and I'd be gone. I have a meeting at the hall.'

Lena didn't reply to that. 'You're looking well,' she said instead.

'Am I?'

'I wouldn't have mentioned it otherwise.'

Mary ignored what she considered to be a jibe. 'I have a cake baked. Would you care for a slice?'

'What sort of cake?'

'Getting fussy in our old age, are we?' Mary riposted sharply.

Lena groaned inwardly. Talk about touchy! 'Not in the least. It's simply that there are some kinds of cakes I like, and others I don't. Surely you remember that?'

Mary now did, though she'd temporarily forgotten the fact. 'Pineapple upside down.'

'Oh, lovely!' Lena enthused. 'Yes please!'

'Cora have some too?'

Mary glanced down at her daughter and gave her an indulgent smile. 'I think you can, poppet. Go and sit at the table.'

Cora hurried to comply.

Lena looked round for Mary and James's elder child. 'Where's Rex?'

'Out playing somewhere. But he'll be home shortly to go with us to the meeting.' Mary added ominously, 'He knows better than to forget or be late.'

Poor little sod, Lena thought. It must be torture for children the age of Mary's to sit through interminable religious waffle. She felt for them.

'Did Mother tell you we ran into each other?' Mary asked.

'Yes she did. Buchanan Street, I believe she said.'

'And is that why you're here?'

Careful, Lena warned herself. 'In a way. I thought that if the mountain wouldn't come to Muhammad, then Muhammad better get her skates on.'

Mary had the grace to laugh. 'It has been a while.'

'Too long. We all miss you, you know.'

'Do you?'

'Yes, we do, Mary.'

'Even Papa?'

'Especially Papa. Don't forget, you were aye his favourite. Naturally he misses you.'

Mary produced the cake from a tin and began to slice it. One slice was larger than the other two, and she handed it to Cora, who immediately began wolfing it down. Mary had lied about overfeeding the child, Lena thought, if that slice of cake was anything to go by.

Mary snorted, a habit she had in common with her sister. 'That was a long time ago. Do you still take sugar in your tea?'

'Please.'

Mary poured boiling water into the teapot, then laid out cups and saucers.

'Can I say something without you flying off the handle?' Lena asked quietly.

'What?'

'You'd be more than welcome back home if you stopped spouting religion. Nobody expects you to change your beliefs. That's your affair. Just stop talking about it when you're with the family.'

Mary glared at Lena. 'Can't they understand I'm trying to save their souls?'

'Yes, they do. But your beliefs are your own, and theirs are theirs.'

'I wondered when you'd get round to religion,' Mary declared, eyes blazing. 'I just bloody well wondered.'

'Now don't lose your rag. Can't we talk sensibly about this?'

'I am talking sensibly, if only one of you would listen,' Mary replied hotly.

'Sensibly to you, perhaps. But not to us. Can't you accept that?'

'No, I can't!' Mary thundered. 'Nor will I ever give up on any of you. I don't want to see you cast into oblivion, or the fiery pits of hell. Not my own family, my own flesh and blood. I'll do everything in my power to make it otherwise.'

Lena, hearing the vehemence with which the vow had been delivered, felt that she'd failed in her task. But then she hadn't really expected anything else.

'More cake?' Cora asked, seemingly oblivious of the argument raging round her.

'You've had enough,' Mary snapped.

Tears filled Cora's eyes. 'Still hungry.'

'I said you've had enough. So be quiet.'

Just then Rex appeared, no one having heard him enter the house. Lena immediately wrinkled her nose in disgust.

'What's that smell?' Mary demanded.

He shrank in on himself, cowering away from his mother. 'I've had an accident,' he replied in a tiny voice. 'I got so excited playing I've done number twos in my pants.'

Forgetting all about tea and cake, Lena quickly made her excuses and fled.

Chapter 4

'Have you been happy doing the same job all your life, Papa?' Tam paused in what he was doing to stare at his son in surprise. 'What makes you ask that?'

'I was just wondering.'

Tam considered the question. 'I honestly don't know. I've never actually thought about it.'

'You've always seemed happy enough to me,' Chrissie chipped in.

'So there's your answer,' Tam declared to Tom.

'What put that into your head?' Chrissie queried.

Tom frowned, and took his time in replying. 'It just seems to me that it must get boring, tedious even, being years and years in the same job. Going through the same routine day after day, that sort of thing.'

'Boring doesn't come into it,' Tam responded. 'My generation are only too pleased to go through the same routine every day because it means we're in work. Earning, able to look after our families. There were many didn't have that luxury when I was younger, and unemployment was rife.'

'True enough,' Chrissie agreed. 'Your papa was considered lucky to get a start at McNair's. There were lots applied who didn't.'

'You've asked me if I'm happy with my job. Are you?' Tam said quietly.

'Oh aye. I enjoy it. And there's so much to learn. But what about twenty years from now? Or thirty, even? Will I still be enjoying it then? Or will I be wishing I'd been able to experience a bit more in life?'

'Like what, son?' Chrissie asked.

'Well, think about it, Mum. I was born and brought up in this house. Some day I'll probably get married and have a house of my own. A house, no doubt, quite close to here so I can walk to and from McNair's. Is my entire life to be just that? Living in the same area, going to McNair's day in day out? It doesn't seem . . . well, very much.'

Lena, sitting at the table, glanced up from the magazine that had been passed on to her from her friend Pet McQueen. 'Pet feels the same way,' she announced. 'She's considering going to Hollywood to try to be a film star.'

'Dear me!' Chrissie gasped, quite taken aback. 'Whoever gave her that idea?'

'No one. She dreamt it up herself.'

'Hollywood?' Tom mused.

'That's right. To try to be a film star,' Lena repeated.

Chrissie had a sudden alarming thought. 'You're not thinking of going with her, I hope?'

Lena smiled, and shook her head. 'I don't believe I'm exactly film star material, do you?'

Embarrassed, Chrissie glanced away. How could any

female who looked like Lena possibly be a film star? She didn't reply.

'Mind you,' Lena went on, 'as Pet pointed out, there are lots of jobs in film studios that don't involve going in front of a camera. A make-up lady, for example.'

'So you are thinking of going?' Chrissie was appalled at the idea. Hollywood was so far away. Why, she'd probably never see her daughter again.

'Who knows?' Lena shrugged. 'Stranger things have happened.'

'Tam, you speak to her this minute. Put your foot down,' Chrissie appealed to him.

'I can't do that. She's old enough to know her own mind. She's not a bairn any more, and no longer under my jurisdiction. If she decides to go then I can't stop her.'

Chrissie opened her mouth to reply, then shut it again. This was terrible.

'They say you can pick a ripe orange or peach from a tree any time you like in California,' Lena continued. 'Imagine that?'

'And it's sunny every day of the week,' Tom added. 'I read that somewhere.'

Tam produced an old pipe and began filling it from an equally old leather pouch.

'Since when have you started on the pipe again?' Chrissie demanded. 'You haven't smoked that for ages.'

'Since today. I found myself missing it. Any objections?'

Chrissie shook her head. 'None at all. In fact, I rather like to see you with a pipe. It makes you look rather distinguished.'

Tam barked out a laugh. Distinguished? What a joke! Still, if that's how Chrissie saw him he wasn't about to disagree.

'You'll never go,' Tom declared to his sister.

'Why not?'

'You aren't the type.'

'And precisely what sort of type am I?' she asked, slightly cross.

'Not that type, and that's for certain. You're not brave enough to take such a leap into the unknown.'

'And you are, I suppose?' she snapped.

'Maybe.'

'Stop it, you two,' Tam admonished them. 'You're giving me a headache.'

'Sorry, Papa,' Tom apologised with a grin, knowing that they were doing no such thing. It was simply one of the things Tam said when he wanted someone to shut up.

Lena, after a final dirty look at Tom, returned to her magazine.

'It would be exciting, though, to go somewhere else for a while,' Tom reflected aloud. 'Though I have to say California is a bit extreme.'

'And how long before you get bored, then?' Tam asked him, striking a match.

'Aye, how long?' Chrissie was worried. She'd be delighted when they both left home, but not if it meant their going to the far-flung corners of the world. That was something she hadn't anticipated for one moment.

'You're missing the point, Papa. I'm only talking about a bit of a change – an adventure, if you like. Not emigration or anything like that.'

'Then you'd come back and settle down?' Chrissie asked hopefully.

'I presume so.'

'And what if you meet someone while you're away and settle down there because she won't leave?' Tam smiled. 'That can happen.'

Tom didn't have an answer to that.

Lena was still fizzing inside. Not brave enough? What a cheek! How did Tom know what she was capable of? He didn't. He might think he did, but he didn't.

Chrissie picked up her knitting and got on with the pullover she was making for Tom. All this talk about California and the like had quite upset her.

Hollywood indeed! What a right load of nonsense.

'Oh, you're awake!' Georgie exclaimed, when she entered their bedroom to find John staring at the ceiling. 'I've brought you a cup of tea.'

'Thanks, darling,' John said, sitting up in bed and accepting the cup and saucer she handed him. 'I've been awake for ages, actually.'

'Then why didn't you get up? It's well past when you usually do.'

He sighed. 'I've had all the sleep I want, but I'm still tired. Bone weary, to tell the truth. So I just carried on lying here.'

Georgie regarded him with concern. 'It's working nights that's done it,' she said. 'It always upsets the system.'

'It's never made me like this before.'

Georgie racked her memory. He was right: it hadn't. There had been one terrible bout of constipation a few years previously, and an attack of boils before that, but never tiredness. 'Tell you what,' she declared. 'Why don't I go to the chemist's later on and get you a tonic. That might do the trick.'

'Good idea, Georgie. Let's just hope it does.'

'Are you going to get up now?'

He nodded. 'Once I've had this tea.'

'Then I'll get your meal on.'

She wished she could feed him on steak, she reflected as she returned to the kitchen. But, sadly, the price of that was beyond them. John earned a decent enough wage, but it didn't extend to sirloin. More's the pity.

Tom spotted her across the dance floor. Twinkletoes, whom he hadn't run into again since the night they'd danced together weeks and weeks ago. He immediately hurried over.

'Hello.' He smiled. 'Remember me?'

She stared blankly at him. 'Should I?'

His heart sank. Damn and blast, she'd forgotten. 'I was hoping you might. We had a few turns round the floor, but it was a while ago now.'

'Oh.'

He could see she still didn't recall him. 'Would you care to dance?' he asked rather formally.

'If you like.'

Hardly an encouraging reply, he thought. Hardly enthusiastic.

She mustn't get too excited, Georgie warned herself. But it did seem, on the face of it anyway, that she was two months gone. Pregnant again, after all this time.

Elation filled her, and a strange warm feeling she remembered only too well from when she was carrying Ian.

Her parents would be thrilled, she thought. Especially Chrissie, who was dead keen for her to have another child, and Chrissie another grandchild. Mary had given them two, of course, but they never saw Cora or Rex now that they were estranged from Mary. She knew how deeply that hurt the pair of them.

A little boy, or a girl? A girl would be nice, as she and John already had Ian. Oh, the fun she'd have with a wee lassie! Dressing her nicely, fussing with her hair, talking to her, eventually, about feminine things. Having another female in the house.

Georgie smiled broadly, guessing what John's reaction would be when she finally told him. He'd be ecstatic. Over the moon.

But she wasn't telling anyone yet. Not till she'd missed another period and was absolutely sure. Then John would be the first to know.

She gently rubbed her stomach. Yes, no doubt about it. A girl was her preference. But as long as all the baby's bits and pieces were in the right places that was the important thing.

'You really are a terrific dancer, Brigid.' Tom smiled at his partner.

'Thank you very much. You're not bad yourself.'

'Well, thank *you*.'

This was their fourth dance together. She had stayed up with him for that length of time, and as far as he was concerned it was a 'click'.

'Can I ask where you live?'

She stared up at him, being shorter than he. 'Why?'

He flushed slightly. 'Oh, I was just wondering if you were local.'

'You mean come from round here?'

'That's right.'

'Do you?'

'Not that far away. About a ten-minute walk.'

'Same for me.'

Good, he thought. He'd definitely try to lumber her later on. The number came to a finish and everyone on the floor applauded.

'Will you excuse me? I have to go to the ladies,' she said.

'Of course.'

She stared him straight in the eyes for a moment, then, turning, walked away.

Lovely figure, he mused as he left the floor. Quite the bobby-dazzler in his opinion. Taking up a position beside a pillar, he awaited her return.

'Someone's home early,' Chrissie commented on hearing the scrape of a key in the outside door. As it was a Saturday night, both Tom and Lena had gone out earlier.

It turned out to be Tom who was back. And in a bad humour, too, judging from his expression.

'What's up, son?' Chrissie asked.

'Nothing, Mum.'

'Would you like a dram?' Tam queried. 'There's plenty left.'

Tom shook his head. 'Thanks, Papa, but I won't if you don't mind.'

'I don't mind at all. It's all the more for me.'

'I think I'll go to bed,' Tom declared, not wanting to face the quizzing about his night at the dancing which was sure to take place.

Chrissie glanced at the clock. 'Aren't you feeling well?'

'I'm fine, Mum. Don't fash yourself. I just thought I'd have a read, that's all.'

'What's wrong with reading in here?'

'Leave him alone, woman,' Tam said. 'If he wants to read in his own room then let him do so.'

'We'll be having a wee bit supper in a minute or two,' Chrissie told him. 'I've got a tin of salmon in as a special treat. Shall I bring you through a couple of sandwiches?'

'No thanks, Mum. I'm not hungry. Goodnight now.'

'There's something up,' Chrissie declared after he had gone.

'If there is he obviously doesn't want to talk about it. Just let him be.'

'But—'

'I said let him be, Chrissie,' Tam interjected. 'Don't go on. Now why don't you get that supper you mentioned? Tom might not be hungry, but I am.'

Tom slumped on to his bed, not quite sure how he felt. Stupid? Probably. Let down? Without a doubt. And bloody angry too, if he was honest.

Just going to the ladies, she'd said. And he, like a right diddy, had stood there patiently waiting for her to re-join him. She never did.

After a while he'd gone looking. But she was nowhere

to be found, which could only mean one thing. She'd bolted, leaving him in the lurch.

He'd liked her, too. A lot.

'Can't you put a sock in it!' James, Mary's husband, said to her in exasperation.

She regarded him with astonishment. It was rare for him, normally so mild-mannered, to have a go at her. 'What's got up your humph tonight?' she retorted.

James sighed. 'Sometimes a man wants just a bit of peace and quiet. Know what I mean? Which there isn't a lot of in this house.'

'I was only reading scripture to the children,' she declared coldly.

'Yet again and again,' he snapped. 'Can't you read them *Little Red Riding Hood* for a change? Or how about *Cinderella*?'

Mary's nose wrinkled in scorn. 'That's the most ridiculous suggestion I've ever heard.'

'Is it?'

'Yes, it probably is. Scripture is far more rewarding and instructive than those stupid stories. No value in them whatsoever.'

'But more entertaining I should say. They're only children, Mary. Let them have some childhood, for Pete's sake.'

Mary glared at him. It never entered her mind for one second that he might be right. Without a further word she turned her attention back to Cora and Rex and began reading from where she'd been interrupted.

James groaned, and rolled his eyes heavenwards. There

was nothing else for it. He was off to the lavatory, in which sanctuary he groped in a pocket to produce a bar of Highland Toffee, his favourite. Sitting, he undid the wrapper, snapped off a piece and popped it into his mouth.

He didn't leave the lavatory again until he'd eaten the whole bar. Which made him feel a lot, lot better.

Lena glanced up from the ledger she was working on to see Hamish Murchison coming in her direction. When she noted he was carrying a ledger she knew what that probably meant.

So handsome, she reflected. And available too. If only . . . But she was only too horribly aware that she had no chance with such a good-looking chap. Pigs would fly first.

'I've come to ask a favour,' he said quietly on reaching her desk.

'The usual?'

'I'm afraid so. I just can't make these figures add up. I've been trying all morning, and failing miserably.'

'And you want my help?'

He leant closer. 'Please, Lena. You'd be saving my bacon. I'm in bad enough odour with old baldy as it is.' Old baldy was Mr Crerar, their head of department, who was, as his nickname suggested, bald as the proverbial coot.

'Have you ever considered changing jobs, Hamish?' Lena smiled at him. 'You're not really cut out for this one, are you?'

'It's just that you're so clever. Everyone says so. I doubt

there's a ledger in the world, no matter how complicated, you couldn't make balance.'

'Flattery will get you everywhere.'

'So will you bail me out?'

Lena took the ledger from him. It was going to be a nuisance, as she had more than enough work of her own to be getting on with, but how could she refuse? One glance into those sexy blue eyes and she was lost. If she'd stood up she'd probably have found she was weak at the knees.

'Of course I will. Come back in an hour or two.'

'Thanks, Lena. You're a darling. I owe you yet again.'

She watched his retreating back, desperately wishing things were different. She'd been called clever Lena at school too, top of the class more often than not. But she'd happily have traded all her so-called cleverness for a new face any day. By God and she would.

'I've come over to apologise.'

Tom turned to find Brigid standing beside him. He couldn't help the scowl that came on to his face. 'Oh aye?'

'Were you cross with me?'

He shrugged.

'You were, then.'

He didn't reply.

'I'm sorry. Truly I am. But let me explain?'

She was pretty, he thought. The figure was as good as he remembered – and he remembered only too well. 'Go on.'

She glanced around. 'Can we find somewhere a little less crowded?'

Tom couldn't see why not.

'Over there,' she said, pointing, and moved off. He followed her. When they reached the quiet corner she'd indicated, she turned to face him.

'This is embarrassing,' she declared, and took a deep breath. 'I had an upset stomach last Saturday night. When I left you to go to the ladies I . . .' She took another deep breath. 'I had terrible diarrhoea.'

He was immediately sympathetic, his face softening.

'I was in there for absolutely ages,' she went on. 'Then, when I was finished, all I could think of was getting home as soon as possible in case there was a recurrence. My stomach really was giving me gyp. Griping like mad.'

'It must have been awful for you,' he said sincerely.

'It was. Believe me. Luckily it cleared up over the rest of the weekend and I was able to go back to work on Monday. So do you forgive me for being so apparently rude?'

'Completely.' He smiled.

'Leaving you standing has been on my conscience all week. I can only imagine what you must have thought of me.'

'Well, let's just say it wasn't very complimentary. I felt a proper charlie.'

Her smile matched his. 'I know it's not a woman's place to ask, but now that's out of the way do you want to dance?'

'With you? I can't think of anything I'd like to do more.'

Hooking an arm round hers, he led her on to the floor.

*   *   *

56

Her mouth was soft, and warm, and by far the nicest he'd ever kissed. It was sheer heaven.

'Hmm,' he murmured when it was over.

'I'd better go on up,' she whispered. 'It's late.'

'Just one more?'

'Just one then,' she agreed.

Magic, he thought when he finally left her to walk off down the street.

That's what she was. Magic.

Chapter 5

'This tea in bed business is becoming something of a habit,' Georgie teased John, who was wriggling into a sitting position.

'And one I rather like. Why, are you complaining?' he asked, tongue in cheek.

She handed him the cup and saucer. 'Not really.'

'Good.'

She stepped back a pace and studied him. 'That tonic I gave you has really worked wonders. You look healthier than you've done in years.'

'I feel it. And not a trace of tiredness when I shouldn't be feeling that way. I'm a new man.'

She leant forward and kissed him on the cheek. 'Hungry?'

'Starving, woman. I could eat a horse.'

She laughed. 'Well, I'll try to do better than that. How do sausages sound?'

'Wonderful.'

'With mash, peas and onion gravy.'

'Better still.'

'And lots of it.'

'Can't wait.' He patted the bed. 'Sit with me for a minute or two.'

She sat where he'd patted. 'Any news yet of you coming off nights?'

John shook his head. 'Afraid not. I'll have another month to do at least.'

She pulled a face.

'Can't be helped, darling. You know that.'

'Of course I do. It just turns things topsy-turvy, that's all.'

'I was talking to one of the drivers the other night. Lucky bugger owns a cottage in the country.'

'How did he manage that?' Georgie queried in surprise. Drivers were well paid, but not that well!

'A relative died and left it to him. He and his family go there on holiday. The rest of the time he's only too pleased to let it out. Which made me wonder, why don't we take it? Next Easter, perhaps, when Ian's off school.'

The idea gripped her, filling her with excitement. 'Whereabouts in the country?'

'Perthshire, he said. It's lovely there, I believe.'

Georgie's eyes glowed with enthusiasm. A real holiday in the country would be absolutely fantastic and it would do them all the power of good to get away: away from Glasgow, though she loved it dearly, with all its smoke and grime; away from soot-blackened tenements stretching off in all directions; away from general heaving humanity and all that went with it.

Away from . . . And then it struck her. April? She did a quick mental calculation. No no, that was fine. April wasn't a problem.

'So, how about it?' John demanded.

'Oh, yes, please. If we can afford it, that is.'

'We'll manage somehow. It's just too good an opportunity to pass up.'

'Ian will love it,' Georgie said rapturously. 'Simply adore it.'

'I'll arrange time off well in advance,' John said. 'Shouldn't be too hard to organise. And of course we'll get there and back free on the railway. So that's a saving.'

Georgie beamed at him, and he beamed back.

'I think we should celebrate,' he suggested.

'How?'

'Why don't you take your clothes off and get into bed?'

'In the middle of the day?' she exclaimed, genuinely shocked.

'Why not?'

Why not indeed, she thought. There were no rules against it after all. And it would be rather exciting. Naughty, even.

'It's been a while,' John reminded her. 'Too long. This night-shift nonsense has been getting in the way.'

She took his cup and saucer from him, and went back to the kitchen, where she removed various pots that had been slowly coming to the boil. Then she returned to the bedroom, stripped, and slipped in beside him.

'You're the best thing that's ever happened to me, Georgie,' he said softly, suddenly serious.

'And you me.'

Moments later they melted into one another.

'Take your time,' Chrissie admonished. 'You'll give yourself indigestion eating as quickly as that.'

'Sorry, Mum,' Tom apologised. 'But I'm going out, which is why I'm in a bit of a rush.'

Chrissie glanced at her husband. This was unusual, as Tom normally stayed in during the week. 'Can I ask where to?'

Tom coloured slightly. 'The pictures.'

'The pictures, eh?' Chrissie mused. 'I take it there's a lassie involved?'

'That's right.'

'What's her name?' Tam asked, amused at his son's obvious discomfiture.

'Does it matter what her name is?' Tom retorted, shifting uncomfortably on his chair. 'She's just a lassie I met at the dancing, that's all.'

'How mysterious,' Lena commented with a smile.

'There's nothing mysterious about it,' Tom replied hotly.

'Then why no name?'

Tom shot Lena a murderous glance. 'I don't pry into your affairs, so stop trying to pry into mine.'

'Now now, don't talk to your sister like that,' Chrissie rebuked him. 'She doesn't mean anything.'

'What's on anyway?' Tam enquired. He liked a good picture himself, though he didn't go all that often as Chrissie wasn't so keen.

'Don't know. We'll find out when we get there.'

'The back seats, of course,' Lena teased. 'Where all the winching couples go.'

Tom coloured again. 'Maybe,' he reluctantly admitted.

'Lots of kisses and cuddles, eh?'

'That's enough, Lena,' Chrissie chided her. 'Leave the lad alone. Can't you see you're embarrassing him?'

Tom hastily finished the little left on his plate. 'Can I leave the table, Papa? I want to get on.'

'You're excused.'

'Thanks. That was lovely, Mum. Thank you.' And with that he hurried from the room.

'Are you enjoying it?' Tom whispered.

'Oh aye, it's great.'

The film was *Safety Last* starring Harold Lloyd who, as usual, was performing all his own terrifying, death-defying stunts. Brigid gave a sudden gasp and her hand flew to her mouth as Lloyd looked as though he was about to topple from the roof of a skyscraper. A moment later she relaxed when he performed yet another amazing acrobatic feat to save himself.

Tom, whose own heart was pumping for reasons that had nothing to do with the film, curled an arm nonchalantly round Brigid's shoulders while he continued to watch the screen. He waited tensely to see if she'd object, but she didn't. There was not even a glance to acknowledge what he'd done.

Tom heaved a small sigh of relief. So far so good. The next step was kissing, which some of the other couples in the back row were already doing. He needn't have worried. Before he could make his next move she

62

turned to face him, closing her eyes invitingly.

The night was a great success, and they agreed to meet up at the dancing the following Saturday.

'Oh no!' Georgie exclaimed softly, bending over in pain. A sharp pain had lanced through her stomach. 'Please, no.' Horribly aware of what was happening, she began to cry.

Through in the bedroom John started to snore.

'So was it a period or did you miscarry?' Chrissie queried, having heard Georgie's tale of woe.

Georgie shook her head. 'I honestly don't know, Mum. I mean, I couldn't rightly look in case . . .' She trailed off. 'I simply cleaned up without paying too much attention and came straight over.'

'You don't usually miss periods, do you?'

'No, never. That's why I was convinced I was pregnant. There again, there's always a first time, I suppose.'

Chrissie wished she had a little whisky or brandy in the house for Georgie. She could always nip out and get some. It wouldn't take long. 'Oh, Georgie,' she sighed. 'I'm so sorry.'

Not as sorry as she was, Georgie thought bitterly. She'd been so looking forward to having another child, to giving her parents another grandchild.

'Where's John now?'

'In bed asleep.' Georgie glanced at the clock. 'I can't stay too long, or Ian will be home for his dinner.'

'And John didn't know you were pregnant?'

'I was waiting to be absolutely certain before breaking the news. Just as well I didn't.'

'But you must tell him,' Chrissie urged.

'No, Mum. It would only upset him and I don't want that. You're not to say anything either, promise?'

'If you wish.'

'I do. Now promise.'

Chrissie nodded. 'I promise.'

Tears welled yet again in Georgie's eyes, and she attempted to brush them away with her hanky. 'I feel so terrible, Mum. So let down.'

'I can understand that. It must be awful for you.' Crossing to her daughter Chrissie raised her out of the chair she was sitting in and hugged her tight. 'You'll get over it,' she crooned. 'It'll just take time. You'll see.'

When Georgie was gone Chrissie broke down and cried herself. The world could be so cruel. She couldn't help but sit and think of the child she'd lost all those long years ago.

So very cruel.

'I've made up my mind. I am going to Hollywood,' Pet McQueen announced.

Lena studied her friend. They were in their favourite café having coffee, and Pet meant it all right. That was obvious from her expression. 'It'll cost you to get there. Won't be cheap.'

'I've already thought of that, and I'm going to start saving right away. I shall also be looking for a part-time job for evenings or weekends. The money from that will help.'

Lena's heart sank. If Pet succeeded in finding more work then she wouldn't be seeing her as much as she usually did. And Pet was her one and only close friend. The pair of them had been pals for years and years. 'I see,' she murmured.

Pet lit a cigarette. 'No more of these either. This is my last packet. They cost far too much anyway.'

'Any idea what sort of job you'll go after?'

Pet shook her head. 'Not yet. But I'll find something in the paper or on the grapevine.'

Pet's day job was in a large department store where she worked on the perfume counter. A glamorous job, Lena had always thought. Certainly far more glamorous than poring over ledgers all day long. That could be tedious, to say the least.

'Hollywood,' Pet mused, a faraway look in her eyes. 'It'll be fantastic.'

Lena regarded her with envy. No doubt it would be.

'So why don't you come along?' Pet demanded. 'Give it a go, same as me.'

Lena smiled. 'I must say I'm tempted. It would be a wonderful experience, if nothing else.'

'Does that mean yes?' Pet said excitedly.

'Not exactly. I'll certainly think about it, though.' This time her smile was rueful. 'My brother Tom says I haven't got the courage to up sticks and go abroad.'

'Nonsense!' Pet exclaimed. 'Of course you have. Don't listen to his prattling on. What does he knew?'

'I keep imagining those orange and peach trees you mentioned when we talked about this before.'

'What about them?'

Lena shook her head in amazement. 'The very idea seems out of this world.'

'Not out of this world.' Pet laughed. 'But in California where the sun shines all the time, and lots of men are loaded.' Her eyes gleamed. 'And when I say loaded, I mean exactly that.'

Not that she'd have much chance with one of those, Lena reflected. But the idea of a life in films, even behind the camera, was certainly very appealing.

'How will you get there?' she asked curiously.

'Boat from the Clyde to New York, I suppose,' Pet replied. 'Then train all the way across America. A long train ride, eh?'

'You can say that again.'

'It takes days, apparently. But eventually it arrives, and there you are. Bob's your uncle!'

Lena glanced out of the café window and saw that it was teeming down again. The Indian summer they'd had was long gone.

Oh, she was tempted all right. Truly tempted.

'Is something wrong?' John asked, watching Georgie making the sandwiches he'd take with him on duty.

Ian was sitting on the floor playing with an array of ancient lead soldiers, most of them missing paint and otherwise damaged in some way. He adored his soldiers and liked nothing more than to play 'battles'. It was his dream that one day he'd have a toy fort to go with them. In the meantime he made do with a cardboard box.

'No,' Georgie replied, looking over. 'Why?'

'It's just . . . well, you've seemed a bit down in the dumps lately. Nothing to do with me, I hope?'

'Of course not, silly.'

He hesitated. 'So, what is bothering you?'

She couldn't tell him about the baby she'd lost, knowing how much it would upset him. She'd convinced herself since the event that she had miscarried and it hadn't simply been a late, and extremely heavy, period.

'Nothing. Nothing at all.'

'Then why the long face?'

She shrugged. 'I wasn't aware I've had one.'

He stared at her in concern, wondering if it had just been his imagination? No, it hadn't been. She'd definitely been out of sorts for the past few weeks. Not at all her usual cheery self. 'Maybe you should prescribe yourself a tonic as you did for me?'

Georgie smiled at him. 'Maybe I will. Certainly wouldn't do me any harm.'

'Buck you up perhaps.'

'The fact this is your last night duty will buck me up more than anything.'

'Aye.' A warm feeling swept through him. 'My last night. Back to normal Monday morning. I can't wait.'

She glanced at Ian and saw he was absorbed with his game. 'Neither can I. It gets lonely in that bed when you're on your own.'

John couldn't have agreed more.

'I start next Wednesday night,' Pet finished triumphantly.

'As a cocktail waitress?' Lena sounded as astonished as she felt.

'That's right. Wednesday, Thursday and Friday straight from work. Saturdays start at six till the finish. Good money, too – plus tips. Apparently there are lots of those.'

'You really have landed on your feet.' Lena said. 'But what about food? If you go to this nightclub straight from work when will you eat?'

'You're forgetting we have a canteen at the store. I'll just eat a lot more at dinnertime there and that'll see me through. I'll possibly be able to grab a sandwich or something at the club, but I'll have to wait and find out. I forgot to ask about that at the interview.'

'Well, well,' Lena mused, highly delighted for her friend.

'I have to wear a costume which is skimpy to say the least. All revealing legs and upthrust bust.'

Pet hardly needed the latter, Lena thought, her bust being the more than generous size it was. Unlike Lena's own modest endowment.

'I'll have my fare saved in no time,' Pet enthused. 'Particularly if the tips are as good as I was told.'

'The club must be frequented by toffs,' Lena guessed.

'So I believe. Rich toffs, too, at the prices it charges. Talk about daylight robbery!'

'That expensive, eh?'

'When I say daylight robbery I mean precisely that. I'm just surprised they don't have the waitresses wearing black masks and carrying horse pistols.'

They both laughed.

On her way home Lena realised she was envious as hell. Absolutely pea green with it.

Georgie glanced over at Ian, fast asleep in his recessed bed. The wee soul had pleaded to stay up and see the new year in with them and she had agreed, knowing full

68

well he'd never last that long. He'd done well though, and it had been nearly ten before John had lifted him from where he'd dozed off and slipped him under the sheets.

'Only a few minutes to go,' John commented, looking at the clock. 'I'd better pour us a drink.'

'Lemonade with mine, don't forget.'

He smiled lovingly at her. 'How could I forget how my wife likes her whisky after all these years of marriage?'

Georgie lit a cigarette while John did the honours. 'Ta,' she murmured when he handed her a glass.

'I wonder what the new year will bring?' he mused.

'Who knows?'

'Happiness and prosperity, I hope.'

'We already have the happiness, John. And we don't do too badly on the money front. Better than many.'

'True,' he agreed.

Another baby, Georgie thought. If she could have a wish granted that's what it would be. A little girl. Bonny as a picture.

Somewhere bells rang out. The new year had arrived. They stared at one another, then John raised his glass in a toast. 'Here's to us in 1925, lass.'

'Us in 1925,' she echoed.

They both drank.

'Now how about a kiss?' he suggested.

'Why stop there?' she teased.

John laughed, laid his glass aside and took her into his arms. The ensuing kiss was long and deep.

'I do love you,' she whispered when it was finally over.

'And I you.'

'Do you think we'll have any first foots?'

'It isn't likely.'

'Then why don't we drink up and go on through?'

Which is precisely what they did.

Chapter 6

Every Sunday morning Tam went for a walk along the banks of the nearby canal. It was something he'd been doing for years. On this particular Sunday Lena had asked to accompany him, which she'd never done before.

It was a bitter January day with the hint of snow in the air. Both of them were wrapped up warm.

'So what do you want to talk about?' Tam enquired as they strolled along.

'What makes you think I want to talk about anything?'

'Why else would you want to come with me? I can't think of any other reason.'

'Perhaps I just like being with you,' she teased.

He smiled. 'Pull the other one, Lena. I'm not daft, you know.'

'I didn't think you were.'

He halted and lit his pipe. 'So, what's on your mind?' he asked as they continued on their way.

'You remember I told you Pet McQueen is going to

America? Hollywood actually. She's saving every penny for the fare.'

He nodded. 'I remember.'

'She's dead keen for me to go with her.'

Tam's eyes slid sideways to fasten on his daughter. 'Do you wish to?'

'I have to admit it's tempting, Papa. It would be a whole new world for me.'

'Aye, it would that,' he agreed.

'And what is there for me here? Not a lot. A boring old job . . .'

'Which you're good at,' he interjected.

'But that's not the point. It's still boring, good at it or not. And it's not as if there are any prospects. I'm a woman, don't forget. Being a ledger clerk is as high as I can get in the company.'

'Which is a pity,' Tam murmured. 'You've a good brain in your head. You could go far if they'd let you.'

'But they won't – as you well know. Only men can progress further up the ladder. It's the same in most fields.'

'Do you think you could do better in Hollywood?' Tam asked slowly.

'There are certainly opportunities there, the Americans being more progressive than us. And if I did get into the film industry, behind the scenes that is, then anything's possible.'

'Where did you get this information?'

'Magazines mainly,' she admitted. 'Pet buys lots and always passes them on. You've seen me reading them.'

'And you believe everything in there is gospel?'

'Of course not, Papa. I'm sure some of the stories are

exaggerated. But there must be a core of truth in those articles. It can't all be baloney.'

He considered that. 'It seems to me that magazines are a rather flimsy basis on which to change your entire life. Don't you agree?'

Reluctantly she did.

'If you were to ask me for advice,' he went on, 'I'd look into this more thoroughly. Do some proper home-work on the subject. I've no idea how you'd go about that, but you'll find a way.'

Lena had to admit it was good advice. 'You're right, Papa. I will.'

'Fine.'

'Let's say I do the homework and still decide to go. How would you and Mum feel about it?'

Tam stopped and put another match to his pipe, which was in danger of going out. 'Well, your mother wouldn't be best pleased for a start. In fact she'd be downright devastated.'

Lena's face fell, although it was more or less what she'd expected to hear. 'And you, Papa?'

'The same,' he said quietly.

They walked a little way in silence before Tam spoke again. 'Parents expect their children to grow up and move out. That's perfectly normal. What they don't expect them to do is leave not only the family home, but the country as well. To go so far away they might be on the moon for all it matters. Perhaps never see them again.'

'I know,' Lena murmured.

'But it's your life to do with as you wish,' Tam continued. 'That's your right. What you mustn't do is let your mother and me hold you back, no matter what the pain involved. If you want to go, then you must. All I ask is that you think long and hard before reaching a decision.'

Lena took a deep breath. 'I will, Papa. I promise.'

Tam stopped again and looked out over the canal. 'I swear that water gets filthier by the week. God help anyone who ever falls in and swallows any. It would kill them stone cold dead.'

Lena took her father by the hand and squeezed it. 'Thanks, Papa.'

John placed the blade of his shovel on the footplate and used it for support as he sucked in breath after breath.

Willie Winning, his driver, frowned at him. 'What's up, John?'

'Came over all funny there for a moment or two. My head spun, and I was suddenly short of breath.'

'That's unlike you.' Willie continued to frown.

John straightened and ran the sleeve of one arm over his face and eyes. 'It must be age,' he joked. 'I'm getting old.'

'Nonsense, man. You're not even thirty yet. *I'm* old. Fifty-eight last birthday.'

'And don't look a day over seventy!'

'Get away with you! None of your cheek, now.'

John grinned. He and Willie were good mates, having often worked together. 'Cheek, me? Never!' he protested.

Willie smiled. 'Only another half-hour and we'll be back in Glasgow and knocking off. Not long to go then.'

Using his shovel John tipped open the fire door and

began heaving more coal inside, the breathlessness forgotten.

'The tips are brilliant,' Pet McQueen enthused. It was the first time she had seen Lena since she'd started at the Green Slipper Club. 'Why, only last week this old chap had a good feel of my arse, then gave me a fiver for the privilege.'

'A fiver!' Lena exclaimed in awe.

'A nice crisp white one. Of course the customers aren't supposed to take liberties, but he or anyone else can feel my arse any time for a fiver. Darn tootin'!'

Lena laughed. 'Tell me more?'

'Usually the tips are in the region of a couple of bob, or half a crown. Occasionally you get a ten-bob note, and once in a while a quid. It soon adds up, I can tell you. And the tips are on top of my wages, which are bloody good to start with.'

'And the customers, what are they like?'

'All sorts really. But all well off. They have to be to be able to afford that place. As I said to you before, it's damned expensive.'

'You're enjoying yourself, then?'

'Immensely. It certainly knocks selling perfume into a cocked hat.'

Lena could well believe that, thinking of the drudgery of her own job, the never-ending entries that had to be made, the columns that had to be added. 'Do you get any single men there?' she asked. 'I mean younger ones?'

'A few. Not many. Mainly they come with their girl-friends or wives on a night out. You know the sort of thing.'

'I can imagine.' It was all she could do, as she'd never been asked out by a member of the opposite sex. Not once. 'What about the clothes these females wear?'

'Expensive, like the prices. There was one woman the other night in an emerald-green dress which was simply stunning. Rather short and showing quite a lot of cleavage, which I thought a bit daring. She certainly got a lot of admiring glances.' Pet described the dress in detail, down to the seed pearls that had been sewn into its waist.

'Gosh,' Lena murmured.

'She was very pleasant, too, when I spoke to her. Some of them turn their noses up at you because you're a waitress, but not her.'

Lena watched as Pet lit up. 'I thought you were stopping smoking?'

'I intended to before I realised how much money I'd be earning. Absolute pots, darling. Absolute pots.'

Lena laughed at the upper-class accent her friend had affected. Not a bad impression, she thought. Pet might have talent as an actress after all.

'Still intending to go to Hollywood?'

'You bet. Soon as possible too. Once I have enough cash it'll be toodle-oo! I'm on my way.' Pet eyed Lena speculatively. 'Any further thoughts on that yourself?'

'Well, one thing's certain: I won't be going with you. I'd never be able to save enough in time, not the way you're raking it in.'

'We could still meet out there though,' Pet declared. 'You having followed on later, like.'

'There's always that possibility.' Lena smiled. She

wondered what it would be like to have a man feel your backside? Rather nice, she decided. Even if he was old.

John was washing at the sink, having just come off shift, when Georgie exclaimed and pointed at his arm. 'How on earth did you get that bruise? It's massive.'

'What bruise, darling?' he asked, turning to face her.

'That one there.'

He glanced down to where she was pointing, and frowned. Georgie was right, it was a big one. 'No idea,' he declared, shaking his head. 'I must have banged it without realising.'

Georgie went over to him. 'Is it sore?'

He touched it gingerly. 'A little. Though I haven't felt it up until now.'

'You'll have to be more careful, John,' she chided. 'I can't have you coming home all black and blue.'

'I'm hardly that.'

'It must have been some whack,' Georgie commented.

'Well, anyway, there's nothing to be done but let it heal of its own accord. Now, what's for tea?'

Tom gaped at the scene which met his eyes. Brigid had persuaded him to a different dance hall from the one he normally used, but she hadn't mentioned this.

There were only four members to the band: brass, piano, drums and vocalist, and the number they were playing – albeit Tom didn't know it at the time – was 'Livery Stable Blues'.

'It's jazz,' he breathed.

'Have you never heard jazz before?' Brigid asked, smiling.

'Once or twice. It's very different.'

'It's meant to be. Quite a change from the traditional stuff you're used to, eh?'

Tom could only agree. Quite different indeed. He studied the dancers, the steps unlike anything he knew.

'I've been coming here for a while,' Brigid told him. 'That's why I wasn't at the other place every Saturday night.'

'Well, the waltz and foxtrot it certainly isn't.'

Brigid laughed. 'You'll soon pick it up. I'll teach you.'

'Are those women supposed to be flappers?'

'They're not supposed to be. They are.'

Most of the dresses on view were skimpy and exuberant. Some had long fringes, many were worn with ropes of gaudily coloured beads. A number of the women sported narrow bandeaux across their foreheads.

The men's attire was varied. Lounge suits were in evidence, such as Tom was wearing, which put him at his ease as he wouldn't stand out. But to his amazement a scattering of men had on sleeveless jerseys atop plus-fours, while a few were clad in Oxford bags which he thought looked truly hideous.

'It's more like a carnival than anything else,' he commented wryly.

'The Bright Young Things is what the *Daily Mail* calls them,' Brigid informed him. 'They're all the rage.'

The number came to an end, and almost instantly the band swung into a new one, this time the 'Dixie Jazz Band One-step'.

'Do you fancy having a go?' Brigid queried. 'And don't worry, I'll talk you through it.'

'I don't want to look a fool,' Tom replied, uncertain.

'You won't. Don't forget we've all got to learn.'

'But so publicly?'

'I'm telling you, it won't matter.'

'All right then,' he agreed, following her on to the floor. At the end of the night he had to admit he'd thoroughly enjoyed himself, while Brigid complimented him on how quickly he'd picked up many of the steps.

'What's all this?' Chrissie demanded as Tam and Tom came through the door carrying a large, boxlike object.

'What does it look like?' Tam replied sarcastically. 'It's a wireless set.'

'Dear me.' Chrissie gasped. 'Where did you get it?'

Tam gave her a fly wink. 'Ask no questions, get no lies. Understand, woman?'

She was shocked. 'Do you mean it's stolen?'

The two men placed the wireless on top of the kitchen table. 'Not at all,' Tam lied. 'Somebody at work owed me a favour and gave it to me to sort of pay that off.'

'Oh!' Chrissie exclaimed, believing him.

Tam had told Tom the same story, but after the incident of the scrap metal Tom wasn't so naive as to take that explanation at its face value. However, he'd said nothing to the contrary, but given the impression of accepting what his father had said.

'Now, where shall we put it?' Tam wondered, glancing round.

When Lena returned from work she was amazed to be greeted by the evening news when she entered the kitchen. It distracted her for a little while, but after tea she fell to brooding again on what had happened at work that day.

She had spotted Hamish Murchison making in her direction and was relieved to note he wasn't carrying a ledger. She had more than enough on her plate as it was.

'How are you today?' He was beaming as he reached her desk.

'Fine. Yourself?'

'In the pink, actually.'

'Oh?'

'You might congratulate me.' He was still beaming.

She had no idea what he was on about. 'Why should I do that?'

'Haven't you heard?'

Lena shook her head. 'About what?'

'I've been promoted into a junior management position, starting next month. A rung up the ladder and more money to boot.'

She stared at him. 'Junior management?'

'That's right.'

She was incredulous. The man was incompetent, to say the least. Why, it wasn't that long ago she'd suggested he find himself another job as he was absolutely useless in the one he had. Now he'd been promoted!

'Well?' he prompted.

'Congratulations,' she replied through gritted teeth.

'Thank you, Lena. I appreciate that.'

He had a few more words with her and then went blithely on his way, while she stared daggers at his retreating back. If anyone should have been promoted it was she. But there was fat chance of that, being a woman.

Bitterness churned inside her, and she actually felt sick. How unfair it all was. How bloody unfair! She might not have minded so much if it had been someone deserving of promotion. But Hamish Murchison!

It wasn't till later she found out Hamish belonged to the same golf club as the chairman, and that the two of them regularly had cosy little chats in the clubhouse, where Hamish had no doubt indulged in some serious brown-nosing.

The news had completely ruined the rest of her day. And now it set her thinking, yet again, about Hollywood, and America in general.

'Look, Mum. Look!' Ian exclaimed excitedly, and pulled Georgie towards the window of a toy shop they were passing.

His eyes grew wide as he stared at the fort on display. It was a cracker, festooned with gaily coloured knights and men-at-arms.

'Very nice.' Georgie smiled, eyeing the price. Nice it might be, but it certainly wasn't cheap.

Ian's mind was racing, imagining himself playing with the fort, and all the fun he would have.

She must speak to John, Georgie decided. He'd said ages ago he'd make a fort for the lad, but had simply never got round to it. She must remind him. On the other hand, Ian's birthday was on the horizon. Perhaps they could buy this one and give it to the lad. Expensive, yes. But maybe they could stretch that far.

She'd have a word later that evening.

*   *   *

'He offered me twenty quid to sleep with him.'

'My God,' Lena exclaimed. 'Someone actually propositioned you?'

'The same old chap who felt my arse. Said we could do it in a swish hotel he'd choose. Bold as brass he was.'

'You turned him down, of course?'

'Of course,' Pet replied indignantly. 'What do you take me for? I wouldn't consider such a thing for a single moment.'

Lena, noticing a glint in her friend's eyes, wasn't sure she believed that. 'Did you report him to your boss?'

Pet shook her head. 'He'd have been barred, which would have been a pity. He's rather a pleasant old coot.'

'Married?'

'He doesn't wear a wedding ring. At least, not in the club. Though who knows? Not all men do, and anyway he might take it off on coming in.'

Twenty pounds, Lena mused. An awful lot of money when you thought about it. It would certainly have boosted Pet's savings, if it hadn't been completely out of the question. You only slept with a man when you were married and he was your lawful husband.

'I still don't mind him feeling my arse though,' Pet said, and giggled. 'As long as I get a fiver afterwards. As far as I'm concerned he can have a good grope any time he likes.'

Lena wasn't at all sure she approved of that. But she could see Pet's point. 'How's the bankbook coming along?' she enquired.

'Handsomely. At a rate of knots. In fact so well I've decided to stay on at the club to make enough to have something solid behind me when I go to the States.'

Lena nodded her approval. 'Good idea.'

'It's so when I arrive there I won't have to rush into anything but will be able to take my time. Where I decide to live, for example. That kind of thing.'

Lena wished she could get a job at the Green Slipper Club and do as well as Pet. But that was a non-starter. They'd never employ anyone with a face like hers. They wanted to attract customers, not scare them away.

'I was wondering . . .' Pet began, and trailed off.

'Wondering what?'

'If he'll up his offer. Twenty-five, thirty. Possibly more. It depends how much he fancies me.'

'Pet!' Lena exclaimed.

'Oh, don't worry,' Pet replied hastily. 'I wouldn't take him up on it. Not even for a hundred quid. I'm just curious, that's all.'

'Well let it stay that way. I don't want to be friends with an immoral woman.'

Pet laughed.

'What's so funny?'

'You saying "an immoral woman". You sounded just like a minister preaching in church. Though God knows, it's been a long long time since I was in one of those.'

'Have you been to the consulate yet to get your immigration forms?'

'Actually, I have. Spoke to a nice bloke there who was very helpful. Explained the forms to me in detail.'

'When do you intend lodging them?'

'Shortly. When I get round to filling them in. The chap told me it can take a while for an application to be processed.'

On her way home Lena thought about their conversation, and Pet's being propositioned by a customer.

She hated to admit it, but why didn't she entirely believe that Pet had turned him down? Or would in the future should the stakes be raised?

She was ashamed of herself for thinking that. But, sadly, she did. Though she'd never find out the truth of the matter. Not in a million years.

Chapter 7

'Just smell that air!' Georgie enthused. 'So clean and pure it almost makes me dizzy.' They were on holiday at the cottage in Perthshire belonging to John's railway colleague.

'It is that,' John agreed.

'Chalk and cheese compared to Glasgow air. No comparison whatsoever.'

'Well, there are no chimneys belching smoke here,' John pointed out. 'Industrial and otherwise.'

'The water's the same. Pure as can be.'

He smiled. 'So you're enjoying yourself then?'

'You know I am. And you?'

'Having a whale of a time. I honestly believe I could stay on for ever. Except I have to go back to work and bring in the pennies.'

Georgie glanced out of the window she was standing in front of. 'I don't know if I could live here. I think I'd miss the bustle of Glasgow too much. Not to mention my family and friends.'

'Aye, there is that.'

Georgie spotted Ian playing amongst a stand of trees. There was no doubt he was loving it, even if he didn't have any of his wee pals to play with. Still, both she and John had tried to fill in for the missing friends and played with him quite a lot. They'd also taken him for long walks, including one to a nearby loch where John had constructed a simple fishing rod for him to try to catch brown trout. Success would have been unexpected, as the hook was in reality just an open safety pin with a worm on it, but Ian had thoroughly enjoyed himself none the less, which was the main thing.

'Do you mind if I go to the village pub for a couple of pints?' John asked. The village was about a quarter of a mile away.

'Not at all. I'll get dinner started while you're there.'

John's face lit up. 'Say an hour?'

'Fine by me.'

'Shall I bring a couple of bottles back for us to have later?'

'Why not? I'd like that.'

Just then the door burst open and Ian flew in. 'I came across a deer in the woods!' he exclaimed. 'Honestly I did. A real live deer. When it saw me it ran away.'

Both John and Georgie laughed. 'Ran away, eh?' John repeated.

'That's right, Dad. It sort of wiggled its ears and then ran off.'

'Well, well.' Georgie smiled. 'You have had an adventure. That'll be something to tell them when you return to school.'

Ian's eyes gleamed. 'Miss Hamilton might ask me to stand up in front of the class and tell them about it.'

'Will that bother you?' John asked out of curiosity. Basically a shy man, he would certainly have hated being asked to do something similar.

'Oh no,' Ian replied. 'I've stood up and told a story before.'

'About what?' Georgie queried.

'Engines. Dad's told me lots about them and I just repeated what he said.'

That amused John, as it did Georgie. He ruffled Ian's hair, then made for the open door. 'Won't be long,' he said, giving them both a small wave.

'Can I come, Dad?'

''Fraid not, son. I'm off to the pub and you're not allowed in there.'

Ian turned to Georgie.' When will I be allowed, Mum?'

'Not for years and years yet. Not until you're eighteen.'

Ian's face fell. 'That's old.'

Georgie had to smile. 'Not too old, I can assure you.'

'I wish I was eighteen now,' Ian declared.

'Don't wish your life away, son. Life's short enough as it is. Eighteen'll come round soon enough, you'll see.'

He wasn't at all convinced.

'You've been going out with this lassie quite a while now,' Chrissie said to Tom one evening.

'That's right, Mum.'

'And we still don't even know her name. Is it a secret or something?'

Tom squirmed in his chair. 'No secret.'

'Then why won't you tell us?'

'Yes, why won't you tell us?' Lena chimed in.

Tom shot his sister a murderous look. 'You keep your nose out of what doesn't concern you. Hear?'

'My, my.' Lena smiled. 'We are touchy.'

'I'm nothing of the sort.'

Lena raised an eyebrow. 'No?'

Tam glanced up from his newspaper. 'Will you two stop it?'

Lena gave a twisted smile. 'Sorry, Papa.'

'Tom?'

'Sorry, Papa.'

Lena lit a cigarette, her eyes dancing with merriment.

'I thought you might like to bring her to tea one evening,' Chrissie said casually after a few seconds' silence. 'It's high time we met her.'

Tom was acutely aware of Lena watching him, waiting for his answer. God, how his sister irritated him on occasion. He knew only too well she did it on purpose.

'I'll mention it to her,' he replied evasively.

'Has she got horns or something?' Chrissie smiled, attempting to be funny.

'Of course not, Mum. She's just an ordinary lassie, that's all.'

'Without a name,' Lena teased, which earned her a disapproving look from Tam.

'I said I'll mention it. Now can we please leave it at that?'

Chrissie rose from her chair. 'I think I'll put the kettle on. Who's for a cup of tea?'

They were on one of their walks when John suddenly came up short. 'Hang on a minute, Georgie, till I catch my breath.'

She stopped to stare at him in concern. It was not the first time this had happened. Going to him, she put an arm round his waist, noticing how pale he was. 'Are you all right?'

'Just a bit breathless. Nothing to worry about.'

She gestured towards a fallen tree. 'Can you make it over there for a sit-down?'

'What's wrong, Dad?' an anxious Ian wanted to know.

'Wheesht now,' Georgie admonished him. 'There's nothing wrong.'

'Then why's Dad all bent over?'

Georgie ignored that as she helped John to the tree, where he slumped on to the trunk.

'Came on without warning,' he said eventually, voice rasping in his throat.

'Maybe you're smoking too much?' Georgie suggested.

'Aye, it could well be that. I must cut down.' He gulped in several more breaths. 'That's better now.'

'Are you sure?'

'Stop fussing, woman. I tell you I'm fine.'

He didn't look it, she thought. Was the light playing tricks or did he have the start of dark bags under his eyes?

'We'd better get back,' she said.

'Nonsense. We'll go on.'

Georgie glanced up at the sky where, thankfully, ominous clouds had appeared. 'I think it might rain and I don't want us all to get soaked. Especially Ian. It would be a shame to end his holiday with a stinking cold.'

John could see the sense in that. 'Right, home it is then,' he declared, coming to his feet.

They had just reached the cottage and gone inside when the heavens opened.

'What do you think?'

Lena gaped at her friend, who'd turned up to their meeting wearing the most beautiful fur coat. 'My God,' she breathed. 'Where did you get that?'

'Bought it, of course.'

'It must have cost a fortune.'

Pet laughed. 'It's musquash by the way. Like?'

Lena could only shake her head in wonder and admiration. 'It's gorgeous, Pet. Absolutely gorgeous. I'd die for a coat like that.'

'I was told it suited my colouring. Do you agree?'

Lena's mind was whirling. Women like them didn't go out and buy fur coats. It was unheard of. Fur coats were for the rich. 'Yes, I do. It certainly does. But where did you get the money from?'

'My savings, naturally.'

'Your savings?' Lena was incredulous.

'I've told you how much I'm making in tips at the club. I'm coining it.'

'Even so . . .' Lena trailed off. A fur coat. Bloody hell! 'What about Hollywood? I thought you were saving up to go there?'

'I still am,' Pet protested. 'But I got to thinking, wouldn't it be better if I arrived there with a decent wardrobe in tow? That way I'll hopefully make an instant impression with the casting directors. The people who hire and fire actors and actresses.'

That sounded reasonable to Lena. A good idea, actually.

'As regards the coat, I didn't pay anything like the retail cost. I got it trade and a discount on top as well. It was just too good an opportunity to pass up.'

'And how did you manage that?' Lena asked.

'The little man who feels my arse turned out to be a furrier. We got chatting one night and he said if I dropped by his shop he'd see what he could do for me. So I did.'

Lena was beginning to smell a very large rat. In her experience people rarely did something for nothing. There was usually a price to be paid. 'And what did you do for him?'

'Nothing at all. I swear.'

Lena looked into Pet's eyes but couldn't see any duplicity there. Either she was telling the truth or she was going to be very good at the profession she intended getting into.

'Not a thing?'

Pet smiled. 'Well, a little bum feel on the way out each time I went there. But where's the harm in that?'

Lena reached across and ran a palm down the fur. As she'd said, it was gorgeous. 'I'm envious,' she admitted.

Pet was delighted. 'Can't you just imagine me parading down Hollywood Boulevard wearing this? Wow, eh?'

'You'll look sensational, and no mistake.'

Pet almost purred with pleasure. 'Now what have you been up to since I saw you last?'

Lena gave her a wry smile. 'Well, certainly not buying myself a fur coat.'

'Come on, wake up. You can't still be tired.'

John yawned. 'What time is it?'

Georgie told him.

'I am getting lazy, aren't I?'

'You can say that again. I've never known you spend so much time in bed.'

'It's the air.' He smiled. 'I'm just not used to it.'

Georgie noticed that the dark bags under his eyes were even more pronounced than they had been, which was worrying. And another bruise had appeared only the other day, this one on his back. Again he'd said he must have knocked himself without realising.

'Will you do me a favour, John?'

'Name it.'

'Will you go and see the doctor when we get home?'

He frowned at her. 'What ever for?'

'Something's not right. You just haven't been yourself for a while now. It's beginning to worry me.'

He took one of her hands in his and gently squeezed it. 'There's nothing wrong, Georgie. I've been a bit off colour, that's all. I'll be right as rain again before you know it.'

'Maybe so,' she conceded. 'But I'd be a lot happier if you went and spoke to the doctor. Please?'

He decided to humour her. Where was the harm in visiting the doctor? None that he could see, apart from the waste of time it would undoubtedly be. 'All right,' he agreed.

'Good. Now, are you going to get up for your cup of tea, or shall I bring it through?'

'I'll get up,' he replied.

'Then I'll go and pour.'

He swung his feet out of bed after she'd left him. It

was their last day at the cottage and they'd had a wonderful time. If they could afford it he'd bring them back the following year, he promised himself. That would be something to look forward to.

Lena was cutting Chrissie's hair, which she did every month or so. Although completely untrained she showed great skill where hair was concerned. Tam and Tom were both working late on a big project which had a deadline to meet.

'Have you seen Pet McQueen recently?' Chrissie asked.

Lena stepped back to appraise what she'd done so far. 'Only the other night, as a matter of fact. You'll never guess what she's gone and bought herself?'

'What's that?'

'A musquash fur coat.'

'Dear me,' Chrissie breathed, visibly impressed.

'She's earning pots of money at this club where she's cocktail waitressing. She says the tips are fabulous.'

'They must be if she can afford a fur coat.'

Lena decided not to elaborate on the story. It was best her mother didn't know about the furrier.

'Is she still intending to go to America?'

'So she says.'

Chrissie hesitated, then asked casually, 'And what about you? Have you made any decisions yet?'

Lena stopped to stare at the back of her mother's head. The question might have sounded casual but she knew there was a lot more to it than that.

'No decisions yet, Mum,' she said softly.

'Will you make your mind up soon?'

'I honestly don't know. What I do know is if I do decide to go it will take me ages to save up for my fare.'

'I see,' Chrissie murmured.

'I promise you one thing, though. When I do make up my mind, one way or the other, you'll be the first to be told. All right?'

'All right, lass. Thank you.'

John breezed into the kitchen carrying various lengths of wood which he placed on the table.

'Well?' Georgie demanded anxiously.

'Fit as a fiddle. The doctor said there was absolutely nothing wrong with me and that you've been worrying about nothing.'

Georgie frowned. 'Did he examine you?'

'Oh aye, the full stethoscope thing. Front and back.'

'What's the wood for, Dad?'

John beamed down at his son. 'Guess what? I'm going to make you a fort – a real humdinger of a fort. But before I start it you and I are going to sit down together and design it.'

'Oh, Dad!' Ian exclaimed, almost beside himself with excitement.

'Was it old Dr McCulloch you saw?' Georgie was still frowning.

'No. He retired recently, apparently. It's a new chap now, Dr Corrie. Young, but seemed to know his stuff. I found him quite affable and easy to talk to, which Dr McCulloch wasn't always, if you recall.'

'And he didn't find anything at all wrong with you? Come on, John, be honest.'

'He did advise I cut down smoking. Just as you did when we were away.'

'Nothing else?'

'No. And that's the God's truth.'

'So how did he explain the breathlessness, the bruising and the bags under your eyes?'

'He didn't. Simply said I was in perfect health, and that was that.'

'You did tell him about those things, didn't you?' she persisted.

'Of course.'

'And he still said there was nothing wrong with you?'

'He did. Now will you please stop fussing. The doctor wouldn't be wrong now, would he?'

'Did you also mention the tiredness?'

John let out an exasperated sigh, not wanting to admit he'd forgotten about that. 'Yes,' he lied.

Georgie stared at him, perplexed. She'd been so certain that something was wrong, but it would seem she'd been worrying unnecessarily.

'Now, we need paper and a couple of pencils,' John declared, turning to a hovering Ian.

'In that drawer,' Georgie informed them, pointing. Ian immediately hurried over and opened it, finding the paper and pencils at once. Georgie went back to her chores, unsure whether or not she was relieved. She still found it hard to accept the doctor's verdict.

'Look what I found on top of the wardrobe when I was looking for something earlier,' Chrissie said, handing Tam a photograph album.

He recognised the album and knew what was inside. Photos of Mary and James's wedding. He stared at it for a few seconds, then slowly opened it, a lump coming into his throat at the sight of the first picture: Mary and James by themselves.

'Seems like only yesterday, doesn't it?' Chrissie smiled.

Before she'd joined that bloody sect, Tam thought. When their firstborn had still been his golden lassie, and apple of his eye.

Lena and Tom watched their father, wondering how he was going to react.

'I said it seems like only yesterday,' Chrissie repeated.

Tam didn't reply. Instead, he turned to the next picture, which was a group one of the family. He'd aged, he reflected. He hadn't been quite as bald then, and he'd certainly been slimmer. Chrissie too had aged, and put on weight. Happier days, he thought. Far happier, at least where Mary was concerned.

'Tam?'

'It was a fine wedding,' he declared at last, in a quiet, reflective voice. 'James looks very smart and upstanding. Quite the bridegroom.'

'I never did like that dress I'm wearing,' Chrissie commented. 'I don't know why I bought it.'

Tam fought back the emotion that was suddenly threatening to overwhelm him. When he next spoke his voice was cracked. 'Bloody religion. It's caused far more harm than good in this world.'

Tom went cold inside to hear him say that. It made him feel sick.

Tam snapped the album shut and stared into space,

his mind full of memories of times long gone. Then he startled them all by suddenly coming to his feet and tossing the album on to his chair. 'I'm off down the pub for a couple of drams,' he declared. 'I won't be too long.'

'It was a mistake showing him that, Mum,' Lena said after Tam had left them.

Chrissie didn't reply, but picked up the album with the intention of returning it to the top of the wardrobe.

'I'm going out for a walk,' Tom said, and got up. He went to a pub as well, but not the one his father frequented.

He knew what had to be done. And it was the last thing in the world he wanted to do.

Chapter 8

'What are you doing?' Georgie asked.

'I would have thought that was obvious.' John smiled back at her. 'Putting another hole in my belt.' With a grunt, he finally managed to push the awl he was using through the leather, and began wiggling it about to enlarge the hole he had made.

'Have you lost weight or something?'

'Must have,' John replied. 'Otherwise I don't suppose I'd need the extra hole.'

'Stand up a minute.'

'Wait till I'm finished here, woman.'

When the job was finally done to his satisfaction he came to his feet and threaded the belt through the loops on his trousers. Georgie studied him. Yes, he definitely had lost weight, and she could only wonder why she hadn't noticed. In fact, he'd become quite thin, though not alarmingly so.

He was eating as much as he always did, she reflected, which wasn't all that much as he'd never been a great eater at the best of times. Unlike her brother Tom, who Chrissie often complained ate them out of house and home.

'There,' John declared, fastening the belt. 'That's better. My trousers were getting so loose on me I was scared they might fall down.' He laughed. 'Imagine that happening in the middle of Sauchiehall Street. I'd probably be arrested for indecent exposure or something.'

If he meant to make Georgie smile he failed to do so. Not a flicker cracked her face.

'Now don't you go worrying again,' John went on, wagging a finger at her. 'I'm absolutely fine. All right?'

'If you say so.'

'I do. Now why don't you get the lad ready for bed and we'll have a nice cup of tea after he's dropped off. How does that sound?'

'Lovely.'

His eyes twinkled. 'Just the two of us, if you get my meaning?'

'What *are* you suggesting?' she teased him.

'As if you didn't know.'

'I don't want to go to bed,' protested Ian, who was in the middle of a game with his old lead soldiers, pretending they were cowboys and Indians.

'You never do.'

'Can't I just stay up a wee while longer? Please, Mummy?'

''Fraid not, Ian. You've got school in the morning, don't forget.'

'Tell you what, son,' John chipped in. 'We'll let you stay up later on Friday night as you don't have school next day. How's that?'

'I suppose so,' Ian replied, knowing there was no use in any further pleading. It had to be bed.

'And I'll have another go at the fort during the weekend,' John promised.

'Can I help?'

'Of course you can. I'd expect you to.'

Mollified, Ian began stripping.

'Did you ever ask that lassie of yours about coming to tea?' Chrissie asked.

Tom looked over at her. 'She's not my lassie any more. We split up.'

Chrissie's expression changed to one of concern. 'I'm sorry to hear that. The pair of you were going out for quite some time. I thought there might have been something in it.'

'Give you the elbow, did she?' Lena taunted, unable to stop herself having a dig.

Tom glared at her. 'No, she didn't. It simply wouldn't have worked out, that's all.'

'And why's that?'

'Just because.'

Lena sniggered. 'Just because!' she mimicked. 'How pathetic is that?'

'Will you shut it!' Tom snarled.

'Enough,' Tam growled from his chair. 'You're forever bickering, the pair of you. Why can't you just try and get on for a change?'

'It isn't my fault,' Tom protested. 'She always starts it.'

'No she doesn't,' Tam contradicted him. 'You're each as bad as the other.'

'The mystery girl with no name,' Lena mused, and lit a cigarette.

'She does have a name,' Tom snapped back.

Lena raised an eyebrow.

'Well, if you must know, her name is Brigid O'Reilly. Which probably tells you why we split.'

Tam, who was putting new soles on a pair of his work boots using the cobbler's last he kept for that purpose, focused on his son. 'What did you say her name is?'

'You heard me, Papa. Brigid O'Reilly. And yes, she is a Catholic. A Fenian.'

'Dear me,' Chrissie breathed. So that was why Tom had always refused to give the lassie a name. It all made sense now.

'And you've split up?' Tam went on, having been only half listening to the conversation while he was intent on his cobbling.

'That's right.'

'Just as well. It could never have got anywhere.'

Lena glanced away, embarrassed to have been the instigator of this revelation, and wishing now she hadn't.

'Not in Glasgow anyway,' Tam added.

'Don't you think I'm aware of that, Papa?'

'Catholics and Protestants don't mix, son. And as for marriage, that's completely out of the question. Try that lark and your lives would have been made hell.'

Chrissie eyed her son shrewdly. 'So it was serious, then?'

Tom nodded.

'I see.'

'You did the right thing by nipping it in the bud,' said Tam. 'And I'm pleased you've finally told us.'

'Brigid and I talked it over,' Tom said slowly, 'and we both came to the same conclusion. She said I'd have to turn Catholic before she'd ever consider marrying me. Which of course I could never do.'

'Quite right, son. It's unthinkable.'

Chrissie's heart was softer than that, though she knew what her husband was saying. She truly felt for Tom. She'd speak to him alone at some point and explain how sympathetic she was.

'Catholics and Protestants.' Tom shook his head. 'Why can't they just get on? It's the same religion, after all. We're all Christian.'

'It's all to do with history,' Tam said. 'And there's a lot more to it than I know about. But as things stand each side hates, despises and mistrusts the other, and many a person has died in the past because of it.

'Anyway, it's over now,' Tom said wistfully. 'Finished.'

'You'll find someone else,' Chrissie declared. 'You'll see. As they say, there's plenty more fish in the sea.'

'Aye, that's true,' Tam agreed.

Were there? Tom wondered. At that moment he couldn't have cared less, for he was missing Brigid more than he would ever have admitted. His sense of loss was profound.

Willie Winning took the controls back from John. 'You're really getting the hang of it now,' he declared. 'You'll be a good driver when you finally get promotion.'

John had thoroughly enjoyed his lesson. It was the custom for drivers to train up firemen to the point where they could apply for promotion, and Willie found John a keen and observant pupil, who caught on quickly and was easy to teach. The engine they were on was a Jones goods engine, number 108, the first 4–6–0 ever to be built in Britain.

'How long do you think I'll have to wait?' John asked.

'You're relatively young yet. A few more years, I'd say. Then make your application.'

'I'll do that.'

'In the meantime I'll let you build up experience. Give you lots of practice and advice.'

'Thanks, Willie.'

'Don't mention it. I remember my days as a fireman. It was my big dream to become a driver, and no doubt it's the same with you.'

John picked up his shovel and flipped open the door to the firebox. Bending to his task, he began to heave in lumps of coal and shale till the inside of the box looked like the gate to hell itself.

Sweat was running off him in rivers.

'I've been meaning to speak to you,' Tam said, when he and Tom were on their way to McNair's.

'What about, Papa?'

'That lassie of yours.'

Tom glanced sideways at his father but didn't reply, waiting for Tam to go on.

'Mary and her religion is bad enough for one family to have to contend with. But if you'd gone ahead and married this Brigid lass . . .' He broke off and shook his head.

'I realised that, Papa,' Tom said softly.

'All I want to say is how sorry I am for you.'

'Thanks.'

Tam sighed. 'Life can be a right bastard at times, and no mistake.'

'What if I had gone ahead, married Brigid and turned? What then, Papa?'

'You'd have been a fool, son.'

'But what would have happened?' Tom persisted.

Tam took his time in replying. 'We'd all have suffered the consequences. Believe me.'

Lena was depressed. She sat at her desk staring blindly at a ledger, thinking about how miserable she was when she should have been hard at work.

It was the same old thing that came back to haunt her time after time. Would she ever meet a man who'd be interested in her? Perhaps even love her? She gave a wry smile. Pigs would fly first.

She loved children, but was probably never going to have any. She might not appear on the surface to be the maternal type, but deep down she was, and she positively ached to have a baby of her own.

Enough of this! she scolded herself. She was becoming maudlin, and that would never do.

Pushing the ledger away she rose and headed for the ladies. She needed a fag, and there she could have one.

John suddenly choked, his eyes bulging, his hand going to his throat.

Georgie looked across the table at him in alarm. 'What's wrong?'

He pushed his chair back and ran to the sink, where he vomited violently into the basin, staring in horror at the bright-red blood which spattered its sides. Again and again he threw up, till at last there was nothing left to come.

'Dear God!' Georgie was standing at his side. What was going on?

Finally John finished being sick. Straightening, he sucked in breath after breath.

'Here, let me,' Georgie said, voice shaking, and began wiping the blood from his lips and chin. Ian was sitting staring at his father as if John had suddenly sprouted horns.

'I'm fine now,' John declared, taking the towel from Georgie and finishing the job himself.

'What brought that on?'

He shook his head. 'Absolutely no idea. I suddenly felt very queasy, and then this.' He glanced down at the blood-spattered sink. 'Fucking hell!' he muttered to himself.

'It's back to the doctor for you this very night,' Georgie said firmly. 'And I don't want any argument about it.'

'All right,' a thoroughly shaken John agreed. That had given him the fright of his life.

'And what's more, I'm coming with you.'

'What about Ian?'

'We'll drop him off at my mum's, and pick him up again later.'

'Just give me a few minutes to pull myself together,' John said. Woozily he made his way back to his chair and slumped on to it. His face had gone completely white, the dark bags under his eyes more accentuated than ever.

Ian, still staring at his father, burst into tears.

*   *   *

'So what did the doctor say?' Chrissie demanded when Georgie and John returned from the surgery. Tam, Lena and Tom were anxiously looking on, their concern obvious.

'He's making an appointment for John to see a specialist,' Georgie replied.

'Has he no idea what the problem is?' Tam asked.

Georgie shook her head. 'If he has he wouldn't be drawn. Just said seeing a specialist was the best thing.'

'Can I sit down?' John queried, attempting a smile that didn't quite come off.

Tom was instantly on his feet. 'Sit here.'

'Thanks.'

'How are you feeling now?' asked Lena.

'Absolutely terrible. I'm so tired it took all my willpower to walk back from the surgery.'

Lena didn't like the sound of that one little bit. None of them did.

'Would a cup of tea help?' Chrissie suggested.

'It certainly wouldn't do any harm.'

'I'll put the kettle on,' Lena volunteered, and set about the task.

'So, when do you think you'll be seeing this specialist?' Tam queried.

'The doctor couldn't be specific,' Georgie answered for John. 'But he did say it should be some time soon.'

'That's good.' Tam nodded.

'And in the meantime he's to stay off work,' Georgie added.

'I don't know about that,' John protested, glancing over at her.

'You'll do as the doctor told you,' Georgie snapped back.

'But my wages . . .'

'We'll manage,' she interjected, her expression resolute.

John sighed. When Georgie spoke in that tone of voice there was no gainsaying her.

'I'll have to let them know at the station.'

'Don't you worry about that. I'll go there tomorrow morning directly after Ian's left for school.' She shuddered inwardly, remembering the mess in the sink which she'd have to clear up when they got home. That wasn't going to be exactly pleasant.

'How about a bite to eat, John?' Chrissie asked. 'I've got some nice newly made scones.'

He shook his head. 'No thanks.'

'Are you sure?'

'They are lovely,' Tom told him, having wolfed down four earlier.

'Honestly, I couldn't.'

When it was time to leave Tom went with them to give assistance to John should it be needed, while Lena cleared the tea things and Tam and Chrissie sat wrapped in their anxious thoughts.

'What do you think?' Tam asked later as he and Chrissie were getting ready for bed.

'He's lost so much weight since I saw him last. I was quite shocked by his appearance.'

'Aye.' Tam nodded. 'I noticed that myself.'

'He's nothing but skin and bone.'

'Georgie must be worried sick.'

'I know I would be if it was you.'

Tam sat on the edge of the bed and put on his pyjama top. 'I wonder what is wrong with him? Could be almost anything.'

'Whatever, I just hope it isn't serious.'

'It looks serious enough to me, girl, and I'm no doctor.' Tam slowly shook his head. 'Vomiting blood. Lots of it. Not to mention the weight loss and permanent tiredness. Makes me wonder if it isn't consumption. There's always a lot of that about in Glasgow.'

'Oh, please God it isn't. That would be terrible.'

'He seems to have all the symptoms that I've heard of.'

Consumption! That would be more or less a death sentence. Some did survive, but precious few. She'd even heard of entire families being taken off by that dreadful scourge.

'Well, all we can do is wait and hear what the specialist has to say.' Tam yawned.

'I'll drop by on them tomorrow morning,' Chrissie declared. 'Georgie might need some help.'

'Good idea. You do that.'

When she was curled up at Tam's broad back Chrissie closed her eyes and prayed for John; prayed he'd soon get over whatever it was and be back to full health again.

'How did you get on?' John asked when Georgie returned from the station next morning.

'I saw the manager, Mr Laidlaw, and explained the situation to him. He was very sympathetic and sent you his best wishes.'

'Aye, he's a decent man is Laidlaw.' John, who was

propped up in bed, where Georgie had insisted he stay, nodded.

'He also said that if you're off for more than a fortnight he'll speak to the Union, and they'll probably send someone round.'

'Good. But I hope it doesn't come to that.'

'Now,' Georgie declared, suddenly businesslike. 'How about some breakfast? I could make you a poached egg. Does that appeal?'

He shook his head. 'I'm simply not hungry, lass.'

'Well, you must have something. What do you fancy?'

'Nothing, Georgie, honestly.'

'Won't you just try, for my sake?' she pleaded.

He took a deep breath. 'All right. A poached egg it is then.'

'Coming right up.' And with that Georgie swept from their bedroom.

In the event John only managed a few mouthfuls before saying he couldn't take any more. He wasn't sure he would, but he did somehow succeed in keeping those few mouthfuls down.

The day had finally arrived for John to be told the results of the extensive tests that had been carried out on him. At the appointed time he and Georgie presented themselves at the specialist's office.

Dr Abrams was considered one of the top men in his field. He was tall and thin, with a sallow complexion and a beak of a nose. His dark-brown eyes had an intense penetrating quality about them as if he was visually dissecting you.

'Please sit down,' he said, indicating chairs in front of his desk. Nervously, John and Georgie sat as instructed. Once they had done so, Abrams also seated himself.

'Your results are in, and conclusive,' he said gently. 'And they're not good, I'm afraid.'

The breath caught in Georgie's throat, and her mouth began to move as she offered up a silent prayer.

'You have leukaemia, Mr Mair. And as I said, the tests are conclusive.'

John swallowed hard.

Stunned, Georgie stopped praying. 'What's the treatment?' she asked hoarsely at last.

'Sadly, there isn't one.'

'There must be!'

'I'm afraid not. Once diagnosed all we can do is let the condition take its course.'

John blinked, and blinked again. 'Am I going to die?'

'Yes. That will be the outcome.'

Georgie sagged. This was her worst nightmare come true.

'How . . .' John swallowed hard. 'How long?'

'That I can't be specific about. But your condition is well advanced, Mr Mair. A year at most. Perhaps only months.' He paused, then added softly, 'I'm terribly sorry.'

John could only smile ruefully at that. 'Not half as sorry as I am, doctor. Not half as sorry.'

Chapter 9

It was at Pet's request that she and Lena went for a walk in the park. She desperately needed to get some fresh air about her, she explained, after nights of working in a smoky nightclub. She came quickly to the point.

'Well, my immigration papers have come through at last,' she announced. 'They arrived in yesterday's post.'

'Congratulations!' Lena beamed. 'You must be excited!'

'Oh, I am. Thrilled to bits actually. Hollywood, here I come with bells on.'

Lena laughed at the picture that conjured up.

'Next thing is to book my passage, which I'll do as soon as possible.'

'You have enough money in the bank, then?'

'Enough, with pots to spare. The Green Slipper Club has been very good to me.'

'And the man who feels your bum?'

'Of course. Which, I'm happy to report, he does regularly at a fiver a grope. God bless the lecherous sod.'

Lena still thought there might be more to it than that,

but had never pressed her friend on the subject. If Pet had taken it further then that was her affair.

'Still not made up your mind?' Pet asked.

'I'm afraid not. There are times when I'm keen as mustard, other times when I think it would be a big mistake. For me, anyway.'

'Well, if you do decide to come I'll always be there waiting with a place for you to stay.'

Lena smiled. 'Thanks, Pet. I'm going to miss you, you know.'

'And I'll miss you, Lena. Not that we'll lose touch. I shall be writing regularly.'

'And I shall be replying regularly. You have my word.'

They walked a little way in silence, each deep in thought.

'Can I ask you a favour?' Pet said eventually.

'Naturally. What is it?'

'Will you come and see me off? I'd like that.'

Lena hesitated for a moment. What if it was during the week when she should be at work? Oh, to hell with it, she decided. She'd lie about being unwell on the day. It was a special occasion, after all.

'I'll be there Pet. Waving from the quayside when the boat pulls away.'

'Thanks. I appreciate that.'

'Who else will be coming along?'

'My parents.'

'It'll be a sad day for them.'

'Aye, it will that. But it can't be helped. I'm on my way and nothing will stop me.'

Lena heard the note of fierce determination in her friend's voice which told her that was only too true.

'I'm off to the land of peach and orange trees,' Pet enthused. 'Hollywood and all its glory.'

How wonderful, Lena thought. How utterly wonderful.

Georgie opened the door to find her sister Mary standing there clutching a sheaf of religious pamphlets and papers published by the sect, and inwardly groaned.

'Mary!' she exclaimed. 'This is a surprise. Come on in.'

'I'm ever so sorry to hear about John,' Mary said as they entered the kitchen. 'You must be devastated.'

Georgie nodded. 'That's one way of putting it.'

'How is he?'

'Not too well, I'm afraid.'

'I thought I might speak to him?'

Shit, Georgie thought. That wasn't a good idea at all. Like the rest of the family John had no time for Mary's religious megalomania.

'It's important,' Mary added, grasping Georgie by the arm.

'How did you hear about him anyway?' Georgie asked.

'One of my neighbours works out of the same station as John. His wife mentioned it a few days ago during a natter we had in the street.'

'Would you like a cup of tea while you're here?'

Mary shook her head. 'Not for me, thanks. Can I see John?'

Oh dear, Georgie thought. This was difficult. 'I don't think that's possible, Mary. He's very frail, and asleep most of the time. I wouldn't want him to get agitated in any way.'

Mary's eyes gleamed with fervour. 'If he's dying, Georgie, I must show him the light before he goes. Save his soul from eternal damnation, for only those who believe will be saved by the good Lord, God Almighty.'

'John has his own beliefs,' Georgie stated quietly. 'And now is not the time or place to challenge those.'

'Nonsense. It's the perfect time!'

Georgie was beginning to get irritated by her older sister. How dare she come crashing in here like this on her so-called holy mission? 'I say it's not, and that's an end of it.'

'You'd send his soul to eternal damnation? The man you purportedly love?' Mary almost screeched.

'Enough of this claptrap,' Georgie replied harshly. 'I want you to leave before you wake John. He needs all the sleep he can get.'

Mary changed tack. 'Please, Georgie? Please let me see and talk to him?' She was squeezing Georgie's arm so hard it hurt.

'No, and that's final. Now on your way, Mary.' And with that Georgie began pushing her from the room.

'At least let me leave this literature and promise me you'll get him to read it.'

'You can leave it. But whether or not he reads it is up to him.'

They were at the front door now. Georgie managed to open it, and with a final push they were both out on the landing.

'Here, take them,' Mary said, thrusting the pamphlets and papers into Georgie's hand. Georgie tore herself free, immediately stepping back inside the house and slamming the door in Mary's face. She's completely off her chump, she thought. A madwoman if ever there was one.

Returning to the kitchen, she threw the pamphlets and papers into the bin. The best place for them, she thought with grim satisfaction.

'It's a lovely cabin,' Lena said, glancing round.

'It'll do me.' Pet opened the suitcase the steward had put on top of her bunk, her musquash coat already hung up on the rail provided.

Lena went to the porthole and peered out at the river and far bank where other ships were moored. 'It's a pity your parents couldn't come,' she said.

Pet sighed. 'They just didn't feel up to it. Wanted to say their goodbyes at home. Ma said she was afraid of making a spectacle of herself by blubbing all over the place in public. As for Da, he said it would break his heart to stand there and watch me steam away out of their lives for ever.'

'I can understand that.' Lena nodded. 'It would have been very hard for both of them.'

'I would still have liked them here.' Pet smiled. 'But there we are, maybe it's for the best they aren't.'

Lena glanced again through the porthole, wondering what she'd feel like if she was the one off to America. Excited, no doubt. And probably terrified as well. It was an awfully big step Pet was taking. A giant leap into the unknown.

'Tell you what,' she said, turning to face her friend again. 'The steward said we could have a cup of coffee and some sandwiches in the salon if we wished. As there's two hours to sailing time why don't we do that and then we'll come back here and I'll help you get settled in?'

*　　*　　*

Lena had watched the ropes being cast off, and now the ship was beginning to stir, seemingly eager, although that could simply be her imagination, to begin its long voyage.

The TSS *Ulysses* was a cargo vessel of roughly eight thousand tons carrying a maximum of six passengers. On this particular trip, it was headed for the port of New York with a cargo of whisky and Shetland ponies, and four passengers.

It was a chilly day, and blowy, with a hint of possible snow or sleet in the air. Lena shivered and pulled the collar of her coat tighter round her neck.

The ship started moving away from the quayside, twin screws churning the water at its rear. Overhead, seagulls were raucously crying as they swooped and soared high above the deck.

There was a huge lump in Lena's throat as she stared at her friend who was gazing back, wearing her musquash coat to keep out the cold.

The ship's horn blew, then blew again, and the ship moved forward on its way down the Clyde to the Atlantic.

'Goodbye! Good luck!' Lena yelled, and frantically waved.

Pet waved back, and seemed to be yelling something as well, which Lena couldn't make out, the words being carried away by the wind, as no doubt hers were as well.

'Good luck, Pet!' Lena repeated in a whisper, a hollow emptiness filling her. Pet was the only close friend she had had in her life, and now she was gone.

After a while she turned and headed for the stop from where a tram would take her home, tears rolling down her cheeks as she walked. The parting had been much worse than she'd anticipated. An awful lot worse.

John came awake to the sound of the front door being shut. A few moments later Chrissie came into the bedroom.

'Oh, you're awake then?' She smiled.

'Just.'

'Georgie won't be long. She's gone out to get the messages. Would you like me to sit with you for a while?'

'That would be nice.'

Chrissie pulled over a chair.

'I was having such strange dreams,' John said in a weak voice.

'Nightmares?'

'Not really. Dreams. I was back with my parents when I was young. They had a newsagent's shop, you know, down Scotland Street. Did very well out of it too. God bless them.' He drew in a deep breath. 'Long gone now, of course. My parents, I mean.'

'It is some years back,' Chrissie agreed.

'Well, they were already getting on when they rescued me from the orphanage, and adopted me. The two of them must have been in their mid-fifties. Never had any children of their own, and then at that age decided to adopt one and I was chosen.'

'They were very nice people, from all accounts.'

'They were. I think you'd have liked them, and they you and Tam. They certainly would have adored Georgie. But sadly they were already gone by the time I met her.' John's eyes misted over in memory. 'Did Georgie ever mention that I'm English?' he asked eventually.

Chrissie frowned. 'No, she hasn't.'

'Well it's true. Though I've no idea whereabouts in England I was born. I've always suspected it was Newcastle, though I've no proof of that.'

'Your parents never told you?'

'I never even knew I was adopted until after they were dead. It was quite a shock when it came to light, I can tell you.' He suddenly smiled. 'But finding out I was actually English was an even bigger one!'

'I can well imagine!'

'English!' He laughed, and shook his head.

'But you're Scots now,' Chrissie declared. 'At least, that's how you've been brought up. And with a good Scots tongue in your head.'

'My surname was Miller, apparently,' he went on. 'So I would have been John Miller and not John Mair.'

'Have you any idea what happened to your original parents?'

'None at all, Chrissie. There was no reference to either of them.' He glanced at her, and guessed what she was thinking. 'Yes, I could well be illegitimate. A bastard. I simply have no way of knowing.'

'That's often the case,' Chrissie mused. 'A lassie has a child out of wedlock and puts it into an orphanage, or some other such institution. Wisely in my opinion. Though it's probably hard on both of them.'

'Aye,' John agreed. 'It probably is. A woman carrying a bastard isn't exactly highly thought of.'

'However, you don't know what your circumstances were. It's all supposition on your part. You might have been placed in the orphanage as the result of some tragedy or other. Don't forget the great influenza epidemics of years ago. Perhaps both your real parents died as a result of one of those.'

'Maybe,' John said quietly.

'One thing I do know: you've been a damn good husband to Georgina, and a fine son-in-law to Tam and me. We're proud of you.'

He closed his eyes for a second or so. 'Thank you,' he whispered.

'Now, how about a cup of tea? Georgie said you might like one when you woke up.'

'That would be lovely.'

'You just stay where you are and I'll put the kettle on.'

He had to smile. 'I'm hardly going anywhere, now am I?'

That made her smile too. 'I won't be two ticks.'

'Of a lamb's tail,' he called after her as she left the bedroom, and heard her chuckle.

Tom was standing outside the dance hall where Brigid had taken him to hear jazz. The place the Bright Young Things frequented. He had intended to go inside, but now he was here he had doubts. What if he should run into Brigid? What then? If she was there he'd have to speak to her; to do otherwise would be rude. But a conversation would only be painful for the pair of them.

Then a new thought struck him. What if she was there with someone else? Someone she'd met since he and she had broken up? That would be unbearable – and highly embarrassing. He'd probably go all red in the face and look a right charlie.

If only he still didn't miss her so much. Not a day went by when he didn't think of her. Recall their times together. The fun they'd had. What a superb dancer she was. How good the pair of them were together.

Hell, he just missed her company.

Gritting his teeth, Tom turned away. He wouldn't go in. Not now, or ever. Instead, he headed for the nearest pub to drown his sorrows. And at the bottom of every glass Brigid's face stared back at him.

'Is Daddy going to die?'

Georgie stopped what she was doing, the question stabbing her like a knife.

'Is he, Mum?'

Georgie sighed. Ian had to be answered. And truthfully too. He had to be told at some point, and now was as good a time as any. But that didn't make it any easier.

'Come and sit down, son,' she said. Taking him by the hand she led him to a chair, and squatted down beside him. God, but this was going to be difficult. She stroked his hair – hair the same colour as his dad's. Then she looked into eyes that also reminded her of John. 'You know your dad's very ill, don't you?'

Ian nodded.

'He's suffering from something called leukaemia.'

'Leukaemia,' Ian repeated, stumbling slightly over the unfamiliar word. 'What's that?'

'It's to do with Dad's blood. It isn't working properly.'

Ian frowned. 'You mean it's gone bad?'

'That's right.'

'So why don't they fix it?'

Georgie longed for a cigarette, but didn't want to move away to get it. 'They just can't, I'm afraid.'

Ian's eyes grew wide. 'So Dad is going to die?'

'Yes, he is. There's absolutely nothing the doctors can do.'

'When is he going to die?'

'We don't know. It could be any time.' Georgie sighed, then took Ian into her arms and hugged him tight, his little chest heaving in her embrace.

'I don't want my dad to die,' he whispered in her ear.

'Neither do I. None of us do. It's simply the way things are.'

She was certain he would cry. But, to her surprise, he didn't, though he was clearly extremely distressed.

'Can I go out and play?' he asked when she eventually released him.

That surprised her too. 'If you wish. Just don't stay out too long. Don't forget you've got school in the morning.'

At the door to the kitchen he stopped. 'Does Dad know he's going to die?'

'Yes, son, he does.'

Ian ran down the stairs as fast as he was able, and then along the street in the same way. There was a secret spot he knew: an old building currently lying empty which you could access through a window that had been left unlocked. And there he went to curl up in a corner all by himself, and stayed until it was time to go home again.

'Do you think he'd like a bottle of whisky? A dram might do him a power of good.'

'I doubt it, Tam. But take one along if you like. I could be wrong.'

Tam nodded that he understood.

Chrissie hesitated, then said, 'You haven't seen him for a wee while, so be prepared for a shock. He's lost even more weight, though I wouldn't have thought it possible. He's now only skin and bone.'

Tam stared grimly at his wife. 'That bad, eh?'

'Worse. Believe me.'

He turned to Lena. 'Are you sure you won't come with us?'

She shook her head. 'I'll visit another night, Papa. Three of us there might be too much for him.'

That wasn't her real reason for not going. She was terrified of death, and had been for a long time. To have been in the presence of someone so close to it would have given her the willies. It was something she shared with her sister Mary.

'Well, we'd better be getting along then,' said Tam.

He bought the bottle en route, but, as Chrissie had anticipated, John declined to have a dram. Even a weak one was beyond him, he informed them. Chrissie had also been right about Tam's emotions at the sight of his son-in-law. He was shocked beyond belief.

Lena eagerly ripped open the letter bearing the Hollywood postmark. It was the first she had received since Pet had left.

Quickly she scanned the three pages the envelope contained. Pet had arrived safely and soon found a nice place to stay, even if it was a little expensive. It was all true about the peach and orange trees, especially the orange ones. They were everywhere. In fact she had two in her back garden, which for some reason the Americans called 'the yard'.

Within a couple of days of arrival she'd registered with Central Casting who supplied extras to all the films. So far she hadn't been given any work, but it was early days yet.

The weather was glorious, the sky a permanent duck-egg blue, with an occasional deeper shade of that colour. She'd already acquired something of a tan, though she was being careful not to get too much of one as it might go against her when casting was taking place.

Oh, but she was enjoying herself. Revelling in the experience. Ever so glad she'd come. It had been a good move, and no mistake. She didn't miss rainy, cold Glasgow one little bit.

After she'd finished the letter Lena re-read it, then laid it aside. She let out a huge sigh, envious to the very core of her being.

Chapter 10

'I'm Miss Hamilton,' the lady at the front door explained with a smile. She was holding an obviously upset Ian by the hand.

'Come in,' Georgie said quickly. 'Is something wrong?'

'Ian's had a bit of an accident,' Miss Hamilton informed her. 'Nothing serious. Simply didn't make it to the lavatory in time.'

Ian hung his head in shame.

'I see.'

'Sorry, Mum,' Ian mumbled.

'Then we'd better get you sorted out, hadn't we?'

Ian nodded.

'Thank you for bringing him home, Miss Hamilton. That was kind of you.'

'Not at all. But while I'm here I would like a little bit of a chat.'

'Oh? Well, of course. Why don't you take a seat while I attend to Ian in our room? We can have a cup of tea when I get back.'

'Lovely.'

Georgie took Ian through to the bedroom, where John was fast asleep. 'What happened?' she asked.

'Are you angry with me, Mum?'

'Of course not. Accidents happen. That's all it was, wasn't it?'

Ian nodded.

'Right then. Get those wet things off and I'll look out some fresh.'

Georgie handed him a towel, then went about producing clean shorts and underwear. She made sure Ian was dry before allowing him to put them on.

'There.' She smiled. 'Good as new.'

'Can I go back to school now?'

'Let's see what Miss Hamilton has to say, shall we?'

Miss Hamilton welcomed the idea of Ian's returning to school as it allowed her to speak to Georgie in private. 'See you again shortly,' she said to him.

'Say thank you for bringing me home, Miss Hamilton,' Georgie instructed him.

'Thank you for bringing me home, Miss Hamilton. I'm sorry for what happened.'

'Don't you worry about that, Ian. Now off you go.'

When Ian had left them a puzzled Georgie returned to the kitchen and put the kettle on. 'That's most unlike Ian,' she apologised. 'In fact I can't remember him wetting himself since coming out of nappies. He's always been excellent where that's concerned.'

'I must say I was surprised as well. There's been no indication of anything like this since he started with us.'

Miss Hamilton was a good-looking woman whom

Georgie judged to be in her mid-to late twenties. She seemed to radiate some sort of inner glow which shone from her face. Georgie had taken an instant liking to her, and was certain she was a very good teacher.

'I have some chocolate biscuits in.' Georgie smiled, wondering what this was all about. 'Would you care for one?'

'Oh, yes, please. I adore chocolate biscuits of any kind. And to be honest, if I'm not careful chocolate itself will be my downfall one of these fine days.'

Georgie laughed. 'I know what you mean. I have to be careful in that direction myself.'

'Anyway,' Miss Hamilton went on, becoming serious. 'This has given me the opportunity to talk to you. I was going to pay you a visit shortly, and Ian's little accident just gave me the excuse to make it sooner.'

Georgie studied her guest. 'Is something wrong?'

'It's Ian's behaviour. He's always been such a sunny little chap. Outgoing, and keen on his lessons. But all that has changed recently. He's become moody and introverted. Sullen, you could even say. And not the least interested in his schoolwork any more. Frankly, he's worrying me, so I've come to ask if there's anything wrong at home. Anything I should be aware of.'

'Do you mind if I smoke?'

'No, go ahead. I don't myself but it doesn't bother me.'

Georgie lit up, and inhaled deeply. She'd had no idea, not an inkling, that Ian was acting up at school, but it was understandable really when you thought about it. Her heart went out to her son. 'It's Ian's dad,' she said slowly. 'My husband.' She told Miss Hamilton what the situation was.

'How awful,' said Miss Hamilton, when Georgie had finished. 'No wonder the wee lad's the way he is.'

'Now you understand.'

'Fully.'

'He . . .' Georgie hesitated, and took a deep breath. 'He's been quite good about it at home, though he has been more reserved than usual. I should have thought about school, though, and perhaps called in and spoken to the headmistress. But to be honest, it just never crossed my mind.'

'And why should it when you've already got so much on your plate,' Miss Hamilton said sympathetically. 'It must be terrible for you. Absolutely ghastly.'

Georgie nodded, emotion suddenly almost overwhelming her. 'Excuse me,' she croaked, and turned away so Miss Hamilton couldn't see the anguish flooding her face.

'Why don't you sit down and I'll make the tea?' Miss Hamilton offered.

Georgie took her up on it.

'How are you doing for money, lass?' Tam asked a few days later.

'We're all right, Papa. The Union, God bless them, are taking care of things.'

'I thought that would be the case, but I just wanted to make sure. You never know. And what about . . .' He shifted uneasily in his chair, thinking this might sound ghoulish. But it had to be asked none the less. He cleared his throat. 'Expenses for . . . well, when it happens.'

'You mean the funeral?'

'Aye.'

'The Union will also take care of that. It's John's due being a fully paid-up member. I've had a representative round here on several occasions. A nice man called Mr Duncan. He's assured me there'll also be a pension. A small one, but welcome anyway.'

'That's something of a relief for you.'

'I'll have to go out and work as the pension won't cover everything. But we'll deal with that bridge when we come to it.'

'It's a dreadful business,' Tam muttered, shaking his head. 'I can't imagine what you're going through. Hell, no doubt.'

That was putting it mildy, Georgie thought. Every time she looked in the mirror it was as if she'd aged even more. At this rate she was going to be an old crone before long.

'Just remember,' Tam went on, 'your mother and I are there if there's anything you need help with.'

'I know that, Papa. Thank you.' She looked away, suddenly overwhelmed by a kind of anger. Why John, she inwardly raged. Why him? He was such a good, upstanding man. Good husband. Good father. Why take him when there were so many rotten bastards around who were being allowed to carry on with their lives? It was so wrong. What was God thinking of to let such a thing happen? 'Oh, Papa!' she wailed.

Quickly going to her, Tam took her into his arms. 'There there, lass,' he crooned in a throaty voice. 'There there.'

She sobbed against his shoulder, filled with a combination of anger and grief.

'Someone once told me life isn't fair,' Tam said quietly. 'How right they were.'

It was as if he'd read her thoughts, Georgie reflected. Just like Papa to do that. She agreed wholeheartedly with what he'd just said. Life was anything but fair.

Lightning lit up the inside of the bedroom, followed a few moments later by a heavy crack of thunder. Rain was lashing against the window.

John threw one arm out, then the other. His body began writhing as though he was fighting invisible demons.

More lightning, more thunder. Rain was driving even harder against the window. Georgie didn't know what time it was, and didn't care. All she wanted was for the storm to stop. It was beginning to scare her.

A flailing arm caught her a blow across the chest, causing her to grunt with pain. That had hurt. Perhaps she should wake him? But deep down she didn't have the heart to – at least not yet. Hopefully he'd soon calm down again.

This time it was a glancing blow across her cheek which knocked her head sideways. A nail had caught her cheek, ripping it slightly to draw a trickle of blood.

She cringed when there was another peal of thunder, this one seemingly directly overhead. What a night, she thought.

'Georgie?'

She was startled, for he'd been sleeping only seconds previously. 'What is it, John?'

'I was having a nightmare.'

'I know. You were thrashing about something terrible.'

'Did I wake you?'

'No, the storm did.' In fact it was a combination of both that had wakened her.

'Listen to that,' he said as another peal of thunder banged out. 'Loud, isn't it?'

'Very.' She hesitated, then asked, 'What was your nightmare about? Can you remember?'

'Oh yes,' he replied very softly.

'Well?' she prompted when he didn't elaborate.

'I don't think I should tell you. You'd only get upset.'

All that did was intrigue her. Now she definitely did want to hear. 'What if I promise not to get upset?'

'You will anyway.'

She wondered what persuasive line of argument she could take. 'John, we're man and wife and as such are supposed to share things. The good and the bad.'

He laughed drily in the darkness. 'I know your game, Georgie. You're trying to weasel it out of me. Well, it won't work.'

'Oh, come on, John. I'm a big girl. Let's hear it.'

He relented, though he knew he shouldn't. 'Give me your hand, Georgie.'

She took hold of his, a hand once plump and strong, now skeletal with protruding bones. A hand that was only a shadow of what it had once been.

'I was dead, Georgie,' he whispered. 'Dead, but alive at the same time. Or at least aware of what was happening.'

She could hear her heart thumping in her chest. 'Aware of what?'

'Worms eating my flesh.'

The picture conjured up in her mind filled her with terror. She wished now she hadn't pursued the subject.

'Nibbling away. My flesh vanishing morsel by morsel, bit by bit. I was screaming for help, but there was no one there. I was in my coffin, deep under the earth. Buried alive.

'Oh, John,' she whispered, not knowing what to say.

'Worms,' he repeated. 'Nasty, slimy things.' He paused for a second, then said, 'Do you know the worst thing about my nightmare?'

'What?' she croaked.

'All the while they were burrowing and nibbling the little bastards were laughing at me. They thought it was terribly funny.'

Outside, the loudest peal of thunder yet boomed out as the storm gathered even more momentum. Neither of them slept again that night.

Miss Hamilton stared in surprise as Ian suddenly got up from his desk in the middle of lessons and headed for the classroom door.

'Ian?'

He neither looked at her nor replied.

'Ian, where are you going?'

He went straight out of the door and down the corridor. He knew the gates to the playground would be shut and locked, but there was another way out of the school and he made for that. Mr Green, the janitor, had a small room where he kept all manner of things: mops, pails, brushes, ladders and the like. There was also a window there, easily opened, from where it was only a short drop to the street.

Minutes later Ian was on the pavement and walking in the direction of his secret spot. He wanted to be alone. No more Miss Hamilton, no more other pupils. Just himself.

Once inside the empty house he lay down and curled up in the same corner as before. Putting a thumb into his mouth, he began to suck.

Lena was delighted to receive another letter from Pet. Sent, as Pet wrote in it, from the land of eternal sunshine.

Work as a film extra was coming in regularly now, and she was employed most days of the week. She'd already made lots of friends amongst the other extras and come to know a few 'important people': in other words, people who could help her with her career. One of them had recommended she take voice lessons with the prime objective of losing her strong Scottish accent. Such lessons would be expensive but she was determined to have them come what may.

She hadn't actually met any of the big stars so far, but she had been in close proximity to several, including Douglas Fairbanks and John Gilbert, no less. Both men were absolutely gorgeous, dishy as could be and, from what she'd heard, extremely pleasant. The actresses were a different kettle of fish entirely. Most of them were out-and-out bitches, who were just as nasty to each other as they were to the female extras they encountered. She'd been advised to stay away from them whenever possible as the one thing they hated most of all was another pretty female, star or otherwise.

Pet had found a better and more convenient place to

stay, an apartment which she was sharing with another extra called Jolene. The two of them were getting along famously.

Pet had kept the juiciest bit for last. She'd met a guy called Dwayne. They'd been out together once, and would shortly be going out again. She'd let Lena know more about Dwayne in her next letter.

'What are you doing up?' Georgie demanded when John appeared in the kitchen carrying Ian's fort.

He grinned. 'Is it against the rules?'

'No, of course not. But you're supposed to be in bed.'

'The doctor never said I had to stay there. Certainly not in my presence.'

She had to admit it was true. The doctor had never actually said that. 'Well, you'd better sit down and I'll put the kettle on.'

John did as instructed. 'Know what I'd really like?'

'What?'

'A proper drink.' He sighed. 'Pity there's none in the house.'

Georgie smiled. 'But there is. The remains of that whisky Papa brought some time back.'

'The very dab. I'll have a dram,' he enthused.

Georgie frowned at him. 'You seem very sprightly all of a sudden.'

'I don't know why but I'm full of beans. That's why I decided to come on through and finish Ian's fort. There's not a lot left to do and I want to get it done.'

Georgie poured his whisky, then one for herself. It was lovely having him up and about like this. A real treat.

'*Slainte*!' John toasted her when she'd handed him his glass. She returned the gesture. 'Now,' he went on. 'I need glue, that sharp knife I use, and the paints and brushes.'

'You just sit there and I'll get them for you.'

He gazed lovingly at her as she moved about, wishing with all his heart that things could have been different. If he'd done one wise thing in his life it was marrying Georgie. He could never have chosen better, not in a thousand years. The pair of them just fitted.

John glanced at the recessed bed where Ian lay fast asleep. The wee fella would take it badly when he was gone. But Ian was young, and the young recovered quickly. At least, he hoped and prayed that would be the case.

Georgie spread newspaper in front of John, and began placing the items he'd requested on it. Soon he was hard at work.

'I'm amazed you're keeping that whisky down,' she commented after a while. 'You've hardly kept any food in your stomach for ages now.'

'Yes, it is a bit of a miracle, isn't it? Just don't knock it, that's all.'

'I'm not!' she protested.

'Fine,' he replied cheerily. 'In fact, that first dram was so good I think I'll have another. If you don't mind, that is?'

'Are you sure, John?'

'Absolutely.'

Georgie rose from the table to refill his glass, while he concentrated on the task in hand.

'I've been meaning to speak to you for some time now,' he said casually a few minutes later.

'About what?'

'Us.'

'What about us?'

'Well actually, it's really about you.'

She was puzzled. What was he driving at? 'I'm listening.'

He cleared his throat, then bent again to the fort. 'You're still a young woman, Georgie. Too young to stay a widow for the rest of your life. I wouldn't want that.'

It was as though she'd been punched in the midriff. 'Go on.'

'I'm hoping, if the right man happens along, that you'll eventually remarry. I would approve of that.'

'Never!' she exclaimed fiercely. 'That will never happen.'

He stopped to stare at her. 'Don't be silly, Georgie. I'm trying to be practical about this.'

'I will never remarry, John, not even if Prince Charming came along. And that's final.'

'There's Ian to consider, don't forget. He'll need a father, or at least a father figure. Surely you wouldn't deny him that?'

'There's Papa. He'll be all the father figure Ian will need. I'll see to it.'

'It's not the same, Georgie. Not by a long chalk, and you know it. What you want is someone who lives in the same house and takes a day-to-day interest in the lad. Tam, with the best will in the world, just couldn't do that.'

Georgie, reluctantly, had to concede he had a point there. But at the moment she simply couldn't think about what he was proposing. 'I'll never find anyone to take your place, John.'

He smiled. 'I'm flattered. But it wouldn't be to take my place. It would be a whole new relationship. Nothing whatsoever to do with me.'

'Nonsense.'

'It isn't nonsense at all,' he protested.

'Yes, it is.'

'No, it is not!'

Georgie lit a cigarette, cross with him, and hurt too. 'I don't want to talk about this any more.'

'Then we won't.'

She smoked in silence, then stubbed out the remains. 'Would you remarry if the positions were reversed?' she asked softly.

'Yes. If I met the right woman, that is. Life goes on for those left behind, after all. And that's a fact, harsh as it may sound.'

She bit back her disappointment. 'You really would?'

'If the right woman came along,' he repeated. 'I may be many things, but I'm not a bloody martyr. And neither should you be. If I'm up there with the angels then I'll heartily approve if you find another bloke. Believe me.' He paused to stare at her, his eyes unblinking. 'And the reason for that is because I love you so much. I'd want you to be happy.'

A lump came into her throat. 'Oh, John,' she whispered.

'There!' he announced with a flourish, laying a small paintbrush aside. 'Finished at last. What do you think?'

'I think it's lovely. Ian will be ever so pleased. Shall we leave it there so he can see it first thing in the morning?'

'Good idea.'

John saw off what was left in his glass, considered having a third, then decided against it.

'I'm suddenly tired again,' he said. 'It's back to bed for me.'

'I'll help you through.'

'I can manage,' he declared, coming to his feet. At the door he hesitated, then said over his shoulder, 'I want you to think about what we were discussing. Promise me?'

'I promise.'

He was smiling as he continued on through to the bedroom.

The next morning when she woke, Georgie found John lying dead beside her.

Part 2

Charlie

1929–1932

Chapter 11

Tam and Tom were bursting with it when they arrived in from work, Tam's face flushed with excitement. 'We've done it. We've bloody well done it!' he yelled and, taking Chrissie by the waist, whirled her round.

Chrissie laughed, as delighted by the news as her menfolk. 'I never thought I'd see the day when we had a Labour government,' she declared when Tam set her down again.

'But only with the help of the Liberals,' Lena pointed out. 'Labour has no overall Commons majority.'

'The fact is we're forming a government, which is all that matters.' Tam was beaming, shaking his head in happy disbelief. This was a dream come true as far as he was concerned.

A curious Ian was looking from person to person, wondering what all the fuss was about. What was Labour?

'Ramsay MacDonald will make a brilliant prime minister. Just you wait and see,' Tom enthused.

'Damn right he will.' Tam nodded. 'And he's a Scotsman too! That's the icing on the cake.'

'Anything to keep that Welshman out,' Tom added.

'Imagine MacDonald appointing a woman as Minister of Labour,' Chrissie said. 'That's a turn-up for the book.'

'I'm not sure I approve.' Tam frowned momentarily. 'But I have to say Margaret Bondfield does have a good reputation.'

'And why shouldn't he appoint a woman minister?' Lena sniffed. 'Honestly, Papa, some of your ideas and prejudices belong in the ark.'

'I quite agree,' Chrissie declared. 'It's high time women got a say in running the country. Let's hope she's just the first of many.'

Tam remained sceptical, but decided not to pursue the argument.

'They said on the wireless that reducing unemployment is to be MacDonald's top priority,' Chrissie informed the men.

'Good idea,' Tam replied. 'It would be my top priority as well if I had the job.'

Georgie arrived to pick up Ian as she did every evening after work. Now that she had a job as a packer in a bleach factory Ian came to his granny's on leaving school to wait for her.

'Have you heard the news, lass?' Tam boomed.

'Aye, I have. It swept round the factory earlier. A few of the girls were actually jumping up and down when they heard.'

Tam laughed. 'Great for them.'

'The manager wasn't too pleased, though. I'm sure he's a Tory.'

'He probably is if he's a boss.' Tam nodded. 'Scum of the earth, that lot.'

'As bad as the Liberals, if not worse,' Tom agreed.

'I've got nothing but contempt for both of them,' Tam declared. 'But it's all change now, thank God. From here on in the working man will get a fair crack of the whip.'

'Anyway, Ian and I will get down the road and leave you to it,' Georgie said, indicating to Ian to collect his things.

They said their goodbyes, and went on their way, Ian quizzing her about what Labour was, and she doing her best to explain. As they walked she noticed him scratching, and when they got home she asked, 'Is your skin acting up again?'

He nodded.

Georgie stared at him in dismay. Ian had developed eczema shortly after his father's death and nothing the doctor had prescribed or suggested had managed to cure it. The skin disease was a continuing bane of both their lives. Thankfully, for the past few months it hadn't been troublesome, but now it would seem to have flared once more.

'Take your shirt off and I'll put some ointment on,' she said. 'And when I've done that try not to scratch.'

All the ointment did was soothe the patches, but at least that was something. It made life more bearable for the lad.

Lena looked up and saw Hamish Murchison heading towards her. She frowned. What did he want? She rarely saw him nowadays since he'd been given his own small department.

He stopped in front of her desk and smiled. 'Hello, Lena. How are things?'

'Fine. And with you?'

'Excellent. Certainly can't complain.'

'Still golfing?' she enquired, her voice dripping sarcasm.

'Of course. Every weekend.'

She could have made a jibe about the chairman, but decided not to. 'So, how can I help? You obviously want something.'

Hamish laughed. 'What makes you think that?'

'Because the only time you ever speak to me is when you do. So, what is it?'

He leant over her desk, his eyes twinkling. 'I was wondering if you'd like to have a drink with me after work?'

That stunned her. 'A drink?' she stuttered.

'That's right. Just the two of us.'

The handsome Hamish asking her out? She couldn't quite take it in.

'Well?'

She nodded, not trusting herself to speak.

'Good. Do you know the Swan Hotel?'

Of course she knew the Swan. It was just down the street. 'Uh-huh.'

'We'll meet in reception. All right?'

Again she nodded.

'See you there then.'

She watched him walk away in complete and utter disbelief.

It was a thoroughly nervous Lena who presented herself in the reception area of the Swan Hotel. To her relief she found him already there and waiting.

He rose to his feet on spotting her. 'You made it.' He smiled.

'And to prove it I'm here,' she replied, with would-be lightness.

He laughed at the typical example of Glasgow humour. 'Shall we go on through?'

It was a lovely feeling when he took her by the arm to guide her. It was the first time any man had ever done that.

'What would you like?' he asked when she was seated at a table.

'A gin and tonic would be nice.'

'Coming right up.'

She still couldn't believe this was actually happening. Halfway through the afternoon she'd almost convinced herself she'd imagined the invitation. At one point her hands had started to shake so badly in anticipation that she'd had to put her pen down and wait for them to stop.

Lena gazed around. She had never been in the Swan before, let alone in the lounge. It was tastefully decorated, she decided. Quite posh, really. A lot of leather, a patterned red carpet, very expensive-looking wallpaper. She had no doubt the drinks would be expensive too. She lit a cigarette, thrilled to bits to be there with someone as good-looking as Hamish Murchison. She silently prayed she wouldn't start shaking again when he re-joined her.

'There we are.' Hamish placed her drink on the table. He'd elected to have whisky and soda. 'I rather like it here, don't you? Beats a smelly old pub any time.'

Lena poured tonic into her gin, then had a sip.

'Cheers!' he said, eyeing her over the rim of his glass as he drank.

'How's the new job coming along?' she enquired politely.

'Not too bad. A few teething problems, though, which I intend to iron out.'

'Oh?'

'And that's where you come in.'

'I don't follow?' She frowned.

He stared at her. 'Lena, you're the best damned ledger clerk in the entire building. Certainly for my money anyway. Which is why I'd like you to consider joining me in my department.'

Her nerves vanished, replaced by the dull ache of disappointment. She'd thought . . . but she'd been wrong, apparently. It would seem this wasn't a social occasion after all. How stupid of her to think otherwise. She should have known better.

'Go on,' she said harshly.

'I want you to be my sort of chief clerk, though without that designation. The company would never wear it.'

Lena knew that to be true enough. All the managers and chief clerks were men.

'If you agree,' Hamish went on, 'I could arrange more money for you. Say ten bob a week. How does that sound?'

'Fifteen bob would sound better.'

'Hmm,' he demurred, not at all certain he could go that far. She was asking a lot.

'Anyway, all this is hypothetical,' she declared. 'Old baldy would never let me go.'

'I believe I can persuade him,' Hamish replied. 'There

are certain pressures I can bring to bear that would make him agree to the move.'

The chairman again, Lena thought bitterly. No wonder Hamish was so optimistic.

'So what do you say?' he demanded eagerly.

Work under him? Lena thought. The man was an incompetent who should never have been employed by the company in the first place. There again, there was the money to consider. The rise was a sweet enticement which would add to her growing savings, for she still hadn't given up the idea of going to Hollywood where Pet was doing extremely well, thank you very much.

'I'd still want fifteen shillings a week extra,' she declared. 'Ten isn't enough.' It actually was, but she wasn't about to admit that.

'If I can get you fifteen will you agree?'

She studied him through cigarette smoke, angry with herself for thinking he'd actually been asking her out on some sort of 'date', as Pet put it in her letters.

'Let me think about it.' She smiled thinly. 'I don't want to make a decision here and now.'

Hamish heard the finality in her tone, and knew there was no point in discussing the matter further.

'So where have you been? You're late,' Chrissie demanded when Lena arrived home.

'Sorry, Mum. I had a drink in a hotel with a head of department who wanted a chat.'

Tom nearly made a derogatory remark, but didn't. 'What sort of chat?' he queried instead.

Lena told them while Chrissie put her tea on the table.

'An extra fifteen bob a week!' Tam exclaimed, and whistled softly. 'I hope you grabbed it.'

'Not yet, Papa.'

'Well, you should have done, my girl. That's a lot of money.'

Lena had already made up her mind to accept the offer, providing old baldy let her go and there was fifteen shillings on top of her current weekly wage. But she wouldn't let on to Hamish until he came back and assured her that both these conditions were in place. Meanwhile, let him worry she wouldn't accept. One thing was certain, for she knew Hamish only too well in some respects: he wasn't doing this out of the kindness of his heart. He needed her.

Later, she sat on the edge of her bed thinking about the day's events, still angry with herself for being so stupid as to think Hamish had asked her out for her own sake.

Would a man never ask her out for that? Not for what she could do for them, but for herself? Black despair filled her, because she doubted one ever would. She was going to die a frustrated old maid, a virgin. She would never know what it was like to have sex, or to be married and have children, all three of which she desperately wanted.

Falling backwards on to her bed, she began to weep, tears running down her face. A face she hated, loathed and detested with a fierce intensity.

It was a fortnight before Hamish again appeared at her desk, smiling like the proverbial cat who'd scoffed the cream.

'It's all fixed,' he announced. 'Old baldy has agreed to

let you go and the cashier to the extra cash. All I need now is to hear you'll take the job and you can start the first Monday of next month.'

'You pulled it off, then?'

'I did. It wasn't easy, mind you, but I got what I wanted in the end.'

How pleased with himself he was, she mused. She wouldn't have been at all surprised if he'd thrown back his head and crowed.

'Well?' he demanded.

'I'll present myself in your department on the first Monday of next month,' she replied with a smile, jubilant inside at the fifteen-shillings rise she would be paid every week – or three pounds a month as she was salaried – and pleased she'd stuck out for fifteen and not accepted the ten he'd initially proposed.

He beamed. 'See you then, Lena.'

'See you then.'

He badly needed her in his department, she reflected. Otherwise why go to all the trouble he had?

She bent again to her work, meticulously carrying on where she'd left off.

Georgie glanced over at Ian, nicely tucked up and sleeping in his bed. How lonely her nights had been since John died, she thought. Oh, there were occasions when her mother dropped by, and sometimes Lena. But usually she spent the nights on her own after Ian had gone to bed.

How she missed John, even after so long. She still half expected him to come in through the door, a cheery smile on his face, demanding to know what was for tea. But most of all she missed his presence in bed, the comfort of his arms, and knowing she was safe and sound while he was there.

She thought back to the little holiday they'd had, and how wonderful it had been. Happy days, true enough. And then how ill he'd been towards the end; dreadfully so. Thin beyond belief. In pain, but never complaining. And then that last evening when he'd come into the kitchen and drunk whisky while finishing off Ian's fort. It was almost as if he'd known he'd never make morning and that was their last chance to be together in this life.

Georgie sighed. Dear John. Dear, lovely, adorable John. Rising from her chair, she went to put the kettle on.

Lena ripped open her latest letter from Pet, or Dawn Ryder as Pet was now known, having been given a new name by the studio. As usual it was full of show business gossip: who was making what film, a rumour about so and so; things of that nature. Pet's latest film had just been released, in which she played a supporting role – a terrific part as a wicked woman. The film was due to come out in Britain the following year, and she, Lena, must go and see it.

In fact Lena had seen Pet – or Dawn Ryder as she must think of her – in several pictures to date. It still amused her to hear Pet speak with an American accent. Though, she had to admit, the accent was good and sounded authentic enough – at least to her ear, anyway.

Pet went on to say the studio had ordered her to diet as she'd gained a little weight recently, so on a diet she was. She remained unattached, though had been out on a number of 'dates' of late. Nothing serious. More to get her face in the movie magazines than anything else.

On finishing the letter Lena refolded it and returned it to its envelope. The same old irresistible Pet who never changed. Good for her. Stardom might not be that far away after all.

Now that would be something.

'Goodnight.'

'Goodnight, Tom.'

More out of courtesy than anything else he kissed the girl, whose name was Alison and who smelt strongly of cheap scent.

'Will I see you again?' she asked when the kiss was over.

'I'll be at the same dancing next Saturday night. I'll probably run into you then.'

'Oh,' she replied, clearly disappointed.

She was rather pretty, he thought, studying her in the moonlight. 'Ta-ra then.'

'Ta-ra, Tom. See you next Saturday.'

'I'll be looking for you,' he lied, and headed off down the street.

Now why had he walked her home, he wondered. He couldn't really say, for he'd known all along he really didn't fancy her. She was nice enough, with a good figure and a sunny nature. By rights he should have been interested enough to take it further, but he wasn't. He knew what the problem was, of course. Brigid. He'd never really got over her.

He'd tried time and time again with the lassies, even

taking a few out several times, but in the end Brigid's ghost always came back to haunt him. To get in the way. The strange thing was he'd never spotted Brigid at the dancing since they'd broken up. He'd been certain he'd run into her at some stage, but it had just never happened.

For what must have been the millionth time in the intervening years he wondered how she was and what she was up to. Was she engaged, or even married? Or still single like himself? Whatever, he hoped she was happy.

Though the thought that she might be happy with someone else was something he found almost impossible to bear. Why oh why had she been a bloody Catholic! Everything could have been so different otherwise.

'I'm just nipping out, Lena. Hold the fort for me if you will.'

Lena watched Hamish clap a bowler hat on his head and make smartly for the door. It was the same every morning: he'd be gone a good two hours at least. And the same in the afternoon.

She knew where he was off to. In a nearby street there was a tobacconist's which had a coffee shop at the rear. That's where he spent his time, either reading the newspaper or chatting with other customers – all men, for it was a strictly male province.

On other occasions he'd announce he was off to a meeting upstairs, meetings she knew to be pure fantasy because she'd checked. It was simply another excuse to skive away from his desk.

The department was running as smoothly as clockwork, thanks entirely to her. It was certainly nothing to do with Hamish, who was one of the laziest men Lena had ever come across. There were four other female clerks whom she'd been put in charge of, all of them diligent workers and good at their job since she had whipped them into shape during her first few weeks in the department.

Lena glanced down at the ledger she was currently bringing up to date. Re-insurance was boring at the best of times, and when it was to do with farming, which was what the department dealt with, it was positively soporific. At least with old baldy there had been some interest, certainly when it came to shipping which she'd rather enjoyed. Shipping had some romance about it: all those different cargoes going to every corner of the world; even the ships themselves with their at times exotic names.

She considered going to the ladies for a cigarette. Why not, when Hamish could disappear off for hours on end? A few stolen minutes in the toilet was nothing by comparison.

Then she remembered she didn't have any cigarettes, having forgotten to buy some on the way in to work. 'Damn!' she muttered. She couldn't even borrow off one of the other girls as none of them smoked.

At least Hamish was easy to get along with, she reflected, unlike old baldy who'd watched everyone like a hawk, and never had a word of praise for anyone. Miserable sod.

Re-insurance. An insurance company takes on a huge risk, then, to ensure they don't come a cropper should they have to pay out an enormous sum, offloads a percentage of that risk on to the re-insurers, paying the proportionate percentage of the original premium to do so.

Re-insurance. Boring as hell. Dry as dust. Non-stop slog with pen, paper and figures – never-ending figures that just went on and on and on till you wanted to scream at the sight of them.

Lena suddenly giggled to herself. What did Hamish look like in that bowler hat? Absolutely ridiculous, in her opinion. A real city-type clown. Quite, quite absurd.

She quickly pulled herself together when she saw one of the other clerks staring at her in astonishment, no doubt because she'd giggled. It was completely out of character.

Oh, but she could murder for a fag!

Chapter 12

Georgie was on her morning tea break, chatting away to Daisy Somerville who worked alongside her, when it happened. One moment they were talking, the next an enormous explosion threw all the women present higgledy-piggledy.

Georgie lay there, stunned, groggily wondering what on earth had happened. Then she heard the screams coming from the factory floor.

Daisy was unconscious, having banged her head when going down. A thin trickle of blood was running from her mouth.

'Jesus Christ!' one of the fallen girls exclaimed, struggling to her feet. Judging from the sounds now coming from the factory floor, pandemonium had broken loose.

'Daisy! Daisy! Wake up,' Georgie muttered, gently slapping Daisy's face.

Daisy groaned, and opened her eyes. 'What happened?'

'Don't know yet. Are you hurt?'

Daisy gingerly felt her body. 'Don't think so.'

'You were knocked out.' Georgie coughed as dust clogged her throat. Glancing up she saw that the dust, and there was a lot of it, was falling in a white shower. She also noticed that a great crack had appeared in the ceiling. 'We've got to get out of here,' she croaked, fearful the ceiling might collapse.

One of the other girls opened the door leading on to the factory floor, and gasped when she saw what confronted her. A huge conflagration was blazing over to her right. And then they smelt it: the pungent aroma of bleach wafting into the room. Within seconds they were all spluttering, their eyes streaming. Another, smaller, explosion further widened the crack in the ceiling.

The girl who'd opened the door stumbled out of it, quickly followed by others as they fled the room. Georgie helped Daisy to her feet, and Daisy cursed as her legs immediately buckled under her.

'Can hardly see,' she whispered, as the bleach fumes grew steadily stronger.

Georgie's lungs seemed to be on fire as she half dragged, half pulled Daisy towards the door. When they reached it the sight that greeted them was of a raging inferno, flames roaring and hissing as the conflagration advanced, trying to encompass and consume everything in its way. The stench was unbelievable, the noxious smell of bleach even stronger than it had been in the room where they'd been having their tea break.

Georgie bent over and coughed violently, her sides heaving as she coughed again and again. Behind her, the ceiling caved in with an almighty crash.

Daisy was staring in horror at the body of a lassie lying prostrate across one of the packing benches. The girl was clearly dead. Daisy recognised her as Ishbel Campbell, a seventeen-year-old. From that distance Daisy couldn't tell what had caused Ishbel's death.

Women were still screaming, while in the distance Georgie thought she could hear the clamour of a fire engine. 'Can you walk yet?' she gasped to Daisy, who nodded that she could. 'Then let's go.'

Daisy started to shake. 'We're all going to die! We're all going to die!' she exclaimed hysterically.

'Shut it. Let's get a move on. Don't just stand there.'

'Can't!' Daisy was still hysterical.

'Can't bloody what?' Despite herself, Georgie was beginning to get angry with her workmate.

'Can't go into that. Too scared.'

Georgie's right hand flashed to crack across Daisy's cheek, a real humdinger of a blow. 'Get a grip, Daisy. For God's sake get a bloody grip. You'll die for certain if you don't make a run for it. Now come on!'

'That hurt.' Daisy's voice was hoarse.

'I was trying to knock some sense into you.'

Daisy's hand went to her throat, then her eyes rolled upwards and she collapsed to the floor, overcome by the fumes.

'Daisy!' Kneeling, Georgie grasped Daisy by the shoulders and roughly shook her, to no avail.

Georgie forced herself to stay calm. What to do? She certainly couldn't carry Daisy; her workmate was far too heavy for that. Nor could she leave her here like this.

Then she thought of Ian. He'd already lost his dad. It was up to her to see he didn't lose his mother as well. She had to save herself for his sake, if nothing else. And that meant leaving Daisy behind.

She gave her friend another shake, but there was still no response. Daisy was out like a light.

'I'm sorry,' she whispered. 'I really am. But there's nothing else I can do.'

Forcing herself to her feet again she stumbled in the direction of the main factory doors.

She was in some sort of dream world which didn't make any sense at all.

'Is that one alive, Charlie?'

'Aye, she is.'

'Then you'd better get her the hell out of here.'

Georgie's eyes fluttered open to stare into the face of a fireman bending over her. He immediately smiled.

'Not to worry, hen. Charlie's here. You're going to be all right.'

She tried to reply, but couldn't. What a lovely face he had, she thought woozily. The face of a cherub.

'Let's be having you now,' Charlie said, lifting her into a sitting position.

The next thing Georgie knew she was slung over his shoulder, vaguely aware of what might have been gunfire but was, in reality, exploding bottles.

Then she passed out again.

'She's awake,' a female voice declared.

Georgie found herself gazing up at a pristine white

ceiling. She had a dreadful headache, her temples pounding. She was also desperately thirsty.

'How do you feel, Mrs Mair?'

The speaker was an elderly nurse whose expression was one of deep concern.

'Water,' Georgie finally managed to croak after several unsuccessful attempts.

A porcelain spout was manoeuvred into her mouth, and she swallowed greedily at the water flowing from it.

'That's enough for now,' the nurse told her, removing the spout. 'I can't give you any more till doctor's seen you, which will be shortly.'

Closing her eyes Georgie thought of Daisy whom she'd abandoned, and who was now probably dead. There was nothing else she could have done, she reminded herself. There was simply nothing else she could have done in the circumstances.

But that didn't make her feel any better. She'd still left Daisy behind to her fate.

'You're a very lucky woman, Mrs Mair,' Dr Almond declared, when he had finished examining Georgie. 'Even a few more minutes in that toxic environment might have proved fatal.'

Georgie gasped for breath, her throat feeling red raw and constricted. 'How many . . . ?' She trailed off to swallow saliva.

'Died?'

'Yes.'

'The figure isn't yet known. Or I should say finalised. But fourteen bodies have so far been recovered.'

159

Dear God, Georgie thought. She wondered who they all were, for it was a small factory and she'd known everybody by sight, and most by name.

'We have three more women here like yourself. Two with bad burns and inhalation damage, the other, like yourself, with inhalation damage.'

At least she hadn't been burnt, Georgie reflected. That was something.

'Now it's best you don't try to speak,' Dr Almond went on. 'Not for a day or two anyway.'

'Son,' Georgie croaked. 'My son.'

'You want to see him?'

'Please.'

'Tomorrow at visiting time, then. I'll have a word with the police and they'll arrange it. But no speaking, mind. Promise?'

'Promise.'

'You just rest. That's the best thing for you at the moment. Let nature take her course.' He added wryly, 'She's often a better doctor than any of us.'

'Thank you.'

'No more speaking.' He wagged a finger at her. 'If you need a bedpan catch the eye of a passing nurse and make this sign.' He demonstrated for her. 'Understand?'

She gave him the smallest of nods, and even that hurt.

She closed her eyes after he'd gone. But there was no peace for her. Over and over, in her mind's eye, she relived the terrible happenings in the factory.

'So how are you today, lass?' Chrissie had been one of the first into the ward when the bell had been rung announcing visiting hour. It was Georgie's tenth day in hospital, and her condition had steadily improved.

'Fine, Mum. I've got good news. Dr Almond has told me I can go home tomorrow,' Georgie replied, her voice newly husky as a result of the fumes she'd inhaled.

'That's wonderful.' Chrissie beamed.

'They're discharging me at ten a.m.'

'I'll be waiting for you.'

'They did offer an ambulance, but I didn't think that was necessary.'

'Are you sure?' Chrissie frowned.

'I'll be all right, honest. There's nothing wrong with my legs, after all. And we'll be in a tram for most of the way.'

'If you're absolutely certain.'

'I am, Mum.' Georgie smiled. 'I can't tell you how keen I am to get out of here. They've all been terribly nice, and the treatment's been excellent. But you know how it is?'

'Oh aye.' Chrissie nodded. 'Home's always best.' She took a deep breath. 'Now, you've not to worry about anything. I'll be there every day to do whatever needs done. Shopping, cleaning, that sort of thing. What's important is for you to get some more rest until you're really fit again.'

'Thanks, Mum.'

Chrissie dropped her gaze a little. 'They're having most of the funerals today. I thought you'd like to know.' At the final count seventeen people had died in the fire.

'Is Daisy Somerville one of them?'

'Yes. She's being buried this afternoon.'

Georgie hadn't told a soul that she'd had to leave Daisy behind. She didn't know if she ever would. Guilt hung heavily within her, and would probably remain there for the rest of her life.

'Such a tragic business, the whole thing,' Chrissie said softly, and shook her head.

'I would have been among the dead if it hadn't been for a fireman called Charlie,' Georgie declared. It was the first time she'd mentioned him. 'I would certainly have never made it out on my own.'

'God bless him,' Chrissie said, extremely grateful to Charlie, whoever he was.

'Aye, God bless him,' Georgie repeated, remembering that cherub-like face staring down at her. 'When I get home I think I'll write him a letter expressing my gratitude.'

'Good idea,' Chrissie approved.

Yes, Georgie thought. She'd do just that.

'I'm nipping out for a little while,' Hamish declared. 'Hold the fort as usual, all right?'

Lena nodded. Right on time for the coffee shop. It was getting so you could have set your watch by him. His leaving, that is – not always his return.

Hamish hesitated. 'I only heard earlier this morning that your sister was involved in that terrible fire which was in all the newspapers. Is that true?'

'Yes, Georgie was in it. Ended up in hospital as a result.'

Hamish cleared his throat. 'She survived then. Was she burnt?'

'Thankfully, no. She suffered from fume inhalation,

which was nasty enough. She's home now and making a good recovery.'

'I'm delighted to hear that,' Hamish said sincerely. 'It must have been a big scare for you and your family. Is she married?'

'Widowed, with a little boy of ten. Her husband died of leukaemia a few years ago.'

'Poor woman. And poor lad. I've lost both my parents. Dad in the Great War, Mum a few years later to influenza. Though in my case I was a lot older than ten when my mum went.'

'I'm sorry to hear that. You losing your parents, I mean.'

Hamish's eyes took on a faraway look. 'I still miss them. Quite a bit actually. But there we are. What's happened has happened and nothing can change that.' He took a deep breath. 'Anyway, I'm off now. And I'm pleased to hear your sister is going to be fine.'

He wasn't such a bad old stick after all, Lena mused when he was gone, wondering if he was presently going out with anyone. Probably, she thought, though he hadn't mentioned it. There again, he rarely talked about anything concerning his private life. All she knew was that he was neither married nor engaged, and, now, that both his parents had passed on. Everything else remained a mystery.

Chrissie sat on the edge of their bed, put her face in her hands and burst into tears.

Tam stared at her in astonishment, then went quickly over. Sitting beside her he put a comforting arm round her shoulders. 'What's wrong, lass? What's wrong?'

Chrissie's entire upper torso was heaving. 'It just suddenly got to me, that's all,' she sobbed.

'What did?'

'Thinking about how close we came to losing Georgie.'

'Aye,' he said slowly. 'It was a near-run thing right enough. The doctor told her that even a few more minutes might have been fatal.'

'The thought of it. The very thought of it . . .' Chrissie trailed off, her mind filled with the horror of what it would have been like if Georgie had died.

'We'll simply have to put it behind us,' Tam counselled. 'That's the best thing.'

'And wee Ian. What would have happened to him?'

'He'd have come here, of course, and we'd have had another bairn to bring up. There would have been nothing else for it. But, as it is, everything's worked out all right.'

'I got such a fright when the polisman told us, Tam. I went cold inside.'

'I think we all did, lass.' He shook his head. 'As they say, you just never know the moment till the moment after.'

'No, you don't,' Chrissie agreed. 'Can you get me a hanky from that drawer over there?'

Tam did so, and handed it to her.

Chrissie sniffed as she dabbed at her eyes. 'Sorry about that. I'm better now.'

'There's nothing to be sorry about. It's perfectly normal. There have been times since the fire when I've been choked with emotion myself.'

Chrissie smiled at him. 'But you didn't cry. Glasgow men don't. They don't consider it manly.'

Tam matched her smile. He had cried, but waited till he was alone before doing so. Not that he would ever let on. Not even to Chrissie.

As she'd said, Glasgow men weren't supposed to be soft.

A new dance hall called La Scala had opened in town and Tom had decided to pay it a visit. He was there with two pals from work, one of whom, from the looks of it, had already 'got off' with a lassie, a tall redhead with a stunning figure.

Tom liked the new dance hall, reckoning that no expense had been spared in doing it out. In the centre of the ceiling a many-faceted crystal ball was revolving, sending off what seemed like a thousand shafts of light in all directions, reflections from the spotlights directed on it.

And then he saw Brigid. In the arms of another man, she was laughing at what the chap was saying, the pair of them apparently very much at ease in one another's company.

Tom was consumed with jealousy. Though, he reminded himself, he had absolutely no right to be. Brigid was nothing to him any more. Only a distant memory. History.

Was she with the chap? Or were they only up for a dance together, having just met? He'd soon find out.

Four dances later when they still hadn't come off the floor Tom was forced to the conclusion that she was with him, though whether the chap was her boyfriend or they'd only just met he couldn't say.

He finally forced himself to take his eyes off her. His night out was completely ruined. He had to get out of there before she saw *him*, he decided. There was nothing else for it.

Ten minutes later he was in a nearby pub drinking pints and chasers, and feeling sick to the pit of his stomach.

Georgie answered a knock on the door to find a smartly dressed man carrying a briefcase standing there. 'Can I help you?'

'Are you Mrs Mair?'

'I am.'

'Let me introduce myself. I'm Mr Brown from Salamander Insurance. May I come in?'

Georgie couldn't think why this Mr Brown wanted to talk to her. She was mystified. 'What's this all about?'

'The fire you were involved in at your place of work, Mrs Mair. My company covered the factory.'

'I see,' she murmured, still uncertain about the reason for his presence here. 'Then you had better come in.'

On entering the kitchen Brown glanced swiftly around, then focused on Georgie. 'You've been in hospital, I understand?'

'That's correct.'

'For?'

She frowned. 'For what?'

'Why were you in hospital?'

'Because of the fumes I inhaled during the fire.'

'Uh-huh.' He nodded. 'And are you now fully recovered?'

Talk about twenty questions, Georgie thought. 'Not quite. I'm still suffering from a sore chest and, as you can hear, my voice has gone all husky. Dr Almond, the specialist who took care of me, says it's entirely possible my voice will remain this way.'

'And your chest?'

'Will be all right given time. I've been prescribed a mixture to help clear it up.'

'Do you mind?' Brown asked, indicating that he wanted to put his briefcase on the table.

'Help yourself.'

'Then let's get down to business, shall we?'

Lena laid down the form, which she'd read from beginning to end. 'This is easy enough to fill in. Do you want me to do it for you?'

'Please.' Georgie smiled. 'You're the expert on insurance.'

'How much will she get?' Chrissie queried from across the room.

'Hard to say, Mum. It all depends. But certainly something; I can almost vouch for that.'

Compensation, Georgie thought with glee. It had never crossed her mind until Mr Brown's visit. Now it seemed she was in for a windfall.

'Have you heard of this Salamander Insurance?' Tam asked Lena.

'Oh aye, They're a very good and respected company. A Scottish company, too, with their head office in Bath Street.'

Tam nodded his approval. The fact they were a

Scottish company was recommendation enough for him.

'Right,' Lena declared. 'No time like the present. Just let me get a pen and we'll make a start.'

Half an hour later the claim form was filled in, ready for Georgie to post back to Mr Brown.

Chapter 13

'Excuse me, does someone called Charlie work here?'
The fireman Georgie had addressed stared at her for a moment or two before replying. 'Would that be Charlie Gunn?'

'I'm afraid I don't know his surname. But I'd like to speak to him, if that's possible.'

'Can I tell him who's asking?'

'Mrs Mair. But that probably won't mean anything even if it is the man I'm looking for.'

'I see,' the fireman murmured. 'Aye, all right. You hang on there, hen, and I'll send Charlie down to you.' And with that the fireman vanished up a flight of stairs.

Georgie glanced at the sky. Damn! she thought. It was going to rain. She'd get soaked if she wasn't careful.

There was a clattering of boots on the stairs, and then her Charlie appeared. He frowned when he saw her.

'Don't you recognise me?' she asked shyly, noting his puzzlement.

'I . . .' And then the penny dropped. 'You're the lassie from the fire at the bleach factory, aren't you?'

'That's right. I've come to say thank you for saving my life.'

Charlie stared at her in astonishment. 'Well! This is the first time anyone's ever done that.'

'I was going to write you a letter till it dawned on me I didn't know your surname or which station you worked at. This is the second station I've called in to enquire about you. The other one had a Charlie as well, but obviously he wasn't you.'

Charlie was tickled pink, and thought she was a lot better-looking than he recalled. There again, she'd hardly been at her best when he'd picked her up off the floor.

'I honestly don't know what to say,' he admitted, still amazed at her having sought him out.

'You don't have to say anything. Just thanks again. I'd have died that day if it wasn't for you.'

Charlie was about to reply when the heavens suddenly opened and it began to bucket down. 'Here, come inside,' he said, and Georgie hurriedly did so.

'Would you like to come upstairs and meet the rest of the lads?' Charlie asked. 'And if you've got time you can have a cup of coffee. At least stay until the rain stops.'

Georgie hesitated. This was the last thing she'd been expecting.

'Oh, come on,' Charlie urged. 'We don't bite.'

'Are you sure it'll be all right?'

'Of course. I wouldn't have asked you otherwise.'

'A cup of coffee sounds wonderful, then. Thanks.'

She followed him up the stairs into a room where the

men of Charlie's watch were taking their ease, waiting for the next call-out. Some were playing cards, others reading, while one chap was sitting in a large comfy chair fast asleep.

Georgie was introduced all round, and the men were delighted when they heard why she'd called in to see Charlie. She thanked them as a group, for they too had attended the fire. Then Charlie ushered her to a chair and fetched her a cup of coffee from a pot already made. He sat opposite her and smiled while she had a sip from the cup he'd handed her.

'Fag?' he offered, holding out his packet.

Georgie shook her head. 'I do smoke, or used to anyway, but haven't had one since the fire. It's my chest, you see. One puff and it's agony.'

'Due to fume inhalation?'

'That's right.'

'I'm sorry to hear it. Were you burnt at all?'

'No, you got me out before that happened.'

'Good. Though fume inhalation is bad enough. How long were you in hospital for?'

Georgie told him. 'This husky voice is another after-effect of the inhalation. My specialist said I might have it for the rest of my life.'

'Well, I like it.' Charlie beamed at her. 'It's sexy.'

Georgie coloured, and glanced away, thinking that the remark was a bit forward on such a short acquaintance.

'Mr Mair must have been . . . how shall I put it? Relieved to say the least that you survived.'

'My husband is dead,' Georgie replied softly. 'He died a few years back from leukaemia.'

'I'm sorry.' Charlie looked stricken. 'Trust me to put my two big feet in it.'

'Don't worry. You weren't to know.'

Charlie sighed. 'As a matter of fact I'm a widower myself. My wife tripped going down the tenement stairs where we live, fell and broke her neck. Died instantly.'

Georgie expressed her sympathy.

'Left me with my daughter Avril to bring up. Which hasn't been easy considering the shifts I do.'

Georgie could well imagine. 'How old is she?'

'Ten.'

'Same as my son Ian. He's ten as well.'

'Really? Now there's a coincidence. It would seem we have a lot in common.

They sat in silence for a few moments, until Charlie asked, 'Does it bother you if I smoke?'

'Of course not. Go ahead.'

She watched him as he lit up. He wasn't exactly a handsome man, but she found his cherubic face most appealing.

'So how do you manage with Avril?' she queried. 'Surely she's too young to be at home alone overnight? You do work night shifts on occasion, I take it?'

'Oh aye. As many night shifts as day ones. I would have had to change my job if it wasn't for my married sister Betty, who lives just round the corner. She takes care of Avril when I'm not there. She also does our washing and ironing, for which I pay her. Betty's been a godsend, I can tell you.'

Georgie finished her coffee, then glanced at a nearby window. 'It's stopped raining,' she observed. 'I'd better be going.'

'What's your first name, by the way?' Charlie asked.

'Georgie. Short for Georgina.'

'Georgie,' he repeated. 'I like it. It suits you.'

'Thank you.'

'It's been a pleasure meeting you, Georgie.'

'And you, Charlie. I'm glad I came.'

'And I'm glad you did. As I said, you're the first one who's ever taken the trouble to say thank you. I'm touched.'

She laid her cup and saucer on the floor, then rose. He did the same.

'I'll see you out,' he declared.

Georgie said goodbye to the rest of the lads, thinking what a nice, friendly lot they were. Then Charlie escorted her down the stairs. At the entrance to the station they halted.

'Goodbye then, Charlie.'

'Goodbye, Georgie. Good luck.'

She extended a hand, and they shook.

'You take care now. Don't get caught up in any more fires,' he joked.

'I'll try not to.'

Turning, she strode away. She'd only gone a few yards when he called after her. Then he was there at her side. 'I was wondering,' he said, and cleared his throat, 'if you'd care to go to the pictures with me on Saturday night?'

She was completely taken aback. 'You mean go out with you?'

'That's right. To the pictures. And we could have fish suppers afterwards if you like?'

'I . . . er . . .'

He mistook her hesitation for a refusal. 'Don't worry,' he apologised. 'It was just a thought.'

Her initial instinct had been to say no. Now she wasn't so sure. 'Can I be honest with you?'

'Of course.'

'I haven't been out with anyone since John died.'

'Coincidence again. I haven't been out with anyone either since Agnes broke her neck. So why don't we give it a go together, eh?'

Her heart was in her mouth as she made a decision. 'Where shall we meet?'

He named a place in the centre of Glasgow, and suggested a time.

'I'll be there,' she promised.

'I'm really looking forward to it.'

'Till then.'

'Till then, Georgie.'

'Going out with a man!' Chrissie exclaimed.

'Well, it would hardly be another woman,' Tom commented, laughing.

'The man who saved my life, don't forget,' Georgie reminded her mother.

'I appreciate that.'

'I, for one, approve.' Tam nodded. 'It's high time you got out and enjoyed yourself again instead of being stuck in that house night after night.'

'Quite right,' Tom agreed.

Georgie glanced down at the floor. 'John told me the night he died that I was too young not to consider marrying again. He was quite insistent about that.'

'Why, are you thinking of marrying this Charlie?' Chrissie asked in alarm.

'Of course not, Mum. I've only just met him. But in order to remarry some day, should it ever come to that, I have to start somewhere. And going to the flicks with Charlie seems as good a point as any.'

Lena was listening, trying to control the jealousy she felt. Her sister had lost one man, and now it would appear she might have found another. Bitterness gnawed inside her as she thought about her own bleak situation.

'So will you look after Ian on Saturday night, Mum?'

'I'd be delighted to, lass. He can bed down in Tom's room and you can collect him Sunday morning.'

Georgie turned to Ian standing by her side. 'You don't mind staying with Granny and Grandpa Saturday night, do you?'

Ian was idly scratching a patch of itchy skin. 'Why can't I come to the pictures with you and this Charlie?' he queried with a frown.

Georgie suppressed a smile. 'Oh, we'll be out far too late for someone your age. You'll be all tucked up and long in the land of nod before I get home.'

Tam winked at his grandson. 'You'll enjoy it here, Ian. We can listen to the wireless. You like listening to the wireless, don't you?'

Ian nodded.

'And I'll bake a cake,' Chrissie declared.

'A chocolate one?' Ian asked eagerly.

'If that's what you want.'

'Oh yes please, Granny!'

Georgie smiled. 'Thanks, Mum. Thanks, Papa.'

'You can tell us all about it on Sunday,' Tom teased her. 'All the gory details, if you know what I mean?'

'Get lost,' she snapped back good-naturedly.

Tom laughed.

On Saturday afternoon Georgie stood by the graveside staring at John's headstone. Ian was already at his granny and grandpa's, and she had felt she had to come and make her peace with John before going out with Charlie later.

'It was your idea, John,' she said softly, as though speaking to him face to face. 'You did give me permission.' She paused, and took a deep breath. 'So I know you'll understand why I'm doing this even though I still love you, and always will.'

Wind rustled in a nearby stand of trees, while overhead two crows cawed raucously.

'Always will,' she repeated.

She was wiping away tears as she left the graveside and made for the main gate out of the cemetery. Daisy Somerville's grave would still be unmarked, or she would have visited Daisy too, and apologised again for leaving her behind in the fire.

'Good God!' Georgie exclaimed.

Charlie turned to her. 'What's wrong?' he whispered.

'I know that woman,' she whispered back.

'What woman?'

'The one who's just come on screen. She's a friend of my sister's who went to Hollywood to become an actress. And there she is.'

Charlie glanced at the screen. 'Which one?'

'The one on the left.' Wait till she told Lena about this, Georgie thought gleefully. She couldn't wait.

'This fish supper is the best I've ever tasted,' she exclaimed later, as Charlie walked her to her tram stop after the film.

'I told you it would be. That one's the best fish and chip shop in all Glasgow.'

She smiled at him. 'So how do you know about it?'

He tapped his nose. 'We firemen get to hear all manner of things. You'd be surprised.'

'Such as?'

'The best fish and chip shop in Glasgow, for example,' he teased.

'And?'

'Which pubs will let you in the back door after hours for another.'

Georgie laughed. 'Trust a man to count that as important.'

She was thoroughly enjoying her night out, finding Charlie easy and relaxing to be with. The more she knew him the more she liked him.

'Can I ask you a question, Georgie?'

'Which is?'

'What did your husband do for a living?'

'Same as you. He was a fireman.'

'Really!' Charlie exclaimed. 'Another coincidence.'

'But he wasn't the same type of fireman as you. He worked on the railway – LMS.'

'Oh, I see.' Charlie nodded. 'He kept the firebox going. Like a stoker on a ship?'

'It was John's great ambition to one day be promoted to engine driver. But he died before that could happen.'

Charlie glanced at her, wondering if it was wise to ask his next question. He decided he would. 'Do you still miss him?'

She took her time in replying. 'Yes, I do, to tell the truth. We were very close. But he's dead, and life goes on. What about you?'

'Do you mean regarding Agnes?'

'Uh-huh.'

'Not really. It wasn't exactly the happiest of marriages. We rowed a lot. It sounds callous to say this, but it was actually something of a relief when she fell down those stairs.'

Georgie was slightly shocked, though she wasn't sure why. She was well aware that not everyone had as happy a marriage as she and John.

'Do you think me terrible for admitting such a thing?' Charlie asked softly.

'No, not really. If that was the case then that was the case. No point in pretending otherwise.'

'Good.'

They continued chatting until they reached the tram stop, disposing of their fish and chip wrappings on the way. They were the only ones at the stop.

'There should be a tram along in a minute.' Georgie smiled at him.

'Have you enjoyed yourself?'

'Oh aye.'

'Me too. A lot, actually.' He spotted a tramcar in the distance. 'You were right about one being along in a minute.'

'If it's mine, that is.'

'Georgie, would you like to go out with me again?'

She'd already decided on her answer, should the question be asked. 'Yes.' She smiled.

'It'll have to be in the week because of my shifts. How would Tuesday night suit?'

'I don't see why not.'

'There's a little restaurant I know. Nothing fancy, mind. Plain cooking, but it is licensed. How about that?'

'Sounds wonderful.'

They quickly arranged a time and place to meet, and then the tram, which was Georgie's, drew alongside.

'Thanks for tonight, Charlie.'

As Georgie moved to board the tram Charlie pecked her on the cheek. 'Thank you, Georgie. 'Bye for now.'

When the tram had moved away Georgie touched the spot where he'd kissed her. To her amazement she didn't feel the least bit guilty.

Tam sighed as he dropped his newspaper on to his lap.

'What's wrong?' Chrissie queried.

'I don't like what I'm reading nowadays. There are hard times ahead, lass, you mark my words.'

'How so?'

Tom glanced up from what he was doing. 'Yeah, how so, Papa?'

'It would seem industry is beginning to feel the knock-on effect of the Wall Street crash last October.'

'But that was in America!' Tom exclaimed.

'None the less, it's going to affect us. We could be in for a bad slump.'

'But we've a Labour government in power,' Chrissie declared. 'Surely they won't let anything happen here?'

'They may not be able to do anything about it,' Tam said. 'Unemployment could just rise and rise. That's how these things work.'

'What about McNair's?' Tom queried, alarmed.

'Who knows?' Tam shrugged. 'We might be all right. There again, maybe not. What do you say, Lena? You're the brains in the family.'

'You're right, things aren't looking too good. Our economy was already fragile before the crash. What I do know is the volume of business at work has been steadily decreasing of late, causing concern amongst the management. It's early days yet, but if I was asked to give a prediction it would have to be a gloomy one. Perhaps even worse than that.'

'Unemployment,' Chrissie whispered fearfully. It was the nightmare of every working-class housewife.

'We'll just have to wait and see,' Tam declared. 'We may be worrying for nothing.'

Maybe, Lena thought to herself.

Georgie's eyes literally bulged when she saw the size of the cheque that had been enclosed with Mr Brown's letter. Two hundred and ten pounds was an absolute fortune to her. A king's ransom.

She shook her head in disbelief. Surely there had been some mistake? There had to be. She'd been hoping for some decent money, twenty or thirty quid perhaps. But two hundred and ten pounds! She'd never dreamt she'd ever have so much.

Raising the cheque to her mouth she kissed it, her mind whirling. What a windfall! What an absolutely marvellous bloody windfall!

First things first, she told herself. She had to get this cheque into a bank, which meant opening an account as she didn't have one. Neither had John, when he was alive. They had lived from one pay day to the next, same as all the families she knew. The sole exception was Lena.

Her hands were shaking as she slipped on her coat, trying to remember where the nearest bank was. Minutes later she was hurrying down the road, the precious cheque secure in her purse.

Chapter 14

It was the second week Hamish had been off with a badly sprained ankle, leaving Lena in charge of the department. She was thoroughly enjoying the responsibility, and as far as she was concerned he could stay away as long as he liked.

She closed the ledger she'd been working on, which brought her own work up to date. She glanced at the other girls, all beavering away, and wondered what to do next. She considered going to the ladies for a fly fag, but decided against it. She'd leave that till later.

Then she remembered something she'd been puzzled about for a long time. Hamish kept several ledgers in a desk drawer which only he ever dealt with. Now why would he do that?

On a whim she decided to investigate. With Hamish off, who was to gainsay her, after all? Curiosity had simply got the better of her. Or downright nosiness, as her mother would have called it. Rising, she went to Hamish's office and went inside, closing the door firmly behind her. With the door shut no one could see what she was up to.

She found the ledgers easily enough, none of the drawers in the desk being locked. Placing them on the desktop, she stared at them. They seemed ordinary enough. No different from the many which passed through her hands. So why did Hamish keep them to himself? It was completely out of character for him to do any work when there were others he could pass it on to.

Sitting at the desk, Lena drew the first ledger to her, and opened it.

Lena was in Hamish's office for well over an hour before she closed the second ledger and sat back in his chair. She was absolutely stunned. Hamish was cooking the books, at least where these entries were concerned.

No doubt about it. He was embezzling. Oh, not a huge amount. But fifty quid a month was embezzlement all the same. No wonder he kept these ledgers in his desk and did all the book-keeping himself. The bugger was at it!

She had to think about this, Lena told herself. Embezzlement was a very serious offence. Not only would Hamish be sacked if she reported him, he could also go to prison.

Replacing the ledgers where she'd found them she left the office and went straight to the ladies, where she lit up. Who would have thought it? Certainly not her. Hamish on the fiddle! If it wasn't so serious she'd have laughed. This was a side to the incompetent Hamish she'd never have dreamt existed.

'Davey McIlwham has been laid off,' Chrissie announced to Tam when he and Tom returned from McNair's that evening. Davey and his family lived up the same close as the McKeands.

Tam regarded his wife grimly. 'How many altogether?'

'Fifteen, I was told.'

Davey was employed in a sheet-metal factory where he'd grafted man and boy. If Tam's recollection was correct the factory employed about thirty men, which meant half the workforce had been laid off. This was bad news indeed. A portent of things to come?

'How are he and Doreen taking it?' he asked.

'You can imagine. Doreen's beside herself. They've got three children to feed, don't forget.'

Tam took a deep breath. 'I'll go down and have a sympathetic word with him later. Not that it'll do much good, but it's the least a neighbour can do.'

'Aye.' Chrissie nodded. 'You do that, Tam.'

'Now, what's for tea, woman? I'm starving.'

Lena was lying on her bed staring at the ceiling, thinking about what she'd discovered earlier in the day and the difficult position it put her in.

She was hardly over-enamoured with Hamish, but at the same time she had nothing personal against him. On the contrary, in many ways she'd become fond of the sod. What on earth had made him do it? He must be paid a reasonable wage after all as head of a department, albeit a small one. Nor did he have a wife and family to provide for.

Idiot! she thought. Bloody idiot! In her mind's eye she gave him a good kick up the backside for being so incredibly stupid.

It seemed to her she had two options. One was to keep

quiet about the whole thing and let matters go on as they had. The only trouble there was what if he got found out in future by someone other than herself? That was always a possibility, even though he did keep those ledgers apart from the others that went through the department. Any sharp-eyed clerk would soon pick up on what he was doing, just as she had. Then it would definitely be the sack for him and maybe prison.

The alternative was to report him and let him suffer the consequences, which she was hesitant to do.

Then a third possibility struck her. She could tell him what she'd discovered and offer to re-do the books so the embezzlement would never be found, the proviso being his promise never to do anything so stupid again. She could save his bacon, in other words.

Out of the blue an idea came to her. An idea so outrageous it simply took her breath away and made her go cold all over. Swinging her feet on to the floor she lit a cigarette with hands that were suddenly trembling.

She couldn't. No, she couldn't. Or . . . could she?

Georgie let herself into the house after another evening out with Charlie. Yet again she'd thoroughly enjoyed his company. The pair of them got on like a house on fire. Things were beginning to get serious, she told herself. The idea pleased her a great deal.

That night she dreamt about Charlie, and in the morning she woke with a huge smile on her face.

'How's the ankle?' Lena enquired when Hamish presented himself. He had been off for three full weeks.

'A lot better, thank you.'

'How did you sprain it in the first place?'

'Haring after a bus, believe it or not. It sort of turned under me, and that was that. Minutes later it was swollen to the size of a tennis ball. Painful as hell, I can tell you. I was in agony.'

Lena nodded her sympathy. 'Well, before you ask, everything's fine here. Up to date and running like clockwork.'

He beamed at her. 'I expected nothing else with you in charge, Lena. You're a treasure right enough.' And with that he went into his office and closed the door behind him.

Later, Lena glanced at the wall clock. Half an hour to go, and she still hadn't made her move. Several times she'd been about to, then changed her mind at the last moment and sat down again.

She didn't have to do it today, she reminded herself. He was only just back, after all. But in her heart of hearts she knew that to be the lamest of excuses. Tom was right when he'd told her she lacked guts. She always had been that way.

But not now. Not bloody now!

Rising, she went to his closed door, knocked, and went in. Hamish looked up in surprise.

'What can I do for you, Lena?'

'I think you and I should have a drink in the Swan tonight.'

He stared at her in puzzlement. 'What? Why?'

'Because I have something important to say to you.'

'Can't you say it here?'

'No. It's too personal for that.'

He continued staring at her, his puzzlement deepening. 'I don't understand.'

'You will. Right after work. That suit?'

'If you insist.'

'I do, Hamish. I most certainly do.'

His forehead crinkled in a frown as she swept away.

Hamish placed a large gin and tonic in front of Lena, who had deliberately chosen an out-of-the-way table where they wouldn't be overheard. 'Now what's this all about?'

She waited till he was seated before replying. 'You're a fool, Hamish Murchison. A damned fool.'

He blinked at her. 'I beg your pardon?'

'You heard me, Hamish. You're a fool.' Surprised by her own calmness, she had a sip of her drink, then lit a cigarette, while he stared at her in astonishment.

'Perhaps you'd care to explain that?' There was a trace of anger in his voice.

'Did you really think you could defraud the company and get away with it?'

His face drained of colour until it was left a pasty shade of white, his eyes out on stalks. 'That's . . . that's . . .' he stuttered.

'Don't try to deny it, Hamish. While you were off I had a look at those ledgers you keep in your desk, which told the story. You've been at it since shortly after becoming head of department to the tune of roughly fifty pounds a month.' She found she was rather enjoying this. His expression was a mixture of terror and sheer incredulity.

'How dare you go through my desk,' he choked at last.

'Not exactly ethical, I admit. But what I found was most illuminating.'

'It's a damned lie!'

She sighed. 'No, it isn't, Hamish. As you're well aware. You've been cooking the books. Thieving, in other words. For which you can be sacked, and most likely sent to prison.' She watched in amusement while he picked up the whisky he'd ordered for himself and drank it in one go. 'Such sloppy book-keeping, too. What you were up to almost leapt off the page at me.'

'What . . .' He swallowed. 'What are you going to do? Are you going to report me?'

She puffed on her cigarette and deliberately didn't reply for a few moments, making him suffer. 'That depends,' she drawled eventually.

'On what?'

'Whether or not we come to an arrangement.'

He was sweating now, trickles of it running down his forehead. 'What sort of an arrangement?' he croaked.

'Embezzlement,' she mused, shaking her head. 'I'd never have thought it of you, Hamish.'

'What arrangement?' he almost screamed.

'Control yourself, man,' she chided. 'You don't want to draw attention to yourself now, do you?'

He quickly glanced round the room, but no one was watching. 'No.'

'Why don't you go and get yourself another whisky? You look as though you could use one.'

He hesitated, desperate to hear what this arrangement was, but his need for another drink momentarily overrode all other considerations. Getting to his feet he strode swiftly back to the bar. Lena was amused to see him ordering two doubles, the first of which he threw down his throat before returning to the table carrying the second.

'This arrangement?'

'I don't think you'd like prison, Hamish. Nasty places, I understand. Then, when you came out, who would employ you? You'd probably end up doing something manual, which doesn't strike me as being you at all.'

He gritted his teeth in fear and frustration. 'What's the arrangement, Lena. Come on, out with it.'

'I'm not exactly a pretty woman, am I?'

He glanced away.

'Well? Be honest.'

'No, you're not,' he admitted.

'Haven't got much of a figure either.'

He didn't reply to that.

'You know what my big dread in life is, Hamish?'

'What?'

'Ending up an old maid. Unmarried, unloved and never having known a man in the biblical sense.'

Dear God, he thought in alarm. Was she about to propose marriage? The idea of being married to Lena McKeand made him feel sick inside. She was the original dog.

'Well, now I'm in a position to sort out one of these things,' she said slowly.

He opened his mouth, shut it. Then opened it again. This was a living nightmare. 'Which one?'

She treated him to a razored smile, the look of a bird

of prey about to pounce on its victim. 'The arrangement is that you sleep with me once a month. That's all I ask. That arrangement to last until the day you get married, at which time it's dissolved. As a bonus for you, and to make this more palatable, I'll allow you to keep on doing what you've been doing, but in the meantime will show you how to do it in a way whereby your chances of being caught in the future are absolutely minimal. And, if you take my advice, you'll re-do the ledgers already in existence in the same manner. In other words, make new books to replace those in your drawer.'

Lena sat back in her chair and studied him. There, it was done. She'd had the courage after all. And, surprisingly, she'd rather enjoyed herself in the process.

'This is blackmail,' he accused hoarsely, mind reeling.

'Yes, isn't it just.' She smiled.

He tried to imagine what it would be like in prison, how it would be to be surrounded by hardened criminals. And, as Lena had pointed out, what would he do for employment on his release? Dig ditches? Him, Hamish Murchison! The very idea made him cringe.

'Well?' Lena prompted.

'You don't give me much choice.'

'Well, it's either one thing or the other. I imagine your golf pal, the chairman, wouldn't be very happy to be informed of your little sideline. It would be the end of a beautiful friendship. Of course, if he doesn't find out, then I would think there's further promotion in the pipeline for you, wouldn't you say?'

'Bitch,' he snarled.

'Sticks and stones, Hamish. Sticks and stones.' She

finished her drink and pushed her glass across the table. 'I'll have another, please.'

He glared at her before picking up the empty glass and returning to the bar. She lit a second cigarette, considering the prospect of being in bed with the handsome Hamish. The images flashing through her mind aroused her, causing her to shift in her chair.

'Thank you,' she said when he returned with another large gin.

'Just once a month?'

'That's right.'

'And the arrangement stops the day I get married?'

She nodded.

'And you'll show me how—'

'Yes, yes,' Lena cut in. 'We've been through all that. You know exactly what the proposition is. So, take it or leave it.'

He stared at her, trying to find something even vaguely attractive in that face of hers. He failed.

'I agree,' he said woodenly.

'The first Saturday of every month,' she said. 'And I leave it to you to fix up where our meetings will take place.'

'All right.'

She'd pulled it off, Lena thought with glee. She smiled at Hamish, who didn't smile back.

Georgie was thoroughly enjoying herself, but then she always did when she was with Charlie. They were at a dinner dance, the first she'd ever been to.

'That was lovely,' she declared, pushing her plate slightly away from herself.

'It is good, isn't it? More wine?'

'Please.' Georgie giggled as he refilled her glass. 'I'm not used to wine. It's making me feel all girly.'

'I like that.'

'Do you?'

'Uh-huh.'

He had gorgeous eyes, she thought. Kind, warm, tender. Occasionally when she caught him looking at her it made her shiver.

He smiled. 'You're an excellent dancer.'

'Thank you. But I'm not nearly as good as my brother Tom. Now he really can dance. He's got magical feet, that one. Fairy feet, my mum says.'

Charlie laughed. 'I don't think I'd like to be told I had fairy feet. Whoever heard of a fireman with those?'

'Or a moulder, which is what Tom does. But that's what Mum says.'

Charlie regarded her over the rim of his glass. 'They sound a wonderful family. Perhaps I should meet them some time?'

'Would you like to?'

'Very much so.'

'Well, I'm sure that can be arranged.'

'I'll look forward to the occasion.' Reaching across the table he laid a hand on hers. 'I'm glad you came to the station that day.'

'So am I.'

'Whoever thought it would develop into this?'

Georgie merely smiled.

'Shall we?' he asked as the band struck up again.

'Of course.'

She sighed with pleasure as he took her into his arms, feeling completely at home there. At home, and totally safe.

Lena took a deep breath before knocking on Hamish's door. He opened it almost immediately.

'Hello,' she said, a slight nervous catch in her voice.

'Hello. Come on in.'

Knowing that he lived on his own, his parents being dead, she'd been expecting a right old tip. To her amazement the inside of the house gleamed like a new pin.

'Gin and tonic?'

'Please.'

As he poured she noticed that the bottle of malt on display was one of the very best. And expensive.

'I thought we'd have a few drinks before . . .' He trailed off, and coughed.

'Good idea.'

She sat, and gazed around. 'If you don't mind me asking, how does a bachelor keep his place so neat and tidy?'

Hamish grinned. 'That's easy. He hires a neighbour, who's a middle-aged widow, to "do" for him. Dust, clean, polish and so on. She also washes and irons, sews, and does other repairs.'

'I see. And you can afford her, plus the best whisky, because of you-know-what?'

'Exactly. It also pays for better clothes than I could normally afford, and lots besides.' Hamish dropped his gaze to stare at the floor. 'Lena, before we go any further I've a confession to make.'

'And what's that?'

'I've never . . . well, to put it bluntly I've never been to bed with a woman. All this will be new to me.'

It pleased her enormously. 'That makes two of us. So it'll be all right then.'

He nodded his relief, feeling a lot better after his admission. He wouldn't be expected to perform like some expert. They had their several drinks, which gradually relaxed them both. 'Shall we go through to the bedroom?' he suggested after a while.

Lena rose, only too eager to do so, yet apprehensive at the same time.

When, later, she left Hamish to walk off down the road she was wearing the broadest of smiles. What had happened had been a bit of a grope and fumble. But they'd got there in the end.

And she wasn't a virgin any more.

Chapter 15

'What an exceptionally nice chap,' Chrissie enthused after Georgie and Charlie had left them. Charlie had been invited for Sunday dinner.

'Decent of him to bring a bottle of whisky along,' Tam commented warmly, and decided to have another dram from what was left.

'They make a good couple, don't you think?' Chrissie asked Lena.

'Aye, I thought so as well.' Lena wasn't nearly as jealous of her sister as she would have been before her arrangement with Hamish. At least, now, she wasn't completely left out of things.

'What did you think, Tom?' asked Chrissie.

'I quite took to him. He's certainly charming enough.'

Ian, who had elected to spend the afternoon with his grandparents, was in a corner playing with an old tin tray, not listening to the conversation.

'Do you imagine it's wedding bells?' Tom mused.

Chrissie looked at Tam, who shrugged. 'Might be.'

'She could certainly do a lot worse.' Chrissie nodded, keen on the idea.

'Ian seemed to take a shine to him,' Tom commented.

'Maybe that's because Charlie brought him sweets,' Lena pointed out cynically.

'No, there was more to it than that. At least I thought so.' Tom was sticking to his guns.

'If nothing else, I'm glad we've met the man who saved Georgie's life,' Tam declared. 'We all owe him a lot for that.'

'No one more than Georgie,' Chrissie muttered.

'Aye,' Tam agreed, sipping the dram he'd just poured. That was true enough.

'Let's just hope she's fallen on her feet and met another as good and kind as John, God rest his soul,' said Chrissie.

Tam's face clouded at the reminder of John, whom he'd liked enormously. What a tragedy that had been.

'Well, I for one approve,' Chrissie went on. 'If they do decide to wed I only hope they make each other happy.'

'I'm sure they will.' Lena smiled.

'What? Get married or make each other happy if they do?' said Tom.

'Both.'

Tam produced his pipe and lit up, thinking about Charlie and what his first impression had been. One thing was certain, it hadn't been a bad one; quite the contrary. That was enough for Tam, who considered himself an excellent judge of character.

'Come on, Lena, let's get these dishes done,' Chrissie urged. 'I'll wash, you dry.'

Lena rose and joined her mother at the sink, while Tam began reading those parts of the Sunday paper he so far hadn't, and Tom fell asleep. The excitement over, it was a normal Sunday afternoon at home.

'How did I do?' Charlie demanded of Georgie the moment they were down the stairs and out on the street.

She linked his arm. 'They liked you.'

'Are you sure?'

'Oh aye, I am that. They all took to you. Thought you were terrific.'

'How about Ian?'

'Bringing him sweets helped. It was a good idea, that.'

'Bribery and corruption, eh?' Charlie laughed.

'A wee bit bribery perhaps, but hardly corruption.'

They smiled at one another. Then, acting on impulse, Charlie kissed her swiftly on the mouth.

'Not in the street!' Georgie exclaimed, pretending to be scandalised. 'What will the neighbours think?'

'Bugger the neighbours. They shouldn't be peeping out from behind their curtains anyway.'

Georgie laughed. 'You'll never stop them doing that. They're a right nosy lot round here.'

'Well, they should find better things to do than spy on each other.'

Georgie pulled herself even closer to him as they headed for Charlie's tram stop. 'When am I going to see you again?'

'How about this Saturday? You can come to my house and meet Avril. How does that sound?'

'Fine by me.'

'She already knows about you so it won't be a bolt out of the blue. Would you like to bring Ian along?'

'Yes, why not?'

'That's agreed, then.'

She stared lovingly into his eyes, and this time it was she who kissed him swiftly on the mouth.

'What about the neighbours!' he exclaimed, tongue firmly in cheek.

'Bugger them. With knobs on.'

They laughed uproariously as they continued on their way.

'Lena, can you come into my office for a minute?'

She glanced up from what she was doing, then got to her feet and followed him.

'Shut the door, will you?' Hamish produced a ledger which he placed on his desktop. 'This is the first of the two I'm re-doing. Will you tell me what you think?'

Lena lifted the ledger, opened it at random, and studied the figures on that page.

He'd learnt well, she thought, although he had not been the easiest of people to teach, not being exactly the sharpest knife in the drawer. He had about as much aptitude for figures as she had for glamour modelling. She flipped over some pages and again studied the figures, while Hamish looked anxiously on.

'It'll do,' she declared at last.

Hamish gave a sigh of relief.

'Where's the one it's replacing?'

'Don't worry, it's at my house. I'll destroy it now you've given that one the all clear.'

'And the second ledger?'

'I shall be starting on that right away. The sooner I've covered my tracks the better, eh?'

She nodded her approval. 'I'll get back to work, then.'

'So must I. Lots to do.'

Like going to the coffee house, Lena thought cynically. At the door she paused. 'You haven't forgotten this Saturday is the first in the month?'

He met her steady gaze. 'I haven't forgotten, Lena. I'll be waiting.'

And she'd be there. Dead on time. She was already counting the days.

'Hello, Avril. I'm delighted to meet you.' Georgie smiled at the curly-golden-haired girl looking up at her. What a beauty, she thought. If Charlie's face was cherubic then Avril's was angelic. She was the prettiest wee lassie Georgie had seen in a long time.

'Hello, Mrs Mair,' Avril replied solemnly, extending a thin white hand.

Georgie had already thought about this introduction, and made a decision. 'I think Mrs Mair is a little formal,' she said, shaking with Avril. 'Why don't you just call me Georgie?'

'If you wish, Georgie.'

Georgie's smile became a beam. 'That's far better. And this is my son Ian.'

Ian already hated this house. He didn't like the way it smelt, or the unfamiliar furniture. He disliked everything about it, particularly the fact that although it was sunny out, it was dark inside. He would later learn that the inside of the house was permanently gloomy which was why the gas mantles were on all the time when anybody was at home.

'Hello, Ian. Nice to meet you.'

'And you, Avril.'

How sweet, Georgie thought. They weren't acting like children but like rather diminutive grown-ups. She thought it touching.

'Why don't you take Ian through and show him your bedroom?' Charlie suggested.

Ian didn't want to visit a lassie's bedroom. It was probably full of dolls and other daft feminine things. Nor did Avril want to take him there. Her bedroom was her private place.

'What a good idea,' Georgie enthused, hoping the youngsters were going to get on together.

Avril glanced at her father and saw the look in his eyes. She'd have to obey. 'All right then,' she declared. 'Come on, Ian.'

Reluctantly, almost dragging his feet, he followed her.

'That seems to have got off to a good start,' Charlie commented.

Georgie thought so too. 'They'll soon warm to one another, you'll see.'

'They're just shy, that's all. Quite natural.'

Georgie dismissed the subject. 'Now, what are we having for dinner?'

'I'm not much of a cook, I'm afraid, Georgie. So if you don't mind, it's just mince and potatoes.'

'My favourite,' Georgie lied. 'And you don't have to worry about cooking. I'll do that. Just show me where everything is.'

He'd been hoping she'd volunteer. 'That's very good of you.'

'Don't mention it.'

'I swear that's the best mince and potatoes I've ever tasted,' Charlie declared, pushing his plate away.

'Thank you,' Georgie acknowledged. 'Are you enjoying it, Avril?'

The wee girl stared at her, face expressionless. 'My mummy was a good cook. Isn't that so, Daddy?'

'Yes, she was, hen. A very good cook,' Charlie replied, eyes flicking to Georgie to see what she was making of this.

'You must miss your mummy a lot, Avril,' Georgie said quietly.

'Can I get down now, Daddy?'

'Not yet. Ian and Georgie haven't finished.'

'I have,' Ian muttered, pushing his plate away as well, wondering when they were going to leave this place and go home. The sooner the better as far as he was concerned.

At that moment there was the scrape of a key in a lock. 'That'll be my sister Betty,' Charlie explained. 'She said she'd drop by.'

The woman who entered the room was unmistakably related to Charlie, having the same cherubic face and similar colouring. 'You must be the Georgie I've heard so much about.' She smiled. 'I'm pleased I get to meet you at last.'

Georgie rose from her chair and shook hands with the newcomer. 'And I'm pleased to meet you. I would have recognised you anywhere as Charlie's sister.'

'Aye, people have always said we look alike.' She glanced at the table. 'Am I interrupting?'

'No, no,' Charlie assured her, coming to his feet. 'We'd just finished.'

Georgie introduced Ian, who got up to shake hands and then more or less hid behind his mother.

'Georgie cooked the dinner,' Charlie informed his sister.

'That's nice.'

'Charlie peeled the potatoes,' Georgie added, feeling awkward.

'That's right, you keep him up to scratch, Georgie. He can be a lazy sod at times. That so, Charlie?'

'According to you, anyway. No one else has ever complained.'

'Agnes did. All the time.' Betty's hand flew to her mouth. 'Sorry. Maybe I shouldn't have said that.'

'No offence taken,' Georgie said, forcing a smile on to her face. 'She was Charlie's wife, after all.'

'Georgie has a funny voice,' Avril said after the visitors had gone.

'That's because the fumes from the fire I saved her from damaged her throat,' Charlie explained.

Avril's expression was one of sheer admiration. 'Were you a hero, Daddy?'

'Of course.'

'You're always a hero, aren't you?'

This was a favourite conversation of theirs. He nodded. 'Always.'

'I love you, Daddy.'

'And I love you, pet. You know that.'

She went to him and buried her head in his lap. 'You won't ever leave me, will you, Daddy?'

'Never,' he assured her.

There was a few minutes' silence, then Avril said, 'Ian has got horrid skin. Did you notice?'

'He has some sort of skin problem. Georgie has mentioned it in the past. The doctors are hoping he'll grow out of it as he gets older.'

'It's still horrid.'

'Tell me, what did you think of Georgie? Did you like her?'

Avril didn't reply.

'Well?'

'Her mince wasn't as good as Mummy's.'

And that's all Charlie could get out of his daughter on the subject.

Lena's eyes opened wide as she gave a loud moan of pleasure. So this is what it's meant to be like with a man, she thought.

And then she found she was mistaken. There was more. Throwing back her head she screamed in reaction to the sensation exploding through her insides.

'That really was something,' Hamish said a few minutes later. Lena was lying staring catlike at him.

'I think we got it right this time,' she said.

He laughed. 'I think so too.'

Lena closed her eyes, reliving what had just taken place, aware that her entire body was glowing in a way it never had before.

'More champagne?'

'Please.'

She sat up when he handed her a glass, her eyes locking on to his over its rim when she drank.

'We seem to have learnt rather quickly,' he commented.

Lena couldn't have agreed more.

Tam was pleased with himself – or dead chuffed as he might well have put it. Another deal with Groves, the scrapman, had been completed, with even more profit than usual as he'd been able to include rolls of copper wire, the price of which was currently extremely high.

Life as a foreman certainly had its perks, Tam reflected. If you were prepared to take the risks, that is. As long as McNair's never found out, mind. And he was damned careful they never would.

He kept fingering the extra notes in his pocket as he and Tom made their way home at the end of their day's work.

Lena laid down the latest letter she'd had from Pet. The big news was that Pet was going out with a famous Mexican actor called Ricardo Martinez, who'd starred in many films as the romantic lead. Pet was terribly excited about this latest liaison, even hinting that it might lead to marriage if things continued as they were. She'd also landed a plum part in a new movie, with shooting due to start in a few weeks' time. She was terribly excited about that too.

As usual Pet ended the letter by demanding to know when Lena was going to join her in Hollywood. Surely Lena had saved up enough money by now to make the trip?

Lena thought about Hamish and their monthly get-togethers. She'd be mad to give those up. Completely insane. It might not be much, but it meant a great deal to her. It was an arrangement she wasn't going to jettison in a hurry. As far as she was concerned Hollywood was now completely off the agenda. And when she replied to Pet's letter she'd tell Pet so. She'd explain that she too was in a relationship, though there would be no mention of how that relationship had come about.

Blackmail.

'I've got some wonderful news,' Georgie announced. She had just arrived at her parents' house with a pale-faced Ian in tow.

'And what's that?' Chrissie wanted to know.

'Charlie and I are getting married.'

Tam nodded. 'Aye, we thought that might happen. Congratulations, lass.'

'Oh, Georgie,' Chrissie breathed, delighted. 'I'm ever so happy for you.'

The entire family crowded round to make a fuss of Georgie, all talking nineteen to the dozen while a silent Ian looked on.

'So, when's the big day?' Tom demanded.

'We haven't settled on that yet, but we will shortly. It'll be the register office, of course, as we've both been married before. And only the immediate family to be there so as to keep down the cost.'

'Very sensible,' Tam acknowledged.

'Does that mean you're now engaged?' Lena queried,

glancing at her sister's left hand to see if there was a new ring on the third finger.

'We decided to forgo that. It'll be marriage plain and simple, with no strings attached.'

'I think this calls for a drink. If I give you the money will you go and get a bottle, Tom?'

'Of course, Papa. The usual?'

'Aye.'

'He's a lovely chap. I quite took to him,' Chrissie enthused. 'You'll be giving up your own house then, I take it?'

'That's right, Mum. I'll speak to the factor as soon as we've settled on a date.'

'A second bite of the cherry, eh?' Lena commented. 'You're lucky.'

'Oh, I know that. I never thought I'd find anyone after John, and here I have. Lucky right enough.'

'So where did he propose?' Chrissie demanded. 'Sit down. I want to hear all the details.'

'In the park, Mum. We went for a walk and he proposed in the middle of it.'

'In the park,' Chrissie repeated. 'How romantic.'

Tam couldn't see how proposing in the park was any more romantic than anywhere else. But then, what did he know? He was only a man.

Ian was in floods of tears. 'I don't want to leave here,' he sobbed. 'And I don't want to change schools either.'

'There there, son. There there. Don't get so upset.' Georgie was upset herself.

'I hate that house. It isn't nice.'

That baffled her. 'What do you mean, it isn't nice?'

'It just isn't.'

'You'll soon get used to it, I promise you. It might be a bit strange to begin with, but that'll soon wear off.'

'And I don't like Avril. She hurt me when we were in her bedroom.'

'How did she do that?'

'She nipped my arm really hard. It was sore.'

Georgie wasn't sure whether or not she believed him. Why on earth would Avril nip Ian's arm? It didn't make sense. 'Are you certain?'

Ian stared at her as the tears continued to roll down his face. 'I'm not fibbing, Mum. I'm not. She was horrible to me.'

If it was true then it was something that would have to be sorted out, Georgie thought. The two children would just have to learn to get along. There was nothing else for it.

'Can't we stay here, Mum? Please?'

'No, we can't, son. I'm marrying Charlie and I'll be living with him in his house. So will you.'

'But I don't want to!'

He was rapidly becoming hysterical, Georgie realised. Well, she couldn't have that. 'If you don't calm down this instant, then big boy or not, I'm going to spank you. Understand?'

Ian stared at his mother in disbelief. She'd never spanked him. Not ever. And now she was threatening to. It was all that Charlie's fault. And that horrible Avril.

He couldn't have articulated it as such, but he felt

as if his entire, secure world was crumbling all around him.

'I now pronounce you man and wife. You may kiss the bride.'

Georgie closed her eyes as Charlie's lips pressed down on hers. Her husband's lips. The lips of the man who'd saved her life, and whom she'd come to love.

As Lena had once said, she was extraordinarily lucky to have a second bite of the cherry.

Chapter 16

Chrissie glanced round in surprise when she heard a key in the lock, and a few moments later Tam and Tom trooped into the kitchen. 'What are you doing home so early?' she demanded. 'Dinner won't be ready for another couple of hours yet.'

'Three-quarters of the workforce has been laid off until further notice,' a grim-faced Tam announced.

Chrissie's jaw dropped. This was awful, though not exactly unexpected. People were being laid off all over the country. And by that she meant Britain and not just Scotland.

'Both of you?' she croaked.

Tam shook his head. 'I'm still there, but only for three days a week as we're now more or less reduced to a skeleton staff. I picked the men in the foundry who got the bullet, and had to choose Tom to be amongst them. You can imagine what would have been said if I hadn't.'

'Three days,' Chrissie repeated. 'Less money, I take it?'

'Oh aye.'

Tom flung himself into a chair. 'Nobody has any idea how long it'll be before we're called back. Weeks. Months. Who knows?'

'Lack of orders, you see, Chrissie. They've been getting less and less of late. And now, apparently, they're on the verge of drying up altogether.' Tam shook his head. 'We've got the Yanks to thank for this. Them and their damned Wall Street crash. Greed was behind that. Sheer bloody greed.'

'You'd have thought the government would have been able to do something,' Chrissie muttered.

'I've no doubt they tried,' Tam replied bitterly. 'But they couldn't.'

Thank God for Lena's pay packet coming in, Chrissie thought, her mind whirling as she wondered how she was going to cope. And Tam's three days, she reminded herself. They'd get by, somehow. But it wasn't going to be easy.

Tam took out his pipe, and lit up. Then he removed it from his mouth and stared at it. 'No more tobacco or fags for me after this lot,' he said. 'Won't be able to afford them. Or my whisky at the weekends. That's something else I'll have to do without.'

Chrissie's heart went out to him, knowing how much he loved his smoke and dram. But he was right, they were both luxuries for which there would be very little cash from now on.

'Maybe I can find another job somewhere?' Tom said hopefully, well aware of how unlikely that was. There again, looking on the bright side, miracles did sometimes happen.

*   *   *

Georgie glanced at the clock, wondering how long it would be before Charlie got home. He had gone out for a drink with some of his pals, while she'd been sitting worrying about her family, who were struggling because of the reduced amount of money coming into the house.

She'd spoken to Charlie about the possibility of his being laid off and he'd laughed, saying that they'd never lay off firemen. Do that and the entire city could burn down. His reassurance had been a big comfort to her. They, at least, were safe from the general slump.

Half an hour later Charlie still hadn't returned. Had something untoward happened, she wondered. Glasgow was a violent place, after all. And then there he was, falling into the room, red-faced, eyes glazed, swaying from side to side. It was the first time Georgie had ever seen him drunk, and it wasn't a pretty sight.

Charlie staggered to the nearest chair and slumped into it. 'I'm pished as a rat,' he slurred. 'I hope you're not going to complain, woman?'

Georgie frowned, not liking his aggressive tone. 'What makes you think I would?'

'Agnes always did. But then she was a bitch. Not sweet-natured like you, eh?'

'I think I should get you through to your bed, Charlie.'

'I want another drink.'

'There's none in the house.'

He gave her a peculiar, leery smile. 'Oh aye there is. Hidden. Planked, you ken.'

This was news to her. 'Where exactly?'

He told her. And, sure enough, when she went to investigate she found a half-full bottle of whisky.

'Pour me a dram,' he instructed her when she returned with the bottle. 'And make it a big one.'

'Why hide the bottle, Charlie? There's no need for that.'

'Habit, you undershtand. From the old days. Had to hide it otherwise Agnes would have had it.'

'You mean she'd have drunk it?'

'And licked the inside of the bottle too if that had been possible.'

'Really?' This was also news.

'Aye, really. She loved the gargle did Agnes.'

She handed him a generously charged glass which he stared at for a few moments before throwing its contents down his throat. He belched loudly.

'Another one, hen. And quickly.'

Georgie wasn't impressed by this side of Charlie. Not one little bit.

He insisted on finishing the bottle before she could get him into bed, where he snored, and intermittently broke wind, throughout the night.

Tom lay in his bed listening to his father and sister getting ready for work. Black despair filled him. He felt useless not working himself. A drain on the family finances because he wasn't earning. A parasite, in other words.

He knew he should get up and join them, but just couldn't bring himself to do so. He didn't feel able to face them when they were employed and he wasn't. He'd been looking everywhere for a job, but there was simply none to be had. Not even the sniff of one.

He'd go for a walk later on, he decided. At least that was something to do.

'Lena, can you please come into my office for a moment?'

Damn, she thought. She was in the middle of a difficult computation which she'd now have to leave and come back to. Most irritating.

'Close the door,' Hamish said when she joined him. Then he sighed, and perched on the edge of his desk, a most unusual informality for him. 'I've had orders from on high.'

'Oh?'

'I've to get rid of one of the girls in the department and I want you to tell me which one.'

That was a jolt. 'I see.'

'You know them and their abilities better than I do. Don't you agree?'

She nodded. That was true enough.

'It's a bad business having to let someone go, but orders are orders.'

'Are the other departments also getting rid of personnel?'

'So I understand. Harsh times, Lena. Harsh times, I'm afraid. Let's just hope and pray it doesn't get to the stage where you and I are also given the boot.'

She smiled thinly. 'I doubt you'd ever be given the boot, Hamish. Your golfing friend, the chairman, wouldn't allow it.'

Hamish had the grace to blush. 'Think about it, and let me know your decision before we leave this evening.'

He was still blushing as Lena returned to her computation.

'Bread and dripping,' Tam said quietly, looking at what Chrissie had placed before him for tea.

'I'm afraid that's all we can afford, Tam. You can't really complain. You had a couple of sausages and mash for dinner, after all.'

Tom stared at his plate in disgust. He absolutely loathed bread and dripping. But he was going to have to eat it; either that or go without.

The so-called meal made up Lena's mind for her. She'd visit the bank the following day.

Chrissie gazed at the wad of notes Lena had handed her as if it was manna from heaven.

'My savings, Mum.'

'You mean . . . your Hollywood money?'

Lena nodded. 'It's needed here rather than lying in the bank.'

Chrissie felt a choke in her throat. 'I never wanted you to go to Hollywood, you must have known that. There again, I don't want your dream to end like this.'

'I'd already made up my mind not to go, Mum, so it's not the end of any dream. I promise you.'

Chrissie raised the notes to her mouth, and kissed them. 'Thank you, lass.'

'Thanks aren't needed, Mum. Don't forget, I'm in this present pickle as well. It's just fortunate that I'm able to help out a bit.'

Chrissie took a deep breath. 'Wait till I tell your father. He'll be right proud of you.'

Lena didn't think pride came into it. But necessity did.

Ian and Avril were on their way to school when she suddenly gripped him by the arm, forcing him to stop.

'You smell,' she said quietly, eyes glittering with amusement. And with that she went running off up the street roaring with laughter, leaving a stricken Ian staring after her.

Georgie had become friends with Gladys Renton, her next-door neighbour, and was now in her house having a cup of tea and a natter.

'Can I ask you a question, Gladys?'

'Aye, sure. What is it?'

Georgie slowly stirred her tea. 'I take it you knew Agnes, my predecessor?'

'Not too well, I have to say. She kept to herself a lot.'

'So you don't know what she was like?'

Gladys stared at Georgie, then nodded. 'I suppose that must interest you. Stands to reason. I know I'd be curious in your circumstances.'

'Well?'

'She was pleasant enough, when sober. Which wasn't often.'

'She drank a lot, then?' Gladys's words bore out what Charlie had said.

'Like the proverbial fish. Whenever she had the money, that was.' Gladys shook her head. 'She'd drink anything alcoholic, that woman. You name it, she'd pour it down her throat. When she was really desperate she'd go on the cheap red wine. And I mean cheap. Other times it would be strong cider. On occasion she'd mix them both, wine and cider in the same glass.'

'How horrible,' Georgie breathed. 'That must have been lethal.'

'That was the whole point, don't you see? It was a sure-fire quick way for her to get out of her skull.'

Georgie hesitated. 'Was she pretty?'

'Might well have been when she was younger. But if so the drink had put paid to that. She was anything but pretty when she died.'

'Fell down the stairs, I understand?'

'Pissed when it happened. They say she tripped, and no wonder, the state she was in. I'd had a brief word with her earlier that day and she was already incoherent. Couldn't get any sense out of her whatever. She was standing there staring at me with dribbles of spit running down her chin. Awful it was. And then later took her tumble. Probably fell over her own feet.'

Poor Charlie, Georgie thought. Imagine being married to a woman like that.

Tom stopped outside a soup kitchen to stare grimly at the queue which had formed there. Poor bastards, he thought. They were really on their uppers. How humiliating having to accept charity.

Most of them would be on the dole, he presumed, though from what he understood the Public Assistance only paid out measly sums. He'd heard somewhere that a married couple with three children got one pound nine shillings and threepence a week. How on God's earth were they expected to live on that? And anything they did manage to earn was instantly deducted from their entitlement. Even a few pence from a child's paper round would be taken off.

At least he and the rest of the family hadn't been reduced to these pitiful levels, thanks to Lena's job, her cash contribution, and his father's short-time. Yes, when you looked at it that way they had a lot to be thankful for.

'What's wrong with you, son?' Georgie asked anxiously at the tea table. Something clearly was.

Ian shook his head, and didn't reply.

'Are you feeling ill?'

'No, Mum,' he answered in a small voice.

'Is it your skin?'

'No, Mum.'

'Then what?'

Avril pushed her plate away. 'I'm going to my Aunt Betty's,' she announced, sliding from her chair.

'I don't want you going there. Your father will be home shortly,' said Georgie.

Avril stared defiantly at her stepmother. 'I'm going to Aunt Betty's. She's a lot more fun than you.'

'No you're . . .' Georgie trailed off when Avril suddenly dashed from the room, banging the outside door closed behind her. What a difficult child, Georgie thought. Was she never going to win her over? Their relationship was rapidly becoming a problem she didn't know how to solve. She felt a complete and utter failure where Avril was concerned. Avril, who doted on her father as if he was some kind of god.

'There's something different about you lately, and I can't quite put my finger on it,' Chrissie declared.

'Different?' Lena queried.

'Aye, different. What do you think, Tam?'

He glanced over at his daughter, frowning as he studied her. He'd been thinking that he could've murdered a pipeful of tobacco, or a fag, for he was still having terrible trouble trying to conquer the urge. Chrissie had refused to give him any of Lena's money to satisfy his craving, saying they had no idea how long the money was going to have to last, so in the meantime he would just have to go without. He'd thought it mean of Chrissie, but in his heart he knew she was right.

'She looks the same to me.'

'She's put on weight,' Tom said.

'You know, I think you have,' Chrissie agreed, having appraised her daughter again.

Lena ran her hands over her hips, which did seem fuller than they had been. Fuller, and rounder. Her bras had been hurting a bit recently, too, which would make sense if her breasts had become larger.

'Your skin's changed as well,' Chrissie commented. 'It's got more colour to it than usual.'

Lena suddenly smiled as the penny dropped. Going to bed with Hamish, albeit only once a month, was having a beneficial effect on her physicality, which delighted her.

'What's causing it, I wonder,' Chrissie said.

'I have absolutely no idea,' Lena lied. 'None at all.'

She began humming as she got on with what she'd been doing. Thank you, Hamish Murchison, she thought gleefully. Thank you very much indeed. She was looking forward to the coming Saturday's session even more now she realised what sex was doing for her.

Charlie had come off duty with a splitting headache, the result of banging his head hard while attending a fire. All he wanted was something to eat and an early night.

'I'd like to talk to you,' Georgie told him as he tucked into his meal.

'What about?'

'Ian. He's being bullied at school.'

Charlie glanced across to where Ian was sitting watching them. Avril was still at her Aunt Betty's. 'Is that right, Ian?'

Ian nodded.

Charlie sighed. He really didn't need this at the moment. 'What are they doing to you? Or is it only one child?'

'It's three boys,' Georgie declared.

Charlie grunted. 'Can't he speak for himself?'

'Ian?' Georgie prompted.

'It's three big boys.'

'And what do they do to you?'

'Hit me. Chase me round the playground. Spit on me.'

'Do you think I should go to the headmaster?' Georgie asked.

'That would only make matters worse. He'd be called a mummy's boy. You don't want that, do you?'

Georgie bit her lip. 'No,' she admitted.

Charlie had another mouthful of food, but he had suddenly lost his appetite. His head was really killing him. Sitting back in his chair, he sighed again.

'It is a rather rough school,' Georgie said.

Charlie stared at her. 'Rough? How do you mean rough?'

'They all seem to be toughies there.'

'And I suppose the school he went to before was a lot nicer?'

'It was actually,' Georgie replied, not noticing the sudden glint of anger in Charlie's eyes.

'Does that mean you think this area isn't as nice as where you used to live?'

'Well, it isn't,' she admitted honestly. 'Surely you can see that?'

'Are you telling me it isn't good enough for you and your son?'

Alarm flared in her. 'No, of course not, Charlie. I didn't mean that at all.' She was unsure of herself now, having heard the aggressive tone in her husband's voice.

'I would remind you,' Charlie almost hissed, 'that my Avril goes to this school you say is full of so-called toughies. She's only a wee defenceless lassie but she gets on perfectly well there. She doesn't get bullied like your precious son.'

'I didn't mean you to take offence,' Georgie retorted swiftly. What was wrong with the man to make him react like this?

Charlie swivelled his gaze on to Ian. 'You say these big boys chase you round the playground. Is that because you run away?'

'Yes,' Ian confessed in a whisper.

The lad's a coward, Charlie thought with contempt. A bloody little coward. No wonder he was being bullied. At school, cowards and the weak usually were. It was the way of things.

'Then don't,' Charlie snapped. 'Stand your ground. If they hit you, then hit back. That's the only thing they'll understand. Hit back and they'll soon stop the bullying. It won't be so much fun for them then.'

'But there are three of them,' Ian protested in a scared voice.

'So?'

'They'll . . .' Ian broke off, the implication clear.

'Knock spots off you maybe. But that's something you'll just have to take until they get the message that you're going to defend yourself.'

'I'm not sure I approve of that,' said a horrified Georgie, having visions of Ian coming home covered in blood and bruises – maybe even with a broken limb.

Charlie decided he'd had enough, and got to his feet. 'I'm going through to bed. So I'll leave you with this little coward of yours.'

Georgie stared at her husband in astonishment and fury. 'How dare you call Ian a coward!' she protested.

'Oh, bugger off, the pair of you,' Charlie snarled, and left them.

Ian started to shake, and then burst into tears.

'Hey, Tom, wait up!'

Tom turned to find Danny Peterson hurrying towards him. Danny was a pal of his from McNair's.

'I was just thinking about you this morning,' Danny announced.

'Oh aye, why's that?'

'Have you found another job yet?'

Tom shook his head. 'And it's not for the lack of trying, I can tell you.'

'Then I might have something that's just the very dab.'

Tom frowned. 'Are you working yourself?'

'Nope.'

'Then why aren't you after whatever it is?'

Danny's face broke into a huge smile. 'Because I've got two left feet, that's why.'

He went on to explain.

Chapter 17

Mrs Simpson, short, plump, immaculately dressed and coiffured, was manageress of the Belgrave, a private club. Her accent was Kelvinside, which is to say Glasgow posh, and her hazel-coloured eyes shone with intelligence.

She studied Tom, sizing him up. Good-looking, she thought. That was in his favour, as was being of middle height. And he had a nice, easy manner about him.

She smiled. 'All right, Tom, let's see what you can do.' She came to stand directly in front of him. 'Shall we start with the waltz? You lead, of course.'

'But there's no music to dance to.'

Mrs Simpson laughed. 'Which makes it all the more difficult, wouldn't you say?'

It certainly did, Tom reflected ruefully.

'Now take me in your arms.'

He did so.

'And off we go.'

In rapid succession they went through the foxtrot,

quickstep, polka, and various other steps that came under the general heading of Old Time Dancing.

Eventually Mrs Simpson stopped and broke away. 'Well, you move all right, I'll give you that.'

'I wasn't really at my best,' he apologised. 'It was the lack of music, I'm afraid.'

'Do you own a lounge suit?'

'I do.'

'A decent pair of dancing shoes?'

'Yes.'

'And are you reliable?'

'How do you mean?'

'Will you turn up every night?'

'Oh yes.' Tom smiled. 'You can count on it. I need the money, you see.'

That was good enough for her.

Tom burst into the kitchen to find the others already sitting down and having their tea.

'Where have you been? You're late,' said Chrissie.

'I've got a job, Mum!' Tom informed her jubilantly.

Chrissie clapped her hands in delight. 'That's wonderful news, son. Absolutely wonderful.'

'Doing what?' Tam asked, impressed that Tom had been able to find employment in the current slump when millions of men were laid off throughout the length and breadth of Britain.

'Promise you won't laugh?'

'Of course I won't laugh,' Tam replied. 'Why would I do that?'

'Because the job's that of a professional dancer.'

Tam stared at his son in astonishment. 'Bloody hell!' he muttered.

'What sort of professional dancer?' Lena asked, amused.

'In a private club called the Belgrave. It's a club for older people where they can have a drink, or whatever. Quite a number of widows, and women whose husbands are away on business, go there, as well as couples, of course. There are four men and three young women employed to dance with the patrons when requested. Money for old rope if you ask me.'

'You'll be dancing with older women?' Chrissie repeated with a frown, not sure if she liked the idea of that.

'It's all above board, Mum. There's no hanky panky or anything of that nature. I just sit there until asked to dance, which I then do. Simple really.'

'What's the pay?' Tam enquired, bemused.

'Almost as much as I was getting from McNair's. And just for dancing, which I enjoy anyway. I can't believe my luck.'

'And the hours?' Lena asked.

'Sunday and Monday off. Tuesday through till Saturday night. Start at six thirty, finish at midnight.'

'I don't know what to say,' Chrissie told him, shaking her head. 'What a bolt out the blue.'

'I've Danny Peterson to thank,' Tom said to his father. 'He put me on to it. There was no use his applying as he can't dance for toffee. I begin next Tuesday.' He sat at the table. 'This means I'll be earning again and not a drain on the family. That's the main thing.'

'Aye,' Chrissie agreed. 'That's the main thing.'

*   *   *

Georgie hadn't laughed so much in a long time. They were at the table, Charlie cracking joke after joke, all of which were extremely funny and some hilariously so.

'Stop it, Charlie,' she gasped at last. 'You'll give me a seizure if you keep on.'

'A last one then.'

It was the funniest of the lot, and brought tears into Georgie's eyes. Ian sat solemn-faced, not having understood any of the jokes. Avril wasn't present; she seemed to be spending most of her time at her Aunt Betty's recently. Georgie hadn't objected, continuing to find the child wilful and difficult. If Avril wanted to be with her Aunt Betty, then so be it.

'I have other ones I could have told you,' Charlie said, a mischievous smile curling his lips. 'But not with Ian here, I'm afraid.' Georgie knew he meant dirty jokes, of which he had a vast repertoire. 'Another time,' he added, and winked at her.

He rose and stretched. 'I'm off out for a couple of pints with my pals from the station. That all right?'

Georgie instantly sobered. 'I thought you were staying in tonight?'

'I never said so.'

'I presumed you were.'

'It'll only be for a wee while, Georgie. I'll be back before you know it.'

She tried to hide her disappointment. This going out with his pals for a drink was becoming more and more frequent. Not that she entirely disapproved; it was just that it would have been nicer if he'd spent more time with her and Ian.

Coming round the table he kissed her on the cheek. 'Did I mention you're looking lovely this evening?'

She was flattered, as she knew she was meant to be. 'Less of the old flannel, Charlie.'

'But you are!' he insisted, and proceeded to blow into her ear, which made her giggle and jerk her head away.

'Not with Ian here,' she admonished him.

'Later, then,' he promised in a whisper.

At the door he turned and winked at her again, before leaving for the pub.

Georgie came awake when the bedroom door opened. God knew what time it was as it had already been late, well past pub closing, when she'd come to bed.

She listened to Charlie stumble into the room, curse when he banged into a piece of furniture then begin to remove his clothes. Moments later he crawled in beside her and immediately started lifting the bottom of her nightdress.

'Are you awake, Georgie?' he slurred.

'I am now. I thought you were coming home early?'

'Forgot it was one of the lads' birthday. We made a bit of a night of it.'

'But the pubs shut ages ago.'

'I told you once I know where to get a drink after hours. That's where we went.'

She squirmed as his hand found her crotch. 'I'm tired, Charlie. Honestly I am.'

'You'll not deny me, will you?'

He stank of booze, the sour fumes from his mouth washing over her. She turned her face away to escape them, and was about to reply when a probing finger found her.

'Charlie!' she hissed.

But it was no use. He was insistent, and she had to let him have his way.

Afterwards she was pleased she had. Despite everything, it had been lovely. Something she'd never have admitted to a living soul, and hardly did to herself, was that Charlie was a far better lover than John had ever been.

Lena sniffed the air. There it was again, the unmistakable smell of perfume. And expensive perfume too if she was any judge. Not hers, of course, as she only occasionally wore a splash of lavender water.

Jealousy at the thought that Hamish must have had another woman in his house stabbed through her. Unjustly so, she reminded herself. Her arrangement with Hamish didn't exclude his seeing other females. But she was jealous none the less.

Hamish, wearing only his dressing gown, re-entered the bedroom carrying two cups of coffee. He smiled. 'All right?'

'Fine.' She regarded him speculatively. If the woman had been in his bedroom did that mean they'd slept together? She rather thought it did. Which probably meant he'd been seeing her for some time.

'Good one, eh?' He handed her her coffee.

'Very.'

'I'll say this for you, Lena. You really enjoy it.'

'So do you.'

'No doubt about that.'

Lena wondered why she hadn't smelt the perfume earlier. Perhaps because her mind had been on other things – like a desperate need for sex. 'Tell me something,' she said.

'What's that?'

'I don't really have the right to ask, but do you have a girlfriend?'

A look of embarrassment crept across Hamish's face. 'What's that got to do with us?'

'Nothing. I'm simply curious, that's all.'

He stared at her, undecided about whether or not to tell the truth. Then he made up his mind he would. Lena would find out eventually, so why not now? 'Yes, I do.'

Lena lit a cigarette, partially turning away from him so he wouldn't see her expression. 'Is it serious?'

Hamish cleared his throat. 'We plan to get engaged next month after I buy the ring.'

Lena felt as though she'd been punched in the stomach, remembering all too clearly that she'd promised these visits of hers would stop when he got married. 'I see,' she murmured, hoping it was going to be a long engagement. 'What's her name?'

'Celia. Celia Cunningham.'

It took a few moments for the penny to drop. 'The chairman's daughter?' she queried in astonishment.

'That's right.'

Realising her mouth had dropped open, she shut it again. 'How on earth did you meet her?'

'The chairman invited some of his golfing friends round for a meal one night and I was placed next to Celia at the table. We got on like a house on fire during the meal, and afterwards. Before leaving I took her aside to ask if she'd like to go out one evening, and she agreed. That's how it started.'

'Is she pretty?'

Hamish was even more embarrassed. 'Extremely.'

'Yes, I'd heard that. They say she's very glamorous.' Unlike herself, Lena thought bitterly. Laying her coffee aside she rose from the bed. 'I'd better get dressed.'

'You're not too upset, are you?'

What a stupid question, she thought. Of course she was upset, and would probably be a lot more so once the news had properly sunk in. 'Not in the least,' she lied with a smile. 'It was bound to happen one day. Though, I have to say, I never for one moment imagined it would be the chairman's daughter.' She added acidly, 'You do aim high, don't you?'

'It wasn't like that, Lena. I swear.'

'No?'

He shook his head.

'But once the opportunity arose you were only too quick to take advantage of it?'

'That's not true.' He was lying now.

'Think of the promotions that'll be coming your way. Why, one day you might even be chairman yourself. Don't tell me that hasn't crossed your mind?'

He didn't reply.

'Do you love her, Hamish? I certainly hope you don't intend marrying her unless you do.'

'Of course I love her,' he replied unconvincingly, blushing as he spoke.

Lena laughed. 'Liar!'

'I am nothing of the sort,' he protested vehemently.

'Oh yes you are, Hamish Murchison. You're lying in your teeth. It's obvious. To me, anyway.'

Again he didn't reply, just stood there watching Lena putting on her clothes.

'Will you be coming back?' he asked when she was fully dressed.

'Damn right I will,' she replied sweetly. 'This doesn't alter matters. Not for the present, anyway.'

To his surprise he found he was rather pleased about that. Though why he should be escaped him.

Tom was nervous as hell when he reported for his first night at the Belgrave, but he began to relax a little after Mrs Simpson had introduced him to the other men and women doing the same job.

Two of the men were considerably older, in their forties Tom judged. Of the women, two were roughly his age while one was, again, in her forties, or thereabouts.

'It's dead jammy here,' Derek, the other younger man, confided to Tom. 'I love it.'

'Money for old rope as far as I'm concerned.' Tom smiled amiably. 'What are the customers like?'

'All posh and monied. It costs a fortune to join the Belgrave, so there isn't any riff-raff.'

Tom nodded that he understood, then gazed out over the main club area, part of which was a dance floor. The decor was gold and heavy tapestry wallpaper. Dotted about were various statues and other items, including huge flower arrangements, that lent, or were supposed to lend, character to the place. The lighting was subdued, giving everything a soft hue.

A few minutes later a three-piece band in black tie arrived. They began arranging and tuning their instruments and when everything was to their satisfaction they struck up.

'There are rooms off here where customers can go and sit in peace, or have a conversation, should they so choose,' Derek informed Tom. 'Not all of them come to dance, you see.'

'So how does a club like this make a profit?' Tom asked, thinking there must be more to it than simply dancing.

'Well, for a start, the drinks are horrendously expensive. Secondly, and keep this to yourself, there's a gaming room where customers often play for high stakes.'

'Ah!' Tom exclaimed. Now it was beginning to make sense.

'Mrs Simpson's a real sweetie,' Derek went on. 'Unless you cross her, that is. Then it's easy to see why she was made manageress. She rules with a rod of iron, but she's fair with it. You do your job well, keep your nose clean, and Mrs Simpson will be your best friend.'

'I'll remember that.' He would too, not having any wish to lose this godsend of a chance to earn.

People had already been arriving, and now even more appeared. Five minutes later Tom was asked by a middle-aged lady to dance.

'Mum, you shouldn't have waited up!' Tom exclaimed. He'd reached home in the small hours, having walked from the club.

'Oh, hold your wheesht. I wanted to know how you got on.' Chrissie took a deep breath. 'Well?'

'It was brilliant, Mum. I thoroughly enjoyed myself.'

'You did?'

'The time just flew past once we got going.' He laughed. 'Some of those women are terrible dancers, truly awful. Others very good indeed. But they were, without exception, nice people.'

'None of them tried to . . . well, make advances?'

'Of course not. I told you, the club is strictly above board. No shenanigans whatsoever.' He regarded her with amusement. 'I must say, I'm surprised you thought of such a thing.'

Chrissie snorted. 'I may be your mother but I'm not unaware of what goes on in the world, you know. I didn't come up the Clyde on a bicycle.'

Clearly she hadn't. 'I'll tell you what though. I could murder a cup of tea.'

'Then I'll make you one. I could use a cup myself.'

While Chrissie filled the kettle and set it on to boil he told her about his night, describing some of the women he'd danced with, mentioning Derek and the others employed as partners, and couples who'd caught his attention.

'I'll tell you something,' he said when Chrissie handed him his tea. 'It sure as hell beats grafting in the foundry, and that's a fact.'

Chrissie didn't doubt it for a minute.

'Ian! Ian!'

Ian, who'd just come out on to the playground, was

startled to hear his name being called. With astonishment he saw it was Charlie doing the calling, and that Charlie had a fire engine with him. Engine and crew.

'Can you get out of there?' Charlie asked when Ian ran over to join him at the railings.

A wide-eyed Ian nodded, wondering what this was all about.

'Go on then. I'll wait for you.'

Ian was well aware he wasn't supposed to leave the playground, but surely this was different.

When he got to the engine a group of pupils had gathered at the spot where he'd spoken to Charlie, all visibly impressed by the sight of the firemen and their machine.

'Right,' Charlie declared. 'Let's put you up in the driving seat, shall we?' And with that he lifted Ian and swung him into the cabin. A fireman already there plonked a helmet on to Ian's head.

Ian was in seventh heaven as he grasped the wheel and pretended to steer. This was magic. Especially as he was being watched by the others gathered on the other side of the railings, a crowd which continued to grow with every passing second.

Charlie took Ian all over the engine, showing him where everything was, and even raising the ladder a bit and allowing Ian to climb a few rungs. The fun only ended with the sound of the bell announcing that playtime had ended.

'Thanks, Charlie.'

'Think nothing of it, son. Now hurry back before you get into trouble.'

Ian had one last look at the engine as it moved away

before re-entering the school building, where he soon discovered he'd become something of a hero.

'Oh, Charlie, that was wonderful of you,' Georgie said later that night when Charlie arrived home. 'Ian's been talking of nothing else ever since he got in.'

'Aye, well, there was a reason for it.'

She frowned. 'What reason?'

'It'll make him somebody at school, somebody to be envied and even looked up to. That's my reasoning, anyway. It might just stop him being bullied if we're lucky.'

Georgie wasn't sure about that, but thought it extremely kind of her husband. 'What can I say? Except thank you.'

'My pleasure, I can assure you. The idea came to me as we were heading back from a call-out. The timing couldn't have been better. We were just passing the school as playtime was starting. A quick word with the lads, and Bob's your uncle.'

She pecked him on the cheek. 'You're a lovely man, Charlie Gunn, and I'm glad I married you.'

'And I'm glad I married *you*.'

In the event his reasoning proved to be correct. Ian was never bullied again. Whatever it was went through the three boys' minds, from that point on they kept their distance.

Chapter 18

Lena glanced up as an elegant young woman swept in her direction, instinctively knowing who the stranger was.

The newcomer stopped at Lena's desk, and smiled. 'If Mr Murchison is free can you please tell him Miss Cunningham is here to see him?'

They hadn't lied about her being a beauty, Lena thought bitterly. The bitch was stunning. Sickeningly so.

'He's alone, so why not just go straight on in,' she replied, forcing herself to be pleasant.

'Thank you.'

Lena watched as Celia tapped the door, then went inside.

'Darling!' she heard Hamish exclaim in surprise. And then the door was shut again.

Those clothes had cost a pretty penny, Lena reflected. And, from the style of them, they might even have come from London's Bond Street itself.

She seethed with jealousy.

*　　*　　*

'Are you all right?' Hamish asked her later, after Celia had gone.

'I'm fine, thank you.'

'I had no idea she was coming. Sorry.'

'There's nothing to be sorry about.'

'Celia was just reminding me I'm to meet her during lunch hour to buy the engagement ring.'

That was something she didn't need to know, Lena thought angrily. Honestly, had the man no tact! 'How nice for the pair of you,' she replied tartly.

'So if I'm late back you'll know what's holding me up.'

She knew what she'd like to hold him up with. A rope with a noose on the end. 'Why don't you take the rest of the day off?' she suggested. 'We can manage well enough without you.'

'Are you sure?'

They could always manage without him, she thought, he being about as useful as a chocolate teapot. It was she who ran the department, not Hamish. Most of his so-called work simply involved signing things.

'Of course I'm sure.'

'Then I'll do that.'

She smiled to herself as he crossed to the hat stand and removed his bowler. One of these days she'd tell him he looked a proper idiot in it, she thought.

There again, maybe she wouldn't.

'Here you are, Mum, my first pay packet from the new job.' Tom grinned, handing Chrissie a small brown envelope.

'Thank you, son.'

Using a finger she opened it and extracted the contents, notes and coins which she swiftly counted. He'd been right; it was only a little less than he'd been earning at McNair's.

Chrissie peeled off several of the notes and returned them to him, keeping the rest. 'You'll be wanting your breakfast now?'

'Please, Mum. I'm starving.'

'I've bought you an egg in anticipation of your wages coming in, so I'll do that for you. Fried or boiled?'

'Boiled. With soldiers if you don't mind.'

Lena, already at the table, snorted. 'Honest to God, soldiers at your age. How pathetic!'

'Leave him alone,' Tam growled.

'But I ask you, Papa!'

'It's always her who starts it,' Tom declared piously. 'And nobody believes me when I say that.'

'You're both at fault,' Chrissie stated. 'Anyway, Tom, you should know better than to rise to the bait. I must have told you that a million times.'

Tam was wondering what to do with the rest of the day. His days off were becoming more and more of a problem for him.

'Now that we've almost as much coming into the house as before I think you can start smoking again, Tam,' said Chrissie.

His face lit up. 'Can I?'

'I just said so.'

'What about whisky at the weekends?'

She glanced over at him. 'Half a bottle instead of a whole one.'

That was better than nothing, he reflected. He hadn't tasted a dram or a pint in months. Nor smoked his pipe or had a fag, come to that. Thank God life, for them anyway, was getting back to normal.

'Look at the time!' Lena exclaimed. 'I'd better be going or I'll be late.'

'Which would never do,' Tom smirked, for no other reason than to annoy his sister.

As she passed him Lena retaliated by giving him a sharp elbow in the ribs.

'That hurt!' he shouted after her.

'It was meant to.'

Chrissie shook her head in a combination of exasperation and disbelief.

'I've hardly sat down all night,' Tom commented to Derek. 'I've been up and down like a demented yo-yo.'

'It gets like that sometimes,' Derek replied. 'But better that than twiddling your thumbs.'

Tom nodded. 'True.' He suddenly became aware of a middle-aged woman, by herself at one of the tables, staring intently at him. He smiled at her, but she didn't smile back, simply continued staring at him. How odd, he thought. And a little disturbing too.

Moments later he was again asked to dance. He glanced to where the staring woman had been, only to find the table empty.

'There's someone here to see you, Lena,' a beaming Chrissie announced, having answered a knock at the door.

Lena stared in astonishment at the figure who brushed past Chrissie. A figure who was almost unrecognisable from the last time she'd seen her.

'Hiya, kid, howya doin'?'

'Pet,' Lena stuttered.

'In the flesh.'

The two women flew into each other's arms, hugging one another tightly.

'And it's not Pet any more,' she declared when they'd disengaged. 'It's Dawn.'

'You'll always be Pet to me. But . . . what are you doing here?'

'Visiting. But first, let me mind my manners.' She went to Tam, gave him a big kiss and had a few words, and then did the same to the hovering Chrissie.

'Where's Tom?' she asked. 'Out on the razzle?'

'He's working,' Lena said. 'I'll explain about that later.' She eyed her friend up and down. 'You look wonderful,' she breathed. 'A real Hollywood star.'

Pet was wearing a grey, waisted suit with a creamy frilled blouse underneath; her shoes were black patent. A simple ensemble, but stunning in its execution.

'Why thanks, honey.'

Lena noted that the once brassy blonde hair had been considerably toned down, and the breasts were not quite so prominent, no doubt due to the bra Pet was wearing. 'So what brings you here?' she demanded, still unable to take in that Pet had just turned up like this.

'It's a long story, hon. Basically, I'm on my way to Europe for a vacation, and stopped off in London to do some promotion for my new movie. And while in London I simply had to come up to Glasgow for a few days to see my folks. And you, of course,' she added with a smile.

'Would you like a cup of tea, dear?' Chrissie asked.

'No thank you, Mrs M. I've only got a few minutes. In fact I've got a taxi waiting downstairs.'

Lena's face fell. 'Only a few minutes?'

'Which is why I thought we might have lunch tomorrow. A long lunch over which we can catch up. What do you say?'

Christ, Lena thought. The next day was her Saturday with Hamish, and she certainly didn't want to miss that. Not the way she was feeling.

'Does it have to be lunch?' she queried. 'How about an evening meal instead?'

'That's OK by me, hon. Where do you suggest, and what time?'

Where? She wasn't used to going to restaurants. Then she remembered the Swan Hotel.

'Seven o'clock then,' Pet agreed. 'I'll be there with bells on. Now I must rush.'

'I'll see you out,' Lena volunteered.

At the door they embraced again, each kissing the other on the cheek.

'Tomorrow night.' Pet smiled.

'Tomorrow night,' Lena repeated.

And then Pet was gone, clattering off down the stairs.

''Bye, Dawn!' Lena couldn't help but call out, thinking it funny. 'Well, well, imagine that,' she went on, returning to the kitchen. 'What a bombshell.'

Hamish during the day, Pet at night. It was going to be one hell of a Saturday!

Charlie arrived home with a face like thunder. 'They sprung it on us just as we were coming off watch. The fucking bastards!' he snarled.

Georgie glanced at Ian and Avril. No matter what had happened, she didn't approve of such language in front of the children, and would take Charlie to task once he'd calmed down.

'Sprung what on you?' she said.

His eyes were blazing when he answered. 'Remember I told you they would never lay firemen off?'

She nodded. 'I remember.'

'Well they've done something else instead. As from next week our pay has been cut by almost half.'

'Oh dear,' Georgie muttered. This was terrible. 'Is there nothing you can do about it?'

'The Union will have something to say, I can tell you. But with the country in such a state at the moment I doubt any argument they might make will have any impact.'

Almost half, Georgie thought. That was indeed a body blow. She didn't know how they were going to manage, but they'd just have to. If the worst came to the worst she always had her insurance money in the bank.

Charlie threw himself into a chair, then jumped out of it again. 'I don't want any tea tonight,' he declared.

'But it's already made. A lovely stew with dumplings.'

'I said I don't want any, woman! What have you got, cloth ears?'

Georgie bit her lip, and didn't respond.

Charlie glanced at his daughter, who unflinchingly gazed right back at him. He grunted. 'What I do want is a drink. And lots of it. By Christ and I do.'

'Shouldn't we be watching what we spend from now on?' Georgie said in a small voice.

'Not tonight. Not tonight! Tonight I'm getting pissed out of my head. Stocious. Hear me?'

'I hear you, Charlie.' She knew there was no arguing with him when he was like this. The way he was at the moment she could easily get a clout if she did. Not that Charlie had ever hit her, but there was always a first time. 'On you go then,' she said, attempting a brave smile. 'I won't wait up if you don't mind.'

Charlie stormed from the house.

Lena opened her eyes to stare at a sweat-slicked Hamish lying beside her. 'It doesn't get much better,' she sighed, with a smile of complete satisfaction.

'No,' he agreed. 'It doesn't.' Reaching across he fondled the breast nearer him. 'These are getting bigger,' he observed.

'You approve?'

'Very much so.' He idly flicked a nipple. Then flicked it again.

'Are you playing a game, or what?' she queried drily.

'I'm just wondering if I can go again if we wait a while,' he answered.

She glanced at his bedside clock. Plenty of time yet before her meeting with Pet. But did she want to go again, as he put it? Truth was, he'd already given her such a pounding she was rather sore. On the other hand, why look a gift horse in the mouth, as the saying went. She also had to remember that these trysts wouldn't go on for ever. Best to get as much as she could while it was available. There would be long lonely years ahead after she finished seeing Hamish, unless someone else came along, which she doubted very much indeed.

'I hope you can,' she purred. Swinging her legs out of bed, she picked up her cigarettes. 'There's something I want to talk to you about,' she said after she'd lit up. 'More of a suggestion really.'

'Oh?'

'Now that you're engaged to the boss's daughter don't you think it would be best to stop fiddling those accounts? I would certainly recommend it.'

Hamish slowly nodded. 'You're right, of course. I'd be daft to continue.'

'I doubt anyone would ever find out. But if they did, well, I don't have to spell out the consequences. Your future's made, Hamish; there's absolutely no need to go on fiddling. Why risk it?'

He stared at her, thinking it was a pity she was so bloody ugly. In other circumstances she would have had a lot to offer. 'Would you like a drink?'

'A little white wine would be nice.'

'No gin?'

'I don't want to get tipsy. I'm having a meal with a famous Hollywood star tonight.'

His eyes opened wide. 'You're taking the mickey, aren't you?'

'Not at all.' She went on to explain about Pet and how

they had been the best of pals before Pet had gone to Hollywood in search of stardom.

'Dawn Ryder,' Hamish mused. 'I've seen her in pictures.'

Lena reeled off a list of those Pet had been in, and then the names of some of Pet's starry boyfriends.

'Imagine you knowing her,' Hamish declared, somewhat awed. 'Who would have believed it?'

'We're going to the Swan. It was the only place I could think of when she asked me to recommend somewhere.'

He laughed. 'Bloody hell! Dawn Ryder in the Swan. I'm almost tempted to turn up just to have a peek. But sadly I . . .' He trailed off, suddenly embarrassed. 'I'll get you that wine.' And with that he hurried from the room.

Lena could guess what he'd been about to say. He was seeing Celia later on. The thought put rather a damper on what had been a lovely couple of hours. Still, she hung on till he was ready again, and exacted a little revenge by clawing his back, and leaving scratches.

Let him explain those to the beautiful Celia, she gloated. If he dared.

'I'd forgotten how much Glasgow smells,' Pet declared quietly after they'd ordered. 'It stinks.'

Lena was immediately up in arms in the defence of her beloved city. 'It does nothing of the sort. It's your imagination,' she snapped in reply.

'It does too, honey. Believe me.'

'It's just a big industrial city, Pet. Not an orange

grove, which is the sort of thing I suppose you're used to now.'

It was obvious to Pet that her friend was miffed by what she'd said. 'I didn't mean to offend, kid. Sorry,' she apologised.

Lena shrugged. 'That's all right. No offence taken.' There had been, but she wasn't about to pursue the subject and spoil their night out together.

'Sure?'

Lena nodded.

'OK. Now, tell me what's new with you?'

'I don't want to talk about me. I want to hear about you,' Lena protested. 'So come on.'

'I told you I was going on vacation to Europe, right?'

'You did.'

'What I didn't mention was that it was at the invitation of an Italian count. How about that, eh?'

Lena was completely taken aback. 'A genuine count?'

'As genuine as they come.' Pet laughed. 'Count Mario Tesccheti, no less. A count and a bachelor worth millions. And I mean good ole Yankee greenbacks when I say that.'

'Wow!' Lena breathed.

'He has a yacht in Cannes, France, on which I'll be joining him and a few others. The plan is that we cruise in the Med, and possibly even the Aegean.'

'Sounds . . . well, amazing.'

'He isn't exactly the best-looking guy around, but who the hell cares?'

'How did you meet him?' Lena asked, thinking it was like a fairy story come to life.

'In Hollywood, natch. I went to a party thrown by

Charlie Chaplin, and there he was. We dated for a while, and then he had to return home on business. But before leaving he pleaded with me to join him in Cannes, which is what I'm going to do.'

'Lucky cow,' Lena said good-humouredly. 'Trust you to meet someone like that.'

'I'm not due to start my next movie for several months yet, which gave me the opportunity to get my ass over here. And when I told the studio they asked me to do some promotion in London, so part of my trip is a busman's holiday, the rest . . .' Her eyes twinkled. 'Sheer unadulterated pleasure. And I say that from experience. He's a real knockout between the sheets. And I mean knockout.'

They stopped speaking for a few moments while their starters were placed before them.

'You've slept with him, then?' Lena said quietly after the waiter had left.

'Darn tootin', kid. On the night we met, the temptation being just too great to resist. Don't forget, it's Hollywood after all; everyone's at it like rabbits. It's how half the female actresses get cast in that town. Putting out to producers, directors and the like.'

'Putting out?' Lena frowned.

'Shagging, honey. The casting couch is no myth, believe me. I could tell you stories that would make your hair stand on end.'

'Does that mean you've been with lots of men?' Lena queried, jealous as anything.

'And some women too, if the truth be known.'

Lena truly was shocked. 'You don't mean that?'

'I do.'

Pet went on to regale Lena with more tales of life in Hollywood, and the goings-on there. Lena, for the main part, listened in rapt silence.

'But enough of me,' Pet eventually declared. 'What's been happening here on the home front?'

Somewhere along the line Lena had decided to lie. To bolster herself in the eyes of her friend. Well, she reasoned, it wouldn't all be a fib. Part of it was true, if embellished.

'I have a boyfriend too,'

Pet sat back in her chair. 'Really? What's his name?'

'Hamish. Hamish Murchison. He's my boss, head of the department. And, you might not believe this, gorgeous as hell.'

Pet was amazed. 'Go on.'

'It's a real love match. He absolutely dotes on me, and I on him. We also . . .' She cleared her throat, then confessed in a whisper, '. . . sleep together.'

Pet was flabbergasted. 'You do?'

'He has his own place, you see. That's where we go. He swears he can't get enough of me.'

'Well, good for you, kid,' Pet managed to say at last. 'Are we talking marriage here?'

'Possibly,' Lena said, managing to blush. 'Though nothing has been said yet.'

'And you're sleeping with him?' Pet frowned, remembering this was staid, Calvinistic Scotland, where morality ruled.

'As often as we can. It's marvellous.'

'Hot damn!' Pet breathed. 'You do surprise me, Lena. You really do.'

It hadn't all been one way, Lena reflected later as she made for her tram stop, having seen Pet off in a taxi. She'd kept her end up, and not been the sad, lonely virgin Pet had been expecting.

At least that was true enough. She certainly wasn't a virgin any more. A fact of which she was extremely proud.

Chapter 19

Georgie arrived home from shopping to find Charlie sitting with Ian bent over his knees, leathering the poor boy's backside with his belt. Ian was screaming his head off, while a smug-faced Avril was watching the proceedings.

'What the hell are you doing?' Georgie shrieked as another blow descended with a loud crack.

'He was naughty,' Avril stated, eyes gleaming.

'Stop that at once, Charlie,' Georgie shouted. Rushing forward, she attempted to pull Ian off Charlie's lap.

Charlie hadn't been there when she'd gone out. Now, from the smell of alcohol emanating from him, she knew where he had been. To the pub. Yet again.

Charlie grunted, and released Ian. 'Be thankful your mother's got back or there would have been more of that,' he snarled at the lad.

Ian, clutching his bottom, tears streaming down his face, was hopping up and down.

'What did he do to deserve this?' Georgie demanded.

If she'd been a man she'd have flattened her husband there and then.

'Tell her, Avril,' Charlie slurred.

'He pulled down my knickers and looked at me,' Avril replied, as though butter wouldn't melt in her mouth.

'I didn't,' Ian stuttered.

'Yes, you did.'

'She asked me to look,' Ian wailed. 'She pulled down her own knickers and asked me to look.'

'Liar!' Charlie shouted. 'My Avril wouldn't do such a thing. She's a good girl.'

'She did!'

'Did not,' Avril said, shaking her head.

Georgie knew which one she believed. 'Whatever, it was no reason for you to be so hard on the boy,' she hissed at Charlie, wondering how many strokes of the belt Ian had had before she'd arrived on the scene.

'Dirty little bastard, trying to interfere with my daughter. I'll have none of that in my house, by Christ and I won't.'

'I'm sore, Mummy. I'm sore,' Ian blubbered, still hopping on the spot.

Georgie suddenly realised she was shaking, and no wonder. 'Never, ever lay a hand on Ian again,' she spat. 'If there's any punishing to be done then I'll do it.'

Charlie regarded her with contempt. 'You're far too easy-going with him. If you're not careful he'll grow up to be a big soft nelly. Or worse, a raving fucking poofter.'

'Don't swear in front of the children,' Georgie said savagely. 'You hear? And what's more, you're drunk again. Drink we can't afford.'

Charlie brandished his belt at her. 'Maybe you'd like a few good wallops across your arse as well! I've a damned good mind to do just that.'

It was the first time he'd ever truly scared her. 'You wouldn't dare!'

'No? Just try me, woman. Just bloody well try me.'

Georgie noticed that Avril was smirking. Little bitch. It was she who'd caused all this trouble. And intentionally so – Georgie had no doubt about that. Avril had laid a trap for Ian and he'd fallen right into it.

'Come on, son, let's go through to your bedroom. Mummy will take care of you there.'

She was certain she heard a snigger from Avril as they left the room, but she did not react. Closing the door of the bedroom behind them, she turned to Ian. 'Right,' she said. 'Take your shorts and undies off, then lie down on the bed so I can see what's what.'

'I'm sore, Mummy,' he sniffled, his tears now drying up.

'I'm sure you are. Now do as I say.

'My God,' she whispered to herself when she examined his bare bottom. What a thrashing he'd had. The flesh was red hot, wealed in places – weals that would very soon turn black and blue. There was even a small dribble of blood where the skin had been cut.

'My poor darling,' she murmured. 'You just lie there until I get some cream that'll soothe it for you.'

'I hate him,' Ian muttered, still sniffling. 'I hate him.'

Georgie had no reply to that.

There she was again, Tom noticed. The staring woman back for the fourth time. Why didn't she speak, ask for a dance, or something? This continual staring was beginning to faze him.

Perhaps he should go over and engage her in conversation? Then he thought better of it. That might cause trouble of some sort, which was the last thing he wanted. Then, to his surprise, she suddenly came to her feet and headed towards him.

'Can I have a dance, please?' she asked, her accent Kelvinside.

'Of course.' He led her on to the floor and they began to waltz. 'I'm Tom, by the way,' he went on.

'I'm Mrs Mulherron.'

'Nice to meet you, Mrs Mulherron.'

'And you, Tom.'

She wasn't a bad dancer, he soon realised. He'd certainly come across far worse. 'I've noticed you looking at me,' he said.

She blushed. 'Oh dear. Has it been that obvious?'

'I'm afraid so. Is there a reason?'

She glanced away, then back at him. 'Yes, there is. You remind me of someone.'

'Oh? Someone nice, I hope?'

'My son Robert.' She hesitated, then added in a tight voice, 'He was killed at Ypres during the war.'

'I am sorry,' Tom said sympathetically.

'The resemblance is quite remarkable. In fact, now I'm close to you it's even more so. Except for the skin – yours is darker-toned than his was. But, apart from that, you could be two peas in a pod.'

That explained the staring, Tom thought. How extraordinary.

'It was a friend of mine who comes here regularly who first spotted you,' Mrs Mulherron went on. 'When she told me I simply had to come and see for myself. And how right she was. It was as if . . . well, it was as if Robert had come back to life.'

Tom didn't know what to say.

Mrs Mulherron suddenly stopped dancing. 'Excuse me,' she choked. 'I've come over all emotional.' And with that she walked swiftly away in the direction of the ladies' room. It was the last Tom saw of her that night.

Tam ran a hand wearily over his forehead. He was worried, and scared too. Another section of men had been laid off at McNair's, to the point where production had almost ceased altogether.

What if they closed the foundry down entirely? That was him out of a job till production started up again, and God knew when that might be. The great slump continued, was going on and on, with no end in sight. No wonder he was scared. In fact, if he was honest with himself, he was downright terrified of joining the ranks of unemployed. The shame would be awful for a chap like him.

They way things stood he couldn't even do a 'trick' by selling off scrap as he had in the past. There simply wasn't enough of it at present due to the cut-backs. And even if there had been, conversely, the reduction of staff meant there were far too many eyes about now to risk anything along those lines. Before, it had all been hustle and bustle, whereas now people had time on their hands. Time to notice things.

Tam sighed. At least Lena had her job and Tom had his, which was something to be thankful for if the worst came to the worst.

Lena wondered what was wrong with Hamish. He'd been agitated in the extreme since coming to work that morning. To put it bluntly, he had a right case of the fidgets.

'What's wrong with you today?' she asked when she had to go into his office. 'Have you got ants in your pants?'

Hamish didn't laugh, or even smile. 'I have to talk to you, Lena. Can we meet after work in the Swan?'

'Talk about what?'

'Not here. In the Swan.'

'Fine.' She nodded. 'I'll be there.'

'Good.'

But he remained agitated for the rest of the day.

'So what's this all about?' she demanded as Hamish laid a drink in front of her.

He sat, but wouldn't look her in the eye. 'I'm sorry, but there's no easy way to say this. Celia and I are eloping at the weekend.'

She stared at him in shock. 'You're what?'

'Eloping at the weekend to Gretna Green where we'll be staying as long as it takes to get married and have a short honeymoon.'

Lena had a swift gulp of gin and tonic, then fumbled for her cigarettes. 'I thought . . . I thought, or rather hoped, you'd be having a long engagement. A year, say, or even more.'

'That was what Celia and I had planned. But the plan has had to be suddenly changed out of necessity.'

It dawned on Lena what he was getting at. There was only one explanation that she could think of. 'Is Celia up the duff?'

Hamish nodded, his expression one of sheer misery.

'Is she certain?'

'Absolutely. It's been confirmed by a doctor.'

'You bloody fool,' Lena angrily hissed. 'How could you be so stupid? Didn't you use a French letter like you do with me?'

'We did,' Hamish protested. 'Always. But on one occasion it split. We didn't realise until it was over, and by then the damage was done. At the time we didn't worry too much. I mean, it only happened once, after all. But once was enough.'

Lena stared grimly at him, though part of her was sympathetic. What had occurred was damned bad luck.

'Celia had hysterics when she was told,' Hamish went on. 'We even discussed an abortion – there are places where these things can be arranged. But, in the end, she decided she wanted the baby. Or, to put it another way, she didn't want an abortion in case something went wrong.'

This weekend, Lena thought in despair. That meant their monthly trysts were over. She felt a sudden dull ache in the pit of her stomach, an ache that grew with every passing second.

'Have you told the chairman and his wife?' she asked.

'Good God no! There'd be hell to pay if we did. Celia and I have talked it all through and decided eloping is the best way out for us. We'll leave a note behind, and then just leave. We'll say we simply couldn't wait any longer to be married, and so we're off to Gretna. Hopefully, they'll think it all rather romantic.'

'How far gone is Celia?'

'Two and a half months.'

Lena raised an eyebrow. 'So, the baby's going to be premature, I take it?'

He nodded.

'Surely the hospital will know to the contrary?'

'We'll sort that somehow. Celia can be most resourceful when she wants to be. The main thing is that her parents don't find out the truth.' He hesitated, then said, 'I'm sure we can pull it off.'

'Excuse me a moment,' Lena apologised and, leaving him, went to the ladies, where she threw up.

Lena lay in the darkness of her bedroom staring at the ceiling, still trying to come to terms with the bombshell Hamish had dropped earlier that evening in the Swan.

It was over, she thought for the umpteenth time. Finished. No more visits to Hamish's house for nookie. From now on sex would only be a memory. Something to be remembered with pleasure, and sadness too.

'Christ!' she whispered to herself. Life could be so bloody unfair. Why did she have to have been born so ugly that she repelled men? For she did, and had known it for almost as long as she could remember.

It was going to be awful continuing to work alongside Hamish day in, day out. Seeing him, thinking of him going home to the beautiful Celia.

Then she had an idea. Perhaps she could get a transfer out of his department into another? Yes, that would help. She certainly couldn't, in the current slump, leave the company altogether. That would be madness with jobs so thin on the ground.

Then she had an even better idea. Perhaps she couldn't leave the company, but she could leave the country. Why not? Hollywood was still there. Pet would surely help her get something when she turned up.

The only drawback was money. She had no savings left, having given them all to her mother, so she'd have to start again from the beginning which would take years the way things were.

Or would it? Dare she? It frightened her to even think about it. But it could be done. Quite easily, too, given her skill and ability as a ledger clerk.

Hamish had got away with it, after all, to the tune of fifty pounds a month. Why, if she embezzled the same amount, in six months she'd have more than enough and could be on her way.

She mustn't rush into this, she warned herself. She must carefully think it through.

A new start. A new beginning. By God and she was tempted.

'I'm sorry I can't offer you a biscuit, or a piece of cake,' Georgie apologised. Gladys Renton had dropped by for a natter and a cup of tea.

'That's all right. I perfectly understand. So how are you doing anyway?' It had been nearly a week since they'd last spoken.

'Fine. Feeling the pinch like everyone else.'

'Aye, aren't we just.' Gladys nodded.

'But you're all right, surely? Your Sammy's still in work.' Sammy was a night watchman whose job was more or less guaranteed as the firm he was employed by feared night-time break-ins by out-of-work opportunists trying to steal whatever. The lead on the company's roof was a particularly tempting target for thieves.

'No, no, I didn't mean Sammy and me,' Gladys hastily corrected herself. 'I meant the country as a whole.'

'Damn,' Georgie swore. 'I'm out of sugar again. Can you take it without?'

'Oh aye. As long as it's hot and wet I'll not complain.'

Georgie hesitated, then said quietly, 'There's something I've been meaning to ask you.'

'What's that?'

'It's about Charlie's wife Agnes. Did he ever . . . well, did he ever hit her?'

Gladys eyed Georgie speculatively. 'Has he been hitting you then, hen?'

Georgie shook her head. 'But he does have a terrible temper, which has made me wonder at times if he's capable of it.'

'I can honestly say I don't know. I never saw any signs that he had, and Agnes never mentioned it. Not to me anyway.'

That was a relief, Georgie thought. 'Thanks, Gladys. I just wanted to know.' She poured boiling water into the teapot. She'd have to go shopping later, she thought. Which meant more money out of the bank to cover the household expenses as she was seeing less and less of

Charlie's pay packet at the end of the week. The majority of his wages went down his throat, leaving her very little to try to manage on.

'There again,' Gladys went on, 'there are some men who hit their women where it can't be seen. On the body like. Some of the bastards can be dead crafty when it comes to hammering the wife, believe me.'

Georgie digested that. 'I see,' she murmured. Had that been the case with Agnes? It was always a possibility.

'While we're asking questions, what do you make of Charlie's sister Betty?'

Georgie took a deep breath, and looked sideways at Gladys who was watching her intently. 'The truth? I can't stand the woman. There's something about her makes my flesh creep.'

'She and Agnes didn't get on, I can tell you that.'

'Oh?'

'Agnes couldn't bear her sister-in-law who, apparently, thought Charlie had married beneath him. Which is a laugh when you think about it. No offence meant, but he's only a fireman after all. Hardly special.'

'I wonder why Betty thought that?'

'Who knows? She's a queer fish right enough. There was talk at the time . . .' Gladys broke off, and bit her lip.

'Talk at what time?'

Gladys sighed. 'Well, I may as well tell you. There was talk at the time, pure speculation mind, that Agnes might not have tripped when she fell down the stairs.'

'I don't understand.' Georgie frowned.

Gladys stared her straight in the eye. 'The talk was that Agnes might have been pushed after some sort of row.'

'Dear God,' Georgie breathed, shocked.

'Betty had been in your house that day. I don't know why, but she'd definitely been there before the accident. I saw her myself. But no one spotted her leaving or knows what time that was.'

'That would have been murder,' Georgie declared, thoroughly shaken.

'There's absolutely no proof it was that. But it's a hard fact the two women loathed each other. And Betty . . . as I said, she's a queer fish. And very nasty with it. A little shove at the right moment, and hey! An accident.'

'She's always been friendly enough to me,' Georgie said.

'Or appeared to be friendly enough. I just don't like her, that's all. She gives me the willies.'

'What I told you is strictly between the pair of us, all right? It was only talk, after all.'

'Strictly between the pair of us,' Georgie agreed. She was still shaken by what she'd just learnt.

'I'm sorry for running away last time,' Mrs Mulherron apologised. 'I was just simply overcome. Please forgive me.'

'There's nothing to forgive.' Tom smiled. 'I understood.'

She gazed into his face, then away again. 'The resemblance really is quite uncanny.'

'Must have been a handsome devil, your son,' Tom joked.

Mrs Mulherron laughed. 'There were those who thought he was. As did I, though I have to admit to being prejudiced.'

'A mother's privilege.'

'Indeed it is.'

'Was Robert an officer?'

'A captain when he was killed. He was with the artillery.'

'You must miss him dreadfully,' Tom sympathised.

'I do. Very much.'

'As must your husband?'

'I'm afraid Freddy's also dead. He passed on several years after the war ended. He never really got over Robert, you see. That was a terrible blow to him.'

'Do you have other children?' Tom was curious.

'No, Robert was our one and only. The apple of Freddy's eye. And mine too, of course.'

The dance came to an end and they politely clapped. 'Can you stay up for another?' she asked hopefully.

'Yes, but only one more. Two at a time is the maximum. House rules.'

'Which is why I have a favour to ask.'

'Which is?'

'I presume you have the days free?'

'That's right.'

'I'd love to have a really good chat with you, which I obviously can't do here, and I was wondering if you'd care to come to lunch next week?'

He was taken aback. 'Lunch?'

'I'd be very grateful if you could. I'd like to show you Robert's photograph so you can see the likeness for yourself.'

Chrissie's warnings about predatory women flashed through Tom's mind. But he couldn't believe Mrs Mulherron was one of those.

Mrs Mulherron noticed his look of concern, and guessed what it was about. 'Don't worry, Tom, we won't be alone. The staff will be in attendance, I promise you.'

Before the dance was over Tom had agreed to go to her house for lunch the following Wednesday.

Lena was hurrying home from work when she was brought up short by a street billboard advertising that evening's newspaper. The headline written on it screamed in large black letters: TRAGEDY AT SEA. FAMOUS HOLLYWOOD ACTRESS DROWNED.

Lena's heart was in her mouth as she bought a copy of the paper and quickly scanned the front page.

The actress was Dawn Ryder.

Chapter 20

'Pet's dead,' Lena announced to the family when she got in. She waved the newspaper at them. 'It's here on the front page.'

'Dead?' Chrissie repeated, shocked. 'How?'

'The paper says she drowned while swimming off the yacht she was holidaying on. It happened yesterday, apparently.'

Tam shook his head in disbelief. He'd always had a soft spot for Pet McQueen.

'I must go and see her parents,' Lena declared. 'They'll be devastated.'

'You'll have your tea first though?'

'I couldn't eat a thing, Mum. I'm just so upset. She and I were . . . well, you know. The best of pals.'

'I'm sorry, sis,' Tom sympathised. He'd also liked Pet.

'I'll just have a tidy up and then be on my way.' Lena suddenly staggered, and had to lean on the table for support. 'Sorry,' she croaked. 'As I said, I'm just so upset.'

'Understandable, lass.' Chrissie nodded.

Lena took a deep breath, and did her best to pull herself together. Leaving them, she went to her bedroom where, within minutes, she broke down and cried.

Poor Pet. Poor, poor Pet. The one consolation was, Lena reflected through her tears, she'd been a Hollywood star when she died. Her dream had come true.

Tom stared in awe at the house where Mrs Mulherron lived. It was more of a mansion than a house, he thought – it was absolutely huge.

Go on, he mentally urged himself. Ring the bell. You are invited, after all. Screwing up his courage, and feeling completely out of place, he mounted a few stone steps and did just that.

There was the sound of footsteps, then the door was opened to reveal a rather ancient butler.

'My name's Tom McKeand,' Tom stuttered. 'Mrs Mulherron is expecting me.'

The butler was staring at Tom as though he'd opened the door to a ghost. 'Quite so, Mr McKeand,' he replied at last. 'Do come in. Mrs Mulherron is in the morning room. If you'll kindly follow me I'll show you the way.'

Tom gazed about him as he walked behind the butler, if anything even more awed than he'd been out in the street. There were antiques everywhere, and gilt-framed paintings on the walls. He had no idea who the painters were, but he presumed they were famous.

Mrs Mulherron rose to her feet the moment he was ushered into the room. 'Ah, there you are, Tom. How kind of you to come.'

He wasn't sure what to do next, being completely out

of his depth. He elected to go to her and shake her by the hand. She looked older in daylight, he noticed. The lighting at the Belgrave was far kinder, particularly for women of a certain age. Which, of course, was the intention.

He smiled. 'I'm delighted to be here.'

'Well, what do you think, Smith? Was I right or wrong?'

'You were right, madam,' the butler replied. 'When I opened the front door I would have sworn it was the young master himself standing there.'

Mrs Mulherron turned her attention again to Tom. 'Now, I'm having a pre-lunch sherry. Would you care for one? Or perhaps something else. A whisky maybe?'

'Whisky would be lovely.'

'Would you care for it neat, sir, or with water or soda?'

'Soda, please,' Tom replied, knowing that was how many of the nobs took it.

'Certainly, sir.'

Mrs Mulherron gestured to the white marble mantelpiece. 'I've laid out a few photographs for you to look at.'

Tom crossed to the mantelpiece to stare at the largest photo, which was set in a silver frame: Robert Mulherron wearing his military uniform. Tom presumed that the photograph had been taken just before his departure to the Front.

He might have been gazing into a mirror. Robert was him to a T. A younger version, but him to a T.

'Do you see the resemblance?' Mrs Mulherron queried with a sad smile.

'Oh, yes. We might have been brothers.'

'You might have been twins,' she corrected.

'Indeed,' Tom mused. They might well have been.

The other photographs were of Robert at various stages in his short life. The resemblance in the younger ones wasn't quite so noticeable, but it increased as Robert grew up. Tom found the whole thing rather spooky.

'How did he die?' he asked quietly.

'Blown up, I was told. One moment he was there, the next gone. He and the entire gun crew.' She paused to compose herself. 'At least it was quick. He wouldn't have known what happened, or felt any pain.'

'That must have been a consolation.'

'Yes, it was. And still is.'

Smith returned with Tom's whisky and soda, offering it to him on a tray. 'Thank you,' Tom said, accepting the drink.

'I don't normally, but I'll have another sherry, I think,' Mrs Mulherron told the butler.

'Certainly, madam.'

'Smith's been with us for years and years,' she explained to Tom when the man had gone. 'He was very fond of Robert. Very fond.'

'He strikes me as a nice man, Mrs Mulherron.'

'Oh, he is. But enough of this Mrs Mulherron business. Far too formal. My Christian name is Dorcas, believe it or not. I hate it. From some Shakespearean play, I understand, and quite the silliest name imaginable. I prefer Dolly, and have insisted on being called that since very early on.'

Tom grinned. 'Then Dolly it is.'

'Good. Are you hungry, Tom?'

'Fairly so.'

'Then we shall shortly go on through.'

The starter was pâté, which Tom had never eaten before, the main course a fish dish which he thoroughly enjoyed. The pudding was something named brûlée, again thoroughly enjoyable, and the meal was accompanied by a choice of red or white wine. Dolly elected to drink white, Tom red.

'If it's not rude to say so, I'm most impressed by your house,' Tom commented halfway through the pudding. He felt quite relaxed, Dolly being the easiest of company. There were certainly no airs or graces about her.

'It is lovely, isn't it?' Dolly sighed. 'I should move to something smaller now that I'm on my own, but I can't bring myself to do so. There are far too many happy memories for me here.'

'Yes, I can understand that.'

Dolly's eyes took on a wistful, faraway look. She was clearly lost in memory.

'Can I ask what your husband did?' Tom was dying to know. Nosy, as Chrissie would have said.

Dolly came out of her reverie. 'Freddy was a manufacturer of nuts and bolts, a very successful one. I sold the business after he died on advice from my advocate. A wise decision, I've always thought. Freddy was the dynamism behind the company. Without him . . . well, who knows what might have happened.'

'Nuts and bolts,' Tom repeated, amused. 'He must have been turning them out by the millions to afford a house like this.'

'Oh, he was. Supplying firms not only in this country, but abroad.'

Tom finished his brûlée, laid his spoon aside, and had a sip of wine.

'Now, tell me about yourself,' Dolly said. 'I want to know everything about you and your family.'

'Everything?'

'Absolutely.'

'That's a tall order,' Tom joked.

'We've got all afternoon, don't forget.'

He shrugged. 'To be honest, there's not that much to tell, really. We're a pretty ordinary family to whom not much happens.'

'Nevertheless, on you go.'

So he did.

'This is Robert's bedroom, which I've left exactly as it was the day he went off to France.'

Tom glanced around. It was certainly a comfortable bedroom, with books and all sorts of mementos scattered around. 'Which school did Robert go to?'

'Glasgow Academy, where he did very well. He was quite bright, if I say so myself.'

'Well that's something I'm not.'

'Oh, I wouldn't say that.' Dolly smiled. 'You strike me as a very intelligent young man. In different circumstances you might have gone far, indeed you might.'

Tom couldn't see it himself. He picked up a rugby ball, throwing it a few inches into the air and catching it again.

'Have you played?' Dolly enquired.

'No.' Tom laughed. 'That's strictly a posh game. It was

football with me. In the playground and on the street. Gangs of us at times. It was great fun.'

Dolly had a sudden idea which caused her to wrinkle her forehead. Why not? she thought. Better they did some good than just hang there in the wardrobe. As long as Tom didn't take offence, that was.

When she made her suggestion, he didn't.

'That must have cost a pretty penny,' Chrissie said, fingering the cloth of the overcoat Tom had brought home with him. 'A real Crombie too,' she added, noting the label.

'Just look at these suits,' Tom demanded, pulling one from the suitcase he'd also brought back.

Chrissie whistled silently. She knew quality when she saw it.

'Three suits and six shirts.' Tom grinned. 'Not bad, eh?'

'I should say so. And that suitcase is crocodile skin. That wouldn't have come cheap either.'

'I've to return the suitcase,' Tom explained. 'She said that way I have to visit her again.'

The clothes were all in excellent condition, Chrissie observed. Almost brand new.

'I was offered shoes as well, but had to turn them down as Robert's feet were smaller than mine.'

'And do these suits fit?'

'Dolly and I both thought so. If I do need an alteration or two I'm sure Lena will help. You know how good she is at that sort of thing.'

'Dolly, eh?' Chrissie smiled. 'On first-name terms now, are we?'

'She insisted. Said Mrs Mulherron was far too formal.'

'And you actually do look like her son?'

'I'm a dead ringer, Mum. We might have been twins.'

Chrissie thought about that. 'What was the house like?'

'Ah!' Tom exclaimed. 'Now you're talking.' He went on to describe the house in detail, inside and out.

'This Mrs Mulherron must be filthy rich,' Chrissie commented when he'd finally finished.

'As Croesus. She even has a butler called Smith. Not to mention a cook, a chauffeur cum handyman, and several maids. That lot must cost more than a couple of quid a week.'

Chrissie could only agree.

Dolly was sitting on the edge of Robert's bed staring at his wardrobe. She'd been right to give Tom those clothes, she thought. Better he had them, and made use of them, than they just continued to hang there.

She hadn't said so to Tom, but the suit he wore at the Belgrave had seen better days. And it couldn't be very nice wearing the same suit night after night. It would wear out in no time, but to buy a new one would be a big lay-out for Tom, who couldn't be on that much money a week.

Now that she'd made a start should she get rid of the rest of Robert's things? She'd avoided doing so since his death, wanting to keep the room exactly as it had been. It would break her heart to do it, but perhaps it would be best in the long run. Coming in here to sit, from time to time, was downright morbid now she thought about it. But she wouldn't make a decision there and then. What if she came to regret chucking everything out?

'Oh, Robert,' she whispered. 'Oh, Freddy.'

How she missed them both.

'Can you please try not to hurt me like that,' Georgie said.

Charlie was surprised. 'Did I?'

'There's no need to grab and squeeze. A little gentleness is what's called for.'

'I'm sorry, Georgie,' he apologised. 'I wasn't aware I was doing that.'

'Well you were. At one point I thought you were going to pull my tit right off.'

'Sorry again. I'll be more careful next time.'

This roughness was a recent thing, Georgie reflected. It hadn't been like that when they were first married. Like everything else in their marriage, lovemaking had deteriorated.

Turning away from him she thought of John. Dear, lovely John. That night she dreamt of him, and how it had once been between them.

A smiling Hamish came breezing into the department on his first day back after the elopement. 'Morning, everyone!' he declared, heading straight for his office. 'Lena, can you please join me for a few moments?'

She mustn't let her feelings show, she thought. She had no right to be angry, or jealous, after all. He'd kept his part of the bargain so she could hardly complain.

His expression was grave when she entered his office

and closed the door. 'First of all let me say how sorry I am about your friend Dawn Ryder. It must have been a terrible shock for you.'

Lena hadn't expected this. 'Yes, it was. How did you find out?'

'It was in the newspapers.'

Of course. She should have thought of that. He read the papers like everyone else.

'Well, I'm sorry, and I wanted you to know that.'

'Thanks, Hamish.'

He took a deep breath. 'Anyway, to business. Has everything been all right here? No problems?'

'No problems,' Lena assured him. She didn't add that there wouldn't be with her in charge.

'And my absence, has that been explained in any way?'

'The chairman sent down a memo saying you'd taken unexpected leave, and to carry on as usual until your return. Elopement or marriage wasn't mentioned.'

'Fine.' Hamish nodded.

'Have you seen Celia's parents since your return?'

'We only got in late last night, and I decided it was best to come straight to work this morning. So the answer's no.'

Lena cleared her throat. She didn't want to ask the question, but felt driven to do so. 'How did it all go?'

He stared at her, then, embarrassed, glanced away. 'As planned. We had the ceremony, which took longer to organise than I'd realised, then had a short honeymoon. I wish I could say the weather was wonderful, but it wasn't. In fact it rained nearly all the time we were there.'

Lena took some grim satisfaction from that. 'Too bad.'

'Still, it could have been worse, I suppose.'

'So now Celia is officially Mrs Hamish Murchison.'

Was it her imagination or did Hamish squirm ever so slightly in his chair?

'That's right. And has a gold band on her finger to prove it.'

'Then I wish the pair of you all the very best.' It wasn't true, but she felt obliged to say it.

'Thank you.'

'There's something else, Hamish.'

'What's that?'

'I'd like a transfer to another department. I'm sure you can understand why.'

He stared at her, aghast. 'You don't mean that?'

'I'm afraid I do.'

'But I rely on you so much, Lena. You know that,' he spluttered. 'You're my right hand. I don't know what I'd do without you.'

'Manage somehow,' she replied, giving him her razored smile.

Hamish came to his feet, walked to the window and stared out. 'Is this some sort of revenge?' he asked quietly over his shoulder.

'Not revenge, Hamish,' she answered. 'But I think it would be for the best, don't you?'

'No I bloody well do not!' he exploded, whirling on her. 'I refuse to transfer you. Absolutely refuse.' He held up a hand. 'And there will be no further discussion or argument about that. Do you hear?'

'What if I went above your head?' she queried, the same arctic smile on her face.

'You can't, Lena. You're forgetting I'm the chairman's son-in-law now. If I say you stay, then you stay.' He glared at her. 'And don't even think of threatening me with our little secret. Because if I go down I'd swear you were in on it. That it was your idea in the first place. Then we'd both be sunk.'

'I had no intention of threatening you,' Lena replied quietly. 'You kept your part of the bargain, and I'll keep mine. Now, is there anything else?'

He shook his head.

A little later he left for the coffee shop, not even looking at her as he strode past.

Tom and Dolly applauded politely at the end of the dance. It had been her second with him, which meant she now had to relinquish him to another partner.

'You seem very perky tonight,' Tom complimented her, having noted the spring in her step, and the twinkle in her eye.

'I feel it.'

'Any particular reason?'

'None that I can think of. I simply woke up in an excellent mood this morning and it has continued throughout the day.'

He smiled at her. 'Will we be dancing again later?'

'Of course. But in the meantime I thought I'd chance my luck in the gaming room.'

'Really? I didn't know you gambled.'

'On occasion, when the opportunity presents itself. Freddy and I used to . . .' She broke off. 'But that's another story which I'll tell you some time.'

Tom re-joined Derek, who'd also just sat down. 'Is the gambling here on the level?' he asked in a whisper.

'As far as I know,' Derek replied.

'Good.'

An hour later Dolly was back asking for another dance, and Tom was only too happy to oblige. He'd become quite fond of Dolly Mulherron, in a friendly sort of way.

'So how did you get on?' he enquired as they took to the floor.

'I played blackjack and won.'

'Good for you!'

'Nearly two hundred pounds.' She giggled. 'Not bad, eh?'

'Not bad at all. I'm impressed.'

The next moment several gaming chips were slipped into his breast pocket. 'Your cut,' she said, smiling.

'But I didn't do anything to deserve a cut!'

'You're getting one anyway.'

From then on, whenever Dolly won in the gaming room, which was often, she shared her winnings with Tom.

Chapter 21

'Thanks for calling round. I'll see you again soon, no doubt.'

''Bye then, Georgie.'

''Bye, Betty.'

Georgie closed the front door and let out a sigh of relief. That had been an unexpected visit from Charlie's sister, and she hadn't enjoyed it one little bit. The woman really did give her the willies. She couldn't have said why, since Betty was always agreeable enough. But there was something in her eyes Georgie found most disturbing.

Had Betty pushed Agnes down the stairs? One thing was certain: Georgie believed her quite capable of it. That was a harsh verdict, perhaps, particularly when there was no proof of any sort, but Georgie believed her capable all right. She found herself watching her back when Betty was around, and being politeness itself.

She shivered as gooseflesh suddenly erupted all over her body. That was the effect Betty had on her.

*　　　*　　　*

'I wonder what she's like?' Derek mused. He was referring to the new young female dancer who was taking over that night from her predecessor, who'd had to leave for personal reasons.

Tom shrugged. 'Search me. As long as she's pleasant, that's all I care about.'

'Aye, true enough.' Derek nodded. All the dancers got on well together, and were hoping the newcomer would fit in. 'There's Mrs Simpson now.'

The manageress had appeared at the far side of the hall, accompanied by a much younger woman.

The newcomer was almost halfway towards them before Tom recognised her. He simply couldn't believe his eyes. It was Brigid. *His* Brigid. The one he'd broken his heart over when they'd split up.

'I'd like you all to meet Miss O'Reilly,' Mrs Simpson announced on reaching the dancers, and immediately began introducing them to Brigid. Tom didn't know what to do. Did he acknowledge Brigid as an old friend, or not mention the fact? He'd be led by her, he decided.

'Brigid, this is Tom McKeand.'

'Pleased to meet you, Tom,' she said formally.

There it was, he'd take his cue from that. 'And I'm pleased to meet you, Brigid.'

'You'll soon get to know everyone,' Mrs Simpson said to Brigid, escorting her back up the line to where she'd be sitting with the two older women.

'Are you all right, Tom?' Derek frowned. 'You look dreadful.'

'Do I?' Tom queried, pretending innocence.

'You've suddenly gone all white and . . . well, I don't know. You just look dreadful.'

'A sudden attack of wind,' Tom lied in a whisper. 'It'll soon pass.'

'Not in my direction, I hope!'

Tom forced a laugh. 'I'll be careful about that.'

His mind was reeling when he sat down again. Brigid! After all these years. It hardly seemed credible. And yet there she was, sitting no more than a dozen feet away, as gorgeous as ever.

During the evening he watched her as she danced, noting she hadn't lost any of her skill and ability. Once he caught her glancing in his direction, looking quickly away again when their eyes met.

He couldn't wait to talk to her when he had the chance.

Tom took his coat from its peg and hurried after Brigid, whom he'd let go on slightly ahead. Out in the street he caught her up.

'Brigid!'

She stopped and turned to face him.

'That was a shock,' he said, joining her.

'For me too. I had no idea you worked there.'

'Have done for a while now.' They resumed walking. 'I got laid off at McNair's and was lucky enough to be told by a pal that the Belgrave was looking for someone. What about you?'

'Same thing. I got laid off too, and heard about the Belgrave only yesterday. I saw Mrs Simpson, and started tonight.'

'God, it's good to see you again,' he breathed.

She glanced sideways at him, then away again. 'How have you been?'

Why hadn't she said she was glad to see *him*? Maybe because she wasn't. 'Fine. You?'

'All right.'

'I must say you're looking well. You've hardly changed at all.'

'Thank you.'

Hardly enthusiastic, he thought glumly. 'And what about me? Have I changed much?'

'Not really.'

'Well, that's nice to know.' This wasn't going at all well. Making conversation was like getting blood out of the proverbial stone.

'What's it like at the Belgrave?' she asked after a moment.

'Terrific. I thoroughly enjoy working there. If you can call dancing work, that is.' He shook his head. 'I still find it hard to believe I get paid for it. It sure as hell beats the hard graft at McNair's. Money for old rope.'

She smiled at that. 'So it would seem. But tell me, is there anything I should know?'

'Like what?'

'The blokes who ask me to dance. Are any of them going to proposition me? That was my worry.'

'Not a chance,' Tom assured her. 'It's a very respectable place. If anyone ever does try it on just tell Mrs Simpson and he'll be chucked out double quick. Mrs Simpson doesn't stand for any nonsense.'

Brigid looked relieved.

'My mother had the same worry when I started there,' Tom went on. 'It quite surprised me that she would think of such a thing, but she did. I was soon able to put her mind at rest.'

280

'I suppose it gets hectic Fridays and Saturdays?'

'It can do. There are some nights when you never get to have a breather from start to finish. On your feet all the time.'

'The other dancers seem nice enough,' Brigid commented.

'They are. A good bunch. You won't have any trouble there either.'

She smiled at him. 'It seems I've fallen on my feet then.'

He smiled back. 'Literally.'

That made her laugh.

When they came to a corner she stopped. 'I go this way,' she said.

'I know.'

'So . . .'

'I thought I'd walk you home,' he interrupted. 'It's not that far out of my way, after all.'

'I'm quite capable of looking after myself, Tom,' she said firmly. 'Nothing will happen to me, even at this time of night. I'll be fine.'

'No doubt, Brigid. I just thought . . . well, I'd like to. There's no harm in it, is there?'

'Are you sure?'

'Absolutely. We are old friends, don't forget. It's not as if I'm going to try to chat you up or anything.'

She stared hard at him, then nodded. 'All right.' They continued on their way.

'I saw you at the dancing once,' he told her. 'Years ago. You were with a chap I presumed was your boyfriend.'

'And why would you presume that?'

Tom was suddenly embarrassed, wishing now he hadn't

referred to the occasion. 'You had three or four dances in a row.'

'I see.' She glanced at him again. 'And?'

'And what?'

'What happened after the three or four dances?'

'I don't know. I left.'

'Because of me?'

'No,' he lied. 'I simply decided to go elsewhere.'

She knew he was fibbing; she could hear it in his voice. Tom had always been something of an open book to her. She wanted to say she hoped it hadn't distressed him, but decided not to.

Tom looked up at the sky. 'I think it might rain. It seems to be threatening.'

Brigid also looked up. It didn't look threatening to her. 'I imagined you'd have been engaged or married by now?' He wasn't wearing a ring, but there again, some men didn't.

''Fraid not,' he answered vaguely.

'Nor am I, before you ask.'

He grinned. 'I'm aware of that. I had a dekko at your left hand earlier to see if you were. I know it's none of my business, Brigid, but are you going out with anyone?'

She hesitated. 'I was, until recently.'

'What happened?'

She decided to be honest. 'He didn't want to see me any more. I think he'd met someone else.'

'The man's an idiot,' Tom muttered.

'What did you say? I didn't catch that.'

'I said the man's an idiot. A bloody fool for giving you up.'

She was pleased. He still cared. 'What about you?'

'No one at the moment.'

For some reason that pleased her as well. She would have been . . . She frowned when she realised what she'd been about to admit to herself. She'd have been jealous.

Tom pulled out his cigarettes and offered her one.

'Not in the street, thank you very much,' she said.

'The street's empty. Who's to know?'

She had to admit she was tempted. She'd have loved a fag, but had been brought up to believe decent women didn't smoke in the street.

'Go on,' he urged. 'No one will see you.'

She gave in to temptation. 'All right, then.'

He struck a match and held it to her cigarette, then his own. He flicked the match to send it spiralling away.

Brigid sucked in a deep lungful of smoke, then slowly blew it out. 'I've cut down to only a couple a day,' she told him.

'Lack of money?'

'That's it.'

'Well, you'll be able to afford more than that once you get your first pay packet.'

'Thank God. That and other things I've had to go without since being laid off.'

Tom realised they had relaxed together somewhere during their walk. They were at ease with one another again. The fact delighted him. They continued chatting, catching up with one another, till eventually they reached her close, where she stopped and turned to face him.

What to do next? he wondered. Peck her on the cheek? Shake her by the hand? No, that would be ridiculous.

Just walk away after saying goodnight? That seemed the safest bet. Though he would much have preferred the kiss on the cheek.

'I'll see you tomorrow night, then, Brigid,' he declared somewhat awkwardly.

She smiled at him. 'Thanks for walking me home, Tom. It was kind of you.'

'Don't mention it. It was nothing of the sort. It was a pleasure, believe me.'

She had enjoyed it too. 'There's just one thing, Tom.'

'And what's that?'

'Don't get any ideas. I'm still Catholic, and this is still Glasgow.'

'I know,' he whispered sadly.

'Goodnight then.'

'Goodnight.'

She was dead right, he thought morosely as he strolled away. She was still Catholic, and this was still Glasgow.

Nothing anyone could do would ever change that.

'What's wrong with you tonight?' Chrissie asked. She and Tam were alone, Tom at work and Lena in her room.

'I've been thinking, that's all.'

'About what?'

'Mary.'

Chrissie sighed, and dropped her knitting on to her lap. She was using wool from an old cardigan she'd unpicked to knit socks for Tam and Tom.

'It's been so long since we've seen her,' Tam went on. 'Years now.'

Chrissie also missed their eldest daughter. Dreadfully

so at times. She couldn't help but feel it was wrong for them to be estranged as they were. She nodded. 'Aye. It is that.'

'The children must have grown quite a bit.'

'I suppose so.'

'And we know nothing of their circumstances. Is James still in work, or has he been laid off too, like so many?'

'I've heard nothing. If I had you'd have been the first to be told.'

Tam wished it was the weekend so he could have had some whisky. But it was still only Thursday. He'd have to wait.

'Do you want to go and see her?' Chrissie asked softly.

Tam glanced sharply at her, then away again. He didn't reply.

'Tam?'

He took a deep breath, then slowly exhaled. 'No, I don't. It's her place to come to us.'

'She won't do that unless she's allowed to try to win us over to her religious views. And you won't allow that.'

'Damn right I won't! If she comes it's as a daughter to her parents without all that guff she spouts about the so-called sect.'

'Then things will just have to remain as they are, I suppose,' Chrissie said, a great weariness in her voice.

The subject was closed.

It was the quietest Tuesday Tom had ever known at the Belgrave. Since his arrival several hours earlier he hadn't been asked up once to dance, nor had any of the others. He was sure they must be as bored as he was.

Derek, sitting beside him, yawned. 'I nearly dropped off there. Mrs Simpson wouldn't have liked that at all.'

'She'd have given you a right flea in your ear.'

Derek grinned his agreement.

Tom had a sudden idea. Why not? He didn't think the manageress would object. On the contrary, she'd probably approve as they were so quiet. He decided to chance it.

Getting to his feet he went to where Brigid was sitting. 'Do you fancy a birl round the floor?' he asked.

She frowned. 'Is that allowed?'

'I don't see why not. The place is all but empty.'

'I'm not sure, Tom. I don't want to get into any trouble.'

'You won't. Now come on.'

Brigid stood up and together they went on to the dance floor. 'It's been a long time,' Tom said quietly as she came into his arms.

'Yes, it has.'

Not that you would have thought it, Tom reflected a few minutes later. It was as if . . . well, it was as if they'd never been apart.

When it came to dancing, anyway.

'So, how's Charlie been lately?' Chrissie queried. Georgie had called in to pay her a visit.

'Much improved, I have to say. He's really been making an effort. Not drinking nearly as much as he was. Nicer too.'

'That's good.'

'Avril's still a right little cow. But then, that'll never change. I've no doubt she'll still be a cow when she grows up. She's that type.'

'And Ian?'

'He's fine. His skin has cleared up a lot recently. Though why, I've no idea. He's getting on quite well at school too, which pleases me.'

'No more thrashings, I take it?'

Georgie's expression became grim. 'No. I'll never forgive Charlie for doing that. Or Avril for instigating it.'

'It was a bad business right enough.' Chrissie shook her head.

'It took Ian a long time to get over it, I can tell you. He's still wary of Charlie. He doesn't say, but I know he is. And I don't blame him either.'

'And you? Are you wary of him?'

'In a way,' Georgie reluctantly admitted. 'He's never yet laid a hand on me. But I always have the feeling it could happen.'

'And if he ever does?'

Georgie shrugged. 'I don't honestly know. I might leave him. There again, that would create a lot of problems. Where would I go, for instance?'

'Here,' Chrissie stated firmly. 'You could have your old bed back in what's now Lena's room. And we could arrange something in Tom's for Ian. We'd cope.'

Georgie's eyes shone with gratitude. 'Thanks, Mum. I'll remember that.'

'See you do.' Chrissie hesitated, then asked, 'Do you regret marrying him?'

Georgie took her time in replying. 'He's certainly not the man I thought I was marrying, and that's the truth. I believed him to be kind and gentle – which he can be, when it suits him. But I wasn't aware of his drinking. That came as quite a shock.'

'You haven't answered my question, Georgie.'

That was because it wasn't a question she wanted to answer. She didn't even want to admit the answer to herself. She stared at her mother, her expression stricken.

'Yes,' she finally admitted. 'I do.'

'What do you do with your days?' Tom asked, having walked Brigid home after work.

'Not a lot, really,' she answered. 'I always have a lie-in during the week, after which I help my mother round the house. Sometimes I go shopping for her. That sort of thing. What about you?'

'Not a lot either. Which is why I was wondering, how about us meeting up?'

'What for?'

'Well, I could buy you lunch for a start.'

Brigid couldn't help but laugh. 'Lunch!' she mocked. 'Since when has it become that? It was always dinner when I knew you before.'

Tom blushed.

'Taking on airs and graces, are we?'

'No, it's not like that. I suppose I used the word because of Mrs Mulherron.'

'And who's Mrs Mulherron when she's at home?'

God, but he wanted to kiss her. That and more, if she'd have let him. 'It's a long story, Brigid, which I can tell you over lunch. So how about it?'

'I don't know,' she replied reluctantly. 'It might not be such a good idea.'

'Of course it's a good idea. You're at a loose end, and so am I. Spending a little time together takes up a bit of slack. It'll be fun. And look on the bright side: you'll get to hear all about Mrs Mulherron. Or Dolly as she insists I call her.'

Brigid was intrigued, as Tom had hoped she'd be. 'Well, maybe,' she prevaricated.

'Which day shall we meet then?' he asked hopefully.

'Hold your horses. I haven't agreed yet,' she protested.

'You name the day and time, and I'll pick you up here.'

Suddenly her resistance crumbled. She could think of nothing she'd like more than to have lunch, as he called it, with Tom. 'No funny business now, right?'

'Right.'

'Sure?'

'Cross my heart and hope to die if I damn well tell a lie.'

She laughed again, then named a day and time as requested.

'I'll be standing here waiting for you.'

What had she got herself into, she wondered as she climbed the stairs to her house. She didn't quite know. But of one thing she was certain: she was looking forward to it.

'Go straight on through, Mrs Murchison,' Lena said, putting on her best smile. 'Your husband's free.'

'Thank you. Miss McKeand, isn't it?'

'That's correct.'

Celia matched Lena's smile before moving ponderously towards Hamish's office.

My God, Lena thought. What a size! Celia was big enough to be carrying a baby elephant rather than a human child. Lena had never seen a pregnant woman so large. And there was still months to go before the birth! As for Celia's bosom, it was simply ginormous, straining at the dress she was wearing. It was going to take Celia a long, long time to get her figure back, Lena gleefully reflected. If she ever did, that was. And after her milk dried she was going to have tits down to her knees.

Oh, life was not all bad, Lena told herself. There was some justice in the world after all.

Chapter 22

It seemed to happen as though by magic. One moment Tom was saying goodnight to Brigid, having walked her home after work yet again, the next they were in one another's arms kissing passionately.

'Oh, Brigid,' Tom breathed when the kiss was finally over. 'That was fantastic.' To his astonishment she broke away from him and burst into tears. 'Brigid, what's wrong?'

'You are. We are,' she sobbed. 'I didn't want this to happen. And it's all my fault for letting it.'

Perplexed, he stared at her. 'I'm sorry. I . . . I don't know what came over me.' He broke off in confusion.

She groped in a coat pocket to produce a handkerchief which she used to dab at her tears. She was furious with herself.

'Can I . . .' He moved towards her and she immediately backed away.

'Damn you, Tom McKeand,' she shouted. 'Damn you. Why did you ever have to come back into my life again?

After all these years of trying to forget you and then . . . The bloody Belgrave. It just isn't fair.'

'You spent years trying to forget me?' he repeated wonderingly.

'Yes, I did. I thought I'd succeeded, too.'

'And I spent years trying to forget you, but never could. You were always there, somewhere, in my mind and thoughts.'

She hiccuped. 'Was I?'

'I never stopped loving you, Brigid. And that's the truth.'

That brought on a fresh outbreak of tears. 'Well, I hate you,' she wailed. 'Hate you for kissing me like that. And saying what you just did.'

Now he was bewildered. 'You hate me for loving you?'

'Yes.'

'But why?'

'Because I'm still in love with you. That's why.'

She hated and loved him at the same time? How could that be? An impossibility, surely. And then it dawned on him what she'd just confessed, and his heart leapt within him.

'You still love me?' he repeated in awe.

'And now we're going to have to go through it all again.'

'Go through what?'

'Breaking up, dope. What else?'

He had no answer to give her, knowing her to be right. What had he been thinking of? What had been going through his mind since she'd turned up at the Belgrave?

'It can't be,' she cried. 'No matter how much we want

it, it just can't be. I've already told you, I'm still Catholic, and this is still Glasgow.'

And with that she turned and fled up her close.

It had been a lovely night out for the pair of them, Georgie reflected as she and Ian made their way home from the pictures. He'd had a good report from school and, as a reward, she'd taken him to see a cowboys and Indians film which he'd absolutely adored. When they came out of the cinema she'd bought them a bag of chips each as a special treat, and they'd just eaten the last ones.

On arriving at their front door she produced her key and opened it. She was still smiling as she entered the kitchen in front of Ian, but what she saw there seemed to turn her blood ice cold, and made the smile vanish abruptly from her face.

Charlie was sitting with a sleeping Avril on his lap. The child was totally naked, and Charlie's half-closed eyes told her just how drunk he was. But it was what he was doing that made her want to scream in horror. His flies were open and he was . . . With Avril on his lap!

Remembering Ian was behind her Georgie reacted swiftly. 'Let's get out of here,' she croaked, turning round and bundling him back in the direction they'd come. In the street again she had to stop for a few seconds in order to throw up in the gutter.

She couldn't believe what she'd just witnessed. It couldn't be true.

But it was.

*   *   *

She re-joined her parents, still in a state of shock. 'Ian's asleep now,' she said.

Chrissie, Tam and Lena still didn't quite know what had happened, only that it was something dreadful. Georgie's garbled story hadn't made much sense, but she had been clear about wanting to stay the night, which Chrissie had readily agreed to.

'Now, what's this all about?' Tam demanded, upset to see his daughter in such a state.

Georgie slumped into a chair. She felt embarrassed about telling her parents and Lena what she'd seen, but tell them she must. They listened incredulously while she described what she'd walked in on.

'Dear God in Heaven,' Chrissie whispered, when Georgie had finished.

Tam's hands were formed into fists. If Charlie had been present, drunk or not, he'd have beaten the bastard senseless.

'The wee lassie was totally naked?' Lena repeated.

'Stark, and asleep.'

'And he was . . .' Chrissie made a gesture.

'That's right, Mum.'

'He's a pervert, that's what he is. A bloody pervert. He should be stuck in jail and the key thrown away,' Tam declared angrily.

'I can't go back there, Mum. I just can't.'

'Of course not,' Chrissie agreed instantly. 'I said only recently that you were always welcome here if anything should happen, and now it has.'

'Thanks, Mum. Thanks, Papa.'

'I'll put the kettle on,' said Chrissie, moving off to

fill it. A cup of tea was her panacea for everything.

'I always worried about him hitting me,' Georgie went on. 'I know he's got it in him. But that! Never in a million years!'

'Did Ian see what he was doing?' Lena asked.

'I don't know. He might have. But maybe not because of the angle and him being a lot smaller. He certainly didn't say anything on the way here, and I didn't probe.'

'Let's hope he didn't,' Lena said. 'It could have an awful effect on him if he did.' She shuddered, her heart going out to her sister and nephew.

'What a mess,' Georgie said quietly. 'What a mess.'

Georgie took a deep breath before inserting her key in the lock. Beside her were Tam and Tom, who had come to help her remove her and Ian's things.

'It's all right, lass; we're with you,' Tam said grimly. 'There's no need to fash yourself.'

They went into the house to discover it empty, as Georgie had predicted. She had known Charlie was supposed to be on duty, but it was always possible he'd taken time off work, or somehow changed his shifts, though the latter was most unlikely.

'You go and do what you have to and we'll wait here,' Tam told her.

Half an hour later they were on a tram heading home again, Georgie's last act on leaving the house having been to post her key through the letter box. She'd have no further need of it, since she never intended to go back there again. As far as she was concerned, hell would freeze over first. In the meantime, at her father's insistence, she was going to have a word with the police.

'I'll leave you here then,' said Brigid, when they reached the street corner where she turned off. Since the night of the kiss she hadn't allowed Tom to walk her all the way home.

'Goodnight, Brigid. You take care now.'

'And you, Tom. Goodnight.'

There was an old tin can a little further down the street ahead of Tom. On reaching it he gave it a good kick to send it clattering away. It didn't help.

He was feeling no better when he went to Dolly's for lunch the following day.

'Why so glum?' she asked, as he pushed yet another half-eaten plateful away from him. 'You've hardly said a word since you arrived.'

Tom sighed. 'Sorry, Dolly. I didn't mean to be rude.'

'Not rude, Tom.' She smiled. 'Introspective, shall we say. Now, what's the problem? For it seems to me you must have one.'

He shrugged. 'It's personal, Dolly.'

'Then it's none of my business.' She paused for a moment. 'Though sharing a problem, personal or otherwise, often helps.'

He suddenly decided he would tell her what was bothering him. It would be good to talk, get it off his chest.

Dolly listened intently as he explained about Brigid and himself, only occasionally interrupting to clarify some point or other.

'I see,' she murmured when he'd finally finished. 'No wonder you're so down in the mouth.'

Tom had a gulp of wine, then another. 'There's simply no solution. None whatsoever. Brigid and I both agree on that.'

'Have you considered leaving Glasgow altogether and going elsewhere? A town where the religious thing wouldn't count?'

Tom smiled thinly. 'Don't forget there's a slump on that affects the entire country. At least in Glasgow Brigid and I have work.'

The latter was certainly true, Dolly mused. It was still an idea, though. 'Are you sure you love her, Tom?'

'Oh aye, there's no doubt in my mind about that.'

'And that she loves you?'

'She told me so only the other night.'

She'd have to think about this, Dolly decided.

'So how was school today?' Georgie asked.

'I'm pleased to be back there, Mum,' Ian enthused. 'It's a far nicer school with far nicer teachers.'

'Good.' She smiled. 'You don't miss the old one then?'

'No,' he declared emphatically. 'I don't miss it at all, and I don't miss Charlie's house either. I hated it there.' He stared at his mother through suddenly soulful eyes. 'I hated it there. And I hated him.'

Georgie could have wept.

Smith ushered Tom and Brigid into the morning room, where Dolly was waiting for them. Tom immediately introduced Brigid to her.

'I'm delighted to meet you, Brigid.'

'And I'm pleased to meet you, Mrs Mulherron.'

'Dolly, please. Now, what would you like to drink? I'm having my usual sherry.'

'That would be lovely.'

'Smith, a sherry for the young lady and, I presume, whisky for Tom?'

'Please.'

'Do sit down,' Dolly said, indicating chairs.

Brigid was overawed by the size of the house, and the quality of its contents. Tom had told her what to expect, but she'd still been taken aback by the actual reality.

'It's most kind of you to come.' Dolly smiled at Brigid when all three of them were seated.

'Not at all. It's kind of you to invite me. Though, I have to say, I can't think why you have.'

'Ah!' Dolly's expression was one of amusement. 'Because I have a proposition to put to the pair of you.'

'Proposition?' Tom frowned. 'What sort of proposition, Dolly?'

Dolly insisted on waiting till their drinks had been brought before explaining. Then she said, 'On Tom's last visit here he told me all about the problem he has in marrying you, Brigid, because of the religious differences, which I fully understand.' She paused to have a sip of sherry, thoroughly enjoying herself. 'You also stated, Tom, that there is a general slump throughout the length and breadth of Britain. Which isn't quite true. It's Scotland and the north of England that are mainly affected. Places where they rely on heavy industry for work, which they don't so much in the south.'

A flicker of hope fluttered in Tom's breast. Was Dolly about to pull a rabbit out of the hat?

Dolly went on, 'My late husband Freddy, God rest his soul, had many business friends and contacts, one of whom I took the liberty of writing to. Ford, the motor car people, have built a new production-line factory in Dagenham, Essex, where they eventually plan to employ seven thousand workers. Freddy's friend is in top-level management there. A man of some importance, you might say.'

Brigid glanced at Tom, then focused again on Dolly.

'I explained the situation to Freddy's friend, who has agreed to take you both on. Tom will be trained up as a foreman of the assembly line, while you, Brigid, will work on that assembly line. Not only that, but if you agree to go he'll arrange accommodation for you to move straight into on your arrival. I may also mention, Tom, that the foreman's pay is very generous in today's climate.'

Tom was stunned. He didn't know what to think. The offer had come completely out of the blue.

'No doubt you'll want to talk it over.' Dolly smiled. 'I'll give you my telephone number before you leave, Tom, and you can ring me when the two of you have come to a decision.'

Tom opened his mouth to speak, but nothing came out. He was literally speechless.

'Go and live in England!' an appalled Chrissie exclaimed. 'You can't do that.'

'Why not, Mum?'

'Because . . . well, it's full of English.' She said the last word as though they were all lepers.

Tom laughed. 'I'm sure many of them are very nice people once you get to know them.'

Chrissie wasn't at all certain about that. The English were the historical enemy, after all. 'I don't know what your father's going to say,' she declared, shaking her head.

'It's the only way I can marry Brigid,' Tom explained. 'And I do want to marry her.'

'I never even knew you were seeing the lassie again. You never said.'

'There was no reason to. I haven't exactly been seeing her as such, not in that way anyway. We simply, quite by chance, ended up working together.'

'Just you wait until your father gets home,' Chrissie muttered.

'It's my life, Mum, and I'm over twenty-one. I can do as I like.'

'But England, son! It's so far away,' she protested.

'It's not the end of the earth. There'll be visits, I'm sure of that.'

Chrissie took a deep breath. 'You haven't made a final decision, though?'

'Brigid will be talking to her parents, and we'll speak again tonight after work.'

'And this Mrs Mulherron is arranging it all?'

'That's right.'

'But why is she going to so much trouble?'

'Because of her dead son, I would imagine. The one whom I'm the spit of. Besides, she genuinely likes me and no doubt wants to help.'

Tears came into Chrissie's eyes. 'Well, you must do whatever you think's best, son.'

'I will, Mum,' he assured her. 'I will.'

*   *   *

'So what did your parents say?' Tom asked Brigid the moment they were out of the Belgrave later that night.

'They weren't exactly pleased, I'll tell you that. And yours?'

'Papa took it more calmly than I thought he would, considering you're a Catholic, that is. In the end both he and Mum agreed the decision was up to me, and if I did decide to go it would be with their blessing.'

'Mine, eventually, said more or less the same. Though they are terribly disappointed I'm not marrying a Catholic, and that it won't be in church. We can't do that with you being a Prod.' She stopped and turned to face him. 'Will you convert, Tom?'

He smiled at her in the darkness. 'I'll do anything it takes if I can have you as my wife. Obviously I can't convert right away. I would imagine that takes time. But once I have converted perhaps we can have another ceremony, this time in a pineapple.'

Brigid laughed, knowing that pineapple was rhyming slang for chapel, which Catholic churches were often called in Glasgow. 'I'll hold you to that, Tom McKeand.'

'Is it agreed, then? We get married as soon as possible, after which it's straight down to this Dagenham place?'

'It's agreed,' she replied, eyes shining.

'Oh, Brigid,' he breathed. 'We're going to be ever so happy together. I just know we are.'

'We've waited a long time for one another, and it certainly hasn't been easy.'

'No, it hasn't. But everything's come right now and that's all that matters.'

*   *   *

Dolly cradled her phone and smiled a little sadly. Tom and Brigid's decision was the one she'd hoped to hear, but she was going to miss dancing with Tom at the Belgrave, and his visits for lunch.

Crossing to the mantelpiece she picked up Robert's picture, the last he'd had taken before going off to France.

Her son, and only child. How cruel and stupid war was. Ask any mother.

Fortunately Tam was home when it happened, otherwise the outcome might have been completely different.

'I wonder who that is?' Chrissie queried when there was a sudden urgent knocking on the front door.

'Well, the best way to find out is to answer it,' Tam said drily, thinking it must be one of the neighbours.

Chrissie hurried off, while Georgie got on with the business of making dinner. She stopped what she was doing when she heard raised voices.

'Tam, it's Charlie insisting on seeing Georgie,' Chrissie called out in a panic.

'Oh, Christ,' Georgie muttered.

'Do you want to see him, lass?'

Georgie glanced over at her father and shook her head. 'No. Never again. I have nothing to say to him. Not now. Not ever.'

'I want to see my fucking wife!' Charlie shouted. 'It's my fucking right. Get your arse out here, woman!'

'He's drunk,' Georgie stated unnecessarily.

Tam rose slowly to his feet, his expression murderous. How dare the pervert come to his house behaving like this?

'Be careful, Papa. He might get violent.'

Tam reached down and picked up the hammer kept on the hearth for breaking large lumps of coal. Holding it in his right hand, he strode from the kitchen. 'Go back through,' he told Chrissie when he reached the door.

Charlie was in a rage, his face puce, the veins standing out. He stank of alcohol. 'I want to see my fucking wife!' he demanded.

Tam never told either Chrissie or Georgie what he said to Charlie that day. Only that no blows had been exchanged.

But Georgie never saw or heard from Charlie again.

'Well, that's that then. We're on our way,' an excited Tom declared, pulling on the leather strap to raise the compartment window and securing the strap on the brass knob provided for that purpose.

Only Chrissie and Dolly had come to see them off. Tam and Lena were at work, and the O'Reillys had declined, saying it would have been too painful for them.

'What an adventure, eh, Mrs McKeand?' Tom beamed at Brigid as he sat beside her. They were the only two passengers in the compartment.

'It certainly is, Mr McKeand.'

It had been a quiet civil wedding, with only Tom's family, the O'Reillys and Dolly in attendance. Dolly had insisted on taking them all out for a meal afterwards.

Tom reached into his inside jacket pocket and extracted an envelope. 'Dolly gave me this in the station,' he told Brigid. 'Said I wasn't to open it till the train was under way.'

'Probably a card,' Brigid suggested.

'Doesn't feel like one.' He ripped open the envelope and took out the single piece of paper it contained. 'Bloody hell!' he exclaimed when he saw what the piece of paper was.

A cheque for one thousand pounds.

Part 3

Bill Bailey

1935–

Chapter 23

'So what does Tom say?' Chrissie asked anxiously.

Georgie sighed, and started to fold up her brother's letter, which she'd just read. 'There's no problem about getting Ian work. Tom can arrange something for him as soon as he shows up in Dagenham. He also suggests Ian stay with him and Brigid until other suitable accommodation can be arranged.'

'That's great, Mum,' Ian enthused. Then, noting her concerned expression, he added, 'Isn't it?'

'I suppose so.'

'Well, I can't get any work round here. You know that. I've tried and tried. Even Grandpa can't get me an apprenticeship at McNair's.'

Ian, now sixteen, had left school earlier that year, and had been scouting round for employment ever since, to no avail. There simply weren't any jobs to be had.

'It's for the best,' Tam declared from where he was sitting. 'The lad has to earn his keep now he's old enough.'

Georgie couldn't help the lump that came into her throat

at the thought of losing her son. Once he left Glasgow, who knew when he might return? If ever. 'Aye, Papa, you're right,' she agreed quietly.

Tam shook his head. 'When will this slump end, that's what I'd like to know. It just goes on and on.'

'But not in some places down south it seems,' Chrissie commented bitterly.

'We should be thankful the south has given Tom employment,' said Tam. 'And now Ian. Better he's in Dagenham than idle here. Better by far. It's a chance for him and he must grab it while it's going.' He swivelled his attention on to Georgie. 'It'll be hard for you, lass, we all appreciate that.'

'Tom will look after Ian all right,' Chrissie assured her. 'You've no worries there.'

Georgie had hated writing to Tom with her request, and had only done so at Ian's insistence. The idea had been Ian's in the first place, and now his eyes were sparkling. 'When shall I leave, Mum?' he queried.

'I'll reply to Tom telling him to expect you. Give it a couple of days and you can be on your way.' Why prolong the agony of his departure? Best get it over and done with.

Tam closed his eyes. Georgie wasn't the only one who'd miss the boy. He and Ian had become quite close since Georgie and her son had come back to live with them. He'd tried desperately to get the lad an apprenticeship at McNair's, but despite his best efforts, including a lot of string-pulling, he hadn't been able to do so. McNair's itself was slowly recovering, now operating at a little over half capacity, and many of the old workers had been reinstated as a result. But there was still a long way to go before it was back to what it had been pre-slump.

'Are you all right, Tam?'

He opened his eyes to smile at Chrissie. 'Absolutely fine, woman. Absolutely fine.' He took out his pipe and began repacking it.

'I can't wait to go.' Ian beamed at Georgie. 'It's going to be fun.'

Georgie made an excuse and left the kitchen.

'You're new!' Georgie exclaimed in surprise. The delivery man who'd appeared in the shop was not the regular one. 'Where's Wally?'

'Broke his leg, so I've been taken on as a replacement. I don't think you'll be seeing him again, either. I'm told he's retirement age, so that's probably what'll happen.'

Georgie was disappointed. She and Wally had been great pals since she'd landed the job at Templeton's, a licenced grocer, nearly two years before.

The new delivery man nodded down at the large wooden tray he was carrying. 'Where shall I put this?'

'In the rear. Come on through and I'll show you.'

'Thanks. I'm Bill, by the way.'

'Pleased to meet you, Bill. I'm Georgie.'

'Pleased to meet you too.'

He seemed a pleasant enough chap, Georgie thought as she led the way. Early forties, she'd have guessed. Maybe a little older.

'So who's this then?' Mr Templeton demanded, making an appearance. 'Where's Wally?'

Bill explained a second time what had happened, and the two men introduced themselves.

'Would you like a cup of tea and a bun?' Georgie asked

Bill when he'd completed his delivery. 'Wally always did.'

'In which case I don't mind if I do,' he said cheerfully.

She led him into the rear of the shop and put the kettle on. In the event, she didn't get much of a chance to chat with Bill while he had his tea, for an influx of customers demanded her attention. She just had time to wave in acknowledgement when Bill said goodbye, thank you very much, and see you again later in the week, as he left.

'Aye, I felt exactly the same way the day I saw Tom off on this very platform,' Chrissie sympathised, seeing Georgie's face was wet with tears. In the distance the train carrying Ian down to England swept round a bend and vanished from sight.

Georgie took a hanky from her pocket and dabbed her eyes. 'He just seems so young to be going away.'

'Young, but already a man. A young man to be proud of. He's got a good head on his shoulders, lass; he won't come to any trouble. Certainly not with Tom keeping an eye on him.'

'I know that, Mum. I expected him to leave home one day, but not to leave Glasgow for the south. Away from me altogether.'

Chrissie thought of Tom, whom she hadn't seen since his departure. He and Brigid had a little boy now, whom they called Robin. An endearing little chap, according to Tom's letters. How she would have loved to see and hold her new grandchild. Maybe one day, God willing. 'Aye, it's hard right enough,' she said. 'But I suppose it's just one of these things in life a body has to put up with.'

'Thanks for coming with me, Mum. I appreciate it. And now I'd better get back to the shop.'

Chrissie pulled her daughter closer and kissed her on the cheek, close to tears herself. 'I'll see you later, then.'

Georgie drew in a deep breath, trying to compose herself. 'At least Ian's skin has been a lot better of late,' she said hollowly. 'That's something.'

'Aye,' Chrissie agreed. 'That's something.'

Tea that evening was a subdued affair, everyone round the table only too aware of the empty chair that had been Ian's, and no one more so than Georgie.

'I'd like you to do me a favour, Lena, if you will.'

She stared at her father in surprise. Asking favours was most unlike him. 'Of course, Papa.'

Tam cleared his throat. He was finding this difficult, feeling it showed a certain weakness on his part. 'I've been thinking a lot about your sister recently,' he began quietly.

'Georgie?'

'No, Mary.'

Lena was more surprised than ever. 'I see.'

Tam gave a heartfelt sigh. 'It doesn't seem right that we've lost touch like we have. It's been bothering me for quite some time.' His expression became grim. 'Why in the name of the wee man did she ever have to get mixed up with that sect of hers and go all holier than thou? They've caused nothing but trouble in this family.'

Lena couldn't have agreed more.

'Your mother hasn't said anything, but I know she worries as well.'

'So what do you want me to do, Papa?'

'Go and see her, lass. You've done it before. Find out what's what.'

'I would imagine things are the same, Papa. Mary up to her neck in religion and spouting non-stop.'

Tam sighed again. 'Probably.'

'If she is, then what?'

'To be honest, lass, I don't know. I really don't. But it would be nice, a relief you might say, to know she and her family are all right. That would at least be something.'

Lena could well understand that. 'Why don't I pay a visit at the weekend? Saturday afternoon, say?'

'Thanks.' Then, hastily, 'Just don't let on you're there on my behalf. Pretend otherwise.'

She smiled, knowing her father didn't want to be seen to be backing down in any way. It was typical of him. 'I won't, Papa. That's a promise.' She hesitated, then asked, 'Does Mum know about this?'

Tam shook his head. 'No.'

'Are you going to tell her?'

He crossed to the window and stared out. It was a lovely day, the sun shining brightly. In his mind's eye he was picturing Mary as a child, a child he'd loved very, very much. 'That depends on what you report when you get back,' he said slowly. 'I might. Or there again, I might not. As I said, it all depends.'

'Saturday afternoon it is then, Papa.'

Lena stopped outside Mary's close and looked up at the grey, scarred building. A typical Glasgow tenement. She wondered what Mary was like nowadays. Had she put on weight, lost some, aged a lot? Well, she would shortly find out.

She plunged into the close mouth, which smelt of boiled cabbage tinged with strong bleach, and began to climb the stairs.

Tam sat upright in his chair when he heard the sound of a key in the front door. Chrissie had gone shopping in town half an hour previously, which meant, he hoped, that this was Lena returned from her visit. It was.

'Well?' he demanded when she entered the kitchen. 'How did you get on?'

This was going to be difficult, Lena thought. It would break her father's heart. And her mother's. Damn Mary for doing what she had. Damn her to hell.

'They emigrated two years ago,' she stated bluntly.

The shock on Tam's face was palpable. 'They've what?'

'Emigrated two years ago,' she repeated. 'A neighbour told me, Papa.'

Tam shook his head in bewilderment. This was unbelievable. 'Where to?' he demanded harshly.

'Canada. Toronto to be precise, according to the neighbour. They just upped sticks and left.'

'But why?'

'It was something to do with the sect which is, apparently, quite big in Toronto. The neighbour had no idea where they got the money from, though she did know James had a job to go to.'

Tam suddenly felt crushed, and old. Older than Methuselah. 'And she never said goodbye,' he managed to whisper at last. 'Just went, without a word.'

'I'm sorry, Papa. Truly I am. But that's Mary all over as far as I'm concerned. Selfish to the core.'

'Don't speak like that about your sister,' Tam said sharply, even though he knew what Lena said to be true.

Lena didn't want to argue, not in these circumstances. Taking out her cigarettes, she lit up. She was furious with Mary for what she had done, the hurt it was causing her father, and the hurt it would cause Chrissie when, inevitably, she found out. To leave the country without saying goodbye. It was despicable!

'I still can't believe it,' Tam said, shaking his head again. 'How could she do such a thing?'

Lena didn't answer, noticing that her father had gone very pale. The pallor was quite a contrast to his normally healthy, slightly ruddy complexion.

Reaching down to the floor Tam picked up his Saturday bottle of whisky and the glass he'd been using. His hands were trembling as he poured himself a stiff one. 'Lena?'

She shook her head. 'Not for me, Papa.'

Tam swallowed half the whisky in his glass, took a breath, then saw off the remainder. 'Your mother's going to be devastated,' he said in a tight voice.

'You'll tell her, then?'

'I have to. I can't keep something like this from her.'

'When?'

Tam considered. 'Are you and Georgie in tonight?'

Lena smiled wryly. When did she ever go out of an evening? Never. And it was the same for Georgie. 'I suppose so.'

'Then I'll tell your mother when we're alone in bed. God help me.'

'I could tell her if you wish.'

He immediately shook his head. 'No, that's my respon- sibility, Lena. I'm her husband, after all. Mary's our daughter.'

Lena watched as he poured himself more whisky. 'Don't get drunk now, Papa. That won't help anything.'

'I've no intention of getting drunk, I assure you.'

'Just go easy, though.'

His eyes became introspective. 'Canada,' he mused. 'A fine country from what I've heard. Lots of opportunities there. They should do well.'

Lena didn't care whether they did well or not. She'd never forgive Mary for what she'd done. Never in a thousand years.

Tam drank his whisky, then came to his feet. 'I think I'll go on through and have a wee lie-down,' he declared. 'I'm suddenly feeling tired.'

'You do that, Papa. It'll be good for you.'

'Aye,' he agreed.

As he left the kitchen it was with a shock that Lena saw he was walking with a stoop. It was something she'd never previously noticed.

'Is there something wrong, Tam?'

He glanced nervously across at his wife. 'What makes you ask that?'

'You've been fidgeting all night. Up and down, up and down. Crossing your legs, uncrossing them. That sort of thing. Not like you at all.'

Tam looked at the clock on the mantelpiece. Still ages to go yet before bedtime. He was absolutely dreading telling Chrissie about Mary.

'There is something different about you tonight, Papa,' Georgie chipped in. 'I noticed it earlier.'

'And you hardly ate any tea at all,' Chrissie went on. 'Even though it was one of your favourites.'

Tam fumbled with his pipe, wondering what to reply. Lena took the initiative. It was best her father talk to her mother now.

'Georgie, can you come through to my room for a bit?'

Georgie raised an eyebrow at this unusual request. She'd been sharing Lena's bedroom until Ian had left, when she'd moved into the one he'd been occupying, which had been Tom's before that. 'What for?' she queried.

'Just come through, will you? I'll explain there.'

Georgie shrugged. 'If you want.'

'I do,' Lena stated emphatically, and left the kitchen, giving Tam a slight nod. A puzzled Georgie followed on behind.

'What was all that about?' Chrissie asked.

Tam cleared his throat. 'I've got some bad news, I'm afraid, lass,' he said quietly, and began recounting the tale of Lena's visit to what had been Mary's house.

'Emigrated to Canada!' an amazed Georgie repeated.

'Two years ago, apparently.'

'Without saying goodbye to Mum and Papa, far less her sisters?'

Lena nodded. 'That's right.'

'The cow. The bloody bitch!' Georgie exploded. 'Isn't that just like her.'

'I said as much to Papa and he told me off for speaking

316

ill of my sister. But you know what he's like where Mary's concerned. She could never do anything wrong. Apart from her religious mania, that is.'

Georgie glanced at the bedroom door. 'I wonder how Mum's taking it?'

'How do you think? Badly, of course. Bound to.'

Georgie sat on the edge of Lena's bed. It was a bombshell right enough. All right, they hadn't seen or spoken to Mary for years. But they'd believed her to be still in Glasgow, not all that far away, easily contactable if need be. And while Mary remained in Glasgow a reconciliation was always possible. But now there would never be one.

'I just can't get over it,' Georgie declared.

'Me neither. Not really.' Lena suddenly laughed. 'All those years Mum had to put up with the idea of me going to Hollywood, which didn't happen. Now it's Mary who's buggered off to Canada.' She shook her head. 'Ironic.'

Tam came awake to the sound of quiet weeping. Reaching out, he took hold of Chrissie's hand.

'Have I wakened you, Tam? I'm sorry.'

'Not to worry, lass. Not to worry.' He squeezed her hand, hoping to comfort her a little.

'The family's breaking up,' Chrissie said, still weeping. 'First of all it was Tom down to England, then Ian, and now Mary and her lot to Canada. We'll probably never see any of them again.'

'We might,' Tam replied. 'Nothing is ever set in stone. You should know that.'

There was a silence. Then Tam went on, 'I blame myself

for this. If I hadn't fallen out with Mary then we would at least have got to say goodbye.'

'You mustn't blame yourself, Tam. How were you to know this would happen?'

He had no reply.

'She might have written us a letter,' Chrissie went on. 'If only to tell us of her intentions. We are her parents, after all. That wouldn't have been such a hard thing to do, surely?'

'No,' he agreed. 'It wouldn't. But the fact remains, she didn't.' He added angrily, 'So much for her precious religious beliefs. Honour thy father and mother, that sort of thing. Even if you disagree with them.'

'Perhaps she'll write some time in the future?' Chrissie speculated hopefully.

'I doubt it, Chrissie. She's been gone two years already, don't forget. Plenty of time to put pen to paper. No, she won't be writing. She's cut us out of her life for good, which we're just going to have to accept.'

Neither of them got much sleep for the remainder of the night.

Hamish's office door was slightly ajar so Lena went straight in without knocking to find him sitting behind his desk with his head in his hands. He looked up when she closed the door behind her.

'What's wrong?' she asked.

'Nothing. I've got a bit of a headache, that's all,' he lied.

'Shall I get you something?'

'I've already taken a powder. But thanks for asking.'

She studied him, thinking how terrible he looked. Like

a man at the end of his tether. 'Are you sure it's just a headache?' she queried. 'If it's something else I'll be happy to talk about it with you, if that would help.'

'It's a headache.' He was still lying, for it wasn't that at all which was bothering him. He suddenly smiled. 'You're a good friend, Lena. I've always appreciated that.'

'Why, thank you.'

'I mean it. A damn good friend. Not to mention an excellent colleague. I couldn't ask for better.'

There was more to this than met the eye, Lena thought. She knew Hamish only too well after all these years, and the intimacies they'd once shared. Something was wrong somewhere if she wasn't mistaken, which she was sure she wasn't.

'How are Celia and the twins?' she asked casually.

'Fine, fine. Never better.'

Again she detected that in his voice which was unconvincing. Trouble at home, perhaps? If so, it was none of her business. He'd made his bed and could now lie in it with the beautiful Celia.

'So, what can I do for you?' he queried.

'I need your signature on these papers.'

'Of course. Right away.'

She wondered if it was money worries that were troubling him. Celia had struck her as the sort who could quite easily spend more than he earned.

She returned to her desk, putting Hamish, and the headache she didn't believe existed, from her mind.

Chapter 24

Georgie smiled when Bill Bailey appeared in the doorway of Templeton's carrying a heavily laden tray. He smiled back at her.

'You're just in time. It's my tea break as well,' she informed him.

'Oh, good oh!'

Georgie turned to Janet, one of the several part-time assistants. 'Can you cover for me while I put the kettle on and have my break? Just give me a shout if it gets busy.'

'All right, Georgie. On you go.'

When she reached the back shop the first thing Georgie did was to light a cigarette. She'd been gasping. Then the kettle was filled and placed on the gas ring Mr Templeton had made available. She was sitting drinking her cuppa when Bill finally joined her, having completed his delivery. 'How are you today?' she greeted him.

'Fine. Yourself?'

'No complaints. Help yourself to a doughnut if you want. Those jammy ones are delicious.'

'How many have you had so far?' he teased.

'Twenty-four,' she replied instantly. They both laughed.

Bill selected a doughnut and sat on an upturned box. 'It's cold out there today,' he commented affably.

'Aye, it is.'

He took a bite from his doughnut. 'You're right, these are good,' he enthused.

'So, how are you settling in with your job?' she asked, genuinely interested.

'No trouble. It's a bit of a doddle actually. Easy as pie.'

That surprised her. 'Really? Wally used to be forever moaning about how hard it was.'

'So I've heard,' Bill replied non-committally.

'Maybe he was just like that.'

'Maybe.'

She realised he wasn't going to be drawn on the subject, which she rather admired him for. He must hear loads of gossip about all sorts of things while doing his rounds.

'Tell me, how did you get the job?' she enquired. 'Did someone tip you off when Wally broke his leg?'

Bill shrugged. 'Luck, pure and simple. I just happened to be in the right place at the right time. Not a moment too soon, either. I was about to give up looking for work and go back into the army.'

'The army!' Georgie exclaimed. Now that she came to think about it there was something military about his bearing.

'I joined as a lad, but over the last few years I'd become tired of it all and decided to come out and try civvy street. Which is what I did some months ago, returning to live with my widowed mum. I had army money which has seen me through, but that was about to run out when this delivery lark came up. So now I don't have to go back in.'

'What sort of rank did you hold?' Georgie asked.

'Corporal.'

'You weren't an officer then?' she teased.

He laughed. 'Not likely. I'm neither posh enough nor intelligent enough for that. Being an NCO suited me just dandy.'

Georgie glanced through to the front shop and saw that Janet was serving a single customer, so there was hardly a rush on. She decided to have another cup of tea. 'Were you in the Great War, Bill?'

His face immediately clouded, becoming pained. 'Oh aye. But I don't want to talk about that if you don't mind. The memories aren't exactly good ones.'

She could well understand that. Many of the soldiers who'd fought in the carnage of the Great War never wanted to speak of it.

'I was in India for quite a spell,' Bill went on. 'Filthy place, but also exciting. Not to mention colourful. Spent nearly six years there in all.'

Georgie was fascinated. 'Where else have you been?'

For the next ten minutes or so he regaled her with tales of life in the army, then had to excuse himself to get on with his round.

What a nice chap, Georgie reflected after he'd gone. She'd thoroughly enjoyed their chat and was looking forward to having more with him.

Tom arrived home from work to be greeted by a beaming Brigid. 'There's someone here to see you,' she announced.

'Oh! Who?'

'Go on through and find out.'

'Sounds mysterious,' he commented as he hung up his coat.

Brigid didn't reply, simply beamed some more.

'Dolly!' he exclaimed in surprised delight on entering their sitting room. 'How wonderful to see you again!'

Dolly rose from the chair she was sitting on and went to Tom, who put his arms round her, then kissed her cheek.

'You're looking well,' she declared.

'And you. Younger than ever.'

Dolly laughed. 'Flatterer.'

'No no, I mean it. Honestly I do.'

His words pleased her enormously. 'Then thank you.'

He released her. 'So, what brings you down to Dagenham?'

'I'm actually on my way to London to do some shopping.' She winked at the hovering Brigid. '*Serious* shopping.' Then she looked back at Tom. 'And I thought, why not make a slight detour and call in to see you all. So here I am.'

'Dolly's agreed to stay to tea,' Brigid told him.

'That's great.'

'I've explained it's nothing fancy. A little bit of plain home cooking, that's all.'

'I'm sure it'll be lovely.' Dolly smiled.

'Where are you staying?' Tom asked. 'We can easily put you up here if you wish.'

'That's kind of you, but I've already booked into an hotel. Brooks and I did that before coming on here.'

'Where is Brooks, by the way?' Tom asked, looking around for the chauffeur.

'I've given him some time off. He'll call back here and collect me later.'

'I'll be in the kitchen if you want me,' Brigid declared, and left them.

Dolly crossed over to the playpen where Robin, now a toddler, was sitting watching them. 'What a gorgeous little lad your son is,' she enthused. 'You must be proud.'

'Oh, I am. Very proud.'

'It makes me feel . . .' Dolly hesitated, then said so softly it was almost a whisper, 'like a grandmother.'

'Then that's how you must think of yourself, Dolly. One of Robin's grandmothers.'

A glint of tears came into her eyes. 'Thank you, Tom,' she said huskily. 'It's very kind of you.'

'Not at all.'

Dolly sniffed, then straightened herself. 'According to your letters you're doing well at Ford.'

'I thoroughly enjoy it there, especially being a foreman. You were certainly right about the company paying well. I simply can't thank you enough for getting me the job.'

She waved a dismissive hand. 'It was the least I can do. I was only too delighted to be able to help.'

'And of course without the move south I wouldn't be married to Brigid, and there wouldn't be a Robin in that playpen. As I said, I can't thank you enough.' He corrected himself. 'Neither Brigid nor I can thank you enough. You're an angel in disguise.'

Dolly laughed. 'Hardly an angel, Tom. I've led far

too . . .' She broke off. 'Well, we won't go into that. Do you miss Glasgow at all?'

He thought about it for a few moments. 'Yes and no. Glasgow is where I was born and brought up. As such, it will always be a large part of me. But we're happily settled here now. Glasgow's the past, Dagenham is the present and future. Tell me, as we're talking about Glasgow, what of the Belgrave? Is it still the same?'

'To be honest, I haven't been there for ages. It lost its appeal after you left. But it was certainly the same the last time I visited it.'

'Did you gamble?'

'Of course. And won. As usual.'

He shook his head. 'You always were incredibly lucky at the tables. I used to marvel at that.'

She smiled secretively. 'Freddy and I, God rest his soul, were frequently at Monte Carlo and other such places. You soon get to know what you're doing. How to calculate the odds. When to bet, and when not to. But yes, luck does come into it and Freddy always said I had the luck of the devil.' A twinkle came into her eyes. 'And maybe he was right, seeing I had the good fortune to marry him.'

'You must miss him a lot,' Tom said quietly.

'I do. And Robert of course. I miss them both terribly.'

The smile she gave Tom was a real heartbreaker.

The evening passed in a flash, and all too soon it was time for Dolly to leave.

Robin was asleep, Dolly having assisted in putting him to bed. She had read him a story, with Brigid looking on, until he'd nodded off. If it had reminded her of when Robert was a child she didn't mention it.

'Will you come and see us again some time, Dolly?' Tom asked in the hallway. 'You're always welcome.'

'Always,' Brigid emphasised.

'You have my word on it.'

'And next time let us know in advance so I can get some sherry and wine in,' Tom added.

Dolly laughed. 'I'll hold you to that.'

'Come on,' Tom said. 'We'll walk you to your car.'

At the car Brooks was standing holding open the door, having turned up precisely at the time he and Dolly had agreed. Like Smith, the butler, he'd been in Dolly's employ for many years, though he was nowhere near as old as the butler.

They stopped by the car door and Brigid gave Dolly a peck on the cheek. 'I hope the meal wasn't too awful,' she said. 'I'm not much of a cook, I'm afraid.'

'It was lovely,' Dolly assured her. 'I thoroughly enjoyed every mouthful.'

It was Tom's turn to kiss her on the cheek. 'Goodbye for now, Dolly. Have a safe journey.'

'Thank you, Tom. You take care of yourself, and your family. Hear?'

'I will, Dolly. You can rely on it.'

She knew she could. Before getting into the car she stared at Tom for a moment, thinking, yet again, what a remarkable resemblance there was to her dead son. It was uncanny.

Tom and Brigid waved as the car drove off, Dolly returning their waves through the rear window.

'Well,' Tom declared, turning again to the house. 'That was a turn-up for the book.'

'Wasn't it just? I couldn't believe it when I answered the bell and found her standing there. What a surprise that was.'

'A lovely surprise,' Tom qualified with a smile.

Arm in arm they went back into the house. The two of them were happy as Larry, and very much in love.

'Have you ever been married, Bill?' Georgie asked. They were in the rear of the shop having the usual cup of tea during his delivery.

He shook his head. 'No.'

'Was that because of being in the army?'

Bill thought about it. 'Not really. I suppose the reason is that I simply never met the right woman. She just never happened along, that's all.'

What a pity, Georgie reflected, certain he would have made a good husband to some deserving female. 'Would you have liked children?'

'Oh, yes.' He smiled. 'I'm very fond of children. Mind you, it must be hard work bringing them up. Not easy at all.'

'It certainly isn't,' Georgie mused aloud.

'You have some then?'

'A boy called Ian. He's almost seventeen now and working with my brother down at the Ford plant in Dagenham, Essex.'

Bill glanced at Georgie's left hand, which didn't sport a wedding ring – a fact he'd previously noted.

'Ian was my first husband's,' Georgie explained, having caught Bill's surreptitious look. 'He died from leukaemia.'

'Oh, I am sorry,' Bill sympathised.

'His name was John and he worked on the railway. It was a tragedy he passed away so young. Ian was only a little shaver at the time.'

Bill had a sip of tea. 'You said your first husband?'

'I was married again to a chap called Charlie, a fireman. I left him a few years back.'

'I see,' Bill murmured.

'He was an alcoholic, amongst other things I don't wish to discuss. I'm well rid of him.'

'It seems I'm not the only one who's been in the wars,' Bill remarked.

Georgie gave a sour, bitter laugh. 'You can say that again.'

He regarded her with an expression of curiosity. 'Do I take it then you're still married to this Charlie?'

She nodded.

'Why haven't you divorced him?' Suddenly Bill was embarrassed. 'I'm sorry. I shouldn't have asked that. It's none of my business.'

'No, that's all right,' she assured him. 'I don't mind speaking about it. For a start, in Scotland you have to be separated for seven years before you can apply for a divorce, which we haven't been yet. Secondly, divorce costs a great deal of money which I don't have.' She paused to draw on her cigarette, then went on wistfully, 'I used to, but at one point Charlie's wages were cut and he was more or less drinking the remainder. I had to use my own savings to keep the house going, and there was very little left when we finally parted. So there you are.'

'This Charlie sounds a right charmer,' Bill commented sarcastically.

'Oh, he was.' A vision of Charlie sitting with a naked Avril on his lap came to her, and Georgie got to her feet. 'I'd better get back behind the counter, Bill. I've been gassing long enough. I don't want Mr Templeton to think I've been taking liberties.'

Bill drained his cup and got up too. 'Aye, it is time to get a move on.'

He could only wonder at the expression he'd seen cross Georgie's face. It had been one of great pain. And, if he was right, disgust.

Lena became aware of Hamish staring at her in the strangest way. He was at a filing cabinet looking for something, or pretending to anyway. It wasn't the first time recently she'd caught him looking at her that way. What on earth was going on, she asked herself. Had she suddenly grown horns, or whatever?

She shifted uneasily on her seat, not liking this one little bit. Should she speak to him about it? Demand to know what he was up to? Why he was staring at her in that manner?

When he walked past her a few minutes later she couldn't help but notice there was a glisten of sweat on his forehead, while his eyes had a dark intensity about them.

It was all very puzzling.

Dolly stood staring out of a window in the morning room at the well-manicured lawn beyond, recalling her recent visit to Tom and Brigid, and how much she'd enjoyed it. Especially meeting the adorable little Robin, as sweet a child as there was.

Why not? she thought. It wasn't as if there was anyone else. In that moment she decided she would go ahead, her mind made up. It was the logical thing to do.

Tam was bursting with excitement when he arrived home from work carrying a bottle of whisky.

'What are you doing with that?' an astonished Chrissie demanded. 'It's the middle of the week. You don't buy whisky until Saturdays.'

'Great news, woman! McNair's is starting to gear up to full production again, and as a result they're taking on all the men they laid off. Starting Monday I'm back on a five-and-a-half-day week.'

'Oh, that's good!' Chrissie sighed in relief.

'Good? It's not just bloody good, it's fucking fantastic!' Tam exploded. Laying the bottle on the table he went to Chrissie, put his hands on her waist and whirled her round and round. Chrissie screeched with surprise, but loved it at the same time. She found herself breathless when Tam planted her on the floor again.

'I bought the whisky because this calls for a celebration,' he declared, and hurried across the room to get glasses.

'Does this mean you're back on full pay as from next week?'

'It certainly does.'

She closed her eyes. 'Thank God for that!'

Tam poured out two hefty ones, topping Chrissie's up

with water which was how she liked it. Not that she was much of a drinker, but she did indulge from time to time. And this was certainly an appropriate occasion for her to do so. He handed her her drink. 'Shall we have a toast?'

She smiled, delighted to see him so happy. 'Of course. Go on, Tam.'

He thought for a moment, his brow creasing in concentration. Then he had it. Holding up his glass he said softly, 'Here's to all the poor buggers throughout the country still laid off. May they be back in full employment as soon as possible.'

Chrissie smiled. How typical of him to think of others at a time like this. It was a fine and suitable toast as far as she was concerned, and she thought it was a lovely sentiment. 'Amen,' she whispered.

'You spoil me, so you do,' Bill declared, having just finished a beautiful pastry he'd been given to accompany his cup of tea. 'That was absolutely delicious.'

'I'm glad you enjoyed it.'

'I most certainly did. Your Mr Templeton is very good to his staff, I must say. Not every boss would be so generous.'

Georgie knew that to be true enough.

'Can I ask you something, Georgie?'

'If you wish.'

'It's a bit personal, so I hope you don't mind.'

Oh, God, she thought. What was he going to come out with? 'On you go.'

'Your voice, it's got a wonderful husky quality to it that

I've never heard in a woman before. It's . . .' He paused to smile. 'Most attractive.'

'You like it, then?'

'Oh, yes.'

'Well, I wasn't born with it this way,' she explained. 'I sort of accidentally acquired it.'

'Oh?'

'Years ago I worked in a bleach factory. There was a terrible fire one day. Horrendous, it was.'

'People killed?'

She nodded. 'And I was very nearly one of them. I was overcome by smoke and fumes while trying to escape the building, and was rescued by the fire brigade, which is how I came to meet Charlie.'

Bill frowned. 'The chap you're still married to?'

'That's right. He saved my life that day. If it hadn't been for Charlie I'd have been another of the victims. We started going out together shortly afterwards.'

'I see,' Bill murmured. 'And the voice?'

'The result of smoke and fume inhalation. It completely changed the way I sound.'

'Well, well.'

'I couldn't smoke cigarettes for a long time. Even a single drag made me cough and splutter. Then one night, when I'd had a gutful of Charlie, I tried again. And on that occasion it was fine, so I've been smoking ever since.'

Bill wondered if he dared. Not yet, he decided. It was still early days. He'd wait a while yet.

But he would. He damned well would when he considered the time to be right.

Chapter 25

Lena closed the office door firmly behind her before rounding on Hamish, who was poring over some papers. 'All right, what the hell is going on?' she demanded, but not loudly enough to be heard by the other women outside.

He blinked at her in astonishment. 'What are you talking about?'

'You and the queer stares you've been giving me lately. You obviously think I haven't noticed, but I have.'

'I've no idea . . .' he began to bluster, then broke off in confusion.

'You're not going to deny it, are you?'

'I'm not aware of having been staring at you,' he said meekly.

'Not just staring at me, but looking as if I was some sort of meat laid out on a butcher's slab, and you one very hungry man. Well?'

'I'm sorry, Lena, truly I am.'

'I don't want sorry, Hamish. I want an explanation.'

'There isn't one. I mean . . .' Again he broke off in confusion, seeming to cower behind his desk.

'I'm still waiting, Hamish,' she persisted. 'And I'm not leaving this office until you tell me what's going on.'

He took a deep breath, then another. 'All right,' he croaked.

'I'm listening.'

'Not here. This is neither the time nor the place. Can you meet me in the Swan after work?'

She studied him, wondering if this was some sort of ruse to get rid of her. Couldn't be, she decided. He must know that if he didn't turn up at the Swan she'd be right back here in his office tomorrow morning.

'I'll be there,' she declared.

'I'll explain everything then. I promise.' He hesitated, then asked, 'Was I that obvious?'

'To me you were.'

'I just hope no one else noticed.'

She treated him to a sharklike smile. 'It's your problem if they have.'

'Oh, shit,' he muttered to himself after she'd gone. But this meeting had been on the cards anyway. He'd planned to have it out with her, just hadn't so far got round to arranging it.

Well, for better or worse, it was arranged now. He wondered what her reaction was going to be.

'There you are, gin and orange,' Hamish declared, setting a glass down in front of Lena and sitting down opposite her. He glanced around, having deliberately chosen a table where they wouldn't be overheard. He just hoped no one came in and sat close to them.

'Now, the first thing is I don't want you to take offence at what I have to say. I mean, please don't get angry or slap my face in public. That would be awful.'

His words immediately caught her interest. 'Go on, Hamish.'

'Promise me?'

She nodded.

Hamish gave a sigh of relief, and had a swallow of whisky. 'This is embarrassing for me, Lena. It really is.'

She didn't reply, instead lighting a cigarette, her gaze riveted on his face with an intensity he found disturbing.

'It all started when Celia had the twins,' he said. 'You'll remember how huge she got before giving birth?'

'I remember.'

'Well, naturally I thought that afterwards she'd slim down again. Or at least attempt to. Which simply wasn't the case. She's still as huge now as she was then.'

That surprised Lena, who hadn't seen Celia since she'd come to the office to speak to Hamish while very pregnant. 'Why's that?'

Hamish shrugged. 'I don't know. I've pleaded with her time and again to do something about her weight, but she totally ignores me.'

Lena frowned. 'You mean she's happy to be that large?'

'Seems so. Not only large, but a right mess to boot. She never wears make-up any more. Never goes to the hairdresser. Buys the most outlandish clothes that make her look even bigger than she is. And . . .' He shuddered.

'And she sometimes goes for days on end without washing or bathing. To be blunt, there are occasions when she smells. Ripe as a piece of French cheese.'

Lena couldn't help herself. She giggled. 'Surely you're exaggerating?'

'I wish I was.'

Lena simply couldn't picture the beautiful Celia in such a state. The idea was mind-boggling.

'She was so pretty too.' Hamish sighed again. 'With a figure to match. Now . . .' He trailed off, and shook his head.

'I'm so sorry.' Lena was genuinely sympathetic.

'Not half as sorry as I am, I can tell you. Every time I look at her nowadays I have the distinct urge to vomit. It's a nightmare, Lena. An absolute nightmare.'

'I had no idea.'

'Well you wouldn't, unless you'd seen her. Which of course you haven't as she hardly ever leaves the house.'

'What about her father? Hasn't he said something?'

'Not that I'm aware of. There again, that doesn't neces- sarily mean he hasn't.'

'And what about her mother?'

'Again, I don't know.'

'You'd have thought her mother would. I've seen her at several official dos and she's always struck me as a well- turned-out woman. And the chairman himself is smart as a new pin.'

'I hate going home at night now, Lena. Absolutely dread it. I sometimes come in here and sit by myself, just putting off the evil hour when I have to see her again. She's become totally repulsive to me.'

Lena had a sip of her gin, sad to hear it. Poor Hamish. He deserved better.

'Her personality has changed as well,' Hamish went on. 'Where before she was outgoing and fun, she's now quiet and secretive.'

'Secretive? In what way?'

Hamish stared into his drink, his face contorted with emotion. 'In all manner of ways. It's as if she's forever hiding something from me. Though God knows what.'

They sat in silence for a few moments. Then Hamish said quietly, 'There's more.'

'Oh?'

He took a deep breath, and slowly exhaled. 'Sex. Or more precisely, the lack of it.'

'I see.'

'Again, it stems from the birth of the twins. She wasn't particularly keen afterwards, which I thought would eventually right itself. Things would get back to normal, so to speak.'

'But they didn't?'

He turned an anguished face towards her. 'Not only that, they got worse.'

'Oh, dear,' Lena murmured.

'It got to the point where she just didn't want to know. Ever. It would suit her down to the ground never to have sex again.'

'Have you suggested she sees a doctor? There must be something wrong.'

'I have, but she won't hear of it. Simply tells me to F off.'

Lena couldn't imagine the well-bred Celia swearing. She just wasn't the type. 'Really?'

'Oh, she uses words worse than that at times. The C one is quite a favourite.'

Lena was amazed. There again, maybe she was being naive. She didn't really know much about the so-called upper classes and their habits. 'Are you telling me you don't get any sex at all?' she asked.

'On occasion. But I literally have to beg for it. And I mean beg. When she does grant me the favour I've no sooner started than she's urging me to hurry up. Hurry up, she says non-stop until I'm finished. Honestly, it's almost as if she was saying, You've got a minute, starting now!'

Despite herself, Lena had to smile. 'If it wasn't for your expression I'd think you were joking.'

'I'm most certainly not, I can assure you. It's humiliating.'

Lena had another swig of her drink while she thought about Hamish's revelations. No wonder he had been staring hungrily at her, considering how his sex life had been. 'What about prostitutes?' she queried. 'Have you considered those?'

A guilty look came on to his face. 'To be honest, I have. Not only considered them, but tried a few.'

'And?'

'I didn't find them very satisfactory, I'm afraid. On one occasion I was so bloody nervous I couldn't even get it up.' He shook his head. 'No, pros are not for me. I want there to be more to sex than that cold-blooded procedure.' He finished his whisky. 'I'm going up for a refill. Do you want another?'

'Just a single this time.'

'Right. Won't be a mo.'

Poor Hamish, she reflected as he made his way to the bar. He'd thought he'd won the jackpot in marrying the chairman's daughter, which hadn't proved to be the case at all. She'd also guessed by now what might be coming next, and why he'd asked her not to get angry, or slap his face in public. A fool could see the proposition a mile off, and she was no fool. Not by a long chalk.

'What was Celia's attitude to sex when you first got married?' she asked curiously when he re-joined her.

'Loved it. Anywhere, any time, swing from the chandelier if you like. Couldn't get enough.'

Lena could well understand what a shock Celia's change of attitude must have been to Hamish after the birth of their twins. His now being desperate was only too understandable. Especially as Celia, by the sound of it, had completely let herself go into the bargain.

Hamish cleared his throat. 'There's something I want to ask you. A sort of favour.'

Here it comes, she thought. 'What is it?'

'Is there any chance, any possible chance, of us taking up again where we left off?'

Lena pretended not to understand. 'How do you mean?'

'The, er . . . arrangement we had.'

'You mean, the one Saturday a month at your place?'

He nodded eagerly. 'That's it.'

'You want to start it again?'

'Please, Lena,' he begged.

'But you don't have a place any more,' she pointed out. 'You live with your family in a different house. I can hardly turn up there on a Saturday afternoon, can

I? Nor can we use my house, as I live with my parents and sister.'

'Ah!' he exclaimed. 'I've already thought of that.'

Lena smiled wryly. She just bet he had. 'I'm listening.'

He twiddled his thumbs, obviously nervous and wanting to get it all out. 'I have a friend who owns a small private hotel. We could go there once a month. And I promise you, he'd be completely discreet.'

'A sort of Mr and Mrs Smith, is that it?'

'Right,' Hamish enthused. 'So what do you say?'

Lena lit another cigarette, her mind racing. This was an offer that needed careful consideration. She certainly wasn't going to turn it down out of hand.

'You've caught me a bit by surprise, Hamish. I wasn't expecting this.'

'I had intended speaking to you soon. And to be honest . . . well, I've been trying to summon up the courage to do so. It's not easy to . . .' He trailed off. 'You know?'

She arched an eyebrow. 'What?'

'Let's just say I wasn't sure how you'd react. I even thought you might laugh at me.'

'And why would I do that?'

'Marrying the chairman's daughter, only to come crawling back to you with such a request. You might have taken deep offence.' He suddenly looked at her in alarm. 'You haven't, have you?'

Lena shook her head. 'No.'

'Oh, thank God for that.'

If anything, she was rather flattered, she thought. More attractive women might well have taken offence, but not her. 'Tell me,' she asked quietly, slightly changing tack. 'Have you ever considered leaving Celia?'

Hamish glanced away. 'Of course I have. But I never will.'

'Even though she's causing you so much unhappiness, not to mention frustration? You could leave her and start over. I appreciate the chairman might sack you if you did, but there are other firms, you know.'

'There's more to it than that.'

'Oh?'

'You may think this soft of me, and I won't blame you if you do, but I love my children very much. It would break my heart to lose them.'

Lena sat back in her chair and studied him. This was a side to Hamish she'd never seen before. 'I don't think it's soft. Not in the least. If anything I think it's admirable, and applaud you.'

He blushed. 'Thanks.'

'I mean that, Hamish. I truly think it's admirable of you. You've gone up in my estimation.'

'Thanks again. But true as that reason is for staying with Celia, there is another. This one, I have to admit, quite mercenary.' He paused, then went on, 'It's not generally known yet, but I'm to be promoted to vice chairman in a few months' time. I don't merit it, of course – you appreciate that better than anyone – but it's going to happen all the same. Call it nepotism if you will, but I have the chairman's word on it.'

'Was it his idea?'

'Of course. He wants me to take over the company when he retires in a few years. My being vice chairman is a way of being trained up for the big job when it finally comes.'

'I see,' Lena murmured. 'Lucky old you.'

'In a way. But the price is Celia. The opportunity would go flying out of the window if I left her. And, there's no denying it, I am ambitious. Always have been.'

'Then I wish you good luck, Hamish.'

'It's your good luck too,' he said quickly. 'If you wish it to be.'

Lena frowned. 'How so?'

'I'm taking you upstairs with me. You'll be my right hand, so to speak. As you've been ever since I became a department head.'

She stared at him in astonishment, momentarily thrown. 'You mean when you become vice chairman?'

'Exactly.'

'But your duties will be totally different from what they are now.'

'Maybe so,' he admitted. 'But whatever, I want you there by my side to ensure I don't muck up and make a fool of myself. I'd probably be out of my depth otherwise.'

Lena had to admit that was probably true. Even as a department head he was out of his depth most of the time. It was because of her that the department ran smoothly. 'It's very honest, not to mention brave, of you to admit that, Hamish,' she said.

He shrugged. 'It's true though, isn't it?'

'Yes,' she stated bluntly. 'It is.'

'So what do you say?'

Lena regarded him shrewdly. 'Does my elevation depend on my answer about resuming our affair?'

'It does not,' he replied emphatically. 'I swear to you it doesn't. Turn me down and you'll still go upstairs with me. Nor am I being kind, or anything like that. I simply need you, and that's the long and short of it.'

Working for the vice chairman as his right hand? She liked the idea of that. And the chairman's right hand given time. 'Will I get more money?'

Hamish smiled. 'Absolutely. Don't you worry, I'll make it worth your while. You'll do very nicely out of it, thank you very much.'

It was a lot to take in at once, Lena told herself. She needed to give it some thought.

'Well?' Hamish demanded.

'There's no problem about me working for you when you become vice chairman. On the contrary, I'll jump at the chance.'

'And the other thing?'

'That needs thinking on, Hamish.'

His face fell. 'You're going to turn me down, aren't you?'

'I never said that. Simply that it needs consideration. I'll give you my decision in a couple of days' time. How's that?'

He nodded. 'It'll have to do, I suppose.'

'Yes, it will. Now let's leave it at that for the time being.'

Tom glanced over at Ian, who'd come for Sunday dinner as he invariably did, although he was now living in a house which he shared with three other bachelors from Ford. 'Have you written to your mother recently?' he asked.

343

Ian shook his head. 'I just never seem to get round to it.'

'Then make an effort. She'll no doubt be worried about you.'

'All right.' Ian nodded. 'I'll do it tonight.'

'See that you do. I'll be asking you tomorrow at work if you did.'

Ian sighed. He hated writing; it was such a chore.

Tom's eyes twinkled mischievously. 'And tell her about that lassie you're courting. Georgie's bound to be interested in that.'

An embarrassed Ian blushed beetroot red.

'You've decided then?' Hamish asked. He and Lena were in the Swan, at the same table they'd sat at three evenings previously.

'I have.'

'And?' He was certain she was going to turn him down.

'The idea of the hotel is out, Hamish. That would be just too degrading, I'm afraid. Going to your place was one thing, an hotel quite another.'

So, he'd been right. She had turned him down. Disappointment welled within him. 'I'm sorry to hear that, Lena. I had hoped . . .' He trailed off, and shrugged his shoulders. 'Never mind. It was worth a try.'

'But I do have a suggestion to make.'

'Oh?'

'A suggestion I believe to be a lot better than yours.' She took her time, teasing it out, taking a sip of her gin before continuing. Enjoying the look on his face.

'Lena?' he urged impatiently.

'Why only once a month? Why not more? Once a week, say. Or even twice. What do you think of that?'

His Adam's apple bobbed up and down as he gulped. This was the answer to his prayers. 'And how would we manage that?'

'Simple, really. I move into a house of my own where you can visit me whenever you like.'

'A house of your own.' He frowned. 'You're prepared to leave home?'

'Well, that's what it would mean. At my age I should have left years ago, but never did because there wasn't any reason to. But now there is. Or could be, if you agree.'

Every week, twice a week! He almost drooled at the thought. It would certainly solve his problem. By Christ and it would!

'There are terms, though,' Lena added quietly.

'Such as?'

'You buy the house, or pay the rent. Also pay to have it furnished. I can't afford to do that by myself, Hamish. I'll need help. You'd also have to stump up for the gas, electric if it's installed, and maintenance,' she added.

'And what do you pay?' he croaked.

She treated him to her razored smile. 'I pay by being your full-time mistress. That's what. Yours whenever you want me.'

Full-time mistress! That certainly appealed. 'And how long would this last for?'

'As long as you like. That's a promise.'

Hamish closed his eyes and pictured Celia, shuddering at the vision he conjured up. True, Lena was no oil painting, but neither was Celia nowadays. And Lena was terrific in bed, as he knew from past experience. Enthusiastic was too tame a word to describe her.

'The question is, can you afford it?' she asked.

Hamish started mentally doing sums. It sounded a big outlay, but it wasn't really. What was more, once he became vice chairman his salary would jump enormously, and that was only months away. He nodded. 'I can afford it.'

'It's agreed then?'

'It's agreed.'

Lena knew it was probably the best she could ever achieve where a relationship with a man was concerned. With her face no one was ever going to marry her, so being a mistress was the next best thing.

She'd settle for that. And be grateful into the bargain.

Chapter 26

'I was wondering,' Bill Bailey murmured, staring at Georgie over the rim of his teacup. He hadn't thought he'd be nervous at broaching this, but he was. '. . . if you'd care to come and meet my mother one night?'

Georgie wasn't entirely surprised. She'd guessed over the past weeks that he was leading up to something. All the signs had been there. 'Oh?'

'I've told her about you. I hope you don't mind?'

'Not at all, Bill.'

'She'll lay on a bit of a meal. That sort of thing.'

'A meal?' She was playing for time.

'Aye. Nothing fancy, mind. Boiled ham, no doubt. That's what my mum usually gives guests.'

Georgie pulled out her cigarettes and lit up, not failing to notice how increasingly nervous he was becoming. 'What's your mum's name?'

'Florrie. Short for Florence.'

'Is she old?'

'Fairly elderly. She's just turned seventy.'

'And your father's dead, is that right?'

'Quite a while ago now. My mum was glad of the company when I came out of the army. She'd been lonely without him.'

'They were close, then?'

'Very. They absolutely idolised one another. He's a great loss to her.'

Georgie could well imagine it would be the same with Chrissie should Tam pass before her. The difference was, Chrissie would still have Lena and herself at home.

'I don't even know where you live, Bill.'

He told her.

A short tram ride away, she thought. Not that far.

'If you come I'll show you my medals,' Bill proposed, tongue half in cheek.

'You have medals?'

'Oh aye. Sometimes they give you one for just having been there. I've got several of those.'

'Any for bravery?'

His eyes took on a peculiar look. 'I have one. But please don't ask me about it.'

'Bad memories?' she sympathised.

He nodded, but didn't elaborate.

It was that little exchange which made up her mind for her, though why, she couldn't have said. 'I'd love to meet your mum,' she declared. 'When?'

'How about this Friday?'

'Suits me.'

He beamed. 'I'll be looking forward to it.'

Georgie just hoped she wasn't making a mistake. There

again, where was the harm in meeting his mother? It didn't mean anything.

'A place of your own!' a shocked Chrissie exclaimed.

'That's right. It's high time I left home, don't you think?'

'But . . . but it's so unexpected.'

'What brought this on?' Tam asked, taken aback.

Lena shrugged. 'Seems a good idea, that's all. You don't want me kicking around under your feet for the rest of your days, do you?'

Tam began studiously packing his pipe. This was a turn-up for the book. Lena kicking around under their feet for the rest of their days was precisely what he'd believed would happen. Now here she was, proposing to fly the coop.

'Have you found somewhere?' Chrissie queried.

'Not yet, Mum. I haven't started looking. But I will shortly.'

'Tam?' Chrissie prompted.

He shook his head. 'There's nothing I can say. She's old enough to go if she wishes. I can't stop her. And why would I try, if that's what she wants?'

Chrissie abruptly sat down. 'This has made my head spin, coming out of the blue as it has.'

'Sorry, Mum. Shall I put the kettle on?'

'Please, Lena. I could do with a cup after that.'

'It'll cost you to get furniture and the like,' Tam commented.

'I plan to use the second-hand showrooms. I should be able to pick up some bargains there.'

Tam grunted his approval. She'd obviously thought this

349

through. But then, he'd expect nothing less from Lena. She'd always had her head screwed on the right way.

'You intend living by yourself?' Chrissie asked with a frown.

'That's right, Mum. I'll enjoy it.'

'Are you sure?'

'Oh, yes. I have no doubts in that department. None at all.'

'What about cooking and cleaning?'

'Don't worry, Mum, I'm quite capable. I'll neither starve nor live in a pigsty, I promise.'

'It just seems queer to me.' Chrissie shook her head. 'Lassies don't usually do that sort of thing.'

'Well, this lassie intends to.'

'Don't argue with her, Chrissie.' Tam smiled. 'You know Lena. Once her mind's made up that's it. Arguing will only make her even more determined. That's the way she is.'

Lena laughed. 'You know me only too well, Papa.'

'Aye, well I would, you being my daughter.'

Lena was still laughing as she went to lay out the cups and saucers. That had gone more easily than it might have, she reflected. Which was something of a relief if she was honest.

'Just call me Florrie,' the old woman said, extending a heavily veined hand covered with liver spots to Georgie.

'Pleased to meet you, Florrie. And I'm Georgie.'

'Pleased to meet you, Georgie. I hope you like boiled ham, for that's what we're having.'

'Love it.'

'Good.'

How stooped she was, and frail, Georgie noticed, as Florrie shuffled over to the gleaming range, which had been newly blackleaded.

'Will you have a seat?' Bill asked, indicating an easy chair.

'Thank you. But perhaps I should help Florrie? Give her a bit of a hand?'

'I may be ancient but I'm not decrepit,' Florrie retorted before Bill could reply. 'If I want your help I'll ask for it. Now, the pair of you sit down, otherwise you'll be in my way.'

Feisty, Georgie thought approvingly. Florrie was certainly that. Already she'd taken a liking to her.

'Tell me all about yourself, young woman,' Florrie demanded from where she was busy at the range. 'Bill has mentioned a few things, but I'd like to know more. If you don't mind, that is.'

Talk about getting right to the point. Georgie smiled to herself. 'I don't mind at all,' she replied. 'If you'll tell me about yourself afterwards.'

Florrie shot her a look, then nodded her agreement. 'Get on with it then. I'm all ears.'

'Is it true what your mother said about me being the first female you've ever taken home?' Georgie asked, when she and Bill were on the way to her tram stop. She coughed, for there was a lot of fog about, interspersed with thick chimney smoke. If she'd spat into a hanky the spittle would have been black.

'Aye, that's right.'

'I'm honoured.'

He chose to ignore that. 'So what did you think of my mum?'

'I liked her. Liked her a lot, actually. She certainly doesn't pull any punches.'

Bill laughed. 'You can say that again. She can be a proper tartar when she gets going. But her heart's in the right place.'

'I can imagine.'

'She took a shine to you too. It was obvious.'

'Really?'

'Oh aye. I could tell. The fact that she offered you a second helping of boiled ham was the proof. She rarely does that to any of our guests. Not that we have many.'

Georgie glanced sideways at him. 'I don't suppose you've got many friends locally, having been so long in the army?'

'A few pals from the old days before I joined up. I bump into them from time to time in a pub I use.'

Thinking of Charlie made her ask, 'Do you drink a lot, then?'

'Not really. I enjoy a pint and a dram as most men do. But I can take it or leave it. Why?' And then the penny dropped. 'I'm not a drunk, like your husband, Georgie. You have my word on that.'

'Sorry for asking,' she apologised. 'It was rude of me.'

'Not at all. I can well understand why you'd want to know after what you went through with that man.'

Georgie smiled gratefully at him. 'I really enjoyed tonight. Thank you, Bill.'

'My pleasure, I assure you.'

How easy-going he was, she thought. There didn't appear to be any side to him whatsoever. 'You forgot to show me your medals,' she teased.

'So I did.'

'You never wanted to in the first place, did you?' she accused him light-heartedly.

'I offered.'

'But didn't produce them. I don't think you have any at all.'

'I do,' he stated emphatically. 'I have some all right.'

She believed him. But then she had when he'd first told her.

'Hey, that's your tram!' he exclaimed as they were approaching the stop. They broke into a run, arriving at the stop just as the tram clanked to a halt.

'Thanks again,' she said breathlessly, and clambered aboard.

'See you next delivery day, Georgie.'

'See you then, Bill.'

Georgie found a seat and slumped into it. She wondered if he'd been going to ask her out again, only to be prevented from doing so by the arrival of the tram. She was not at all sure what her reply would have been.

There again, there was always the next delivery day.

'Lena!'

She glanced up to find Hamish beckoning her into his office. Once she was inside he closed the door behind them.

'This is for you,' he declared, picking up an envelope

from his desk and handing it to her. The envelope was open and contained a wad of notes, a number of them white ones. 'To get you started with your house,' he explained. 'Have you found anywhere yet?'

She shook her head. 'I've been watching the ads in the papers but haven't spotted anything that might be suitable. Not so far, anyway. But when I do I might need time off from here to view. And then, when I have the house, more time off to arrange matters.'

Hamish nodded that he understood. 'Just speak to me first, then go and do what you have to. Understand?'

'Thank you, Hamish.'

'Do you fancy a drink in the Swan after work?'

'For any particular reason?'

He gave a dry, bitter laugh. 'Because I'd much rather spend an hour with you than with Celia. That a good enough reason?'

She was strangely touched. 'It's enough.'

'Good.' As she was turning away he said, 'Lena?'

'What, Hamish?'

'On the other hand, we could spend a few days at that hotel I mentioned. Get the ball rolling, so to speak.'

She could hear the pleading in his voice, and realised how desperate he must be. She also noticed that a sudden faint sheen of perspiration had appeared on his brow during the past few seconds. Be that as it may, she wasn't going to stoop to acting like a common tart, even if she did want sex as much as he.

'We'll stick with the drink, Hamish,' she replied. 'I've already made plain my feelings on going to that, or any other, hotel.'

He sank back into his chair, his disappointment obvious.

'Don't worry, though. The time will come soon enough. You'll see.'

She felt immensely powerful as she left his office. It was a sensation she liked. Very much.

'You're getting very friendly with the delivery man,' said Janet, during a lull when there weren't any customers in the shop.

Georgie affected surprise and innocence. 'Am I?'

'It looks that way. You have your tea break with him every time he comes. The pair of you sit in the back shop nattering away like a couple of old fishwives.'

'He's easy to talk to,' Georgie prevaricated with a smile.

'Is there anything in it?'

'In what?'

'The pair of you? He certainly fancies you all right. That's clear enough.'

'Not to me it isn't.'

'And you seem quite keen yourself, I've noticed.'

'Have you now?' Georgie replied coldly.

'He's not bad-looking, either. Rather handsome, really.'

'I suppose,' Georgie grudgingly admitted. 'If you like that type.'

'Which you obviously do.'

Georgie glared at her colleague. 'Aren't you taking a lot on yourself saying something like that?'

Janet was instantly contrite. 'Sorry, Georgie. I didn't mean to upset you. I was only commenting, that's all.'

'Then I'll thank you to mind your own business, and I'll do the same.'

Further conversation was interrupted by the arrival of a customer.

Little madam, Georgie thought later. How dare she presume? Even if she was right.

'Is this a new boyfriend Georgie's got?' Tam asked Chrissie one night when they were alone. Lena was out somewhere, and Georgie had gone to the pictures with Bill.

'She says not. She says they're only friends. Nothing more.'

'Hmm,' Tam grunted.

'Why do you ask?'

Tam folded the newspaper he'd been reading and dropped it to the floor. 'Because she's had two bad experiences, I suppose,' he said quietly. 'I wouldn't like her to get her fingers burnt again.'

'No,' Chrissie replied slowly. 'I wouldn't either. But she's a grown woman, and a mother, Tam. She'll know her own mind. It's certainly not up to us to interfere.'

'I have no intention of interfering, woman. But I can be concerned, can't I? She is my daughter, don't forget.'

There was silence between them for a few minutes, then Tam asked, 'What do we know about this chap anyway?'

Chrissie sighed. 'You won't let it go, will you?'

'I'm simply curious. Surely there's no harm in that?'

Chrissie laid her darning aside. She'd had enough of it anyway, and her eyes were hurting. Not for the first time she wondered if she should visit the optician for a test.

'Well?'

'Well what?' She frowned.

'What do we know about him?'

Persistent, Chrissie thought. That was Tam all over. 'Not a lot really. Just a few bits and pieces.'

Tam was clearly irritated. 'Which are?'

'He's ex-army. Joined as a lad, and came out only recently. He lives with his widowed mother and works as a delivery man servicing Templeton's, where he met Georgie. That's it.'

'How old is he?'

'No idea. Georgie has never mentioned it.'

'Has he been married?'

'Again, Georgie has never mentioned it. Though I did get the impression he hasn't. Honestly, Tam, stop worrying. Georgie's quite capable of looking after herself.'

'Aye, like getting herself hooked up with that pervert Charlie. She looked after herself there all right.'

'Aye, well. We all make mistakes.'

'And I just don't want her to make another one.'

'Let me remind you, Georgie said they were only friends. Nothing more.'

Tam eyed his wife balefully. 'In my experience that never works between a man and a woman. It simply isn't natural. One thing is eventually bound to lead to another. Unless he's queer, that is.'

Chrissie was genuinely shocked. 'How could he be that when he was in the army? What a suggestion!'

'Take my word for it, lass, not all queers flounce and walk around with limp wrists. Some of them can be hard as nails, believe me.'

'And how would you know about such a thing, Tam McKeand?'

'I just do, that's all.'

'Huh!' she snorted.

'Don't huh me! I hate it when you do that.'

'Huh!' she snorted again, taking a rise.

'Huh yourself.'

She made a mental note to tickle him when they got into bed. If he hated her snorting then he hated that even more, being ticklish in the extreme.

'I've had a thought,' she declared.

'Oh aye?'

'This Bill invited Georgie home for tea to meet his mum. Why don't we suggest to her she invites him here for tea to meet us? A sort of return gesture, you could say.'

Tam considered the suggestion. 'What an excellent idea,' he enthused. 'Then I can judge him for myself.'

Chrissie was alarmed. 'You won't put him off, will you? Or start quizzing the poor man?'

'I promise.'

'A promise I'll hold you to, Tam. I'll be furious if you subject him to some kind of interrogation.'

'I can ask questions, can't I? What it was like in the army, and so on?'

'As long as you keep it to that sort of thing.'

'I will.'

'Anyway.' Chrissie shrugged. 'Georgie might not want to invite him.'

'Why not?'

'She might just not want to, that's all.'

'I don't see why she wouldn't. She went to his house, surely it's only polite for her to invite him to ours?'

'We can only suggest it to her. The decision will be hers.'

When they spoke to Georgie later that evening she was all for it. Bill was to be asked to tea.

Lena went to the large window dominating the room and stared out, thinking what a lovely area Hillhead was. Far smarter than where she currently lived with her parents, and where she'd been brought up.

The 'apartment', as the factor so grandiosely called it, was light and airy, with large rooms and high ceilings. She'd fallen in love with it the moment she'd walked through the door.

There were trees in the street, she noted, and the street was devoid of any rubbish or debris. The facing terrace, which was identical to the one containing her 'apartment', was constructed of stone that positively shone in the sunlight.

Her apartment, she realised she'd thought. And so it would be, for there and then she decided to rent it, knowing it would be a place where she'd be happy.

Hillhead! Who'd have ever thought she'd be moving into such a posh area? Certainly not her. But why not? With Hamish funding her she could afford it easily.

'Right,' she declared out loud. It was straight back to the factor and sign whatever had to be signed, and pay whatever had to be paid as a deposit. Hamish's envelope stuffed with cash was burning a hole in her handbag.

She was euphoric as she locked the front door behind her and hurried off down the stairs. She'd found her new home. And it was an absolute cracker!

Chapter 27

Lena closed Hamish's office door behind her, then whirled to face him, her eyes blazing with excitement. 'I've got some wonderful news!' she declared.

He came to his feet. 'So have I.'

That threw her slightly. 'You first, then.'

'My promotion has been brought forward. I start as vice chairman next Monday.'

'Oh, Hamish!' she breathed, delighted for him.

'You'll be starting your new job then as well. I've decided that your title will be personal assistant to the vice chairman. What do you think?'

'I . . .' She broke off, lost for words.

'Pleased?'

'Of course I am. But shouldn't a personal assistant be able to type and take shorthand? Neither of which I can do.'

He shook his head. 'I'll have a secretary who'll do that. No, your duties will be more or less to check everything that arrives on my desk. Keep me on the right lines, so to speak. Ensure I don't make any balls-ups.'

Which was precisely what she did now. 'I see.'

'That all right?'

'Fine.'

He then mentioned a sum that far exceeded what she currently earned. 'Big promotion, big pay rise. For both of us.' He beamed. 'Any complaints?'

She knew he meant the latter as a joke. 'None.'

'Sure?'

If they hadn't been at work, she'd have given him a hug. 'Absolutely, Hamish. Absolutely!'

'I can't tell you how thrilled I am, Lena. I'm bubbling inside with it.'

'And so you should be. You're very lucky.'

'Aye.' He nodded. 'I'm well aware of that. On two counts. One, marrying Celia. And two, having you to rely on. For which I can't thank you enough.' He suddenly remembered something. 'Oh, and by the way, you'll have your own office right next to mine. An office all to yourself.'

'Really?' She was amazed.

'Really. It's not long been refurbished, either. Tastefully, too, in my opinion.'

'And your office?'

'Twice the size of this with a carpet on the floor and a drinks cabinet.' He laughed. 'Imagine, a bloody drinks cabinet! Can you beat that?'

'When's the announcement going to be made about your promotion?' Lena enquired.

'A memo is being put round this afternoon which'll cause quite a stir, I shouldn't be surprised.'

'And about me?'

'No memo. You just report upstairs next Monday and that'll be that. I'm sure we'll both settle in fairly quickly.'

Lena, frankly, couldn't wait. She rather enjoyed her present job, but the new one should be far more interesting. And certainly far more financially rewarding.

Hamish's eyes twinkled. 'I'll tell you what. As soon as we can we'll christen the drinks cabinet. I'll enjoy that.'

'I'll bet you will,' she teased.

'There's another thing. As from next Monday the chairman is going into semi-retirement in order to play more golf. He intends coming in only one day a week from now on, and probably only half a day at that. In other words, I'll be more or less running the company.'

Better still, she thought. Hamish's cup was certainly running over. 'When was all this decided?'

'At the weekend. Or at least that's when I was told. Celia and I were over there for Sunday lunch, and the chairman dropped his bombshell in the middle of it.'

'Well, you did know it was coming,' she pointed out.

'I did. What was so unexpected was bringing forward the date. That took me completely by surprise. You could have knocked me over with the proverbial feather.'

'I've got some good news as well.'

'You said. What is it?'

'I've found the most perfect place. At least I think it is. I'm certain you'll love it.'

'When are you moving in?'

Lena laughed. 'Hold your horses. It needs doing up first. And then I've got the furniture to buy. It'll take a few weeks at least.'

'Where is it?'

'Hillhead. A lovely street. I fell in love with the apartment the moment I walked into it.'

'"Apartment".' Hamish chuckled. 'Sounds very posh.'

'The factor's description, not mine. And yes, I suppose you could call it that. Certainly a lot posher than I'm used to.'

'There are going to be a lot of changes to what you've been used to.' Hamish smiled.

Lena could only agree, well aware she was about to move into a whole new lifestyle, including the increase in salary coming her way. It was going to be lovely.

'Tell you what,' Hamish said. 'Why not a drink in the Swan after work to celebrate both sets of news?'

'I'll be there. Now I'd better get on. There's plenty to be done.'

A little later, as was his habit, Hamish skived off to the coffee shop to meet up with the regulars.

'I insist. This round's mine,' Lena declared, pushing a ten-shilling note at Hamish. 'Think of it as a sort of thank you for what you've done for me.'

'A lady shouldn't pay for the drinks. But in this instance, I gracefully accept your offer.'

Lena studied him as he went up to the bar. He'd changed considerably since they'd first met. The sexy blue eyes were the same, if a little duller than before, while his hair was definitely thinning, and had begun to show the first strands of grey at the temples. He'd also put on weight, though not drastically. All in all, he was still a damn good-looking man.

'So, how's Celia?' she asked when Hamish re-joined her.

He pulled a face. 'Fatter than ever. She's now so portly she's started waddling like a duck.'

Lena laughed. 'Surely you're exaggerating?'

'Nope. She waddles just like a duck.'

'Is she taking any better care of herself?'

'Hell will freeze over first. Fat and unkempt. My darling wife who used to be so beautiful.' A catch came into his voice. 'It's a tragedy, that's what it is. One of Greek, or Shakespearean, proportions. As I said, my price for getting where I am today. And a heavy price it is too.'

'You've still got the twins to be thankful for,' Lena reminded him.

A smile crept across his face. 'I wouldn't change them for anything. Not for all the tea in China. And that's a fact.'

When they finally left the Swan they were both slightly tipsy, Hamish even staggering a little.

'I enjoyed that,' he slurred.

'So did I.'

His eyes narrowed in concentration. 'You know something, Lena?'

'What?'

'You really are terrific company. A man feels relaxed in your presence. Very . . . relaxed.'

She was touched. 'Thank you, Hamish. Shall I call you a taxi?'

'You do that and I'll drop you off.'

'Are you sure about that?'

'Absolutely. It isn't any trouble.'

'But what if we're seen?'

'That could have happened any time in the Swan.

364

Besides, what's wrong with the boss taking a colleague out for a drink? Or dropping her home in a taxi after they've both been working overtime? I don't see anything wrong in either.'

Neither did Lena, albeit they hadn't been working overtime. Just then a taxi came into view which she promptly flagged down. Having given the driver her address she sank on to the leather seat beside Hamish. As the taxi moved off, to her surprise, he took her hand and held it, at the same time giving her a smile in the darkness.

For the first time in her life Lena felt cherished by a member of the opposite sex.

It was a glorious feeling.

'Come in, come in.' Chrissie beamed, ushering Georgie and Bill into the kitchen, where the table was already set for the meal that was to follow.

Tam rose from his chair. This was a moment he'd been waiting for: meeting his daughter's new 'friend'.

The first thing he noticed was how completely at ease Bill was. Not nervous in the least. Confident in himself, Tam thought, unsure whether he liked that or not.

Introductions were made all round, then Tam offered their guest a dram, which Bill accepted. Georgie glanced at Lena, who gave her an almost imperceptible nod of encouragement.

'I'm told you were in the army,' Tam began. 'And in the war?'

'Bill doesn't like talking about the war,' Georgie put in hastily. 'And don't ask why, he just doesn't, that's all.'

'Sorry,' Tam apologised. 'I didn't know.'

Not a good beginning, Georgie thought. Damn!

Georgie clicked the front door shut behind Bill and returned to the kitchen, where Chrissie and Lena were already busy at the sink.

'Did you have to give him the third degree, Papa?' she said. 'For a while in here it was like the Spanish Inquisition.'

'I didn't give him any third degree,' Tam blustered. 'I was only making conversation.'

My arse! Georgie thought angrily, though she didn't say so in front of her parents.

'You were a bit harsh, Papa,' Lena commented over her shoulder.

'Nonsense.'

'You were, Tam,' Chrissie declared grimly. 'I felt right sorry for the poor chap.'

'Then you should have said something.'

'I tried to, several times. But you just weren't listening.'

'We all tried to steer the conversation in different directions,' Lena added. 'Except you kept coming back to whatever you were droning on about at the time.'

Tam was upset. He hadn't realised he'd been that bad. 'I was only doing my job,' he replied gruffly.

'And what job's that?' Georgie demanded.

'Being your father. Trying to protect you, that's what. I thought you needed it after the almighty mess you made with Charlie Gunn.'

Georgie burst into tears and fled the room.

'Idiot!' Chrissie snapped. 'Bloody stupid idiot.'

'I'll go and talk to her.'

'Leave her for now,' Lena advised. 'And for what it's worth, I liked Bill. I thought him a genuinely nice bloke.'

'Me too,' Chrissie said.

Tam dropped his head to stare at the floor. He too had taken a shine to Bill, but only after he'd got to know a bit about him, and been in his company for a while.

Taking out his pipe Tam slowly began the procedure of filling it and lighting up. Bill's visit wasn't mentioned again for the rest of that day.

Chrissie exclaimed in delight and waved the letter that had just arrived at Tam and Lena, who were having breakfast. 'It's from Tom,' she explained. 'Brigid's expecting again.'

Tam's face lit up. 'Is she, by God? That's wonderful news.'

'How far gone is she?' Lena asked.

'Four months, it says here.' Chrissie shook her head. 'I couldn't be more pleased.'

'A wee lassie would be nice this time,' Tam commented. 'A sister for Robin.'

'Aye, true enough,' Chrissie agreed. 'Unfortunately we don't have a say in such matters. What comes along comes along.'

Georgie appeared in the kitchen. 'What's all the commotion about?' she demanded.

'Brigid's going to have another baby,' Chrissie informed her.

'Good for Brigid.'

'I'm sure Tom had something to do with it,' Lena observed.

Georgie laughed. 'I'm sure he did.'

Suddenly Lena was depressed, knowing she'd never have any children of her own. Marriage would never happen for her. Pushing her plate away, she came to her feet. 'I'd better get going or I'll be late. It's a big day for me, don't forget.'

'Good luck then,' Tam declared.

'Aye, good luck, Lena,' Chrissie added. Crossing to her daughter she kissed her on the cheek. 'You can tell us all about it when you get in tonight.'

Lena stared around her, having just entered her office for the first time. It was a little male for her taste, but lovely all the same. As Hamish had said, it had clearly only recently been refurbished.

Crossing to her desk, she sat behind it. It was a larger desk than she'd previously had, and the chair was far more comfortable.

'Personal assistant to the vice chairman,' she said aloud, and smiled. She'd certainly come up in the world.

'What do you think?' Hamish asked from the doorway that connected their offices.

'It's wonderful.'

'Come and see mine.'

His was just as large as he'd said it was, the Wilton underfoot a pattern of blues and reds. Her desk might be big, but his was positively enormous. There was also a pretty chaise longue, presumably for him to lie on should he feel like doing so.

'Look at this,' he declared, and led her to an ornately carved cabinet which he opened to reveal myriad bottles and glasses. 'Nothing but the best, eh?'

'I'm impressed.'

He leant closer to her and whispered, 'So am I.'

He was like a kid with a new toy, she thought. And why not? It was a huge achievement on his part. Even if he'd had to marry the boss's daughter to get there.

'We'll have that drink I promised you before going home tonight.' He smiled.

'I'll look forward to it.'

He suddenly became all businesslike. 'Now, we'd better at least appear busy. Make a start, eh?'

'What would you like me to do?'

He gestured towards some files on his desk. 'We'll go through those and see what's what. And when we've done that we'll take it from there.'

'Right.' She nodded, and added, 'Just one word of advice, Hamish, if you don't mind.'

'What's that?'

'Forget the coffee shop for a while. At least until you get settled in and everything's running smoothly.'

'Good idea, Lena.'

She was pleased he'd agreed, for she was safeguarding her own job as well as his.

'We've had a letter from Dolly,' Brigid announced to Tom when he got in from work. 'She's over the moon at our news.'

Tom beamed at his wife, whose bump was now quite obvious. From the look of things it was going to be a large child. 'I thought she might be.'

'She's promised to come and see us again after the baby's born. Which would be marvellous. The only worrying thing is she says she's been unwell. Nothing too serious according to her, but the doctor's advised she stay in bed for a while until she recovers.'

Tom frowned. 'Does she say what's wrong with her?'

'No, only that she's been unwell. She thinks the doctor's being a bit melodramatic, but has decided to stay in bed just to be on the safe side. According to her it's driving her mad.'

'Well, it would do,' Tom said. Dolly wasn't the sort of woman who enjoyed being inactive. 'Anyway, what's for tea and where's that son of mine?'

Later that evening Tom wrote back to Dolly, telling her he hoped she'd be better soon. And to let him know once she was up and about again.

Georgie glanced at the wall clock, thinking Bill was late with his delivery. This would be the first time she'd seen him since he'd come to tea.

Half an hour later she began to worry as he still hadn't shown up. Usually Bill was prompt to within five or ten minutes.

He arrived a quarter of an hour later. 'Sorry, I can't stop for a cup of tea today, Georgie,' he apologised. 'I'm having trouble with the van.'

She watched as he bustled in and out several times until the delivery was complete. Then he was gone with a wave of a hand, and a muttered 'See you next week.'

Her heart sank as she heard his van roar off. There didn't appear to be anything wrong with it to her. In fact it sounded just as it normally did.

Georgie bit her lip. Had it simply been an excuse for

not joining her for a cup of tea? Had he taken offence when he'd visited them? In her opinion Papa had been rude; was this a consequence of that rudeness? In other words, was her friendship with Bill over?

She sighed. There was nothing for it but to wait till next week and see what happened then.

It was going to be a long week.

Hamish came awake to the realisation that he was alone in bed. Where the hell was Celia? He lay there for a full ten minutes before deciding to get up and investigate.

He found her in the kitchen guzzling the substantial remains of a steamed pudding she'd dished up earlier. She stared at him, a heaped spoon halfway to her mouth, her eyes blazing hate and loathing. Unblinking eyes that narrowed as she continued to stare.

Pig, he thought. That's what she'd become. A pig!

He said nothing, nor did she. Turning on his heel he left her to her gorging.

'That'll be one and threepence ha'penny,' Georgie said. The customer she was serving handed over the money and she rang it up on the till. She was about to have a word with Janet when a bobby came into the shop.

'Mrs Gunn?'

She was taken aback. 'Yes?'

'You're Mrs Gunn?'

'I am.'

'Is there somewhere we can talk privately?'

What in God's name was all this about? 'Come with me,' she said. 'You all right by yourself for a few moments, Janet?'

'Of course.'

In the back shop, Georgie turned to face her visitor. 'So what can I do for you?' she asked.

'I understand you and your husband are separated, Mrs Gunn. However, you are still his next of kin.' The bobby paused for a moment, then went on, 'I'm sorry to have to tell you that your husband was killed in the early hours of this morning whilst in the performance of his duties.'

Georgie's mouth went dry. 'Killed?' she echoed.

'He and a colleague, when a section of wall collapsed on them.'

Charlie dead? She was stunned by this bolt from the blue. 'I see,' she muttered.

'Would you care to sit down?'

'No, I'm fine, honestly.'

Charlie dead! She didn't know whether to laugh or cry.

Chapter 28

'A telephone as well?'

Lena was nervous about her mother's visit, but had felt she had to agree when Chrissie had all but insisted. 'I'll need it for work, Mum,' she lied.

'Is that a fact?'

'It was Mr Murchison's idea. My boss. The company are paying for it.' Lena was only too horribly aware of how unconvincing she sounded.

'My my. You really must be important now,' Chrissie commented, a trace of sarcasm in her voice.

Lena shrugged, and didn't reply.

'And most of your furniture appears to be new. I thought you were going to be buying from the second-hand showrooms?'

'That was before my big promotion, Mum. Don't forget I'm earning a lot more now.'

'Aye, that's true enough. But you've hardly started the job and couldn't possibly have saved up enough money in the time to pay for all this.'

'I did have savings.'

'Must have had a lot, then.'

Lena felt wretched, hating having to lie to her mother. 'Would you like a cup of coffee?'

'In a minute. I haven't seen everything yet. Now, where's your bedroom?'

'This way. I'll show you.'

Chrissie followed Lena into the bedroom. Like the rest of the 'apartment', it was newly decorated, Lena having had the painters in. Immediately, Chrissie eyed the brand-new bed, which hadn't yet had its wrappings removed. 'A double, eh?'

'More comfortable, wouldn't you say, Mum?'

'Oh aye, no doubt about it. Though you've never complained about the single you've been used to all these years.'

Lena couldn't hold her mother's piercing gaze, and dropped her own to stare at the floor.

Chrissie crossed over to the bed and sat on it. 'Come here, lassie. Join me.'

Lena did so.

'Will you tell me what's going on? For there's something here that isn't right.'

Lena, again staring at the floor, didn't reply.

'Well? I'm waiting.'

'What makes you think something isn't right?'

Chrissie sighed. 'I'm your mother, and know you through and through. Just as I know Georgie through and through. So, are you going to explain?'

'There's nothing to explain.'

'Lena, don't lie to me. I may be a poor, uneducated

working-class woman but I didn't come up the Clyde on a bicycle. Nor am I as green as I'm cabbage-looking.'

Despite herself, Lena smiled.

'I'm still waiting,' Chrissie stated patiently after a few seconds had ticked past.

Lena knew then she'd have to tell her mother the truth, that there was nothing else for it. In her heart of hearts, it was what she really wanted to do.

'Mum,' she said, starting off slowly. 'It's never mentioned in the house, but we all know I'm ugly as sin.'

'That's not true!' Chrissie protested vehemently. 'I admit, you're no great beauty. But ugly as sin? Never!'

'That's very kind and loyal of you, Mum, but you know it *is* true. I wish it wasn't, but the fact remains that it is.'

A hint of tears crept into Chrissie's eyes. 'So what's that got to do with this so-called "apartment"?'

'I'd love to get married, Mum, and have babies, but that'll never happen. No man will ever propose to me.'

This maternal side of Lena was new to Chrissie. 'One might,' she argued.

'It's highly unlikely. And the idea that I'll end up as an old maid isn't exactly an appealing one, I can tell you.'

Reaching across, Chrissie took hold of her daughter's hand, and gently squeezed it.

Lena took a deep breath, and went on. She told Chrissie everything, with the exception of having blackmailed Hamish into having an affair in the first place.

'So there you have it, Mum. I'm to be Hamish's mistress. A kept woman.' Shaking slightly, Lena detached her hand and crossed to the small fireplace where her cigarettes and lighter were on the mantelpiece. Taking out a cigarette, she lit up. 'I suppose you're ashamed of me now?' she queried in a small voice.

Chrissie studied her daughter. She hadn't known what to expect, but certainly not this. Life certainly was full of surprises. 'Is this Hamish Murchison a good man?' she asked quietly, not replying to Lena's question.

Lena couldn't yet look her mother in the face. She was too embarrassed. 'It depends what you mean by good. He's not the brightest spark around, and only got where he is today by marrying the chairman's daughter. And with help from me, I have to add. But yes, I suppose, on the whole, he is a decent enough chap.'

'And his wife won't . . . well, you know . . . any more?'

'Only rarely, according to him. And then he's had to plead with her first. Go down on his hands and knees, so to speak.'

Chrissie shook her head. 'That's awful.' She sounded genuinely sympathetic.

'And, as I just said, she's let herself go dreadfully. Fat as anything nowadays. Sometimes he even has to tell her to have a wash because she smells.'

Chrissie made a face. 'How disgusting.'

Lena wished she had some drink in. She could certainly have used one right now. 'It's my one chance to have anything like a normal life, Mum,' she choked. 'Can you understand that?'

'Aye, lass.' Chrissie sighed. 'I can.'

'I appreciate I'll only be second fiddle, and that I'll never have children. But surely that's better than the alternative? That's how I see it, anyway.'

Chrissie's heart went out to her daughter. The ugly

duckling who'd never turned into a swan. She and Tam had often wondered where she'd got her looks from and never succeeded in coming up with an answer. 'Will this set-up make you happy? For surely that's the important thing.'

Lena considered the question. 'Yes, I believe so, Mum. As happy as I'll ever get a chance to be.'

'And he's paying for everything?'

'That's right. It was part of the deal.'

'Have you . . .' She broke off, and coughed. She was still unclear on this particular point.

'Lots of times, Mum. I lost my virginity to him quite some time ago.'

Chrissie's face flamed. She was unused to talking about such matters, particularly to members of her own family. 'I see. Was it . . . agreeable?'

'Very. We get on exceptionally well in that department. If you know what I mean.'

Chrissie did, only too well. She and Tam were just the same, if perhaps not as frequently as they'd once been. 'Your father must never find out about this,' she said. 'He'd go off his chump if he knew.'

'He'll only find out if you tell him, Mum.'

'Have no fears about that. He'll never hear of it from me.'

'That's fine, then.'

Chrissie got to her feet. 'I think I'll have that cup of coffee now. If it's still on offer, that is?'

'Of course it is, Mum.' Lena looked Chrissie full in the face for the first time since her explanation. 'I don't ask for your approval, Mum. Just your understanding.'

Chrissie went to Lena and took her into her arms. 'You have that, lass. I don't condemn you for what you're doing. It's your decision, after all. As for approval, let's just say I don't disapprove. You're entitled to a wee bit of happiness just like everyone else. And if this is the only way for you to get that happiness, then so be it.'

'Thanks, Mum,' Lena said huskily, a huge wave of relief washing through her.

'It feels like a comfortable bed,' Chrissie commented as they left the room.

Which made Lena laugh.

Georgie glanced at the wall clock. Bill should be showing up any minute now and she would find out what was what about their friendship.

The door opened, but it was not Bill who came in. Instead, Wally, the previous delivery man, appeared carrying a tray. Georgie stared at him in surprise.

'Morning, Georgie.' He beamed. 'How's tricks?'

'Where's Bill?'

'Oh, very nice,' Wally retorted. 'No nice to see you again, Wally, how's your leg sort of thing.'

'I'm sorry,' Georgie apologised. 'I was just expecting Bill, that's all. Anyway, I thought you were retired?'

'I am.'

'So what are you doing here?'

He rested his tray on the counter. 'I've been asked to take over the round for a while as this Bill is ill.'

'Ill?'

'Aye, the influenza, I hear. Bad with it too. He'll be laid up for several weeks, I expect.'

Alarm flared through Georgie. Influenza could be a killer. She'd read somewhere that fifteen million people had died from it during the great worldwide pandemic of 1918 to '19. 'He's bad, you say?'

'That's what I was told. Now, I'd better get on. I take it I'll still be offered a cup of tea when I'm finished?'

'Tea and a sticky bun if you like.'

'That's the ticket, Georgie. You're a real gem.'

She stared at his retreating back as he headed for the rear of the shop, worried sick about Bill.

'What's wrong with your face tonight?' Tam demanded. 'Have you got the bellyache or something?'

Georgie shook her head. 'No, I'm fine, Papa.'

'Then cheer up, for God's sake. You've been a right misery since you got in from work.'

'Sorry.'

'Hard day at the shop?' Chrissie enquired.

'Not really, Mum. It's Bill. He's off with a bad dose of influenza.'

Chrissie's expression immediately became one of concern. 'I've heard of other cases recently. Mrs McGuire, further up the street, has it. I understand she's in a right old state.'

'Why don't you go and see him?' Tam suggested.

'I've been considering it, Papa.'

'And?'

'You don't want to catch it yourself,' Chrissie warned. 'Best to keep away. At least until he's over the worst of it.'

'Sound advice.' Tam nodded. 'I should have thought of that.'

Georgie couldn't make up her mind whether to go or not. 'I'll leave it for a few more days,' she said rather unconvincingly, wondering how Bill's mother was coping. She was quite an old woman, after all.

And what if Florrie was down with it as well?

'How much longer before this "apartment" of yours is ready?' Hamish asked.

Lena smiled. 'Getting impatient, are we?'

'Just a bit.' From the hungry look in his eyes it was obvious to her just how randy he must be. 'Surely you've got everything more or less organised by now?'

'I have, and shall be moving in, lock, stock and barrel, this weekend. So how's that?'

'Excellent,' he enthused. 'When can I pay a call and be shown round? I'm dying to see what it's like.'

'I'll be in a mess unpacking, but how about Sunday night? Can you manage that?'

'Try and stop me. Shall I bring anything?'

'A bottle would be nice.'

'I'll bring several as a house-warming present.'

She laughed. He was keen. There again, if she was honest, so was she. It had been a long time. 'Will you have any trouble getting away?'

'I'll make up some sort of excuse for going out. Not that Celia will enquire. She's always more than happy to see the back of me.'

How sad, Lena thought. 'Between seven and eight. Will that be all right?'

'I'll be there. With bells on,' he added meaningfully.

'I'm sure you will.'

'Ting a ling.'

Lena couldn't help but laugh again. Ting a ling. How ridiculous! Yet somehow apt.

Georgie stood looking up at the tenement where Bill lived. Should she visit or not? He was a friend, after all, so why was she holding back?

It wasn't fear of catching flu herself; that wasn't it at all. It was to do with her and Bill and the possibility that he might read more into her visit than she intended.

Somehow it had been easy when she'd been married, for there could be nothing between her and Bill other than friendship. Even though she was separated, she was still a married woman. But that state of affairs had abruptly changed with Charlie's death.

She was confused by the situation she now found herself in. And even a little scared, if she told the truth, though what there was to be scared about regarding Bill was beyond her. You couldn't have found a nicer or more gentle man. There again, hadn't she thought that about Charlie? She had only found out differently after they'd wed.

She hadn't gone to the funeral. Hadn't wanted to. It would have been hypocritical of her if she had. Anyway, she hadn't known when it was taking place, or where, though she could easily have found out if she'd wanted.

She presumed Avril had gone to live with her Aunt Betty; hardly a big change for the girl, who'd spent most of her time there as it was.

No, she'd leave her visit for a few more days, she suddenly decided. Turning round, she retraced her steps back up the street, but she had only gone a hundred yards or so when she stopped. This was nonsensical, she told herself. She was being downright daft. Bill was her pal, and her pal was ill. That's all there was to it. Turning again, she headed back to his close, plunging inside when she reached it.

'Oh, it's you, Georgie,' Florrie declared on opening the door. 'Come on through and I'll put the kettle on.'

'How's Bill? I hear he's got influenza.'

Florrie sighed. 'He has indeed. But he's now on the mend, I'm pleased to say.'

Florrie looked awful, Georgie thought. Tired and drawn, and even frailer than she recalled. 'That's good. How have you been coping?'

'Surprisingly well, considering. The neighbours have been a great help, mind you. In and out all the time to see how I am, and if there's anything they can do. I don't know how I'd have managed without them.'

'There's nothing like a decent neighbour.' Georgie nodded. 'We're fortunate like that ourselves.'

'The worst bit was when Bill was delirious,' Florrie said quietly. 'Thrashing around, sweat pouring off him. Out of his mind most of the time. But that's past now, thank God.' She gave Georgie a shrewd glance. 'He'll be pleased to see you. He's mentioned you on a couple of occasions.'

Georgie was surprised. 'Has he?'

'Aye, when he was delirious. At one point he called out your name as if he thought you were in the room with him.'

Georgie glanced away, not knowing what to make of that. Florrie smiled.

She put the kettle on, then set out cups and saucers. 'Would you care for a slice of fruit cake?' she asked. 'One of the neighbours handed it in earlier.'

'No, thank you. The tea will be fine.'

'Watching your figure, are you?' Florrie teased.

'Not at all,' Georgie protested. 'Why do you ask?'

'Relax, lass, don't fash yourself. I'm only having a wee joke.' Florrie ran a hand over her forehead. She was dreadfully tired. Bill's illness had taken a lot out of her.

'Are you all right?'

'Aye, fine. There's nothing wrong with me. Strong as a horse, even if I don't look it.'

Georgie could only wonder if that was true.

'Shall I take you ben, and bring the tea on through when it's ready?' Without waiting for a reply Florrie led the way. Georgie followed.

Bill's face lit up when he saw who his visitor was. 'Georgie!' he exclaimed in delight, struggling into a sitting position.

If Florrie looked awful, he looked ten times worse, Georgie thought. He'd clearly lost a lot of weight. His collar bones were protruding, and his face was almost emaciated.

'This is kind of you,' he said with a smile.

'So, how are you, Bill?'

'Getting better. Getting better. That right, Mum?'

'Aye, he is. This time last week I thought he was at death's door, and that's a fact.' She sighed, a sigh that came from deep within her. 'The doctor said things might have turned out differently if he hadn't been so fit.'

'At least that's one thing I can thank the army for!'

'I'll get the tea,' Florrie declared, and left them to it.

'Sorry I'm unshaven,' Bill apologised. 'I just couldn't face the thought of a razor on my skin. For some reason it's become extremely tender.'

'Don't worry about that. I'm used to seeing men first thing in the morning.' Oh dear, she thought. Maybe she shouldn't have said that. 'I do have a brother and father after all,' she added lamely.

'I still feel embarrassed. You haven't exactly caught me at my best.'

'You've been ill,' she said. 'What else would I expect?'

He smiled, but didn't reply.

'Do you mind if I sit down?'

'Of course not.' He patted the edge of the bed. 'There isn't a chair, I'm afraid, so will this do? How's the shop?'

'The same. It never changes. Oh, by the way, Wally has been hauled out of retirement to do your round while you're off. It was him who told me you had influenza.'

'I just hope he doesn't think he's getting his old job back on a permanent basis, that's all.'

Georgie could see he was concerned. 'I wouldn't worry if I were you. The job will be there waiting when you return. Which you mustn't do until you're fully well again. Hear?'

He grinned sheepishly. 'I hear you, Georgie.'

'Return too soon and you could have a relapse or something. People make that mistake all the time.' She suddenly flushed. 'Sorry, I shouldn't be telling you what to do. It's none of my business.'

'But I like it. Shows you care.'

Their eyes locked for a few seconds, then she glanced away.

384

'It's good to see you again, Georgie,' he said, his voice loaded with sincerity.

'And you, Bill.'

'I've missed you.'

'I've missed you too, Bill,' she confessed, and meant it every bit as much as he did.

'I'm pleased about that.' Reaching out, he touched her hand, then drew his own away again at the sound of his mother approaching with their tea.

Georgie felt strangely elated when she walked to the tram stop. It was as though she'd suddenly won an unexpected prize.

Chapter 29

'Well, you've certainly made a good job of this,' Hamish declared in admiration. They were in the sitting room, which had been painted cream throughout, including woodwork and ceiling. There was a burgundy-coloured carpet on the floor, and the combination was quite striking. Lena thought it worked a treat, and so too, apparently, did Hamish.

'Modern furniture,' he noted. 'Goes well in here.'

'Thank you.' She smiled. 'I'm glad you approve.'

He glanced at the drawn curtains. They too were cream, sporting swags and tails with flashes of burgundy to match the carpet. 'You've been quite adventurous really.'

'I've always hated the flock wallpaper you get in so many houses. And old Victorian furniture you need two strong men to move.'

Hamish laughed. 'You've just described the chairman's house to a T.'

'And yours?'

'Somewhere in between, I'd say. Celia is a little more traditional than you.'

'And how is she?'

'Immersed in a novel when I left her. Didn't even look up when I said goodbye.'

'What did you tell her about where you were going?'

Hamish shrugged. 'I didn't. Merely said I was off out, and that was that.'

Lena was already excited at the thought of what was going to happen, and had been for most of the day. She was almost twitching with it.

'Shall I open the champagne?' he asked. He had brought two bottles.

'Please. I'm afraid I don't have any proper glasses. In fact, all I have are tumblers.'

'That doesn't matter. You get a couple while I do the honours.'

'Don't spill any, now,' she warned.

He grinned. 'Don't worry, I won't spoil your nice new carpet. Now on you go.'

Quite masterful, she thought. She liked that.

He waited till she returned with the tumblers before popping the cork, and she exclaimed excitedly as he poured the frothing wine.

'A toast, Lena?'

'What to?'

'Us,' he declared firmly. 'And your "apartment".'

They drank.

'Christ!' Hamish swore softly. 'That was unbelievable. Out of this world.'

Lena couldn't have agreed more. It had been indeed. 'You were heroic,' she purred.

'Was I?'

'Absolutely.'

He ran a hand over her thigh, thinking about what had just taken place. So far the 'apartment' had cost him a pretty penny, but it was going to be worth it.

Bending his head, he flicked a nipple with his tongue. 'I don't know about you, but I'm exhausted.'

'Not too exhausted, I hope.'

'Why's that?' he teased, knowing exactly what she meant.

'A lady's expectations, Hamish.'

He laughed. 'You're insatiable. Always were.'

She took it as a compliment. 'Why don't I get us another drink while you revive?'

'Good idea.'

He watched her slip from the bed and throw on a brightly patterned kimono. 'That's pretty,' he commented.

'Glad you like it.'

'I like what's inside it even more.'

Her eyes twinkled with amusement. 'What a silver-tongued smooth talker you are, Hamish Murchison. You could quite turn a girl's head.'

He continued to watch as she padded from the room. By God, she was a terrific shag. Fabulous in fact. It made him shiver just thinking about it.

Lena returned with more champagne and sat alongside him. 'When will you come again?' she asked.

'I haven't left yet!' he protested.

'I'm aware of that. But when will you come again?'

'Keen, aren't you?' he teased.

'As mustard.'

Pushing the flap of her kimono aside he began stroking her leg, which was still sweat-slicked from their recent exertions. 'How about Wednesday night?'

'If you come straight from work I'll cook for you.'

'Are you any good?'

'Try me and find out.'

'I've already tried you and found out.'

She laughed. 'Cooking, idiot. Not the other.'

'Well, if you're half as good at cooking as you are at that then I can't wait.'

'I'm good at all manner of things,' she said. 'You might be surprised.'

He studied her, then shook his head. 'I don't think I would, Lena. You're an extremely talented woman, especially at work. I'd be lost without you there.'

'Thank you,' she whispered. 'I appreciate that.'

He thought of what Celia had become, and then of Lena. There was just no comparison. None at all.

He laid his champagne aside, then took hers and did the same with that. 'Guess what?'

'What?'

'That revival you were hoping for. It's taking place.'

She glanced down. 'So it is. In such a short time, too.'

Moments later they were again locked in each other's arms.

'So how was Bill tonight?' Chrissie enquired when Georgie arrived home after her second visit. Tam was still at McNair's, overseeing a big order that had to be filled urgently.

389

'Much improved, I'm happy to say. Out of bed and sitting in the kitchen. He's also put on a little weight, I noticed.'

Chrissie didn't fail to hear the enthusiasm in her daughter's voice. 'Does he know about Charlie?'

'He hasn't mentioned it. So I presume not.'

'So why haven't you told him?'

Georgie shrugged.

'There must be a reason, Georgie. It's as plain as the nose on your face, at least it was to me, that the man dotes on you.'

Georgie still didn't reply.

'Don't you care for him that way? I thought you made a splendid couple. There again, I thought the same about you and Charlie.'

'Aye, me and Charlie,' Georgie said. 'That was a mistake if ever there was one.'

'You can't let that mistake ruin the rest of your life,' Chrissie told her. 'It seems to me you have another chance here, so why not grab it while you can?'

Georgie thought about it. 'Bill has never said anything to me about an intimate relationship. Not really.'

'That's because he believes you to be a married woman,' Chrissie pointed out.

Georgie became agitated. She lit a cigarette, blowing the smoke fiercely away. 'The truth is, Mum,' she said at last, 'I'm scared. Scared and confused.'

'Scared and confused about what?'

'Oh, I don't know!' Georgie exclaimed. 'I just am.'

'Scared of Bill?'

'Not in any physical way. But on an emotional level, I suppose.'

'And confused?'

'Because I don't know my own mind.'

'Hmm,' Chrissie murmured.

'I've only ever thought of him as a friend, you see. Nothing else. I couldn't because of my situation.'

'But now you can, Georgie. Your situation's changed.' Chrissie studied her daughter for a few seconds, then asked, 'Have you ever kissed him?'

'No, I haven't.'

'Then maybe you should. It could well be the indicator you're looking for.'

'Indicator?'

'Come on, Georgie, don't be so dense. A kiss can tell you all manner of things. It certainly did me the first time I kissed your father. I felt . . .' She hesitated. 'Well, we won't go into that. But I'm sure you understand what I'm getting at.'

'And what if it leaves me cold, Mum?'

'That's an answer, isn't it?'

'And what if it doesn't?'

'Then that's another answer. But I think in your heart of hearts you already know which one it's going to be. Don't you?'

'No,' Georgie lied. 'Now if you don't mind I'm going through to my room. I've a few things to do there.'

Like think, Chrissie mused as Georgie left the kitchen. Not that she was trying to get rid of her daughter, not at all. But Georgie was too young to remain a widow for the rest of her life. That would be a tragedy.

In her opinion, if happiness was round the corner, then get walking.

*   *   *

'You weren't joking when you said you could cook. This is delicious,' Hamish enthused.

'Thank you.'

'What exactly is it?'

'Veal with orange. It's got all sorts in it. Stoned raisins, currants, nutmeg, oranges, and so on and so forth.'

Hamish shook his head in amazement. 'I don't mean to be rude, but how did a woman from a working-class Glaswegian background learn to cook a dish like this?'

'What were you expecting, mince and tatties?'

He laughed. 'Not quite. But the question stands.'

'I went to evening classes for a while some years back. No reason, really – it just appealed. Afterwards I thought it had been a waste of time as I could never have served up anything fancy to my parents. They're strictly plain-food people. Especially my father. His favourite meal is toad in the hole, would you believe. No disrespect to Papa, but to him that's the height of culinary achievement.'

Hamish laughed again. 'Doesn't know what he's missing.'

Lena tasted the red wine, a fine claret she'd laid in for the occasion. 'What's Celia like as a cook?'

Hamish also had a sip of wine. 'To be honest, she's quite talented. When she puts her mind to it, anyway.'

Jealousy stabbed through Lena. 'Oh?'

'Never been taught, but just seems to know what to do. She's particularly brilliant at sweets. Makes a wonderful thing with fresh cream and brandy snaps. I always make a glutton of myself when that turns up on the table.'

Lena's jealousy intensified. 'Just cream and brandy snaps?'

'Sherry is involved as well. She turns the whole business into a sort of log.'

'I see,' Lena murmured.

Hamish stared at her, then glanced down at his plate. 'Sorry. I shouldn't have told you that.'

'Not at all,' Lena protested. 'I'm only pleased she's good at something.'

There and then Lena decided she was going to work very hard at her cooking, improving her knowledge and her ability. She was damned if fat Celia was going to be better than her in the kitchen.

As for the bedroom, she had no worries there. None whatsoever.

'I shall be reporting back to work on Monday,' Bill declared. Florrie had gone to a neighbour's for a cup of tea within minutes of Georgie's arrival, her intention being, as Georgie and Bill had both guessed, to leave the pair of them alone.

Georgie frowned. 'So soon?'

'I asked the doctor when he was here yesterday and he says that'll be fine. I'm quite recovered.'

'You still need to put on more weight.'

'Aye.' He nodded. 'You're right there. But that'll come, given time.'

'Wally won't be best pleased. He's enjoying himself doing the round.'

'Wally can take a running jump,' Bill said vehemently. 'The job's mine, and I'm keeping it. He can go back into retirement where he belongs.

Georgie smiled.

'I have to say, Georgie, your visiting me has done me a power of good. I can't thank you enough.'

'You're more than welcome, Bill.'

'I just wish . . .' He trailed off, and shrugged.

'What, Bill?'

'Nothing. Pipe dreams, that's all.'

Her heart began hammering. She was suddenly aware that this was the moment she'd been waiting for. 'I've something to tell you, Bill,' she murmured, in a voice that was only just above a whisper.

'There's nothing wrong, is there?'

'No, nothing wrong.' She took a deep breath. 'Charlie's dead.'

Bill stared blankly at her. 'Dead?'

'Killed while attending a fire. Apparently a section of wall fell on him and a colleague, killing them both. It was covered in the papers, but you wouldn't have read about it as you were ill at the time. If Florrie saw it the name clearly didn't ring a bell.'

Bill was stunned. 'So you're a widow again?'

'That's right.'

'Free?'

'I suppose so.'

'If you're a widow again, then you're free.' He wanted to say it was brilliant news, but he thought it would be tasteless. A man was dead, after all. Even if he had been a bastard who'd caused Georgie a load of grief. 'How do you feel about it?' he asked tentatively instead.

'Relieved. It means Charlie isn't lurking in the background any longer.'

Bill nodded at her honesty. 'So what about us?'

She glanced away.

'Georgie?'

'That depends on you.'

'No it doesn't,' he contradicted her. 'It depends on us.'

True, she thought.

'Well?'

It was time to put it to her mother's test. Was it mere friendship between them, or could it be more? At that point she remained undecided. 'I'd like you to kiss me,' she said in a voice huskier than usual.

Bill didn't need to be asked twice. Going to her, he took her into his arms, gazed deeply into her eyes, then did as she'd requested, aware of her trembling as their lips met.

'I've wanted to do that for a long, long time,' he said when the extended kiss was finally over.

Georgie sighed with contentment. She'd stopped trembling and her insides were positively glowing. It felt so right being in his embrace, so warm and comforting. She knew now, without the shadow of a doubt, that they could be a couple.

'I think you'd better do that again,' she said. 'Just to be certain.'

He frowned. 'Aren't you already?'

'Of course. But I'd like to play a little hard to get.'

'I thoroughly enjoyed that,' she declared as they left the Variety Theatre. 'I haven't laughed so much in ages.'

'Me neither.'

'Some of the jokes were rather blue, though. I found myself blushing more than once.'

395

'You're not some sort of prude, I hope?' he teased.

She blushed again at the suggestion. 'I don't think so. At least I've never considered myself one.'

'That's good. For I'm certainly not.'

She glanced sideways, wondering what it would be like with Bill. He'd never been married, after all, and she'd never thought to question him about past experiences, of which she was sure there must have been some.

She hooked an arm through his, and drew closer to him. 'As it's such a lovely night why don't we walk for a wee bit before catching a tram?' she suggested.

He looked up at a cloudless sky dotted with stars like so many diamonds winking down. It was indeed a lovely night. 'We'll walk if you wish. It'll do us both good.'

He and Georgie had been seriously courting for a number of months now, seeing one another two or three times a week. Learning more about one another, building and strengthening their relationship. Their previous friendship had deepened into something much more than that.

They walked a little way in silence, each savouring the other's company, revelling in just being together.

'I've had a thought,' Bill said finally.

'And what's that?'

'I'm fed up with feeling sad every time I have to say goodnight to you.'

A sense of warmth blossomed inside her, and she pulled herself even closer to him. 'I feel the same way.'

'Then perhaps we should do something about it.'

She glanced at him again, a tightness replacing the warmth in her belly. 'Such as?' she queried softly.

'Get married.'

She came to a sudden stop to stare at him. 'Are you proposing, Bill Bailey?'

'Well, don't look so surprised. You must have guessed I was going to at some time.'

She had, of course. 'Then do it properly.'

He raised his free hand and placed his fingertips against her cheek. 'Will you please marry me, Georgie?'

'And if I say no?' she teased.

'Then I'll shoot myself.'

She laughed. 'Dope.'

'So, what's the verdict?'

Georgie couldn't have been more certain of anything. She and Bill were made for one another. It was, in her opinion, a perfect match. She considered herself extremely lucky to have a third chance with someone. 'I'll marry you, Bill,' she breathed. 'I'll be delighted to.'

Neither cared that they were in the street with people passing in both directions.

They kissed, oblivious of everything around them.

'Getting married!' Florrie exclaimed.

'That's right, Mum.'

'Thank God for that. Off my hands at long last. I thought I was never going to get rid of you.'

Georgie laughed, knowing the old woman was joking.

'Thank you very much,' said Bill, pretending to be hurt.

'Mind you, I've seen it coming for a while now. I'd have had to be blind not to.'

'You approve, then?' Georgie asked.

'What do you think, lassie?'

'Thanks, Mum.'

'Don't thank me. Thank Georgie for taking on a big lump like yourself. She must be mad.'

'I'd be mad to pass him up,' Georgie declared, eyes shining.

Florrie beamed. 'Now, when's the big day?'

'We'll have to organise a house first,' Bill replied. 'We'll name the day after we've found one.'

'Well, you already have. If you want it, that is.'

Georgie frowned. 'I don't understand.'

'This house. It's yours. And more or less everything that's in it.'

'But what about you, Mum?' Bill protested. 'Like Georgie, I don't understand. Are you staying here or going somewhere?'

'I shall be going to live with your Aunt Pru in Helensburgh. She'll jump at the chance of having me there – she's been lonely ever since your Uncle Archie was killed in the war. And I'll enjoy being by the sea, which I've always rather fancied after a lifetime in dirty old Glasgow.'

Bill turned to Georgie. 'What do you think?'

'I'm all for it. And I can't thank you enough, Florrie.'

'That's settled then,' Florrie declared enthusiastically. 'I move out and you two move in. Perfect.'

Georgie thought so too. Absolutely perfect. It was the icing on the cake.

Chapter 30

'There's a letter come for you,' Brigid told Tom on his arrival home from work.

'Oh aye?'

'Official-looking, too. Your name and address have been typed. Posted in Glasgow according to the franking.'

Who could be sending him an official letter from Glasgow? 'Where is it?'

'On the sideboard.'

'Daddy, Daddy, Daddy!' Robin yelled, careering into the room and heading straight for his father. Tom grabbed hold of the lad and swung him aloft, tipping him from side to side as Robin squealed with delight. It was the nightly ritual when Tom got in from Ford.

'One of these days he's going to be sick all over you when you do that,' Brigid prophesied.

'Never. You wouldn't be sick over me, would you, son?'

'No, Daddy.'

'See?' Tom smiled at Brigid, who raised a disbelieving eyebrow. 'And how's my daughter?'

'Sleeping, I'm happy to say.'

Sarah was now two months old, and a lovely child, at least according to Tom and Brigid.

'Has she been fed?'

'Half an hour ago, so she'll stay down for a little while.'

Tom put Robin back on the floor, then crossed to the sideboard to find out what the letter was all about.

'I'm hungry,' Robin announced.

'Tea will soon be on the table. You'll just have to wait.'

Robin pulled a face, then ran from the room.

'I don't know where he gets his energy from,' Brigid declared, shaking her head. 'It makes me tired just watching him.'

Tom picked up the letter, which indeed had a Glasgow postmark. He ripped the envelope open and extracted the single sheet it contained. Quickly he scanned the contents.

'Oh, dear,' he whispered.

'What is it?'

Tom glanced over at his wife, whose expression was one of concern at the tone he'd used. 'Dolly's dead.'

Brigid's hand flew to her mouth. This was dreadful news. 'How?'

'The lawyer doesn't say. It seems she's left me a substantial amount of money and this Mr . . .' Tom looked again at the letter, 'Mr Bird wants me to go up to Glasgow to sign some papers.'

'Go to Glasgow?' Brigid frowned. 'Can you get time off?'

Tom thought about it. 'We are a bit slack at the

moment. If I go to management and show them this letter it should be all right. They're usually fairly reasonable about matters concerning bereavement.'

'Poor Dolly,' Brigid whispered. 'She was such a nice woman.'

'And good to us. It was lovely the times she called in to see us en route to London on her shopping trips.'

Brigid nodded her agreement. 'Substantial amount,' she mused. 'I wonder how much?'

Tom exhaled heavily. 'I have absolutely no idea. But whatever, it was kind of her to remember me in her will.'

Dear Dolly, he thought. He was going to miss her.

'Lena, I'm off out now,' Hamish said, putting his head round the door of her office. She knew that meant the coffee shop. 'And I won't be in for the rest of the afternoon as I'm playing a round of golf later.'

'Well, enjoy yourself.' She glanced at the window where sunshine was streaming in. 'You've got a lovely day for it.'

'Exactly. Now, is there anything you want me to do before I leave?'

She smiled indulgently at him. 'There's nothing, Hamish. You just toddle off.'

He lowered his voice. 'I'll call in this evening, if that's all right by you?'

'Of course it is. I'll be waiting.'

'Good. See you then.'

Lena sighed when he'd gone, and leant back in her chair. The chairman might still be the chairman, and Hamish vice chairman, but it was she who literally ran the company nowadays. The thought gave her a great sense of achievement. Naturally, only she and Hamish knew what the real situation was, but so what? As far as she was concerned that didn't matter.

Who would have thought she'd ever get into a position like this? Certainly not her. She was a woman, after all, and women were kept pegged to a particular level, not allowed to advance into positions of power. Those were strictly men only.

Taking out her cigarettes, she lit up. By God but it felt good to be where she was. Fulfilling, too. The boss in all but name.

She couldn't help but laugh to herself.

'Surprise!'

Chrissie's eyes popped out on stalks, or so it felt like to her. She couldn't believe what she was seeing. 'Tom,' she croaked.

'In the flesh.' He pulled her into his arms and hugged her tight. 'Hello, Mum. How are you?'

'Why didn't you warn us you were coming?'

'I wanted to surprise you.'

Detaching herself, Chrissie wiped tears from her eyes. 'Well, you've done that all right.' She patted her bosom. 'My heart's jumping about like billy-o.'

'Can you put me up for a couple of nights?'

'Aye, of course. Silly to ask. Now come in. Come in.' She shouted through to the kitchen. 'Tam, it's Tom. He's home!'

Tom picked up the small suitcase he'd brought, and the bottle of whisky he'd bought nearby. When he entered the kitchen it was to see Tam standing beaming at him.

'Hello, son.'

'Hello, Papa.'

They shook hands, and Tom gave the bottle to his father. 'I thought we might have a dram?' he suggested.

'Grand idea.'

'So what brings you here?' Chrissie wanted to know. 'Or is it just a visit to see your old mum and papa?'

'A substantial amount of money, you say,' Tam repeated a few minutes later. 'Any notion how much?'

'None at all, Papa. A few hundred, I should imagine.'

'A nice little windfall.'

'Mrs Mulherron was a good woman,' Chrissie commented. 'I fair took to her. How old was she, do you know?'

Tom shook his head.

'And you're seeing this lawyer tomorrow?' Tam said.

'That's right. Half past eleven. He's got offices in Gordon Street.'

Chrissie had a sudden thought. 'Are you hungry, son? I haven't much in, but I could do you an omelette if you like.'

'That would be smashing, Mum. I am a bit peckish.'

'Right then!' She began bustling about.

'It's grand having you back, son,' Tam declared quietly.

'It's good to be back, Papa. Though we are well settled in Dagenham. We enjoy it there.'

'No religious problems, I take it?'

'None.'

Tam nodded his approval.

'Now tell us all about wee Sarah,' Chrissie commanded from the sink. 'There's only so much you can put in a letter. I want to hear everything from your own lips.'

Tom was completely stunned. 'How much?' he eventually asked in a tight voice.

Mr Bird, the lawyer, repeated the sum he'd just mentioned.

'Jesus Christ,' Tom gulped.

Mr Bird, bald, spectacled and in his early forties, smiled at Tom. 'I did advise you in my letter it was a substantial amount.'

Tom shook his head in amazement, still unable to fully take this in. 'A substantial amount to me is obviously very different from a substantial amount to you, Mr Bird. I thought we were talking hundreds, not a bloody fortune.'

'You are her main beneficiary, Mr McKeand. And Mrs Mulherron was an extremely rich woman. By the way, that figure doesn't include the house and contents, which will realise considerable equity in their own right.'

The house as well! Tom couldn't believe it. His mind was reeling. 'But . . . why me?' he stuttered. 'Are there no relatives?'

'I'm afraid not. Mrs Mulherron was quite alone in this world.'

'I see,' Tom murmured.

'Now,' Mr Bird went on, 'there are certain arrangements that have to be made, papers to be signed and so on. So shall we make a start?'

When everything had been completed for the time being, Tom left the lawyer's office and headed straight for the nearest pub. He badly needed a drink while he tried to absorb the bombshell that had just exploded in his life.

Why, he need never work again if he chose not to do so, he realised. In fact there were all sorts of things he could choose whether or not to do. From now on almost anything was possible – financially, anyway. His head was still spinning when he reached the pub and plunged inside.

'So how did you get on?' Chrissie queried anxiously when he finally returned to his parents' house. He wasn't drunk, but not exactly sober either.

'You'd better sit down before I tell you, Mum.'

'Oh aye. A disappointment, eh?'

He waited till she was ensconced in an armchair before relating his conversation with the lawyer.

'Oh, son,' Chrissie whispered when he told her the amount he'd inherited, her face draining of colour. 'Are you sure there's no mistake?'

'Quite. That's what Dolly left me. That plus the house and all its contents.'

Chrissie shook her head in wonder. It was simply incredible. 'Aye, well, you won't be short of a bob or two from now on,' she said. Which must have been the understatement of the year.

'Mr Bird, the lawyer, informed me it was a heart attack,' said Tom.

Smith, the ancient butler, smiled sadly. 'That's correct, sir. Madam was in the morning room and had asked me for her usual glass of sherry. When I returned with it she was sitting with her eyes closed, as if she'd just dropped off to sleep. Thinking that to be the case I left her to it. It wasn't until later that we discovered the truth – that she had in fact passed on.'

'There wouldn't have been any pain, then?'

'I shouldn't think so, sir. It must have been all over in a moment. At least that's what I'd like to believe.' The butler turned away so Tom couldn't see his expression, which was one of profound grief. After a moment he turned back to Tom. 'Sorry about that, sir.'

'That's all right. I understand.' Tom cleared his throat. 'What's going to happen to you now, Smith?'

'Oh, I'll be absolutely fine, sir. Madam was kind enough to leave me a sum that will see me through to my final days. She was extremely generous, I have to say.'

'And the rest of the staff?'

'The same with them, sir. Everyone received something. No one was left out.'

'That's good.'

Smith glanced sadly around the morning room, a thousand memories flitting through his mind. 'Can I enquire what you intend to do with the house, sir?'

'Sell it, I'm afraid. I live in England now, as you know, and have no intention of returning to Glasgow. So the house is surplus to requirements.'

'I thought as much, sir. We all, the staff that is, did.'

'I shall be having valuers in to appraise the contents, which will then be sold, or auctioned off. When that's done the house will go on the market. It's so beautiful I shouldn't imagine it'll take long to be snapped up.'

'No, sir,' Smith agreed.

'In the meantime I wish you and the others to stay on

until such times as you find new employment, or the house is sold. Whichever comes first.'

'That's kind of you, sir.'

Tom regarded the ancient butler. 'I presume you won't be looking for another job, but retiring?'

'Quite correct, sir.'

'Where will you go?'

'I've already considered that, though I haven't yet come to any decision. But I shall find a place all right, don't you worry about that.'

'You're going to miss being here,' Tom said softly. 'It'll be an awful wrench to leave. I can only say I'm sorry, being the cause of it.'

Smith shook his head. 'You're not the cause, sir. Madam's dying is.' He hesitated, then said, 'It never crossed my mind that she'd go before me. And yet she has. One of life's little ironies, I suppose.'

'Yes,' Tom agreed.

'It was a lovely funeral, sir. All the staff were there, plus a few of Madam's friends. It was a tearful farewell right enough.'

'Dolly was buried before I found out about her death, otherwise I too would have attended.'

Smith nodded that he understood.

'There's something I'd like to do before I go,' Tom declared.

'Which is, sir?'

'See round the house. Is that possible?'

'Of course, sir. It is yours now, after all. You're perfectly entitled. Where would you care to begin?'

'I'll let you decide that.'

'Very good, sir. If you'll just follow me.'

It turned out to be even bigger than Tom had thought. Absolutely huge, in fact. What a pity he had to sell, he mused on leaving. But he had no intention of returning to Glasgow and its religious bigotry. No, he and his family were settled down south, and that's where they'd stay.

'So what are you going to do with all that money?' Tam asked. He and Tom were having a drink in a local pub.

'I have no idea, Papa. And that's the truth.'

'Will you keep on working at Ford?'

'Maybe, maybe not. One thing's certain, I'm not jumping rashly into anything. That would be stupid.'

Tam nodded his agreement. 'Very wise of you.'

'Once everything's settled and the money's in my account, I want to send you and Mum a cheque. I hope you're not going to be all stiff-necked and say you'll refuse?'

Tam had a swallow from his pint while he considered that. He had his pride to think of, after all. There again, Tom was his son, and he wanted to share some of his good fortune with him and Chrissie.

'Well, Papa?'

'For your mum's sake, eh? Maybe make life a wee bit easier for her.'

'Exactly.'

Tom extended a hand and the two of them shook on it.

'I have to admit, you've made a beautiful job of your "apartment",' Tom said. He had arranged by telephone to pay Lena a visit.

'Thank you.'

He stared at her, thinking there was something different about his sister. Something he couldn't quite put his finger on.

'Drink?'

'Please.'

'Whisky or gin?'

He smiled. 'Whisky, please. I hate gin.'

She hadn't known that. 'Have you seen Georgie and her new husband since you got back?' she asked, busying herself with the glasses.

'Last night, as a matter of fact.'

'What did you think of Bill?'

'Seemed a decent enough chap to me. It was obvious the pair of them get on well enough.'

Lena handed him his whisky. 'I like him too. Georgie seems to have landed on her feet this time after the one she had before.'

'Aye,' Tom muttered. 'That Charlie was a bad lot right enough. Bloody pervert.'

Lena raised her glass in a toast. 'Here's to Georgie and her new marriage, may it be a long and happy one.'

They both drank. 'Now, what about you?' Tom queried.

'What about me?'

'Well, for a start, how are you getting on living alone?'

If only he knew, Lena thought. If only he knew. Hamish was with her three evenings most weeks nowadays. She might not be married like Georgie, but she had the next best thing. A lot more than she'd ever thought would come her way. And she was profoundly grateful. It was enough to satisfy her.

She smiled. 'Just fine.'

'That's good.' He didn't add that it wouldn't have suited him.

'And how does it feel to be Mr Moneybags?'

He laughed. 'I still haven't really got used to the idea. I certainly don't feel any different.'

'No?'

'Not really. I half expect to wake up one morning and find it's all been a dream.'

'And what does Brigid think?'

'She had hysterics when I told her on the phone. I had quite a job convincing her I wasn't pulling her leg.'

'Understandable, I suppose,' Lena mused. 'It's not every day you're left a fortune completely out of the blue.'

'No, it isn't,' Tom agreed.

How much more relaxed his sister was than he recalled, Tom thought. Previously she'd been permanently wound up, on edge, bad-tempered. But all that had now seemingly disappeared. There again, maybe he'd just caught her on a particularly good night.

'You've put on a little weight,' he commented. 'It suits you.'

'Thank you.'

He noticed her bust was fuller too, but didn't mention that. The Lena of old would have snapped his head off if he had, telling him to mind his own bloody business. She would have thought it was far too personal a remark to make.

All in all it was a very pleasant visit, and then it was time for Tom to leave. At the door they hugged, and kissed cheeks, she telling him to take care, and give her love to his family, he wishing her all the very best for the future.

How strange, Tom thought as he strode off down the road. Why on earth had there been a man's collar stud on Lena's dressing table? If she had a chap in tow why hadn't she mentioned it?

How very strange.

Tom carefully laid the wreath he'd brought along on Dolly's grave, which already boasted several other wreaths and flower arrangements.

'I just wanted to say thank you personally, Dolly. You were a wonderful human being and I'll miss you.'

He stood there in silence for a few minutes, remembering the Belgrave and how good she'd been at gambling, and other things.

There was a choke in his throat, and a hint of tears in his eyes, when he finally left the graveside and made his way out of the cemetery.

Tom was on the train home again when the idea suddenly came to him. An idea which instantly appealed. Appealed a great deal. In fact, an idea he considered inspirational.

He'd set up his own business, a manufacturing one. He'd produce nuts and bolts as Freddy, Dolly's husband, had so successfully done. Start small, and then, as he got established, expand. With his contacts at Ford surely he could become a supplier to them? He'd told his father he wasn't going to rush into anything, nor would he. There would be a lot to learn before striking out on his own.

No, not quite on his own. He'd take Ian, Georgie's son,

with him. Eventually put him into a managerial position. Georgie, not to mention Ian himself, would love that.

Oh yes, what a brilliant idea. And one, he was sure, of which Dolly would wholeheartedly have approved.

Twilight Time

FOR PAT

WISE AGENT, DEAR FRIEND

Here's looking at you, kid!

Chapter 1

'Chocolate!' Maggs Fletcher paused for a moment to glare at her mother, face flushed with indignation and outrage. 'You've never ever made me a chocolate cake, not even on my last birthday, which was my twenty-first.'

Lavender Fletcher sighed. 'I simply thought I'd do something different this time round, that's all. So just calm down and don't spoil your sister's big day.'

The glare was turned on Crista, the sister in question. 'Spoilt brat! They've always favoured you.'

'That's not true,' Crista retorted.

'Yes it is.'

'No it's not.'

'It is so.'

'Oh for God's sake shut up, the pair of you,' Lavender interjected, beginning to get angry. 'No one's been favoured over the other. Your father and I have always been careful about that. Right, Davey?'.

Davey had been sitting watching this exchange, an amused glint in his eyes. Not for the first time he was thankful for having a sense of humour. In his opinion you certainly needed one living with three women as he did. He agreed with a nod.

'The only reason I made the cake chocolate was because I came across a new recipe I wanted to try out,' Lavender explained.

'Huh!' Maggs snorted, not believing a word of it.

'Why don't you open your present, maid,' Davey suggested to Crista, hoping to change the subject.

'It's on the mantelpiece,' Lavender declared, smiling at her daughter, who'd turned seventeen that day.

Maggs's expression became one of suspicion. Crista had better not get something better than she'd got on her twenty-first or there would be all hell to pay.

So far there was only a single present for Crista, but no doubt there would be others later from the various relations who lived in the village. They'd probably be popping by after tea.

Crista tore open an envelope and read the card it contained. 'Thanks, Mum and Dad,' she beamed. She opened the second, and final, envelope, which held a card from Maggs. 'Thanks, Sis.'

'I would have bought you something but I'm broke.' Maggs shrugged. 'You know how it is.'

That annoyed Lavender, but she didn't say anything. Maggs had been well aware that Crista's birthday was coming up and could surely have made provision. She earned a decent enough wage after all, with more than enough left over after she'd paid for her 'lodge', the contribution she made to the house. One thing was certain: when the boot was on the other foot, Crista always had a present for her sister.

2

'That's all right,' Crista replied good-naturedly. 'A card is just fine.'

'Come on then, do the honours,' Davey urged.

Inside the paper wrapping was a small cardboard box, and inside the box three dainty ladies' handkerchiefs of finest Irish linen. 'Oh, they're lovely,' Crista enthused, genuinely thrilled.

'Your initial is embroidered on a corner of each,' Lavender pointed out. 'Did them myself.'

Crista went over to her mother and kissed her on the cheek. 'Ta, Mum.'

Davey cleared his throat, indicating he too wanted a kiss, which he duly got.

For a moment Lavender's eyes misted over in memory of her son Wilf, the eldest of their three children, who'd been killed in action while fighting in Palestine during the final stages of the Great War. How she missed her darling boy. Not a single day went by when she didn't stop and think of him, remember him, grieve for him.

'I don't know about you but I'm starving,' Davey declared, coming to his feet. 'And there's that cake to look forward to afterwards. I want an especially big piece myself.'

Lavender smiled affectionately. Her Davey had always had a sweet tooth. Sweet as the man himself.

'What's for tea then?' Maggs queried, for she too was hungry after a long hard shift at the mill where she, Crista and Davey all worked.

'Tripe and onions,' Lavender teased, smiling inwardly to see Maggs's face fall. Maggs absolutely loathed tripe and onions.

'You're joking, Mum!' Maggs wailed.

'Why would I do that?' Lavender asked, straight-faced, thinking, Serves you right for not buying Crista a present.

'Nothing wrong with tripe and onions,' Davey stated, himself quite partial to the dish.

'I love it when it slips and slithers down your throat,' Crista said, a hint of laughter in her voice, smiling when she saw Maggs wince. 'But it's best of all when you chew it.'

Maggs felt sick, her stomach having just flipped over. Tripe was disgusting, the slimy taste it left in your mouth simply horrendous. As for chewing it! She shuddered at the thought.

'Please say you're joking, Mum?' she pleaded. 'Please say you are?'

Lavender relented, deciding not to take the tease any further. 'It's liver, actually. Liver and onions.'

Maggs let out a huge sigh of relief. 'Thank God for that.'

'With chocolate cake for afters. Now, if you'll all come through we can eat.'

Maggs wasn't madly keen on liver either, but it was preferable – anything was preferable – to the dreaded tripe.

Crista groaned when their alarm clock started to jangle. Five a.m., the start of another working day. Well, she consoled herself, it was nearly the weekend when she could sleep in for a bit. And there was a dance on Saturday night, which was something to look forward to. She supposed it would be the same old faces: people she'd grown up and gone to school with. And who, for the main part, also worked at the

4

mill, the village's largest employer. Still, you never knew, there was always the chance that a stranger or two might be there. It did occasionally happen.

'Maggs, Crista, are you both awake?' Lavender demanded from the landing outside their shared bedroom.

Maggs swung her feet on to the floor. 'I'm up, Mum,' she replied wearily, and yawned.

'Me too, Mum,' Crista added, throwing back her bedclothes.

Forty-five minutes later found them, father and daughters, leaving the cottage and joining the stream of workers heading for the mill that lay on the outskirts of the village.

Lavender sensed something was amiss when she saw three of her neighbours talking animatedly outside the bakery.

Mavis Davis looked up at Lavender's approach. 'Have you heard the news, Lavender?' she called out.

'What news?' Lavender queried on reaching them.

'Old Doc Mumsford was found dead in his bed this morning, having passed away in his sleep during the night. It was Terry, the postman, found him.'

'Dear God!' Lavender whispered, deeply shocked.

'Dead as a dodo,' Mrs Green added, wanting to get her ha'p'orth in.

'Terry knocked and knocked because he had a parcel for the doc,' Mavis went on. 'He thought it strange when there was no reply, as he knew the doc should be in getting ready for morning surgery. Anyway, to cut a long story short, Terry went inside, the door always open as you know, realised something wasn't right, and eventually discovered the doc dead in bed.'

'Lovely man,' Mrs Radmore said, shaking her head. 'Delivered all my children. Was kindness itself.'

'He'll be missed all right,' Mrs Green added. 'And him such a good doctor too.'

It was taking Lavender a few moments to digest this thunderbolt. Why, she'd spoken to Doc Mumsford only a couple of days ago, when he stopped her in the street to inquire how she and the family were.

'Terrible, isn't it?' Mavis said to Lavender.

'Awful.'

'He was a good age mind you, well into his seventies I believe,' Mrs Radmore, the eldest of them, declared. 'But he was never the same after his wife died all those years ago. Lonely years for him in many ways, I should imagine.'

Lavender recalled Fay Mumsford well, a tiny creature with the sunniest of natures. She and the doc had been madly in love, he absolutely heartbroken when she'd succumbed to the cancer that carried her off.

'He was in this practice for almost fifty years, Terry said. Terry was terribly upset. Well, you can understand. It was doc saw his boy through the diphtheria. Terry always reckoned they'd have lost young Harry if it hadn't been for Doc Mumsford at their house night and day till the crisis was finally over. God bless him.'

'A saint,' Mavis declared quietly. 'He was truly a saint.'

'Has a date been set yet for the funeral?' Lavender queried.

6

'Too early for that,' Mrs Radmore replied. 'But I for one will be going. Wild horses wouldn't keep me away.'

They all agreed it was the same with them. They'd definitely be there no matter what.

The news went round the village like wildfire and for the rest of the day it was the main topic of conversation in every shop, pub and wherever people stopped or gathered. Old Doc Mumsford was dead. May he rest in peace.

'Have you heard . . .'

'About Doc Mumsford?' Davey interjected. 'This morning. Everyone's been talking about it the length and breadth of the mill.'

'Does anyone know yet what happened?' Maggs asked. She, Crista and their father had just arrived in from work.

'The word is it was a heart attack,' Lavender replied. 'But I'm sure that's just guesswork. It won't be known for certain until after the post-mortem.'

Davey slumped into a chair and ran a hand over his face. 'I wonder who'll replace him?' he mused. 'Whoever, I hope he arrives soon. The village can't go for long without a doctor.'

Lavender nodded her agreement. She knew at least three women who were expecting imminently, one at any time. No doubt the mothers-to-be would cope if necessary, with help from female neighbours and the like, but it was always best to have a doctor handy in case anything went wrong.

'He was such a nice old man,' Crista commented, remembering how he used to give her the occasional

7

sweet when she was younger. As indeed he'd done with most of the village children.

'Well he's gone now,' Davey said darkly, thinking death hadn't exactly been a stranger in the village over the past few years. The Great War, which had ended the previous year, had seen to that. Fifteen sons of the village, including their Wilf, had gone off and never come back. Lovely lads every one. Damn all warmongers to hell!

'Can you keep my tea for a while, love?' he asked Lavender. 'I'd like to go down to the pub for a bit. If you don't mind, that is.'

It was very unusual for Davey to go to the pub during the week but Lavender could understand why he wanted to go now. Doc Mumsford had been everyone's friend. 'Of course I don't mind. It's stew, which I can dish up whenever, so don't feel you have to hurry back.'

'Thanks. I won't be too long.'

'So how was the mill today?' Lavender inquired cheerily of the girls after Davey had gone, wanting to get away from the subject of Doc Mumsford.

'Nothing ever changes there. It's the same day after day,' Maggs answered.

'Never changes,' Crista agreed disconsolately.

The gloom returned.

Crista didn't know why she ever bothered coming to these dances held once a month in the village hall. They were always the same, boring beyond belief. There again, it was something to do, somewhere to go. The alternative was to stay home, yet again.

'Hello, Maggs. Crista,' said Tom Woolocombe, a lad

8

who'd been in Maggs's year at school. Unlike many of the others he hadn't gone to work at the mill but become an apprentice butcher.

'Hello, Tom,' Maggs replied, while Crista smiled in greeting. 'How are you?'

'Fine.'

'Been down the pub?'

'Of course, maid. It's Saturday night, tain't it?'

'Who was there?'

He reeled off a list of familiar names. 'Haven't seen you there for ages?'

Maggs shrugged. 'I used to go with Betty Saunders, but she won't go in any more and I can't on me own. I'd be talked about if I did. Get a reputation.'

Tom grinned. 'True enough. There again, why not take Crista along?' His eyes twinkled as he made the suggestion.

'She isn't old enough, as you well know, Tom Woolocombe. Spanish John would refuse to serve her and ask her to leave right away. You know how strict he is about that sort of thing.' Nobody knew why Spanish John was so called as he had no Spanish connections whatsoever. It might have been because he was swarthy in appearance, but no one knew for certain.

'There's another pub, maid.'

'It would be the same in them. Come back when you're eighteen, until then stay out.'

Tom winked at Crista. 'I've got a bottle hid out back. Scotch. Fancy a swig or two?'

'No she does not!' Maggs retorted hotly. 'And she's certainly not going out the back with you or anyone else. So there.'

9

'All right, all right, don't get excited,' he protested. 'I was only being friendly like.'

Maggs laughed. 'Believe that and you'll believe pigs can fly.'

Crista was annoyed with her sister for interfering. She was well capable of looking after herself, thank you very much.

'I've seen flying pigs,' Tom declared, tongue firmly in cheek.

'Have you indeed,' Maggs replied acidly.

'I have. I swear.'

'Don't be daft, Tom Woolocombe, tain't no such things.'

'There can be after eight or so pints of strong cider,' he retorted, and laughed. 'Flying pigs, pink elephants, all sorts.'

Crista found that funny.

'Get on with you,' Maggs snorted, also amused.

'Don't work with Scotch though, only cider,' Tom went on, slightly belabouring the joke.

Maggs glanced across the floor to where a group of chaps were talking loudly and generally larking about. 'That bunch look as though they've been at the cider.' Even as she spoke one of the lads lost his balance and went crashing to the floor to end up on his backside, provoking loud guffaws and much thigh-slapping from his companions.

'I reckon they have,' Tom agreed.

'There'll be some sore heads in the morning,' Crista commented.

'Tain't a good Saturday night unless you have a headache next day,' Tom riposted lightly.

'Oh really?'

'Really,' he nodded. 'Take my word for it.'

Utter nonsense, Crista thought. But that was young men for you. Half of them would have lived in the pub if it had been possible.

The band, an even worse lot than usual, struck up, having just returned from a break.

'How about a dance then, young Crista?' Tom queried, the twinkle back in his eyes.

That surprised her. 'With you?'

He pretended to look about him. 'I didn't hear anyone else speak.'

'I don't know,' she prevaricated.

'What don't you know, maid? I've asked ee to dance. The answer's simple enough, yes or no.'

Oh, why not, she thought. It would be rude not to accept his invitation. Not that she fancied him, not in the least. He just wasn't her type, whatever that was.

'As long as you don't step on my feet,' she said. She knew from painful experience that village lads had a bad habit of doing that. Most of them couldn't dance for toffee.

'How about if I promise to be extra careful?'

'All right then.'

He extended a bent arm to her. 'Then shall we, Cristabel Fletcher?'

That took her aback a little. It wasn't often she was called Cristabel. 'Certainly, Thomas Woolocombe.'

Maggs watched them join the other dancers, slightly miffed that it wasn't she who'd been asked up. Tom was one of her peer group, after all. Oh well, she mentally shrugged. Plenty more fish in the sea.

It was about five minutes later, Tom and Crista still

11

dancing, when a voice said quietly beside her, 'Hello, Maggs. It's been a long time.'

She turned to find herself staring at a somehow familiar face, a face badly disfigured with scars and puckering. The left eye was pulled right down and out of shape.

'In case you don't recognise me, it's Dickie Trippett. Remember?'

The breath caught in her throat. Of course she remembered Dickie Trippett. They'd been childhood sweethearts, of the most innocent kind, when in their early teens. She now saw with a shock that he was also missing an arm.

'Hello, Dickie,' she croaked. 'The grapevine said you got back some time ago.' She meant back from the war.

'I haven't felt like coming out too much.' He glanced down at the floor. 'Embarrassed, I suppose.'

Her heart instantly went out to him. Poor Dickie. He'd been such a handsome lad, too. Quite gorgeous and a great favourite amongst the girls. 'I heard you'd been wounded,' she nodded.

'Blown up, actually. I'm lucky to be alive.'

Oh my God, she thought. What on earth to say? 'What are you doing nowadays?'

He gave a hollow laugh. 'Not a lot. Living with my folks, and . . . well, not a lot.'

'It's good to see you,' she said simply, her voice ringing with sincerity.

'Thanks, Maggs. It's good to see you too.' He gazed around. 'It was my mum talked me into coming here tonight. Though I'm beginning to think it might have been a mistake.'

'Why so?'

His mouth tightened. 'People staring, that sort of thing. And when I do speak to someone there's . . .' He broke off, reluctant to go on.

'There's what, Dickie?' she prompted quietly.

'Pity,' he said in almost a whisper. 'Pity in their eyes. It makes me squirm inside.'

She could well understand that. Both the pity in people's eyes, and his reaction to it. 'How long were you in hospital for?' she asked.

'Absolutely ages. They tried to do things with my face, but, well, they weren't exactly successful. Though I suppose it could have been a lot worse. Some of the chaps in the hospital with me, particularly the burns cases, ended up a frightful mess. Two of them committed suicide when I was there. Both hanged themselves.'

The dance number ended, followed by general applause. Maggs noted that Crista appeared to be staying up with Tom. 'Fancy a shuffle?' She smiled.

He looked at her in surprise. 'I've only got one arm, Maggs.'

'So? You've still got two feet, haven't you?'

That made him smile, a sort of horrible twisted grimace. 'Could you cope with a one-armed man?'

'I've no idea. But I can try. I'm game if you are?'

Dickie studied her for a moment. 'Are you certain?'

'Absolutely. Now come on.'

It was difficult for the pair of them, but somehow they managed. Maggs stayed up with Dickie for a full half hour. For old times' sake if nothing else.

★ ★ ★

13

Davey was furious, absolutely livid. And he wasn't the only one. It was the day of Doc Mumsford's funeral and none of the work force at the mill had been allowed time off to attend, even though Doc Mumsford had been the mill doctor in addition to his other duties.

Various foremen had been spoken to, and their requests had gone to management, right up to Mr Swain the owner. Back had come the decree: no time off, with no exceptions. It was a work day and that was that.

Ford Paper Mill was a large, sprawling affair, built in mid-Victorian times by the Swain family, and remaining in their possession ever since. The Swains were landed gentry, also owning four large farms in the area, and by far, so the story went, the richest family in that part of Devon. Another Swain, cousin to Miles Swain the mill owner, was the local Liberal Member of Parliament.

Davey glanced up at a wall clock close to the paper guillotine he was operating. The funeral would have started by now, and how he wished he was there and not where he was. It was a consideration of respect after all, something he'd had a great deal of, as had many others, where the old doc was concerned.

'Bloody capitalist bastards,' he muttered angrily to himself. It would have been an entirely different matter if it had been Miles Swain's funeral. A very different matter. Then the whole place would have been closed down for the day. Perhaps even longer.

Seething inside, Davey got on with the job in hand. As always, he was extremely careful. Guillotines were dangerous things.

★ ★ ★

'Dear Lord and Father of mankind,
Forgive our foolish ways!
Re-clothe us in our rightful mind,
In purer lives thy service find,
In deeper reverence praise.'

Mavis Davis, who'd been softly singing, now sighed. 'I just love that hymn, don't you, Lavender?'

Lavender nodded. 'It's very pretty.'

'And moving.'

Lavender and Mavis, with others in front and behind, were leaving the church on their way to the Angel pub where Spanish John and his wife Dee Dee were laying on a free buffet for anyone who cared to join in.

'I think it's a disgrace the mill people weren't allowed to attend, don't you?' Mavis went on.

'I couldn't agree more.'

'Those money-grabbing, hifalutin, noses-in-the-air Swains, it's typical of them to have done something like this. No wonder they're hated. Each and every last one of them.'

Again, Lavender couldn't have agreed more. But even so, she reflected, it had been a great turnout, the entire church packed. Sadly, there were no relatives present, for the simple reason that it had transpired Doc Mumsford didn't have any, not even a single offspring. The Mumsfords had never been blessed. Doc Mumsford had been quite alone in the world.

They went into the Angel where, sure enough, Dee Dee had laid out a magnificent buffet of sandwiches, sausage rolls, pickled eggs, cheese, sliced Scotch eggs

15

and the like. 'I say, that looks wonderful,' Lavender enthused to Spanish John, who was behind the bar.

'He was a good customer, old Doc Mumsford,' John replied. 'It was the least we could do.'

Folk were piling in now so Lavender hastily placed their order, a gin and orange for herself, a half of beer shandy for Mavis.

'Still no word of a replacement doctor?' Mavis asked as they made their way to a table.

'Nothing that I've heard. But I believe the doctor in Clyst Barton is going to take a surgery once a week and be on hand for emergencies should they crop up.' Clyst Barton was a village about five miles away from Ford. There had always been great rivalry between the two places.

Mavis sniffed. 'Don't like ee. My sister lives in Clyst Barton as you know, and she says ee's a proper pig. No manners whatsoever.'

'At least it's something. Better than no one at all,' Lavender pointed out, to which Mavis had to reluctantly agree.

'Lovely service, didn't you think?' Mrs Radmore declared, joining them.

'The vicar spoke well.' Mavis nodded.

Lavender noted that Mrs Green had appeared to head straight for the food without first buying a drink. Not very polite, she thought.

Spanish John and Dee Dee were now extremely busy behind the bar, the pub quickly filling up. The men present either didn't work at the mill or were retired.

'I see the Greeds have managed to come despite her not being well recently,' Mavis said, having been scanning the crowd. The Greeds were a retired couple.

'And the Towsers,' added Mrs Radmore, nodding in their direction.

There was a few moments' hush while Dee Dee announced that everyone was just to help themselves to food and not wait on ceremony.

'Have you noticed something?' Mavis asked Lavender.

'Noticed what?'

'Not one member of the Swain family here. Nor did I see any of them in the church.'

'Typical,' Lavender muttered crossly. 'Just typical.'

'Did you expect anything else?' Mrs Radmore queried with a frown.

They had to admit they hadn't.

Chapter 2

'Oh, Mrs Fletcher! Can you wait up?'

Lavender stopped and turned on hearing her name, recognising the voice as belonging to the vicar. She was on her way home from the butcher's, where she'd bought some lovely skirt of beef for their tea that evening.

The Reverend Tricknell came hurrying alongside. 'Can you spare me a few moments?'

'Of course, vicar.'

He gestured that they should resume walking. 'I have a favour to ask.'

'Oh! Which is?'

'I was wondering if you, and a few other ladies from the village, could spare some time to clean and tidy up the doctor's house. I've been in there and unfortunately it's a right tip.'

Lavender could well believe it. Doc Mumsford had lived by himself, without the assistance of a house-keeper which he'd always refused to have, so it was hardly surprising the place was in a mess.

'Of course, vicar. I'll be only too happy to help.'

He nodded his appreciation. 'Thank you, Mrs

Fletcher. It wouldn't do for the new doctor to arrive and find the house in its present state.'

'New doctor!' Lavender exclaimed. 'So they've found one, then? We'd all come to the conclusion it might take some time, there not being any relatives or the like to tackle the legal side of things, which we thought might cause some problems.'

'And so it might have done,' the vicar agreed. 'Except Doc Mumsford was far-sighted enough to arrange matters in his will.'

'I see.'

'Doc had consulted a solicitor in Exeter some years back, apparently. On his death the practice, with house included, was to be advertised in the relevant medical journals, the proceeds of the sale to be bequeathed to the trustees of the village hall, the money to be used for total and complete refurbishment. Which the hall desperately needs, as you're aware.'

It certainly did, Lavender reflected.

'So matters were able to proceed forthwith, without any delay,' Reverend Tricknell went on. 'The practice has now been advertised and bought, and the new doctor will be arriving sometime in the next week or two.'

This was wonderful news, Lavender thought. The entire village would be pleased. 'Do you know his name yet?'

The vicar shook his head. 'I know nothing whatsoever about the gentleman. Neither age, marital status or where he's coming from.' He cast a shrewd eye at Lavender. 'You're the first I've told so far, so no doubt you'll want to spread the word.'

Lavender flushed slightly. 'I don't gossip as a rule. But this is hardly gossip, is it?'

'Not at all,' Tricknell replied with a small grin. Unless he was far mistaken the news would be round the entire village by that evening. Perhaps even sooner. That's how villages were, gossip a staple diet amongst the women.

'I'll mention it to whoever I bump into,' Lavender declared.

Tricknell just bet she would. 'I thought this Thursday for the cleaning. About ten a.m. Would that suit?'

'Fine by me.' Lavender nodded.

'Four women should be enough, I'd imagine.'

'More than enough.'

'Then I'll arrange it.'

They parted outside the Fletchers' cottage, Lavender saying goodbye and then going in to start preparing the evening meal.

On second thoughts, she decided to leave that until later. Mavis Davis would be her first port of call to have a chat with.

As Tricknell had foreseen, there wasn't a household in Ford which didn't know about the imminent arrival of the new doctor come teatime.

'Usual?'

Dickie Trippett nodded. 'Please, John.'

Spanish John began pouring a pint. 'Lovely day again.'

Dickie glanced out of the nearest window. 'It is that. If it keeps up harvesting will be early this year.'

'That'll keep the farmers happy, eh?'

Dickie laughed. 'I suppose so. Which'll be a change,

they're usually such a miserable bunch. Being miserable is a way of life with them.'

'Nothing ever right. Or rarely. All gloom, doom and despondency. Not to mention tight with their pennies. They're Scrooges one and all.'

Dickie groped in his pocket and placed the correct money on the bar. That was the last of his cash for a while, the thought of which made him despair. 'Do you get many in here?' he inquired, referring to farmers.

'Not often. As I said, they're all Scrooges who hate putting their hands in their pockets unless they absolutely have to.'

Their conversation was interrupted at that point by the arrival of a motor car outside. Motor cars were something of a rarity in Ford. Spanish John raised an eyebrow, wondering who it might be.

A few moments later a young man breezed in, his clothes – cravat, hacking jacket, well-tailored corduroy trousers and brogues – indicating he was a 'toff'.

'Good morning, landlord,' the toff boomed in an upper-class accent.

'Good morning, sir.'

'Large Scotch if you please.'

'Any preference, sir?'

Dickie was amused. He'd never before seen John being deferential. Well, perhaps deferential was too strong a word. Obviously respectful might be a better way of putting it.

'Not really. Unless you have some Chivas?'

'Sorry, sir. I don't run to that.'

'Then whatever.'

The toff produced a silver cigarette case and lit up,

21

using what appeared to be a very expensive lighter. Having done that he produced a wallet and placed a pound note on the bar. 'One for yourself, landlord?'

'Not for me, sir. Far too early. But thank you all the same. Water?'

'Any soda?'

'Indeed I have, sir.'

'Just a splash then.'

The toff accepted his drink and immediately saw off half of it. 'Thirsty work, driving, what?'

'I wouldn't know, sir. I don't have a motor car myself.'

'Well take my word for it, it can be.'

The toff swivelled round to stare good-naturedly at Dickie. 'Would you care to join me?'

'No thank you.'

For a moment something painful flickered across the toff's face, and then was gone. 'I don't wish to be rude, but did you lose your arm in the war?'

Dickie nodded.

'Thought so.'

'At Ypres. The third battle.'

The toff's expression became grim. 'Bloody business from what I understand. Bit of a shambles. Though our chaps were brave as always.'

The toff finished his Scotch and asked for another. 'Devons?' he inquired.

'That's right.'

'Was in the Household Cavalry myself.' He broke off, his brow furrowing. When he continued it was very quietly. 'Nearly bought it myself on several occasions.'

Dickie didn't know what to answer to that, so didn't.

'Are you sure you won't have a drink with me?' the toff asked, brightening a little. 'And we'll have a toast. Absent friends, what?'

Dickie couldn't refuse when that was the toast. 'I can't buy you one back, I'm afraid. I'm skint.'

'No need,' the toff assured him. 'I'm off after this anyway.'

Dickie finished his pint which John duly refilled. The toast was made, the toff draining his glass in one swallow.

'Right then. That's me. Cheerio.'

'Cheerio.' Dickie smiled, grateful for the second pint.

'Goodbye for now, sir,' John said as the toff left with a backward wave.

'I wonder who he was?' Dickie mused after the car had driven away.

'Rupert Swain,' John informed him. 'Lives in London now, I believe. He's the youngest son.'

'So he's been in before?'

'A number of times. Always en route to the family home. Never stays long. A quickie, or a couple of quickies, and that's it.'

'Seemed a reasonable enough bloke. For a Swain, that is.'

Spanish John smiled to hear Dickie qualify what he'd thought about Rupert. 'Always been pleasant enough to me, which is how I judge a customer. Had the old man in once and he's a very different kettle of fish. A complete bastard through and through in my opinion. The sort you just naturally want to hit.'

'Sounds about right, from what I've heard of him.'

John had been washing Rupert's glass during this

exchange, and now began polishing it. 'Any luck in finding a job?' he asked casually.

Dickie barked out a bitter laugh. 'There aren't many openings, it seems, for one-armed men. Even if that arm was lost fighting for King and Country.'

'You were at the mill before, weren't you?'

'Training as a machine operator. That's gone by the board now, of course. Nor did they have anything else they felt they could offer me.' Dickie gazed moodily into his pint. 'I do have a small pension from the army, but God knows how I can survive on that. I'd be right up shit street if I wasn't living with my parents.'

'So it's pretty bad, eh?'

'Just a bit,' Dickie replied morosely.

'How about working here then?'

That took Dickie completely by surprise. He gaped at John. 'Here?'

'As a barman.'

'But . . . ?' Dickie shook his head. 'How could I be a barman with only one arm?'

John stopped what he was doing to stare at Dickie. 'I knew a one-armed landlord once. It didn't seem to bother him. He coped all right.'

'Really?'

'Really. I'm not saying it'll be easy, especially to start with – I'm sure I'll have a few broken pint pots. But I'm willing to give it a go if you are?'

Dickie was dumbstruck.

'Just one thing though. If it doesn't pan out I don't want any hard feelings on your part. Is it a deal?'

'Yes please,' Dickie replied in a cracked whisper, his delight, not to mention relief, all too evident.

'The wages aren't great, but certainly enough to

get by on. You can live in too if you wish, have your own room. The board and lodge would be reflected in your wage, of course. Or you can continue staying with your folks. I don't mind either way.'

'I'll have to talk to my mum about that.'

'You do that, Dickie.'

'When can I start?' he queried eagerly.

'Monday morning, eleven o'clock. And we'll go from there.'

Dickie shook his head. 'I don't know what to say. Truly I don't.'

John smiled. 'You don't have to. I think I can guess. Now how about a pint on the house to settle the deal.'

When Dickie finally returned home he felt he was walking on air. He'd found a job at long last! Miracles did happen after all.

The vicar hadn't exaggerated, Lavender reflected. Doc's house was in a right old state. Talk about a pigsty!

'This'll take some doing,' Mavis observed, and Lavender nodded her agreement. The other two women present were Mrs Tricknell, the vicar's wife, and Dolly Tyler, all four having brought their own cleaning materials. Lavender didn't have much time for Dolly, who somehow always succeeded in rubbing her up the wrong way. Lavender also suspected Dolly had volunteered for the job so she could have a good old snoop around doc's house. That was Dolly all over.

'Best get started,' Mrs Tricknell declared.

'I think we should take a room each,' Lavender suggested, which the other three agreed was a good idea. They wouldn't get under each other's feet that way.

'I'll take the study,' Dolly announced, for Lavender was right: she was there for a good old snoop and thought the study might be the best place for that. At least to begin with.

The house was a large one with six bedrooms, a dining room, drawing room, kitchen and scullery. It also boasted a combined bathroom and lavatory, considered a luxury in Ford where the majority of houses had outside conveniences.

Lavender's heart dropped when she went into the kitchen. There were stacks of dirty dishes everywhere, some of them looking as though they hadn't been washed in years. 'Dear God,' she whispered, deciding the first thing for her to do was boil up some water. She was going to need a lot of that.

Meanwhile Mavis was rolling up a rug, intent on hanging it over the washing line so she could give it a good bashing with the cane carpet beater she'd brought along. Seconds after Mavis began whacking, which she did lustily, she was surrounded by clouds of swirling dust.

About an hour later Mrs Tricknell appeared in the kitchen, sweat running down her face. 'This is going to be a bigger job than I anticipated,' she said to Lavender. 'You don't want to even see the state of the bedlinen.'

Lavender could well imagine. Doc Mumsford may have been a great doctor, but he'd certainly been a total loss at keeping house. 'The copper's over there,' she declared, pointing.

'I'll fire it up,' Mrs Tricknell stated. 'And when I've done that how about a cup of tea?'

'Wonderful. But I'll have to wash some cups first. Probably in bleach.'

Mrs Tricknell shuddered, having already spotted the stacks of dirty dishes. 'I don't know why he didn't take on a housekeeper. He must have been able to afford one.'

'Maybe he simply didn't want another woman in Fay's house. Do you think that could be it?'

Mrs Tricknell's face softened. 'I do believe you've hit the nail on the head, Lavender. He was such a sentimental man, after all.'

The vicar's wife was in the process of firing up the copper, Lavender attacking the dishes, when Dolly entered the kitchen carrying a medium sized cardboard box. 'You'll never guess what I've just found?' she proclaimed, eyes glittering with amusement.

'What's that then?' Lavender queried.

'A box crammed full of . . .' She broke off to snigger. 'I nearly died of embarrassment when I saw what was inside.'

'Well?' Mrs Tricknell, on her hands and knees, prompted.

'This is full of male contraceptives. Hundreds of the little buggers.'

Mrs Tricknell blushed scarlet. 'Dearie me,' she muttered.

'What would doc want with those?' Dolly smiled. 'Surely he was past that sort of thing.'

'Of course he was,' Lavender snapped. The very idea of Doc Mumsford having those for his own use was totally ridiculous. 'They must be for patients. What else?'

'Are you sure?' Dolly teased.

27

'Of course I'm bloody sure. Don't you start trying to stir up trouble, Dolly Tyler, by making insinuations, either here or elsewhere in the village. That would just be malicious gossip.'

'I don't gossip!' Dolly retorted hotly, for the moment actually believing it to be true.

'They must be for patients,' Mrs Tricknell, still blushing, stated. 'Though I never knew, hadn't an inkling, he dispensed such things.'

'I wonder who those particular patients are?' Dolly mused, further wondering if there might be a list somewhere. Now wouldn't that be a find!

'I'm not interested, and neither should you be,' Lavender admonished. 'I suggest you return them to wherever they were and let the new doctor deal with them. If Doc Mumsford gave them out then I'm sure the new doctor will too.' God, how the woman irritated her! She'd cause trouble in an empty room.

'I agree.' Mrs Tricknell nodded.

Dolly snorted. 'If you think that's the right thing to do.'

'We do,' Lavender and Mrs Tricknell replied in unison.

Dolly flounced from the room thinking she'd expected a good laugh out of that, which hadn't happened. She returned the box to its place and then took one of the packets from inside it and secreted it about her person. She'd never seen a sheath and wanted to examine the one she'd just pinched.

She smiled, wondering if she could persuade her Arthur to try it out. It would be a new experience for the pair of them.

She giggled at the picture conjured up in her mind.

★ ★ ★

Sorting out the rags which would eventually be made into paper was essentially a boring task but one Crista, none the less, rather enjoyed. It certainly didn't need any brain work.

Her job was to remove buttons, hooks, eyes and any other metal pieces along with any elastic. All pieces of silk, wool and artificial fibre had also to be removed if the best paper was to be produced.

Her adept fingers moved with practised speed. She was one of a long line of girls standing beside the slow-moving conveyor belt that took the rags to a machine which cut them up into three-inch squares.

Crista glanced down the line to where Maggs was also sorting. Both of them were hoping that in time they'd be promoted to something more responsible and the added money that would go with it.

When she'd first started at the mill Crista had found the roar of machinery almost unbearable, and for the first few months it had given her a more or less permanent headache. But gradually, as she'd got accustomed to the din, the headaches had disappeared and now she hardly noticed it.

Not long now till tea break, she thought, looking forward to it as she always did. Tea and a bit of a natter with the other girls. It was forbidden for them to talk, except about the job in hand, while at the conveyor belt.

Her fingers continued to move, her mind elsewhere, not thinking about anything in particular, just whatever popped into her head.

* * *

29

'Are you certain hiring Dickie Trippett is a good idea?' Dee Dee asked Spanish John during their meal prior to evening opening.

John looked up to stare at his wife. 'I thought you agreed it would be? At least that's the impression I got when we discussed the matter.'

Dee Dee shifted uneasily on her chair. 'I know. It's just . . . well, I've been thinking about it.'

'And?'

'The one-armed thing doesn't bother me. It's his face. That's pretty repulsive, John. What if it puts off customers?'

'It won't.'

'How can you be so sure?' she persisted.

John sighed, disappointed in his wife. 'Dickie's local, born and bred in the village. And the vast majority of our customers are local. They'll all remember Dickie as he was, and how he came to be as he is now. He's one of them, don't forget, one of their own. A village is just like an extended family, after all, and he's part of that family. And a highly thought of one at that. I can't see his face being a problem. You no more stop loving, or accepting, him because he's come back from the war disfigured than you would your own brother.'

Dee Dee suddenly felt ashamed. John was right, but then he nearly always was. She was the one at fault for not showing compassion. 'I'm sorry I brought it up,' she mumbled contritely.

'This fish pie's good,' John declared, changing the subject.

Dee Dee took the hint. The matter of Dickie Trippett was closed.

★ ★ ★

It was the afternoon of the second day cleaning Doc Mumsford's house and Lavender was in his bedroom gathering his clothes together to hold in store and then sell off at the next jumble sale, proceeds going to the church as proceeds from that particular event always did. Lavender and the others had been certain doc would have approved.

She opened another drawer in the tall chest that stood against a wall and started to go through it. It contained mainly cardigans and pullovers, of which doc had had many.

She was in the process of removing them when she came across a bundle, tied with blue ribbon, of what appeared to be letters. There were no envelopes, just the letters themselves.

Frowning, Lavender crossed to the bed and sat with the bundle in her lap. What to do? Should she take them through to Mrs Tricknell to deal with, or what? That was the trouble when there was no next of kin to pass things on to. After several moments' hesitation she decided she'd read the top letter to see what it contained.

My dearest darling Fay, the letter began, in the neat copper-plate writing for which the doc had been known.

There was a lump in Lavender's throat when she reached the bottom of the first page, for it was a letter from doc to his wife during their courting days.

How desperately he'd loved Fay, Lavender reflected when she came to the end of the letter. What an outpouring of loving and tenderness, a poignant declaration of true, and what would turn out to be abiding, love.

She had no right to read any further, she told herself, it was far too personal. To do so would have been an intrusion. Carefully she placed the letter back on top of the bundle and retied the blue ribbon. She sat for a while gazing at the bundle, remembering her and Davey's own courting days, a sweet memory if ever there was one. There hadn't been any letters between the pair of them, no such legacy of a time long gone, though still vibrantly alive in memory.

'Lavender, where are you?' Mavis Davis called out from the hallway.

'In here,' Lavender replied, hastily picking up the bundle and pushing it under a pile of clothes already laid out on the bed. Those letters were too intimate to be read by others, she decided. They should be destroyed as there was no one for them to go to.

Which was precisely what she did that evening at home, putting the bundle on the fire and watching it crisp, char and go up in flames. Sending them back to doc and Fay, she told herself. Which might be a little fanciful, but was how she wanted to see it.

Sending them back to doc and Fay.

'Nice and early, good,' Spanish John said to Dickie, who'd arrived for his first day. He then smiled. 'You look nervous?'

'This job means a lot to me. I want to do well in it.'

John nodded his approval. 'That's the ticket. Keep that attitude and you and I will get on just fine.'

Dee Dee, who had been out at the back, popped her head into view. 'Anyone fancy a cup of tea?'

'I'll have one,' John replied. 'Dickie?'

'Oh, yes, please.' He suddenly laughed. 'A bit different from the mill, this. Tea before I've even started.'

'Sugar and milk?' Dee Dee queried.

'Milk and two sugars. If that's all right?'

'Of course it is.' Dee Dee disappeared.

'Right,' John declared. 'Ever pour a pint?'

Dickie shook his head.

'Then we'll begin with that.'

To Dickie's delight, and amusement, a chocolate biscuit accompanied the tea when it arrived.

Crista was coming out of the general store when a motor car drew up alongside and a young man quickly got out. 'Excuse me,' he said. 'Can you tell me which is Fore Street?'

Handsome, Crista thought. And not from round here. 'That one,' she replied, pointing.

The young man noted that the street appeared to go in two directions from where they were standing. 'Where would I find number thirty-six?'

He had an accent, she realised, though she wasn't sure what sort. He certainly wasn't Devonian. Up north somewhere, she guessed. 'You mean the doctor's house?'

'That's right.'

She regarded him quizzically. 'Why do you want to go there? It's empty right now. The doctor died.'

'I know.' The young man smiled. 'I'm the new doctor. Let me introduce myself. I'm Dr Murray, Jamie to my friends. I'll be taking over the practice.'

The new doctor! And she was the first to speak to him. Crista was thrilled.

'And you are?'

'Crista Fletcher. We live four doors down.'

'Then we'll be neighbours, Crista. May I call you that?'

'If you wish. It's up to you.' She found herself flushing slightly. 'Welcome to Ford.'

'Why, thank you. Now, I wonder where I can collect a key?'

'You don't need one. The door's open. Old Doc Mumsford never locked it.'

'Really!' Dr Murray exclaimed in surprise. 'Why not?'

'You don't need to in this village. Lots of people never lock their doors.'

'Well, I'm going to have to get used to that.' He smiled again. 'Coming from a large city as I do.'

Crista wondered what large city that was, but didn't ask.

'Goodbye for now then, Crista. Pretty name.'

'Goodbye, doctor.'

After the car had driven off Crista hurried home to tell her parents that the new doctor had finally arrived, which would be a relief to everyone.

And to tell Maggs he was a real dreamboat.

Chapter 3

Jamie Murray didn't know what he'd expected, but not something as positively antediluvian as this. Why, the damned house didn't even have electricity!

It had taken him almost five minutes, but eventually he'd managed to light one of the many lanterns dotted around. Not only no electricity but no gas either, apparently. He hadn't been able to find a gas mantle in any of the rooms he'd been in so far.

Sinking into an armchair – Christ, there was a spring right up his backside! – he lit a cigarette and wondered just what he'd let himself in for.

Had he made a terrible mistake? Too early yet to make a decision on that; only time would tell. But so far he was most unimpressed. Grant you the house was tidy enough, and in the bedroom the bed was freshly made up. A sniff of the sheets had confirmed that. However, he hadn't yet explored the actual surgery, and he dreaded to think what he might find there.

He thought back to his parents' house in Edinburgh, a veritable palace compared to this. There again, he reminded himself, he wasn't exactly short of funds. And it might be fun, an adventure even, to modernise what was going to be his home from here on in. If he stuck it, that was.

Jamie yawned. It had been a long hard journey down from London, the last leg of his trip south. He should have stopped somewhere along the route and eaten, but hadn't because of his eagerness to get to Ford before it was very late, not wanting to arrive in the middle of the night.

He could go to a pub, he supposed, providing the village had one. Surely it did! There he might be able to buy a filled roll or something of that nature. Then again, it might give the locals the wrong idea if he pitched up at the pub on his first night here.

He was still cogitating matters when there was a knock on the front door. Surely not a patient or an emergency already? he thought, lurching to his feet. He carefully stubbed out his cigarette before going out into the hallway, having to return when halfway there for the lantern he'd lit.

'It's me, Crista.' She smiled when he opened the door.

'Oh, hello!' The pretty girl from outside the shop, he remembered.

She indicated the plate she was carrying, which was covered by a clean tea towel. 'My mum sent me with this. She thought you might be hungry after your long journey.'

'How kind!' He beamed. 'I am hungry. Starving in fact. Come in.'

Crista hesitated. She'd only been told to deliver the meal, not go inside.

'Truth is, I could use a bit of help and advice,' he explained.

'Oh!' That was different.

They went into the kitchen and she set the plate on the table there. 'It's only cold meat and things,' she said, removing the tea towel to reveal several slices of thickly cut ham, a pork pie, slices of tomato and a chunk of cheddar. 'Not much, I'm afraid.'

'Looks like a feast to me. Please thank your mother on my behalf.'

'I will, doctor.'

He placed the lantern beside the plate. 'Tell me, Crista, am I right in assuming there isn't any gas in this house?'

She laughed. 'None in all the village, doctor.'

'Then how on earth do you cook?'

'On a range.' She pointed to a contraption fixed into the far wall. 'That burns coal, wood or both, whatever. Mum left it set; all you have to do is put a match to it.'

'I see,' he murmured, mystified. 'Is your mother connected to the practice in some way?'

Crista laughed. 'No. But she and several other ladies of the village came in to clean the place after Doc Mumsford died. It was a right tip, you see, filthy according to mum. They cleaned it, and, well, did everything they could. A sort of welcoming gesture I suppose you could call it.'

Jamie was touched. 'I shall be thanking them at the first opportunity.'

'Oh, you'll get that soon enough. Everyone is proper curious about the new doctor so they'll be making it a priority to give you the once-over and have a chat if possible.' She recalled his saying he came from a large city. 'Have you ever lived in a village before?'

He shook his head.

'Well, everybody likes to know what's going on, everyone else's business in other words. As you're new, and a doctor into the bargain, which makes you special, they'll be sniffing about like dogs round a bone. So you'd best be prepared for that.'

Crista paused for a few moments in thought. 'Tell you what, why doesn't mum come here tomorrow morning, introduce herself and show you how everything works, and where things are. Would that be helpful?'

'It certainly would,' he enthused.

'Sometime in the morning, then.'

'I'll look forward to it.'

They both started when his stomach suddenly rumbled loudly, Crista laughing at his stricken expression. 'You are hungry.'

'I'm terribly sorry about that,' he apologised. 'It caught me quite unawares.'

'Don't bother me none, doctor. It's just nature's way after all. We're quite earthy in Devon, you know. Especially in the villages and countryside. We call a spade a shovel, if you understand what I mean.'

He was smiling now. What a charming girl. He liked her.

'Oh one last thing,' she declared. 'I almost forgot.' Crossing to a cupboard, she opened it. 'There are some bottles of beer in here, and an opener. Left by Doc Mumsford. One of the ladies came across them when they were cleaning and it was decided to leave them. Mum thought you might like a bottle with your meal.'

38

'I would indeed. Doc Mumsford wasn't teetotal then?'

'No fear of that. He was always popping in and out of the pubs for a quick one. The village liked that about him. It made him somehow more approachable and not the aloof, distant figure I'm told some doctors can be.'

'A tradition I shall try to uphold.' Jamie smiled.

'Folk will take to you a lot more quickly if you do. It'll make them feel you're one of them.' Crista drew in a deep breath. 'Now I'd better be going. Mum and dad will be wondering what's happened to me.'

Jamie saw her to the door, where he thanked her and repeated that he was looking forward to meeting her mother in the morning. He watched her walk away into the black velvet night, there being no moon or stars, and realised that his earlier despondency had now quite disappeared.

On returning to the kitchen the first thing he did was open one of the bottles of beer before sitting down to his meal.

Whatever else, he mused, he'd certainly got off to a welcoming start.

'Well didn't you spend a long time with your dreamboat!' Maggs mocked the moment Crista got home.

Crista glared at her sister. 'And what if I did? We were only chatting. Nothing more.'

'Chance would be a fine thing.'

Davey sighed. 'Put a sock in it, Maggs. You're being unfair.'

'Bitchy more like,' Crista declared. 'She's just jealous, that's all. She wishes it had been her sent up the road and not me.'

'Will you two stop it,' Lavender said firmly. 'The pair of you are always at each other's throats. You've no idea how tiresome it is.'

'It's always her starts it,' Crista complained. 'Never me.'

'That's a lie!' Maggs retorted hotly. 'And you know it is, Crista Fletcher.'

'Shut up the two of you or you can go off to bed right now,' Davey warned them. 'Your mother's right. Night after night it's squabble, squabble, squabble.'

Maggs glared at Crista but refrained from saying anything further, knowing her father to be quite capable of ordering them to bed. She might be twenty-one but, he would point out, it was his house and his rules applied to everyone living there. Twenty-one or not she'd have had to do as he said.

'Was he pleased with the meal?' Lavender asked.

'Delighted. Starving hungry he was. I did laugh when his stomach rumbled, he was ever so embarrassed.'

Lavender could imagine.

'He invited me in for a few minutes as he wanted my help and advice, as he put it.'

Lavender raised an eyebrow. 'Oh?'

'He's clueless about running a house, mum, absolutely clueless. I got the impression he was shocked there was no gas or electricity. As for the range, I don't believe he's ever seen one before, far less knows how to use one.'

'Dear me,' Lavender murmured.

'He's very nice, though. Positively charming. A cut above the village lads and that's for sure.'

'He's certainly made an impression on you,' Maggs commented drily.

'So? Nothing wrong with that.'

'Nothing at all.' Maggs smirked. Crista had been right about her wanting to take the plate up the road. She was dying to see this 'dreamboat' for herself.

'He's never lived in a village before, Mum. Told me that.'

'Oh?'

'So he's going to find things a bit different from what he's used to, I should imagine.'

'Did you find out where he came from?'

Crista shook her head. 'All I know is what he told me outside the shop, that it's a large city somewhere. Up north I think. He's got a funny accent, one I've never heard before.'

'He must be Scotch,' Davey chipped in.

'Why that, Dad?' Crista frowned.

'Jamie is a Scotch name. I don't know about Murray, but Jamie certainly is.'

Scotch, Crista mused. She'd never met any Scotch people before. 'One thing, mum, I said you'd drop by tomorrow morning to show him how everything works. I hope that's all right?'

'I suppose so,' Lavender replied, taken aback.

'Now you've had a better look at him how old do you think he is?' Maggs probed.

Crista considered that. 'I could be wrong but I'd say late twenties. Maybe thirty. Certainly no more.'

'That's awfully young for a doctor.' Lavender frowned.

41

'They've got to start somewhere,' Davey pointed out. 'Perhaps he's straight from medical school, or wherever it is doctors learn their stuff.'

'It won't go down well,' Lavender murmured. 'His age is bound to go against him.'

Davey smiled in amusement, knowing exactly what she meant. People would have been expecting an older, more experienced man. Someone you wouldn't be embarrassed to talk about certain things with. 'Put it this way,' Davey stated. 'He's the only doctor we've got. People will have to accept him or not bother using his services. If he knows his job they'll soon come round. Mark my words they will. Besides, it'll be like a breath of fresh air in the village. I quite approve myself.'

Lavender wasn't at all sure about that. 'What time have I to go there?' she asked Crista.

'Didn't fix a time. Just during the morning, whenever you decide to turn up.'

Later in the morning, Lavender decided. He'd probably want a lie-in after his journey. Between eleven and twelve sounded about right to her.

'How about a cup of tea?' Davey proposed, firmly ensconced in his chair before the fire.

'Maggs, put the kettle on,' Lavender instructed absent-mindedly, still thinking about the morning's meeting.

'Why can't Crista do it?'

A warning look from her father told her not to argue further. She got up to comply.

'Hello. You must be Crista's mum?'

'Good morning, doctor. Yes, I am.'

42

'Come in. Come in.'

What Jamie saw was a middle-aged woman carrying a bit more weight than she might. One thing was certain, there was no doubt where Crista got her looks from.

'Thank you.'

'I believe I have to thank you and some other ladies for tidying the place up.'

Tidying! There had been a lot more to it than that. If the poor man had seen the house in the state Doc Mumsford had left it he'd probably have turned tail and run. 'That's all right. We're a friendly lot round here. Always ready to lend a helping hand.'

Jamie ushered her inside. 'You're my second visitor this morning. The minister has already called by to introduce himself.'

Minister! 'You mean the vicar, Mr Tricknell?'

Jamie instantly realised his mistake. 'Sorry. We call them ministers where I come from.'

'And where would that be?' she queried, intrigued. Like Crista she couldn't place his accent.

'Edinburgh in Scotland.'

'Ah! So you are Scotch, then. My husband said you must be with a name like Jamie.'

'Scots, Mrs . . . ?'

'Fletcher.'

'Of course, of course,' he quickly apologised. 'Your daughter did mention. It just slipped my mind.'

'Understandable in the circumstances.' She smiled, thinking Crista had been right in saying he was handsome. He certainly was that. No wedding band either, she'd already noted. A bachelor. That was going to cause some excitement in the village. Indeed it would.

43

'When are you going to have your first consultation?' she asked, curious.

'I don't know yet. I'll need at least a couple of days to settle in and see what's what.'

Lavender nodded that she understood. 'Crista said you wanted me to show you how things work?'

'Yes please. I'm afraid I . . ' He shrugged. 'Have little experience in these matters.'

They went into the kitchen. 'It's all very easy really. Shouldn't be a problem when you get the hang of it.'

'Let's hope so.'

She gazed around. 'We'll start with the range, shall we?'

'If you will. It looks a fearsome contraption.'

Lavender laughed. Fearsome indeed! What utter tripe. 'Have you lit it yet? I did leave it set. All you had to do was put a match to it.'

Again he shrugged. 'I thought it best to leave matters as they were until you arrived.'

Lavender sighed. This might prove more difficult than she'd thought. 'Right,' she declared. 'Now pay attention.'

It was more than two hours later before she left.

Davey knew the moment he heard the terrible scream ring out that there had been another accident. He immediately stopped what he was doing and ran towards the source of the scream while all around him co-workers were looking grimly at one another.

Who was it this time, they were all wondering.

The surgery was even worse than Jamie had anticipated, and that, after seeing the rest of the house, was saying something.

He shook his head in disbelief when he saw the various coloured potions and concoctions on display in glass bottles and jars that might have come straight out of the Ark. Had Mumsford updated anything in the last twenty or thirty years? He doubted it.

The instrument drawer was a nightmare, everything old and way out of date. Luckily he'd brought his own instruments with him, but they would have to be supplemented as soon as possible.

There had to be a medical suppliers in Exeter, he presumed. He would contact them directly he'd made up a list of what he needed. A very long list it was going to be too.

What amazed him was that those he'd spoken to so far had nothing but praise for Mumsford who, to put it mildly, might have been practising in the Middle Ages. All he could think was that the man must have had a great bedside manner.

He was startled out of his reverie when the phone rang, the one he'd already spotted on Mumsford's bureau. There was another phone in the house, one of the two obviously an extension.

'Hello? Dr Murray speaking.'

Jamie frowned as a garbled voice assailed his ear. Something about an accident at the mill, a chap with a crushed arm.

'I'm new here so you'll have to tell me how to get to the mill,' Jamie stated quietly, thankful that his medical bag was all packed and ready. There was nothing to write on, or with, so he had to commit the directions to memory.

'Right, I'm on my way,' he declared when, after gentle probing, he had a rough idea of the severity of the problem. Returning into the main part of the house he picked up his bag and headed for the car. The directions were simple enough. He shouldn't have any trouble finding the mill.

All work having come to a standstill, Crista and Maggs were amongst those watching Jamie attend to Dan Starling, the chap who'd been hurt. Mr Langdon, from management, was also there, hovering at Jamie's side.

'Ring for an ambulance. This man will have to go into hospital,' Jamie instructed, concentrating hard on what he was doing.

'Is that absolutely necessary?' Langdon queried anxiously.

'Yes, it is,' Jamie snapped in reply, thinking, What a stupid bloody question!

'If you insist.'

Jamie paused for a moment to glance up at Langdon, his eyes glittering. 'It is. Now get a move on or you could have a corpse on your hands.' That enough to send Langdon scuttling away.

Jamie smiled thinly while around him there were nods of approval at how the young doctor had stood up to management. Jamie knew there was little fear of the patient's dying, certainly not after he'd finished with him, but the man badly needed the facilities a hospital could provide and he couldn't.

Taking a deep breath, he brought his attention back to the task before him.

'Dan Starling was screaming blue murder when Dr Murray got there,' a wide-eyed Crista related to her mother on arriving home that evening. 'And next minute Dan was unconscious. Completely out of it.'

'He tore Dan's shirt sleeve, produced a whopping huge syringe, and that was that. Dan's eyes just rolled upwards and he was gone,' Maggs elaborated.

'Poor Dan,' Lavender murmured, shocked by the news of the day's events.

'You should have seen the speed with which the doctor worked,' Crista went on. 'Unbelievably fast. Isn't that so, Dad?'

Davey nodded. 'He was like a demon. Most impressive.'

'And he stood up to that bully Langdon,' Maggs declared. 'Sent him away with a right old flea in his ear and no mistake.'

'He stitched the arm himself,' Crista continued. 'In three places too. There was blood everywhere.'

Maggs went white at the memory. 'It was terrible,' she breathed.

'The accident should never have happened,' Davey stated angrily. 'Again and again management have been warned about not having safety devices in place. But they ignore that advice because they claim it will lead to a loss in production. Never mind the safety of the workers, production is everything. Bastards!'

'Language, Davey,' Lavender admonished gently.

'Sod the language. It's only a matter of time before some poor bugger gets killed. And it'll be their fault, mark my words it will. The whole mill is a deathtrap.'

'Will Dan lose his arm?' Lavender asked, thinking about Dickie Trippett whom she'd seen earlier in the street.

47

'The doctor said no,' Davey informed her. 'Though I think Dan might well have done if the doc hadn't been so quick in getting there or knowledgeable about what he was doing.'

That was the second accident this year alone, Lavender reflected. It was indeed worrying. Davey was right, safety devices and guards should be installed on all the machines. But Swain was hardly likely to do that. Not only might it slow production, it would also cost, and Miles Swain was notoriously tightfisted in that direction. At least as far as the mill and its workers were concerned. Not so for himself and his family. That was something else altogether.

'What we need is a union,' Davey declared. 'A union that would bring pressure on the management and which they couldn't ignore.'

Alarm flared in Lavender. 'Don't you start that talk again, Davey Fletcher. Form a union and Swain will sack every man jack, and woman, who joins it. You know that.'

'And bring in outside workers from other parts of the country where there's a lot of unemployment to replace those sacked. It's been done before, Dad,' Crista reminded him.

It was true, Davey thought miserably. That's precisely what Swain would do. The man was despicable and didn't give a tuppenny damn for his workers. Profit was all he cared about. Profit and more profit.

'We could stop those newcomers getting in.' Davey rumbled defiantly. 'Fight the buggers if we had to.'

'And then what?' Lavender queried. 'Well I'll tell you. Swain would have the police on to you and you'd all be locked up for affray, or something similar. He'd get his way in the end, no doubt about it.'

Davey's shoulders slumped. Life was so bloody unfair at times. So bloody unfair! All he and the others wanted was a safeguard against injury while at work. Surely that was reasonable? Apparently to Miles Swain it wasn't.

'I don't want to hear any more about unions, or fighting, in this house,' Lavender warned him. 'It's difficult enough making ends meet without bringing disaster on ourselves.'

Davey stared at his wife, loving her dearly. 'And what if it's Maggs or Crista gets hurt next time?' he queried. 'Will you still feel the same way?'

Lavender turned away so he couldn't see her stricken expression. Damn him for bringing that up. Damn him.

'Well?' Davey persisted.

'I'll put the tea on the table,' Lavender persisted, voice thick with emotion.

Davey, not wanting to upset her any further, let the subject drop.

He'd open next Monday morning for his first proper consultation, Jamie decided. The Isca Medical Supply Company he'd been in touch with by telephone had been as good as their word and delivered everything he'd ordered, with a few exceptions, the following day. Which had been a big relief.

In the meanwhile he'd had several patients call in at the surgery asking for attention, including one old chap who'd demanded a new bottle of Doc Mumsford's special tonic for the relief of gout.

49

On quizzing the old chap – there weren't any patients' records, none at all – all he'd learned was that the tonic was a purple colour and tasted bitter, like the very blazes! But it didn't half help the gout.

Jamie suspected, having tested some of Mumsford's potions and concoctions, that the tonic was no more than coloured water laced with quinine, of which he'd found a huge amount in a cupboard. A placebo, in other words.

On inquiring further he'd discovered that the old chap drank eighteen pints of strong cider every day, and was inordinately proud of the fact he could still do that at the ripe old age of eighty-three. His suggestion that the old chap, a Mr Newell, might relieve the gout himself by cutting down on the cider had been met with a furious outburst, and a renewed demand for Dr Mumsford's tonic.

Jamie had then lied – well, it was partially true – by saying he had no idea what was in the tonic, a secret mixture of Mumsford's obviously, so couldn't oblige. He could however give Newell pills which should have the same effect.

Newell hadn't been best pleased, but had eventually accepted that Jamie couldn't prescribe what he hadn't got. Grumbling mightily, Newell had taken the pills but only after declaring roundly that he doubted they'd be any damned good, and that Mumsford's tonic had been the only thing that had ever relieved his discomfort.

On seeing Newell to the door Jamie had repeated his suggestion that the old chap might cut down on his drinking, which had set Newell off again, and he hobbled away cursing and swearing, shouting he was damned if he was going to do any such thing.

Jamie sighed when he closed the door again. Then laughed, thinking the whole episode quite a hoot. My God, what a charlatan Mumsford had been. Through and through.

There again quinine, if that's what had been in the tonic, was a powerful drug in its own right. Perhaps . . . just perhaps . . . ?

He'd have to think about that one.

Chapter 4

The hum of conversation stopped, and every eye, or so it seemed, swivelled on to Jamie the moment he set foot in the Angel pub. It was a Saturday night and, being lonely, he'd decided to go out for a walk culminating in a few drinks.

He noted there were two men behind the bar as he walked towards it. The older was swarthy in appearance, almost gypsyish, the younger had only one arm and a badly scarred face.

'Can I help you?' the swarthy man asked.

'Large Scotch please.'

'Certainly.'

'Hold it right there, John.'

The swarthy barman turned to face the speaker. 'What's up, Charlie?'

'Nothing's up.' He came to stand beside Jamie. 'You're the new doctor. I saw you at the mill.'

Jamie nodded.

'Your drink's on me. And no arguing. Dan Starling is my brother-in-law and I saw what ee did for him. Ee saved his life, we all reckon. So this is my way of showing my gratitude.'

A muttering of approval, accompanied by nods, went round the room.

'Well, thank you very much. I appreciate that.'

'I'm Charlie Veal, and that's the landlord there, Spanish John we calls him.'

Jamie acknowledged John. 'Pleased to meet you.'

John gestured to Dickie. 'This is Dickie Trippett. Got wounded in the war as you can see.'

'Nice to meet you too, Dickie.'

Dickie replied with a broad smile, which looked somewhat frightening on his scarred and twisted face.

Charlie stuck out a hand. 'We also liked the way you stood up to that bastard Langdon. He's a proper bully, my word and he is. You did well there.'

Jamie shook with Charlie. 'Your brother-in-law needed the hospital. It was simple as that.'

'You've made friends here, doc. Remember that.' Abruptly striding away, Charlie rejoined some cronies sitting round a table.

John placed the Scotch in front of Jamie. 'And there's another of the same to follow. Compliments of the house.'

'Why, thank you.'

John beamed at Jamie, then went off to attend a waiting customer, Dickie busy pouring a pint.

Jamie sipped the Scotch – he preferred it neat – and gazed about him. They certainly seemed a friendly bunch, he thought. Though things might have been different if it hadn't been for the accident at the mill. That had got him off to a good start, even if it had sadly been at Dan Starling's expense.

'I hear you're a Scotsman,' John said, addressing Jamie again.

53

'That's right. From Edinburgh.'

'What brings you all the way down here then?'

Jamie took a moment in replying, considering whether or not to divulge the real reason. He decided against. 'The practice was up for sale, and the location appealed.' He shrugged. 'Simple as that, really.'

John was no fool. He could see Jamie was holding something back. 'You'll find Devon very different from Scotland, I'd imagine.'

'No doubt about that. Different sort of countryside entirely. A much softer landscape. I like it. What I've seen so far, that is.'

'Settling in all right?'

'Sort of.'

'Oh?'

'A few teething problems, that's all.'

John picked up a newly washed glass and began wiping it. 'Well, if I can help in any way you only have to ask.'

'That's very kind of you.'

'All part of being a landlord. Excuse me again.' John moved off to serve a customer who'd just come up to the bar.

By the time Jamie left he'd had four double Scotches and two pints of scrumpy cider, none of which he'd paid for. Dan Starling's name had been mentioned more than once.

He'd enjoyed that, he decided. It had been fun. He'd certainly be going to the Angel again.

Lavender raised an eyebrow in surprise. 'Where are you off to this time of night?'

'Out.'

'Well I can see that,' she replied sarcastically. 'Out where?'

'To visit someone.'

Why was he being so evasive? she wondered. The bugger was up to something. 'Someone who?'

Davey sighed, knowing this was going to cause trouble. 'Andy White.'

Lavender's face hardened. 'And what would you be going to visit Andy White for? As if I can't guess. Are you the only one going?'

Davey shook his head.

'Who else?'

He reeled off a short list of names.

'Just as I thought. You're going to be talking about forming a union, aren't you?'

'There's no harm in talking,' Davey protested.

'None at all,' she admitted. 'It's what the talking might lead to that worries me.'

'Something has to be done,' Davey declared, a tremble of anger in his voice. Not anger at Lavender, but at conditions at the mill.

'That's as may be,' Lavender replied hotly. 'I don't deny things at the mill are a disgrace. But I don't want you involved, hear?'

'But Lavender . . .'

'Don't but Lavender me, Davey Fletcher. I told you the other night what'll happen if you start this union nonsense again. You'll be out of work and I won't have enough money coming in to run this house. What then, eh? What then?'

He had no answer to that.

'Do you want us all to starve? And what about the rent for here? If we don't pay that then we're out on our ear. We'd probably be out on our ear anyway as it's Swain who owns the house.'

Davey knew all this to be horribly true. 'As I said, we'll only be talking. Nothing more.'

'Then why bother in the first place? Waste of time such a meeting'll be.'

Davey dropped his head to stare at the floor.

Lavender decided to change tack. 'Don't go, Davey. Please don't go. For my sake if nothing else,' she pleaded.

He could feel his resolution melting away. He'd never been able to deny Lavender anything. 'I promised,' he whispered.

'So break your promise. If those hotheads want to get into trouble, let them. I just don't want you getting in it up to your neck.'

Again Davey didn't answer.

'You'll never win against Swain. He's far too rich and powerful. Going up against him you'd be lambs to the slaughter.' She put a hand on his arm. 'If I thought you had any chance of being successful I'd be right behind you. But you haven't. None at all.'

'We have to try,' he mumbled defiantly.

A sudden idea came to Lavender. A bloody good one too, she thought. 'Listen, why don't you go behind his back by writing an anonymous letter to the newspapers. State your case publicly and then see what happens. Who knows what the results might be.'

That caught Davey's imagination. 'If we did that there wouldn't be any personal risk involved.'

'Exactly!' she declared triumphantly. 'So what do you think?'

'I could put it to the others. See what they say.'

'They must realise the sense in it. I mean, why stick your necks out if there's a way round it? But the letter has to be anonymous so that Swain can't get back at the writers.'

'In my book it's certainly worth a try,' Davey enthused, beginning to get excited.

'But that's all,' Lavender warned him. 'No deputations to Swain or anything like that. He'd have your guts for garters.'

'I'll put it to the others then. So now can I go?'

Lavender nodded. 'And tell me all about it when you get back.'

'I will.'

Putting his arms round her he kissed her lightly on the mouth. 'Thanks, Lavender. You were always a lot smarter than me.'

'I'm nothing of the sort,' she protested. 'It's just that women think differently from men, go about things a different way, that's all.'

'Ta ra then.'

She was smiling as she watched him leave the house, but deep down she was still worried. This whole business was a minefield as far as she was concerned.

She could only hope and pray her Davey didn't step on one of the damn mines.

Jamie swore volubly, and resisted an almost overwhelming urge to kick the range. The bloody thing had gone out yet again! Why oh why wouldn't it stay alight, he inwardly raged. What was he doing wrong? It had all seemed so simple when Mrs Fletcher had explained it to him, child's stuff she'd called it.

Jamie took a deep breath, and slowly exhaled. He was starving, absolutely starving. He hadn't had even as much as a cup of tea all day. And he was fed up to the back teeth of surviving on cold things bought from the shops. He desperately, desperately, wanted a hot meal.

He stared moodily at his arch enemy, the range. That was the trouble with being brought up in a house where everything was done for you. Even in France he hadn't had to cope with anything like this. France might have been rough and ready, not to mention downright basic at times, but again it had all been laid on for him as a doctor and an officer.

There was nothing else for it, he decided. He'd have to drive into Exeter and find a restaurant. The very thought made his mouth water.

One thing was certain. He wasn't going to give up on the range, he'd learn to use it if it was the last thing he did. Besides, he had to. There was no alternative.

Jamie was just shrugging into his coat when the telephone rang. Not now! Not now! he inwardly wailed. Please God don't let it be a call-out.

But it was.

'Why so worried-looking, Mum?'

Lavender glanced across at her younger daughter. 'Am I?'

'You appear to have the cares of the world on your shoulders. Isn't that so, Maggs?'

Maggs nodded. 'I was just thinking the same thing myself.'

'It's your dad,' Lavender replied hesitantly.

'What about him?' Crista queried.

Maggs frowned. 'Is he ill? He seemed all right to me when he went out.'

'No, he's not ill. In fact he's in fine health. Never better.'

'What then?' Crista prompted.

Lavender slowly explained about Davey's involvement in trying to form a union, and that he'd gone for a meeting of those with like minds. She did not mention the letter the men were composing to send to the newspapers.

'Dangerous,' Maggs commented after Lavender had finished speaking.

Lavender shook her head. 'I just wish your father would let this thing go. He's playing with fire.'

'Well I personally think he's daft to get involved in the first place,' Maggs declared. 'We all know what Swain's like.'

Crista nodded her agreement.

Lavender glanced at the clock ticking on the mantelpiece. Davey had been gone a good hour. It would be at least that again before she could expect him back.

She continued to brood.

Well, this was it, Jamie thought. His first official surgery. Best get on with it.

Putting a smile on his face he opened the door connecting the surgery to the waiting room to find himself confronted by a veritable sea of faces.

Ouch! he thought. It looked as though half of Ford was there. Surely they couldn't all be ill! And then it dawned on him. Most of the ailments would be minor or downright phoney. They'd come to give him the once-over, and form an impression.

'First patient please,' he requested, continuing to smile.

An extremely fat woman creaked to her feet and lumbered towards him.

'It's me feet, doctor,' she declared when they were in the surgery and the door was closed again. 'I'm a martyr to them.'

He was exhausted when the surgery was finally over and would have given anything for a nice cup of tea, unfortunately an impossibility as he still hadn't conquered the intricacies of the range.

Nor the copper, which he'd also been attempting to light.

It was during morning break that Abigail Nicholls, a former school friend and co-worker of Maggs, came across to her. 'What are you doing tomorrow night?' she asked casually.

Maggs shrugged. 'I've nothing planned.'

'Fancy going to the Angel for a drink?'

It had been ages since she'd been out, Maggs realised. It would do her good. 'Why not? I could do with a laugh.'

'Good.'

Maggs caught a sly expression flitting across Abigail's face. 'Any reason the Angel in particular? Why not the Salmon and Pig?' That was the other pub Ford boasted.

Abigail glanced round to make sure they weren't being overheard. When she spoke again her voice was lowered. 'Because I heard the new doctor was in there last Saturday night and I thought he might turn up again tomorrow.'

'Really?'

Abigail nodded. 'You saw him that day when he came here, a right handsome bugger ee be. And single too, I'm told.'

Maggs smiled. 'And you think . . . ?'

'It's possible, tain't it? I ain't bad-looking myself, after all. Who knows what might happen if I give him the eye.'

Dr Murray, Maggs mused. A dreamboat Crista had called him. And her sister wasn't wrong either.

'If nothing else we'll have a good drink and a bit of fun. But that's the reason I want to go to the Angel.'

Maggs nodded. 'What time and where will we meet?'

An arrangement was made for eight p.m.

'The letter was posted this morning,' Davey informed Lavender. 'So we can only wait and see if it's printed.'

'There were no names to it?' Lavender asked anxiously.

'None. It was anonymous, just as you suggested.'

'Saturday I would imagine if they're going to print it. But there again, it could be any day.'

'If it's printed,' Davey repeated.

Lavender nodded. 'If it's printed.'

Jamie came out of the Salmon and Pig disappointed to say the least. The customers had been mainly farming types who'd glared suspiciously at him from the moment he'd gone in to the moment he'd left. As for the landlord, he was another rustic with no

61

sense of humour, at least none Jamie could detect. A lugubrious, baleful-eyed man whose conversation, what little there had been of it, was both stilted and pedantic.

On mentioning he was the new doctor, which he'd done so the landlord didn't think he was merely passing through the village, the response had been, 'Oh yes.' That and nothing more. No welcome to the village, or pleased to meet you, or anything at all that could be construed as welcoming.

What a contrast to the Angel, Jamie mused, as he made his way down the street. Chalk and cheese. No comparison whatsoever. Well one thing was certain, he would be in no hurry to go back there again.

He realised then the landlord hadn't even introduced himself so he had no idea what the man's name was. Not that it mattered.

Surly bastard.

Dickie Trippett's face lit up with surprise and delight, if it did come out a little grotesquely, when Maggs came through the door. 'Hello, Maggs,' he enthused when she and Abigail came up to the bar. 'Lovely to see you.'

Abigail was busily looking around, but there was no sign of Dr Murray. Early yet though, she consoled herself. He might still show up.

'So what'll it be?' Dickie asked Maggs, who ordered a gin and orange. Abigail said she'd have the same.

Should he or should he not continue on to the Angel? Jamie wondered. Then he thought better of it. He'd had enough at the Salmon and Pig for one night.

Besides, he had some reading to do and he wanted to write to his mother. He needed her advice.

Ten minutes later found him busy with pen and ink.

Dickie glanced over to where a seated Maggs and Abigail were deep in conversation. If he'd been able to get married, Maggs, out of all the village girls, would have been his choice. He'd had a special soft spot for her since school.

But of course no woman would marry him now, not looking as he did. Marriage was out of the question. What woman could possibly be interested in a one-armed man with a hideously scarred face? None. None in her right mind anyway.

No, he was on the scrapheap where women were concerned. There would be no marriage for him, or children come to that. Those were beyond him now. Something that would simply never happen.

Pity, he reflected sadly. He believed he would have been a good husband and father.

He abruptly snapped himself out of his reverie. If he kept this up he'd become maudlin, which would never do. He'd been self-pitying enough in the past. He must just accept the reality of what his life had become and get on with it.

He musn't forget, despite what had happened to him, he was one of the lucky ones. He'd come back from France. Not quite the man who'd gone, but come back none the less. There were plenty who hadn't.

He should be grateful for small mercies. Difficult as it might be at times.

★ ★ ★

'Hello, ladies.' Tom Woolocombe, the butcher's apprentice, smiled at Maggs and Abigail. 'Mind if I join you?'

'Do you have to?' Abigail smiled thinly, and sarcastically, in reply.

Tom laughed. 'Always the charmer, Abigail. Always that.'

'Of course you can join us,' Maggs declared. 'Come to chat us up, have you?'

'Maybe.'

'No chance, Tom Woolocombe,' Abigail said, but this time in a teasing tone. She and Tom had a long-standing love-hate relationship.

'Where's your gorgeous sister then, Maggs?' Tom jibed. 'Why didn't you bring her with you?'

'She's under age, as you well know,' Maggs replied, miffed that Crista had been brought up.

'I keep forgetting that,' Tom lied.

Abigail's gaze swivelled to the door when it opened, but she was disappointed. It wasn't Jamie who came in but a couple of other young chaps. Maggs finished her drink, and waited, hoping Tom might offer to buy her another. He didn't.

'Give her my regards,' Tom said, coming to his feet. 'Tell her we'll have a natter next time she's in the shop.'

Maggs sniffed. 'That doesn't happen very often. Mum does most of the shopping.'

'Give her my regards anyway.' And with that he strolled off to join the two who'd just entered.

'Aggravating sod,' Maggs murmured, still put out that he'd been more interested in her sister than in her.

'Couldn't agree more. Thinks far too much of himself. Believes he's a right ladykiller.'

They both laughed.

'That'll be the day,' Maggs commented scornfully. Ladykiller indeed!

'But I have heard he's . . .' Abigail dropped her voice and leant conspiratorially closer, 'very well endowed.'

'Really?'

'So I'm told.'

'By who?'

'You'd be surprised. He was described to me as a donkey. And they weren't referring to what's between his ears either.'

'Dear me,' Maggs murmured, mind running riot. Being country girls they were both well aware of sexual matters and everything relating thereto. They could hardly be anything else with the village surrounded by so many working farms.

'Donkey,' Abigail repeated, and giggled.

Maggs glanced over at Tom, seeing him in a completely different light. To say she was intrigued would be putting it mildly.

'Dr Murray, this is a surprise,' Lavender exclaimed, hastily wiping her hands on her apron.

'I wonder if I could have a word?'

'Certainly. Come in.' What was all this about? Lavender wondered. 'Would you care for a cup of tea while you're here?'

'Oh yes please,' he replied enthusiastically, following her into the kitchen. 'In fact in a way tea's what I've come to see you about. Or part of it anyway.'

'I'll make a fresh pot.'

Jamie gazed about him. Cosy, he thought. And

immaculately tidy, exactly what he would have expected of a woman like Mrs Fletcher, if he was any judge of character.

'So, how can I help you, doctor?'

'To be honest, Mrs Fletcher, I thought I could cope on my own, but simply can't. That range is quite beyond me. As for the copper . . .' He trailed off and pulled a face. 'I haven't been able to get to grips with either.'

Lavender hid a smile. 'Is that so?'

'Child's play, you called it. Well, I'm afraid I must be some sort of idiot.'

'Surely not!' Lavender exclaimed, highly amused by this. Talk about men being domestically useless! Dr Murray appeared to be a prime example.

'Anyway, I wrote to my mother about the problem and she's suggested I take on a housekeeper. Which I intend now doing.'

'Very wise, doctor.' Lavender nodded. 'We all thought Doc Mumsford should have done the same after his wife passed away. But I think he had his reasons not to.'

'I was wondering if . . . well, if you'd be interested. I'll pay the going rate, I promise you that.'

Lavender was astonished. 'But why me?'

'Because I know you. And you seemed extremely capable in the way you tidied up the house before my arrival.'

'I see,' Lavender murmured, completely taken by surprise.

'Well?' Jamie prompted.

'Let me think about it for a few minutes.'

'Of course. Of course. But I would like an answer

as soon as possible. Things are becoming a bit difficult for me, to say the least.'

Lavender could well imagine they were if he hadn't
been able to light the range. 'Exactly what duties do
you have in mind?' she queried hesitantly.

'The usual. Washing, ironing, cleaning. Oh, and one
hot meal a day. I don't care when I have it as long
as it's served outside surgery hours.'

'That would be seven days a week then?'

He raised his eyebrows. 'I suppose so.'

Lavender digested that. 'And what do you call the
going rate?'

'Whatever it is. I've no idea what wages are expected
down here.'

Lavender named an hourly sum.

'That would be absolutely fine.'

What he was talking about was a full-time job,
Lavender reflected. Could she manage that on top of
what she already did? One thing was certain, the extra
wage would come in handy, no doubt about it. Why,
she'd be earning as much as Davey. It was tempting,
very much so.

She crossed to the kettle as it began to boil.

'I am pretty desperate, Mrs Fletcher,' he confessed
quietly. 'I'd want you to start as soon as possible.
Tomorrow perhaps?'

Lavender reluctantly made a decision. 'I'm sorry,
doctor, but I have to turn you down.'

His disappointment was obvious. 'I can't say or do
anything to change your mind?'

Lavender shook her head. 'It's nothing personal, but
I simply couldn't manage to run two houses, which
is what it would amount to. Don't forget I have a

husband and daughters to take care of as it is. That's a lot of work, doctor.' She paused for breath. 'But I do have a suggestion to make?'

'Which is?'

'Put a postcard in the newsagent's window advertising the position. There's bound to be some woman in the village who'll snap it up. And quickly too.'

Jamie grabbed at this sensible proposal. 'Then that's what I'll do. Thank you for the advice.'

'As I said, I'm sorry, doctor, but you can appreciate my position. However, I thank you for thinking of me. I'm flattered.'

On leaving the Fletcher household Jamie went straight to the newsagent's where a postcard was duly placed in the window.

Chapter 5

'It's in, it's finally in!' Davey exclaimed excitedly, waving a copy of the *Gazette*, the local rag, at Lavender. 'And the *Western View* too. A huge article in both papers.'

Davey placed the *Gazette* on the table and quickly opened it to the appropriate page. With Lavender by his side he began to read.

'A good picture of the mill,' Lavender commented.

The unedited letter had been printed in full, above a profile of Miles Swain.

'What do you think?' Davey asked when Lavender had finished.

'This is going to cause a stir, to say the least.'

'Won't it just,' Davey enthused. They then turned to the *Western View*, which had a far larger distribution that took in most of the West Country. That also had excellent coverage.

'Well well,' Lavender sighed, after she'd read it.

'What's going on?' Crista demanded, coming into the room.

'Someone's written an anonymous letter to the papers about safety conditions at the mill,' Davey informed her. 'It gives Mr High And Mighty Swain a proper roasting.'

Crista came over and glanced at the articles. 'He's not going to like it.'

'Damn right he won't!' Davey laughed.

'I wonder who wrote the article?' Lavender pretended to muse, not wanting Crista to know her father had been in on it. The fewer people who knew that the better.

'Whoever, they're brave. If Mr Swain finds out their identity it'll be the sack. He won't stand criticism of any sort.'

Davey rubbed his chin, taking Lavender's cue and also pretending innocence. 'I don't suppose we'll ever find out.'

Crista quickly skimmed the letter. 'It's all true, of course. As Dan Starling could tell you.' She frowned. 'I wonder if it was him?'

'Not very likely,' Lavender declared. 'He's still in hospital with his arm in splints, I believe. He wouldn't be able to write a letter even if he wanted to.'

'True.' Crista nodded.

'Whoever wrote it has done us all a favour. Maybe now Swain will be forced to install safety devices.'

'I doubt that very much.' Crista laughed. 'He's not the sort to be forced into doing anything.'

Davey frowned. 'This time he might.'

'And pigs might fly,' Crista declared. 'Still, I hope you're right, Dad. Something has to be done to stop the accidents.'

Davey sat at the table and began rereading the articles, savouring every word. He chuckled inwardly, thinking of Swain's reaction when they were brought to his attention.

The bloody man would have a fit!

'Good morning, doctor. I've come in reply to your advertisement for a housekeeper.'

Jamie's first impression was that she seemed likeable enough. 'Come in, please.'

Still smiling, the woman stepped inside.

It was the middle of the following week that Davey spotted Langdon, from management, speaking to Andy White. As he watched, Langdon moved away, with Andy following him. Davey saw the pair of them climb the stairs to where the offices were.

Now what was that all about? Surely management hadn't found out about Andy's involvement with the letter? They couldn't have done, Davey assured himself. No no, it must be about something else. Though what, he couldn't imagine.

'Oh, Mrs Fletcher!'

Lavender, en route to the greengrocer's, stopped and turned round as Jamie came hurrying up. 'Good morning, doctor.'

'Good morning, Mrs Fletcher. And a lovely one it is too. If somewhat cold.' He didn't really think it cold but he'd already learned that cold to a Devonian was a very different matter from cold to the Scots, who were used to far lower temperatures.

'It is chilly,' Lavender agreed.

'I wanted you to know I've found someone for the housekeeper's job. She started yesterday.'

Lavender was pleased to hear that. 'Can I ask who?'

'A Mrs Tyler.'

'Dolly Tyler!'

'Yes, that's her Christian name.'

Lavender's heart sank. Dolly Tyler of all people. The last person she would have recommended. Dolly was a born snoop, and on top of that she didn't have a particularly enviable reputation. There had been stories, but only that. Nothing had ever been substantiated. Still, and Lavender firmly believed this – certainly in Dolly's case – where there was smoke there had to be fire.

'She seems very capable,' Jamie enthused. 'And she told me she was one of the ladies, with yourself, who tidied up my house before my arrival.'

'She was there.' Lavender smiled thinly.

'So, that's that then. Thank you very much again, Mrs Fletcher. Now I have to dash. I have a call to make.'

Oh dear, Lavender thought as she continued on her way. She could only hope Dr Murray hadn't made a big mistake.

'Dad's going to be late home from work,' Maggs announced as she and Crista arrived in.

'Why's that?' Lavender queried, thinking she'd now have to take the meal out of the oven.

'Andy White's been sacked. It seems he was behind that letter in the newspapers,' Crista informed her.

Cold fear clutched at Lavender. 'Sacked?' she croaked.

Crista nodded. 'He was taken to the management offices, sacked, and then escorted off the premises. Everyone's talking about it.'

'How . . .' She had to force herself to ask the question. 'How did they find out?'

Maggs shook her head. 'No one knows. But they did.'

Oh my God, Lavender thought. If they'd found out about Andy did they know about Davey? 'Was he the only one sacked?' she queried, the slightest of tremors in her voice.

'As far as I'm aware,' Maggs replied. 'Crista?'

'The only one,' she confirmed. 'Why, Mum, do you think there might have been more men involved?'

'I've no idea. I just asked, that's all. So why has your dad gone to see Andy?'

'Well they are quite pally,' Maggs pointed out. 'I suppose he felt he should go round there and see if there was any way he could help. At least that's what I presumed, dad never said. Just to tell you he'd be late home.'

Lavender fought to control the sense of overwhelming panic that was threatening to engulf her. It would be an absolute disaster if Davey too was sacked.

What in God's name would they do?

'Everything all right?'

Jamie glanced up from his meal and smiled at Dolly Tyler. 'Fine, thank you.'

'Shepherd's pie is one of my specialities. My husband Arthur swears I make the best shepherd's pie in all Ford.'

The man either had no taste buds or was lying, Jamie reflected grimly. What he was eating was awful.

'Now you just leave the dishes and I'll deal with

them in the morning,' Dolly went on. 'So tooraloo, I'm off.'

'Goodnight, Mrs Tyler.'

When she was gone he stared distastefully at his plate. Oh well, he told himself. It was better than nothing. Certainly better than going hungry.

Cooking wasn't one of Mrs Tyler's strong suits, he'd come to realise. But he supposed he'd just have to get used to what she dished up.

Lavender looked yet again at the clock on the mantelpiece. What was keeping Davey? He was taking absolutely ages.

She and the girls had finally had their tea an hour previously, what was left for Davey placed on top of the range to keep it warm. Though after this amount of time it was surely ruined.

She started and immediately came to her feet when she heard the front door open, her eyes locking on Davey's when he came into the room. As Maggs and Crista were both present they couldn't say anything yet.

'How's Andy?' Lavender asked.

'Terrible. Really taking it badly. As for Sally, I've never heard a woman rant and rave like that.'

He gave Lavender an almost imperceptible shake of the head to indicate he didn't want to discuss this further for the present.

A fearful Lavender took the hint.

'Well?' Lavender demanded the moment they were alone in their bedroom.

'Not to worry, love. Andy didn't say a word about

74

the rest of us. Took the entire responsibility for the letter on himself.'

Relief surged through Lavender like a tidal wave. 'Are you sure about that?'

'Of course I'm sure,' Davey replied irritably. 'Andy wouldn't lie.'

'So how did they find out about him? That's what I want to know.'

Davey shook his head. 'Would you believe the silly sod got drunk in the pub one night, absolutely legless, and started boasting about the letter. Or his being behind it anyway. Someone, no doubt trying to curry favour, reported him to management and that was it.'

'And no other name was mentioned?'

'In the pub? Apparently not or they too would have been for the high jump. No, our secret's safe as long as no one else opens his mouth.'

Lavender sat on the edge of the bed and stared at her husband. How she now bitterly regretted suggesting that letter, but at the time it had seemed a good idea. Certainly better than a deposition going to management.

'I've been out of my mind since the girls got home and told me what had happened,' she said quietly.

Davey nodded. 'I can imagine. But I had to go and see Andy to find out what was what. And once there I couldn't easily get away. Andy kept pleading with me to hang on as a sort of buffer between him and Sally. In the end we went and sat in his shed for a while in the hope she might cool down a bit.'

'And did she?'

'Nope. She was still as angry when I left as when I arrived.' Davey suddenly smiled. 'You should have

75

heard her language. And in front of the children too! The air was blue.'

'I don't blame her,' Lavender commented. 'Writing the letter was one thing, but to get drunk and brag about it quite another. He must have been out of his head.'

'He was. With drink.'

'He never could hold his beer or cider. You've always said that.'

Davey sighed. How very true that was. 'He's quite the hero at work, you know. Though a lot of good that'll do him now he's unemployed. One thing's for certain, he'll never get another job round here. Swain will make sure of that.'

'So what's he going to do?'

'He's no idea, Lavender. Not yet anyway. Move away, I suppose. There won't be anything else for it.'

'But he's Ford born and bred. And so's Sally. Move where? He's lived here all his life, like most of us.'

'It'll be a huge upheaval for him. And the family. I certainly wouldn't care to be faced with the same prospect.'

Leave Ford! The thought appalled Lavender. Why, in her case she'd be nothing more than a fish out of water. 'Do you think he could get something in Exeter?'

Davey shrugged. 'Possibly. It just depends with who. Swain's net is cast far and wide, don't forget. He has a great deal of influence throughout the entire county.'

'Are you suggesting Andy may have to leave Devon altogether?'

'It could well come to that.'

'Dear God,' Lavender murmured.

'At least we're safe.'

'Unless someone else blabs.'

'They won't. Not after this. Not now they've seen what's happened to Andy. Poor bastard.'

'*Poor* Sally and children,' Lavender qualified. 'They're quite innocent after all. Now they too are having to pay the penalty.' She took a deep breath and gave Davey a steely stare. 'I want you to promise me one thing.'

'What's that?'

'No matter what happens at the mill, no matter how many accidents, you'll never get involved in anything like this again. Promise?'

He nodded.

'Say it. I want to hear you say it.'

'I promise, Lavender. My word of honour.'

'And you won't go back on that, right?'

He smiled. Trust her to be so pedantic. 'I won't go back on that. I've given my word of honour, after all.'

Lavender stood and began undressing. 'I doubt I'll get any sleep tonight. So don't blame me if I keep you awake by tossing and turning.'

'Well at least you won't snore,' Davey replied, trying to inject some humour into the situation.

'I don't snore!' Lavender retorted hotly.

'Oh yes you do.'

'Rubbish.'

'In fact,' Davey declared airily, deciding to really take the mickey. 'You do a lot worse than that in bed.'

'Such as?'

'Oh . . . What Crista used to call windy waffles when she was young.'

Lavender was outraged. 'I do nothing of the sort, Davey Fletcher.'

'How do you know? You're asleep,' he teased.

Her expression was horror-struck. 'Do I really? How awful.'

He couldn't contain himself any longer and burst out laughing. 'I'm only joking, love. But I did get you going there.'

'You mean I don't?'

'Well . . . a little snore from time to time. But that's all.' Still laughing, he too began to undress.

'Daft bugger!' Lavender chided, but she was smiling when she said it.

On a sudden impulse he took her into his arms and held her tight. 'I'm glad I married you, woman. It's the best thing that's ever happened to me.'

She went all soft and warm inside. 'I feel the same about you.'

The love and tenderness they were exuding between them was almost palpable.

'Good morning, landlord!' Rupert Swain boomed, breezing into the Angel. 'The usual, please.'

'Large Scotch and soda?'

Rupert beamed. 'Good chap.'

'Back again then?'

Rupert leant on the bar. 'For a few days. See the jolly old parents, what?'

Spanish John could think of many words to describe Miles Swain, but 'jolly' certainly wasn't one of them. 'That's nice.'

Rupert placed a ten shilling note on the bar and then lit a cigarette. 'Filthy weather coming through

78

Wiltshire. It was so bad I very nearly stopped and booked in somewhere.'

John tried to look sympathetic. 'Nasty business at the mill since you were last here,' he casually commented.

'Rather. Pater told me all about it over the telephone. He was quite upset.'

'Not half as upset as the chap he sacked,' John said drily.

'What did the man expect?' Rupert waspishly replied. 'Stupid thing to do anyway.'

'There again, he may have had a point.' Careful, John warned himself. Don't stick your neck out too far.

'Perhaps he did, I've absolutely no idea. But what I do know is you don't publicly criticise my father. Privately either come to that. He simply won't tolerate it, what?'

John started polishing the brasses, a job Dickie Trippett would normally have done, but for the moment it was a bit of a distraction. He didn't want the anger he felt to show. 'I take it from what you just said you don't know much about conditions at the mill?'

'Not really. Years since I've been in there. My elder brother Giles is the one who'll take over when pa retires so I really don't have any interest in the place. No need.'

'Another, sir?' John queried, noting Rupert's glass was empty.

'Better not. Only came in for a quickie.' He ground out the butt of his cigarette. 'Thank you, landlord.'

'Call again, sir,' John declared, forcing a smile on to his face.

'No doubt. No doubt.' And with that he was gone through the door, a motor car engine bursting into life seconds later.

Spanish John stopped polishing to stare after him. 'Prat,' he muttered. 'Upper-class toffee-nosed prat.' He'd just revised his opinion of Rupert Swain.

Jamie slit open the envelope which had arrived in that morning's post and extracted the note it contained. He frowned as he read what had been written.

Well, he thought, laying the note down on his desk. He'd been invited to drinks at the Swains' this coming Sunday. He hadn't expected that.

There again, he was the new local doctor after all. It did make sense that the Swains would want to meet him socially. To judge him, probably. And ensure he knew where the power in the land lay.

Of course he would go. It might even be amusing.

'I've dropped by to find out if you've heard the latest,' Mavis Davis declared to Lavender on entering the Fletcher kitchen.

'And what's that?'

'The bailiffs have been round to visit the Whites and told them they have to be out by this weekend.'

'No, I hadn't heard,' Lavender replied slowly, thinking the news was terrible. 'I haven't been out yet today.'

'I suppose it was only to be expected,' Mavis ploughed on. 'Swain does own the cottage after all.'

Lavender nodded her agreement. It had always been on the cards. Still, confirmation that it had actually happened was something else again. She couldn't even begin to imagine how distraught Sally White must be.

'He's a bastard, that Swain. He might have given them more time.'

Lavender put the kettle on. 'Have they any idea what they're going to do?'

'Fortunately they'd seen this coming, or the possibility of it anyway. Sally and the children are moving in with her parents while Andy's going off job hunting in Plymouth.'

'Plymouth!' Lavender exclaimed. A filthy, dangerous city by all accounts.

'To try and find work on the docks. If he does he'll send for Sally and the children once he has a house for them.'

Lavender crossed two fingers. 'I can only wish them the best and hope he's lucky.'

'Amen.'

A country dweller all her life, as Sally and Andy were, the thought of going to live in a big, smelly, overcrowded city was complete anathema. Her heart truly went out to Sally.

'He should never have written that letter,' Mavis stated grimly. 'That was just asking for trouble.'

'Not so much writing the letter,' Lavender corrected her friend. 'But getting drunk and boasting about it in the pub. That was pure idiocy.'

'I couldn't agree more.' Mavis's face took on a sly, cunning look. 'There are rumours going around that Andy wasn't the only one behind the letter.'

Alarm flared in Lavender. 'How do you mean?'

'The rumour is a number of men ganged together to write it and that Andy's covering for them.'

81

Lavender turned away so Mavis couldn't see her expression. 'Is that what they're saying?'

'Yes it is.'

Lavender crossed to the bin where she dumped out the leaves in the teapot in preparation for making fresh.

'I wondered if Davey was one of those Andy was covering for?' Mavis queried, eyes glittering in anticipation.

Lavender whirled on her. 'No he isn't!' she exclaimed harshly. 'And don't you go gossiping round the village speculating that he might be either. If Swain got to hear then Davey could also get the sack.'

Mavis recoiled at the savagery of Lavender's attack. 'Sorry,' she stammered. 'I'm not out to cause any trouble. I was only wondering, that's all. He and Andy being pally like.'

'Davey had nothing to do with that letter. And that's the God's honest truth,' Lavender lied.

Mavis held up her hands. 'All right! All right! Keep your shirt on.'

'And you watch what you say in future, Mavis Davis. You know what this village is like, your wondering out loud becomes hard fact by the end of the day. And then how long before Davey is summoned up to the management offices as Andy was?'

Mavis dropped her gaze. 'I'm just an old fool, Lavender. Please forgive me. I didn't mean any harm. I swear.'

Lavender relented. Mavis wouldn't do any more idle speculating now she realised what the consequences could be. 'Why don't you sit down?' she said. 'You're getting in my way standing there.'

Mavis was only too pleased to change the subject. 'Can't. Or I don't want to.'

Lavender frowned. 'Why ever not?'

'Because I've got a sore arse, that's why.'

'How do you mean, sore?'

'I thought it was a boil to begin with so I had a look with a mirror. Tain't no boil, that's for sure. Nothing like.'

'Then you'd better go to the doctor.'

Mavis's face set in defiance. 'I can't go and see Dr Murray. He's far too young.'

'Young or not, he is the doctor.'

'I'm not showing him my arse. I'd be mortified with shame.'

Lavender did her best to suppress a smile. 'I doubt yours is all that different from the many he must have seen.'

'Well he ain't seeing mine. Now, if it had been Doc Mumsford that would have been different.'

Lavender had to admit Dr Murray was young, but even so! This was daft. 'What does it look like?' she asked.

'My arse?'

'No, the bit that's painful.'

Mavis knitted her eyebrows. 'Sort of whitish grey-ish, with cracks in it.'

'And how big is it?'

'The size of a ha'penny.' Mavis pointed to her left buttock. 'Right here she be. Isn't half giving me gyp.'

'Well I think you should go and see Doc Murray. I certainly would.'

Mavis suddenly became all coy. 'At that age he might take liberties.'

Lavender couldn't believe she'd heard that. 'What sort of liberties?'

'Well . . . you know?'

It took all Lavender's willpower not to burst out laughing at the sheer ludicrousness of the idea. How old was Mavis? Mid to late sixties, perhaps even older.

'My Robert was a great liberty taker up until the day he died,' Mavis confessed, blushing. 'Men are all the same.'

'He's a doctor, Mavis. They don't do that sort of thing.'

The coyness became even more apparent. 'He might. Men can't control themselves when they're suffused with lust. That's my experience.'

Lavender recalled Robert Davis, as meek and mild a man as you could meet. He'd obviously had hidden qualities. 'I'm sure you'll be safe. In fact I'd bet a five pound note on it.'

Mavis shook her head. 'I don't know. And there's the embarrassment of it. We'd have to have the light on.'

'Well of course you would. He wouldn't be able to examine you otherwise.'

'That's my point.'

Lavender sighed in exasperation. 'Tell you what. I can't do anything about your embarrassment, but would it help if I went with you to make sure no liberties were taken?'

'You mean into the actual surgery itself?'

Lavender nodded.

Mavis thought about it.

'Well?' Lavender prompted.

'I would be safe then, I suppose.'

'And you can just pretend it's Doc Mumsford examining you and not Dr Murray.' As a final persuader she added, 'Best get that attended to in case it gets even worse.'

'All right then,' Mavis reluctantly agreed. 'We'll go together. And I warn you, I'm not taking a foot inside that surgery unless you're there.'

'I'll be there. I promise.'

Dear God in heaven, Lavender thought after Mavis had gone. What went on in that woman's head?

Unbelievable.

Chapter 6

Abigail Nicholls glanced up at the bar clock, and frowned. 'He still isn't here yet,' she muttered to her companions, Maggs and Gemma Gatsby, another of their friends who worked at the mill. When Gemma had heard they were going to the Angel that Saturday night she'd asked if she could tag along. A reluctant Abigail had agreed, thinking Gemma's being there just meant more competition.

'Plenty of time before closing,' Maggs replied. Tom Woolocombe was standing at the bar and she couldn't help remembering what Abigail had said about him. Donkey! The vision that suddenly sprang to mind caused her to blush and squirm in her seat.

Dickie Trippett appeared beside them holding a pint pot crammed full of change and a few notes. 'We're collecting for the White family,' he announced. 'Andy in particular really as he's going to need a couple of quid behind him when he's looking for work in Plymouth.'

All three girls immediately reached for their purses. They might not have much but what little they had they'd share with Andy. Dickie was right, he'd need money to get by until he found a job.

'He's off tomorrow morning, isn't he?' Gemma queried.

Dickie nodded. 'John will cash this up after the pub's closed and take it round to Andy before he leaves.'

Maggs noticed her father coming into the pub. She was surprised, because he hadn't said at teatime he was going out that evening. She presumed it must have been a last-minute decision.

'Evening, lads.' Davey affably greeted those already at the bar. To John he added his would be a pint of the usual, scrumpy cider. The 'lads' all muttered a welcome in return.

'We're having a collection for Andy,' John informed Davey as he poured. 'A little something to help him on his way.'

'Good idea,' Davey replied, thanking God Andy had kept his mouth shut otherwise he might have been being included in the collection.

When some minutes later Dickie asked him for a contribution Davey put ten bob into the pot. More than he could really afford but he felt he owed Andy. Even if it was the stupid bugger's own fault for getting drunk and letting the cat out of the bag.

'Why, hello?'

Crista, who'd been lost in thought as she walked down the street, found it was Jamie addressing her. 'Hello, doctor.'

'And where are you off to?'

'I'm running an errand for mum.'

'I'm going to the pub. I rather fancied a pint.'

'The Angel?'

He nodded, falling into step beside her.

'Dad's there. And so's Maggs. Being a Saturday it'll be busy.'

'I don't plan to stay long. I just thought it would be nice to have a little bit of company.'

Crista regarded him shrewdly. 'It must get lonely living on your own? It certainly wouldn't suit me. But then, I've never had to.'

Jamie smiled. 'It does get lonely at times. It's a big house to rattle around in by yourself.'

'That didn't seem to bother Doc Mumsford none. There again, I suppose he'd become used to it over the years.'

'From what I gather he was well liked by everyone.'

'Oh, he was!' she exclaimed. 'He was a real sweetie. It's sad that he's gone.'

'Well, I only hope I can fill his shoes in time.'

'Oh, I think you will. People seem to have taken to you. Especially after the Dan Starling business and standing up to that bully Langdon. The man's a real menace.'

That people had taken to him pleased Jamie enormously. It was extremely important when you were a local doctor that you were both liked and trusted.

'Can I ask a question?' Crista queried.

'Of course. Go straight ahead.'

'Why did you come to Devon? It's an awful long way from Scotland. Hundreds and hundreds of miles.'

He didn't know why, but decided to tell her the real reason, a reason he hadn't so far divulged to any other villager. 'I was in the war, you know.'

'As a soldier?'

'No, doctor. I served all over France and Belgium, often quite near the Front.'

Her expression darkened. 'I lost a brother, Wilf, in the war. I still miss him. The whole family does. Particularly mum. She still cries occasionally. Just breaks down and cries.'

'I'm sorry,' Jamie murmured.

They walked a little way in silence. 'When I came home from France I could easily have found a practice in Edinburgh,' Jamie said quietly. 'But everywhere I went in the city I saw ghosts of lost friends and acquaintances who'd been killed over there. Some days it seemed like all around, forever present. Chaps I'd been to school with, university with, neighbours. All sorts. I'd walk into a pub and . . .' He trailed off, and shrugged. 'I'm sure you get the picture.'

A sympathetic Crista nodded.

'That's when I knew I had to leave Edinburgh and go far away. Somewhere there weren't any memories, where I'd never been before. Where there wouldn't be ghosts.'

'So you chose Devon?'

'Yes, I chose Devon,' he replied, wistfulness in his voice. 'A new start. A new beginning. Far away from where I'd been born and brought up, and where there were so many painful memories. My parents understood when I explained it to them. They weren't very happy about my leaving Edinburgh, and Scotland. But they understood.' Jamie paused to take a deep breath. 'So there you are. Now you know.'

Crista looked into his face and saw how troubled he was about what he'd just told her. How deeply ran his emotions on the subject. She felt somehow privileged that he'd confided in her.

Jamie groped in a pocket for his cigarettes, then remembered he'd run out. He seemed to be smoking far more than he used to these days. He'd buy more in the Angel.

They came to a crossroads, where Crista halted. Jamie stopped too. 'I'm afraid I have to leave you here. I'm going that way.' She smiled, pointing.

'Crista . . .' He was suddenly uncomfortable. 'Perhaps it would be best if you kept what I've just said to yourself. Will you?'

'If it's what you want.'

'I do. I don't know why it came out like that. Bit of a mystery really.'

'Perhaps it's been bothering you and you just had to speak to someone about it. There are times when we all have to do that.'

What a wise young lady, he thought. An old head on young shoulders, as his mother would have said. 'Maybe you're right.' He smiled.

'Anyway, I must be off.'

'On your errand.'

'On my errand,' she agreed.

He thought about Crista Fletcher, and how pleasant she was, during the remainder of his walk to the Angel.

'He's here,' Maggs whispered to Abigail, whose head immediately snapped in the direction of the door. Sure enough, there was Jamie heading for the bar.

'What'll it be, doc?' Spanish John queried.

'A pint of beer. Doesn't matter which. And a large Scotch.'

Jamie glanced around. As Crista had predicted, the pub was busy. There were a number of faces he recognised, which pleased him. He waved back when Charlie Veal, Dan Starling's brother-in-law, waved to him.

'Evening,' Davey Fletcher said.

'Good evening.'

'We haven't met. I'm Davey Fletcher, Lavender's husband.'

Jamie shook hands with him. 'I've just been having a chat with Crista on my way here. Lovely girl.'

Davey visibly swelled with pride. 'That's my other daughter, Maggs we call her, short for Margaret, sitting over there with some pals from the mill.'

Jamie looked across, but wasn't sure which one was Maggs.

'There you are, doc,' John declared, placing two glasses on the bar. 'That jug's got some water in it if you wish some.'

'How about you, Mr Fletcher? Can I get you another?'

'It's Davey. And yes, thank you. I won't say no.'

'Did you see him looking at us,' Abigail whispered.

'I saw,' Maggs whispered back.

'I wonder how we get to meet him?' Abigail mused, fully intending that to happen.

'Excuse me, Dr Murray.'

It was Dickie Trippett who'd spoken, and he now explained to Jamie about the collection being taken up.

'Did you see the letter in the papers?' Davey asked casually after Dickie had moved away, the pint pot richer by half a crown.

''Fraid not. I missed it.'

'There was a lot of truth in what Andy wrote,' Davey went on. 'Conditions at the mill, safety conditions that is, leave a lot to be desired.'

'And he was sacked for writing this letter?'

Davey nodded, but before he could go on he was interrupted by Maggs. 'I didn't know you were coming out tonight, Dad?' A smiling Abigail, eyes fixed on Jamie, was by her side.

'I decided after you'd already left.'

Jamie could see the similarity to Crista now, though it wasn't heavily pronounced. Older, he noted, and quite pretty.

'Have you met Dr Murray?' Davey asked.

'No, I haven't.'

'Then let me introduce you.'

As soon as the formalities had been completed, an eager Abigail, but trying not to show it, engaged Jamie in conversation.

Crista lay staring at the ceiling, unable to sleep, which was unusual for her. On the other side of the bedroom Maggs was long gone and reeking of alcohol, which Crista could smell despite the distance between them.

She thought back to earlier in the evening and her conversation with Dr Murray. It was clear the war had deeply affected him, and continued to trouble him. All that talk of ghosts might have been scary in other circumstances, but not with him. It had been downright sad if anything.

She tried to imagine what it must be like to lose so many friends, as he had done, and couldn't. Not to the point where you were haunted by them. There had been quite a few men in the village killed during the conflict, but that wasn't the same. They'd all been older than her, some considerably, and she hadn't been particularly close to any of them, with the exception of her brother Wilf.

Dear, lovely Wilf, gone for ever. The brother she'd grown up with, a little bit of a hero to her. She still found it hard to believe she'd never see him again, that one day he wouldn't come strolling in through the door, back just as though he'd never left. A lump came into her throat, and her eyes misted over as she wondered again how he'd been killed, for they'd never been told. Probably because the authorities simply didn't know. Only that he was dead.

She wondered, too, what he would have been like if he had returned from France. Would he have been haunted by ghosts as Dr Murray was? That was a question that would for ever remain unanswered.

Again she thought of the conversation between her and the doctor, and how he'd confided in her. It gave her a warm glow inside to think he had. It also made her feel very grown up, a true woman and not just a slip of a girl. Well, she was seventeen after all. She certainly felt like an adult so perhaps she actually was one.

He'd confided in her, which somehow made her feel special, for now didn't they share a secret together? A secret because he'd asked her not to tell anyone else.

She was still thinking about Jamie when she eventually drifted off.

★ ★ ★

Jamie halted his car in the driveway leading up to the Swain house to stare at it. He hadn't been sure what to expect, but certainly nothing like this.

Squat, ugly, with a sort of brooding, ominous almost, presence about it. He loathed the house on sight.

Jamie slipped back into gear and continued on his way.

'Everyone else will be down in a moment,' Rupert Swain declared. 'Let me pour you a drink in the meantime. What's your poison?'

'Scotch if you have it.'

'Good man. The very thing. I'll join you in that.'

Jamie took a surreptitious glance at his watch to see if he was early. He wasn't. If anything he was ever so slightly late.

'How are you settling in?' Rupert inquired politely.

'Fine.'

'And what do you think of the village?'

'Quaint, I suppose is the right word.'

Rupert laughed. 'Yes, it certainly is that. Many Devon villages are. I suppose it's the thatch that does it, gives them that impression. Jolly pretty though, what?'

Jamie didn't reply, just smiled his agreement.

'Ah there you are, Dr Murray. How nice to meet you at last. I'm Alys Swain, Rupert's mother.'

Middle-aged, elegant, extremely well – and expensively – dressed, Jamie noted. She must have been something of a beauty in her day.

'What would you care for, Ma?' Rupert asked.

She considered that. 'A dry sherry, I think.'

She and Jamie proceeded to chat for a few minutes

and then another man entered the drawing room, this one a coarser version of the handsome Rupert. Somewhat shorter, too.

'Giles, come and meet the new doctor.' To Jamie she explained, 'Giles is our elder son who'll be taking over the mill when Miles retires.'

A strong grip, Jamie thought as they shook. 'Pleased to meet you.'

Giles muttered something indistinct in reply. 'Gin and ton for me Rupert. And make it a strong one.'

Jamie sipped his whisky, observing the reddish-purple veins already evident in Giles's nose albeit he couldn't have been more than thirty. A heavy drinker, Jamie surmised.

'A Scotchman, eh?' Giles said, a trifle unpleasantly, staring hard at Jamie.

'Scots actually,' Jamie corrected him. 'Scotch is what I'm drinking.'

That annoyed Giles. 'Whatever.'

When Rupert lit a cigarette Jamie presumed it was all right for him to do likewise.

'It was you tended that careless fool at the mill, I take it?' Giles said to Jamie.

Careless? That wasn't what Jamie had been led to believe. Obviously the Swains saw things differently. He nodded.

'Was it really necessary for him to be taken to hospital?'

Jamie stared Giles full in the eyes. 'Yes. Otherwise you could have had a corpse on your hands.'

'Couldn't you have dealt with it there and then?'

'Given the right equipment and facilities. But those were at the hospital, not at the mill.'

Giles grunted, but didn't pursue the subject.

'Sorry I'm late, Alys. Got held up at the stables. That damned idiot farrier again. Time I replaced him with someone else.'

Jamie turned towards the speaker and knew instantly this was the Miles Swain he'd heard so much about. Middle-aged, like his wife, with white hair and matching bristling eyebrows. He was short, squat in fact, and ugly. A human version of the house, Jamie thought. And, as with the house, he disliked the man on sight.

Alys introduced Jamie, but Miles didn't offer a handshake. He merely glared suspiciously at Jamie. 'You're very young,' he snapped.

Jamie didn't reply.

'Well?'

'Well what, Mr Swain?'

'I said you're very young.'

'I'm old enough,' Jamie answered softly, refusing to be dominated or browbeaten. He was already sorry he'd come, but it had seemed politic in the circumstances. Out of the corner of his eye he spotted Rupert watching this exchange with an amused expression on his face.

'What's your background, son?' Miles demanded.

Jamie's back was now well and truly up. Don't do anything stupid, he cautioned himself. He couldn't afford to make an enemy of Miles Swain. Even if the man was a rude and obnoxious pig.

'What would you care to know?' Jamie replied, again softly. 'And by the way, I haven't been called son since the day I accepted the King's Commission.'

Miles blinked. He wasn't used to being faced down. 'You were in the war, then?'

Jamie nodded.

'Where did you serve?'

'France and Belgium. All over.'

'As a doctor, I presume?'

'Uh-huh.'

'That would explain what I heard,' Miles said after a few moments' thoughtful pause.

'And what exactly did you hear, Mr Swain?'

'How incredibly quick you were when dealing with Starling. They said your hands positively flew. Learned to do that over there, I suppose?'

Swain may be obnoxious, but he was no fool, Jamie realised. 'That's right. In many cases it was necessary to save a man's life. The man on the table and those waiting to be seen to.'

Miles grunted. 'So, despite your age, you're hardly inexperienced.'

Jamie gave a languid smile. 'Quite correct.' His tone held the vaguest traces of sarcasm.

'Pa, you're wanted on the telephone.'

Jamie, concentrating on Miles, hadn't heard the newcomer enter the room. Turning, he found himself staring at an extremely beautiful young woman somewhere in her early twenties. A typical English rose, was his first impression. Blonde hair that was almost white, peaches and cream complexion, and a slim figure. Her eyes were a sort of washed-out blue, and even at that distance quite mesmeric.

'Blast!' Miles swore. 'What now?' Without uttering further he stamped bad-temperedly away.

'This is our daughter Helen.' Alys smiled at Jamie. 'Helen, this is Dr Murray.'

'If you'll excuse me, I've just remembered I've got

something to attend to that can't wait,' Giles apologised, and followed his father from the room.

Jamie was pleased, and a little relieved, to see the pair of them go. 'How do you do, Miss Swain?' He smiled.

Her hand was cool in his, her smile warm and welcoming. 'I hope my father didn't daunt you, doctor,' she said. 'He can do that to people.'

'Not in the least.'

She looked into his face and saw he meant it. 'Good.'

'Drink, Helen?' Rupert queried.

'A little white wine.'

'Shall we sit?' Alys was indicating chairs.

Jamie wondered what Helen's perfume was. Whatever, it was delightful.

Jamie had stayed longer than he'd intended, simply because Miles and Giles – they sounded like a music hall double act! – hadn't returned, which had made the atmosphere far more congenial.

He'd been quite taken by Helen Swain, an absolutely charming young woman, utterly unlike her father and brother. He'd been genuinely sorry to say goodbye to her.

Well, that was an experience, he thought as he drove away from the awful-looking house that so accurately reflected its owner. Miles Swain had certainly proved to be everything he'd heard about the man, and worse. As for Giles, he was another out of the same mould.

Rupert had been different, more his mother than his father. And weak with it. A philanderer, Jamie guessed. A dilettante. More stage-door johnny than anything else. Rupert hadn't impressed him at all.

Helen, on the other hand, most certainly had. There was nothing weak about her. He'd sensed steel behind that beautiful face and figure. He'd found her fascinating, and entertaining to be with. Intelligent too, no doubt about that. He suspected if she'd been born a man she too would have been successful in business, but without the rude, bullying tactics employed by her father.

Jamie wondered if she ever came into the village and if he'd bump into her there.

'What did you think of the doctor, dear?' Alys Swain asked Miles over lunch.

'Liked him.'

'I did too.'

Miles nodded. 'Stood right up to me. There's not many do that. Or are willing to. He's got spunk, and that's a quality I admire.'

Helen smiled. She too had liked the new doctor. Rather a lot, really.

'Oooh, doctor, your hands are cold!'

Lavender smothered a laugh. Just listen to Mavis! Talk about being coy and winsome. She was acting like a young maid a quarter her age.

'I'm sorry about that, Mrs Davis.'

'That's all right, doctor. You're being ever so gentle.'

Lavender glanced over at the screen behind which Mavis was lying stretched out having her examination. All that nonsense about not letting the doctor see her with her knickers off. She was positively revelling in it!

'Is that painful, Mrs Davis?'

'Not really, doctor. As I said, you're ever so gentle.'

'And that?'

Mavis giggled. 'That's tickly.'

'I'm going to have to spread your buttocks slightly. Just so you know what I'm about to do.'

Another giggle.

'Hmm.'

'What does that mean?'

The old cow was flirting, Lavender thought. Actually flirting with him! It was ever so funny.

'Just that I'm thinking, Mrs Davis.'

'Diagnosing like?'

'That's correct.'

Lavender was certain she detected laughter in the doctor's voice. Thank God he had a sense of humour. The way Mavis was carrying on it could have been positively embarrassing otherwise.

'I do believe I've finished now, Mrs Davis. You can put your things back on.'

'Oh?' Her disappointment was clear. 'Are you sure, doctor?'

'Quite sure, Mrs Davis.'

Jamie emerged from behind the screen and crossed to a sink where he washed his hands. A little over a minute later Mavis, face flushed, also appeared.

'Are you all right?' Lavender inquired innocently.

'Fine, thank you. It wasn't too much of an ordeal.'

If he asked you to go back behind the screen again you'd be there like a shot, Lavender thought.

'Any ideas, doctor?' Mavis asked, sitting on a second chair provided in front of his desk.

'Yes. It's an ulcer.'

'Ulcer!' she exclaimed. 'On my *arse*?'

Jamie's mouth twitched in amusement. 'I'm afraid so.'

'How did it get there? I mean you don't normally get ulcers on your . . .' She cleared her throat. 'Bottom.'

'It can happen.' He opened a cupboard and took out a large bottle.

'Dearie me,' Mavis muttered.

'Don't worry. We'll soon have it cleared up,' Jamie declared, transferring some yellow ointment from the bottle into a pot. Returning to his desk, he sat and pushed the pot across to Mavis. 'I want you to put that on it morning and night. It's a bit messy, I'm afraid, so it's going to add to your washing.'

'And this'll cure it?'

'No, it won't do that. It'll act as a barrier to prevent the infection from spreading, though. The ulcer should clear of its own accord.' Jamie beamed. 'I don't think you need to come back. Unless it persists, which I doubt.'

Mavis's face fell. 'Very well, doctor.'

Jamie rose to his feet. 'Good day, Mrs Davis. And you, Mrs Fletcher.'

His eyes were twinkling.

'You old fraud!' Lavender exclaimed the moment they were outside. 'You enjoyed that.'

'No I didn't,' Mavis protested. 'It was humiliating.'

'Oooh, doctor, your hands are cold!' Lavender declared, imitating Mavis. And started to laugh.

Mavis blushed bright red. 'What are you laughing at?'

'What do you think? As I said, you're an old fraud,

Mavis Davis. It's probably just as well I was there –
to protect the doctor from you and not the other way
round.'

Mavis continued her protestations all the way down
the street.

Chapter 7

Davey returned home from work to find a grim-faced Lavender waiting for him. She indicated the newspaper lying on his favourite chair. 'You'd better read that,' she declared. 'I've left it open at the appropriate page.'

'What's it about?'

'Read it and see.'

Crista glanced at Maggs, they too having just arrived in. Maggs merely shrugged.

'By Gerald Swain, Liberal MP.' Davey read aloud. The MP for that area.

Davey read slowly, his mouth pursing about halfway through the full-page feature. The article was in defence of Miles Swain, and intended to be a full vindication of Miles's policies at the mill. Miles and Gerald were full cousins.

'Well well,' Davey breathed when he'd finally finished.

'What does it say, Dad?' Crista asked.

'According to this, and I'm not sure I believe it, Miles Swain has been struggling to keep the mill open, let alone install safety devices that would cost

103

a packet. The article states he simply can't afford improvements.'

'Can't afford them!' Maggs exclaimed. 'The man's one of the richest in the county.'

'True,' Davey mused. 'But there's an old saying that you don't throw good money after bad.'

'Isn't the mill making a profit then?' Crista queried with a frown.

'Not according to Gerald Swain. He says there's been a steady decline in the need for all types of paper since the war, which means, again according to him, profits have been dropping month by month until the mill is actually losing money because Miles Swain has been doing his best not to lay off workers.'

Lavender laughed cynically. 'If you believe that then you'd believe pigs can fly and the moon's made of green cheese. Miles Swain is as ruthless as they come. If it was a choice between his losing money and people their jobs his wallet would win out every time. The whole thing's a smokescreen, I tell you. In other words, damned lies.'

Davey shook his head. 'I haven't noticed any drop in demand for paper. A few hiccups from time to time, perhaps, when production has been eased, but no more than that.'

'Exactly,' Lavender snapped. The mention of lay-offs had shaken her to the core. The thought of Davey, their main breadwinner, being unemployed was a nightmare. It wouldn't happen, of course, but even the vaguest suggestion of the possibility was enough to frighten the life out of her.

'It's clearly a reply to Andy's letter and accusations,' Davey mused.

Lavender nodded her agreement.

'Do you think it might be some sort of threat?' Crista queried.

Lavender regarded her daughter through troubled eyes. She hadn't thought of that.

'It could be,' Maggs murmured, and bit her lip.

'There again, we might, just might mind you, be doing the man an injustice,' Davey said slowly. 'After all, we've no idea what goes on in the management side of things.'

'But you yourself said there hadn't been any fall away in production, apart from the odd hiccup here and there,' Lavender reminded him.

'True. But now I think about it, there's more to it than that.'

'How so?' she demanded.

'He may have had to lower his prices to keep that full production, undercut other mills. And if he's been doing that then profits will certainly have gone down.'

Lavender hadn't thought about that either.

'The simple truth is we don't know,' Davey declared.

'One thing we do know for certain is that Miles Swain is a twister through and through,' Lavender hissed.

Davey couldn't argue there. 'I just wish we had some way of finding out what's really what.'

'We haven't, though,' said Lavender.

'I tell you what,' Davey declared. 'After tea I'll go to the pub and find out what's being said there. There are bound to be a few blokes in to discuss the matter.'

'Good idea.' Lavender nodded.

'Do you want to come with me?'

She considered that. She was up to date with all her ironing, and nothing else needed doing. 'I think I will.'

And with that Lavender got on with putting out the tea. Worried as they all were, it didn't stop them being hungry.

Dolly Tyler, in the middle of cleaning, picked up a packet of Jamie's cigarettes that he'd left lying around. What a careless man he was, she thought, opening the packet to see how many it contained.

Thirteen, she counted. That was good. He wouldn't miss one. Or two, she thought, changing her mind.

She quickly extracted two and put them in her apron pocket for later.

Having replaced the packet exactly as it had been she began humming and got on with her work.

'You're so messy. I can't stand it any more,' Crista complained hotly to Maggs, kicking a discarded cardigan in her sister's direction. They were in the bedroom they shared.

'I'm not messy!' Maggs protested.

'Don't make me laugh. Just look at this place. And it's all your stuff lying about. Not mine.'

'Miss Goody Two Shoes, are we?' Maggs sneered.

'I'm nothing of the sort. Neat and tidy, that's all.'

'I've seen your things on the floor as well,' Maggs accused. 'Just like mine.'

'If you did it was only temporary.'

'Ha!' Maggs retorted sarcastically.

That infuriated Crista. Maggs was only trying to

paint her as black as she was herself. And it wasn't true.

'Just look at that!' Crista declared, pointing to the small dressing table they both used. 'Hair pins all over it, not to mention the spilled face powder. I'm sick to the back teeth of cleaning up after you.'

'No one asked you to.'

'You're nothing but a dirty slut, Margaret Fletcher.'

Now Maggs was furious. 'I won't have you calling me that, you sanctimonious cow.'

'At least I'm not dirty.'

'I am nothing of the sort! I wash regularly, just like you.'

Crista shook her head. 'I don't mean personal cleanliness. I mean in your habits. Especially in here. You're an absolute disgrace.'

Maggs's eyes sparked fire. 'You take that back.'

'I will not.'

'Oh yes you will or I'll claw your face.'

'Try that and I'll biff you one.'

'You and whose army?'

'I don't need any army. I'm quite capable of doing it all by myself. Biff you good and proper.'

'That'll be the day.'

At which point the bedroom door flew open to reveal an exasperated Lavender. 'Are you two at it again?' she thundered. 'You're making so much noise they can probably hear you right across the street.'

'She started it!' Maggs accused, pointing a finger at Crista.

'No I didn't. You did, leaving all this mess about. It's like living in a pig sty.'

'That's ridiculous. I'm just a little untidy, that's all.'

'A little! That's the understatement of the year.'

'Stop it this minute!' Lavender commanded.

'I . . .' Maggs started to say.

'Be quiet, girl.' The voice was a whiplash.

Maggs's mouth snapped shut.

Lavender took several deep breaths, then said, 'Now, Crista, what's this all about?'

Crista explained.

'I see. And what have you got to say, Maggs?'

'She's exaggerating. But then she always does.'

Lavender glanced about her. 'Is most of this clutter yours?' she asked.

Maggs nodded.

'Then it seems to me Crista has a point.'

'It's just not fair,' Maggs moaned.

'What isn't?'

'Having to share such a small room. We're always getting under each other's feet.'

'Well I'm sorry about that, but that's how it is, I'm afraid.'

'It doesn't have to be, Mum,' Crista said in a very quiet voice.

Lavender frowned. 'What do you mean?'

'Why doesn't one of us move into Wilf's room?'

A stricken expression came over Lavender's face. Wilf's room was exactly as he'd left it on going off to war. Nothing had been touched, or moved. To Lavender it had become a sort of shrine to her dead son, a shrine she visited from time to time to recall memories, and sometimes silently weep.

'It would make life a lot easier for Maggs and me,' Crista added, again very quietly.

'Will you at least think about it, Mum?' Maggs

pleaded, knowing it to be the perfect solution to the problem. It was the first time either of them had made that particular suggestion. But would her mother agree? She doubted it.

Lavender nodded. Then she turned and walked away.

Crista looked at Maggs, the pair of them knowing full well the significance of what they had asked.

'I'll clear some of this lot up,' Maggs declared, and started on the task.

Like Maggs, Crista didn't think Lavender would agree either. But she felt she'd had to ask.

'What are you going to do?' Davey asked Lavender, when the pair of them were in bed.

Lavender knew exactly what he was referring to. 'I don't know,' she answered truthfully.

'It makes sense.'

She didn't reply to that.

'And perhaps it would even be for the best. Wilf is dead, darling. It's time you faced the fact.'

Anger stirred in her. 'I'm well aware he's dead. I have faced that fact. It's just . . .' She trailed off.

'Where you go to remember him.'

Tears welled in her eyes. 'If you sniff the pillows and sheets on his bed you can still smell him, Davey. Even after all this time you can still smell him.'

He groped for her hand under the bedclothes and squeezed it. 'I wasn't aware of that.'

'Of course not. You're a man. Men wouldn't think to do such a thing.'

Davey sighed. 'Isn't it just a little morbid, love? Unhealthy even?'

Was it? Perhaps.

'Sharing a room was all right for the girls when they were young, but they're both grown up now. It would be one thing if we didn't have that extra bedroom. But we do. It seems such a pity to let it go to waste when we could use it.' Davey had an inspiration. 'I believe if there was some way of asking Wilf about it he'd tell us not to be so silly, keeping the room as it is. Memories are in the mind after all, there until the day we ourselves die. We don't need material things to remember them.'

Lavender knew Davey was right. If they had been able to ask Wilf he'd have told them to go right ahead and get on with it. Of course he would. She'd just never thought of it that way before.

'I miss him so much,' Lavender said huskily.

'So do I. We all do. He was a lovely lad, and one I was extremely proud of.'

The tears were flowing down her face now. 'Davey?'

'What, love?'

'Don't say any more. Just cuddle me.'

Pulling her into his arms he did exactly that, holding her till they eventually fell asleep.

Lavender sat in what had been Wilf's bedroom, staring about her. It was the middle of the morning so Davey and the girls were at work.

There, to the left of his chest of drawers, were his old football boots, alongside an equally old bladder that he'd been given as a present on his eighth birthday. She didn't have to open any of the drawers in the chest to know what they contained. She could have recited the contents of each one by heart.

Standing propped against the other side of the chest was his fishing rod. Wilf had been a keen angler, always ready, when he had the chance, to fish the local rivers and ponds. It was a pastime he hadn't shared with Davey, who considered fishing boring.

For well over an hour she sat on his bed, thinking, remembering, occasionally smiling at some memory or other that came into her head.

Eventually, for she had to get on, Lavender came reluctantly to her feet and smoothed down the front of the skirt she was wearing where it had become rumpled.

She'd made up her mind.

'Maggs, being the eldest you'll move into Wilf's room once I've cleared it out and got it sorted,' Lavender announced that night during their meal.

Three pairs of eyes swivelled on to her, all registering surprise. Even Davey had been convinced she'd never agree.

'Thank you, Mum,' Maggs mumbled.

'I'll make a start on it at the weekend.'

'I'll help you if you like?' Crista offered.

'And me,' Maggs added hastily.

Lavender dropped her gaze to stare at her plate. 'No thank you. If you don't mind it's a job I prefer to do by myself.'

'Of course, Mum. I understand.' Crista glanced at Maggs, who nodded. 'We both do.'

'Can I make a small suggestion, Lavender?' Davey asked, trying to sound casual.

'What's that?'

'How would you feel about me redecorating the

room before Maggs moves in? New wallpaper and a lick of paint, eh?'

Lavender took her time in answering. That would mean all traces of Wilf's occupancy really would be gone.

'It's only a suggestion.' Davey smiled. 'Entirely up to you.'

'All right.' Lavender sighed. 'After I've finished clearing it out.'

'Fine.'

Crista realised only too well how difficult it had been for her mother to agree both to Maggs's moving in and to the redecoration. Tactfully, she changed the subject.

'God, you look bloody awful this morning,' Spanish John said when Dickie Trippett arrived for work. Dickie's face was pale, washed out, and there were dark purplish patches under his eyes.

'I didn't sleep very well last night,' Dickie explained.

'Oh?'

'I had a nightmare.'

Dee Dee appeared from the back. 'Anyone care for a cuppa?'

'Please,' said John.

'And me,' Dickie added.

Dee Dee hurried off again.

'Do you want to sit down for a few minutes?' John queried. 'You look knackered.'

Dickie shook his head.

John, extremely concerned, regarded him curiously. 'Do you often have nightmares?'

A faraway look came into Dickie's eyes. 'Pretty frequently.'

112

'About the same thing? Or am I being too nosy?'

'No, that's all right. Not always exactly the same. Different incidents. All horrible.'

It suddenly dawned on John what Dickie was talking about. 'The war?'

Dickie nodded. 'Yes,' he croaked.

'Do you want to speak about it? Would that help?'

Dickie forced a smile on to his face. 'There isn't time, we've got too much to do. But thanks anyway.'

'As you wish.' John hesitated, then said, 'Perhaps you should pay the doc a visit. See if he can give you something. It's worth a thought.'

'Maybe I will.'

'I believe he was in the war himself, served at the Front as a doctor. So I imagine he'd be sympathetic.'

Dee Dee arrived back with two steaming cups. 'Here we are.'

That broke the mood between the pair of them. 'Thank you.' Dickie smiled at her. 'And when I've finished this I'll do the bottling up.'

Poor sod, John thought. Poor bloody sod. Because of his age, and the fact he had a slightly deformed foot as a result of a childhood accident, he hadn't made it into the Forces.

He'd heard tales though. Tales to make your hair stand on end.

One chicken, a duck, potatoes, swedes, leeks, plus various other assorted vegetables, all left by grateful patients, sometimes in lieu of payment when cash was short, placed on the doorstep for the doctor.

Not a bad morning's haul, Dolly Tyler thought as she brought the last of the offerings into the kitchen.

113

The previous day a fine rabbit had been left, and two days before that a brace of pheasants which were even now hanging from a hook.

Far too much for one man, Dolly told herself, not for the first time. When she went home she'd be taking some of this lot with her. It would only go to waste after all, and that would never do.

There was no point in bothering Dr Murray about such matters, though. As long as he was well fed and watered she needn't bore him with domestic details.

She'd have the duck, she decided. Her Arthur was very partial to duck. It would make a lovely meal for the pair of them.

'Can you describe the last nightmare you had?' Jamie asked, when Dickie finally got round to seeing him. 'I ask that for a reason.' It would give him an indication of the severity of the problem, on which the strength of the pills he intended prescribing depended.

'You were "over there", weren't you, doc?'

'Yes,' Jamie replied softly.

'You must have gone through a lot yourself?'

Jamie nodded grimly. 'I saw things that will be with me to my dying day. Things that would haunt most men.'

Dickie felt himself relax a little. He was with someone who knew the horrors that had taken place. 'Do they haunt *you*?'

Jamie knew he had to be honest. There was nothing else for it. 'I don't get nightmares. But I do have waking flashbacks that just come into my head from seemingly nowhere. Those can be difficult, as you can imagine.'

Dickie could, only too well. 'You asked about the last nightmare?'

'Please.'

'You know the effects of mustard gas.'

'Oh yes,' Jamie breathed softly.

'There were twenty-three of us in that section. At least I think it was twenty-three. The gas just suddenly hit us. No warning, nothing like that. I was at one end of the section, the end opposite to where the gas came from. Normally it would have come slowly, rolling gently in. But this time was different. There must have been a wind carrying it. I don't know. I was busy.'

Dickie paused, and swallowed hard. 'I said there were twenty-three of us. Well, because of where I was, I was the only one to get his gas mask on in time.' He closed his eyes for a moment. 'I stood there watching them die. Clawing at their throats, faces contorted. Some running away from the gas, but it was too late by then. Others lying on the ground having convulsions. Eyes starting, arms and legs flailing. A vision, doc, straight out of hell.'

Dickie stopped and shook his head. 'I was the only one who survived that attack,' he mumbled. 'God help me.'

Jamie pulled out his cigarettes. 'Do you smoke?'

Dickie shook his head.

'Do you mind if I do?'

'Go right ahead. Don't bother me none.'

Jamie lit up, thinking about what Dickie had just told him. 'Do you feel guilty about surviving?' he eventually asked.

Dickie considered that. 'I'm not sure. Maybe.'

Jamie had a long draw on his cigarette while regarding Dickie pensively. 'First thing is there's no shame in surviving when others around you don't. It's simply the luck of the draw. Luck that went in your favour. Understand?'

'I suppose.'

'The second thing is, in any war there are two kinds of wounds, physical ones and those of the mind. Heaven knows, you suffered enough of the physical variety, but also, it seems, of the latter.'

Jamie paused before going on, to let that sink in. 'We doctors can do something about the physical side, but little about the mental. Most of what goes on in the mind is simply beyond our current knowledge. Perhaps one day it won't be, but for now it is.'

'Does that mean you can't help me, doc?'

'They say time is a great healer, and I believe that. The best thing to do is try and let your mind heal itself. And pray that it does. However, in the meantime we have these nightmares to deal with. And there I can help a little. I'm going to prescribe you some tablets which I want you to keep by your bedside. When you wake up from your next nightmare take two with water. I think you'll find you'll sleep like a baby for the rest of the night. In other words, the tablets won't take the nightmares away but will assist you in coping with the after-effects.'

'Thank you, doctor.'

'And another thing.'

'What's that, doctor?'

'I'm here whenever you need me. No matter when, night or day. I'm always available.'

116

'That's very kind of you.'

'Not really.' Jamie smiled. 'Don't forget, I was there.' He stubbed out his cigarette and rose to get Dickie's tablets. He desperately wished there was more he could do for the lad. But there wasn't.

Jamie didn't recognise her to begin with because the distinctive blonde, almost white, hair was neatly tucked up into a hard hat.

Helen Swain reined in the horse she was riding, and smiled. 'Morning, doctor.'

'Good morning. Out for a hack, I see.'

'Indeed. Do you ride yourself?'

Was it his imagination or was there more to that question than appeared on the surface? 'I used to, but haven't for years now. Simply don't have the time.'

'Pity. You could have borrowed one of our horses and accompanied me on occasion.'

She really did look extremely fetching in the outfit she was wearing, Jamie thought. It showed off her figure most effectively. He felt a small tingle of excitement pulse through his veins.

'Perhaps I still might. Who knows?' he teased.

'So where are you off to?'

'A house call on a bedridden patient. An old lady who's suffering from just being old.'

The mare became restless and Helen gently patted her quiet again. 'I really do envy you your job,' she declared.

'Oh?'

'It's such a useful one. Tending the sick, relieving pain, that sort of thing. Have you always wanted to be a doctor?'

'Always,' he admitted. 'My father would have preferred me to follow him into the family business, but I wasn't interested. It was going to be medicine for me as long as I can remember.'

Helen was curious. 'And what sort of family business is that?'

'Import–export. We're quite big actually.'

'How fascinating.'

He wondered what she found fascinating about it. 'Do you dance?'

That caught him by surprise. Riding, dancing, what was this? 'Moderately. I can get round the floor but I'm hardly any great shakes.'

She laughed. 'Modesty. I like that.'

'Not modesty,' he replied ruefully. 'The plain truth.'

She stared at him thoughtfully for a few moments, then said, 'We have an annual event at the house every Christmas called the Butterfly Ball. Would you care to come?'

Again he was caught by surprise, his mind racing. 'That would be very nice. But tell me, why the Butterfly Ball at Christmas? There aren't any butterflies around then. Wrong season.'

Her horse was restless again, wanting to get on with the hack. 'It used to be held during the summer,' she explained. 'But for various reasons it was changed to Christmas several years ago. We simply decided to keep the name, that's all.'

'I shall look forward to it.'

'It's black tie. You do have one, I presume?'

He wasn't certain whether that was a dig or a tease. 'You presume correctly.'

'Then I'll send you an invitation. Goodbye now.'

'Goodbye.'

He watched her ride away. She had an excellent seat, he noted. And smiled.

Yes, she certainly had that.

Chapter 8

'Why don't you just give up? He clearly doesn't fancy you,' Maggs said to Abigail Nicholls, who'd been trying to catch Jamie's eye ever since he'd come into the Angel.

Abigail pouted in disappointment, knowing in her heart of hearts that what Maggs said was true.

'Not his type,' Gemma Gatsby added, a trifle cattily.

'And you think you are?' Abigail sniffed in reply.

'Not at all. But be realistic, he's a doctor. He isn't likely to be interested in a mill girl. We're way below the likes of him. When he gets married it'll be to someone posh. Some female with a bit of cash.'

'He is rather gorgeous though.' Abigail sighed wistfully.

'If you're going to set your sights on someone he should be a local lad,' Gemma went on.

'Such as?'

Gemma nodded towards the bar. 'Tom Woolocombe isn't bad. Not in the doctor's class I admit. But not bad all the same.'

'Tom Woolocombe!' Abigail exclaimed derisively. 'You must be joking! I wouldn't touch him with the proverbial barge pole.'

'I would. Given half the chance.' Gemma smiled.

'You would?' That was Maggs.

'Certainly. But he's never shown any interest in me. Not that way anyway.'

'Have you heard the rumour about him?' Abigail queried in a whisper.

'You mean about him having a huge willy?' Maggs sniggered.

'That's the one.'

'Of course I've heard it. I've no idea if it's true, but I have heard it.' Her eyes took on a speculative gleam. 'I'd certainly like to find out for myself.' In a suggestive voice, she added quietly, 'Very much so.'

'Dirty cow,' Abigail mocked.

'Damn right. Aren't we all? We just pretend not to be as it would probably shock the men. But deep down, oh yes.'

Maggs found herself squirming in her seat, and not through embarrassment either. It was as though she had an itch she desperately wanted to scratch.

'I wonder if he'll come over?' Abigail mused.

'Who, the doctor?' Maggs frowned.

'No, Tom, stupid. If he does I might just ask him.'

That shook Maggs. 'You mean about his . . . willy?'

Abigail shrugged. 'Why not?'

'Because being a chap he'd probably say the rumour was true, whether it was or not. Of course he would!' Gemma stated. 'No, there's only one way to find out, and we all know what that is.'

All three of them stared at one another, then simultaneously began giggling.

★ ★ ★

Jamie was about to finish his pint and leave when he was tapped on the shoulder. Turning, he found himself facing a bandaged Dan Starling.

'I'd like to buy you a drink. Ee saved my life and I want to show my appreciation, doc.'

'There's no need for that, Dan. May I call you that?'

'Ee can call me anything ee cares to after what ee did for me. Scotch is it, doc? I'm told ee drinks that.'

Jamie couldn't see any reason not to accept the offer. And it would be bad manners to refuse. 'Well, thank you very much.'

Dan called Dickie over and ordered a large Scotch.

'Aren't you joining me?' Jamie queried.

'I got friends down t'other end. I should be with them.'

'How's the arm?'

'It'll never be the way it was, the hospital doctor told me that. But I've still got it, and that's something.'

'Good.' Jamie nodded. Despite what he'd done at the mill he'd worried that the arm would have to be amputated. He was glad it hadn't.

Dan paid for the whisky when it arrived. 'Anything I can ever do for you, doc, just say. I owes ee.'

'Not at all. I was only doing my job.'

'And doing it damn well. I thanks ee again.'

And with that Dan moved away.

Maggs's heart skipped a beat when bully Langdon stopped beside her. 'I want a word with you, Miss Fletcher. Come to my office during your afternoon break.'

'A word . . . with me?' Maggs stammered.

'That's what I said. You know where my office is, don't you?'

'I've never been there, but I'm sure I'll find it all right.'

'The afternoon break. I'll be waiting,' he declared, and strode off.

'What was that all about?' Crista asked. The pair of them were working side by side that day.

'God alone knows. I don't.'

Whatever, it couldn't be good, Crista thought. Not when Langdon was involved. They both remembered only too well the last person Langdon had taken upstairs. Andy White.

And he'd been sacked.

'You'll never guess what, Mum?' Maggs announced when she arrived home that evening. She'd already told Davey and Crista.

'What's that?'

'I've been asked to be a waitress at some sort of fancy "do" the Swains are having over Christmas.'

'A waitress!' Lavender exclaimed. 'How did that come about?'

'I've absolutely no idea.'

'Four of them had to report to Langdon's office, apparently,' Davey chipped in. 'All for the same thing.'

'I could hardly refuse,' Maggs continued. 'Langdon would have held it against me and I don't want to cross him.'

'But why you?' Lavender frowned.

'Search me.'

'Are you to be paid?'

Maggs shrugged. 'He never said, and none of us

asked. We were all too frightened, I suppose.'

'So who are the others?'

Maggs named them.

'I see,' Lavender mused. They were all girls roughly the same age.

'I thought I was for the high jump,' Maggs said. 'I really did. Though I haven't done anything wrong that I know of.'

'Well at least it wasn't that,' Davey commented, and sighed. This was a turn-up for the book.

'What sort of waitressing?' Lavender queried.

'Just taking drinks round the guests and collecting empty glasses. Nothing difficult.'

'She's to wear a black skirt and white or cream blouse,' Crista informed Lavender.

'Well, you've got those,' Lavender said to Maggs.

'Waitressing at a posh "do" for the Swains,' Davey thought out loud. 'Should be worth ten bob, I'd say.'

Lavender gave him a withering 'don't be so silly' look. It was unknown, at least in the village, for Miles Swain to be generous.

Maggs would be lucky if she was paid anything at all.

Tom Woolocombe, face pink with embarrassment, took the chair in front of Jamie's desk.

'And you are?'

'Tom Woolocombe, doctor.'

Jamie jotted that down, then requested a few more relevant details for his files. Finally he had all he needed. 'So, how can I help you, Tom?'

Tom refused to meet Jamie's gaze. 'I've come to buy some more sheaths. I've run out.'

Jamie glanced at his notes. Tom was a single man. 'I see,' he murmured. This explained the large box of them he'd found on taking over the practice. Tom was the first to make such a request.

'Old Doc Mumsford always sold me them,' Tom went on, feeling Jamie should know that.

'Uh-huh.'

'So can I have three packets, please?'

Mumsford had been a more enlightened doctor than he'd thought, Jamie reflected. Good for Mumsford, considering his age.

Tom shifted uneasily in his chair when Jamie didn't immediately reply. 'Is there a problem, doctor? I can get them in Exeter but I don't go in there very often. That's why Doc Mumsford kept them.'

'There isn't a problem, Tom. Far from it. I whole-heartedly approve of your responsibility in using sheaths. As for the morality of it, that's the vicar's business, not mine.'

'You won't tell him, will you?' Tom asked in alarm. 'He might speak to my folks and mum's a great churchgoer.'

Jamie smiled. 'Don't you worry, what passes between us is strictly confidential.'

Relief flooded through Tom. Thank God for that!

Jamie came to his feet. 'If you just wait there I'll go and get what you want.'

What a decent chap, Tom thought as Jamie left him. He'd been worried that the new doctor might not be as obliging as the old one had been, but he was.

That was all right then.

★ ★ ★

'Lavender!' Davey smiled at his wife when she appeared. 'It's finished. What do you think?'

Lavender, a lump coming into her throat, gazed around what had been Wilf's bedroom. Maggs and Crista were both out at a local dance.

The room was transformed, the new wallpaper a completely different design from what had been there before, the paintwork bright and shining.

'You've done a grand job,' she told him. 'Maggs will be pleased.'

'She'd better be.' Davey pretended to growl. 'There's a lot of hard work gone into it.'

Lavender thought of all Wilf's things that she'd had to get rid of, most of which had gone to the rag and bone man who came round once a month. She'd considered passing some of Wilf's clothes on to those in the village who'd have appreciated them, then decided against it when she'd realised she might come face to face with them in the street. That was just too awful to even think about.

'Are you all right, maid?' Davey queried in sudden concern, seeing the look that had come on to Lavender's face.

She nodded, but didn't reply.

'It's for the best. I'm sure of it.'

'That doesn't make it any easier,' she said huskily.

'I know. I know.' He put an arm round her. 'Listen, I've had an idea. It's early yet. Why don't we go down the Angel and have a couple? Buck us both up.'

'I've got things to do, Davey.'

'Nothing I'm sure that can't wait. Anyway, I'd like to take my favourite girl out. Show her off a bit.'

Despite herself, Lavender smiled. 'I think I'm past the age of being shown off.'

'Not to me you're not. And never will be.'

How lucky she was to have a man like Davey, Lavender reflected, not for the first time. He was one in a million as far as she was concerned. She could have named many women in the village who'd been nowhere near as fortunate.

'So, what do you say?' he prompted.

'All right. But just for a little while.'

'That's my girl.' He kissed her lightly on the lips. 'Give me a few minutes to clean myself up and then we'll be off.'

A little make-up would be in order, she decided. And she'd better give her hair a comb. Maybe even a dab of lipstick, which she rarely wore.

Yes, lipstick would be nice. Davey always liked it when she put some on.

'Can I speak to you, doctor?'

Jamie glanced up from the medical book he was reading to refresh his memory on an unusual condition one of his patients had developed and he'd never previously treated. 'Of course, Dolly. What is it?'

'I'm afraid I've done it again, doctor. Scorched a shirt.'

Damn! he inwardly swore, irritated. That was the second this month, and the fifth since he'd taken her on. The woman was lethal where shirts were concerned.

'Badly?'

Pulling a face, she nodded. 'It'll have to be thrown away. I really am terribly sorry.'

That meant he'd now have to make a special trip into Exeter to buy some more, which was a nuisance. Expensive, too; shirts weren't cheap. Certainly not at the rate Dolly went through them.

'I feel I should pay for this one, doctor.' Knowing his character, as she'd come to, Dolly was certain he wouldn't take her up on this offer. And she was right.

Jamie waved a hand dismissively. 'There's no need for that. Just try to be more careful in future.'

'Thank you, doctor,' she gushed. 'I will.' She hesitated, then went on. 'I'll leave you to it then.'

'Thank you.'

Jamie sighed and sat back in his chair, his concentration completely gone. When would he have the time to get into Exeter? He simply didn't know. But he'd have to get in as soon as possible. More shirts had suddenly become a necessity.

He reached for his packet of cigarettes, and took one out. He really must stop smoking so much, he chided himself. He was getting through them like sweeties of late.

After a soothing cigarette he resumed his reading.

Lavender waited till Davey had finished his tea before breaking the bad news. 'PC Munny called on Andy White's wife this morning,' she said slowly.

'And why was that?'

'Andy's been killed in a dockside accident.'

Davey stared at her in shock. 'Killed?'

Lavender nodded. 'Munny didn't have any details. Only the fact Andy's been killed.'

'Christ!' Davey swore softly.

Crista laid down her knife and fork, suddenly not hungry any more. This was terrible.

'How's Mrs White taking it?' Maggs asked.

'As you can imagine. She was still in hysterics when I called in to give her our condolences. It went round the village like wildfire.'

'No one at the mill knew,' Davey said, his expression one of disbelief. 'I'd have heard if they had.'

Lavender blamed herself. If she hadn't suggested that letter then Andy wouldn't have got the sack and had to go to Plymouth for work. There again, if she hadn't then Davey and the rest of them might have gone to Swain as a deputation and all got the boot, in which case Andy might still have gone to Plymouth and been killed.

'I suppose it's too early to talk about a funeral,' Davey mused, still stunned.

'Or where it will be held even,' Lavender added. 'It could well be in Plymouth to save the expense of bringing him home.'

Davey was remembering Andy, whom he'd known all his life. It seemed unbelievable that he was gone. 'It's a bit ironic really,' he declared eventually.

Lavender frowned. 'How so?'

'He got fired for complaining about the lack of safety measures at the mill, then goes to Plymouth where he's killed in an industrial accident himself.' Davey shook his head. 'Poor bugger.'

'Poor Mrs White and children,' Crista qualified grimly.

Davey nodded. 'Of course. You're right. It's going to be hard on them. Bloody hard.'

129

Harder than most men would realise, Lavender thought. A lot harder.

'Hello, Tom.' Abigail smiled, stopping beside him. It was another Saturday night at the Angel. 'How are you tonight?'

'Fine. How about yourself?'

She contrived to flash her eyes at him. 'Not bad. A bit bored, though. I thought you might come over and cheer us up.'

Tom glanced across to where Maggs Fletcher and Gemma Gatsby were sitting. 'I would have thought you three would have enough to say to one another not to get bored.'

'That's female talk, Tom Woolocombe. A man present would spice things up.'

He regarded her steadily. 'Is that so?'

'Oh yes,' she breathed huskily, and flashed her eyes again.

This was a new Abigail, Tom thought. If he hadn't known better he'd have sworn she was trying to get off with him. But that couldn't be right. Not Abigail Nicholls, not with him.

'Are you short of money and wanting me to buy you a drink? Is that it?' he asked suspiciously.

'Certainly not!' she protested. 'The thought never entered my mind.'

'No?'

'No,' she stated emphatically. 'I've got enough cash to buy my own, thank you very much.'

He wasn't convinced that was true. 'I'll maybe come over later,' he replied. 'See how things go.'

Abigail chucked him under the chin. 'Do

130

try to. I, for one, always enjoy your company.'

Was she playing games, trying to make a mug of him? he wondered. Knowing Abigail it was quite possible. 'Since when?'

'Since always.'

He snorted.

'Honestly!'

'It's never seemed that way. You often look at me as if I'm some sort of bad smell under your nose.'

Abigail was enjoying this. 'That just shows how little you know about women.'

'Oh?'

'Have you never heard of playing hard to get?'

He was suddenly starting to see Abigail in a new light. 'Of course.'

'Well?'

'Well what?'

She sighed, as if in exasperation. 'Honestly, Tom, you can be so slow at times.'

That made him even more confused. 'Can I?'

'It's pretty obvious, I should say. I mean, what does a girl have to do to get your attention?'

'They don't seem to have had any trouble in the past,' he countered.

'Then perhaps I'm different. Do you think I'm different?'

She was playing games, had to be. He glanced again at Maggs and Gemma, who were watching them attentively. Had some sort of bet been made. Was that it? 'Are you?' He couldn't think of any other reply to make.

'Why don't you try and find out?' Abigail was amazed by her own audacity. This was fun.

131

Tom had a sip of his pint while he furiously thought. 'Where are you off to anyway?' he queried, for she'd stopped beside him clearly en route for elsewhere. At least that's how it had appeared.

'The lav.'

'Then you'd better get on before you have an accident.'

She laughed. 'Cheeky! But you're right. Toodle-oo, Tom!' Both coyly and provocatively, she added, 'For the moment anyway.'

He watched her retreating figure, which was a rather nice one he had to admit. Lovely bum, and well built up front. He began wondering what it would be like to shag Abigail.

And would she?

'Can I join you?'

Abigail indicated the empty seat beside her. 'Help yourself. I was beginning to think you were stuck to that bar.'

He was drunk, he realised. But not drunk enough not to know what was going on. If the girls thought they were going to take the mickey out of him then they were mistaken.

They made small talk for a little while, the three girls being amiable enough. Occasionally Abigail would lean towards Tom and place a hand briefly over his.

Eventually Maggs excused herself, saying she wanted a word with a couple of friends sitting in another part of the pub, and Gemma declared she'd go with Maggs, which left Abigail and Tom on their own.

132

Abigail moved in for the kill. She wanted to find out if the rumour was true.

Music from the funeral service was playing as Jamie strode past the church on his return from a house call. None of the people from the mill would be in attendance as Miles Swain hadn't allowed anyone time off work to be there, which had caused a great deal of bitterness in the village even if it wasn't unexpected. To compensate, the vicar was holding a memorial service for Andy White that coming Sunday. It was bound to be jam-packed, Andy having been a popular man.

Jamie thought of Mrs White, whom he'd had to sedate on the day she'd received news of her husband's death, and the following one as well. The distraught woman had been beside herself with grief.

Jamie shook his head in sadness as he continued on his way.

'I still can't get over that Tom Woolocombe,' Abigail declared to Maggs during the walk home from work. 'So much for his reputation as a ladies' man!'

Maggs smiled. 'It must have been a bit of a let-down.'

'You can say that again. A "Bye Abigail, it was nice talking to you", and that was that. I was right miffed, I can tell you.'

'Maybe he's taking things slowly? Don't forget there have been times in the past when the pair of you have almost been at daggers drawn.'

'True,' Abigail acknowledged.

133

'Let's see what happens next Saturday night. Whether or not he follows it up.'

'Do you think he will?'

'I have absolutely no idea. Who knows what goes through a chap's mind? They just don't think like us.'

'Thank God,' Abigail suddenly giggled. 'It would be boring if they did.'

The two of them went a little way in silence, then Abigail suddenly said, 'Tom did surprise me the other night.'

'You mean by not taking you home?'

Abigail shook her head. 'No, in that he really is quite a nice chap underneath. I'm beginning to think I had quite the wrong impression of him.'

'Oh?'

'He's actually rather sweet. And interesting to talk to. At least that's what I found. As I said, I was most surprised.'

'Perhaps he saw a new side of you too?'

'Perhaps,' Abigail mused. 'I'd like to think he did.'

Maggs glanced sideways at her friend. 'Do I detect a budding romance here?'

Abigail considered that. 'It started as something of a joke, as you know. I simply wanted to find out for myself if the rumour was true. But now? Well, who's to say.'

Maggs thought about herself and the fact she didn't have a boyfriend at the moment. Not that she'd ever been in a serious relationship, but there had been chaps along the way, plus the kissing and cuddling that went with it. She wished . . . well it would be nice to meet someone. Someone special. Someone she could fall for and who fell for her.

A yearning filled her. A yearning for something she'd never yet had.

'Why, hello, Dr Murray.'

Jamie, thinking about a patient he had to call on later that day, started out of his reverie to find he was being addressed by Helen Swain. He raised his hat. 'Good morning, Miss Swain.'

She indicated the brown paper parcel he was carrying. 'Been shopping?'

'For shirts.' He then related how Dolly Tyler kept burning and scorching his shirts, which made Helen laugh.

'Dear me. I shouldn't care to have her in my employ.'

Jamie pulled a face. 'She is something of a liability at times, I have to admit. She's not a very good cook either. Quite dreadful really.'

Helen's eyes bored into his. 'Then you must get rid of her. Replace her.'

Jamie wasn't sure he wanted to go that far. 'I'll have to think about it.' He smiled. Helen really was her father's daughter, he reflected. There had been steel in her voice when she'd said what she just had.

'By the way, I'm heading for Tinley's tearooms. Perhaps you'd care to join me? They do delicious cakes and pastries if you like that sort of thing.'

He really should get back to Ford, he told himself. On the other hand mid-morning tea with Helen Swain might be quite delightful. Oh, why not! 'That would be lovely, Miss Swain.'

'I don't think we need be so formal now we know one another. Helen, please.'

135

'And I'm Jamie.'

'Shall we, then . . . Jamie?'

'You'd better lead the way. I'm still fairly unfamiliar with Exeter.'

As he'd anticipated, their time together was most enjoyable.

Chapter 9

'Maggs, will you hurry up or you'll be late!' Lavender called out from the kitchen, having noticed what the time was. Maggs was getting ready to go waitressing at the Butterfly Ball.

Davey shook his head. 'Women!' he muttered. 'They're all the same.'

Crista grinned at her father. 'Are we?' she teased.

'Oh yes. Take my word for it.'

'Don't listen to what he says.' Lavender smiled. 'He's talking nonsense as usual.'

'I'm nothing of the sort!' Davey retorted good-humouredly.

'Oh yes you are. Stuff and nonsense. Like most men.'

'Rubbish.' He winked at Crista, expecting a further comeback from Lavender, but there wasn't one.

'So there you are,' Lavender declared as Maggs appeared in the doorway. 'Let's have a look at you.'

'Well?' Maggs demanded, having turned slowly round.

'You'll do. Though I'm not so sure about the make-up.'

'It's only a little powder, Mum. That can't hurt.'

Lavender snorted. 'There's more on your face than powder, as you well know, lady.'

'Stop nagging her,' Davey interjected. 'The maid's fine.'

Crista sighed. 'I wish I was going to a ball. They must be wonderful.'

'Maggs won't be there to enjoy herself,' Lavender reminded her younger daughter, 'but to serve drinks and whatever else they tell her to do. It's strictly work, not pleasure.'

'I can still wish, can't I?' She focused on Maggs. 'Now, you will tell me all about it when you get back?'

'I promised, didn't I?'

'I want you to describe all the dresses, and jewellery, but particularly the dresses. They're bound to be dazzling.'

'You're being picked up in the square, aren't you?' Davey queried.

'That's right. Some kind of transport, there and back, is to be provided.'

'You'd better be on your way,' Lavender declared. 'Otherwise you'll miss it, and you don't want that.'

'Bye everyone!' Maggs cried gaily, and swept from the room.

Crista stared after her sister in envy. Lucky beast, she thought. She'd have given anything to be in her shoes.

'Now, who fancies a cup of tea?' Lavender asked as the front door banged shut.

Tea, Crista thought, wrinkling her nose. It would be champagne where Maggs was going. She'd never tasted champagne. But maybe one day . . .

She could only dream.

* * *

Rupert Swain was bored stiff. The same old faces, the same old inane conversations. If he could have got out of coming to the ball he would have.

He'd just been chatting to Annabel Courtney, who had a wandering eye and the biggest feet imaginable. Feet like veritable boats. Very horsey she was, so he'd had to put up with an interminable ten minutes about her latest acquisition, a hunter called Blackie apparently. Surely they could have come up with a more inspiring name than that!

'Enjoying yourself, dear?'

Rupert smiled broadly at his mother. 'Having a wonderful time, mater.'

Alys matched his smile. 'Liar,' she whispered.

Rupert shrugged.

'Do try harder, dear. For me?'

He kissed her lightly on the cheek. 'I will. Promise.'

'I know some of them can be stuffy. But there are interesting people here as well. The new doctor, for example. He's rather jolly, in my opinion.'

'I'll speak to him later. If I get the chance.'

'You do that, dear. In the meantime, do cheer up. You've got a face like curdled milk.'

Rupert laughed at the analogy, knowing only too well it was probably true.

What he needed was a proper drink, he decided after Alys had moved on. He'd had enough of insipid punch and dreary white wine, all that was on offer. Yes, that was precisely what he needed. Bound to buck him up.

'I say, old boy, how are things in London, what?'

Redvers Ffoulkes had his arm round a female Rupert didn't recognise, whom Redvers introduced as Cynthia, currently visiting some relations from Wiltshire.

Another tiresome conversation ensued.

'Can I help you?' Rupert had sneaked off to find some Scotch and run into Maggs in one of the many corridors.

'I'm sorry, sir. I'm lost. I had to go to the lav and now can't find my way back again. I'm completely confused.'

Rupert suppressed a smile. What she said was perfectly understandable; the house was a bit like a rabbit warren. Getting lost was easily done if you didn't know your way around.

'Shall I direct you?'

'Oh yes please.'

Good-looking female, he thought, eyeing her over. Quite a popsy really. He indicated her freshly starched apron. 'I take it you're not one of the guests.'

Maggs giggled. 'No, sir. I'm waitressing for the night.'

'Local?'

'Yes, sir. From Ford.'

'Do you know who I am?'

She nodded. 'I have seen you. You're Rupert Swain. One of the boss's sons.'

'Boss?'

'I work at the mill, sir.'

'Ah, I see.'

Maggs put her hands together in front of her and fiddled with her fingers. She was finding his frank gaze most disconcerting.

'What's your name?'

'Margaret Fletcher, sir. My friends call me Maggs.'

'Maggs,' he repeated slowly. He liked it. It had a good, honest, unpretentious ring about it. 'You did find the lavatory, I take it?'

'Yes, sir.'

'Good.' He winked at her, not wanting to let her go. For the first time that evening he was enjoying himself. 'Can you keep a secret?'

'Yes sir. I hope so, sir.'

He lowered his voice. 'I've bunked off from the others so I can get myself a decent drink. I can only take so much of that punch and white wine.'

'I understand, sir.' She nodded.

'Do you?'

'Oh yes sir. I would imagine that's the sort of thing gentlemen do.'

How charming, he thought. How absolutely charming. 'Tell me more about yourself, Maggs.'

She looked blankly at him. 'Me, sir?'

'Yes you.'

Maggs swallowed hard, thinking she really should be getting back before she was missed. 'There's nothing to tell, sir. I was born in Ford, went to school there, and now work at the mill. That's about it.'

'What about boyfriends? Do you have one of those?'

She shook her head.

'I find that hard to believe, a pretty girl like you. The local lads should be falling over themselves.'

Maggs coloured slightly at this flattery, loving every moment of it. 'Maybe I'm just choosy,' she prevaricated.

'As you have every right to be. I know I would in your position.'

She didn't know what to reply to that, so kept silent.

'What about your family, Maggs?' he queried, prolonging the conversation.

'My father works at the mill as well, and so does my younger sister. I had an older brother who also worked there but he was killed in the war.'

'I see,' Rupert murmured, his mind flashing back to France. 'A lot of good men died "over there".' He added reflectively, 'Far too many.'

'I've heard you were in the war, sir.'

'Yes, indeed I was,' he replied quietly. His brother Giles had failed the medical, thanks to intervention from their father – string-pulling, in other words. Giles was the heir after all. Having got one son off the hook their father had decided that the other had to go, otherwise it wouldn't have looked good. The pair of them failing the medical would have been just too much of a coincidence. So it had been up to him. The short straw. For his sins.

Reflecting on this gave Rupert a sudden idea. With a gasp, he bent over clutching his stomach.

'Are you all right, sir?' Maggs queried in alarm.

'Old war injury, nothing to worry about. I'll be fine once I sit down.' He gestured along the corridor. 'There's a small sitting room there. Will you help me to it?' It was where he'd been heading when he'd bumped into her.

'Of course, sir.'

'Thank you.'

She put an arm round him as he hobbled in the direction he'd indicated. Reaching the door, she opened it so they could go inside. The gas mantles were already lit, and a fire was burning in the grate.

Rupert sighed as he sank on to a sofa. 'That's better.'

'Is it terribly painful, sir?'

He gave her a bleak smile. 'Not now. It soon passes once I sit down. Nothing really, just comes back to haunt me from time to time.'

'Were you badly injured, sir?'

'Only slightly compared to many. That young Dickie Trippett in the village, for example. Poor sod.'

Maggs gazed at him in concern. 'Is there anything else I can do, sir?'

He pointed to a decanter and glasses on top of a sideboard. 'Pour me a decent Scotch if you will.'

He watched her keenly as she busied herself, admiring her figure, all sorts of fantasies going through his head. 'A dash of soda from the syphon, Maggs. And would you care for a drop yourself?'

'Oh no sir. I couldn't do that. Not while working.'

'But you do indulge, I presume?'

'Gin, sir. And sometimes cider when I'm hard up. But never Scotch. Can't stand the taste of it myself.'

He patted the sofa beside him when she'd handed him his drink. 'Join me for a few moments. I'm enjoying chatting to you.'

'I can't, sir. I'm bound to be missed.'

'Don't worry. I'll see everything's all right when you get back. A quick word and that'll be that.'

Maggs reluctantly sat, knowing it to be wrong, but what else could she do? He was a Swain after all.

The evening was certainly brightening up, Rupert reflected. Fortune had been kind to drop this little poppet into his lap.

Yes indeed.

★ ★ ★

'I thought you said you couldn't dance very well?' Helen Swain accused Jamie.

'I can't.'

'Well you're certainly doing fine as far as I'm concerned.'

'Why thank you.'

'Are you enjoying yourself?'

'I'm enjoying dancing with you.'

Helen laughed. 'I like that. Very smooth.'

Jamie raised an eyebrow. 'I am disappointed about one thing, though.'

'Oh! What's that?'

'Not a butterfly in sight. Not even a paper one.'

'I did explain to you we originally held the ball during the summer when there were a lot of butterflies around, thanks to what's been planted in the gardens over the years. At least during the day.'

'And now?'

'They're still there in the summertime.'

'But not at Christmas?' he teased.

'No.' She frowned. 'We'd never thought of paper butterflies as adornments. I must suggest it next year.'

'Large ones could be fun. Suspended from the ceiling. All colours of the rainbow. It should be a pretty sight.' He hesitated, then added, 'Talking of which, you're a pretty sight yourself tonight. Very much so.'

'Why thank you. You're most gallant.'

Her almost white, blonde hair was curled into a chignon, or French pleat, her dress a bluey, metallic green that caught the light and relected it in an almost shimmering effect. The dress itself was made of silk messaline trimmed with iridescent bead motifs. Its generous girdle was adjusted in a novel way, the long fringed streamer slipped through a loop to give the appearance of a knot. The sleeves came to the wrist, the hem to midway between knee and ankle. It would have been overgilding the lily for Helen to have worn jewellery round her neck, which remained bare.

When the music stopped they disengaged and applauded. 'Shall we have another?' he proposed.

'Why not?' Helen replied, eyes twinkling.

But it wasn't to be. 'Dr Murray?'

The speaker was the butler, a tall thin man called Westcott.

'Yes?'

Westcott had a few words with Jamie, who then turned to Helen. 'I'm sorry, but I have to go. Duty calls.'

Her face fell in disappointment. 'Do you really?'

'I'm afraid so. An emergency that can't wait.'

He had time to offer further apologies to Miles and Alys Swain before hurriedly taking his leave.

Unknown to him, Helen was standing at a window watching him drive away.

A bleary-eyed Maggs was the last to appear for breakfast next morning.

'Bacon and eggs?' Lavender queried, busy with the frying pan.

'Please, mum.' Maggs poured herself a badly needed cup of tea.

'Well?' Davey demanded. 'Did they pay you?'

'Half a crown, dad.'

Davey shook his head. 'The Swains always were a tightfisted lot. It should have been more.'

'I'm just surprised she got anything,' Lavender declared. 'It would be just like them to let her go whistle.'

'I hope I didn't wake anyone when I got in,' Maggs apologised. 'I tried to be as quiet as I could.'

'What time was that?' Lavender asked. 'You were certainly late. I fully intended waiting up but simply couldn't in the end. I was that tired.'

'After two,' said Maggs.

'So?' Crista prompted.

'So what?'

'What was it like? Did they all drink masses and masses of champagne?'

'They didn't serve champagne. It was punch and white wine.'

'Told you they were tightfisted,' Davey muttered, getting stuck into his breakfast.

Oh God, if they knew what had happened all hell would break loose, Maggs thought. She still couldn't believe that Rupert Swain had kissed her. And what a kisser he was too! Not only kissed her but arranged to meet her that coming Wednesday evening.

She smiled softly at the memory, his words from the night before still ringing in her ears. How pretty she was, how attracted he was to her. What a gorgeous mouth she had, and absolutely stunning legs. Talk about flattery! The man was an expert at it. But in a nice, plausible way.

She closed her eyes for a moment, remembering their embraces, his hand flitting over her breast, then gently squeezing. He had attempted to go further but she'd stopped that, asking him what did he think she was? How contrite he'd been, saying he hadn't

146

been able to help himself. She was just so lovely and desirable.

'Maggs?'

She looked at her sister.

'Something wrong? You've got ever such a funny expression on your face.'

'Nothing's wrong,' Maggs replied quickly. 'A touch of wind, that's all.'

'It's the change of routine that'll have given you that,' Lavender declared knowledgeably. 'It does it to me every time.'

'Tell me about the dresses,' Crista urged. 'I want to hear every last detail.'

Maggs sighed and sipped her tea. It was the last thing she wanted to do.

'Well?' Crista prompted.

Maggs did her best to comply.

'Morning, doctor. You're up nice and early.' Spanish John had run into Jamie in the street.

'Walking the dog, I see,' Jamie muttered.

'Do every morning. A good mile there and back. Parsley loves it.'

The mongrel, one of the strangest-looking mutts Jamie had ever clapped eyes on, wagged its tail as though in agreement.

'I'm not up nice and early,' Jamie informed John, falling into step beside him. 'I haven't been to bed yet. I've been out on a call all night.'

John could now see that Jamie was unshaven, and somewhat grey about the gills. 'So what was that all about? Or shouldn't I ask?'

'Childbirth. Mrs Clarence. Do you know her?'

147

John nodded. 'They come in occasionally. I thought she wasn't due till next month?'

'She wasn't. But the baby had other ideas. Anyway, he's here now. A bouncing baby boy, as they say, weighing in about six to six and a half pounds. Mother and baby both fine.'

'That's good.'

'You know, I can't believe that since arriving in this village I've delivered so many babies in such a short space of time. You really are a most fecund lot.'

John frowned. 'You got me there, doc. What's fecund?'

Jamie laughed. God, he was tired! 'Fertile. It means fertile.'

'Oh, I understand now.'

'I have a theory,' Jamie went on. 'Nonsense probably, but a theory none the less, that this is happening all over Britain, and that it's Nature's way of redressing the balance after the war.'

'You mean more than the usual number of children being born to replace those men who were lost?'

'That's it. As I said, nonsense probably, but it is a possibility.'

John chuckled. 'I suppose it is. Maybe more than you realise, doc. We country folk know all about Nature and how she can make things right again after some disaster's struck. And if the war wasn't a disaster then I don't know what is.'

They stopped outside the pub. 'You off home to bed now?' John queried.

Jamie nodded. 'I'm dead beat.'

'Fancy a drink first?'

'At this time of the morning?' Jamie asked incredulously.

'It's still last night as far as you're concerned. Look at it that way. And I'd be happy to oblige.'

'But you're shut,' Jamie pointed out. 'What if PC Munny was to find out you'd served a customer at this hour?'

John found that highly amusing. 'There'll be no complaint from Munny. My word and there won't. It wouldn't be the first time he's been standing at my bar when we're officially closed. Besides, I own the pub and you'll be drinking as my guest. That's allowed.'

He didn't need to be asked twice. 'Then I'll take you up on your offer.'

'Round the back. That's my private door.'

A few minutes later found John placing a pint in front of a grateful, and very thirsty, Jamie. 'Do you the world of good,' John declared.

'Will you join me?'

John shook his head. 'I won't if you don't mind. Never touch a drop before ten p.m. Couldn't do my job otherwise.'

Jamie had several welcome gulps of beer, then lit up. 'Christ, that hits the spot.'

'The pint or the fag?'

'Both.'

John smiled, a smile that slowly vanished as his expression became thoughtful. 'May I give you a word of advice, doc?'

'Go ahead.'

'I don't want you to think I'm sticking my nose into your business, but people are talking.'

That baffled Jamie. 'About what?'

'You.'

'Me! Why ever are they doing that?'

'They're worried that you're getting thick with the Swains. And, as you well know, the Swains are hated in these parts. Positively hated. No one more than the old man himself.'

Jamie thought about that.

'I hope you don't mind me saying. I felt . . . well, I felt you should be told.'

'I see,' Jamie murmured.

'It was all round the village the day after their annual Christmas "do" that you'd been there. That and the fact you danced with the daughter.'

Jamie laughed. 'Bloody hell! The day after?'

''Tis a village, doc. Hard to have secrets here.'

'It wasn't meant to be secret,' Jamie protested. 'They asked me and I accepted. End of story.'

John eyed him shrewdly. 'That's as may be. But folks have interpreted it differently. You see, around here it's us and them, them being the Swains. There's no crossover line. You're either one of us, or one of them.'

'Do you think like that, John?' Jamie queried with a thin, cynical smile.

'I run a public house, doc. I deals with whoever walks through the door. Everyone's welcome if they don't cause no trouble.'

Jamie was in a quandary. He enjoyed Helen's company, quite a lot actually. And she seemed to enjoy his. It also annoyed him he was being dictated to. Surely it was his affair whom he was friendly with or not?

'You are a figure of importance in the village, doc. People look up to you, just as they did to old Doc Mumsford. They think of you as one of their own.

150

You'd lose their trust, and respect, if you cosy up to the Swains.'

'I'm not cosying up to anyone,' Jamie persisted. 'Least of all the Swains. Nor do I wish to alienate them either. That would be stupid.'

'Suit yourself,' John said slowly. 'I just thought you should know what's being said, that's all.'

'And I thank you for it. It's certainly given me a great deal to mull over.'

'Village life, doc. Not quite as straightforward as it might appear. Rather complicated really. Everyone sort of living in everyone else's pockets as they do.'

Jamie drank some more beer, his mind whirling.

'Another?' John asked when Jamie had drained his glass.

'No no, one's enough.'

'Then I'll let you out the back. I hope you didn't mind . . .'

'Not in the least,' Jamie interjected. 'I'm glad you spoke. Thanks again, John.'

'Only trying to help, doc. Take care of yourself now.'

And with that Spanish John was gone, leaving Jamie to trudge thoughtfully home where a welcome bed awaited him.

Maggs hoped Rupert wasn't going to be late as it was a bitterly cold night to be standing around in. The place they'd agreed to meet was a lane a little way outside the village. Maggs had insisted on that, as she didn't want anyone spotting her with Rupert. You couldn't be too careful.

She breathed a sigh of relief when headlights

appeared, and moments later the car had pulled to a halt beside her.

Rupert leant across and opened the door. 'How are you?'

'Fine.'

He gazed at her in the darkness. 'I can't see what you're wearing but you smell delicious.'

Maggs laughed. 'Do I?'

'You most certainly do. My head's swimming with it.'

It was only some lavender water of her mother's that she'd pinched. 'Where are we going?'

'A little out-of-the-way pub I know where no one will recognise us. Does that sound all right?'

'Sounds wonderful.'

'I'm glad you could make it, Maggs. I thought you might change your mind.'

She very nearly had, on several occasions. Apart from anything else she still couldn't believe that Rupert Swain was interested in the likes of her, a common mill girl.

'I'm here, Rupert. So shall we go?'

He drew her to him and pecked her on the cheek. 'Let's.'

Maggs had expected to be nervous, but surprisingly she wasn't. She couldn't have felt more relaxed.

Going out with Rupert Swain! Pity she'd never be able to tell anyone.

There again – and she smiled – who knew how the cards might fall?

Chapter 10

Crista was in a lighthearted mood as they made their way to work, the first day back after the New Year's holidays. It was rare that it snowed in Devon, but it was snowing now, swirls of thick flakes gusting and blowing. If it kept up, and she hoped it would, there'd be a completely white landscape before very long.

'This is fun, isn't it?' she enthused to Maggs, walking alongside.

Maggs shivered. 'I'm freezing.'

'Oh, come on! It isn't as bad as it was last night. That was really cold.'

Maggs had to grudgingly admit her sister was right.

The holiday had been a treat, Davey was thinking. Lying late in bed with Lavender, enjoying the private time together. He grinned to himself. They'd certainly done that.

'I think I might make a snowman when we get home tonight,' Crista declared to her sister.

'At your age! Don't be so soft. Snowmen are for children.'

Crista laughed. 'I don't care.'

'Hmmh!' Maggs snorted.

'Will you help me?'

'I will not. If you want to indulge in such foolishness, then that's up to you. But I'm certainly not joining in.'

Maggs spotted Abigail Nicholls and gave her a brief wave. Abigail's romance with Tom Woolocombe, to everyone's amazement, had really taken off during the holidays. The pair of them had become thick as thieves.

As for Rupert, that had been difficult. But they had managed to meet up once more, driving to a quiet spot where they'd canoodled. She smiled at the memory. What a kisser he was! She got goosebumps just thinking about it. Sheer heaven. Absolute bliss!

'Hello, something's up,' Davey declared, pointing ahead to where a group had gathered at the mill gates. They appeared to be reading some kind of notice. He frowned, wondering what it was all about.

They soon found out.

'What are you doing home?' Lavender demanded in surprise when Crista appeared back at the house.

'I've been laid off indefinitely, Mum.'

Surprise turned to shock. 'What!'

'I've been laid off,' she repeated dully. 'Me and quite a few others. Our names were posted on the mill gates.'

Alarm suddenly seized Lavender. 'What about your father and Maggs?'

'They're all right, Mum.'

'Thank God for that.' It would have been a disaster if Davey, the main breadwinner, had also been laid off. Then they really would have been in trouble.

Crista slumped miserably into a chair. 'It was so

unexpected. So out the blue. No warning, nothing.' She shook her head. 'Especially coming after the holidays like that.'

Lavender was already thinking that she'd have to be more careful with what she spent in future now there was one less wage coming into the house. Sometimes it was difficult enough to make ends meet as it was.

'Was there any indication as to how long this will last for?' Lavender queried.

'None. But I'm sure dad will try and find out.'

This was a real blow, Lavender thought, mind buzzing. And as Crista had said, so unexpected. No warning whatever.

'What am I going to do, Mum?' Crista asked, almost tearfully.

'I've no idea, maid. Try and find something else in the meantime, I suppose. Though that's going to be hard with others laid off as well. They'll all be on the look.'

Lavender sat opposite Crista and the pair of them stared at one another.

The letter, Lavender thought, and suddenly it all made sense. This was Swain's revenge for the letter to the newspaper.

The bastard.

'You're late,' Lavender said when Davey and Maggs came in that evening.

Davey's expression was grim in the extreme. 'People weren't just laid off. There's more.'

'What?' she queried, hand flying to her mouth in anticipation.

'Those still working have had an hour added to the shift without anything being added to their pay packet. That's why we're late.'

'Another hour,' Lavender breathed.

'Every day. And not an extra farthing to show for it.'

'How do you feel, Crista?' Maggs asked.

'Terrible. I still can't believe it.'

'It's the letter, of course, Davey. This is Swain getting his own back.'

Davey nodded. 'Has to be. It's a load of nonsense that demand has fallen away. Something he's concocted. None of the other mills in the valley are short of work. At least none that we know of. Every one is working to full capacity.'

'So what Swain has actually done is have those still employed make up the shortfall of those laid off.'

'That's right,' Davey agreed, anger in his voice. 'We'll be producing the same volume of paper for cheaper overheads, which means more profit to him.' He clenched his fists. 'I swear to God if the man was to walk in this room right now I'd knock him flat and to hell with the consequences.'

Lavender gave a heartfelt sigh. 'Be that as it may, all we can do now is make the best of things. There's nothing else for it.' She shot Davey a warning glance. 'And I don't want to hear any further talk of deputations and the like. That would only make everything worse. And you can bet whoever made up the deputation would be straight out on their ear.'

Davey knew she was right. Swain had them exactly where he wanted and there wasn't a damn thing they could do about it. Not if they wished to continue working at the mill, that was.

'There was mention of a strike,' Maggs said fearfully. 'But no one that I heard was keen on the idea.'

'Of course they wouldn't be,' Lavender snapped. 'They've got their families to consider. Swain would turn a strike into a lockout, and before we knew where we were we'd all be starving.'

'I heard of a strike that took place not long before the war,' Davey said slowly. 'And that's exactly what the owner did. He sacked the entire workforce, threw them out of their homes – which he owned, of course – and brought in a new team from up country somewhere. That's the last thing we want happening here.'

Lavender closed her eyes. The thought of losing their home was enough to frighten her out of her wits. It simply didn't bear thinking about.

Davey, seeing the state she was in, went to her and took her into his arms. 'We'll be all right, maid. I promise. Swain has just moved the goalposts, that's all. We'll survive.'

'Please God we do,' she whispered. 'Please God we do.'

'Am I going to die, doctor?'

Jamie tried to hide a smile. What a fatuous thing to ask. 'No, Miss Peabody,' he declared solemnly. 'There's no chance of that for many years yet.'

'Oh, thank goodness. Do you hear that, Amelia? Not for many years yet.'

'So what's wrong with her, doctor?' a concerned Amelia Jelly asked, fluttering at the bedside.

It was the first time Jamie had been called to these

157

two maiden ladies, who lived by themselves and had telephoned to say it was an emergency. Some emergency!

'A slight chest infection,' Jamie explained. 'Nothing to worry about. It'll soon clear up of its own accord.'

Amelia Jelly fluttered some more. 'I do think you should give poor Grace something, doctor. To be on the safe side.'

Jamie could see the anxiety written all over the woman's face. 'Perhaps you're right,' he conceded, pretending to look grave. 'You can't be too careful, after all.'

Grace Peabody buttoned up the front of her nightdress and sank into the pillows piled behind her. 'Dr Mumsford always gave us something when we were ill. He was most understanding,' she declared.

A placebo no doubt, Jamie mused. Just as he would prescribe one to keep the old girls happy. 'Is there somewhere I can wash my hands?' He smiled.

'Of course,' Amelia Jelly responded. 'Out of the door and on the left. There are fresh towels laid out in anticipation.'

'Thank you.'

The bathroom was an up-to-date one with all mod cons including running hot and cold water, Jamie discovered. That would have cost a bob or two. Whatever else, the ladies apparently weren't short of money.

On leaving the bathroom he paused to glance around. A small cottage, even by Ford standards, but neat and compact. It had rather a nice atmosphere to it.

'Would you care for a cup of tea before you go? I shall be making one for us,' Amelia Jelly queried when Jamie returned to the bedroom.

'And there's some delicious cake that Amelia made,' Grace added, beaming at her friend. 'She's ever such a good baker.'

'I bake and Grace cooks,' Amelia elaborated. 'We each do what we're best at. Isn't that so, Grace?'

'That's so,' Grace acknowledged with a tiny nod of her head.

'I won't if you don't mind,' Jamie replied. 'I'm afraid I have to get on.'

'What a pity,' Amelia sighed. 'We get so few visitors. Isn't that so, Grace?'

'So very few,' Grace agreed sadly.

'But there we are. I suppose we should get out and about more.'

'We must try, dear.' Grace nodded.

'Yes, we must.'

'Just send us your bill, doctor. We always pay promptly.' Grace smiled.

'Always promptly,' Amelia agreed.

'We prefer it that way.'

'In case we forget.'

'We can be a bit forgetful at times,' Grace explained.

'Getting on, you see.'

'Getting on,' Grace agreed.

Amelia sighed, and so did Grace.

'I shall expect you to be up and about this time next week,' a highly amused Jamie told Grace.

'So soon?'

'I should imagine so.'

Grace shook her head. 'I really did think I was dying. That my time had come.'

'She really did,' Amelia assured Jamie.

'Well she's not. Now, I really must go.'

'Of course, doctor,' Amelia fluttered. 'Let me escort you to the front door.'

'There's no need for that,' Jamie protested mildly.

'Oh, I insist. Manners, you know.'

'Manners indeed.' Grace nodded.

Grace Peabody said goodbye to Jamie in the bedroom, and Amelia at the front door, adding that she'd call in at the surgery later to collect the medicine.

Something was bothering Jamie as he walked off down the street. Niggling at him. Something he couldn't quite put his finger on.

He came up short as it suddenly dawned on him. 'Of course!' he muttered. That was it.

On entering the house he'd seen a small kitchen, a lounge, and upstairs the bedroom and bathroom. Just one bedroom. There hadn't been any other door to indicate a second. One bedroom, and one bed.

He laughed aloud, totally bemused. Who would have thought it in a quiet Devon village? Certainly not him.

Life truly was full of surprises.

Maggs couldn't sleep for thinking about Rupert. This lay-off business had further complicated matters. How could she possibly continue seeing someone whose father was responsible for what had happened at the mill?

And yet . . .

Why should he pay the penalty for being Miles Swain's son? That wasn't fair. Rupert wasn't at all like Mr Swain. He was kind, gentle, thoughtful and very loving. These were all qualities of his that she'd come to recognise and appreciate in a very short time.

And he was keen. Very much so. To the point where she'd begun to wonder what it would be like to be Mrs Rupert Swain.

Rich, that went without saying. Clothes, jewellery, a beautiful house. All sorts. Closing her eyes she imagined herself got up as the fancy ladies at the 'do' had been. The picture envisioned in her head made her positively ache with longing.

What was there for her otherwise? Marriage to one of the local lads, who'd probably work at the mill, or in some other low-paid job. Scrimping and scraping, trying to make ends meet as her mother so often had to. Poverty, in other words.

Well, there was nothing wrong with honest poverty, her father often said so. But there again, he didn't have an alternative. Nothing wrong with poverty indeed! Her backside. That was working-class claptrap. Honeyed words to convince the lower orders to put up with their miserable, backbreaking lot.

Hard-working, keeping down a job, honourable: all words her father used from time to time. An attitude that, up until now, she'd also subscribed to. Honourable, proud . . . The list went on and on.

But what if, *what if,* she could escape from all that? Live a life of ease and luxury, not want for anything, have servants at her beck and call. Never have to worry about money ever again? Be somebody, a lady. Not just a woman, a lady!

And Rupert was lovely. Truly lovely. It would be a wonderful marriage.

'Mrs Rupert Swain,' she whispered, and smiled.

★ ★ ★

'Hello?'

'Jamie, it's Helen Swain.'

'Why hello, Helen. How are you?'

'Fine. In the pink. And you?'

'The same. Soldiering on.'

She laughed. 'Don't you mean doctoring on?'

'I suppose so.' He grinned.

'Anyway, I'm ringing to find out what you're doing Saturday afternoon?'

'Nothing I can think of,' he replied slowly, frowning.

'Oh, good. I've been invited to cocktails at a friend's house and I was wondering if you'd care to accompany me?'

'Cocktails, eh?' He repeated the word as he thought desperately.

'And canapés. That sort of thing.'

'Sounds marvellous.'

'You'll come then?'

He needed time to consider this after his conversation with Spanish John. It was a subject he'd put to the back of his mind. 'It's difficult for me to commit myself right now, Helen.'

'Oh?'

Did he detect an iciness creeping into her voice? His thoughts were racing. 'The fact is I'm to deliver a baby either Friday or Saturday. At least that's when it should be due. But you know how these things are?'

He paused, but there was no reply. Just the sound of her breathing. 'Helen?'

'I'm still here.'

He was right. Her voice had gone icy. He suddenly

realised she was a woman probably used to getting things all her own way. People jumping, and grateful to do so, on her slightest wish or command. 'That's the position I'm in, Helen. I must be on hand when the call comes.'

'Can't a midwife deal with it?' Now her voice wasn't only icy, but cross as well. Petulant even.

'There's the possibility of complications which merit a doctor being in attendance.'

'I see.'

'However,' he added brightly, leaving the door open, 'the birth might occur on Friday in which case I'd be happy to go along with you.'

'When will you know?' she asked after a few moments' hesitation.

'If it hasn't happened, or at least started, by Friday night, I'll have to hang on in the village.'

Again there was a few seconds' hesitation. 'That being so, I think it best we forget the whole matter.'

'I . . . Well, I'm sorry, Helen.'

'Not to worry. It was a good idea. Goodbye then.'

'Goodbye, Helen. Have a . . .' He broke off when there was a click indicating she'd hung up.

Jamie replaced his receiver and stared at it. 'Damn!' he muttered. That had been most unfortunate. His own fault really. He should have thought the matter through after the conversation with John. Now he was left in a bit of a quandary.

Maggs stared at the house where the Swains lived, taking in it and the surrounding acres, which were also theirs. It was a Sunday afternoon and, with nothing else to do, she'd decided to go for a walk. Normally

163

Crista would have come with her but Crista wasn't feeling too well and had elected to stay at home.

What would it be like living in such a grand mansion? Maggs wondered. Not that Rupert would ever inherit it; the entire estate would go to his brother Giles. That much she'd already gleaned from Rupert.

But Rupert would inherit money, and a lot of it according to him. Provision had already been made. Certainly enough to buy a fine house in London, as opposed to the apartments he presently stayed in, with servants.

Living in London would suit her down to the ground, for her name would be mud here if she married a Swain. Worse than mud. She'd be held in total loathing and contempt. God knows how her parents would react if the marriage ever took place. But that was a bridge she'd cross should she ever reach it.

She was seeing Rupert again tonight, this time her intended excuse to the family being that she was visiting Gemma Gatsby. She smiled in anticipation of being in his arms, his mouth on hers.

'Maggs?'

Hearing her name spoken roused her out of her reverie. 'Why, hello, Dickie,' she responded, turning to face him. 'What are you doing out here?'

Dickie Trippett laughed. 'I could ask the same of you.'

She shrugged. 'Having a walk, that's all. I don't normally come this way, but decided to do so for a change.'

'Same here. Out for a walk while the pub's shut.' He gazed at her in open admiration. 'I saw you looking at the Swains' place. Some house, eh?'

164

'Huge.'

'Not very pretty in my book. But yes, huge. It must cost a fortune to run. Not that old man Swain has to worry about money. He's absolutely rolling in it.'

'I imagine they all must be,' she replied softly.

Dickie was congratulating himself on his luck at meeting up with Maggs. Being in her company was always a pleasure. Always had been. 'I'm on my way back,' he said. 'What about you?'

She nodded.

'Then shall we walk together?'

'If you like.'

That thrilled him.

'So how are things?' she asked, making conversation, as they moved off in the direction of Ford.

'All right, I suppose.'

'Still enjoying working in the pub?'

'Very much so. I fell on my feet there. It was kind of John and Dee Dee to give me the job.'

That was true enough, Maggs reflected. Job prospects must be strictly limited for a man with only one arm and a badly scarred face. Poor Dickie. He hadn't been a bad-looking lad either when he went off to war. She dug her hands deeper into her coat pocket, for it was bitter out. She promised herself a nice cup of tea when she got home.

'I must say you're looking well,' Dickie commented. 'Positively glowing.'

'Am I?'

'Unless it's the cold causing it.'

Maggs laughed. 'Possibly.' She knew it wasn't the weather at all, but because she'd been thinking about Rupert and what their life together could be like.

That was enough to make any girl glow with well-being.

She and Dickie continued chatting, he in seventh heaven, as they went on their way.

'No, darling, no!' Maggs protested, when she and Rupert had parked in a quiet spot for a bit of canoodling.

He reluctantly removed his hand from underneath her skirt where it had finally reached her inner thigh. 'What's wrong?' he said huskily.

'I'm not that sort of girl. You should know that by now.'

Rupert swore inwardly. 'And what sort of girl would that be?'

'Easy. Cheap.'

'I've never considered you either easy or cheap, Maggs.'

'Then don't treat me as if I am.'

Rupert drew apart and lit a cigarette, his heart pounding – and not only his heart. 'I'm sorry,' he mumbled. 'It's just . . . well, that I fancy you so much.'

'Do you?' she asked softly.

'Very much so. You wouldn't be here if I didn't.'

She regarded him steadily in the dark. 'Is that all? Just fancy me?'

Damn! he thought. Why did they always want you to say that? 'I more than fancy you, there.'

'Oh, Rupert!' she breathed. 'How much more?'

All right, he told himself. If that's the way it has to be. 'I believe I'm falling in love with you.' His voice was quavering as he spoke.

'My darling! I'm in love with you. Totally and utterly.'

166

He decided he didn't want the cigarette after all. Not now. Rolling down his window he flicked it away.

This time she didn't stop his hand. But she wouldn't let things go further than that.

Lavender let out a cry as she caught her heel on a cobble, her ankle twisting under her. She desperately tried to break her fall as she pitched to the ground.

Jamie, who was across the road, immediately dashed over to her. 'Are you hurt, Mrs Fletcher?'

'My ankle, doctor.'

A quick examination revealed a bleeding gash on the ankle. 'Best get you home,' he declared, assisting her to her feet. Lavender's face screwed in pain as she got up.

'I think it's twisted as well,' she said, grimacing.

Luckily there was only a short distance to go before they were there. Jamie opened the door and helped her inside.

'What's wrong, Mum?' a horrified Crista demanded as they entered the kitchen. Jamie hastily explained as Lavender sank on to a chair.

'Now let's have a proper look,' he said, kneeling. To Crista he added, 'Could you please boil me some water? But before you do that I'd be obliged if you'd nip down the road and collect my bag. I had to leave it there while I assisted your mother.'

Crista was gone less than a minute, running all the way. 'Is it bad?' she queried on rejoining them.

'Well, the gash won't need stitches,' Jamie replied, 'though your mother will be hobbling for a while.

Unfortunately there's nothing I can do about that except strap it.'

When the kettle was boiled Crista poured water into a basin and placed it beside Jamie along with a clean towel and flannel, watching in concern as he bathed the wound and then applied some ointment. After that he bandaged the ankle tightly.

'How's that?' he asked at last when everything was to his satisfaction.

'Better, thank you,' Lavender answered, though her leg was still throbbing.

'If I leave the ointment can you change the dressing every day until the gash is healed?' He smiled at Crista.

She nodded. 'Of course.'

'You must make it as tight as your mother can bear. Understand?'

'Yes, doctor.'

'And I'll come back in a couple of days to check on things.'

'I can't thank you enough, doctor,' Lavender declared, smiling her gratitude.

'Just fortunate I was on hand, eh?'

'It was that.' She turned her attention to the hovering Crista. 'As the kettle's just boiled, brew us all a pot of tea. I, for one, could certainly use a cup.'

Jamie was about to refuse when he had an idea. 'Thank you. That would be lovely.'

'Sit down, doctor. Sit down.'

He repacked his bag first, then sat. 'Can I ask you a question, Mrs Fletcher? It's about the Swains.'

Her face hardened. 'What do you want to know about them?'

When Jamie finally left he was in no doubt – Lavender having confirmed everything that Spanish John had said – about how hated and detested the Swains were in the village and surrounding area.

Or how people would view him should he become involved with one of them.

Chapter 11

Maggs was wishing she hadn't let Abigail talk her into coming to the monthly local dance. It was proving just as dull and dreary as she'd feared. The only reason she'd agreed was because Rupert was in London for several weeks and she'd thought it best to keep up what would have been her normal routine, which included going to the dance.

She smiled to herself thinking about Rupert, itching for his return, to be in his arms again, his mouth on hers. And other things too, she reminded herself, her smile broadening. Oh yes, very much those other things too!

'Would you care to dance, Maggs?'

The speaker was Arthur Chappell, a lad roughly her own age who worked as a farm hand. Why not? she thought. And then she'd go home. She'd had enough for one evening.

Arthur was a well-meaning dancer, which was about all you could say for him. She wrinkled her nose slightly. She didn't know what preparations Arthur had made before coming out, but having a bath clearly wasn't one of them.

She wondered what Rupert was like as a dancer. Terrific, probably. With his background he was almost certainly bound to be. She fantasised it was he she was up with and not the clumping Arthur.

When the number was over Arthur asked her to stay on. She declined, saying it was time for her to leave, but thank you very much. Arthur didn't argue, simply thanked her for the dance they'd had and went looking for another partner.

Now where was Abigail? Maggs wondered, glancing around. She really should say goodnight to her and Tom. The pair had been dancing together nearly all night long.

Try as she might she couldn't spot either of them, which puzzled her. Surely they hadn't left without a cheerio? It would be unlike Abigail to do so. Maybe they'd both gone to the toilets? Yes, that might well be it. She headed that way herself, intending to speak to Abigail there. But Abigail wasn't in the ladies, which puzzled her even further. She couldn't believe they'd gone outside for a kiss and cuddle; it was far too cold for that. She decided to pop her head out of the back door anyway, just in case.

But she never reached the back door. She was passing the cupboard where cleaning materials were kept when she heard a frenzied moaning coming from inside. Maggs frowned. What on earth was going on? Someone being tortured? And then the penny dropped, causing her face to break into a broad smile. She'd found Abigail and Tom.

She should go straight back to the dance, she told herself. Leave them to their privacy. But somehow she couldn't. Not straight away, anyway. Curiosity was getting the better of her – that and a lasciviousness which was part of her nature.

'Oh my God!' Abigail whimpered softly in a contorted voice. 'It's so good. So good.'

Maggs bit her lip, her own body having quickly reacted to what she was overhearing. She was sopping wet.

A banging sound started up, as if something was being slammed against a wall. Maggs could only guess it was Abigail.

She could almost feel the heat emanating from inside the cupboard. Tom was muttering now, though she couldn't make out what. But the sense of urgency in his voice was all too clear. And then Abigail gave a loud, strangulated cry of exultation, which slowly tailed away into a series of sobs.

Maggs took a deep breath, then another, finally forcing herself to return to the dance. Once there she collected her coat and left.

She was shaking during her walk home. Shaking from all manner of emotions churning inside her. One thing was certain, and that surprised her a little. Though perhaps it shouldn't.

She deeply envied Abigail for what had just taken place.

That Monday morning Maggs excused herself to Davey and hurried across to where Abigail was also making her way to the mill.

'Well, is it?' she eagerly demanded.

Abigail looked blank. 'What are you talking about?'

'Does Tom really have a huge willy?'

That startled Abigail. 'How should I know?'

172

'Because you do. I went searching for you at the dance to say goodnight and overheard the pair of you in the cleaner's cupboard.'

Abigail went bright red. 'Oh Christ! Did you?'

Maggs nodded gleefully.

'How long did you listen for?'

She wasn't admitting to that. 'Long enough.'

Abigail swallowed hard. 'How embarrassing.'

'You were certainly enjoying yourself,' Maggs teased.

'Stop it, Maggs. This is awful.'

'So?'

'So what?' she asked, trying to pretend innocence, and totally failing.

'Is it huge?'

'Well, how can I say? I've no comparison.'

'Oh, come on. Stop mucking about. Tell me.'

Abigail glanced around, but there was no one close by. 'It's pretty big,' she reluctantly admitted.

'So it *is* huge?'

Abigail giggled, and suddenly became all intimate. 'I nearly died when I saw it. It'll never fit was all I could think.'

Maggs's eyes gleamed. 'Was that the first time?'

Abigail shook her head. 'We've been doing it for a while now. But I wouldn't have done it unless he'd agreed to get engaged.'

'So you're engaged?'

'Not officially. I'm not really going to tell anyone until we get the ring. Tom is saving up. It won't be much of a ring, I'm afraid, not on what he's paid. But it'll be a ring none the less, and that's all that matters.'

Maggs sucked in a deep breath. 'And what did it feel like? You know?'

'Being shagged?'

Maggs nodded. They were rural girls after all, the subject of sex more open than it often was in the city.

Abigail thought about that, wondering how she could describe what Maggs had just asked. 'You know what it's like when you diddle yourself?'

Maggs gave another nod.

'Well it's similar, only a hundred times better.'

'A hundred times . . .' She broke off in astonishment.

'Well, that's how it is for me. Honestly.'

Maggs closed her eyes for a brief second. Would it be the same between her and Rupert? She fervently hoped so.

Abigail clutched Maggs by the arm. 'Swear you won't tell anyone. Please?'

'You have my word. Not a soul.'

Relief flooded Abigail's face. 'It might be different after we're officially engaged. But not now. Not yet.'

'I understand.'

'Not a soul, Maggs. You've sworn.'

'Cross my heart and hope to die.' She hesitated. 'How huge is it actually? I'm fascinated.'

Abigail brought her hands up and indicated a length.

Maggs's eyes nearly popped out of her head. 'Bloody hell!' she exclaimed, which made Abigail laugh.

Maggs's mind went into overdrive.

'Dr Murray! This is a surprise.'

'Could I have a word, Mrs Fletcher? Is that possible?'

'Of course. Come in. I've got a fresh pot of tea on the go. Will you have a cup?'

'Thank you. Yes, I will. By the way, are you alone?'

Strange question, Lavender thought. 'Quite. I've sent Crista out on an errand and she won't be back for a while yet.'

'Good. I was hoping to catch you by yourself.'

Lavender led the way into the kitchen and told Jamie to sit while she sorted out the tea. He refused a slice of cake when offered.

'Crista's still without work I take it?' he inquired, making small talk.

'That's right. It's not for the lack of trying but there's just nothing to be had locally. It's got so bad, and her so fed up, she's talking about looking for work in one of the Exeter hotels. Chambermaid, waitressing, that sort of thing. The only trouble with that is she'd have to live in, which she doesn't want. Me neither for that matter. But it might come to it yet. She feels dreadful about not bringing money into the house, you see, not earning her keep. But that's not her fault. And we are managing. Perhaps not quite as well as we were, but still managing.'

Jamie accepted his tea, and Lavender sat down opposite him. 'So, what can I do for you, doctor?' she asked.

'To be utterly frank, it's a delicate matter, Mrs Fletcher.'

'Oh?'

'Very.' He had a sip of tea before going on, choosing his words carefully. 'I have a problem which I don't quite know how to resolve. I've thought about who might be able to give me advice, and finally decided you're my best bet.'

Lavender raised an eyebrow. 'Sounds serious.'

'It is. And what I say next must be in strictest confidence between the pair of us. Is that agreed?'

She was intrigued. 'Of course.'

Jamie studied his teacup. This was difficult and he was hating doing it. But done it must be. 'It's regarding Mrs Tyler,' he said slowly.

Lavender's lips tightened. 'What's she been up to, then?'

'Do I detect a note of disapproval in your voice, Mrs Fletcher?' he queried.

'You do. Let's just say I don't hold Dolly Tyler in particularly high regard. And neither do many in this village. She has a certain reputation.'

'For what, may I ask?'

Lavender shrugged. 'This and that. She's known to be rather underhanded in many of her day-to-day dealings. People don't like that.'

'Would these dealings include theft?' Jamie asked quietly.

Lavender stared at him, her eyes diamond hard. So that's what this was all about. 'I have to admit I've never heard that. But I certainly wouldn't put it past her. What's she taken?'

'Do you mind if I smoke?'

'Not at all. Just use your saucer there as I don't have any ashtrays. The saucer will wash easily enough.'

Jamie set his tea aside while he lit up. 'These, for a start. I had begun to think I was becoming a heavy smoker, at least heavy by my standards, until I started keeping count. I have a bad habit of leaving my packet lying about. Anyway, once I kept check I soon realised that cigarettes were vanishing out of my packet. Two

176

here, three there. Nothing substantial, but vanishing none the less.'

'And you think she's been taking them?'

'I don't see who else it could be. I do have the occasional visitor, but I'm always present when the visitor's there. Whereas she has access to the house at all times, whether I'm there or not.'

'Go on,' Lavender prompted.

'Other things too. You'll appreciate that, as a doctor, I get left presents of food. All manner of things, some-times in lieu of fees. Well, on a number of occasions I've been stopped in the street by patients asking how I enjoyed such and such. A duck, brace of pheasants, rabbit. A fruit tart, a particular kind of cake, et cetera et cetera. Things that never appeared on my table when they should have done.' Jamie shook his head in sadness. 'If she'd only asked I'd have told her to take whatever she wanted that was surplus to my needs. But she never has. And, to echo what you said about the villagers, I don't like that.'

Neither did Lavender. If true, and she could well believe it of Dolly Tyler, then Dolly was letting the whole of Ford down. And that was unforgivable.

'But the worst thing of all are the tracheostomy tubes,' Jamie went on.

'Tracky what?'

He smiled. 'They are used in a throat procedure. In certain cases where a patient is choking, or the air supply impaired, an incision is made in the windpipe, called a tracheostomy, and a tube inserted to allow the patient unrestricted breathing.'

Lavender nodded that she understood, though it sounded horrible to her.

'On arrival at the practice I found seven of those tubes wrapped in a soft cloth at the back of a drawer. I have absolutely no idea why Dr Mumsford had seven of them. Mementoes perhaps? It's anyone's guess. But the point is, the other day I was rearranging my surgery and decided to include one of those tubes in the rearrangement. When I opened the cloth there were only five where there had once been seven. In other words, two were missing.'

'But why would Dolly take two of those?' Lavender frowned.

'Perhaps because they're made of solid silver and therefore valuable.'

'Dear me,' Lavender muttered. This was far worse than stealing a few fags or a bit of food.

Jamie flicked ash into his saucer as Lavender had instructed him to do.

'So what kind of advice do you want from me, doctor?'

'She simply can't remain in her post, Mrs Fletcher. Do you agree?'

Lavender nodded.

'But how do I get rid of her? That's the question. If I sack her she'll want to know why, and then it's her word against mine. God knows what she'd put round the village about me. And I'm the newcomer, don't forget, while she's a born and bred local.' He paused, then went on. 'But maybe she wouldn't be believed so much, considering what you've told me about her character and reputation, which I was unaware of.'

'Have you thought of speaking to PC Munny?'

'Indeed. But I don't want to do that. What I do

want is for her to simply hand in her notice and leave, allowing me to engage someone else. Someone trustworthy.'

Lavender pursed her lips while she thought about it. 'How would it be if I talked to her?' she eventually suggested. 'I'm fairly certain I can get her to agree to that.'

His face brightened. 'Would you?'

'I think the threat of PC Munny becoming involved would frighten Dolly out of her wits. I'm sure she'll see the sense of keeping the whole matter hush hush, strictly between the three of us and no one else.'

'I'd be ever so obliged, Mrs Fletcher. I can't thank you enough.'

Lavender smiled. 'She hasn't agreed yet. But knowing Dolly as I do I believe it's a forgone conclusion after I explain to her the whole business will be forgotten, and never mentioned again, as long as she hands in her notice.'

Jamie set his now empty cup aside and came to his feet. 'I'm in your debt, Mrs Fletcher.'

'Not at all.'

'How's the ankle, by the way?'

'As good as it's ever been. I have a small scar from that gash, but nothing to worry about.'

She saw him to the front door, where he thanked her again before going on his way.

Dolly Tyler thieving, Lavender reflected after he'd gone. She wasn't at all surprised. Not at all.

The Tyler family were a bad lot and always had been.

★ ★ ★

'There we are,' Rupert declared, placing Maggs's drink in front of her, and then sitting down with his own. 'Cheers!'

She lifted her gin and orange, a large one as it always was when she was out with Rupert. 'Cheers.'

They were in the quiet, out-of-the-way pub that Rupert brought her to where they were unknown to the locals.

'My friend Abigail is to get engaged shortly,' Maggs announced after she'd had a sip. 'To a chap in the village called Tom. They make ever such a handsome couple.'

'Oh?'

She sighed dreamily. 'I think the whole thing is just so romantic. I know they'll be happy together. You can just tell.'

'Really?'

'Oh yes. They're only waiting till he saves up enough to buy the ring before making it official.'

She was looking even prettier than usual tonight, Rupert thought. If he could he'd have pounced on her there and then.

'What do you think about engagements?' Maggs asked with a smile.

'What's there to think about? You get engaged, then married. At least that's what's supposed to happen.'

Maggs's eyes twinkled. 'Have you thought about it?'

'Me?'

'Yes you.'

He laughed. 'Engaged to whom?'

Maggs didn't reply to that. 'He's shagging her, you know,' she said instead.

The baldness of the statement took Rupert aback. 'Who is?'

'Tom and Abigail. She wouldn't let him until he promised to get engaged. Then she did. She says it's wonderful.'

Alarm bells went off in his brain. What was she getting at? Surely she didn't think . . . ? His eyes narrowed ever so slightly as he stared at her afresh. 'No doubt.'

'Have you ever shagged anyone, Rupert?'

He didn't reply for a few seconds. 'That's not the kind of question you should ask someone. It isn't polite,' he prevaricated.

'Does it embarrass you?'

'Yes, it does.'

'Then that means you have.'

'I never said so.'

'I can see it in your face.'

What sort of conversation was this turning out to be? Lively and frank if nothing else. 'Then aren't you the clever one,' he teased.

'I'm still a virgin. I hope you appreciate that?'

'Of course. I'd expect nothing else,' he smoothly lied. Damn! He'd been sure she wasn't. He'd thought all village girls were fairly promiscuous. At least so he'd been led to believe. He smiled inwardly. Though not as promiscuous as some of the so-called upper-crust ladies of his acquaintance.

'Just so you know.'

'Oh, Rupert, I do love you,' she said huskily, wrapped in his embrace. On the way back from the pub they'd stopped in the secluded spot they normally chose.

181

He didn't answer, his hand busy.

'Tell me you love me, Rupert. Tell me you do.'

At that moment he'd have told her the moon was blue cheese if she'd asked. Christ, but he was randy. 'I do.'

Her eyes shone triumphantly in the darkness. Truth was, she actually was in love with Rupert Swain. The thought of him and what he represented, anyway. 'Are you sure?'

'I'm sure,' he croaked, trying to pull off her lower undergarment.

'Does that mean we'll get engaged?'

'If you want,' he lied with a groan.

Elation filled her as she moved her bottom, releasing the undergarment which was swiftly tugged down her legs. She was *engaged*! The words thundered round and round inside her head.

'I want you so much, Maggs,' he pleaded. 'You've no idea how much.'

A feel with her hand confirmed his words. Deftly she began to undo his flies, wanting to hold him, to know what that was like. She caught her breath when she found out.

'Oh God,' he groaned as her hand started to move.

'You won't change your mind, will you?' she whispered.

'About what?'

'Us being engaged.'

'No, I won't.'

Her exposed breasts were now heaving, her breathing coming in short, sharp pants. 'There's no room in here to do the full thing,' she whimpered, her insides on fire.

182

But she was wrong. There was. Rupert somehow managed it.

'Dr Murray is going to need a new housekeeper,' Lavender commented during tea a few evenings later.

'Why's that?' Davey queried through a mouthful of food, a habit of his which irritated Lavender, and one she'd never got him to break.

'Dolly Tyler is leaving him. Says she can't run two households, it's become too much for her.'

Lavender smiled, recalling her conversation with Dolly, a memory she'd treasure for the rest of her life. Dolly's face had been an absolute picture throughout.

'That so?' Davey mumbled, not really interested.

'The doctor has asked me if I know of anyone to take her place, someone I can recommend.' This time Jamie had no intention, if he could possibly avoid it, of advertising in a shop window and taking on someone he didn't know anything about. That had been his explanation to Lavender, who'd agreed to help.

'There must be plenty of housewives in the village who'd jump at that job,' Maggs declared.

'I'm sure,' Lavender mused. 'But who?'

Crista was staring at her mother, her brow creased in thought. 'Does it have to be a housewife?' she asked.

Lavender shrugged. 'I don't suppose so. Any woman who fitted the bill would be acceptable.'

Maggs glanced at Crista. 'Why do you ask? Do you have someone in mind?'

'Yes, I do.'

'Who?' Lavender inquired.

Crista stared her mother straight in the eyes. 'Me.'

'Are you the last one, Crista?' Jamie queried, glancing round the waiting room which was empty at last. It had been a long surgery. Sometimes people nipped outside for a smoke until it was their turn.

'Yes.'

'Then come in. Take a seat.' Once he too was seated he formed his hands into a pyramid shape and smiled at her. 'So, what's wrong with you?'

'Nothing, doctor. I'm right as rain.'

He frowned. 'Then why are you here?'

'I want to apply for the job as your housekeeper.'

'You . . .' He broke off in astonishment, his mind racing.

'I know I'm rather young,' she went on hurriedly, 'but there's nothing round a house I can't do.'

His smile returned. He was finding this amusing. 'Is that so?'

She nodded.

'Does your mother know you're here?'

'Of course. I wouldn't have come without telling her first.'

'And has she explained the duties involved?'

'Yes, she has.'

'You know how to cook, wash, iron?'

'I do everything like that at home when helping mum, so why not here for you?'

She had a point. 'Regarding the cooking,' he said slowly, referring to a matter of particular concern. Dolly Tyler's meals had been excruciatingly bad. He'd suffered so many attacks of indigestion that he'd taken

184

to keeping a bottle of peppermint by his bedside. 'Are you any good at that?'

'I do believe so, doctor. No one in our house has ever had any complaints, anyway. Mum taught me.'

'Hmm,' he mused. 'There is the question of age, you being so young. I hate to mention this, but do you think people in the village might read more into your being here than was the actual case?'

'Mum and I discussed that. They might gossip to begin with, but then when they thought about it they'd realise mum would never let me work here if there was even the hint of any shenanigans.'

That made sense, he thought, warming to the idea of Crista as his housekeeper. She was certainly easy on the eye, and had to be better than Dolly Tyler whose work had fallen away over the last months.

'Can I ask what you pay, doctor?'

He told her. 'That's the same as Mrs Tyler was getting. Would it be acceptable to you?'

'Oh yes!' she replied excitedly. 'It's more than I earned at the mill.'

He made a decision, since no one else had as yet applied for the job. 'Why don't I give you a month's trial and see how you get on?'

Crista beamed at him. 'When do I start?'

'Monday morning?'

'I'll be here nice and early. And thank you, doctor. I appreciate this.'

Well, he was indebted to Lavender, he reflected. Giving Crista a trial run was one way of repaying her.

★ ★ ★

185

'Vegetable soup,' Crista declared, placing a bowl in front of Jamie. 'And there's some nice fresh crusty bread in the basket.'

'Right then,' he said, and picked up his spoon.

Crista watched anxiously. This was the first proper meal she'd cooked for Jamie. She offered up a silent prayer it was all right.

Jamie's face broke into a broad smile. 'Delicious,' he pronounced. 'Absolutely delicious. What's the main course?'

'Lamb chops with vegetables and two kinds of potatoes.'

That too proved a huge success with Jamie, particularly the gravy which, Crista informed him, she'd made with jam, a recipe of her mother's. In his opinion it knocked spots off the thick, yellow muck Dolly had consistently served up.

After a month Crista was duly confirmed in the job.

Chapter 12

Maggs lay back in the grass basking in the afterglow of lovemaking. With the arrival of summer she and Rupert had been able to find secluded spots, far from prying eyes, where they could indulge themselves. Overhead the sun shone fiercely down out of an azure sky.

This particular place, one of their favourites, was masked by trees behind, with the bank of a river only feet away. It was truly idyllic and ideal for their purposes.

Rupert lit up, smiling as he looked at her prostrate form. 'Shouldn't you pull your skirt down now, you brazen hussy?' he teased.

'Why, don't you like what you see?'

He laughed. 'I could sit staring at it for hours.'

'Then don't complain. And don't call me a brazen hussy. I'm nothing of the sort. What I am is a woman madly in love.'

'Good,' he nodded.

'And you?'

'Equally madly in love.'

She sighed with pleasure, listening to the buzz of

bees, her nostrils filled with the sweet scent of wild flowers growing nearby.

'Rupert?'

'What, darling?'

She brought herself up on to one elbow. 'It's getting harder and harder for me to find excuses to get away. I'm simply running out of them.' She hesitated, then went on. 'I think mum's beginning to suspect, if she doesn't already, that I'm seeing someone.'

'Oh?'

'What will be puzzling her is not that I am, but not mentioning it or telling her who. It won't be long before questions are asked.'

He drew deeply on his cigarette while he thought about that. 'And of course you can't say it's me.'

'Christ, no! They'd both have a fit. Particularly dad. Me going out with a Swain! He'd blow his top. And that's putting it mildly.'

'I can understand the problem,' Rupert mused. Well, it was no skin off his nose. He was starting to tire of her anyway. Trouble was, there was no alternative in the offing for him to have his fun with.

'So I've come up with an idea,' she stated slowly.

'Which is?'

'I've given this a lot of thought, Rupert. I want you to appreciate that.'

'I'm listening.'

'Why don't we elope to Gretna Green?' she suggested, eyes shining and full of hope.

'Elope!' This was the last thing he'd been expecting.

'Yes, why not? And after that we live in London at your place until we can find a house of our own.'

188

She hurried on. 'Think of the advantages. For a start I won't have to face my parents about you, and secondly you won't have to face your father, for I'm sure he's not going to be best pleased at us marrying.'

Dear God, Rupert thought. This was a bombshell. Elope with Maggs to Gretna Green? He'd never heard anything so ludicrous. This relationship was going to have to be terminated sooner than he'd wanted. But not yet, not yet. She had such a gorgeous body, even if she was a trifle dim. But what did dim matter in someone so lovely and enthusiastic between the sheets? Not that there had ever been any sheets in their case. A while longer, he decided. He'd play for time before getting rid of her.

'Well, Rupert?' she demanded eagerly.

'It's certainly worth considering,' he prevaricated, trying to sound enthusiastic.

'Shall we do it, then?'

'I must think about this, Maggs. It's not something to do lightly. You must appreciate that.'

Her face fell. 'I was hoping we could go within the next week or two.'

He glanced again at her lower nakedness, feeling himself stir and twitch. Damn, but she was desirable. As seductive a popsy as he'd ever put a leg over.

'That's a bit soon, I think. I mean, I'd have to organise matters first.'

'What's to organise?' she asked with a frown. 'We just get in your car and go. I'll leave a note behind to explain and presumably you'll do the same.'

He regarded her curiously. 'From what you've told me it would mean you might never be able to return to Ford. Are you prepared for that?'

189

Her expression became one of defiance. 'If that's how it's to be then yes.'

'Never see your parents again?'

A lump came into her throat. 'I love my family dearly, Rupert, and would never willingly wish to hurt them. But you're the man I love, the man I intend sharing my life with. And to do that I'll sacrifice anything no matter how much it hurts or costs me.'

A teensy bit melodramatic, he thought. But impressive. He really had got through to her. Then he thought wryly, for he was no fool, or his money and position had. Cynical bastard, he chastised himself. But it was true.

'I see,' he said quietly.

'So?'

'Well, I certainly can't slope off in the next few weeks. I have business to attend to in London that needs me to be there. What I suggest is we discuss this further when I return. It's a big step, Maggs. We mustn't rush into it without thinking it through.'

Her disappointment was obvious.

'That doesn't mean I'm against the idea,' he lied. 'I'm not. It's simply . . . well, you've caught me a bit on the hop, I suppose.'

'But we will do it?'

He moved closer to her and stroked her buttock. 'I wonder what Gretna Green's like?' he mused. 'I've never been to Scotland.'

'And I've never been anywhere further than Exeter.'

'Would you enjoy living in London, Maggs? I mean, it's very different from here. Couldn't be more so.'

'I'll be happy as long as I'm with you, Rupert.'

'Will you?'

She nodded.

'Dear Maggs,' he smiled. 'Dear beautiful Maggs.'

She also smiled when she correctly read the look that had come into his eyes. 'Again?'

'If you're up to it?'

'Oh, I'm up to it all right,' she replied throatily, dropping on to her back.

He was going to miss her, he reflected. He'd just have to make the best of what time they had left before he was forced to end it.

And that would be as long as he could draw it out between them.

Jamie took a shirt out of his cupboard and shook it out prior to putting it on. He could hear Crista through in the kitchen preparing breakfast.

She was a brilliant ironer, he thought as he slipped into the shirt. Far better than Mrs Tyler had been. But then she was far better at every aspect of housekeeping than Dolly had been. He'd certainly fallen on his feet in hiring her.

Dickie Trippett came suddenly awake to find himself shaking and covered in cold sweat. Hastily he groped for the pills Dr Murray had prescribed and swallowed two. He sat up in bed, his chest heaving, knowing it would take at least twenty minutes for him to settle down again.

It had been another nightmare, this time a really bad one. They'd been advancing when a shell had dropped right in amongst them, momentarily blinding him with the flash of the explosion.

This was it, he'd immediately thought as he was

191

hurled to the ground. But amazingly it wasn't. What was more, he hadn't suffered any injuries, as he quickly ascertained on regaining his sight.

All around him were dead, dying, and badly wounded, the groans of the latter horrible to hear. Rifle fire crackled while the big German guns continued to roar.

'Dickie, Dickie,' a voice croaked.

He crawled over to where Sidney Dennis, a good pal of his, lay. Both Sidney's legs had been blown off, a pair of white thigh bones all that remained. Beneath him was a pool of ever-spreading blood.

'Do me a favour, Dickie.'

'What's that, mate?'

'Straighten my legs out, there's a good chap.'

Dickie could see that death was already creeping into Sidney's eyes. It was a look he'd come to know only too well. 'Sure thing, Sid. Just give me half a mo'.'

He had to force himself to do it but somehow he touched both protruding thigh bones. 'How's that then?'

'Better. More comfortable like.'

'Good.'

'Take me packet out and light a fag for me too. I could murder a ciggie.'

Dickie located the packet and a box of matches. Extracting a cigarette, he lit it, and then gently placed it between Sidney's lips.

Sidney inhaled, then smiled. 'Ta.'

'Think nothing of it. That's what mates are for.'

'I'm going to miss my Gwenda, you know. I loved that woman.'

'Don't talk like that, Sid. You're going to be fine.'

'Am I?' Sidney chuckled, a rattling sound in his throat, and died, his eyes, now blank and glazed, remaining open.

'Goodbye, mate,' Dickie whispered, hoping there would be someone there to comfort him in his last moments. If there were last moments, that is, and he wasn't killed outright.

Catching up his rifle he came to his feet and continued on towards the enemy.

It was the only thing to do.

'Would I be in your way if I sat down and read?' Jamie inquired politely. Crista was busy dusting and polishing.

'Not in the least.' She hesitated. 'Or would you prefer it if I left the room?'

'No no, that's not necessary.'

Jamie plonked himself into a chair and opened his newspaper, which he hadn't yet had a chance to look at. But instead of reading he soon found himself watching Crista, admiring her figure and the graceful way she moved. She certainly was a pretty thing.

'I'm going to the pub tonight,' she informed him over her shoulder.

That surprised Jamie. 'Are you old enough?'

'I am as of today. It's my birthday.'

'But you should have warned me! I'd have got you a card or something.'

It was sweet of him to say that, she thought. 'It'll be my first time in the Angel. I'm looking forward to it.'

'Just make sure you don't get drunk,' he teased. 'That would never do.'

Crista laughed. 'I'll try not to.'

'What'll you be having, then? Pints of beer and cider?' He was still teasing her.

'A half pint of either will suit me, thank you very much.'

He had an idea. 'What time are you going?'

'About eight, I'd imagine.'

'With your boyfriend?'

'I don't have a boyfriend. Not at the moment, anyway.' Of late she'd been approached by several of the village lads but the truth was she hadn't fancied any of them. And she certainly wasn't going out with someone just because he'd asked her. That would have been silly.

For some reason Jamie was pleased to hear there was no boyfriend. He was smiling as he returned to his newspaper.

'Are you putting on weight, Maggs?' Lavender queried with a frown. 'That skirt is cutting into your waist.'

'I've noticed it too,' Crista commented. 'But I didn't like to say in case Maggs thought I was having a go at her.' It was that evening and the two girls were getting ready for the pub.

An expression of guilt came on to Maggs's face. 'I suppose I am. I can't think why.'

'Well, you have been eating a lot more recently,' Lavender said, pursing her lips in disapproval. 'Perhaps you should cut back a little. There's nothing wrong with a healthy appetite, mind you. But you can take things too far.'

'She doesn't seem any different to me,' Davey piped up from where he was sitting.

'Huh!' Lavender snorted derisively. 'So much for your powers of observation, Davey Fletcher.'

'I have put on weight, Dad. Mum's right,' Maggs confessed. 'My skirts have been tight on me for weeks. I suppose I've just been pretending otherwise. Trying to kid myself.'

'Well you still look the same to me. So there.'

Lavender rolled her eyes heavenwards. 'Men,' she declared. 'About as useful as a bicycle to a fish.'

An amused glint came into Davey's eyes. 'You don't always say that, do you, darling? Quite the contrary on occasion.' He laughed quietly to himself.

Lavender coloured when she realised his meaning. And then coloured even more.

Crista grinned at her sister, who grinned back. They too had realised what their father had meant. No wonder Lavender was embarrassed. Davey would undoubtedly cop an earful when they'd left for the pub.

Crista was thoroughly enjoying herself, having decided pubs were fun. Spanish John had challenged her on their arrival, and then bought her a drink when she'd explained it was her eighteenth birthday. She'd thought it was a terribly nice thing for him to do.

There were four of them grouped round the table, Crista, Maggs, Abigail Nicholls and Gemma Gatsby, all talking away nineteen to the dozen, when Jamie came into the pub and crossed straight to the bar.

Abigail frowned when she caught sight of him. 'You know, I don't understand what I ever saw in Dr Murray. He isn't a patch on my Tom.'

'Where is Tom anyway?' Maggs asked, surprised he hadn't turned up with Abigail as he usually did.

'Playing skittles at the Salmon and Pig. I've promised to join him later, though I don't want to because of Surly Sorley. I loathe being served by that man.'

Alec Sorley was the name of the landlord there, but he was known throughout the village as Surly, and had been for years. It described exactly his attitude to his customers. Needless to say, albeit people used his pub, he wasn't much liked. Most folk went in there because of his wife Janet, who was as pleasant and cheerful as he was churlish.

'Hello, here comes the doc,' Gemma said quietly. And sure enough Jamie, holding an envelope in one hand and a drink in the other, was heading in their direction.

'Good evening, ladies.' He smiled on reaching them.

They all thought it rather funny to be addressed as ladies. How posh!

'This is for you, Crista,' Jamie declared, handing her the envelope. 'And this. It's what Dickie says you're drinking.' And with that he placed a half of beer shandy in front of her.

Crista flushed with pleasure and embarrassment. 'Why thank you, doctor.'

'On you go, open your card,' Maggs urged.

'Nothing startling, but the best I could come up with in such a short time,' Jamie apologised.

'It's wonderful,' Crista declared, absolutely thrilled. 'Thank you very much.'

'Happy birthday.' And with that he was gone, returning to the bar and the pint he'd ordered for himself.

'Wasn't that kind,' Gemma commented. 'What a proper gentleman.'

Crista glanced over at Jamie, eyes shining. 'He is a

gentleman, through and through. Lovely to work for too.'

Maggs was about to add to that when her forehead was suddenly beaded with sweat and an awful feeling of nausea gripped her. 'Excuse me,' she muttered, and hurried, as fast as she could without actually breaking into a run, to the toilet where she was violently sick.

She leant against the cubicle wall when it was all over, and closed her eyes. It wasn't that, she tried to convince herself. The weight gain and now sickness were simply a coincidence.

Or were they?

'Doctor, this pile of papers has been here for ages. Can I put it somewhere out of the way?'

Jamie frowned. 'Sorry, Crista. I've been meaning to attend to that lot for weeks but just haven't had the time. They're all waiting to be filed.'

'Filed?'

'Patients' notes, invoices. Oh, all sorts. Every time I think I'll make a start on them I get called elsewhere. But don't worry, I'll do something about them shortly.'

How harassed he looked, she thought. Tired too, as if he wasn't getting enough sleep. 'I never realised how busy doctors are.' She smiled. 'It seems to me you're always run off your feet.'

He nodded. 'It is a hectic life, and that's a fact. Ford could actually do with two doctors and there'd still be enough work for both of them.'

'Would you like me to file those papers for you?' she asked softly.

His face brightened. 'Could you? I mean, it's not part of your normal duties.'

'I'd be delighted to. All you have to do is show me where they're to be filed and I'll get on with it.'

'I'd be ever so grateful.' He hesitated, then said, 'I think we know each other well enough now for you to call me Jamie. But only when we're alone. That would be best.'

'If you wish. Though it'll seem strange at first.'

'Will it?' He laughed. 'Don't forget I'm a man as well as a doctor. And we have become friends during your time here. Haven't we?'

'I suppose so,' she agreed. Of course they had, now she thought about it.

'Then Jamie it is.'

He gathered up the papers, surprised at how many had actually accumulated. Far more than he'd thought. 'If you follow me I'll show you what to do.'

'Yes, Jamie,' she replied, enjoying the sudden intimacy of addressing him by his Christian name.

Maggs lay in bed worrying a nail as she stared into the darkness. There was still another week to go before Rupert returned from his latest trip to London. A week she knew would seem like an eternity.

There was no doubt about it now. She was pregnant. Up the duff. Had a bun in the oven. Or whatever else you cared to call it.

He loved her, she reminded herself. He'd sworn it on a number of occasions. There was no doubt in her mind that he would stand by her.

London, she thought. How was it going to be,

living there? He'd warned her it would be different. But she'd cope, of course she would. It might just take a bit of getting used to, that was all.

She tried to imagine what their house would look like. Large, of course, with perhaps not lots of servants but certainly some. Her eyes gleamed at the prospect.

'Mrs Rupert Swain,' she said aloud, and squirmed with pleasure. She couldn't wait for the day she became that.

It was going to be awful leaving everyone behind, her mum, dad and Crista. But there was nothing else for it. Her parents would simply never accept her marrying a Swain. Nor would the village. She'd be an outcast, a figure of hate just as they were.

Carefully she felt her breasts, which were beginning to get larger. Tender too. As for her stomach . . . well, she and Rupert just had to leave as soon as they could before it became apparent she was expecting. Any more weight gain round her middle and tongues would be wagging. That's how it was when you lived in a village, where everyone, bar none, was under constant scrutiny. Any change caused comment and possible speculation.

'Rich,' she murmured, and smiled. That's what she was going to be. It was a dream come true. She would have fine clothes, jewellery, and everything else that went with having lots of money.

But the best part would be never having to work at the mill again. God, how she loathed that place and the mind-numbing toil she endured there. Day in, day out, the same thing over and over again till you wanted to scream.

She thought of the note she'd write to her parents. What a shock it was going to be for them. More than a shock.

Maggs hardened her heart, refusing to think further on the subject. Or the consequences for them of her actions in running away with Rupert. What would be would be and that's all there was to it. They might never forgive her but they'd get over it in time. The anger would die away to eventual acceptance. At least she hoped so. For their sake.

As for her, it was the life of Riley from now on. The life of bloody Riley!

'Jesus Christ, that was the best yet,' Rupert declared, rolling off Maggs. She was wild when warmed up, and certainly didn't need much warming.

'Was it really?' She almost purred with contentment.

He lit a cigarette as he always did directly afterwards. 'I'd say so. It was for me anyway.'

'Good.'

Rupert shook his head. 'You really are something, Maggs.' He stopped himself just in time from adding she was the best shag he'd ever had. By a mile.

'You do love me, don't you, Rupert?'

'Of course I do, Maggs. In spades.'

'And I love you.'

He smiled in acknowledgement.

'Rupert?'

'What?'

'I'm pregnant.'

It took a few moments for it to sink in. 'You're what?' he exclaimed, totally aghast.

Her smile was verging on beatific. 'Pregnant. Expecting a baby. *Our* baby.'

'But you can't be,' he protested vehemently. 'You just can't be. I've always been careful.'

'No you haven't. There have been times when you simply couldn't wait. And once when . . . well, you lost the johnny inside me. Remember?'

'But . . .' He broke off, lost for words.

'I'm three months gone.'

'Are you absolutely certain?' he stuttered.

'Of course I am, silly. There's no mistake. I have missed the occasional period in the past, but not three in a row. Besides, there are other signs. No, I'm certain all right.'

'Damn!' he muttered angrily.

His saying that made her suddenly nervous. 'We are still going to get married at Gretna Green, aren't we?'

'Married?' He let out a large guffaw, all pretence having vanished. 'Don't be ridiculous, you stupid little tart.'

The look of rage on his face held her transfixed, her entire world, with that one sentence, simply blown apart. 'You don't mean that, Rupert. Please tell me you don't,' she pleaded.

'Of course I bloody well mean it. Did you actually think, really believe, that I would marry you? If you did then you must be dimmer than I thought.'

Tears welled into her eyes. 'Oh, Rupert,' she whispered, voice quavering.

He regarded her steadily. 'Anyway, how do I know the baby's mine? Half the lads in the village might well have had you by now.'

'You were the first. I was a virgin. I swear!'

'Huh!' he snorted. 'You're hardly likely to admit otherwise, are you now?'

'The baby is yours, Rupert. On my life it is. Oh, please don't do this to me.'

The smile he gave her was cruel as could be. 'Can you just imagine me telling my father I'd married a common as muck mill girl? He'd take a horsewhip to me and then have me certified.' Rupert paused for effect, actually beginning to rather enjoy this. 'I was only shagging you because you were available. No other reason. And I fully intended getting rid of you soon anyway. This has only brought matters to a head, that's all.'

Maggs began to cry, dollops of tears running down her now reddened cheeks. She felt cheap, degraded, dirty.

'I simply used you, woman,' Rupert snarled. 'But I have to admit, to be totally honest, you are good at it. I've never come across better. But it's finished now. You hear? Finished. Done. Over.'

'But the baby . . .'

'That's got nothing to do with me,' he brutally interjected. 'Go and drink a bottle of gin and have a stinking hot bath. That's my advice.'

He laughed as he climbed into his trousers, and then started to put on his socks and shoes. Maggs watched numbly. Without another word he stood up and strode away, returning to where he'd parked the car.

'Rupert!' Her cry was heart-rending, coming from her very soul.

Rupert never answered, or looked back.

Maggs collapsed on to the grass where they'd so

202

recently made love, while her tears continued to flow. She couldn't believe what had just happened. That he'd said what he had.

It was a nightmare come to life.

Chapter 13

'You look tired, dear.'

Davey yawned. 'It's been a long hard day at the mill. I'm absolutely whacked.'

Lavender gazed at him in concern. 'Is there anything I can get you? A cup of tea?'

He shook his head.

'Do you want to turn in early then?'

'Probably.' He glanced at the clock on the mantel-piece. 'But not quite yet.'

Lavender returned to her darning, thinking to herself that this particular pair of socks had almost had it.

Maggs was sitting at the table watching her parents, while Crista was reading a novel that had come to Lavender from Mavis Davis. When they'd finished with it Lavender would pass it on.

'You're very quiet tonight, Maggs,' Lavender commented without looking up.

Maggs bit her lip. She was going to have to take the plunge sooner or later and tell them. Why not now? She really couldn't put it off much longer, thanks to Nature's taking her course.

This time Lavender did look up. 'Maggs?'

'I heard you, Mum. I suppose I've just got a lot on my mind.'

'Oh?'

There was only one way to do this and that was come straight out with it. She took a deep breath. God only knew what the next half hour or so was going to be like. It didn't bear thinking about.

'What's worrying you, then?' Lavender prompted.

'Mum, Dad, I've got something to tell you. Something important.'

Lavender stopped darning and frowned. 'What's that?'

'Dad, you're not paying attention.'

'I am. I am,' he protested. He hadn't been.

Maggs dropped her gaze to stare at the table, her pulse racing. 'I'm pregnant. Three months gone.'

The ensuing silence could have been cut by the proverbial knife as Davey, very slowly, sat upright in his chair.

'I hope I misheard you,' he said at last.

Maggs shook her head. 'You didn't.'

A goggle-eyed Crista, her interest in the novel completely forgotten, was riveted.

Lavender had gone white. 'Are you sure?'

'Yes, Mum. I am.'

Davey was stunned, to say the least. He knew both girls were grown up but they'd always be children in his eyes. His little moppets. His lovely darlings.

'Oh my God!' Lavender whispered.

Bloody hell! Crista thought, but didn't utter it aloud. Like her parents, she hadn't even known Maggs had a boyfriend.

'I'm sorry. Truly I am,' Maggs said quietly, and contritely.

Rage that came from nowhere suddenly erupted inside Davey. 'I'll give you sorry,' he shouted, coming to his feet. 'Do you know what this means? It'll be the talk of the village once it gets out. I can just hear the sniggering, the dirty laughter, the crude comments. The family's reputation will be in tatters. We'll be a complete laughing stock.'

Maggs cringed under this verbal assault. She daren't look at either of her parents, least of all her dad. She realised she'd begun to shake.

Lavender forced herself to think. 'Hold on, Davey. It might not have to come to that.'

He whirled on her. 'How do you mean?'

'Not if the lad, whoever he is, married her more or less right away. After all, it wouldn't be the first time that had happened in Ford, would it?'

Davey, boiling inside, swallowed hard. Lavender was right, that would solve the problem. Get them out of this unholy mess.

'And when the baby comes it's arrived early. That's a common enough occurrence as well,' Lavender went on.

Davey nodded. It was the only solution.

Lavender's gaze was hard as granite as she stared at her elder daughter. 'How could you let us all down like this, Maggs? I'm thoroughly ashamed of you.'

Maggs cringed even further into herself.

'I thought we'd brought you up properly. To have morals. To know right from wrong. And now this.'

Maggs desperately wished she could jump up and run away. Hide somewhere. Be anywhere else. But that was impossible. She just had to sit there and take it.

Davey clenched and unclenched his fists, trying to contain the fury threatening to engulf him. 'I should take my belt to you. Leather you within an inch of your life,' he hissed. Taking his belt to either Maggs or Crista was something he'd never ever done, though he had threatened it once or twice. But that's all it had ever been, a threat.

'Oh, how could you, you ungrateful little madam,' Lavender suddenly cried out. 'Did you ever stop to think of the shame you could bring on all of us, let alone yourself? What possessed you, Maggs?'

Maggs was too terrified to reply.

Lavender regained her composure. 'Now then, who's the father?'

Maggs had to force herself to speak, and when she finally did it came out as a strangulated croak. 'I can't say, Mum.'

'What do you mean you bloody well can't say!' Davey shouted. 'Of course you can. Or are we dealing with some sort of immaculate conception here?'

In other circumstances that might have been funny. But not now.

'Have you told him you're . . .' Lavender took a deep breath before going on, finding it excruciatingly difficult to articulate the word. 'Pregnant?'

Maggs nodded.

'And he'll stand by you? Do the right and proper thing?'

Maggs shook her head. 'He won't marry me, Mum. He's refused to do so.'

'What!' Davey exploded. 'Refused! Well, the bastard

will stop doing that when I get hold of him. I'll beat him to a pulp if he doesn't walk you down the aisle.'

'Perhaps the lad is just scared,' Lavender said, hoping against hope that might be the case. 'I'm sure he'll listen to reason once we have a word with him. Or his family will. They'll make him go through with it.' Desperation was in her voice now. The alternative was simply unthinkable. The shame and humiliation of one of her daughters producing an illegitimate child just couldn't be allowed to happen.

'He won't marry me. And no matter what you do or say he won't change his mind.'

'Then why on earth did you . . . go with him?' Lavender's voice was a whiplash.

'Because I thought we were going to get married. But when I told him I was expecting he said there was no chance of that happening. That he'd never intended to marry me in the first place.'

Davey's face had gone puce. 'The rat. The rotten fucking rat to take advantage of you like that. I'll kill him. I'll strangle him with my own bare hands.'

'Try and calm yourself, Davey. I know this is difficult, but try and calm yourself. We'll sort it out somehow.' Lavender knew she was clutching at straws. If Maggs didn't marry, their good name and standing in the village would be for ever destroyed. Falling pregnant and marrying was one thing, falling pregnant and not marrying quite another.

But Davey was now beyond reason. Striding over to Maggs he stuck his face into hers. 'Who is he? I'm damned if he's getting away with this. Who is he?'

Maggs recoiled. She'd never seen her father like this before. He'd turned into a raging monster. 'I can't say, Dad. I can't. Please don't go on.'

She screamed when Davey grabbed hold of her blouse and hauled her to her feet. 'His name, Maggs? His bloody name!'

Lavender was on her feet now. 'Davey, Davey, let her go.'

'I'll have his name!' Davey roared in a thunderous voice. 'Who is he, Maggs?'

'I . . .'

She screamed again when Davey slapped her hard, his complexion now the colour of boiled beetroot. 'Who is he?'

The breath whooshed out of Maggs as yet another slap knocked her head sideways.

Lavender was tearing at Davey's clothes. She couldn't let this continue. He'd do the girl a mischief. 'Stop it! Stop it!' she pleaded.

'I'll have his name, by God and I will,' Davey roared again, oblivious to his wife and her entreaties.

All resistance had melted out of Maggs. 'Rupert Swain,' she choked.

Davey went very still. 'Who?' he whispered in disbelief.

'Rupert Swain. I met him the night I went waitressing at their house.'

It was a Swain that had made his daughter pregnant. A hated, detested, loathed, reviled Swain. Davey's eyes misted over as though a red fog had suddenly inhabited them.

He let Maggs go and stumbled away a few steps. His face, though it seemed hardly possible, was even

209

redder than it had been. Of all the families in the village, out of all of them, a *Swain*!

Davey gasped and clutched his throat as something in his brain seemed to explode. Terrible pain shot right through the rest of his body. He was dimly aware of falling, toppling over, but not of hitting the floor, for by then he was unconscious. His legs twitched several times and then went still.

Lavender, Maggs and Crista stared at him in horror.

It was Lavender who reacted first. Throwing herself down beside him, she quickly cradled his head in her arm. When she put the back of her free hand against his mouth she could detect he was still breathing.

'Crista, run and get Dr Murray. Hurry, girl. Hurry!'

Crista was out of the door like a shot and running as fast as she could. As she ran she prayed that Jamie was home and not out on a call.

Jamie was doing the daily crossword and enjoying a glass of whisky when he heard a sudden commotion out in the hallway. Seconds later a wild-eyed Crista burst into the room. He looked at her in astonishment.

'Jamie, Jamie, you've got to come straight away. Dad's had some kind of seizure,' she blurted out.

Instantly Jamie was on his feet. 'I'll get my bag and be right with you.'

'What sort of seizure?' he demanded as they left the house.

'He was having an argument with Maggs when his face went all red and purply. Next moment he was unconscious on the floor.'

They found Lavender where Crista had left her,

on the floor with Davey's head cradled in her arm. Jamie knelt beside her and felt for a neck pulse. There wasn't one.

'He's dead,' Lavender announced in a strange, faraway-sounding voice. 'He went a couple of minutes ago. Just sort of sighed, and that was that.'

He was dead all right, Jamie thought. No doubt about it. 'I'm sorry,' he said.

Lavender gave a rather comical, lopsided smile. 'That's what Maggs said shortly before it happened. She said *she* was sorry.'

Jamie glanced around, but Maggs was nowhere to be seen. Odd, he thought, as from what Crista had told him she'd been in the room when the seizure occurred.

Crista had slumped into a chair where she was silently crying, her body shaking with grief. Lavender, on the other hand, was dry-eyed and fully composed. Like a character out of a Greek tragedy, Jamie reflected. 'Do you have a sheet or blanket to cover Davey?' he asked quietly.

'I don't want him staying on the floor like this. I want him to be put into his own bed. That would be more dignified,' Lavender replied hollowly.

'Right. I understand.'

Lavender shook her head and appeared to come to her senses. 'Will you help us do that, doctor? He's a bit heavy for just Crista and myself.'

'Of course. Will we do it now?'

Lavender glanced over at Crista. 'Are you up to it, maid?'

Crista wiped her nose with the back of her hand, and then got up. 'I'm all right, Mum.'

211

Lavender smiled at Davey. 'He was a good husband, you know,' she said to Jamie. 'One of the best. One of the very best. Unlike some in this village I could name.'

Jamie didn't reply to that.

Eventually Lavender released Davey's head and the three of them set about moving him.

From Maggs's bedroom came the sound of anguished sobbing.

Jamie had just finished getting dressed the following morning when he heard activity in the kitchen. Frowning, he went through to discover Crista there.

'What are you doing?' he queried, genuinely surprised.

'It's still my job to make breakfast for you,' she replied.

'But not this morning. I didn't expect you in today. Or for a few days, come to that.'

'You still have to eat, don't you?'

'Yes, but . . . in the circumstances.' He paused for a couple of seconds, then asked, 'How's your mother?'

'As you'd imagine, I suppose. She stayed with my father all night, sitting on the edge of the bed. She never slept a wink.'

'And you?'

'A little. Maybe more than I realised.'

'I'll give your mum a sedative later. If she'll have one.' Lavender had refused the previous night.

'PC Munny has been round again to say the under-taker will be coming about noon to . . . take dad away. I want to be there when they do.'

'Then you must.'

She attempted a smile that didn't quite come off. 'Bacon and egg all right?'

'Sounds wonderful. Have you eaten yet?'

Crista shook her head.

'Then perhaps you'll join me? I'd enjoy that.'

'I don't think I could eat anything, Jamie. I've no appetite at all.'

He was having none of it. 'I can understand that, but you must try. And that's an order from the doctor.'

She smiled wanly. 'Doctor's orders, eh?'

'Correct. You must at least try.'

'If you say so then,' she replied in a voice little above a whisper. 'It won't be long.'

'But before that a cup of good strong tea. You can't beat one first thing in the morning.'

She didn't know why, but suddenly she felt a lot better. As if her load had been lightened somewhat.

To Jamie's amusement, and relief, when she finally sat down she not only cleared her plate but had two slices of toast on top of that.

Despite her grief Jamie found breakfasting with Crista an absolute delight.

As usual, those who worked at the mill weren't given time off to attend the funeral itself, but they came on later to the pub to have a word with Lavender and pay their last respects.

It had been a good service, the vicar recounting Davey's life and saying how well liked and respected he was in the village. Lavender sat throughout with her head bowed, wincing ever so slightly when 'respected' was mentioned. That was a word that would probably never again be applied to their family once Maggs's secret got out.

Maggs herself was distraught, blaming herself for

her father's death, and cursing Rupert Swain for the bastard he was. She also cursed herself for being so bloody stupid as to believe he would marry her. What had she been thinking of! Men in Rupert Swain's position didn't marry mill girls, as he'd so cruelly pointed out when she'd told him about her condition.

Unknown to Lavender she had taken his advice and drunk, not an entire bottle of gin as she simply couldn't manage it, but the best part of one. But neither the gin nor a steaming hot bath had had the desired effect, and she was still pregnant.

Maggs desperately didn't want to go to the Angel after the service, but knew she had to. It would have been seen as an affront if she hadn't. Abigail and Tom had turned up, but not stayed long. Tom was unwilling to spend much money as he was still saving up for the engagement ring. Gemma Gatsby hadn't put in an appearance, but Maggs hadn't expected her to, knowing Gemma to be laid up at home with a bad cold.

The pub had been jam-packed after the mill closed, but the crowd was now thinning out as people left in dribs and drabs. Maggs wished she too could leave but felt she had to stay on until her mother made a move. She glanced over to where Crista was talking to a young village chap, the pair of them seeming to be enjoying themselves despite its being a wake.

All might have gone well enough, in fact, if Maggs hadn't suddenly caught sight of Lavender across the room surreptitiously giving her a venomous, hate-filled look.

The shock of that look, the recognition of her

mother's feelings towards her over what had happened, made her crumble inside. Tears sprang into her eyes and she knew she had to get out of there fast in case she broke down.

'Excuse me. Excuse me,' she muttered, as she made her way through the crowd in the direction of the toilets.

'Maggs?'

Someone called out her name, possibly noting her distress, but she ignored whoever it was. Then she was through the door leading to the toilets, but momentarily could get no further. Leaning her back against the wall she let out a soft, tormented wail as the tears turned into a flood. Bending over, she clutched her stomach, which was churning from remorse.

'Dear God, Maggs, are you all right?'

The speaker was Dickie Trippett, whose approach she'd neither seen nor heard. 'Of course I'm not fucking all right, you daft bugger,' she heard herself reply.

Dickie ignored the rudeness. 'There's a small sitting room through the back. Why don't I take you there and you can have a sit-down for a few minutes?'

Suddenly that seemed like a good idea. She didn't want anyone else to see her in this state, even if it was understandable after her father's funeral. 'Please,' she mumbled.

'Here, let me help you.' Dickie stared at her in concern as he assisted her along the passageway and through the door into the sitting room. 'Can I get you something? A brandy, perhaps?'

'That would be lovely. Thank you.'

'I won't be a tick.' And with that he hurried off.

Her mother hated her, Maggs thought in despair.

And why shouldn't she, after what Maggs had done? Not only got herself pregnant, but caused Davey's death as a result. Not only bringing shame on to the family but killing her father into the bargain. Inconsolable grief and guilt threatened to engulf her as she stuffed a fist into her mouth. All she wanted to do was die herself.

'Here you are, Maggs. Get that in you.'

She gratefully accepted the large brandy and gulped it down.

'Here, steady on, Maggs,' Dickie exclaimed in alarm.

'Can I have another, Dickie? Please? I'll pay for it.'

'Don't worry about that.' He took the glass from her and hurried off again.

Maggs fumbled for her handkerchief and dabbed at her tear-soaked face. What was she going to do? She simply didn't know. If there was an answer to all this mess and tragedy it was beyond her.

'Now take it easy with that,' Dickie counselled on his return, wondering how much she'd had already and if there was any danger of her throwing up.

'Everything fine in here?' an inquisitive Spanish John asked, appearing in the doorway.

'It's Maggs. I thought it best she have a few minutes on her own,' Dickie explained.

Poor maid, John thought. God, she was upset! 'She can take as long as she likes. You stay with her, Dickie. We can manage behind the bar for a while.' John left them to it, clicking the door quietly shut behind him.

'It's all my fault, Dickie,' Maggs suddenly sobbed. She hadn't been able to confide in anyone since this nightmare had begun, the whole thing building and building inside her till it had reached the point where she just had to unburden herself to someone or else go out of her mind. Why not Dickie? They'd always been pals, and he was a good soul.

'What's your fault?' he frowned, wondering what on earth she was going on about.

'I killed him.'

The frown deepened. 'Killed who, Maggs?'

She stared at him through tortured eyes. 'My father.'

He was flabbergasted. 'That's nonsense. He had a seizure. We all know that.'

'What you don't know is the seizure was because of me and the argument we had.' She paused to try to collect her wits. 'If I tell you something, Dickie, will you promise never to let on to anyone? And I mean that. Not a single, solitary person.'

He nodded. 'I promise.'

Maggs had a sip of her brandy. 'I'm pregnant, Dickie,' she stated quietly.

'Oh shit,' he whispered. 'By whom?'

'That was the bit that killed dad. Rupert Swain.'

'Rupert . . .' He broke off in astonishment. 'How? I mean, I know how, but how did you become involved with him?'

Maggs took a deep breath, and slowly began telling Dickie the full story, starting with the night she waitressed at the Swains' house.

Dickie listened in amazement, and then anger as she related how Rupert had ditched her because of her pregnancy. When she got to the bit about Davey's seizure the tears began to flow afresh.

They remained closeted in the sitting room for well over an hour, Dickie trying to comfort her and offer advice, though in truth there wasn't really any advice he could offer. One thing they both agreed upon. It must never become known in the village who the baby's father was. That would be catastrophic for the remaining Fletchers.

In the end Maggs had regained something of her composure, thanking Dickie for listening to her babblings, and making him promise again to remain silent about what he'd learnt that night.

When she finally reached home Lavender had already gone to bed.

'Penny for them?' Spanish John smiled. 'You look lost in thought.'

Dickie shrugged. 'I suppose I am.'

The pub had just closed for the night, and the three of them were having their usual staff drink. They had become quite close since Dickie started working there. Dee Dee lit up one of the black Russian cigarettes she indulged in every night after work. To Dickie's amusement, she occasionally alternated them with a small cigar from the box she'd buy every so often from a splendid tobacconist's in Exeter.

'Want to talk about it?' John asked. 'Or not, as the case may be.' He was worried about Dickie, who hadn't been himself since the Fletcher wake a few days previously.

Dickie had a sip of his pint while he considered that. 'Can I ask you a question, Dee Dee?' he said eventually.

'Go ahead.'

'It's a bit personal. I don't want to embarrass you.'

She gave him a broad smile. 'It takes a lot to do that after so many years in the pub trade.' She jabbed her cigarette in John's direction. 'And having been married to him all this while.'

John laughed. 'Steady, girl. Don't you go giving away any family secrets now. You might make me blush.'

With John's swarthy skin colouring Dickie didn't think that was possible. He rose from his chair. 'I'm going to have a Scotch, if you don't mind.'

'Help yourself,' John replied, thinking this must be serious. It was rare for Dickie to touch the top shelf.

Dickie resettled himself in the chair he'd been occupying and regarded Dee Dee keenly. It took him a further few seconds to screw up enough courage to speak.

'It's simply this, Dee Dee. Do you think a woman might take me on having only one arm and a scarred face?'

Christ! she thought. It was the last thing she'd expected. For some reason she'd imagined it might be money troubles. 'Do you have someone in mind?'

He shrugged. 'Maybe.'

John's thoughts were racing, trying to work out who it might be. The only possible answer he could come up with was Maggs Fletcher, because of their long conversation after the wake plus the fact that Dickie was always pleased to see Maggs and be in her company. John had noticed that quite some time ago. There was no one else, to his knowledge, Dickie showed that reaction to. There again, he might be barking up the wrong tree entirely.

'Women are funny creatures,' Dee Dee mused. 'Quite unlike men in so many different ways, and not

219

just physically either, which I think is blindingly obvious. Wouldn't you agree?'

Dickie nodded.

'Men are usually attracted to a female, at least in the first place, by what she looks like. Her figure, hair, eyes, those sorts of things. That's why the attractive ones have men buzzing round them like bees round a honey pot. All shallow, of course; looks fade, figures go south, especially after childbirth, which can cause havoc with women's bodies. Stretch marks, crêpe patches, you name it. And just because a woman is pretty doesn't mean she'll make a good wife or mother, far from it. Whereas the not so pretty ones often do because they've had to work that much harder to land a chap. It hasn't been handed to them on a plate, so to speak.'

Dickie was intrigued. He'd never thought of it like that.

Dee Dee had paused for a puff on her cigarette. 'Women, on the other hand, see matters quite differently. They're looking for what's inside, as opposed to the outside. Certainly a handsome chap is nice to be with, to show off and impress other women. But will he be a good provider, a good father and husband, be faithful? Is he someone you can rely on, who'll care for you, look after you when you're ill? Does he have a sense of humour and make you laugh? Now that's very important, believe me. All these qualities are considerations.'

'I make Dee Dee laugh every night when I take my clothes off,' John quipped.

'Ssshh, you,' Dee Dee admonished. 'I've been asked a serious question and I'm trying to answer it.'

John grinned at his wife, the pair of them as much in love at that moment as the day they'd got married.

'Make her laugh?' Dickie mused. That was something else he'd never thought of.

'I suppose what I'm trying to say, in a rather convoluted way, is that physical appearances aren't nearly as important to women as they are to men. If I loved a bloke a few scars wouldn't make any difference, or the loss of an arm. The man would still be what he is inside despite those imperfections, for want of a better word.'

Dickie smiled, or his version of one. The only trouble with that was Maggs didn't love him.

'I suppose again,' Dee Dee went on slowly, 'it all boils down to the female in question. And I'm afraid that's the best I can do.'

'Thanks, Dee Dee. I appreciate your views on the subject.'

'Do they help?'

Dickie saw off the rest of his Scotch, briefly toyed with the idea of having another, then decided against it. 'Yes, I think so,' he replied. 'I simply don't want to make a fool of myself, you know.'

'I'm sure you won't do that,' Dee Dee said softly. 'And good luck. Whoever she is, I hope she deserves you.'

Dickie had no reply to that. 'Well, time to be off,' he declared, coming to his feet.

He thanked Dee Dee again before leaving and heading out into the lonely night.

It was Crista who answered the knock. 'Why, hello, Dickie. This is a surprise.'

221

'Is Maggs home?'

'We're in the kitchen. Come through.'

He found Maggs and her mother sitting in chairs by the range. The atmosphere was decidedly chilly.

'Hello, Dickie.' Maggs smiled. 'Shouldn't you be at work?'

'It's my day off. Good evening, Mrs Fletcher.'

'Good evening, Dickie.' She was clearly puzzled. 'To what do we owe this honour?'

'I was wondering if I could have a private word with Maggs? It's important.'

'I see.' Lavender's gaze momentarily flicked in Maggs's direction, and then back to Dickie. 'Well, I suppose it won't do any harm if the pair of you go into her bedroom and chat. And as you're here, would you like a cup of tea? I was just about to make fresh.'

Dickie shook his head. 'No, I won't, thanks.'

It was obvious to Lavender that Dickie was nervous, which made her wonder even more what this was all about.

Maggs too was puzzled, though guessed it might have something to do with their previous conversation. 'All right, then,' she agreed, getting up. 'This way.'

Once inside the bedroom Maggs closed the door and sat on the edge of her bed. She patted a spot beside her.

'I'll stand if you don't mind, Maggs.'

'Suit yourself.'

He coughed. This wasn't going to be easy. And Lavender was right, he was nervous as hell.

'Well?' Maggs prompted.

'I've been thinking about what we talked of at the

Angel the night of your father's funeral,' he began hesitantly.

Maggs's face clouded over. As if she needed reminding about her predicament! 'Go on, Dickie.'

'This is difficult for me, Maggs. I suppose I'm worried you might laugh, but I have a suggestion to make.'

'About me being pregnant?'

He nodded.

Hope suddenly flared in her. 'Do you know someone who might be able to abort me? Is that it?'

'No no, nothing like that. It's something else.'

The hope faded as quickly as it had flared. There was nothing, absolutely nothing, that Dickie could say that might help the situation. Or was there? He'd always been a bright chap; perhaps he had come up with a solution. Though she was damned if she could imagine what it might be.

Dickie cleared his throat. 'I want you to think this through before you say yes or no, Maggs. All right?'

'All right, Dickie,' she agreed.

'You and I were great pals before I went off to war. In fact I'd like to think we were maybe a little more than that. The truth is, I always harboured, in those days anyway, aspirations about you.'

Maggs smiled. 'You were a good kisser, I remember.'

He flushed. 'You weren't bad yourself.'

'And we did have a few laughs.'

'More than a few, I'd say. I always thought, believed, we got on tremendously well together.'

'I think we did. Still do as far as I'm concerned.'

That gave him encouragement. 'Let's take a hard

look at this thing, Maggs. You're pregnant and the bastard who made you that way has ditched you. Right?'

She winced.

'Right, Maggs?'

She nodded.

'And we both know what this village is like if you give birth to a baby without a gold band on your finger. Your reputation will be in ruins. You'll be seen, and talked about, as some sort of scarlet woman. It'll also affect your mother and Crista as well. Unfair perhaps, but that's village life for you. Hypocritical when you think about it considering some of the things that go on behind closed doors here. But that's how it is. Everyone is only too quick to be judgemental, and point the finger.'

Maggs had gone white. 'My dad said something similar the night he died.'

Dickie nodded. 'And your dad was right.' He hesitated, then went on. 'It's not going to be easy for the baby either. Not when he or she grows up a bit and starts school. You know how cruel children can be. Whatever you have is going to be in for a hell of a time. The taunts, the jeers, the name calling. Poor little sod.'

Maggs dropped her head to gaze at the floor. How true, she reflected. How very true. It was going to be murder for the child. Why oh why had she gone and slept with Rupert Swain? she inwardly raged, only too well aware of the answer. What a fool she'd been. What an absolute, stupid, bloody fool! If only she could turn the clock back. But that was impossible. She'd been a fool and now she'd have to live with the consequences.

'Maggs?'

'I'm listening, Dickie.'

'I know I'm not the chap who went off to war. That my face is hideous and I've only got one arm. But I do care for you, enormously. More than care. So here it is. I'll happily marry you if you'll have me. And not only that, I'll treat the child as if it was my own flesh and blood.'

Maggs was stunned. 'Are you proposing?'

'I thought that's what I just did. I appreciate I'm hardly a catch, but your reputation would be saved. And the child would be legitimate and have a father.'

She was lost for words.

'Maggs?'

She looked up at him, thinking what a good man he was. Her saviour if she wanted him to be.

'As I said, I don't need an answer right away. Take a while to consider it. But not too long, for if the answer's yes we should get wed as soon as possible. Everyone would still talk, of course, the haste of it all, and so shortly after your dad dying. Speculation will be rife. But no matter what's said no one would know the real truth, would they?'

'Rupert Swain would.'

A look of sheer contempt flitted across Dickie's face. 'Damn him! Besides, he's scarcely likely to open his mouth, is he? It would hardly be in his interests to do so. No, he'll keep quiet and be thankful his name hasn't been mentioned in connection with any of this.'

That made sense, Maggs thought. Bitterness and fury lanced through her as a vision of Rupert momentarily flashed across her mind. She took a deep breath.

225

Dickie's proposal was certainly a turn-up for the book. She'd been a fool to get herself into this state and would be an even bigger one to turn down Dickie's offer.

'Where would we live?' she queried.

'I've already considered that. I'm sure my parents wouldn't object to putting us up for a while until we can get a place of our own. Or how about here if you don't fancy that?'

'No, Dickie, certainly not here. That simply isn't a runner. Mum's been . . . well, cold to say the least towards me since dad died. In fact, I believe she now hates me.'

Dickie frowned. 'Surely hate's too strong a word? I mean, how were you to know your dad would have a seizure?'

Maggs gave him a cynical smile. 'I wasn't. But it was my fault none the less. If I hadn't come home pregnant, and not only that but pregnant by a *Swain*, then it would never have happened.'

'I suppose you're right.' He sighed.

'So you see, living here is quite out of the question.'

'Then it would have to be with my parents.'

'Are you certain they'd agree?'

'Oh yes, no doubt about it. I think they've written me off as a marriage prospect, so if I did get married they'd be over the moon and thrilled to help in any way they could.'

Maggs knew she had to be honest. It was only fair. 'I could never love you, Dickie. You have to be aware of that before I make a decision.'

'I know,' he replied softly. 'But as you've admitted,

we both like one another and get on well together. That must be worth a lot.'

'And you'd treat the baby as your own flesh and blood?'

'I've promised, haven't I? And I never go back on my word, Maggs. Never.'

She could believe that.

'Do you want me to go now so you can think it over?'

'No, wait. Whatever my decision I'll give it to you before you leave.'

Dickie glanced away. 'I'll understand if you refuse me, Maggs. There'll be no hard feelings. I appreciate it's not an easy decision for you to make. Taking me on as I am, that is.'

Why was she hesitating? She should jump at the chance of being let off the hook. And there was her mother and Crista to think about. It would let them off the hook as well. Stop their lives being blighted.

Maggs closed her eyes. Could she bear to be made love to by Dickie? Have that face staring down at her? And what about his only having one arm? Married to a cripple. A man who could never even hold her properly.

'I earn a decent wage at the Angel,' Dickie went on quietly. 'John and Dee Dee are very generous. So there's no question I can't afford to keep you and the child. It'll be tight, of course, but there again, that's nothing unusual in Ford, is it?'

'No,' she agreed.

'And given time, depending how many children might happen along, you might get yourself a little job to help matters. If you wanted, that is.'

Still she hesitated. How her world had changed since meeting Rupert Swain. Before him she'd never have entertained Dickie's proposal in a thousand years. Not in a million. What bright hopes she'd once had of love and marriage, particularly with Rupert.

Suddenly her mind was made up. There was no other decision she could make. 'I'll marry you, Dickie,' she declared.

He bit his lip. 'Are you sure about that?'

'And be proud to,' she lied. 'We'll make a go of it, you'll see. I'll be the best wife ever.'

'It's settled, then.'

She forced herself to rise, cross over and kiss him. 'It is now.'

'Shall we tell your mother?'

'Yes, let's do that.'

Hand in hand they went back to Lavender and Crista.

'We have an announcement to make,' Maggs stated, staring Lavender full in the eye. 'Dickie and I are to wed.'

'Push, Maggs, push!' Jamie urged.

'What the fuck do you think I'm trying to bloody well do!'

Jamie smiled to himself. It was amazing the language even the best-bred women came out with during childbirth. It could often be quite ripe to say the least.

'Almost there,' he crooned, gently assisting the baby on its way.

Maggs screamed for the umpteenth time, the agony unbearable but somehow having to be borne. She'd known it would be painful but never realised it would be this bad.

'Ah!' Jamie breathed as the baby finally slipped free into his waiting hands. A pop-eyed Crista, who'd been helping, was watching.

'It's a little boy,' he told Maggs, and gestured to Crista to hold the baby while he cut the cord.

Maggs grunted as the afterbirth followed. She was suddenly more tired than she'd ever been in her entire life.

Jamie took a few minutes to sort out the baby and dispose of the afterbirth. 'You can tell Dickie he can come in now,' he instructed Crista.

'Let me see him,' Maggs croaked. 'Are all the bits and pieces where they should be?'

'They are. He's perfect,' Jamie assured her. 'And you can hold him if you like.'

She somehow found the strength to do that. 'We agreed that if it was a boy we'd call him David after my father.'

'That'll certainly please your mother,' Jamie said, nodding his approval. 'I'm just surprised she isn't here.'

Maggs glanced away, a strange look coming into her eyes. 'She's squeamish, doctor. Always has been.'

It was a lie, of course. Lavender had refused point blank to be present at the birth.

Chapter 14

'That's your father off to the pub,' Jamie's mother declared. Sheena Murray and her husband Cameron were down from Scotland on a visit, the first they'd made to Ford. 'Now how about a drink? I could certainly use one.'

Jamie glanced up from the patient's notes he was studying. 'If you want a drink, then why didn't you go with dad?'

'Because I wanted a quiet word with you, that's why. Now shall I pour or will you?'

Jamie laid his notes aside. 'I will.' The measures his mother poured tended to be lethal.

Sheena sat and watched him. 'Thank you,' she said, when he handed her a glass. If Jamie thought her measures were far too large, she thought his were stingy. She'd come to the conclusion it was because he lived amongst the English, the Sassenach, who were known for being mean where alcohol, especially spirits, was concerned.

'Now then,' she said, settling back in her chair. 'I have a question for you.'

He knew from her tone of voice, and long experience, that some sort of interrogation was coming up. 'Which is?'

'To begin with, how long have you been here now?'

He did a rapid mental calculation. 'Three and a bit years. Doesn't seem that long. Time has simply flown by.'

Sheena fixed him with a beady, penetrating stare. 'So why is it in that three and a bit years you've never mentioned a ladyfriend in any of your letters, eh?'

'Haven't I?' He smiled, affecting innocence.

'You know fine well you haven't.' She paused, then asked somewhat dramticatly, 'Is there something I should know about? Something you might want to tell me, eh?'

He was mystified. 'Like what?'

'You're no one of thae queeries, are ye, Jamie?'

He couldn't help bursting out laughing. How incongruous that had sounded coming from his mother. 'Do you mean homosexual?' he teased.

'That's what I said, queeries. If you are I want to know. And now's the time to tell me, face to face, while I'm here.'

'And what if I was?' He was beginning to enjoy this.

'Oh, Jamie, me lad. Tell me you're only joking. For God's sake tell me that.'

He stared at her stricken expression, and didn't have the heart to continue teasing her. 'No I'm not, Mum. I swear it.'

Sheena crumpled slightly in relief. 'You had me worried there, son,' she declared, shaking her head.

'I'm just surprised you could have thought it of me.'

231

'I didn't think it! It just, well, sort of crossed my mind, that's all. Though if you were I don't know where you'd have got it from. Certainly not your father. He's a man's man and no mistake. And not from my side of the family either. There's nothing queer about any of them, eh?'

'Not that I've ever detected.'

She drank her whisky, seeing off about half what was in the glass. Jamie winced. He'd forgotten what Scottish drinkers, including their women, could be like.

'So why no mention of a ladyfriend?' Sheena went on. 'It's not as if you're getting any younger. None of us are. And I would like a grandchild or two before I die.'

Jamie thought about that. 'I have been out with several women since coming to Ford. But nothing that lasted.'

'Perhaps you're not trying hard enough, eh?'

'It's difficult, Mum.'

'How so?'

'Meeting them, I suppose. The hours of a country doctor are long, not to mention tiring. I never quite seem to get the chance to socialise much.'

'I can understand that,' Sheena mused. 'But it's your own fault for taking up a country practice anyway, albeit I understand your reasons. Things would have been far better, and easier for you, if you'd stayed put in Edinburgh and not gone gallivanting to foreign parts.'

He frowned. 'You mean France? But that was the war.'

'No, I mean England, daftie. It's a foreign country to us. You haven't turned native, have you?'

'Is that what you think?'

'Well have you, eh?'

'Mum, I was born and brought up in Scotland, and will always be Scots no matter what or where I live. That satisfy you?'

'I should hope so.' She finished off her dram. 'I'll pour this time,' she stated firmly, getting up. 'What about you?'

'I'm fine for the moment.'

He watched his mother pour what in an English pub would have been considered a quadruple. 'A bit heavy-handed there, aren't you, Mum?'

'Och, wheesht your havering. That's what I mean about you turning native, when you make daft comments like that.'

Jamie sighed, and dropped the subject.

Sheena sat down again. 'There must be some lassie round about that's caught your eye.'

'You mean in Ford?'

'I've seen some lovely ones. Take Crista, for example. She's a real looker and no mistake.'

'Crista?'

'That's who I said. Are you getting deaf or something?'

He smiled. 'No, Mum, there's nothing wrong with my hearing.'

'Then don't repeat what I've just said. Well?'

'Crista works for me, Mum.'

'So?'

'She's too young for a start.'

'Too young! I wouldn't say that. How old is she?'

'Twenty, I think.'

'What's young about twenty? She's certainly

233

capable round the house. She's impressed me with her abilities.'

Jamie couldn't argue with that. The place had run like clockwork ever since she'd taken over from Dolly Tyler.

'Has she got a laddie then?'

'Not that I know of. But I'm not certain. She might have. She's never said.'

'If she hasn't then I know why.'

That surprised Jamie. 'You do?'

Sheena became all smug. 'Of course I do. I'm just amazed you don't. But then even as a child you were never very observant.'

Jamie laid his glass aside and lit up a cigarette. Sheena remained silent, staring at him.

'All right,' he finally conceded when she didn't go on. 'Are you going to tell me or what?'

'It's obvious. If only you had a pair of eyes in your head.'

He was beginning to get an inkling about what she was driving at. But surely that wasn't right? Couldn't be.

'The lassie's in love with you, son.'

'You're joking!'

'Do I look as if I am?'

She didn't.

Jamie thought about that, then shook his head. 'No, I don't believe it.'

'She damn well is. Take my word. It's written all over her face every time she looks at you. Plain as day. Except to you, it would seem.'

Crista in love with him and he hadn't noticed? His mother had an uncanny habit of being right about these things that had driven his father to distraction down the years. So was she about this?

'I think I'll have another drink after all,' Jamie murmured, coming to his feet.

Sheena simply smiled benignly.

Jamie sighed as he closed the door behind him. God, that had been a long, and somehow irritating, surgery. He was whacked and just wanted to put his feet up for half an hour.

'The usual coffee, Jamie?' Crista queried, ceasing what she was doing.

'Please.'

She frowned in concern. 'Are you all right?'

'Just tired, that's all.' He shrugged. 'I haven't slept well the last couple of nights.'

'And why's that?'

Because of you, he thought, but didn't say. 'Just a phase, I imagine,' he prevaricated, sinking into a chair. He studied her as she made the coffee. 'Are you having one as well?'

'I've still got an awful lot to do.'

'Go on, I insist. Sit down and talk to me. I enjoy your company.' With a jolt he realised the truth of what he'd just said. Having a chat with Crista was often one of the highlights of his day. He found it . . . comforting. She was so easy to get on with, so sympathetic.

He lit a cigarette as he continued to stare at her. There was no question she was damned attractive, figure as well as face. And easy-going with it.

'You've never said, Crista,' he asked casually. 'Have you got a chap? Anyone I'd know?'

She blushed. 'No, there isn't anyone.'

'I just wondered,' he replied, as if he'd simply been curious, nothing more.

'Here you are,' she declared, setting his coffee on a small table by his chair. 'Would you like a chocolate biscuit to go with it?'

He shook his head. 'But you have one if you wish.'

'Not for me, thanks.'

She sat facing him. 'It must be nice for you to have your parents here.' She smiled.

'It is.'

'I think they're lovely. Your father doesn't half make me laugh with some of the things he comes out with. Especially in that accent of his.'

'He can be quite a character at times. Mother too. I shall miss them when they leave.'

Her expression became serious. 'I can understand that. I'd hate to live away from my family.'

He could see how much she meant it. A typical Ford person, he reflected. Very few of them had any desire to go out and explore the world, being happy enough to live and die in Ford. To spend all their days in the village and environs.

'Tell me something,' he began slowly, hoping he wasn't going to make a hash of this. 'Would you agree that you and I have become friends over the past few years?'

'Friends?'

'That's what I said.'

'But you're my employer. That wouldn't be right.' A sudden flash of panic crossed her face. 'I haven't been taking liberties, have I? Overstepping the mark because you allow me to call you Jamie?'

236

He laughed. 'Of course not. You haven't over-stepped any mark. I just thought . . . well, we'd gone a bit further than a simple employer–employee relationship. That we'd become friends.'

'Is that what you want?' she asked softly, a look in her eyes he couldn't decipher.

'Yes, it is.'

'Then I suppose we're friends.'

That pleased him enormously. He was about to pursue the subject when the telephone rang. 'Damn!' he swore, thinking it must be a call out.

But it wasn't. It was Sheena saying she and Cameron would be staying on for dinner in Exeter, where they'd gone shopping, and would he care to join them. He declined, saying he had several calls to make later but would no doubt see them sometime that evening.

When he returned to the kitchen it was to find that Crista had gone upstairs where, from the sound of things, she was changing his bed.

He swore again, having wanted to continue their conversation.

'Good morning, Crista.'

'Good morning, Mrs Murray. How are you today?'

'Fine. I must say I do sleep well down here in Devon. Must be something in the air. Jamie doing his surgery?'

Crista nodded. 'Would you like your breakfast now?'

'Please. Mr Murray will be down shortly. He's still shaving.'

Sheena went to the window and gazed out. It was going to be another wonderful day, their last in Ford.

237

They were off the following morning on their journey back to Scotland. She turned to look speculatively at Crista. 'Jamie worries me, you know,' she said quietly.

'Oh? Why's that?'

'I think he's working far too hard. Never seems to stop. Night and day. Wouldn't you agree?'

Crista nodded. 'But that's the job, I suppose. I must say, I never realised the hours a doctor puts in until I came here.'

'But there is one thing pleases me.'

'What's that, Mrs Murray?'

'That he's got you to look after him. I can't imagine where he'd be without you.'

Crista blushed. 'Thank you,' she stammered.

'And I mean that. I'd be a lot more worried if it wasn't for you. The pair of you seem to complement each other ever so well. If I didn't know better I'd have taken you for man and wife.'

Crista jerked as though suddenly stabbed, but didn't reply.

'I must say I'd heartily approve if that was the case.' There, she couldn't put it more bluntly than that.

'Would you?' Crista queried hesitantly.

'I most certainly would. Cameron thinks the same. He mentioned it to me only the other night.'

Crista busied herself with the breakfast, her mind whirling. 'But that could never be, Mrs Murray. I'm working class, whereas Jamie – well, he's a doctor and all. Far above the likes of me.'

'Stuff and nonsense, my girl. Don't forget we're Scots, and the Scots don't have the same class-ridden attitudes that you English have. We judge people for themselves, not who they are or how much money they have in the bank. Nor who their ancestors were. Most of the upper classes, or so called upper classes anyway, are descended from cut-throat robber barons and the like, so where's the pride and snobbery in that? Nothing to be snooty about in my opinion.'

At that point Cameron Murray came striding into the room. 'I'm starving,' he announced, rubbing his hands together.

'If the pair of you sit down I'll serve up in a tick.' Crista smiled at him, and was rewarded with a wink.

She stared thoughtfully into the frying pan where the eggs were cooking nicely. In fact she stared so long and hard at them she came perilously close to burning the damn things, which would have been most unlike her.

'Now don't cry, Mum. I can't bear that,' Jamie chided gently. He'd driven his parents to St David's station from where they'd travel to London, intending to spend a few days there before continuing northwards.

'I'm not crying. I've got a piece of grit in my eye, I think,' she lied.

'The luggage is on board and the porter tipped,' Cameron declared, joining them. He was trying to be bluff and hearty, though he too was deeply saddened to be saying goodbye to Jamie. 'We had a wonderful time, son. Thank you very much.' The two men shook hands.

Sheena did her best to compose herself. 'You will write soon, won't you, Jamie?'

'I promise, Mum.'

'And we'll telephone the moment we get home.'

'Shall we get into the carriage, dear? The guard looks as if he's about to wave his flag.'

Sheena threw her arms round Jamie and hugged him tight. 'You take care now. And try not to work so hard.'

'I will, Mum,' he promised, though the latter was impossible.

'Don't forget the conversation we had about Crista,' Sheena whispered in his ear. 'She's a fine lass. Don't be shy in coming forward, if you know what I mean.'

He did. Only too well.

More goodbyes were said, and then the train was pulling away, the visit over.

As he walked down the platform Jamie made a sudden decision to stop off in town before returning to Ford.

Jamie cradled the telephone. Well, he thought, that was a surprise. It had been Miles Swain himself summoning him to the Swain house tomorrow. It was the first time he'd been invited to attend any of the Swain family since setting up practice in the village.

He'd tried to probe into the nature of the complaint or illness, but Swain had been evasive, simply agreeing a time at Jamie's convenience. That too had surprised Jamie. At *his* convenience. From what he knew of the man he would have expected to be given a time and told to turn up.

How curious.

It was Helen Swain who answered his knock. He had expected a servant to do so. 'Hello, stranger.' She smiled.

Pretty as ever, he noted, her white-blonde hair cut

in a fashionable bob. 'How are you, Helen?' he asked pleasantly as he stepped inside.

'Never better. And yourself?'

'As you see me.'

He glanced casually at her left hand but there was no ring in evidence so she was still apparently unattached. 'I have an appointment with your father.'

'I know. He told me. That's why I answered the door myself.'

'So what are you up to nowadays?'

'This and that. I spend more time in London than I used to, which I enjoy. But apart from that it's the usual country pursuits. And you?'

'Work, work and more work. Life is never dull. I did spot you once, a couple of months ago, out riding. I waved, but you couldn't have seen me.'

She seemed about to comment on that, then apparently changed her mind. 'I'll take you to pa. He doesn't like to be kept waiting.'

Miles Swain was in the study, sitting at his desk wearing a silk embroidered dressing gown clearly with nothing underneath. He threw down his pen and rose the moment Jamie entered the room. 'Ah, doctor, how kind of you to come.'

Having shaken Jamie by the hand he crossed to the door and locked it. Turning, he stared directly at Jamie. 'Perhaps you're wondering why I've sent for you and not one of the doctors in Exeter that I normally use?'

'I've no idea who you normally consult, Mr Swain. Only that you haven't asked for my services before.'

Swain took a deep breath. 'This is a most delicate matter, doctor. Embarrassing, even. The thing is, you

241

see, I socialise with those people and, because of that, in this particular case, don't wish to patronise them.'

Jamie was intrigued, wondering what on earth was wrong with Swain.

'You are discreet, I take it?'

'Always, Mr Swain. Every doctor should be.'

Swain gave Jamie a cynical smile. 'True. True. But sadly *not* always the case. Particularly where I might be involved. Therefore I'm going to pay you triple your usual fee to ensure that discretion.'

That slightly angered Jamie. 'There's no need, I assure you.'

'But I insist. And that's all there is to it.'

Jamie placed his bag on the desk. If the man wanted to waste his money then why should he argue? 'So what seems to be the problem, Mr Swain?'

A look of abject fear suddenly appeared in Swain's eyes, and then was swiftly gone. 'I appear to have something wrong with my waterworks, Dr Murray. I'd appreciate your opinion.'

'Of course.'

Jamie glanced around and noted a chaise longue against one wall. 'If you'd care to lie on that and open your dressing gown I'll see what's what.'

One glance caused Jamie's heart to sink as he recognised the symptoms only too well. None the less he carried out a rigorous examination, interspersed with probing questions.

'Is there somewhere I can wash my hands?' he asked when he was finally finished.

Swain rose from the chaise longue and retied his dressing gown. 'Out of the door, turn right and it's two doors down.'

'Thank you.'

When Jamie returned, having vigorously and thoroughly washed his hands, he found Swain sitting at his desk pouring himself a large brandy.

'Care for one, doctor?'

'Not for me, thank you.'

'I thought all Scotsmen drank?'

'Well, I certainly do. But not right now. I have other calls to make and evening surgery to take.'

Swain nodded that he understood. 'So what's the verdict, then?'

'It's not good, I'm afraid, Mr Swain.'

Swain didn't reply, simply had a large gulp of brandy.

'You have syphilis.'

Swain fixed Jamie with a penetrating stare. 'Are you absolutely certain?'

'I saw and treated hundreds of similar cases amongst the troops during the war. There's no mistake.' Most of the poor buggers hadn't cared all that much that they'd become infected, their attitude being they'd probably be dead soon anyway. Killed at the Front.

The look of abject fear Jamie had seen previously flashed through Swain's eyes a second time. 'You say "treated" them?'

'There are various treatments but no cure, Mr Swain,' Jamie replied grimly, knowing he'd just delivered a death sentence.

Swain slowly nodded, then drank more brandy. 'How long?'

'A few years, perhaps more. It depends.'

'I see.'

Jamie watched Swain pour himself another hefty brandy. 'Did you have any idea?'

243

'I guessed. But I hoped I was wrong. It might just have been something else, after all.' He gave a heartfelt sigh. 'What happens next? I mean, how does it progress?'

'Gradually the infection will take a greater hold of you. Your mind will eventually start to deteriorate until finally . . .' Jamie trailed off, unwilling to go on.

'I become a mindless idiot,' Swain finished for him.

'I'm sorry. But that's more or less what happens.'

'Dear God,' Swain whispered, and shuddered.

'There are a few things I now have to ask you,' Jamie said quietly.

'Go on.'

'How long since you and Mrs Swain had relations?'

Swain barked out a laugh. 'Don't worry about her, doctor. We haven't had those since the birth of our last child. She'll be as clear as a bell.'

He got up and walked over to the window where he stood with his back to Jamie. 'She had an exceptionally hard and difficult time with that birth. Terrible, actually. And when it was all over she swore never to go through it ever again. It had also destroyed all her desires in that direction. They were gone, completely.'

Jamie had heard of that happening before. It wasn't all that unusual; more common than many people realised.

'I was still a relatively young man at the time, Dr Murray. And much as I loved and adored my wife, which I still do, I found it impossible to be celibate so I therefore made arrangements to satisfy my needs. Only now it would appear, despite having been most careful in my choice of partners, I've become unstuck.' He suddenly turned and smiled wolfishly at Jamie. 'Damned bad luck, eh?'

244

Jamie could only nod his agreement. Despite Swain's reputation he felt sympathy for the man.

Swain turned again to stare out of the window. 'I'd like to be alone now, doctor, if you don't mind. And thank you for coming. I appreciate it.'

Jamie couldn't think of anything further to say, so simply left, closing the study door firmly behind him.

'Are you doing anything on Saturday night, Crista?'

Crista paused in her polishing of the silver. 'Why do you ask?'

'I've come by two tickets for a variety show in Exeter and wondered if you'd care to accompany me?'

She didn't answer right away, her mind racing. 'I've never been to the theatre, Jamie,' she replied eventually.

'Then now's your chance. There are some good turns on the bill, I believe. Should be a laugh.'

'I don't know,' she prevaricated. 'What would people say if we were seen?'

'To hell with what people say. I simply have two tickets that were given to me and think it would be a shame to waste them. I certainly don't want to go on my own.' That the tickets had been given him was a lie. He'd bought them himself after seeing his parents off at St David's station.

Go out with Jamie! Her heart was thumping at the prospect. It would be a secret dream come true. 'I'll have to speak to my mother first.'

'Of course,' Jamie nodded. 'Quite right too. I'm sure she won't object.'

Crista wasn't at all certain about that.

★ ★ ★

'Go to the theatre with Dr Murray?' Lavender repeated suspiciously. 'Why would he ask *you*?'

'I explained, Mum. He's been given two tickets and doesn't want to waste one.'

Lavender, who'd worked full time behind the counter of the local dairy since shortly after Davey's death, remained suspicious. She just couldn't understand Jamie's asking Crista, his housekeeper. It seemed so unusual, to say the least.

'Well, Mum?'

'I suppose it's all right,' Lavender grudgingly agreed, shaking her head in bafflement. 'If you wish to go, that is.'

'Oh, thank you, Mum. Thank you!'

'But make certain you're home at a reasonable time. You know how people talk.'

'I will, Mum. I promise.'

Crista was thrilled to bits and couldn't wait to tell Jamie she'd be accepting. Then she frowned as a thought hit her. What was she going to wear?

Jamie and Crista were laughing as they left the theatre at the conclusion of the show, both having thoroughly enjoyed themselves.

'Some of it was ever so funny,' Crista enthused. 'Particularly that comic Ben Wilton. He had me in stitches.'

She was positively radiant, Jamie noted, proud that she was with him. He should have done this a long time ago.

'I think it's going to rain though,' Crista declared, glancing up at the leaden night sky. 'I can smell it.'

All around them people were streaming past as they

too exited the theatre. 'As it's still relatively early would you care to go for a bite of supper?' Jamie proposed. 'I know of a few places close by that cater for the after theatre trade.'

Oh, she was tempted! But instead she shook her head. 'I'd love to. Truly I would. But then I'd get home late and I promised mum I wouldn't do that.'

Jamie bit back his disappointment. 'Fair enough. Shall we go to the car, then?'

Crista had been right about the rain. Halfway to Ford the heavens opened and it bucketed. Jamie slowed right down and peered anxiously through the windscreen, trying to see ahead. Every so often Crista would glance at him, her expression one of admiration. And more.

Eventually Jamie drew up outside her cottage. 'Here we are.'

'I can't thank you enough for tonight, Jamie. I thoroughly enjoyed every moment of it.'

'So did I.'

She caught a tone in his voice reflecting what she was thinking. 'I'll see you in the morning.'

'I'll look forward to it.'

At that precise moment, because of how he'd said that, she knew beyond doubt this was no passing fancy on his part. The realisation sent an almost electric tingle through her. 'So will I,' she whispered.

They stared into one another's eyes, and something intangible passed between them. An understanding of what was what. Would he kiss her? she wondered. But Jamie, playing the gentleman – it was their first time out together, after all – didn't.

'Goodnight, Jamie.'

'Goodnight, Crista.'

In a flash she was out of the car and across the pavement, and had vanished indoors.

Jamie yawned, and suddenly realised that what he wanted was a pint. A glance at his watch told him there was still plenty of time before closing.

He was approaching the Angel when an older woman, clearly nine sheets to the wind, came staggering out to stand swaying on the spot. On getting closer he recognised her to be Mavis Davis.

Mavis peered at him. 'Is that you, doctor?' she slurred.

'It is, Mrs Davis.' He tried not to sound too disapproving.

She almost fell against him, saving herself by grabbing and holding on to his lapels. 'Have you heard the wonderful news?' she queried.

There must be some sort of party going on at the Angel, Jamie now realised. The place was positively humming, punctuated by sounds of loud raucous laughter. 'No. What's that?'

'Mr Miles bloody Swain killed himself this afternoon. Shot his ugly sodding head off!'

Jamie went cold inside.

Mavis shook him. 'Isn't it fantastic? The whole village is celebrating.' She suddenly let go of him and hiccuped. 'I think I've had a drop too much,' she apologised, patting herself on the breastbone.

'I think you have, Mrs Davis. Will you be able to get home all right?'

She waved a hand at him. 'Don't you worry about me, doctor. I'll be hunky dory.'

'Then you'd best get along.'

'I'll do that.'

Jamie watched her lurch on her way, her feet all over the place. He continued to watch until she was lost to view, and all the time he was thinking about Miles Swain.

It was sheer bedlam inside the pub, which was packed to bursting. He nearly changed his mind and left again, but he decided to stay when he spotted Crista in a far corner with friends.

It took him ages to get to the bar but finally he managed it. 'What do you think of the news then, doc?' Dickie Trippett beamed as he poured Jamie's pint.

'Unexpected, I would have thought.'

'You're damn right it was. Imagine him doing that! No one knows why, and no one actually cares. He did it and that's all that matters.' A perspiring Dickie placed Jamie's pint in front of him. 'First one's on the house. John's treat.'

For some reason that disappointed Jamie. He'd thought more of John. There again, he wasn't a villager in the sense John was. And to be fair, it might simply have been a shrewd business move by the landlord, who knew his clientele only too well.

'Thank you, Dickie.'

Somewhere at the rear of the pub male and female voices began to sing. Jamie couldn't make out the words with the exception of what appeared to be the shouted chorus, which was THE OLD BASTARD'S DEAD! THE OLD BASTARD'S DEAD!

Suddenly Jamie felt sickened, and just wanted to be out of there, Crista or no Crista. To him, these goings-on were totally obscene.

★ ★ ★

249

'Jamie? Jamie, where are you?'

He came into the kitchen to discover Crista there. 'Why, hello.' He smiled.

'I saw you in the pub. One moment you were there, the next gone. I wondered if everything was all right?'

His face clouded over. 'Would you like a Scotch? I'm just about to have one. Or there is some gin.'

'Gin would be nice. Any tonic?'

'A bit.'

'So what happened?' she asked as he began pouring.

He took his time in replying, and when he did he spoke softly. 'I suppose it's to do with the war and my experiences in it.'

She accepted her drink from him. 'Want to tell me about them?'

'I honestly don't know if I can, Crista. Or even if I want to try.'

He looked into her eyes and saw that she was only trying to help, that she cared. He also saw the enormous tenderness there. 'You see so many dead, Crista. Thousands and thousands of them. All young men, or mostly young men anyway, whose lives have suddenly been snuffed out, and you wonder where the sense in it all is. You also appreciate the true sanctity and preciousness of life. Of everyone's life. Even the Germans.'

He took a deep breath while she continued to gaze at him. 'It does something to you, that's all. And then tonight I go into that pub and everyone's celebrating the fact a man shot himself. All right, I know Swain was hated, and probably deserved to be, but none the less. What I witnessed tonight sickened me to the pit of my stomach.' He took a mouthful from his glass. 'I probably haven't explained anything.'

'I think you have,' she replied gently.

He could very easily have reached across and stroked the softness of her cheek. 'Maybe partially, no more. As I said, the war isn't a subject I care to discuss.'

'I can see it's affected you an awful lot.'

Jamie could smell her now. No perfume, no scent. Just the sweetness that was her. 'Crista?'

'What?'

Neither of them knew how it happened, but suddenly they were in each other's arms, kissing passionately, yet tenderly at the same time.

When it was finally over Crista rested the side of her face against his shoulder. 'I've wanted you to do that for a long, long time now,' she whispered.

'Have you?'

'Oh, yes.'

He ran his fingers through her hair, then pressed her head even more tightly against him. 'I was a fool not to realise what was in front of my very nose,' he said huskily.

'And what was that, Jamie?'

'My feelings towards you. How stupid of me. How very stupid. And how blind.'

Crista wondered if she dared say what she wanted to, and decided she would. 'I love you, Jamie. But I never dared hope . . .'

Love? Yes, that was the right word. Now that he thought about it he simply couldn't imagine life without her. She'd become part and parcel of his very being without his being aware of it. Thank God his mother had had the sense to pull the blinkers from his eyes. 'I love you too, Crista.'

She went rigid. 'Please don't say that if it isn't true, Jamie. I couldn't bear it.'

It was as if all their years together had suddenly crystallised within these past few minutes. He'd just been walking the road to Damascus.

'I do, Crista. I swear. I love you with all my heart.'

'Oh, Jamie!' The face she lifted to his was tear-stained, her eyes closing as he gently kissed her again.

'Don't cry, darling.'

She managed a smile. 'They're tears of happiness that this has actually happened.'

'Will you marry me?'

The words rang round her brain like a peal of joyous bells. 'Of course I will, Jamie. I'd marry you tomorrow if . . .' She suddenly broke off and, to his surprise, disengaged herself from their embrace.

'What's wrong?'

'Of course I'll marry you, Jamie,' she repeated. 'But if we're going to do this it must be done right.'

'How do you mean "right"? I don't understand.'

'There must be a proper engagement before the wedding. Over nine months. And during that time there mustn't be any . . . well, of that. You know.'

'You've lost me, Crista. No, I don't know.'

She blushed furiously. 'Shagging. I want to be a virgin when I go to the altar. I owe mum that.'

It was beginning to dawn on him what she was getting at, what her reasons might be. 'Is that because of Maggs?'

Crista nodded. 'The tittle-tattle round the village was awful when Maggs suddenly got married and then had a so-called premature baby. It was sheer agony for mum knowing what was being said. I owe it to her that there's no breath of scandal, not even the hint of one, when we get wed. It's important to me.'

He could see the anxiety written all over her face, and a look of desperate pleading. 'If that's how it's to be then that's how it'll be.'

'You won't mind? About the shagging, I mean? You can wait?'

'It seems I'll have to.'

'Oh, Jamie,' she whispered, face now filled with gratitude.

'But as that's the case I suggest we get engaged as soon as possible. First opportunity we get we'll go into town and choose a ring. How about that?'

She was back in his arms again, heart wildly pounding. He holding her as tightly as he could without hurting her. 'I love you so very much, Jamie,' she whispered.

'And I love you just as much.'

Her instincts told her that was true.

'Would you like us to go down the road and tell your mother what we've decided?'

Her eyes were shining bright as stars. 'Can we?'

'I don't see why not. But not yet. Not quite yet. Let's just savour this moment. Not break the spell for a little while.'

She couldn't have agreed more. And they didn't.

What's more, he kept his word. Crista was still a virgin when she walked down the aisle.

1967

Chapter 15

For Crista it was always the worst day of the year. This one was particularly poignant, being the tenth anniversary of Jamie's death. She lay in bed staring at the ceiling, her mind full of memories, nearly all happy ones.

She recalled with crystal clarity walking into Jamie's office to find him slumped over his desk. Despite frantic efforts on her part it had been impossible to revive him. A subsequent post-mortem had revealed that death had been due to a blood clot on the brain, which, she'd been assured, would have taken him instantly, without even a moment's warning or pain. That had always been of enormous comfort to her.

Dear Jamie, how she missed him. Theirs had been a wonderful marriage. There had been a few ups and downs along the way, but that was only to be expected. He hadn't only been her husband and lover, but her very dear friend, as she'd been a friend to him.

Later in the morning she'd go to the cemetery, as she did every year on this day. Always alone. She'd never wanted anyone else there, not even the children, when she talked to him as if he was still alive and could hear her. Sometimes, and maybe it was her imagination, he even seemed to reply, his voice echoing in her mind.

Crista came out of her reverie when she heard the front door click open, and then shut again. She smiled, knowing it would be Ez, her younger daughter, come to bring her a cup of tea in bed. A ritual Ez performed faithfully every year on this day of days.

It was about ten minutes later that Ez came into the bedroom carrying a cup of tea and toast. 'Morning, Mum. The sun's shining and it's lovely out.'

'And how are you?'

'Fine. Yourself?'

'So so. The usual.'

'Nothing changed there then.'

Crista smiled as she sipped her tea. Strong and well sugared, just the way she liked it. 'Pete get off to work OK?' Pete was Ez's husband, a bricklayer by trade.

'Oh yes. He was even quite good-natured about it.' The women exchanged knowing looks, Pete being notoriously grumpy first thing in the morning.

Ez sat on the edge of the bed. 'I've been thinking, Mum.'

'Oh?'

'About you and this house.'

Crista guessed what was coming next. 'I'm not moving, if that's what you're going to suggest.'

'But it would make sense,' Ez argued. 'The house is far too large for a single person. All you do is rattle around in it all day long. A smaller place would be far more comfortable and easier to manage.'

A look of determination came over Crista's face.

'I have no intention of leaving here, Ez, not now or ever. This is the family home where your dad and I brought up you and Sally. It's where I belong and where I fully intend to remain. All right?'

'If you say so.'

'I do,' Crista replied emphatically. 'And I certainly don't rattle around, as you put it. It's not like that at all.'

Ez sighed. 'Sorry, Mum. I was only trying to be helpful. Think of what's best.'

Crista's gaze softened. She'd never have admitted it in a thousand years but Ez was her favourite. She loved the older Sally, but Ez had a special place in her heart. Ez's character had a great deal to do with it, for she was far kinder, and certainly warmer, than her sister. And Ez had a lot of Jamie about her, particularly in looks and facial expressions. 'I know that, dear. And I thank you for your concern about my well-being. It's just . . . if I left this house I'd be a fish completely out of water. Can you understand that?'

Ez nodded. 'I suppose so.'

'Good. And that's the last I want to hear on the subject. Agreed?'

'Yes, Mum. Agreed.'

Crista watched as Ez, a smoker like her father, lit up a cigarette. 'Nick will be off to university soon,' she commented between mouthfuls of toast. Nick was Ez's eighteen-year-old son, Anne, sixteen, her daughter.

Ez shook her head. 'I can't say I'm looking forward to it. We'll all miss him dreadfully.'

'That's only natural, Ez. But he's only going to Bristol, which is hardly the other end of the earth,

259

and he'll be back during holidays. Just be thankful he's bright enough to have been accepted. The only one to go to university since your dad.'

Ez smiled in recollection. 'Dad was disappointed, though he never said, that neither Sally nor I went, but I personally wouldn't have wanted to even if I could have got in. Living in Ford, getting married and being a housewife, not to mention a mum, has always been enough for me. Sally too, according to her.'

Crista knew Ez was right. Jamie had been disappointed — more, she suspected, than he'd ever let on — that neither of his daughters had made university, and would have been absolutely delighted to know his grandson Nick was going. But, as Jamie would have wisely said, happiness comes first and foremost, and if they were happy to stay home in Ford then so be it.

'That was lovely. A real treat.' Crista smiled, setting her cup and plate aside. 'Thank you.'

'Would you like me to run your bath?'

'I'm quite capable, Ez. I'm not decrepit yet.'

'I'm aware of that, Mum. I was just . . . well, trying to be . . .'

'Helpful?' Crista cut in, and they both laughed.

'Sometimes I think you missed your vocation by not becoming a nurse,' Crista commented. 'You'd have been a wonderful one.'

'Washing bums is not for me,' Ez replied jocularly. 'Nor bed pans, thank you very much.' She screwed up her face in mock disgust. 'How very nasty.'

'That wasn't what I was getting at, as you well know. However, I do take your point. Neither of those things you mentioned would have been my idea of fun either.'

'So will I run the bath or not?'

Crista relented. 'Oh, on you go. Just this once I'll play the invalid.'

'No, Mum,' Ez admonished. 'It's me playing the doting daughter.'

'Then you dote on while I get up.'

Ez was laughing as she left the room.

'Christ, I'm glad that's over for another night,' Maggs declared tersely as she locked the door of the Angel. She and Dickie had taken over the pub years previously when Spanish John and Dee Dee had retired to Torquay.

'It wasn't that bad,' Dickie replied, busy with dirty ashtrays.

'Bad enough. Neither of us is getting any younger, don't forget. More and more I feel my age, and that's a fact.' Maggs, who'd put on an enormous amount of weight since her youth, waddled to a bar stool and perched on it. 'I'm dying for a drink,' she announced.

'The usual, love?'

Maggs nodded, and watched him pour out a large brandy which he placed in front of her. He then poured himself a pint of a new local beer that had only recently come into existence. The brewery, a one-man affair, was situated on the edge of the village.

'That barrel any better than the last?' Maggs queried after Dickie had tasted it.

He shook his head. 'If anything it's worse.'

'Then why serve it in the first place? He's not even a nice bloke to deal with. Obnoxious, in my opinion, and always has been.'

Dickie shrugged. 'I only support him 'cause he's

local. Besides, some of the customers quite like it.'

'Only because it's cheaper than everything else.'

Dickie couldn't argue with that, as it was true. 'We'll stay with him a while longer and then he can't say we didn't give him a fair crack of the whip. OK?'

'Suit yourself. But if it was up to me that's the last barrel we'd have on the premises.'

'You do look tired,' Dickie acknowledged, concern in his voice.

'I'm dead beat at the end of every night. I'm telling you, Dickie, it's all getting too much for me. I just wish we could retire and put our feet up for a change.'

So she was back on about that again, Dickie thought in despair. 'You know we can't afford to retire Maggs. We need the income to make ends meet, it's as simple as that.'

Maggs fixed him with a steely glare. 'You don't want to retire because you enjoy working. Go on, admit it for a change.'

He couldn't meet her gaze, for she was right. He did enjoy working. The pub was his life. At the same time it was also true that they couldn't afford to retire. They were managers working for wages, unlike Spanish John and Dee Dee who'd owned the pub before selling it to a brewery chain.

Maggs saw off the remains of her brandy and pushed the glass towards Dickie for a refill. She knew she drank to excess and had done for a long time now, but she didn't give a damn. It was the alcohol which had piled on the pounds and she didn't care about that either. Why should she? As far as she was concerned there was nothing in her life but unending drudgery. The alcohol helped her cope.

Dickie refilled the glass without being asked to do so, wishing she didn't drink so much. It was another bone of contention between them. He had tried to get her to cut back, to no avail. In the end he'd given up, tired of the arguments it caused.

'Life just isn't fair,' Maggs commented sourly.

'And what makes you say that?'

'I'm thinking of Crista and the easy ride she's had of it.'

Dickie inwardly sighed. This was another hobby horse of hers.

'She's worth pots since Jamie died. Absolute pots, thanks to what he inherited from his parents. You'd have thought she'd have passed some of it on to her only sister.'

'Why should she, Maggs? It's not as if we're in financial trouble of any kind. From her point of view it must seem we're sitting pretty.'

'Sitting pretty! How can we be that when we can't afford to retire decently?'

'It's not Crista's problem,' Dickie wearily explained. 'It's ours. And one I'll someday find a solution to.'

'Huh!' Maggs exclaimed in disbelief. 'And pigs might fly, Dickie Trippett. Pigs might fly.'

'Crista was just lucky, that's all,' Dickie reminded Maggs. 'It's not as if she married Jamie for his money. That was a true love match if ever there was one. And she worked hard for him when he was alive. Don't forget she was his receptionist as well as his wife for all those years. And it isn't easy dealing with the public, as we both know only too well.'

'She was still bloody lucky,' Maggs grumbled. 'Given

263

to her on a plate it was. Nothing like that has ever happened to me.'

Dickie turned away so she couldn't see his expression. Why did Maggs always succeed in making him feel such a failure! That had been the case right from the word go. Anything he accomplished was never quite good enough. He was second best, a second-rater, a ball and chain round her neck that she had to put up with.

And yet he'd never regretted marrying Maggs for one single moment, still loved her as much as he'd ever done. That, despite the fact – and he'd tried, oh how he'd tried! – that she'd never come to love him.

Maggs finished her second brandy and pushed her glass across the bar for a third. She knew she was becoming maudlin, not that it mattered. Again, she simply didn't care.

Dickie was thinking that things might have turned out different if they'd had children together, but that hadn't happened. David, who wasn't his, had remained their only child.

They hardly ever saw David any more. He was now married with children of his own and living in Plymouth. He'd joined the Merchant Navy at an early age, eventually achieving the position of Master, or ship's captain. During his time in the Mercantile Marine he'd travelled the world, most recently to Singapore from where they'd received a postcard only that week. To this day David had no idea Dickie wasn't his real father, or who was.

'It would be nice to have a proper holiday sometime,' Maggs mused aloud.

'But we do go places,' Dickie reminded her.

'Like Sidmouth?' Maggs sneered. 'Some holiday that. Right on our own doorstep.'

'But I thought you liked Sidmouth? You've always said you did.'

'But it's not a real holiday, is it?' she argued. 'I mean, it isn't even out of Devon, for Christ's sake!'

Dickie became uneasy. 'You know I don't like to go too far away.'

'Because of this bloody pub!' she accused. 'I swear you start to twitch the moment you're away from it. And when we do go it's never for more than a week, with you itching to get back after the first day. Not only that, you're for ever on the phone checking that everything's OK and that the damned place hasn't burned down or something equally ludicrous.'

'I can't help it,' Dickie admitted rather pathetically. 'I'm sorry. It's just how I am.'

'As if I didn't know that.'

'So where would you like to go?' he asked, dreading the answer.

'Somewhere on the continent maybe. Somewhere we can be guaranteed sun. And not for a week, either! A fortnight at least to make it worthwhile.'

The thought of a fortnight abroad appalled him, filled him with dread.

'Well?' she demanded angrily.

'It would be very expensive. I doubt we could afford it.'

Money again. The look she gave him was one of sheer contempt. She fought back the urge to call him a useless cripple, something she'd done twice during their married life, on both occasions with devastating effect.

'Perhaps the Channel Islands,' he muttered. That wasn't too far away, and shouldn't cost all that much. But certainly for no longer than a week. A fortnight was quite out of the question.

'The Channel Islands,' Maggs mused, her interest caught. Hardly exotic, but better than Sidmouth.

'We could take a boat there and back. And I hear the food is excellent, lots of fish which I adore. From what I understand there's quite a French influence albeit the islands are British.'

Maggs was warming to the idea. The only trouble was, when the time came, would Dickie actually commit himself to going? She knew him only too well of old where leaving the pub was concerned.

'When?' she demanded.

'Next year. Perhaps in the spring before the tourist trade gets going?'

She could understand the reasoning behind his suggestion. He didn't want to miss the tourist trade in Devon, which was expanding all the time, and it would be cheaper, considerably so, to go out of season.

'Well, Maggs?'

'Will there be any sun that time of year?'

'Bound to be. You'll see.'

'For a fortnight?'

His face dropped. 'A week, Maggs. Can't possibly manage more than that.'

'It'll be a fortnight and no argument,' she declared with finality. 'Now pour me another brandy while we discuss the matter further.'

She smiled with grim satisfaction as he poured.

Somehow, someway, she was going to hold him to this. And God help him if he even tried to renege.

She'd make his life a living hell.

'Hello, Nick!' Crista exclaimed in surprise as her grandson came into the room. 'What brings you to see your old nan?'

'I just thought you might like some company.'

She attempted to rise. 'I'll put the kettle on.'

'No no no, you sit where you are. I'll do it.'

He filled the electric kettle and plugged it in. All the appliances in the kitchen were now mod con. The range Jamie had so hated had long since been ripped out and replaced by an up-to-date gas fire and cooker. There was even a fridge, of which there were still only a few in Ford.

'So what are you up to lately, nan?' Nick asked cheerily as he fiddled with the teapot.

'Oh, the usual. The WI, helping sew costumes for the dramatic society when they have a production on, involved with the fête when that comes round. Don't worry, I keep myself busy.'

'I'm off soon, you know. Three weeks.'

'Your mum and I were talking about it just the other day. She says they're going to miss you dreadfully.'

Nick shrugged. 'I'll miss them too. And you, of course. In fact I'll miss Ford generally. But if I want to go to university it can't be helped, can it?'

'I'm afraid not.' Crista suddenly frowned. 'You're not having second thoughts, are you?'

'Not really. But it is an awfully big step, after all. Leaving home for the first time, going to live in a city after village life, that sort of thing. Daunting to say the least.'

'You'll cope all right,' she assured him. 'I know you will.'

'Let's just hope so, eh?'

'There's some cake in that tin if you'd care for a slice,' she said, pointing.

'Not for me, thanks. How about you?'

She was tempted, but resisted. She'd managed to keep a reasonable semblance of her figure over the years, unlike poor Maggs, and fully intended it to stay that way. She'd never had to diet but always kept a strict watch on what she ate, and tried, except perhaps at Christmas, never to overindulge. 'Me neither.'

'To be honest, Nan,' he suddenly confessed, 'I've suddenly got the jitters about Bristol. Silly really. As you said, I'm sure I'll cope.'

'It's fear of the unknown, I expect.' Crista nodded. 'When your grandpa talked about the Great War, which he only ever did occasionally, he always said that was the worst thing. Fear of the unknown. He said it could turn the stomach of the most coura-geous man to jelly.'

'At least I don't have to worry about being shot or blown up in Bristol,' Nick joked.

Crista smiled. 'I hope not.'

When the tea was ready Nick placed a cup and saucer on the small table by her chair, then sat oppo-site holding the mug he'd selected for himself. He knew Crista hated being served tea or coffee in a mug, but did keep a few in the house for others.

'I have another reason for coming today,' he said slowly.

'Oh? And what's that?'

'I know I've already thanked you for funding me going to university, but I want to again. It would have been impossible otherwise.'

Crista's features softened. 'It was the least I could do, Nick, when it became apparent you were bright enough. Your grandpa would certainly have approved.'

'But thanks again, just the same. I do appreciate it.'

'I know.'

He regarded her shrewdly. 'Talking of grandpa, don't you get lonely all alone here since he's gone?'

Crista wagged a finger at him. 'Now don't you start. I get enough of that from your mother. Why can't I convince people that I'm happy as Larry living by myself? I have the wireless, the television, visitors – what more do I need?'

'I was just asking, Nan, that's all. We worry about you.'

'Then don't. It's not necessary. If I felt lonely, or otherwise, I'd be the first to say. OK?'

'OK, Nan.'

'There is one thing, though. Something you can do for me.'

'Name it.'

'Make sure you write regularly when you're away. I want to hear all your news, how the studies are going. That you're eating properly and generally taking care of yourself.' Her eyes sparkled mischievously. 'Also about any girlfriends you might get involved with.'

Nick blushed. 'Nan!'

'I mean it. About the girlfriends, that is.'

'Everything about them?' he teased.

She knew precisely what he was getting at. Honestly,

this modern generation, it had no shame. Not like in her day. She wondered what Nick's reaction would be if she told him she'd been a virgin on her wedding night. He'd probably think it hysterical. But there you were, things had changed dramatically down the years.

'A censored version, I think,' he conceded. 'You are my nan, after all.'

'That'll do. But not too censored. I want to enjoy the juicy bits.'

Nick shook his head in disbelief. 'You're amazing, you truly are.'

Was she? She didn't think so. Just someone trying to keep up with modern life. Surely there was no harm in that? Of course not. Simply a little fun in what could otherwise be a rather humdrum existence.

She may be old – well, oldish – but she wasn't dead yet. Not by a long chalk. By heavens she wasn't.

When Nick came to leave she made him promise he'd call in again before setting off to Bristol, which he assured her he would.

Crista felt a real rosy glow of pleasure after Nick had gone. He was such a lovely lad. Jamie would have been proud of him, as indeed she was.

Very much so.

Maggs came awake to find Dickie thrashing around beside her. Every few seconds he'd mutter something about guns, explosions and the dreaded gas. Even after all these years he continued to have nightmares about the Great War, although nowadays it was rare for him to wake screaming and shouting the place down. He still had pills to take should he wake, but that didn't happen very often now. The nightmares had become more subdued, and less frequent.

A glance at the luminous dial of her bedside clock told her it was just gone four a.m. 'Christ!' she muttered. It was still the middle of the night as far as she was concerned.

Maggs grunted in pain as a suddenly flung out arm smacked into her ribcage. That was it, she thought. Enough. She'd get up and make herself a cup of tea while waiting for him to settle down again. It was something she'd done countless times before.

She slipped from bed and into her dressing gown, grimacing from the soreness where he'd hit her. Quiet as anything, having put on her slippers, she padded from the bedroom.

She was halfway down the stairs when the idea came to her, making her smile. To hell with tea. She'd have a drink all right, but brandy.

When she finally returned to bed she was drunk as a lord. Later, she told Dickie she was having a lie-in for a while because he'd kept her up half the night with one of his nightmares. She'd really enjoyed that, she thought as she drifted off again. Drinking alone and at that time of the morning had made her feel deliciously wicked. As an added bonus, Dickie hadn't been there to watch, and comment, disapprovingly.

'Can I help you?' Crista asked the stranger who'd knocked her door.

The man raised his hat. 'Mrs Murray?'

'Yes.'

'I believe you do bed and breakfast? I inquired at

the Angel if they did and the landlord there recommended I come to you.'

Well dressed, Crista noted, the suit clearly an expensive one, as obviously were the shirt, tie and shoes. She couldn't place his accent but he certainly wasn't from these parts.

'Do you have a room currently available?' the man queried.

'How long for?'

'A few nights, no more.'

'Come in, then.'

Crista had been doing bed and breakfast, mainly for tourists during the summer, for a long time now. She didn't need the money; it was simply rather nice, and often entertaining, to have guests for short periods. They were invariably good company, too.

'Let me introduce myself. My name is Max Rubin,' the stranger declared once he was inside.

Round about the same age as herself, maybe slightly older, Crista guessed. Well spoken and polite, too. 'How do you do, Mr Rubin? Are you on holiday?'

'Partly. But mainly here on business.'

'I see.' She couldn't help but wonder if he was a foreigner. He had that look about him. 'May I ask where you're from?'

'London. Born and bred there.'

So much for his being foreign. Still, he could easily have foreign blood in him. From the little she knew of London they were a mixed lot in the capital.

'If you follow me I'll show you the way,' she said.

'Thank you.'

'Come down today?'

'Yes, I drove. That's my car outside.'

'Well, you had lovely weather for it.'

'Indeed I did. The journey was a delight.'

It didn't take Rubin long to make up his mind and agree Crista's letting price. Less than ten minutes after knocking the door he was unpacking his case.

Chapter 16

'That's the freshest egg I've had in years,' Max Rubin declared with relish at breakfast the following morning. 'You just can't buy them like that in London.'

'Really?'

He shook his head. 'It's impossible, Mrs Murray. Take my word for it.'

'Is that because of the travelling time eggs take to get there?'

He considered that. 'I suppose so. It's the same with fish. Not a patch on those straight from the sea. A world of difference, actually.'

'More tea, Mr Rubin?'

He beamed at her. 'Please. This country air has given me quite an appetite.'

'Would you care for another egg then?'

'Could I?'

'Of course. Have as many as you wish.' She laughed. 'It's all included in the price.'

She got busy with the frying pan, and the beef dripping she always used to give added flavour. 'As a matter of interest, do you know how to tell how fresh an egg is?'

'No idea.'

'The yolk gives it away. A fresh egg's yolk stands proud, whereas the yolk of an old egg is flat.'

'Goodness gracious!'

'It's the same with the colour of the yolk. The more yellow it is the better fed the chicken's been, and the more goodness there is in it.'

Max laughed. 'You are a mine of culinary information, Mrs Murray. I'd never have thought to look at the colour of a yolk.'

'There you are then. You've learnt something new.'

'Indeed I have,' he agreed.

'What are your plans for today?' she asked casually, not wanting to appear nosy.

'Exeter on business. Probably till early evening. I thought I'd eat something round about then after which I'll come back here. If that's all right with you?'

'Suits me. You can do as you like, come and go as you wish. If you do come back and find I'm out feel free to watch television or listen to the wireless. They're easy enough to work.'

'Thank you.'

'And I'll give you a key before you leave.' Crista paused for a moment, and sighed in recollection. 'It's sad really. There was a time in this village when you never thought to lock your door. It was always left open, whether you were in or not. Unfortunately that's not the case any more. And hasn't been since they built the estate.'

'I haven't noticed any estate?' Max frowned.

'Well, it depends which way in or out of the village you go. But it's there all right. Virtually doubled our population when it was completed.'

'You don't approve, I take it?'

Crista picked up the frying pan and lifted the egg on to his plate. 'Some of the new people are OK. But others . . . Well, they were townies and don't quite fit in with our ways. Now we get vandalism and all sorts which never happened before. It's most distressing to those of us who remember the village as it was. As I said, sad really.'

Max nodded his understanding as he reached for another slice of toast. 'It must be.'

'But there we are, there's nothing we can do about it.'

'I suppose not,' he murmured.

'We used to have a village policeman. Now we hardly see one from one week to the next.'

'It's the same in London,' he informed her. 'You still have bobbies on the street, but nowhere near as many as there were. The latest gimmick is for them to drive round in cars. Daft idea if you ask me. The old beat bobby knew exactly what was going on in his manor, who was up to what, who was ill, who had fallen on hard times, everything. You can't get that kind of information driving about in a car. It divorces you from the populace at large.'

Somewhere during that morning Crista had decided she liked Max Rubin. He was an extremely pleasant man. He thanked her as she refilled his teacup.

'Aren't you having some?' he asked.

'I've already had my breakfast.' It was her policy never to eat with her paying guests. PGs, she called them. To her way of thinking it was the right way to conduct matters.

'You must have been up early?' He smiled.

'I usually am. It was a habit I acquired when young and working at the mill.'

'Oh yes. I did notice that. Tell me, is it still operational?'

'It certainly is, though not employing anything like the number of people it used to. Demand has fallen away considerably since the last war, I understand, and the workforce has been reduced to about a quarter of what it was when I was there.'

'I see. What kind of mill is it exactly?'

'Paper. There used to be a lot of them in this area, but many have closed down in recent years.'

'Fallen demand again?'

'That's right. I've no idea why that should be so, but apparently it is.' Crista smiled. 'At one time nearly every man in Ford worked there, and many of the women too. It was either that or go on the land. But there too employment has been vastly reduced due to new farming methods and the introduction of modern machinery. Where a farmer employed a dozen, maybe more, folk in the past he's now employing only one or two. Sometimes none at all if he can do what's required by himself.' She shook her head. 'There have been some incredible changes round here since I was born.'

'So what do the village men work at now?' Max was intrigued.

'You name it. Where once they were tied to the village through lack of transport they can now get out and about thanks to the general use of motor cars. In the old days cars were a rarity, but not any more. There are hundreds in the village.'

'Progress, eh?' He smiled.

'You could call it that, I suppose. One thing's for certain, it's all but destroyed the old village way of life. It just isn't the same nowadays.'

'Would you turn back the clock if you could?' he queried, curious as to her answer.

Crista thought about that. 'Not really. There were some good things about the old days, and some very bad. And it's the same today. Life is just different, that's all.'

'But surely better when you take the overall view?'

'I have to admit it is. Telly, wireless, improved living conditions, more money about. And certainly less poverty of the sort that was common then. But that doesn't mean I don't miss being able to leave my front door unlocked and not worry about it.'

Max laughed. 'I take your point.'

Crista removed his now empty plate and placed it in the sink. 'The reason I'm going out tonight is because I'm playing skittles at the Angel.'

'Skittles?' He frowned. 'What's that?'

She explained.

'Sounds fun.'

'It is. Or at least we think so. If nothing else it gives the women a chance to get out by themselves for an evening.'

'Don't the men play too?'

'Oh, yes. But on a different night. We get to have a right good gossip and they have a right good drink. Everyone's happy.'

'Sounds ideal,' he said approvingly.

'That's what we think. Now, how about more tea?'

He shook his head. 'I couldn't take another drop. I'm full to bursting.'

'Excellent. Proper job.'

His gaze followed her to the sink as she set about washing up. 'I was wondering . . .'

'About what?'

'If I am back early would it be all right for me to drop by the Angel and watch the game? I'd like to see it in action.'

'Of course you can. You'll be most welcome.'

'Then I might just do that.' He nodded.

As he had said, it sounded fun. He was looking forward to it.

Maggs finally snapped. 'Can't you talk in a normal voice like everyone else?' she barked at the customer she'd just served. 'I'm fed up to the back teeth with you whispering everything as though it was a state secret. It's downright irritating to say the least.'

'Whispering' Smith, as he was nicknamed, blinked at her, completely taken aback by this outburst.

'Not only irritating but bloody bad manners,' Maggs went on. 'It's not as if you were ever talking about something important, you never are. So why don't you just speak naturally?'

Whispering cleared his throat. 'I'm sorry, Maggs. I didn't realise I was upsetting you.'

'Me and everyone else. For years I've had to put up with you acting as though you were a spy imparting classified information. You're no spy and even if you were you couldn't keep a secret to save your life.'

Dickie, who'd overheard this exchange, came strolling across. 'What's the problem, Maggs?'

She took a deep breath, then shook her head.

'Nothing. It's sorted now.' And with that she hurried off.

'Bit touchy tonight, isn't she?' Whispering commented, well aware he'd gone red in the face.

'Hasn't struck me that way,' Dickie replied, backing his wife.

For a moment Whispering's eyes glittered maliciously. 'Maybe she's been on the sauce again. That would explain it.'

Dickie stared at Whispering while he made up his mind whether or not to temporarily ban him for making that remark. As it so happened Maggs hadn't been. But even if she had it was no business of anyone else's.

'Now you're being rude,' Dickie said slowly. 'But then that's nothing new from you. You have a name for it.'

Percy Matford, a friend of Whispering's who was sitting beside him, giggled just like a girl, thinking that extremely funny.

'I don't have to come in here, you know,' Whispering blustered in retaliation.

'That's right. You don't.'

Percy giggled again, which earned him a glare from Whispering.

'Think about it.' Dickie smiled, and moved away back up the bar, leaving Whispering staring daggers at him.

'Sorry about that,' Maggs apologised quietly to Dickie. 'He just got under my skin once too often, that's all.'

Dickie fought back his laughter. For it was absolutely true. Any anger he felt towards Maggs for having a go at a customer, and a regular at that, simply melted away.

Moments later Max, coming into the pub, was barged aside by Whispering bustling aggressively out.

'Don't take any notice of him,' Dickie said when Max got to the bar. 'He's out of sorts tonight, that one.'

Max shrugged. 'No harm done.'

'Now what's it to be?'

'A pint of Bass if you have it.'

'We do indeed.'

While Dickie was pulling the pint Max glanced around wondering where the skittles were, for the game Crista had described was nowhere in evidence.

'Out the back in the skittle alley,' Dickie informed him when asked. 'Through that door there.' He indicated. 'Up the corridor and then through the door at the top. It's ladies' night, though.'

'I know. Mrs Murray told me. I said I might come along and watch.'

'Brave chap,' Dickie commented in amusement.

'Why so?'

'Ladies' night means there are only women in there. You'd be the sole bloke.'

'Ah!' Max hadn't thought of that.

'You got fixed up with her, I take it?'

Max nodded. 'Thank you. The accommodation is excellent.'

'Good. She's my sister-in-law.'

'Is she really?'

'It's a village, chap. Nearly everyone is related in some way or another. At least, it was like that before the estate was built. Still, you get the idea.'

Max smiled. 'I get it.'

'Excuse me,' Dickie apologised, and moved off to serve another customer.

Women only, Max mused as he sipped his pint. He didn't fancy that at all. Particularly as he was a stranger hereabouts.

No, he'd give the skittles match a miss and go back and watch television instead. Pity, though. He was sure he'd have enjoyed the experience.

'I really am sorry about tonight,' Maggs said contritely to Dickie as they were getting ready for bed.

'You mean the words you had with Roger?' Roger was Whispering's real name.

Maggs nodded.

'Don't worry about it. He'll be back.'

Maggs sighed. 'It gets harder and harder having to be nice to everyone all the time. Especially puffed up idiots like him. I tell you, if he had another brain cell he'd be a plant.'

Dickie found that highly amusing. It described Whispering to a T. The man was one of those people who thought himself terribly clever when in fact the exact opposite was the case.

Maggs went to Dickie and put her arms round him. 'Thank you for being so understanding.'

'I try to be.'

'I know I'm difficult to live with at times, Dickie. But that's just how I am.'

'We're all difficult in some way or another.'

'Not you,' she said softly. 'They don't come any easier than you.'

'Dear Maggs,' he whispered, suddenly very

emotional. How he loved her. Always had and always would. No matter what.

'Sleep well?' Crista asked as Max came into the kitchen.

'Like a top. It must be the country air again. I never sleep nearly so well in London.'

That pleased her. 'How would you like your eggs this morning? Fried, boiled or scrambled?'

'I think boiled.'

'With soldiers?' she teased.

Max laughed. 'I haven't had those in years. But why not?'

'Help yourself to tea or coffee.'

She placed a small saucepan on the cooker and slipped two eggs into the water it contained. 'You didn't make it last night,' she remarked casually.

He decided honesty was the best policy. 'I did, actually. Or into the pub, anyway. Then your brother-in-law told me I'd be the only man amongst a load of women. I changed my mind when I heard that.'

'Coward, eh?'

'You could say that.'

'Pity. It was a good night.'

'Lots of gossip, I presume?' Now it was his turn to tease.

'Oodles and oodles of it.'

'Such as? Or can't you say?'

'No point in telling you as you wouldn't know any of the people involved.'

'I see.'

'But some of it was rather juicy.' She laughed. 'You'd be surprised what goes on in villages beneath

283

the guise of propriety and general respectability. Shocks even me at times.'

'Really?'

'Oh, yes. A lot of the gossip is sheer nonsense, of course. No truth in it whatsoever. Simply made up. There again, some of it actually is true.'

'Fascinating.'

'I thought only women found gossip fascinating,' she teased.

'Oh, I don't know. I'm sure some men do.'

'Does that include you?'

He knew he was being mocked. 'Possibly. Or, there again, possibly not.'

He was a handsome chap, Crista reflected. Nose a little large, but somehow it fitted his face. His eyes were blue and penetrating, his grey hair neatly groomed. There was a distinguished look about him, as though he might be a company director or something similar. She wondered what he did for a living, or if he was retired. She certainly wasn't going to ask; that would have been impolite.

'So what's it today, more business in Exeter?'

Max shook his head. 'Pleasure actually. I'm going to motor down to Exmouth and spend the day there.'

That surprised her. 'I didn't realise you knew Devon. I got the impression this was your first time here.'

'No, I have been before. On several occasions, with my wife. We spent a couple of holidays in Exmouth, which is why I want to return there. Revisit old memories, you might say.'

'I did notice you were wearing a wedding ring,' she remarked casually.

'My wife's dead now. Eight years ago. She was called Rebekah.'

'That's a nice name. I like it.'

He sat for several moments lost in thought. 'Those holidays were a long time ago now. We had them when we were both relatively young. I always meant to take her back, but somehow never got round to it.' He shrugged. 'You know how it is. Always putting off until tomorrow what you should be doing today.'

Crista smiled in sympathy. 'Soft or hard boiled?'

'Soft please.'

Crista put toast into a rack and set that on the table alongside butter, marmalade and jam. 'You clearly still miss her.'

'Yes, very much so. We were extremely close.'

'Same with me and my husband. He died ten years ago. There's not a day goes by that I don't think of him.'

'And yet life goes on.'

'I suppose.'

He suddenly grinned. 'Well, we're here to prove it.'

Crista watched him as he buttered a slice of toast. What elegant hands, she observed. Long, slim, the nails beautifully manicured. The hands of an artist.

'My Jamie died of a blood clot on the brain. I was assured it must have been more or less instantaneous so there would have been no pain involved. I've always been thankful for that,' she said.

Max was staring at her, a strange expression on his face. 'A blood clot on the brain?'

'That's right. I found him in the office slumped over his desk. He was the village doctor. A Scotsman from Edinburgh who bought this practice after the previous doctor passed on.'

Max laid the slice of toast he was holding back on his plate. 'What an extraordinary coincidence,' he said slowly.

'What is?'

'That's what my Rebekah died of. A blood clot on the brain. And like your husband her death was instantaneous.'

A cold shiver ran through Crista. 'Dear God!' she whispered.

They both stared at one another till Crista roused herself, remembering the eggs. If she left them much longer they'd be rock hard.

'Rebekah was also home when it happened,' Max went on. 'We were sitting listening to some Chopin when she suddenly stiffened, muttered something I couldn't make out, and then was gone. Just like that. As if an internal switch had been flicked off.'

Crista's hands were trembling as she conveyed the eggs into eggcups and took them over to Max. 'There you are. Fresh as can be. Laid yesterday,' she muttered, attempting a smile which didn't quite come off.

Max's appetite had completely disappeared. The last thing he wanted now was anything to eat.

'As you said, an amazing coincidence,' Crista choked.

'Yes.'

'Will you excuse me for a few minutes?'

'Of course.'

And with that Crista fled the kitchen leaving Max gazing after her, as shaken by the revelation as she.

★ ★ ★

'Have a safe journey back to London,' Crista said the following morning, when Max's car was loaded up and ready to leave.

'I've thoroughly enjoyed my stay, Mrs Murray. Thank you for putting me up.'

'The pleasure was all mine.'

'No no, Mrs Murray, it was most certainly mine.'

They smiled at one another, then shook hands. 'You've got decent weather for travelling anyway,' Crista commented.

'Indeed. I've been lucky with that.'

'Cheerio now.' Crista smiled again as he opened the car door and slid inside. 'And take care you don't break those eggs.' She'd given him half a dozen as a present.

'I'll do my best not to.'

He gave a farewell wave, and the car moved smoothly away down the street.

What a nice man, Crista reflected as she went back inside. As PGs went he'd been a joy.

'Cooeee!'

'I'm in the living room.'

Crista's heart sank when she saw the state the room was in. Talk about untidy! But then her elder daughter's house was always a right tip. Untidiness was a trait Sally certainly hadn't inherited from her.

'Hello, Mum. I'm just having a sit down and cup of tea. Do you want one?'

'That would be nice.' Crista handed Sally a paper bag she'd been carrying. 'Put that in the kitchen, will you? It's a cake I thought you'd like.'

'Honestly, Mum, I'm quite capable of baking myself, you know. What sort is it?'

'Lemon sponge.'

'Daniel'll love that.' Sally promptly vanished out of the room to fetch the promised tea.

Typical, Crista reflected bitterly. No "thank you, Mum", or any other show of gratitude. Just the rebuke that Sally was capable of baking herself. She sighed. That was Sally all over. She doubted it would ever change.

'Here you are,' Sally announced breezily on her return and handed Crista a mug. Crista was sitting, having had to clear things off a chair in order to do so.

Crista gazed at the mug in dismay. Sally should have known better. She hated mugs.

'So, to what do I owe the honour?' Sally queried, resuming her own chair.

Crista inwardly winced. No "lovely to see you, Mum", or "how are you, Mum?" Straight to the point had ever been Sally's way. 'Daniel out working with his dad?' Daniel was Sally's son, apprentice to her husband Ben, a painter and decorator by trade.

Sally nodded. 'They'll be back at teatime.'

'Well, it's Daniel I've come about. His birthday is in a couple of weeks and I wondered what I could get him?'

'God, I don't know, Mum. You know what twenty-year-olds are like to buy for. Difficult to say the least.'

Crista thought about that. 'So what are you and Ben getting for him?'

'I was hoping you wouldn't ask that. You won't approve.'

'I was considering clothes. Youngsters that age always need more of those.'

Sally shook her head. 'Whatever you bought would be wrong. Kids are so pernickity nowadays. I simply let him buy his own and that's an end of it.'

'Well, there must be something he wants!' Crista declared irritably. Sally was being most unhelpful.

'Oh, sure. Money.'

A look of disapproval came over Crista's face. 'I never give money. That's the easy way out and shows a lack of thought.'

Sally shrugged. 'You asked and I'm telling you. That's what he'd appreciate most. He's saving up.'

'Oh? What for?'

'Something you'll disapprove of.'

'And you don't?'

'He's a sensible lad. Ben and I agree on that, which is why we're giving him money towards it.'

Crista was becoming exasperated now. 'You said I'd disapprove. Well, I'd like' to make up my own mind about that.'

'OK. Suit yourself. But keep your hair on. It's a motorbike.'

'A motorbike!' Crista exclaimed. 'You can't be serious?'

'I appreciate they can be dangerous, we've been through all that. But as I said, Daniel is a sensible lad. He'll treat the bike with respect and not go daft on it. We have his word on that.'

'Have you now?' Crista commented cynically. She knew young people only too well. They'd promise anything to get what they were after.

'Yes we have,' Sally snapped. 'And now we'll drop the subject if you don't mind.'

Crista glanced down at the carpet, not wishing to

fall out with her daughter as she'd done so often in the past. There were times she could easily have believed that where Sally was concerned there'd been a mix-up at the hospital.

Except that Sally had been born at home, delivered by Jamie.

Chapter 17

It was a cold October evening. Crista was dozing in front of a blazing fire when the telephone rang. Wearily, for her arthritis was acting up again, she came to her feet to answer it.

'Hello?'

'Is that Mrs Murray?'

'Speaking.'

'It's Max Rubin. Remember me?'

A warm glow that had nothing to do with the fire spread through her. 'Of course I do, Mr Rubin. How are you?'

'Fine. Couldn't be better. And yourself?'

'In the pink,' she lied, having no intention of mentioning arthritis.

'That's good. Now, I was wondering, could you put me up for about a week? Maybe longer. I have to come down to Exeter again on business.'

It was unusual for her to have PGs during the winter; in fact she couldn't even remember the last time. But why not? The room was lying empty, after all. 'I'd be delighted to. When would you be arriving?'

'Sometime on Sunday. Would that suit?'

She had plenty of clean linen in the airing cupboard, so she had no problem there. 'Perfectly.'

'Excellent. Another thing, could I have an evening meal with you? That would save me the trouble of having to go out again and search for a restaurant.'

She didn't normally provide evening meals for PGs, but she'd make an exception in this instance. 'If you wish, Mr Rubin. I warn you now, though, I only do plain English cooking. Nothing fancy, you understand.'

He laughed. 'Sounds wonderful.'

'Then I shall look forward to seeing you.'

'If everything goes according to plan, between five and seven I'd say.'

'Then between five and seven it is. Goodbye, Mr Rubin.'

'Goodbye, Mrs Murray.'

'And oh, Mr Rubin?'

'Yes, Mrs Murray?'

'I shall make sure I have fresh eggs in for your breakfast.'

He laughed a second time. 'I can't wait. I haven't had a decent egg since I stayed with you earlier in the year.'

Crista hung up and stared at the telephone. Well, that had been a surprise. A very pleasant one too.

It would be nice having Max Rubin around the house again. He was such good company.

Crista had bumped into Abigail Woolocombe, Nicholls that was, and the pair of them were having a good old chat together, as they hadn't seen one another for a while, when their conversation was interrupted by the roar of a motorbike careering past.

Crista stared at the driver in dismay, recognising both machine and crash helmet as belonging to her grandson Daniel. She watched as he screeched round a corner to be lost to view.

'Is that who I think it is?' Abigail frowned.

'Daniel, Sally's son. The young fool, driving like that in these conditions.' There had been several falls of snow during the past few days, unusual for Devon, some of which had now formed into patches of black ice.

'He'll come a cropper if he's not careful,' Abigail commented.

Crista wondered if she should speak to Sally, then decided against it. For what possible good would it do? She'd only be told to mind her own business. Daniel could do no wrong in his mother's eyes.

'Let's hope and pray he doesn't,' Crista replied slowly, fearing the worst. Even if the lad had been driving carefully he shouldn't be out on a motorbike in weather like this. It was sheer lunacy.

With a heavy heart Crista resumed their previous conversation.

Maggs had her back to the bar, dealing with some minor paperwork, when she heard the door *ting*, announcing the arrival of their first customer of the morning. Dickie was down in the cellar changing barrels and cleaning the pipes.

'With you in a moment,' she said over her shoulder.

'Don't worry. I'm not in a rush.'

Maggs paused momentarily, thinking that the voice

293

sounded familiar. For the life of her, though, she couldn't think to whom it belonged.

With a flourish she finished what she was doing and turned to smile at the customer. 'What can I get you, sir?'

'A large Scotch, please. And do you have soda?'

'Of course.'

Recognition hit her like a sledgehammer blow. He was a lot older, well of course he was, the hair now grey, the skin leathery where it hadn't been before, the eyes slightly sunken, the skin round them deeply creased. But there was no mistaking. It was Rupert Swain, whom she hadn't seen since he'd broken it off between them and left her pregnant with David.

You bastard, she thought. You bloody bastard. How dare you come in here!

Her hand was trembling as she lifted a glass to the gantry, quite thrown by this totally unexpected turn of events. 'Come far?' she asked casually as she placed the glass in front of him and then indicated a nearby soda syphon he clearly hadn't noticed.

'I'll say. All the way from Rhodesia, what?'

'Do you live there?'

'Live and farm. Have done for donkeys'. But it's not so clever now, all these political shenanigans making life sticky. Don't agree with Independence myself, but that puts me in the minority over there. Most people are red hot for it.'

He didn't recognise her, she realised. There wasn't even a flicker of recognition on his face. There again, she had changed a lot, her huge weight gain not the least of it.

'I haven't been in this pub for absolute yonks,' Rupert declared.

'Oh?'

'It used to be run by a chap called John in my day. Can't recall his surname.'

Rupert was speaking just as he had in the twenties, Maggs realised. It was as if the man was caught in some sort of time warp. Nobody — well, not in this country — spoke like that any more.

'We took over from John and Dee Dee,' she said.

'And you are?'

She looked him straight in the eye. 'Mrs Trippett.'

'Pleased to meet you, Mrs Trippett. I'm Rupert Swain. My brother owns the mill.'

She didn't reply to that.

'Come back to see the old bugger before he pops his clogs, what? Extremely ill, I'm advised.'

She didn't reply to that either.

'Have you heard about that?'

Maggs shook her head, which was a lie. She knew full well Giles Swain was a dying man. The entire village knew.

'My sister and I will have to sell the mill when Giles does go. Neither of us is interested, you see, so what else can we do? It's not as if Giles has a family to pass it on to. Never married, don't you know.'

'So I believe,' Maggs murmured. Well, that was one piece of news she'd soon put round. The mill was to be sold, the end of an era where the Swains were concerned.

She wondered if Rupert was aware of the stories that had persisted for years about his brother, to the effect that Giles Swain preferred men to women, and young boys in particular. Nothing had ever been proved, but the fact remained that Giles had never married. Nor ever had a ladyfriend, as far as was known.

'Another?' she queried, seeing Rupert's glass was empty.

He shook his head. 'Just wanted a snifter, that's all. Got to be careful driving in this country these days, I'm told. Don't want the jolly old chaps in blue hauling me off to clink, what?'

'That would never do,' she replied drily, but the sarcasm was lost on him.

'Probably see you again, Mrs Trippett. Cheerio!'

She sagged when he'd gone, the shock of his visit beginning to take effect. Rupert Swain! Who would have believed it! He might still be rotten rich, but she couldn't help thinking he'd turned out to be something of a joke.

For some inexplicable reason tears seeped into her eyes.

'I do believe that to be the best casserole I've ever tasted,' Max declared, placing his knife and fork on his empty plate.

'Get away with you.' Crista smiled.

'I mean it. That meat just melted in my mouth. Quite wonderful. If that's what you call plain English cooking then give it to me every time.'

'Flatterer.'

'Not at all, Mrs Murray. I simply tell the truth. It was absolutely delicious.'

She was delighted by his praise. 'Why thank you.'

He indicated the bottle of wine he'd provided. 'Can I top up your glass?'

Crista was about to reply when the telephone rang. Now who on earth could that be? she wondered. 'Excuse me.'

Max took the opportunity to pour himself a refill while Crista was out of the room. He'd brought a case down with him and intended opening a bottle every night. Good wine was a passion of his and had been for a long time.

A few minutes later a clearly distraught Crista returned. 'I'll have to leave you, Mr Rubin, I'm afraid. There's been an accident.'

He was instantly on his feet. 'What's happened?'

Crista took a deep breath to try to calm herself, her mind whirling. 'It's my sister Maggs, the one who runs the Angel with her husband. She's fallen down the stairs and badly hurt herself. That was Dickie saying he's waiting for the ambulance to turn up and can I run the pub for them this evening. The thing is, I've never been behind a bar before, but Dickie says there's no one else. He phoned my daughter Ez but they must be out somewhere as they aren't answering. Ez has often worked part-time in the past so she was the obvious one to ask.'

This was terrible, Max thought. 'Perhaps I can come with you? I've served behind the bar in a club I belong to many times. It's a private club run by the members so we all take a stint there.'

'Oh, Mr Rubin, that would be wonderful. But I shouldn't intrude . . .'

He waved her protestations into silence. 'Shall we get our coats and be on our way?'

Crista glanced at the table. 'I'll just leave things as they are for now. I can do the dishes later, or in the morning.'

'Right,' he declared. 'Let's go.'

They arrived at the Angel just as Maggs was being stretchered into an ambulance. 'How is she?' Crista demanded.

'Not good. The ambulance chaps think she banged her head and probably has at least one broken rib. I'm going with her to the hospital. Can you cope?'

'Of course I can, Dickie. You go with Maggs and don't worry about this place. I've got Mr Rubin with me who's kindly offered to help. He has experience running a bar. Isn't that so, Mr Rubin?'

Max nodded. 'Everything will be fine.'

'I wouldn't have opened, which I'm due to in five minutes, except there's a men's skittles final tonight. I can't let them down. Not unless I absolutely have to, anyway.'

'You won't have to,' Max assured him. 'Mrs Murray and I will take care of everything. Now I think you'd better get in there with your wife. The ambulance looks ready to leave.'

'Thank you. Thank you both,' Dickie said earnestly, his gratitude only too evident.

'Ring me here when you know what's what,' Crista pleaded.

'I'll do that.'

Moments later Dickie had disappeared into the back of the ambulance. The doors were hastily closed and the ambulance, siren sounding, quickly sped away.

'Dear God. I hope Maggs is all right,' Crista whispered, her tone anguished.

Max took her by the elbow and guided her inside, where the first thing they did was hang up their coats.

'Now let's see what the prices are,' he declared, taking charge.

To their relief all prices were marked at the back of the pumps, and on the gantry. The soft drinks were unfortunately not priced, so they decided they'd have to take a flyer on those.

'The best thing is to ask the customers,' Crista decided. 'I'm sure most people who use them will know.'

Max stared at Crista in concern. Her anxiety was obvious. 'I'm certain your sister will be OK.' He smiled, trying to be positive.

'Oh, I hope so, Mr Rubin. I hope so. Maggs and I have never been the closest of sisters, but she's still my sister after all.'

He understood that. 'Listen, to make things easier why don't you call me Max? We're going to sound silly calling each other Mr and Mrs all night.'

Crista could see the sense in that. 'All right, Max. And I'm Crista.'

Their first customer arrived.

'Damn!' Crista swore.

'What's wrong?'

'This barrel has run out and it's the beer Dickie sells most of.'

'Not to worry. Where's the cellar?'

'Can you change a barrel?'

'I have done in the past so I should be able to, unless it's some sort of new system I'm not familiar with.'

Crista gave him directions and he hurried off.

What a brick, she thought. It would have been a complete shambles without his help. He'd assumed charge with a calm assurance, jollying the customers along when he wasn't quite sure of something, and generally making things flow smoothly. She couldn't have done it without him.

Crista glanced at the clock above the bar. Still no word from Dickie, but she supposed it was early yet for that. For the umpteenth time since getting his phone call earlier, she prayed Maggs was all right.

'OK, let's see what's what.' Max had returned from the cellar. Picking up the zinc pail that lived beneath the bar, he began drawing off the newly connected barrel. Crista stared at him in admiration. You could almost believe Max had been doing this all his life.

After a pail and about a quarter Max took a glass and tasted a sample.

'Well?' Crista queried.

'Seems fine to me.' If there was uncertainty on his part it was because the beer was unknown to him.

'Let me have a drop and I'll soon tell you,' a regular waiting to be served offered.

Max poured a little into a wine glass and handed it over.

'She'll do nicely,' the regular confirmed with a nod of his head.

'I think we're winning,' Max whispered to Crista, and laughed.

It had just gone half past eight when Ez came bustling into the pub. 'What's this I hear about Aunty Maggs having an accident?' she asked.

Crista recounted what had happened.

'How bad is it?'

'No idea yet. Uncle Dickie has promised to phone us here when he knows.'

A look of amusement came across Ez's face. 'I never thought to see you serving behind a bar, Mum. It's a turn-up for the book right enough.'

'Well, Dickie couldn't get hold of you so I was the only one left to ask. There was no point in trying Sally, you know what she's like. There would have been some sort of excuse.'

'True.'

'By the way, this is Max Rubin who's my current PG.' Crista went on to explain about Max's having had past experience. Ez and Max shook hands, each saying they were pleased to meet the other.

'So how did you find out about your aunt's accident?' Max asked, curious.

'My next-door neighbour was in here earlier. When he heard us get home he knocked the door and told me. I came straight over.'

'How kind of him.'

'That's how it is in a village, Mr Rubin. Or one aspect of it anyway.'

'Another is people sticking their noses into other folk's business,' Crista added. 'That can be very annoying, believe me.' She caught her breath as the telephone rang. 'That might be Dickie,' she said, and hurried to answer it.

'Ez is an unusual name,' Max commented. 'Is it a contraction?'

'You mean shortened?'

He smiled, and nodded.

'Yes, it's short for Elizabeth. It's a habit in our family to shorten names. Mum's full one is Cristabel, and Aunt Maggs is Margaret. My sister Sally was called Sal when she was young but insisted on Sally when she grew up.' Ez suddenly laughed. 'Someone else whose name was never shortened was my Granny Fletcher, that's mum's mum. She was christened Lavender, but could hardly be called Lav, could she?'

'As in toilet?'

'Exactly. As in toilet. So she was always Lavender, the full shebang.'

'Yes, it would have been most unfortunate to have been referred to as Lav,' Max agreed, eyes twinkling.

'I'll just hang up my coat, if you'll excuse me,' Ez said. 'I'll work through to closing time. That'll take some pressure off mum.'

'Which she'll appreciate, I'm sure.'

'Whatever else mum is, she was never cut out to be a barmaid. Though I'm sure she did her best.'

'And very good it was too. Being asked for a Black and Tan did faze her at one stage, but I soon explained what it was.'

'Guinness and bitter.'

'Or sweet stout and bitter, depending on your preference. Same with a bitter top. I had to explain that as well. But she's quick, your mum, she soon picks things up.'

302

'I'm impressed with your knowledge of bar work,' Ez admitted. 'Have you ever been a pub landlord?'

'Good grief no. I'm strictly amateur.'

Crista returned, still looking worried.

'Well, Mum, what's the score?' Ez demanded.

'No news, I'm afraid. The doctors have sedated Maggs for the night, and she's asleep now. According to Dickie they can't do an X-ray till the morning, so all they can do is keep her comfortable until then. The doctors apparently agree with the ambulance-men that she's got at least one broken rib, and they're almost certain she's suffering from concussion. Again, they can't verify that till morning when they'll carry out some additional tests.'

Ez looked at Max, then back at Crista. When she next spoke she'd lowered her voice. 'Was aunty drunk?'

That startled Max, who tried not to show it. What was this all about?

Crista shrugged. 'I can't say. But, according to Dickie, she was certainly smelling of alcohol.'

'She was drunk then.' Ez nodded. 'That's why she probably tripped and fell. The stairs aren't difficult ones, after all. Pretty straightforward.'

'We don't know she was drunk,' Crista admonished sharply. 'So let's give her the benefit of the doubt until proved otherwise. All right?'

Ez shrugged. 'If you say so.'

'I do.'

Crista glanced at Max. 'I'm sorry. This shouldn't have been mentioned in front of you. It's a family concern.'

'I shan't be repeating anything, Crista. I learnt to be discreet years ago.'

'Thank you, Max.'

'Can I make a suggestion, Mum?'

'What's that Ez?'

'I can easily look after the bar for now. Why don't you and Mr Rubin go into the kitchen and have a cup of tea or coffee? I'd imagine you could also use a sit down.'

'Suits me. My feet are starting to ache a little. I'm not used to standing around so much.'

'Then off you go. And will you take my coat with you? I haven't had a chance to hang it up yet.'

'Of course.'

'Are you serving, Ez, or just looking pretty?' a waiting customer, whom they hadn't noticed, called out.

'Both,' Ez replied.

She was crossing to serve the man as Crista and Max made their way into the kitchen.

'I'm totally and utterly whacked,' Crista declared when she and Max finally got home at almost quarter to one. 'And it's well past my bedtime.'

Dickie had eventually returned to the pub at closing time, having had trouble getting hold of a taxi at that time of night. There was nothing he could tell them that he hadn't already said on the telephone. Nothing further could be done for Maggs, who was in a stable condition, till the morning.

He'd been effusive with his thanks for helping him out, and had insisted they all have a drink with him, which they'd duly done. A drink which, in Dickie and Max's case, had become three.

'I hope you didn't mind hanging on a bit, but I

thought your brother-in-law needed to unwind a little,' Max apologised.

'It was the right thing to do. Poor chap was in a terrible state. And I don't blame him either. Maggs could easily have been killed falling down the stairs as she did.' Crista shook her head. 'She's her own worst enemy that one. Always has been.'

Max tactfully didn't reply to that, remembering what had been said about the possibility of Maggs's being drunk. It had seemed obvious from the conversation that that was a regular occurrence.

'Damn!' Crista swore, spying the table they'd left earlier, which still had the dirty dishes and other meal things on it.

'I'd leave those till the morning if I were you,' Max advised. 'It's far too late to begin washing up.'

'I'll just pile them in the sink and get them out of the way, though.'

'I'll help.'

Crista stopped and smiled at him. 'That's what you've been doing all evening. Helping. I can't thank you enough.'

'Forget it, Crista. There's no need.'

'It was sweet of you all the same.'

When the table was cleared and the dishes were in the sink they said their goodnights and went off to bed.

Max was smiling as he dropped off to sleep.

Crista was horrified when she woke and saw the time. Throwing off the covers, she quickly got out of bed and whipped on her dressing gown. Aware she must look a mess, but not able to do anything about it for the moment, she hurried downstairs. What on earth would Max think of her!

'Max, I'm ever so sorry,' she apologised, bursting into the kitchen and finding him there. 'I've overslept. I must have forgotten to set my alarm last night.'

Max was already bathed and dressed and, to her amazement, wearing a pinny. 'Not to worry, Crista. I guessed what had happened so have tidied up and got the breakfast ready to put on.'

'Tidied up?' She frowned.

'The dishes are washed, dried and put away. The kettle's boiling, and the fire's going. Have I forgotten anything?'

Crista was aghast. 'You shouldn't have done these things. You're a guest here. Those were my jobs.'

'Well, they're done now. And I'm starving. How would you like your eggs?'

'I'll do those.'

He held up a hand. 'No you won't. Just for once I'll do what's necessary. Do you intend going to the hospital this morning?'

She nodded.

'How are you getting there?'

'A bus. Well, two buses actually. I'll have to change.'

'Then forget about that. I'll drive you.'

'But your business appointment?'

'I'll still have plenty of time to make that. Never fear. Now do you want to eat before your bath, or afterwards?'

She couldn't believe this was happening. 'After, I think. That's what I usually do.'

'Then toddle off. Just give me a shout when you're nearly ready and I'll have breakfast on the table waiting. So, I'll ask again. How would you like your eggs?'

'Boiled please,' she replied meekly. 'And only one.'

'You prefer them hard, I recall?'

'That's right.'

'Then off you go and don't forget to shout.'

A bemused Crista did as she'd been told.

Chapter 18

'Hello, Crista.' Maggs smiled weakly. 'Dickie said you were waiting in the corridor.'

Crista sat on the single chair provided. 'It's a bit of a pain that there's only one visitor allowed in the ward at a time, but there we are. It's my turn now. So how are you?'

'Shaken, and sore. I also have a thumping headache.'

'I'm not surprised, with two broken ribs and mild concussion. But cheer up. You'll be out of here soon enough. The end of the week, the doctors said. If all goes well, that is.'

Maggs sighed. 'Imagine me doing a daft thing like falling down the stairs. Silly, eh?'

'Pretty,' Crista agreed.

Maggs stared at her sister. 'I know what you're thinking, that I was drunk. Aren't you?'

Crista hadn't intended to bring that up, considering this to be neither the time nor the place. 'Dickie did mention you smelt of alcohol.'

'It's true, I'd had a few. But I wasn't drunk. I suppose I simply wasn't concentrating on what I was doing.'

Crista wasn't sure whether or not to believe her.

Maggs had lied too often about her drinking in the past. 'So why was that?'

A strange look came across Maggs's face. 'He came into the pub, Crista. I was behind the bar while Dickie was downstairs in the cellar. I served him, we chatted, and then he left without recognising me.'

Crista frowned. What was she on about? 'Who, Maggs?'

'You'll never guess.'

'All right, I won't guess. So who?'

'After all these years to suddenly turn up again like that. It gave me quite a shock, I can tell you.'

This was becoming irritating. 'Who, Maggs? You still haven't said.'

There was a long pause, then Maggs whispered, 'Rupert Swain. That's who.'

'Dear God,' Crista muttered.

'He didn't recognise me at all, Crista. Not even a flicker. It was as if he'd never seen me before in his life.'

'Oh, Maggs,' Crista breathed, knowing how hurtful that must have been for her. Both Rupert Swain's appearing and his not recognising her.

'He told me he's been in Rhodesia all this while, farming he said. He's only back here now because his brother is dying.'

'I see,' Crista murmured.

'I recognised him almost straight off. He looks a lot older, of course, but underneath the age the old Rupert was still there. In a funny way it was as if he'd never been away.'

'Did you tell Dickie?'

'Don't be ridiculous!' Maggs rebuked her sharply.

'I wasn't about to do that. The trouble is, Rupert said he'd probably call in the pub again and I hate to think what Dickie will do if he realises who he is.'

'Aah.' Crista nodded. 'I'd forgotten Dickie knows he's David's father.'

'Or how Rupert treated me when he found out I was pregnant by him. The rotten bastard.'

There was a few moments' silence between them, then Maggs spoke again. 'He's turned into a bit of a joke, Crista. Talking exactly as the toffs did in the twenties. The way he used to. Listening to him I couldn't help but think he might have stepped out of a time warp.'

Crista took a deep breath. 'How did you feel about him? Seeing him again, that is?'

Maggs smiled thinly. 'If I tell you something will you promise to keep it strictly to yourself? Not confide in another single soul?'

'You have my word, Maggs.'

'It isn't easy.'

'Then take your time.'

'Rupert is the only man I've ever loved. Even after he ditched me and I thought I hated him I really loved him deep down. And all these years I've thought, and wondered, about what might have been if we'd married and I'd become Mrs Rupert Swain.'

Crista knew her sister only too well. 'Are you sure you really loved Rupert, or was it the money and position he had to offer? Come on, be frank.'

'I have to admit the money and position were a huge attraction in the beginning. I'd be a liar to say otherwise. But I did love him too, Crista, and always have.'

'Oh, Maggs,' Crista said sympathetically. 'And what about Dickie?'

Maggs thought about that. 'Dickie's a good man, there's no denying it. He certainly saved my bacon, and the family's, when he took me on and made an honest woman of me. But I've never loved him, Crista. I've always hoped I might come to one day, but it never happened. Dickie was my ticket back to respectability and that's all he's ever meant to me.'

'How sad, when you mean all the world to him.'

'I know,' Maggs replied, her expression one of guilt. 'Don't think that hasn't bothered me. It has. I'm not so heartless.'

'You at least like him, surely?'

'Oh, I like him all right. And admire him too, the way he's carved out a life for himself with the disability of having only one arm. But like isn't love, and never will be.'

They both reflected on that.

'Can I say something else you must keep to yourself?' Maggs asked eventually.

'Go on.'

'Women don't normally talk about these things. At least not the women I know. It's personal, understand?'

Crista nodded.

'Having sex with Rupert was unbelievable. He did things that . . . well, I can't really describe it. But it was simply wonderful, Crista. When we were together it was like walking on cloud nine. A bit trite that, but that's how it was.'

Crista smiled. 'It was the same with me and Jamie. We sort of fitted, if you know what I mean.'

'It was never the same with Dickie,' Maggs went

on slowly. 'Not for me anyway. There's never been any magic. None at all. He – well, to put it bluntly, simply isn't very good when it comes to that.'

'So you've never loved him and he's bad in bed.'

'Exactly. Can you understand now why I dreamt of Rupert all these long, despairing years? He was the complete opposite to what I ended up with.'

'I'm so sorry,' Crista whispered. 'Truly I am.'

'And now Rupert comes waltzing back into Ford, and what? I find out he's turned into something of a joke. A parody I think the word is. That one short conversation destroyed me, Crista. Not only that, it made me feel a complete fool.'

'You're never that,' Crista tried to assure her.

'No? Well I think I am. And it's painful, believe me it is. Incredibly so. Oh yes, I loved Rupert and we had terrific sex together. But would either have lasted if I had married him? I don't believe so now. The man I spoke to recently in the pub was an idiot, a rich idiot perhaps, but still an idiot all the same. The hard, unpalatable truth is, I'd probably have been as unhappy with him in the long run, if in different ways, as I've been with Dickie.'

Crista didn't know what to reply to that, so kept quiet.

Maggs gave Crista a bitter, cynical smile. 'Do you realise what this means? I've wasted my life over a stupid, and impossible, dream. You know how when you see a romantic film it usually ends up in marriage or at the bedroom door? All very dewy-eyed and lovely. But it ends there, you see. What the film doesn't do is go on and tell you what happened after-wards. What their life together was like. Or even if the marriage lasted and what their relationship became during that time. Oh, they might have continued being happy enough. But for many that wouldn't have been the case, a rot between them setting in. Well, that was my downfall. I stopped at the bedroom door and in my imagination saw only the good things that might have been.'

'You're being too hard on yourself,' Crista admonished softly.

'Am I? I don't think so.'

Their conversation was interrupted by the ringing of a bell announcing visiting time to be over.

'I'll come again tomorrow,' Crista promised. 'Is there anything you need?'

'No.'

'Are you sure?'

'I'm fine, Crista. Honestly.'

'And don't worry. I'll keep everything you confided to myself. I swear.'

'I know you will. You're someone who keeps her word. Perhaps that's one of the reasons I've always envied you.'

Crista frowned. 'Why would you envy me?'

'Because for you the dream came true when you met Jamie. The pair of you fell in love, and that was how it stayed till his dying day. And I've always envied the person you are. Kind, considerate, caring, forgiving. Not at all like me. You got all the gifts, Crista, whereas I consider I never got any, or very few anyway. Now you'd better go before Sister appears and starts shooing you out.'

On impulse Crista, standing, bent over and kissed Maggs on the forehead. 'Till tomorrow then.'

'Take care, Sis.'

'I will.'

Crista turned round and walked slowly up the ward, fighting back tears. For the first time in her life she'd begun to understand, and even like, Maggs. Like – and pity her too.

'Ah, there you are. How's your sister?' Max asked anxiously when Crista arrived home.

'Two broken ribs and a mild concussion. They're talking about letting her out at the end of the week.'

That surprised him. 'Bit soon, isn't it?'

Crista shrugged. 'I presume they know what they're doing. The doctors that is. Anyway, patients aren't kept in hospital as long as they were. A change of policy, I presume.'

'Must be. In the old days she'd certainly have been in far longer. How is she in herself?'

'Not too bad. Angry that she'd been so silly as to fall down the stairs. Said her mind must have been elsewhere.'

Max wondered if that was a euphemism for being drunk. But he certainly wasn't about to ask. If Crista mentioned it, fine. But she didn't. Instead, she glanced at the clock above the mantelpiece, noting as she did so that Max had restarted the fire. 'That must have been a quick business meeting. I didn't expect to see you again till later.'

'It was quick,' he confirmed. 'And as there didn't seem to be anything to keep me in Exeter here I am.' He hesitated. 'That is all right, isn't it?'

'Of course it's all right. Now, how about a nice cup of tea?'

'Sounds good to me. By the way, I wasn't sure how long you'd be at the hospital so I took the liberty of buying some things for the evening meal. Loin chops OK?'

Crista stopped filling the kettle to stare at him in amazement. 'You've been shopping for this evening?'

'That's right. Chops, potatoes, veg. And a few other items I thought might go with them. Ever such a pleasant butcher, Mr Woolocombe he said his name was.'

'That's Tom. Ford born and bred. Known him all my life. He's married to a good friend of mine.'

'Well, Tom and I had a very nice chat, me being the only customer at the time. I was most impressed with him and his shop. And I must say, the meat on display looked exquisite. Far better quality than what's on sale round where I live in London. I also bought some cream cakes from the little supermarket. If you fancy it we could have one each with the tea.'

Crista laughed. 'You are full of surprises, Max. I've never known a man like you.'

'Really?'

'Really. Country men aren't so thoughtful. Most of them would never dream of doing women's work, and that includes shopping. As for buying cream cakes for tea, the moon would turn blue first.'

Max frowned. 'Am I that different from the men round here?'

'Well I think so.'

'That's a compliment, I hope?'

'Very much so.'

'Good.'

'I'll pay you back for what you've spent,' Crista declared. 'I'll get my purse in a moment.'

'You'll do nothing of the sort!' Max exclaimed, affronted. 'I won't hear of it.'

'But you're my PG. I'm supposed to do the providing. That's included in the bill.'

'Well not for me it isn't. You'll charge me as per normal, or I'll be cross and never come back again.'

Crista lit the gas under the kettle. 'Does that mean you intend to come back?'

'If things work out as I'm hoping. And to date they are.'

That news pleased her. Somehow Max had become more than the usual PG, he'd also become something of a friend. It was certainly less lonely in the house with him about, which surprised her. She hadn't realised how lonely she'd actually been since Jamie's death.

'Is that all right?' Max queried. 'Me coming back again, that is?'

'Of course.'

'It'll probably be after the new year. Sometime in January I'd think. It all depends on how quickly my solicitors expedite matters.'

Solicitors? This was the first mention of those. Up until now she'd only known he went into Exeter on business of some sort.

'After tea I think I'll go for a walk, if you don't mind? I rather fancy a breath of fresh air,' he declared.

'It is cold out, and damp, don't forget. It's late October after all.'

'I'll wrap up warm, Crista, don't you worry. And a brisk walk will do me the world of good. By the by, when are you visiting your sister again?'

'I promised I'd go in tomorrow.'

'Then I shall drive you there.' He held up a hand when he saw she was about to protest. 'Please? I'm not planning to do anything for the entire day anyway, so it would be my pleasure.'

'If you're sure . . .'

'I'm absolutely sure, Crista. Agreed?'

She smiled. 'Agreed.'

Max stood on the embankment running alongside one of the roads in and out of Ford, staring at a section of land on which a few sheep were grazing.

It was perfect, he thought. With a stunning view covering the length and breadth of the valley.

He closed his eyes for a moment, envisioning the bungalow he intended to have built there, imagining himself living in it. How gloriously peaceful it would be after the hustle and bustle of London, how quiet.

Opening his eyes again he took a deep breath of clean, fresh air, which was so different from that in London.

London, he reflected. Would he miss it? Well, he'd thought long and hard about that and the answer was no. London, where he'd been born and brought up, held many fond memories for him. But the time had come, at least he felt so, to move on. Leave all that behind him for an idyllic retirement.

He watched a crow, or it might have been a rook for he couldn't tell the difference, wheel and dive, swooping over the land, before flying gracefully, malevolently, off into the far distance.

Excitement gripped him when he saw a rabbit make a sudden dash from behind a tussock to disappear into a stand of long grass. You didn't see many rabbits in London, he mused. Unless they were hanging in a butcher's window.

No, he wasn't making a mistake. He was convinced of that. This was the ideal place to spend what years were left to him.

Reluctantly he turned away and started back to Crista's. She'd been right to say it was cold out. It was bitter.

'Is something wrong, Crista?' Max asked the following morning.

'How do you mean, wrong?'

'The way you've been moving about since you got up. Sort of stiff and as if you're in pain.'

'It's that obvious, eh?'

'Well I noticed it.'

Crista sighed. 'It's arthritis,' she confessed. 'Doesn't half give me gyp at times.'

'I'm sorry to hear that.'

'It might ease off in a few hours, it often does. First thing in the mornings are usually the worst, though why that should be having been warmly tucked up in bed all night I've no idea.'

He nodded his sympathy. 'If it's any consolation I suffer from it too.'

'You do?'

'Part of the price you pay for getting old, I suppose.'

'Then just be thankful you don't live in Devon, Max. It's very damp here, which aggravates it a lot.'

That surprised him. 'I didn't know Devon was particularly damp.'

'Well it is, take my word for it. It's not too bad

318

hereabouts; there are other parts of the county far worse, indeed there are.'

'I really had no idea,' he mused, then laughed. 'I suppose my vision of Devon was never-ending sunshine and sandy beaches lapped by deep blue sea.'

'That's what the posters advertising the holiday resorts would have you believe. Well, it can be like that in summer, but in winter, that's something else again.'

'Do you take anything for your arthritis?'

'A couple of aspirins. Jamie used to say there was nothing better. Forget all the lotions, potions, tonics and tablets, aspirins are what you need.'

'I must remember that.'

'What do you take, then?'

'I have some medication prescribed by my local GP. It can help, but not much really.'

'Well if you heed my advice you'll switch to aspirins and bin the medication. I swear by them.'

A sudden thought struck Max. 'That's something else we have in common.' He smiled.

'Is it?' She couldn't make the connection.

'Yes, you know?'

Crista shook her head.

'My Rebekah and your Jamie. How they died.'

Crista glanced abruptly away. 'Of course,' she whispered. 'I'd forgotten about that for the moment.'

Max cursed himself for bringing it up for it obviously distressed Crista. He should have known better. 'What time shall we leave for the hospital?' he queried, changing the subject.

'As soon as we're both ready.'

'I am. All I need to do is put on my coat,' he replied, trying to be upbeat.

'I'll just see to my make-up,' Crista mumbled, and hurried from the room.

'Damn!' Max swore quietly to himself. He'd made a right bloomer there.

Late in the afternoon two days later Max arrived back from Exeter to find a grim-faced Crista and an equally grim-faced Ez waiting for him. 'What's up?' he asked, wondering if something terrible had happened to Maggs.

'Sit down, Max,' Crista instructed.

He did.

'Just one question. Are you negotiating to buy a piece of land called Sarah's Portion?'

Max nodded. 'I am.'

'Right. Ez, repeat to Max what you overheard in the pub at dinnertime. And use the words you heard.'

'Part of it is slightly offensive, Mr Rubin. If I'm to use the exact words.'

'Go on, Ez,' he said. 'I understand.'

Ez took a deep breath. 'I was doing the dinnertime shift, as I have been since Aunty Maggs went into hospital, when these three farmers came in. Now that's unusual in itself as the village farmers mainly use the Salmon and Pig, but for some reason they came into the Angel. What's even more unusual for farmers is that they were already well bevvied as they'd obviously been drinking elsewhere. Maybe they'd been to the Salmon and Pig and decided to visit us as well.'

Max frowned. 'Is that so unusual?'

'It was the time, you see. Middle of the day. Believe me, for farmers that's almost unheard of round here, unless it's a wedding or a funeral or the like.'

'I understand now.' Max nodded, wondering what this was leading up to.

'Well one of them, Rendle Westacott, started boasting about how he was going to make a killing out of a piece of land he was selling to an old London Jew boy who intended building on it.'

Max went very still. 'Did Mr Westacott indeed,' he said softly.

'Rendle said you were stinking rich, rolling in it, and knew nothing of the prices round here. The three of them thought it all very funny.'

'I'm so sorry, Max,' Crista whispered. 'How offensive to call you that. I'm ashamed of them.'

'Thank you for telling me about this, Ez. I'm in your debt.'

And with that Max rose and left the room, ice cold inside with anger.

Chapter 19

'I don't need to ask why you're so quiet tonight,' Crista commented later as they were having their evening meal.

'What Ez told me has given me a lot to think about.'

'I can well understand that.'

They ate for a few moments in silence before Crista went on. 'I'm curious as to why you never mentioned about buying land with the intention of building on it?'

Max smiled. 'Simple enough really. Until I signed on the dotted line it was all so much pie in the sky. It's always been my way never to discuss things until they're fact. That's how I've always conducted my business dealings.'

'I see,' she murmured.

'The idea was that I'd retire to Ford. I've been looking round the county and decided Ford was where I liked best, and where I'd settle.'

'So are you going to build a house, then?'

'A bungalow to be precise. Something brand new with all mod cons where I'd spend my retirement years.'

'Sarah's Portion does have planning permission, I take it?'

'Oh yes. I wouldn't have been interested otherwise. Has had for some time, actually. It all seemed straightforward enough, Westacott wanted to sell, I wanted to buy, and that was that. My solicitor assured me the price was fair.'

Crista's eyes narrowed fractionally. 'Can I ask who your solicitor is?'

'A Mr Vickery of Thomson, Vickery and Read.'

'Paul Vickery?'

'That's right. Do you know him?'

'Of him, Max. He's Rendle's cousin.'

Max stopped eating to stare at her. 'Is he really?'

'Did you contact him looking for a suitable piece of land, or was the land already advertised somewhere?'

'I contacted him. I simply chose the firm out of the number available. It seemed as good as any other.'

'And so it probably is. Are you really rich?'

Max shrugged. 'Depends what you call rich. I'm certainly comfortable. In fact more than that, I suppose.'

'In other words you are.' Crista gave him a cynical smile. 'People from the big cities somehow think we rural folk are soft in the head. Naive. Country bumpkins. Well nothing could be further from the truth. Particularly where farmers are concerned. They're far more shrewd, and certainly more unscrupulous, than you would imagine. The gormless act many of them go in for is exactly that, an act. There's nothing gormless, or simple, about them. There is an expression down here, and I apologise for saying it at the table, but they'd skin a turd if they could make a profit on it.'

Max laughed. He'd never heard that one before.

'And believe me, it's true.'

'It seems I'm the one who's been naive,' Max declared.

'To an extent. But then who'd think a solicitor would set you up like that? I believe that's the modern way of putting it?'

'Yes, Crista, it is.'

'I'm sure if you go into it you'll find nothing illegal has taken place. You were looking for a piece of land with planning permission and Vickery came up with one which suited. As the buying price hadn't been previously advertised there was no wrong-doing in asking for a lot more than it was actually worth. You merely accepted the price in good faith.'

'Like a prize mug,' Max said bitterly.

'Well thanks to Ez no harm's been done. Has it?'

Max shook his head. 'Though it was a near run thing. I was supposed to sign the relevant documents in a few days.'

'Was there any sort of down payment?'

'No. I wasn't asked for any.'

'So you're free to back out of the deal without losing anything then.'

Max laid down his knife and fork, having completely lost what little appetite he'd had. 'It's such a shame. Sarah's Portion would have been ideal. It's a beautiful situation, just what I'd had in mind.'.

'So what will you do now?' she asked casually.

'I don't really know. Start searching all over again, I suppose.'

'For another piece of land?'

Max nodded.

'Is there nothing else going in or around Ford?'

'Not with planning permission there isn't. Sarah's Portion is the only available site.'

What a pity, Crista reflected. She'd really taken a shine to him. 'Can I ask you something, Max?'

'Go ahead.'

'I don't want to sound rude, I'm merely curious. Are you really Jewish? I hadn't realised.'

He found that amusing. 'With a name like Max Rubin and you didn't realise?'

Crista blushed. 'I just didn't. I thought you might have foreign blood in you of some sort, but I hadn't twigged that you were actually Jewish.'

He regarded her quizzically. 'Well I am, Crista. Does it make a difference?'

'Not as far as I'm concerned. I've simply never known a Jewish person before. There aren't any others in Ford. At least not that I know of.'

'Now you do. What do you think?'

She didn't understand that. 'How do you mean?'

'Apart from my religion am I any different from your Christian friends?'

'No.'

'Do I have horns coming out of my head?'

He was teasing her, she realised. 'Now that you mention.' She pretended to peer at him. 'Perhaps they're invisible.'

Max laughed. 'There aren't any, I promise. Nor is there a tail coiled in the back of my trousers. I assure you of that as well.'

'So you're quite human, just like the rest of us?' She was enjoying the daftness of this.

'Quite.'

'That's all right then.'

'Good.'

'Oh dear!' she suddenly exclaimed. 'I've given you bacon for breakfast while you've been here. Jews don't eat pork, do they?'

'I don't practise my religion any more, Crista. So the bacon didn't matter.'

'Thank goodness for that.'

'If I was practising I wouldn't have eaten it and explained why. OK?'

She smiled. 'OK.'

Max's mood changed again and he became introspective. 'I suppose I'd better leave in the morning as there's nothing to keep me here now. I'll telephone Vickery before I go and inform him the deal's off.'

Disappointment bit into Crista. She wished he was staying longer. It was good having him about the house. 'Will we ever see you again?' she asked quietly.

Max shrugged. 'I don't know. I've simply no idea.'

'Oh well.' She sighed deeply, thinking all good things must come to an end. She was going to miss him. Quite a lot really.

'Enjoy that?' Max asked later that evening as the musical programme they'd been listening to on the radio finished.

'Yes, I did.'

His eyes twinkled. 'Classical music isn't exactly up your street, is it, Crista?'

'I wouldn't say that. I can't pretend to be an expert or anything, but when I do listen to it I tend to like what I hear.'

'I find it wonderfully soothing at times. And on

326

occasion exhilarating. I have it on a lot when I'm at home.'

'By yourself?' she asked casually.

'Well of course. Who else is there?'

'I don't know. You just don't speak about London all that much. In fact you never speak of it at all.'

He sat up straighter in his chair and smiled at her. 'So what would you like to know?'

'Whereabouts in London you live, for example.'

'Golders Green.'

She racked her memory. 'I've never heard of it.'

'A middle-class area, posh in parts. It also has a large Jewish population. The house is pre-war, built between the wars actually. A mock Tudor design, which isn't everyone's taste, but we found it pleasant enough. Lounge, ample kitchen, three bedrooms, the master en suite, a separate bathroom and toilet. It also has a decent-sized garden which, I must confess, I neglect dreadfully. Every so often I have someone in to give it a good going over. Anything else?'

'Now you make me sound like I'm prying.'

He laughed. 'Not at all. A woman's natural curiosity, to be expected. I'm only surprised you haven't asked me more about myself before now.'

Crista rose and switched off the radio, then returned to her chair. 'You've been talking about building a bungalow to retire to. Does that mean you're already retired, or what?'

'I'm retired, Crista. I sold my shop six months ago.'

'Shop?'

'Where I conducted my business. I'm a jeweller by trade, and had eight staff working for me. They've been retained by the company who bought me out.

And a very handsome sum I made on the transaction, as well. More than I'd expected.'

'A jeweller,' Crista mused. 'It must have been a fairly large shop to employ eight people beside yourself.'

'Not really. I specialised in making jewellery, you see. And most successful I was too. The shop was "By Appointment".'

Crista was amazed. 'You mean you sold to royalty?'

'Indeed we did. Including our present Queen.'

She didn't know what to say to that.

'I inherited the business from my father, and he from his father before him, who started the business when he arrived in this country from Poland many years ago now.'

'So you actually made jewellery, didn't just buy it and sell it on?'

'That's right. We were, and still are, craftsmen of the old school. We would be approached, by whomever, to discuss the creation of a piece, or pieces. Consultations would follow, then designs for approval, after which we would fashion whatever was ordered. We were extremely exclusive simply because of the quality of what we produced. It cost a great deal of money to buy a piece, any piece, from the shop of Max Rubin.'

'And you were bought out?'

Max shrugged. 'Rebekah and I were never blessed with a family so there was no one to carry on after me. The end of a line, you could say. So I decided to retire and sold the shop. I simply walked out one day and that was that.' He hung his head. 'A sad day, I have to admit. Very sad indeed. I'm not ashamed to own that I cried. But not until I'd actually left the shop and was walking away.'

'Do you miss it, Max?'

'Of course I miss it. It was my life. But what I did was the right thing, for me and the business. I'm convinced of that.'

'And now you want to live in Devon.' She smiled, impressed by what he'd just told her.

'Very much so. A fresh start somewhere completely different from what I've been used to. A new world to experience and explore.'

'I knew you were an artist of some sort,' Crista declared.

That astonished him. 'How so?'

'Your hands. They're artist's hands. I thought that from the first moment I saw them.'

Max held up his hands and regarded them thoughtfully. 'Well, they certainly aren't those of a labourer, and that's a fact.'

They both laughed.

'Max, I've had an idea,' Crista announced when he appeared for breakfast next morning.

'And what's that?'

'I want you to hang on for a few hours more while I have a chat with Rendle Westacott. Will you do that?'

He nodded. 'A chat about what?'

'That needn't concern you for now. But I may, just may, be able to make him change his mind about the price of that land.'

'I see,' Max murmured. 'Then I'll certainly hang on.'

'Good. I'll leave for the farm directly after break-fast.'

Max could only wonder what she had up her sleeve.

Directed by his wife, Crista found Rendle in the barn tinkering with his tractor. 'Morning, Rendle.'

He jerked his head up to stare at her in surprise. 'Morning, Mrs Murray. What brings ee here?'

'You do. I want a word.'

His eyes narrowed in speculation. 'Does ee now. And what would that be about?'

But Crista wasn't to be rushed. 'What's wrong with the tractor?'

'Damned if I knows. 'Tis always giving me trouble. A right old bitch she be.'

'Thinking of replacing her, are you?'

That further surprised him. 'How did ee know that?'

'Two and two, Rendle. Nothing clever.'

Two and two what? She'd lost him there.

'How's your son Arthur by the way? Haven't seen him round the village for a while.'

'He's fine. Jim dandy. He's about here somewhere, or else out feeding the livestock. ''Twill be one or t'other.'

Crista nodded, but didn't say anything.

'Why, ee want to talk to him as well?'

'No. I just wondered how he was, that's all.'

'Never better, Mrs Murray. Apple of me eye, that lad. Though I'd never tell him that. I wouldn't want to spoil the bugger.'

'He's well, then?'

'In the pink as they say.'

'Pleased to hear it.'

Rendle wiped his hands on a dirty rag, waiting for Crista to come to the point of her visit.

'I was thinking about Arthur only the other day,' Crista eventually said, which was a lie.

'Oh?'

'Remembering that time as a child when he was very ill and nearly died.'

Rendle leant against one of the tractor wheels. ''T was touch and go for a spell, I recall.'

'Croup complicated by a chest infection, Jamie told me afterwards.'

Rendle nodded. 'Thank the good Lord for your husband and what ee did, Mrs Murray. Hadn't been for ee young Arthur would have been a goner and no mistake.'

'The village was cut off for a whole week due to flooding. No one could get either in or out.'

'That's right. Worst flooding in my lifetime. Quite a few beasts got drowned in it too.'

'When Jamie saw Arthur he said the lad had to be taken immediately to hospital. But of course that was impossible. Arthur, like the rest of us, was stranded.'

Rendle's expression tightened. 'The missus cried her eyes out. Fair beside herself she was.'

'Arthur needed round the clock attention under correct medical supervision. Hospital was the place for him. His only hope.'

'So Doc Murray said. Bless his memory. Four days he stayed in our house, four long days and nights. The only time he left the lad's side was to attend to a call of nature. He was heroic, Mrs Murray, that's exactly what Doc Murray was, heroic. Thanks to him Arthur pulled through and grew up to be the man he is today.'

'Soon to be married, I understand?'

Rendle's face lit up. 'He is indeed, Mrs Murray. And a fine maid she be too. Tansy Passmore. You must know the family?'

'Of course I do. He works for the gas company, doesn't he?'

'That's right. And the maid's a typist in Exeter. Pretty little thing. Arthur's done well for himself there.'

'Then all I can do is wish them the very best of luck.'

'Thank ee, Mrs Murray. That be reet kind of ee.'

'I shall be one of those standing outside when they leave the church. I'll want to see the bride in her dress.'

'You can come tae service if ee wants. That's the least I can do after what your husband did for Arthur. Come to the wedding and reception afterwards. I'll make sure ee gets an invite.'

'We'll see,' Crista murmured. She made as if she was about to leave, then hesitated. 'There's one more thing, Rendle.'

'What be that?'

'I believe you're selling Sarah's Portion.'

His face immediately closed down to become suspicious. 'I is. Be that of any interest to ee?'

'It is, Rendle. You see, the buyer you have at the moment is a personal friend of mine.'

They stared at one another while the seconds ticked slowly by. 'Is he, by God,' Rendle said eventually in a low voice.

'Mr Rubin. Mr Max Rubin.'

'I had heard he'd been staying at your house as lodger or summat. But I didn't know he was a friend.'

'Well he is. A very good one too. I just thought you should be aware of that.'

A medley of emotions played across Rendle's face, though embarrassment wasn't one of them. 'Business is business, Mrs Murray.'

'Of course. I can't disagree there.'

''Tis a fair price if that's what you're on about.'

Crista didn't reply, simply raised a disbelieving eyebrow.

'Well 'tis,' he persisted, though unconvincingly.

Again Crista didn't reply, just continued to stare at him till finally Rendle dropped his gaze to the ground.

'Well, I must be off,' Crista declared. 'Good day to you, Rendle.'

'Good day, Mrs Murray.'

'And do give my regards to Arthur, won't you?'

This time it was Rendle who didn't reply. Nor did he look up again until after Crista had left the barn.

'Well, Crista?' Max demanded the moment she arrived home.

'I don't know. Honestly I don't. Farmers are a funny lot when it comes to money. They'll do anything to make a shilling, and rather die than lose one. However, be that as it may, what you must do now is telephone Vickery and inform him you've lost interest in Sarah's Portion. Say you've decided the price is way too high. Emphasise that. I'll put the kettle on while you ring.'

'Aren't you going to tell me what you said to Westacott?'

'After the call, Max.'

She watched him as he walked from the room, hoping her timely reminder to Rendle of his debt to Jamie had worked. At least it had been worth a try.

'That's done,' Max announced a few minutes later on his return.

'How did Vickery take it?'

'He sounded quite shocked to me. I believe he thought the deal was cut and dried.'

'And so it was until Ez paid us a visit.'

Max shook his head. 'I would have been taken for a right Charlie. I'm obliged to your daughter. Truly I am.'

Except it might yet mean he wouldn't be coming to live in the village, Crista thought sadly. But if it wasn't to be then it wasn't to be.

'Now are you going to tell me what you said to Westacott?' Max prompted.

'Sit down while I pour the tea and I'll explain while we're having it.'

'You did your best, Crista. You can't do more than that.'

Three days had passed since Crista had gone to see Rendle and still Vickery hadn't rung back. She and Max had agreed the previous evening he might just as well return to London.

'Thanks, Max.'

They were standing outside the house, his luggage already loaded into the car boot. Max gazed wistfully around, then back at Crista. 'I shall miss Ford,' he declared, attempting a smile.

'And I, for one, will miss you coming here.'

'You've been kindness itself, Crista. I can't thank you enough.'

'It's been a pleasure, Max. You've become a friend.'

'And you, Crista. And you.'

Damn! she thought. She was going to cry and that would never do. 'Well, you'd better be off then,' she declared rather brusquely. 'You've a long way to drive.'

'Yes, I'd better.'

What he did next surprised her. There was a brief peck on her cheek, and then he was climbing into his car. He gave her a final wave, which she responded to, as he drove away.

'Goodbye, Max. Take care,' she whispered.

Turning, Crista went back into a house which somehow now felt strangely empty.

Chapter 20

Rendle Westacott stopped what he was doing to watch his son Arthur driving the tractor which, between them, they'd finally managed to fix. He hadn't been exaggerating when he'd said to Crista that the lad was the apple of his eye.

Rendle sighed. Crista's visit had put him in a right old quandary. On the one hand he owed Crista for what her husband had done all those years ago, there was no denying that, on the other he desperately wanted the money selling Sarah's Portion would bring in.

Of course he had tried to cheat Max Rubin, but business was business after all. If he could charge a price and get away with it, then fair enough! Rubin was a grown man who should be able to take care of himself.

Now Crista had stuck her oar in and the deal was off, much to his disappointment and disgust. The thing was, if he continued to hold on to the land who was to say another mug might not happen along in time who'd pay the sort of price Rubin had been prepared to until tipped the wink by Crista?

There again, another mug might not appear no matter how long he hung on for, and the land would have to be sold eventually for its true worth. A worth that might just decrease if the value of agricultural land fell in the future.

One thing was certain, he didn't owe this Rubin anything. Except, Rubin was Crista's friend and he owed her for what Jamie had done for Arthur.

He also had to take into consideration the fact that he'd lose face if he backed down, and that was completely unacceptable. He'd be a laughing stock amongst his cronies, especially those he'd boasted to about how he was taking the rich London Jew boy to the cleaners, for it was bound to leak out eventually if he didn't get his original asking price. These things somehow always did.

He decided there was nothing else for it. He was going to have to talk this over with his wife Meg, explain the situation to her. Meg would know what to do.

Mind you, he didn't have to take her advice. But he could at least listen to what she had to say.

With a shrug of his shoulders he bent again to work.

'How are you feeling, then?' Crista asked. Maggs was now home from hospital.

'Well, the ribs are still painful, and will be for a while, I'm told. It's simply a case of taking it easy and waiting for them to mend.'

'And your head, Maggs?'

'I get a dull ache occasionally, but nothing more. That too will pass in time.'

Maggs had lost weight, Crista noted. Which could only be a good thing. Nor could she detect any smell of alcohol, which was even better.

'So, what's new in the village?' Maggs queried with a smile. 'Any juicy gossip to tell me?'

Crista shook her head. 'Nothing that I've heard of.'

'Don't tell me everyone's behaving themselves!' she exclaimed incredulously. 'That would be a first for Ford.'

'I doubt it. It's simply that I haven't heard.'

'Oh well.' Maggs sighed. 'I'll soon catch up once I get behind the bar again. You hear everything there.'

'I can imagine.' Crista smiled.

'It's surprising how indiscreet people are when they've got a drink in them. You cease to exist as far as they're concerned. Except when they want something, that is.'

'Don't go back to work too soon now,' Crista cautioned. 'That wouldn't do you any good at all.'

'Always the practical one, eh?' Maggs smiled thinly. 'The one with common sense. Unlike her sister.'

Crista inwardly groaned. After their chats in the hospital she'd thought she and Maggs had buried the hatchet, let old enmities go. Perhaps she'd been wrong.

'Well?' Maggs prompted.

Crista shrugged. 'If you say so.'

Maggs eased herself into a different position. If she stayed in the same one for too long it became uncomfortable.

'Dickie must be pleased to have you back,' Crista commented in a neutral tone of voice.

'Oh, I don't know. He seemed to be doing pretty OK without me.'

That angered Crista, but she didn't show it. 'He's been worried sick on your behalf, Maggs. What happened gave him a terrible fright.'

Maggs glanced down, and didn't reply to that.

'I should have thought, hoped, it's drawn you closer together?'

'Perhaps,' Maggs mumbled. Crista wanted to snap back at her, but refrained from doing so. Maggs suddenly brightened. 'I'm really looking forward to our holiday next year. I can't wait.'

This was more like it, Crista thought. 'You haven't mentioned you're going on one?'

'To Jersey. Dickie wasn't keen — well, you know what he's like. He hates spending even a minute away from his precious pub. But I got him to agree. I don't know when, though; that hasn't been decided yet.'

'I hear the Channel Islands are very nice. A bit Frenchified, I understand.'

'I want to stay for a fortnight, but Dickie insists a week is long enough. Well he would, wouldn't he? A couple of days there and he'll be champing at the bit to come home again.'

Crista smiled. 'That's Dickie to a T.'

'Well tough luck on him. I want a proper holiday and that's what we're going to have. And it'll be for a full fortnight if I have my way. Which I usually do. You wait and see.'

Crista had no doubt about that. Maggs had always been able to twist Dickie round her little finger.

Maggs's eyes gleamed. 'Sun and sand, it'll be glorious. Wait till you see the tan I'll have when I get back. You'll think I'm a black woman.'

Crista simply couldn't imagine her sister in a

swimming suit, not at her size. The vision conjured up in Crista's mind was grotesque.

Maggs squirmed in her chair with anticipation, wishing the intervening months would fly by. 'It'll be a good hotel too,' she went on. 'Something expensive where we can wallow in luxury. Be attended on hand and foot.'

'Sounds wonderful.'

'It will be, Crista, I promise you. You'll be jealous as hell when I show you the snaps I intend taking.'

Jealous? Crista didn't think so. She and Jamie had never been people to take holidays, though they had gone to Scotland once which she'd enjoyed, even if she had found the Scots a somewhat strange race, and almost impossible to understand at times. On occasion it had seemed as if she was listening to a foreign language. Having said that she'd certainly been made welcome. They hadn't been able to do enough for her.

'Changing the subject, how's that nice Mr Rubin who was staying with you? Is he coming back again?'

Crista's face clouded over. 'He won't be as far as I'm aware. The business deal he was working on fell through and so there's no need for him to return.'

'Pity,' Maggs commiserated. 'He must have been company for you when he was here.'

'He was that. Good company too. We got on quite well together.'

'It was kind of him to help out the night I went into hospital. I never saw him to thank him.'

'Oh, Dickie did that. And excellent help he was too. I don't know how I'd have coped otherwise until Ez finally showed up.'

340

'Well, if you are ever in touch with him again make sure you thank him on my behalf.'

'I'll do that.' Crista nodded, though she doubted the opportunity would ever present itself.

While Maggs and Crista were talking upstairs Dickie was behind the bar dealing with the dinnertime session which, after a short flurry, had gone quiet.

He was polishing a glass and thinking about the paperwork he'd have to get on with later when the door opened and a customer breezed in.

'Morning, landlord. Scotch and soda if you don't mind. Better make it a large one.'

Well dressed, Dickie noted, and a toff from the accent. 'Certainly, sir. Any particular brand?'

'You wouldn't have Chivas, I don't suppose?'

Dickie smiled. 'Not much call for that in Ford, sir. We only stock the more popular brands, I'm afraid.'

The customer was staring at where Dickie's missing arm should have been. 'Here, I say. I remember you.'

Dickie frowned. 'Do you, sir?' Now he thought about it, the man's face was vaguely familiar.

'You worked here years and years ago when John had the place. Ain't I right?'

Dickie nodded.

'Lost your arm in the Great War, what? I remember you telling me.'

'That's right, sir. Were you in it too?'

'Was indeed, old boy.' The customer stuck out his hand to shake Dickie's. 'Rupert Swain's the name. Can't recall yours I'm afraid.'

Dickie went rigid, and then terrible anger erupted

in him. This was the bastard who'd got Maggs pregnant and then refused to marry her. The man who'd treated Maggs appallingly, causing her untold grief.

Rupert's extended hand remained unshaken while a look of puzzlement gradually crept over his face. 'Something wrong, landlord?'

For a few frozen moments Dickie debated with himself about having it out there and then, but decided against it. Apart from Crista no one else in the village knew David wasn't his son, and that's how he wanted it to remain.

'Your money's no good here, Mr Swain,' he said tersely. 'And I'd be obliged if you'd leave my pub.'

'Leave your pub!' Rupert spluttered. 'For what reason?'

'I don't need to have one. It's my privilege as landlord to serve only those whom I wish to, and I don't want to serve you. That's final.'

'But . . .' Rupert was at a complete loss for words.

'Now get out. And never, ever, come back again. Understand?'

'This is preposterous,' Rupert blustered.

'I don't give a monkey's what you think it is, just get out or I'll call the police.'

Rupert drew himself up to his full height. 'I've never been so insulted in my entire life! And I have no wish to stay here a moment longer.'

'Good. Now piss off.'

Rupert wheeled and strode away, violently throwing open the door to head for his car.

'You all right, Dickie?' Percy Matford, one of the few regulars present, asked. ''Tain't never seen you like this before.'

'I'm fine, Percy. Don't worry about it.'

'You're shaking, chap. Positively shaking.'

He was too, Dickie realised. Reaction to what had happened, no doubt.

Percy suddenly giggled like a girl. 'Imagine chucking a Swain out on his ear. My God, that would never have happened in the old days when Mr High And Mighty Miles Swain ruled the roost hereabouts.'

Dickie didn't reply to that, knowing the incident would be all round Ford before the day was out. Well, that's as may be, but no one would ever find out the reason he'd done what he had. That would remain his secret.

Maggs and Crista would understand without asking, but they'd never say. Not in a million years.

'I've brought you half a dozen cream cakes from the shop,' Sally announced gaily. 'I thought we might have some with tea.'

Crista was taken aback by this unexpected visit from her daughter, and already suspected the motive behind it. It was a rare event for Sally to drop by, and invariably it was only when she wanted something.

'How are Ben and Daniel?' Crista inquired.

'Oh, fine. Fine. Though short of work. Well, it's that time of year, isn't it? Not much call for painters and decorators in the run up to Christmas. Or directly afterwards come to that. It's always the same.'

Money, Crista thought. That's what this was all about. She'd have bet on it.

'Now shall I put the kettle on, Mum, or will you?'

'I will.'

Sally placed the box of cakes on a table and slumped

heavily into an armchair, from where she gazed around. 'Talking of painting and decorating, isn't it time you had this room done? The whole house, come to that. It's been years.'

'The house suits me as it is, thank you very much,' Crista replied somewhat tartly. Sally might be her daughter but she couldn't say she liked her. Loved her, yes. But not like.

'Mind if I smoke, Mum?'

'Go ahead.'

'Can you get me an ashtray?'

Crista bit back telling her to get off her backside and fetch it herself. She made Sally wait until the kettle was on and the cups and saucers set out.

'So how are you, Mum?'

'A bit arthritic, but not too bad apart from that.'

'You look terrific, I must say.'

Soft soap, Crista thought. Flannel. 'Do I?'

'Oh, yes. Though I would suggest you go to the hairdresser's a little more often. It's not as if you can't afford it, after all.'

'And how often do you go, Sally?'

'Every other week without fail.'

'Somewhat excessive for someone whose husband is currently out of work, wouldn't you say?'

A look of irritation flashed across Sally's face. She absolutely hated being criticised, though she was the first to criticise others. 'That's a matter of opinion, Mum. Don't forget I've got to keep looking good for Ben. He likes a woman to take care of herself, always appear her best. And what's what I try to do.'

'Still, you have to live within your means. It's folly to do otherwise.'

Sally was beginning to get angry now. 'That's easy enough for you to say, dad leaving you stinking rich as he did. You can afford more or less anything you want.'

Crista sighed with exasperation. 'That's hardly the point, Sally. If your dad had left me otherwise I'd have to do what I've just been saying to you.'

Sally puffed nervously on her cigarette. This wasn't going at all how she'd planned. She was hardly in the door and already she and her mother were at each other's throats. And over what? Nothing at all, in her opinion.

'How much is it you're after anyway?' Crista asked casually as she placed plates beside the cakes.

Sally gaped at her in astonishment. 'How do you mean?'

'Oh, come on, Sally. I'm not a fool, you know. Ben's out of work, as too is Daniel who works for him, Christmas is rapidly approaching and, knowing you, you'll be short of cash again because you spent it all when it was freely coming in. You've never been one to put by for a rainy day.'

Sally was blushing, raging inside that her ruse had been so easily seen through. 'I think you're being most unkind,' she sniffed.

'Not unkind, darling. Simply realistic. That's why you've come today, isn't it?'

'What I didn't come for was a lecture, Mum.'

'Of course you didn't. You came to freeload as you have so often in the past.'

Sally was squirming with embarrassment. Part of her wanted to get up and leave, but if she did that there certainly wouldn't be any money forthcoming.

'It was only a temporary loan I had in mind,' she lied.

'Nice clothes,' Crista said suddenly, catching her daughter off guard. 'They look expensive.'

'You only get what you pay for,' Sally blustered. 'Buy cheap and it always costs you more in the long run.'

'True enough. But that hardly applies to you as the turnover in your clothes is so quick. You hardly wear something before you've thrown it out and replaced it.'

Sally had no reply to that. Instead she sat in grim silence while Crista made the tea.

'We'll just let that mash for a minute or two,' Crista observed when the pot was filled.

'Did you get out of bed the wrong side this morning?' Sally queried waspishly.

'Not that I'm aware of, dear.'

'You're in such a foul mood, Mum.'

'You surprise me. I thought I was in a rather jolly mood actually.'

'Hmmh!' Sally snorted in disbelief.

'So how much did you have in mind?'

'Do you mean money?'

'Well I wasn't referring to potato crisps. I assume you came with an amount you were going to ask for in mind.'

'Christmas is so expensive, Mum. You know what it's like.'

'Doesn't have to be. It certainly wasn't in the old days when there simply wasn't spare cash available to lash around. And yet we enjoyed ourselves just the same.'

'That was then, this is now.' Sally sneered. 'A lot more is expected nowadays.'

'So it seems,' Crista replied casually.

'The fact is, we're pretty broke. And Ben has absolutely no work in the offing. Nothing at all. It's pretty scary.'

'You're drawn to the limit at the bank, I take it?'

Sally nodded. 'Couldn't be helped.'

'And yet you still go every other week to the hairdresser's and wear fancy clothes.'

'I bought these clothes ages ago,' Sally protested.

Crista looked her firmly in the eye. 'When would that be?'

'I can't recall exactly,' she prevaricated.

'No?'

Sally couldn't hold Crista's gaze and looked away. 'A couple of months, I think.'

Crista knew from her tone she was lying. The clothes were newer than that. 'Really?'

'Maybe even longer.'

'I see.'

'Isn't that tea ready yet?'

Crista poured, using a strainer. She had no use for the modern teabags; tea made from them wasn't quite the same in her opinion. 'Still one sugar and milk?'

'Please, Mum.'

'Would you care to select your own cake?'

'You do it for me. It doesn't matter which. They all look rather yummy.'

On inspecting them Crista had to agree. She decided to have one with a little chocolate square on top.

'What do you think?' Sally asked when they were both settled and had sampled their cakes.

'About what?'

'The cake, of course.'

'Very nice.'

'I told you they were yummy.'

They didn't speak again until after the cakes were eaten and the tea drunk.

'Another, dear?' Crista queried.

'Are you having another?'

'Not for now. Perhaps later.'

'Then I won't have one either.'

'More tea?'

'Please, Mum.'

If Crista had thought Sally would get up and do the honours, she was disappointed. Sally sat fast and allowed her to do that.

Maybe she should go to the hairdresser's more often, Crista reflected when she was seated again. The passing of years had made her a little negligent in that department, as with Jamie gone it hadn't seemed to matter very much. She decided to book an appointment early in the new year. Spruce herself up a bit. Why not? But she certainly wasn't going to get into the habit of going every other week like Sally. That was completely excessive. Not to mention a waste of good money.

'I made a decision after the last time I gave you money,' she declared.

Sally's eyes narrowed in suspicion. 'Oh?'

'That I wasn't doing you any favours by continually baling you out.'

'Now hold on a minute!' Sally retorted hotly. 'It isn't true that you've continually baled me out. Just not true at all.'

'No?'

'I admit you have, very kindly, given me money on occasion. But only that.'

'Your opinion, Sally, not mine.'

'Well, when was the last time?'

'August, have you forgotten? A little matter of the bank pressing you to do something about your overdraft.'

'That wasn't my fault, Mum.'

'It never is, according to you.'

Sally placed her cup and plate on the floor. 'If you recall, one of Ben's clients took for ever to settle up, months and months in fact. And that left us short.'

'Perhaps so, dear, but the point I'm making is you're going to have to learn to handle your finances better so that you can overcome blips like that without always coming running to me. It's quite simple really. Stop being a spendthrift and then you'll cope.'

'I am not a spendthrift,' Sally snapped. 'I can be quite careful when I want to be.'

'Which is never. And you are a spendthrift. It's high time you accepted that and changed your ways. I'm actually doing you a good turn, though I doubt you'll see it that way for now.'

Sally's expression was one of sheer incredulity. 'Are you saying you won't give me anything?'

'That's right.'

'But I'm your daughter!'

'I can't argue with you there. And I should know, I gave birth to you. And a difficult birth it was too. I remember only too well.'

Sally shrugged that aside. 'I only want two hundred pounds. What's that to you? Nothing. Not a damned thing.'

349

'Only two hundred?' Crista smiled. 'That's quite a bit.'

'Not to you it isn't.'

Crista suddenly felt old and very tired. 'No matter what you think, Sally, you're not getting another penny out of me. Not now, not ever. I've been far too indulgent as it is. From here on in you'll have to learn to stand on your own two feet. Nor will I be changing my mind. You can rely on that.'

'But what about Christmas?' Sally wailed. 'We'll have nothing!'

'Except each other, which is the most important thing after all. Why not try going to church and celebrating the real meaning of Christmas? That's what it's all about, you know. Not turkeys, puddings and lots of expensive presents.'

Sally was appalled, unable to believe she was actually hearing this. Her mother had been so easy to 'tap' in the past.

Crista saw tears well in Sally's eyes. 'And don't try that on me,' she chided. 'I know you can turn the waterworks on and off at will.' She took a deep breath. 'Now, I think you'd better go. I have lots to do.'

A stunned Sally came to her feet. 'Mum . . .'

'Goodbye, Sally,' Crista interrupted, also coming to her feet. 'Don't forget to shut the door on your way out.'

'I . . .'

'Bye, Sally.'

She hadn't enjoyed doing that one little bit, Crista reflected after Sally had gone. But it was for the girl's own good, and something she should have done years ago.

It was with a heavy heart she set about the house-work she'd promised herself to get on with.

Maggs stopped and sucked in a lungful of clean fresh air, thoroughly enjoying the experience after the stuffiness of the pub. This was her first outing since coming home and she was off to the local shops to buy a few things.

She'd just reached the village square when a car drew up at the lights there, almost right in front of her. With a shock she realised the driver was Rupert.

He started to talk to his passenger, a woman roughly her own age with what appeared to be badly dyed blonde hair and a deeply tanned, leathery face. Not at all attractive. She might have been once, but constant exposure to harsh sunlight had put paid to that.

The woman was Rupert's wife, Maggs just knew. The fact was obvious from their body language together. And the realisation made Maggs feel sick. She was in a daze when she entered the shop where, suddenly, she knew what she wanted to buy above all else. When she'd finished her shopping she crossed the road and walked up a pathway that took her into the cemetery.

She located a bench she knew of and sat, despite the freezing cold wind whipping viciously amongst the gravestones. Moments later she'd opened the half bottle of brandy she'd bought and taken a gulp.

She only left the cemetery when the bottle was finished.

Chapter 21

How kind, how lovely, Crista thought when she saw that the Christmas card she'd just opened was from Max. She was in the middle of reading the sentiment it contained when the phone rang.

'Hello?'

'Crista, it's Max. Max Rubin.'

She laughed. 'I've only this minute received your card. Thank you very much.'

'My pleasure.'

'I fully intended sending you one then realised I don't have your address. I very much doubt a card addressed to M. Rubin, Golders Green, London would have reached you.'

Max thought that funny. 'I doubt it too. I can't think why I never gave you my address. I should have done. Anyway, that's beside the point for now. I have some brilliant news. At least I hope it's brilliant.'

'Oh?'

'I've had a letter from Vickery, the solicitor in Exeter, saying Westacott is willing to drop his asking price and quoting a new one.'

Excitement raced in Crista. Max might be coming

to live in Ford after all. How wonderful! 'That *is* brilliant news, Max.'

'Before replying I wanted to check with you that the new price is fair. I'm sure you'll know whether it is or not.'

'I'm no expert on land prices, Max. But what's he asking now?'

Max told her.

'Hmm,' Crista mused.

'Well?'

'It's still a bit high in my opinion. But of course nothing like it was.'

'I see.'

Crista's mind was whirling. 'I'm guessing, but I think I might know why that is.'

'Go on.'

'Well, Rendle has already boasted to his cronies that he was taking you for a ride. With this latest quote he still is, but by a far lesser margin. I believe he's trying to save face by still being able to maintain he got a better price for the land than it's worth. Understand?'

Max did only too well. 'So what do you recommend?'

'That's up to you and how badly you want the land. It isn't much over the current value, Max. Not much at all. But, as I said, enough to save Rendle's face.'

She waited patiently while Max thought about that.

'I'm going to accept, Crista,' he declared at last. 'As you said, it depends on how badly I want that land and I do.'

353

She couldn't have been more delighted. 'That's terrific, Max. When will you notify Vickery?'

'I'll do so later today which means, hopefully, the deal should be finalised sometime early in the new year. I hate having to pay over the odds, but occasionally there's no other option and this appears to be one of those times.'

'So you'll be back here shortly, then?'

'Indeed I will. I presume you'll still be able to put me up?'

'Of course I will,' she enthused. 'I won't hear of you staying anywhere else. You've become part of the family.'

There was great tenderness in his voice when he next spoke. 'I'm looking forward to it, Crista. More than you might imagine.'

His tone caused her insides to flutter. 'Just let me know the date of your arrival and I'll have the bed aired and the freshest of eggs waiting for you.'

Max laughed. 'Thanks for your help, Crista.'

'Don't mention it.'

'And see you soon.'

'See you soon, Max.'

Crista hung up and smiled to herself. It would be good to have Max back again.

No. It would be a lot more than that.

Whispering Smith and Percy Matford were the first into the Angel when Dickie opened for the evening session.

'Have you heard the latest?' an excited Whispering demanded of Dickie, for once talking in a normal voice.

354

'Not until you tell me.'

'Giles Swain popped his clogs a couple of hours ago.'

Dickie stopped what he was doing to stare at him. 'Are you sure?'

'It's gospel. Believe me.'

'Well well,' Dickie mused, remembering the celebrations when old man Swain had died. There would be nothing like that with Giles's passing, not because Giles was better liked but simply because the Swain family held nothing like the influence over the village that they once had.

'Does that call for a free pint?' Percy asked hopefully.

'You'll be lucky,' Dickie retorted, causing Percy's face to fall.

'I wonder what they'll do with the Big House?' Whispering mused, plonking himself on to a stool at the end of the bar.

'You're drinking the usual, I take it?' Dickie queried, and got a nod from both men.

'My money's on the brother and sister selling,' Percy declared. 'He lives abroad now and she elsewhere. Tain't got no need to keep it.'

'True enough,' Whispering agreed.

'House and mill I reckon,' Percy went on. 'That'll net them a shilling or two.'

Whispering pursed his rather blubbery lips. 'I should say so.'

As Dickie pulled the second pint he hoped Rupert Swain would sell quickly and get the hell back to where he'd been all these years. The sooner the better.

'What was the sister's name again?' Percy frowned.

355

'Helen, I seem to recall,' Whispering informed him.

'That's right. Helen. Pretty thing she used to be. Though every bit as stuck up as the rest of them. Right la-di-da she was.' He suddenly giggled. 'Probably all fat and horrible these days with nellies down to her knees.'

Percy and Whispering both laughed, finding that extremely funny. Dickie didn't, but said nothing, certain there hadn't been any dig at Maggs intended. If there had been he'd have slung them both, regulars or not, out on their ears.

Then more 'early doors' customers arrived and Whispering fell back to doing just that. The main topics of conversation, of course, were the demise of Giles Swain and speculation about the house and mill.

'I'm stuffed, absolutely stuffed,' Crista sighed, sinking into a comfy armchair. She'd been invited to have Christmas lunch with Ez and family and they'd just finished.

'Would you like a drop more wine, Mum? Or how about a glass of port?' Pete, Ez's husband, asked.

'Not for me, thanks. Any more alcohol and I'll be tiddly.'

Pete, an affable, bluff man, smiled broadly. 'You are allowed at Christmas, you know. It's quite acceptable.'

Crista returned his smile. She liked Pete, even if he could be a little dense at times. But he suited Ez, and that was all that mattered. Crista had always thought that Nick had taken after Ez in the brains department, whereas Anne, their daughter, took after Pete, particularly in looks, both of them blond-haired with slightly ruddy complexions that surely denoted a Saxon heritage.

'I simply couldn't, Pete. But thanks all the same.'

'Excuse me,' Nick apologised. 'I'm off to my room. Is that OK, Mum?'

'If you wish.'

'Give me a shout when you get round to the dishes and I'll come back down and help.'

'Don't worry, you're not getting off with not doing them,' Anne told him. 'We've had enough of your skiving during these holidays.'

'Skive? Me?' Nick mock-protested. 'Never!'

'Oh yes you have been!' Anne stabbed a finger in his direction.

Nick's reply was to stick out his tongue at her, then swiftly leave the room.

'Kids,' Ez grumbled good-naturedly. 'Who'd have them?'

'You weren't exactly little Miss Perfect when you were young,' Crista reminded her. 'Far from it.'

'So you say.'

'So I know. I was there, remember.'

Ez sank on to a matching chair to Crista's and proceeded to light up a cigarette. 'Lovely turkey, I thought,' she commented.

'It was that,' Crista agreed. 'Everything was lovely, spot on. Couldn't have been nicer.'

'I helped with the cooking,' Anne chipped in. 'I prepared most of the vegetables, didn't I, Mum?'

Ez nodded. 'She'll make an excellent wife in time, won't you, dear?'

'I hope so. When Mr Right finally comes along.'

Crista laughed. 'Don't be too hasty to rush into

marriage, that's my advice. Enjoy yourself first before taking the plunge.'

'Is that what you did, Nan?'

'Oh, things were different in my day. Very different. We never had the opportunity to enjoy ourselves the way your generation do. I'm quite envious at times.'

'But you don't regret anything, do you?' Anne frowned.

'Not really, if I'm honest. I might have done if I hadn't met your grandpa when I did. But certainly not after that. He was my life, I his, and that's all there was to it.'

Pete was finding this boring. 'I think I'll go out to the shed for half an hour, Ez. I've things to do there,' he declared.

'On Christmas Day?'

He shrugged. 'I hardly see that makes a difference.'

'You should be staying here, with your family.'

'Half an hour, Ez, that's all.'

'I sometimes think you've got another woman out there,' she teased.

Pete winked. 'Maybe I have. A bit of fluff on the side.'

'Get on with you.' Ez laughed. 'If it keeps you happy.'

'So,' she said when Pete was gone. 'I bumped into Sally earlier in the week and she told me the pair of you had a run-in.'

Crista nodded. 'Sort of.'

'I heard her side of the story, what's yours?'

'Sally, yet again, wanted money from me and I had already decided enough was enough. I said no, she had the vapours and left in a huff.'

'How much was she asking for?'

'Two hundred pounds.'

Ez shook her head. 'You did the right thing, Mum. Sally's always been of the belief that money grows on trees. It's about time she faced reality like the rest of us.'

'Well she'll have to now for she'll get no more out of me. The next money coming her way won't be until they read out my will. Till then she'll just have to learn to manage on what comes into her house.'

'Delusions of grandeur, that one,' Ez said, shaking her head. 'Always has had.'

'Well she certainly didn't get it from me, and that's a fact.' Crista hesitated. 'Did she mention what sort of Christmas they were going to have? According to her the cupboard was well and truly bare.'

'She didn't say. But her shopping basket was full, I did notice that.'

Crista smiled. 'I didn't think things were as bad as she made out. Tight, perhaps, but nobody was going to starve.'

'It must have been quite a shock when you refused her.' Ez suddenly grinned. 'I'd love to have seen her face.'

'It was something of a picture, I have to admit.'

'It was dad who always spoilt her,' Ez stated quietly. 'She was his favourite.'

'That's not true!' Crista protested. 'It simply isn't. Your father didn't have a favourite.'

Anne, listening avidly, was fascinated by this turn in the conversation.

'He did, Mum. Maybe you never noticed, but I was aware of it. He favoured Sally whenever he could.'

Crista was deeply upset to hear this. 'I certainly never saw any favouritism. I'd have spoken to him if I had.'

'Anyway.' Ez sighed. 'It's all in the past now that dad's gone. But it did hurt me when I was young. I always felt I wasn't somehow good enough. That Sally was better than me. She was, and still is, far prettier.'

'Nonsense.'

Ez smiled indulgently. 'That's a mother speaking.'

'Well you were the brainier one, there's no contesting that. You consistently got higher marks at school.'

'It wouldn't be hard going up against Sally. She's thick as the proverbial plank.'

'Now you're being bitchy, Ez,' Crista admonished.

'Maybe,' Ez mused. Then, 'Were you really never aware of his favouritism?'

'I swear it. This is the first I've known there was such a thing.'

Ez slowly lit another cigarette, making a mental note to use the pumice on her fingers, which were nicotine-stained. She smoked far too much but couldn't break the habit, probably because she didn't really want to. 'In a way I'm pleased about that,' she replied softly.

'Why?'

'Because you'd have gone down in my estimation if you had been aware of it.'

Crista didn't know what to say to that. This whole conversation was a revelation.

'Now,' Ez suddenly declared, changing the subject. 'How about a nice cup of tea? I could murder one.'

'Please.'

'I'll put the kettle on.'

Crista watched her daughter as she went about

making tea. Ez had given her a lot to think about. She'd had no idea. None at all.

'Here we are, home sweet home,' Crista declared, back at her house. She and Anne had linked arms for the journey, Anne having been detailed to go with her because of the icy pavements.

'Can I come inside for a few minutes?' Anne asked. 'I'd like a word with you.'

'Of course, dear.' Crista wondered what Anne had in mind. 'So, what is it?' she asked once their coats were off and they were comfortably settled.

Anne was suddenly looking uneasy. 'It's about Nick, Nan. He's worrying me.'

Crista frowned. 'In what way?'

'He hasn't been the same since he came back for the holidays. In all sorts of ways.'

'Such as?'

'He seems to be permanently tired and is for ever in his room sleeping. And did you spot the dark rings under his eyes?'

Crista nodded. She had.

'And another thing, he hardly eats any more. Bits here and there, playing with his food more than anything.'

Crista had noticed that as well. Most of what he'd been dished up had been left on his plate, which she'd thought strange for a young lad his age. They were normally ravenous most of the time. 'Maybe he's ill,' Crista murmured.

'I asked him that and he said he was absolutely fine. Mum spoke to him as well and got the same answer.'

'Perhaps it's just a reaction to all the studying he's doing at university,' Crista speculated. 'That could explain the tiredness.'

'And what about loss of appetite?'

Crista shrugged. 'Upset tummy?'

'No, it's not that. He's been back a couple of weeks now; an upset stomach doesn't last that long. Besides, he would have mentioned it to Mum if that had been the case.'

'It could be he's ill and just doesn't realise it? I suppose that's possible.'

Anne fidgeted in her chair. 'There's something else, Nan. Something I daren't tell Mum or Dad.'

'And why's that?'

'Because if I'm right Dad would kill him.'

Crista sat further back in her chair and studied her granddaughter. 'But you can tell me, I take it?'

Anne nodded.

'Well, go on. What is this terrible thing?'

Anne fidgeted some more before replying. 'The trouble is, I could be wrong, you see. Maybe I made a mistake about what I smelt.'

'And what do you think you smelt?' Crista probed.

'I was passing Nick's room a couple of days ago. Mum was out and Dad was at work, so there was only Nick and I in the house. Anyway, I was passing his room when I thought I smelt the faintest whiff of dope.'

Crista looked blankly at her. 'Dope?'

'You know, Nan. Marijuana, cannabis, pot, dope.'

'Dear God,' Crista breathed. Nick was on drugs! The very thought chilled her heart. 'How would you know what it smells like anyway?' she queried, eyes narrowing.

362

'For goodness' sake, Nan, it's 1967. There are kids in the village smoke the stuff.'

'There are?' It surprised her.

'Only a few. But some. There's one actually grows it, or so he says.'

Crista was rocked to say the least. 'And you've smelt it when you've been around them?'

'They're not people I normally mix with. But yes, I do come into contact with them from time to time. It's inevitable in a village.'

'I see.'

'As I said, I couldn't be absolutely certain that's what I smelt – it was only a faint whiff, after all. But it would explain Nick's sleeping so much, the dark rings under his eyes and his loss of appetite. Wouldn't it?'

'I'm no expert on the subject, Anne, far from it. But yes, I suppose it might.'

Anne, having said her piece, fell silent, fervently hoping she was wrong.

'Doesn't dope lead to stronger drugs?' Crista queried after a while.

'I understand it can do.'

'But there's been no sign of that, has there? No syringes or the like?'

Anne shook her head.

Which didn't mean a damn thing, Crista thought. This was awful. Absolutely terrible. And Anne was right: if Nick was smoking dope and Pete found out there would be hell to pay. Pete would knock Nick for six. And that would only be for starters.

'I had to speak to someone, Nan. You understand that?'

'Of course I do. In the meantime I think you'd better leave this with me and I'll see what I can do. When is Nick due to return to Bristol, by the way?'

Anne told her. 'Don't forget I could be wrong, Nan.'

Crista regarded her shrewdly. 'But you don't think you are, do you?'

Anne dropped her gaze to stare at her lap. 'No,' she replied in a quiet voice. 'But I still could be.'

'We'll see.' Crista made a gesture dismissing the subject. 'So, would you like a cup of tea while you're here? That was a cold walk we just had.'

'I'd love one, Nan. I'll make it.' Anne jumped to her feet.

Now, Crista wondered. How was the best way to go about this?

Crista had been tossing and turning ever since she'd come to bed, her mind churning from what she'd learned that day.

She'd had no idea, none whatsoever, that Jamie had favoured Sally above Ez. How stupid of her, how incredibly blind, never to have noticed. Now she came to think back there had been signs, intimations, but it had simply never registered with her what was going on.

And now there was this thing about Nick to worry about, and it was worrying her sick. She was going to have to read up on the subject before she tackled Nick, and would start with Jamie's old medical books, which she still had. They might prove helpful.

One thing was certain: she held the trump card where Nick was concerned, if he wanted to continue at university, that was. And she was sure he did. She prayed to God he wasn't on anything stronger than dope, that it hadn't come to that. If it had then she had a real problem on her hands.

Information, that's what she needed. What would be really helpful would be to talk to someone who knew all about these things. But who? There was no one of her acquaintance to turn to. At least none she could think of.

Or was there?

She may not know anyone, but Max might. Living in London Max must know all sorts. At least it was worth a try.

She'd telephone him first thing in the morning.

Chapter 22

Maggs was sitting at an upstairs window of the pub staring out at the church where the funeral of Giles Swain was taking place. Even at this distance she could hear the sound of singing.

Rupert was in there, she thought. No doubt with his wife, the leathery-faced hag she'd seen him with that day. The woman who had what she'd so coveted all those years ago.

She smiled in memory of their lovemaking and how wonderful it had been. Going to bed with Dickie had never even remotely been a patch on that. But Rupert had turned into a relic from a bygone age, a clown talking as if it was still the twenties. A living dinosaur from the past. A joke of a man.

And yet . . . It had been so good between them once, certainly sexually. The sort of sex she'd never again experience. Sex that even now made her smile and sent tiny shivers coursing through her insides.

Soon Rupert would leave again, go back to Rhodesia with the hag, and probably never return to the village of his birth.

She wished with all her heart he'd never come

back to see her as she now was, a fat lump whom he hadn't even recognised. That had hurt, by God it had. There again, she'd at least been spared his shock if there had been recognition. Yes, that was something.

Maggs picked up her glass of brandy and had a sip. She had a bottle secreted away which Dickie knew nothing about, so there'd be none of that nonsense about her drinking so much.

Dear, sweet, crippled Dickie. Useless in bed and always had been. If she'd been cruel she'd have called him the one-minute man, which was more or less right. That was hopeless for any woman, and certainly her. It was like being given a bar of chocolate only to have the bar snatched away again after you'd had the first nibble.

The mourners were coming out now, the vicar having appeared at the church doorway, shaking hands and having a quiet word in all his pious glory.

There wasn't to be an interment. The body was to be taken away for cremation so presumably Rupert and the hag would be going on to that. Not for the first time she wondered what the hag's name was. She'd probably never know. Not that she cared that much anyway.

What dreams she'd had when being so-called courted by Rupert! Money, position, a life of ease. And then she'd fallen pregnant with David and that had been that. Finish. Goodbye Maggs. And brutally so.

She couldn't help but think of the old Doris Day song, 'Que sera sera, whatever will be will be . . .' Or the poem by Robert Burns she'd come across in a magazine article while in hospital. 'The best laid plans of mice and men . . .' Wasn't it the truth, though. Wasn't it just.

Maggs sighed, suddenly filled with a terrible loneliness and . . . and what? Regret, was that it? Possibly. Loneliness and regret, terrible twins.

She drank more brandy, noting she'd have to refill her glass after another swallow. At least she didn't have to worry about Dickie's coming up and finding her drinking. He was busy in the bar and she'd have gargled with strong mouthwash before being in his company again.

'Rupert Swain.' She said his name aloud, and smiled. Yes, the sex had been fantastic. But that was then, and this was now. A lifetime later.

A long and bitter lifetime.

'I'm disappointed I had to summon you to visit me and that you hadn't already come of your own accord,' Crista admonished Nick.

'Sorry, Nan. I kept meaning to pop by and somehow just hadn't got round to it yet.'

'Same with the letters, I suppose? You promised me faithfully to write regularly and when was the last time I got one? Months ago.'

'I have so much studying and practical work to do, Nan. It's all much harder than I'd imagined. When you finish for the day the last thing you want to do is write a letter, believe me.'

Crista had already decided what strategy she'd use to get a confession out of him. Attack right from the start, catch him off guard, no pussy-footing about but go straight for the jugular.

'Is that why you've taken to smoking dope?' she snapped, eyes blazing.

He gaped at her in astonishment. 'What?'

'You heard me. Is that the excuse for taking to smoking pot?'

His expression was one of total confusion and guilt. 'I don't know what you're talking about, Nan.'

She stabbed a finger at him. 'Oh yes you do. I can see it in your face plain as day. Well?'

'I've never . . .'

'Don't lie to me, Nick. I won't have it. I'm not some gullible fool, you know. I may be old but that doesn't mean I don't know what's going on.'

'I've never . . .'

'I said don't lie!' she thundered.

He caved in. 'OK, Nan. I have.'

Crista didn't reply to that, just stared at him.

'It doesn't do any harm. Honestly. It's not as bad as alcohol.'

'Except it can lead on to harder drugs. Isn't that so, Nick?' she said softly.

'Not in my case. I swear.'

'You've already tried to lie to me once, so why not again?'

'I haven't.'

'No experimenting with coke, heroine'

He was flabbergasted. 'Where did you learn about these things, Nan?'

'Don't forget I was a doctor's wife,' she replied sternly. 'You learn a lot when you're one of those. And that includes the misuse of drugs.'

Nick shook his head in amazement.

'Now take off your jacket and roll up your shirt-sleeves,' she ordered.

'What for?'

'I want to see your arms.'

'Bloody hell,' he muttered. He'd thought he was coming to visit his dear old Nan and walked into the Gestapo instead. He couldn't believe it was his grandmother talking to him and not some Nazi monster.

'Come on, get on with it,' Crista commanded.

The jacket came off to be thrown on a chair, then one shirtsleeve was rolled up to the elbow.

Crista immediately grabbed the arm and examined it. To her profound relief there were no puncture marks. 'And the other one.'

That too was clear of marks.

'I told you,' Nick stated in a surly, offended tone of voice.

'What about pills? Those purple things and the like. Have you ever popped one of those?'

'Only once or . . .'

Crista lashed out, hitting him as hard as she could. He spun away, uttering a cry of surprise.

'You bloody idiot,' Crista snarled. 'Have you any idea what those pills can do to you? What the lasting effects can be? People have actually died from taking them. Do you hear, DIED!'

Nick hung his head, unable to hold Crista's gaze. Although he knew it to be true it was a reality he'd never really faced up to. Well, he'd reasoned, it wouldn't happen to him, would it? That sort of thing always happened to someone else.

Crista's chest was heaving, such was her fury. It took all her self-control not to go over to Nick, take hold of him, and give him a right good shaking.

'So what have you got to say for yourself?' she demanded.

Nick swallowed hard. 'Sorry, Nan.'

'Is that all, a pitiful "sorry, Nan"?'

He seemed to shrink in on himself.

'I always thought you intelligent, Nick, but this . . . This is an act of gross stupidity.' She shook her head in despair. 'Smoking cannabis and popping pills. God help you if your father ever found out.'

Nick's face drained of colour. 'You wouldn't tell him, Nan, would you?'

She'd keep the frighteners on him for a little while longer, she decided. 'I might. For your own good.'

'Oh please, Nan, don't?'

'As I said, for your own good.'

Nick might be a grown-up young man, but he knew he was no match for his father if it came to a fight. Pete was far more powerful than he. He would simply flatten him.

'Please don't,' he begged.

'It's your mother I'd be more worried about. Could you bear to see her crying her eyes out, saying how much you'd disappointed her, how much you'd let the family down? Could you bear to give her that much grief and pain? To know she's lying awake at nights worried sick about you? That she keeps asking herself again and again where she went wrong?'

Nick felt as though he was about to cry himself. He idolised his mother and wouldn't hurt her for the world. So why had he been so incredibly thought-less? When he'd started it had all seemed a joke, a bit of a lark. Just joining in what a lot of others were doing.

'I want you to promise me you'll stop all that,' Crista declared. 'Will you?'

Nick nodded.

'I want to hear you say it.'

'I'll give up the smoking and pills, Nan. I swear.'

'Your word of honour?'

'My word of honour.'

Crista wasn't finished yet. 'I'd like to remind you that I'm funding you at university. If I find out, and I will, that you've gone back on your word then that funding will immediately stop. Understand?'

'Yes, Nan.'

'Which would mean you'd have to leave university and get a job, either in Bristol or Ford. I would imagine either as a clerk in an office somewhere or else manual work. You're not qualified for anything else.'

Crista smiled inwardly, aware how much Nick hated the idea of working with his hands, which was why she'd mentioned it.

'I won't break my word, Nan.'

'To ensure you don't I will be paying periodic, and completely unannounced, visits to Bristol during the next few years. I shall just turn up at wherever you're living to see what's what. And don't for one moment think you'll be able to pull the wool over my eyes, for you won't. If you're on drugs of any kind then I'll know about it. Call it feminine intuition if you like, but I'll know about it. Just as I knew you were smoking dope during these holidays.'

She was awesome, Nick thought in admiration. Truly awesome.

372

'Right,' she announced. 'You'd better be off home again. And I shall expect to see you at least once more before you return to Bristol. OK?'

He came to his feet. 'OK, Nan.'

'Now on your way before I change my mind and tell your mother and father anyway.'

Nick fled.

Crista sank into a comfy chair as soon as he was gone. She'd hated doing that, absolutely loathed it. But sometimes in life you had to be cruel to be kind. Jamie had taught her that.

She felt drained, completely done in, now it was all over. She only hoped she'd succeeded in scaring the pants off the silly sod. And she thought she had.

She smiled to herself. Thank God for Max. She'd telephoned him and explained the situation, her concern about what Nick was up to, and asked if he could be of any help.

He'd do his best, Max had instantly replied, saying he didn't personally know much about drugs, but did have friends who he was certain could assist. Two days after that telephone conversation he'd rung back with all sorts of information for her, some of which she'd found very depressing indeed.

She owed him for that, Crista thought, looking forward to his arrival back in Ford in a few weeks' time.

She'd have a little sleep first, she decided. Forty winks, and then she'd ring Max to tell him the outcome of her confrontation with Nick.

★ ★ ★

A round of applause, led by the gargoyle-faced Whispering Smith, greeted Maggs's first appearance behind the bar since her accident.

Hypocrite, she thought, smiling at Whispering. The same went for his pal Percy Matford. Another hypocrite if ever there was one.

'Now, who wants what?' she demanded, while Dickie looked anxiously on.

Soon she was busy as could be, the dull ache of her ribs not at all a problem. Just as she'd assured an over-protective Dickie it would be.

'Max, welcome back!' Crista beamed when he appeared in the hallway carrying a case.

'And great it is to be back. I've missed you.'

Crista coloured slightly on hearing that. She'd missed him too. 'Now why don't you put that case in your bedroom and I'll make a nice cup of tea before you begin unpacking.'

'Wonderful,' he enthused. 'Though coffee would be better.'

'Becoming particular are we now?' she teased.

He was instantly contrite. 'Tea's fine if coffee's a problem.'

'Don't be silly. Of course it isn't.'

They stared at each other for a few seconds, both smiling. Then Max bustled through to his bedroom. A few minutes later he returned carrying two long, flat jewellery cases; one red, one blue. He offered the red one to Crista. 'This is for you. A small gift.'

Crista frowned, completely flustered. 'For me!'

'As a thank you. If it hadn't been for you and Ez I'd have been taken to the cleaners over Sarah's Portion.

And it was also because of you speaking to Rendle Westacott that he dropped his price.'

'But you don't have to give me anything for that, Max.'

'None the less, I wish to.'

Crista, heart pounding, took the case and opened it, gasping when she saw what was inside. 'Oh, Max, it's beautiful.'

The bracelet was made of interwoven gold links, each link delicately patterned. Crista carefully lifted the lovely thing from the case and held it dangling.

'Why don't you try it on?' he suggested.

'Max, I can't possibly accept this.'

Now it was his turn to frown. 'Why not?'

'It must have cost a fortune.'

'Not really. I made it myself, you see.'

She gaped at him. 'You made it yourself?'

'I told you I was a jeweller who made pieces as well as sold them. I made that in my workshop at home over the holiday period.'

Crista draped it over her wrist. No one had ever given her anything like this before, anything so precious. Jamie hadn't been a great one when it came to buying presents, sometimes because he simply forgot, other times because money was tight. Despite his having been a successful local doctor there never seemed to have been much cash in the bank in the early days.

She smiled. 'It truly is beautiful.'

'Then allow me. Let's see how it looks on you.' Crista watched as he engaged the clasp. 'A perfect fit, I'd say.' He nodded in approval. 'Which is more by good luck than design. I had to guess the size.'

'Well, you certainly got it right.'

'I'd be offended if you don't accept it, Crista. Please?'

How could she possibly refuse after a plea like that?

'It's eighteen carat, by the way.'

Crista didn't care how many carats it was, she simply adored it. 'What can I say, Max?'

'You don't have to. The look on your face is enough.'

Crista laughed. 'You can be an old smoothie, you know.'

He wagged a finger at her. 'Less of the old if you don't mind. I prefer to think of myself as a man in his prime. As for smoothie? I refute that as well. Merely loquacious and well mannered when I so choose.'

Crista laughed again. 'Exactly, an old smoothie.'

'And this,' Max declared, holding up the blue case, 'is for Ez as a thank you for her part in the business.'

'The same as mine?'

'Not quite. Let me show you.'

The design was identical, Crista noted, only in silver as opposed to gold. 'It's *very* kind of you, Max.'

'Nonsense. Will she like it?'

'I've no doubt about that.'

'Good.' He snapped the case shut again. 'I'll let you give it to her when the pair of you next meet. In the meantime, did you mention something about coffee?'

For the rest of that day Crista's eyes were forever straying to the bracelet on her wrist, entranced by the way it sparkled and shone. By the sheer opulence of it. On going to bed that night she briefly considered taking it off, but decided against.

It was the first thing she looked at when she woke next morning.

'I haven't forgotten that holiday in Jersey you were so keen on,' Dickie suddenly said to Maggs as they were getting ready to go downstairs and open the pub for the midday session.

That jolted Maggs. Picking up the reins of her job in the bar had driven it right out of her mind. 'Oh?'

'In fact I've been making some inquiries. I thought the first two weeks in April might be suitable.'

Maggs stared at him. 'You did say *two* weeks?'

'That's right. It's what you wanted, in fact insisted on, isn't it?'

She'd fully intended to go away for a fortnight but had expected far more opposition from Dickie. She was amazed, and delighted, that he'd so easily agreed. 'Will there be any sun then?'

'Bound to be. Lots of it, no doubt. It's just off the coast of France don't forget.'

Maggs would have preferred to go later, June or July, but knew there was no chance of Dickie's agreeing as those months were slap bang in the middle of the tourist season. 'Let's just hope there is.' She smiled.

'We'll go by boat, just as we discussed. And stay in a top-class hotel.'

Maggs raised an eyebrow. 'That'll cost, Dickie. The hotel, I mean.'

'Nothing's too good for you, darling. Besides, I think you deserve it after recent events.'

'You mean my accident?'

'Exactly.' He shrugged. 'Maybe it's time we did splash

377

out a bit. Perhaps I've been too careful in the past where money's concerned.'

An unexpected warmth flooded her at that. Warmth and affection, both of which surprised her. 'Have you any hotels specifically in mind?' she asked.

'I do have several brochures. And more are on the way.'

'Then let's see those we have.'

'The final choice will be yours, of course. That's only right, after all.'

'Come here, Dickie.'

He did and, to his complete astonishment, she kissed him on the mouth. He couldn't remember the last time she'd done that. Usually it was he who kissed her.

A whole fortnight in Jersey, Maggs thought. It was going to be glorious. She just knew it.

Crista spotted Sally walking towards her at the same moment Sally spotted her. This would be their first encounter since Crista had refused her daughter the two hundred pounds.

'Hello, Sally. How are you?' she asked, smiling, when they came face to face.

There was no smile in return. 'Fine, Mum. And you?'

'Can't complain.'

'Off to the shops, I see.'

'That's right.'

'I've just been and am now on my way home again.'

Crista was only too aware that Sally was exuding sheer hostility, which saddened her enormously. But she had been right in what she'd done, she reminded herself. It had been long overdue.

The conversation lasted a scant couple of minutes, and then they parted, Sally's hostility never having wavered.

She would come round in time, Crista consoled herself. Of course she would.

Chapter 23

Max's eyes lit up when Crista handed him a very large, buff-coloured envelope bearing a London postmark which had just arrived with the morning post.

'Ah!' he beamed. 'I hope this is what I think it is.'

Crista was curious, but said nothing as he hastily tore open the envelope and extracted several folded sheets of flimsy paper which she could see were covered in what appeared to be drawings of some sort.

'The plans for my bungalow,' Max informed her, still beaming with pleasure.

'That's nice.'

Max moved his breakfast dishes further up the table and attempted to spread out the plans. 'Let's see what they've done,' he murmured, already engrossed. Crista proceeded to clear the table. 'Excellent,' Max muttered. 'Excellent.'

Crista left him to it while she did the washing up. He was still apparently engrossed when she finished.

'Are they all right?' she asked quietly.

Max looked up at her and nodded. 'More or less.

There are a few things I'll want changed, but nothing really major. Come and have a dekko.'

Crista crossed over to stand directly behind him, from where she could clearly view the plans.

'Well?' he queried eagerly.

Crista shrugged. 'Can't make head nor tail of any of it, to tell the truth. It's all just a jumble of lines and squiggles to me.'

Max laughed. 'It's a lot more than that, Crista. Here, let me try and explain.'

She listened intently as he pointed out what this was, and that, and gradually the plans began to make sense to her.

'Only two bedrooms, Max?'

'Why more? I'd never need them.'

She leant over and placed a finger on a room at the rear. 'And that's your workshop?'

'Have to have that, Crista. I may be retired but I'll continue dabbling. Make the odd piece, amusing myself.'

'I approve. I've known men look forward to retirement all their lives, and then when it finally came they fell apart after a couple of months when it didn't turn out to be what they'd expected.

He nodded his agreement. 'So, what's your overall opinion?'

Crista considered that. 'It's difficult to tell. I mean, I'm obviously not used to judging something from a plan. But it seems fine.'

'It'll be a great deal more than fine when I'm finished, Crista. It'll be a palace. You see if it isn't.'

'I'll take your word for it, Max,' she replied, smiling at his enthusiasm.

'Everything will be top of the range, the best money can buy.' He winked at her. 'As you've probably guessed I'm not short of a bob or two. In fact, without boasting, I'm rather wealthy. Especially after selling my business.'

Crista had already surmised this from their previous conversations.

Max glanced at the plans again, and sighed. 'I'll have to take these back to London so I can personally explain to the architects the small changes I want made. I'll ring them in a few moments and arrange a meeting.' He had a sudden idea. 'Have you ever been to London, Crista?'

She shook her head. 'No, I haven't.'

'Then why don't you come with me? You'll enjoy it.'

That took her aback.

'Of course you might want a day or two to think about it,' he added.

Go to London, with Max? 'And where would I stay when there?' she queried, a peculiar tone in her voice.

He realised what she was driving at, which he hastened to clarify. 'My intentions are strictly honourable, Crista. I'd put you up in an hotel while I stayed at my house. How about the Ritz, would you fancy that?'

'I don't know,' she murmured. 'It's certainly tempting.'

'I'll give you the grand tour while we're there. Buckingham Palace, Madame Tussaud's, Eros in Piccadilly Circus. We could also take in a show or two and go out to supper afterwards in Soho. How about it?'

She really was tempted, but reality stood in the

way. 'I'm sorry, Max. I have to turn you down.'

'But why?'

'This is a village, Max. Can you imagine how tongues would wag once it got out that I'd gone to London with you? The gossips would have a field day and my reputation would be mud.'

'They needn't find out,' he protested. 'We'll just slip off quietly.'

Crista shook her head. 'Slip off quietly or whatever, it would sooner or later get out, I promise you. It's like that in a village.'

His disappointment was obvious. 'But surely they couldn't say anything if it was all above board?'

'Don't be naive, Max. The gossips would never believe that. It's potentially too juicy a story. No, by the time they'd finished, and trust me, most of it they'd simply conjure out of thin air, you and I would have been up to all sorts in London.'

That bemused him. 'Do they say anything about me lodging here with you?'

'That's different. Everyone knows I take in paying guests. It's accepted. But London would be quite a different kettle of fish.'

Max shrugged. 'So be it. A pity, though.'

'Yes,' Crista agreed softly.

'To change the subject slightly, I shall be wanting to engage a local builder in the near future and wondered if you had any suggestions?'

'Ez's husband Pete is the man to ask about that. He knows everyone in the building trade round here so he's the one to advise you.'

'Then perhaps I can speak to him when I get back from London?'

'I'll arrange it.'

Max returned to studying his plans while Crista got on with what she had to do. Her accompanying Max to London was never mentioned again.

'How was Exeter?' Dickie inquired when Maggs came home laden with parcels.

'Terrific. Just wait till you see what I've bought for our holiday in Jersey. I was ever so lucky in what I found.'

Dickie noted the sparkle in her eyes and the healthy brightness of her cheeks, so different from how she'd been before the accident and directly afterwards. The thought of their forthcoming holiday had certainly bucked her up, which pleased him enormously.

He watched her begin to unwrap the parcels to reveal all manner of summer clothes and outfits. He tried not to dwell on how much it must have cost. 'What do you think?' she queried, holding a very pretty floral patterned dress with short sleeves against herself.

'I like it.'

'It's not too young, is it?' she asked anxiously.

'Just right, I'd say.'

'I had the usual problem of getting things to fit. But that new ladies' shop that's opened up in the High Street has a decent range of larger sizes, which helped a lot.'

'Good.' Dickie nodded.

'I shall certainly be going there again.'

He had no doubt she would.

Maggs suddenly eyed her husband. 'I think we should get a few new togs for you as well. Spruce you up a little.'

384

'Me?'

'And why not? You've been wearing those same scruffy old things for years now. It's high time you had a new wardrobe. Make you look presentable.'

'Are you saying I don't?' he queried wryly.

'Oh, come on, Dickie, you know what I mean. It'll all be part of the fun.'

Dickie knew he couldn't refuse, so some new clothes it was going to have to be.

'A nice blazer and flannels perhaps,' Maggs mused. 'Or there again, something trendy.'

That alarmed him. 'Forget the trendy if you don't mind. If I went behind the bar like that I'd have the piss taken out of me no end.'

Maggs laughed; that was true enough. 'All right, I take your point. But we're certainly going to smarten you up. The pair of us are going to look the bee's knees when we go away. OK?'

'OK,' he agreed in a resigned tone.

Sarah's Portion really did have a beautiful view, Crista reflected, standing staring out over it. She had often passed the plot of land in the past but had never actually stopped to consider it.

She wondered where Max would site his bungalow. Facing out over the valley would be her choice, with a private road at the rear giving him access for his car and any other vehicle wishing to get to and from the house.

Yes, it was a wonderful spot. Max had chosen wisely. And she was sure that whoever Pete recommended would make a good job of building the bungalow. A 'proper job' as they said thereabouts.

385

Turning, she headed for home, wondering how Max was getting on in London, and wishing she'd been in a position to have gone with him, be given the grand tour he'd so kindly offered. It would have been nice. Very nice indeed.

A cold February wind began whipping up, causing her to shiver, and pull her coat even more tightly about herself, thankful for the scarf and warm woolly beret she was wearing.

She was missing Max, she thought as she walked. Her own house seemed terribly empty in his absence and, with something of a shock, she realised he really had become part of the fabric of her life. She'd never felt lonely before his arrival. Well, perhaps at times, the odd moments, something neither Ez nor Sally had appreciated. But that had changed now she was used to having him about, talking to him, making his meals, just having him there.

Another two days and he'd be back again, she reflected, hurrying on her way. She must plan a special treat for his evening meal.

Ez accepted a cup of tea from her sister and sank further into the chair she was sitting on. 'So,' she began. 'Still upset with Mum, I understand?'

'That's right. And don't you start, Ez. I'm not in the mood.'

'Suit yourself.'

'I'll just never forgive her for what she did. We had a rotten Christmas, you know that? Absolutely rotten. And all because she wouldn't lend me a miserable two hundred quid.'

Ez ignored the use of the word 'lend', well aware

that Sally had never even attempted to pay back any of the money she'd had from Crista in the past.

'After all,' Sally continued hotly, 'what's two hundred quid to her? Nothing. Nothing at all.'

'I don't think it was the money Mum was on about,' Ez said quietly.

Sally blinked at her. 'How do you mean?'

'Wasn't it more about you living beyond your means? At least, that's what she told me. Living beyond your means and learning to budget.'

Sally stared hard at her sister. 'I do not overspend, which is what Mum accused me of.'

'Then why do you often need extra to pay off your debts?'

'You sound like you're taking her side,' Sally said accusingly.

Ez was in full agreement with her mother, but didn't wish to say so. 'That wasn't my intention,' she prevaricated.

'I should hope not.'

Ez had a sip of her tea and didn't reply, knowing full well Sally wouldn't leave it there.

'I'm only ever asking for a little of what's going to be mine one day after all,' Sally blustered. Then, when she saw the look on Ez's face, she added, 'And yours too, of course.'

Again Ez didn't reply.

'What good is money lying in a bank when I can put it to good use here and now?' Sally demanded.

'That money's there for Mum's old age,' Ez pointed out. 'What's left after she dies is what comes to us. And who knows? It might be little enough if Mum lives to be a hundred.'

The thought of such an eventuality had never crossed Sally's mind. 'Do you think she might?' she asked, both seriously and anxiously.

Ez fought back the urge to go over and slap her sister. Honestly, the woman was appalling at times. 'It's always possible.'

Sally leant back in her chair to consider that dreadful reality. 'Dear me,' she whispered.

Me, Ez thought. Yes, it was always that with Sally. Me me me me me. 'Surely you hope Mum's going to live for quite a while yet?' she asked grimly.

'Of course I do,' Sally snapped back. 'What would make you think otherwise?'

It was on the tip of Ez's tongue to reply 'money', but she didn't.

'It's unlikely though,' Sally mused. 'I mean, not many people live to that age.'

'I hope you'll make it up with her soon,' a quietly seething Ez stated.

'And why should I do that?'

'It's never a good thing when families fall out. Especially over such a small thing.'

'Small my arse!' Sally exclaimed. 'It wasn't small to me. Not at the time it wasn't. Mum let me down and that's all there is to it.'

Ez had had enough of this. She'd come here to try to patch matters up between Sally and Crista, and failed miserably. She should have known better. 'I must be getting on,' she declared, placing her cup and saucer by the side of her chair.

'Before you do, what do you make of this old guy who's been staying with Mum? He seems to just keep coming back.'

Ez involuntarily glanced at the silver bracelet she was wearing. 'What about him?'

'He and Mum are becoming awfully friendly by all accounts.'

'So, what's wrong with that?'

Sally shifted uneasily. 'I don't know. It just seems strange, that's all.'

'He's in the area on business, Sally. All right?'

'And there isn't anything else?'

'Like what?' Ez frowned.

'Mum is rich, don't forget.'

So that's what she was bothered about. Money again. 'I don't think Max is the least interested in that. He's simply lodging with Mum while he has a house built. And as for them being friendly, Mum would hardly have him back again if she didn't like him or they didn't get on, would she?'

'I suppose not,' Sally reluctantly agreed.

She really had had enough, Ez decided, getting up. 'Don't worry, I'll see myself to the door.'

Sally didn't move. 'Fine.'

What a tip her sister lived in, Ez reflected as she went to collect her coat. It was disgusting.

'Right. I'm going to leave you two to it,' Crista declared. 'I'm off to my WI meeting.'

'Enjoy yourself,' Max replied.

Crista pulled a face. 'Some hope. It'll probably be boring as usual.'

'At least you'll get a good gossip afterwards,' Pete teased.

Crista drew herself up to her full height. 'I don't gossip, Pete Chudleigh. And I despise those who do.'

'Don't get on your high horse, Mum,' he protested. 'I thought all women gossiped.'

'Well I don't.' She softened slightly. 'I may discuss certain village happenings. But I refuse to get involved in anything malicious, speculative or hurtful. Understand?'

Pete's eyes were twinkling. 'Yes, Mum. You're white as the driven snow.'

Max was thoroughly enjoying this good-natured banter, finding it highly amusing.

'I'll ignore that. And now I'm off.'

Pete laughed as Crista swept away. 'She's a wonderful old bird, isn't she?' he said to Max.

'I wouldn't argue with you there,' Max replied quietly. 'I have a great deal of respect for your mother-in-law. She's certainly been kindness itself to me.'

'Now,' declared Pete, rubbing callused hands together. 'Where are these plans of yours and let's get down to brass tacks.'

'How did you get on?' Ez asked when Pete got home.

'Fine. I was able to make a few suggestions and Max will be contacting the firms in question for quotes. I steered him well clear of the dodgy buggers, of whom there are far too many round here nowadays. I was happy when he agreed with me that the lowest quote isn't always the one to go for, that quality counts above everything else.'

'Have you been drinking?' Ez frowned, having caught a whiff of alcohol.

'Max insisted we go to the Angel for a few pints when I refused to take anything for giving him the advice. I was hardly going to say no.'

390

'Hardly,' Ez repeated drily.

'The pair of us had a right old chinwag. Very knowledgeable he is, and a good sense of humour. The two of us got on like a house on fire despite the difference in ages and backgrounds.'

'You liked him then?'

'Very much so.' Pete suddenly smiled. 'He told me that he's going to insist that whoever he takes on will employ me on site for the duration of the job. He will too if I'm any judge of character.'

'That'll give you a decent spell of work when the time comes.'

'Which I'll be grateful for. As you know there isn't much on the horizon, so this'll be a godsend.'

Ez was thrilled to hear this news as it meant she didn't have to worry for a while about future wages coming in. There wasn't much building work scheduled in the area, at least that Pete knew of, for the coming spring and summer.

Pete winked at her. 'How about we have an early night?'

'We could do.' She smiled. 'But it depends when Anne gets home.'

And just then they heard their front door click open and shut announcing that their daughter was back.

Pete matched Ez's smile. 'I'm terribly tired, aren't you?'

'Terribly,' she echoed.

'Half of beer shandy please.'

Dickie thought the older woman who'd ordered was somehow familiar as he poured her drink. 'There we are,' he declared, placing it in front of her and telling her the price.

The woman opened her purse and counted the correct amount on to the bar. 'It's Dickie Trippett, isn't it?'

He nodded.

'Don't you recognise me?'

'You are familiar,' he mused.

'Gemma Catchworthy. Gatsby that was. I used to live in the village.'

'Of course! Of course!' he exclaimed. 'You were a friend of my wife's. I'm married to Maggs Fletcher.'

'I remember. You were married before I left.'

They began a bout of reminiscing before Gemma came to the point of her visit. 'I was wondering if you were looking for any staff either full or part time?'

Dickie was about to say he wasn't, then paused to think. It might be a good idea if Maggs didn't do so many hours behind the bar, and there was their holiday coming up. 'Have you any experience, Gemma?'

She laughed. 'Tony – that's my husband, who's now dead – and I used to run a pub, the last one in Godalming, Surrey. We ran pubs for years.'

'I'm sorry to hear about your husband's death,' Dickie commiserated.

'Stroke. Had it one day, was gone the next. Very sudden. After it was all over I decided to return here where I was born. Where my roots are. And so here I am. I've rented a little cottage and am now looking for work.'

'Then you've found it,' he responded, to her obvious delight. An hourly rate was quickly agreed between them.

'When can I start?' Gemma asked.

'Next Monday evening? Here for early doors.'

'You can count on me, Dickie.'

He was certain he could. 'Now I'm going to give Maggs a shout and the pair of you can have a good old natter.'

Chapter 24

'That's it!' Maggs declared, brandishing a letter. 'The hotel's confirmed our booking. All that's left for us now is to turn up and enjoy ourselves.'

How happy she looked, Dickie thought. And excited. She'd become a different woman entirely since he'd agreed on the fortnight's holiday.

'You don't think I'll look silly in a swimsuit, do you, darling?' she asked. It had taken her a while but she'd finally found one in Exeter that fitted.

'Not in the least,' Dickie assured her. For in his eyes, loving her as he did, she wouldn't.

'I probably won't go in as the sea is bound to still be cold, but I can certainly stretch out on the beach and get the sun.'

'You'll have to be careful about that,' Dickie warned her. 'It's been years since you last sunbathed.'

'Don't you worry, I'll have all the necessary creams and lotions. I've no intention of turning into a lobster after my first day and spoiling the rest of the holiday.'

Dickie was pleased to hear it.

'I simply can't wait,' Maggs enthused. 'I only wish we were going tomorrow.'

'Well we aren't, so you're just going to have to contain yourself.'

'Wasn't it lucky Gemma turning up as she did after all these years? Her being an ex-landlady, that is. Between her and Ez the pub will be in safe hands while we're away.'

'It was lucky,' Dickie agreed. 'She certainly knows her way round a bar, and the customers have all taken to her. Of course it helps that she already knew some of them from the old days.'

'Sad about her husband, mind. Just keeled over and that was more or less that. It must have been terrible for her.'

Dickie nodded his agreement. 'At least she was able to collect a decent-sized payout on his life assurance. As she told us, that together with what she can earn will keep the wolf from the door.'

'I wonder if Crista knows she's back yet?' Maggs mused. 'They were quite pally once upon a time.'

'I'd be surprised if she doesn't. You know how word gets round in Ford. Quicker than any flash flood.'

Maggs laughed, for that was true enough. 'If you put Gemma on dinnertime shift this Saturday that'll give us a chance to get into town together and buy those clothes for you that we discussed.'

Dickie groaned inwardly. Shopping was not exactly his favourite pastime. But in this instance it had to be done. Maggs would never let him off the hook.

An amused glint came into Maggs's eyes. 'I wonder how you'd look in shorts?'

Dickie's face was a picture.

★ ★ ★

Crista came to the end of Nick's letter, his second since returning to Bristol. Everything was fine, he said. He was working hard and had changed his circle of friends. (Something she entirely approved of.)

He mentioned this and that, merely chatting on paper, ending by hoping she was well and he'd see her at Easter when he intended coming home again.

All very satisfactory, Crista thought, laying his letter on the mantelpiece. He was telling her he was on the straight and narrow as far as dope was concerned, and she believed him. She could only hope and pray it stayed that way.

She turned her attention to Max, who was studying three different sets of quotes for building the bungalow that had arrived in the post. 'Any good?' she queried.

He glanced up at her. 'I believe so. But I think it best I consult Pete before I make a decision. He knows these people, after all, whereas I don't.'

Crista had a sudden idea. 'Why don't you ring him later when he's home from work and suggest the pair of you meet up in the Angel for a drink? You can show him the quotes there and ask for his recommendation.'

'Good idea,' Max enthused.

'And if you don't mind I'd like to tag along.'

'Of course, Crista,' he replied quickly, thinking it was fairly rare for her to go to the pub. In fact this was the first time he could remember her suggesting it.

Crista just hoped Gemma would be working.

'Crista!' Gemma squealed when she walked into the pub with Max and Pete. 'I'd have recognised you anywhere. You haven't changed a bit.'

Crista went straight to the bar and leant across, Gemma doing the same, and they hugged each other joyfully. 'And I recognised you right away too.'

They beamed at one another. 'A long time,' Crista stated happily.

'Isn't it just.'

'And you're a widow, I believe. I'm sorry to hear that.'

'You too. Ten years ago, Maggs told me.'

Crista nodded. 'A lifetime ago in some respects. As if it was only yesterday in others.'

'Well, it's eight months for me so I'm still getting used to the idea.'

Crista could well understand that, and sympathised. 'How does it feel being back?'

'So many changes, Crista. I was amazed.'

'When you're living here they happen gradually so I suppose you don't notice them so much. But yes, there have been a lot.'

'Are you ladies intending yipping all night or can a thirsty chap get a drink round here?' Pete queried in a friendly, good-humoured way.

Crista introduced him, then Max. 'Now, the first round is on me. And I won't have any argument,' she declared firmly.

'You won't get one out of me,' Pete riposted. 'I'll gladly take a drink off you.'

Max was less keen, but wasn't about to argue. He didn't consider it gentlemanly to accept a drink from a lady.

'I have a ciggie break coming up shortly,' Gemma informed Crista. 'I'll come over and join you if I may.'

'I'll be cross if you don't.'

'Lots to catch up on, eh?'

'Lots,' Crista agreed, absolutely delighted to see her old chum again.

It struck her then that she should have had the foresight to buzz Abigail and invite her along. That would have been a real reunion.

But she hadn't thought about it. Pity.

It was about a week later, and Max was in Exeter, when the phone rang. 'Hello?'

'Mum, it's Ez. I've just heard that Daniel has come off that motorbike of his.'

Fear gripped Crista. 'Has he been killed?'

'No no. But I understand he's hurt. Listen, Mum, I'm just about to leave and go round to Sally's. Do you want to come?'

'Of course I do. He's my grandson.'

'Shall I pick you up or meet you there?'

It only took a moment to decide. 'I'll meet you there, Ez. I'll get my coat and be straight on my way.'

'OK, Mum.' And with that the phone went dead.

A few minutes later a worried Crista was hurrying up the road in the direction of Sally's house. As chance would have it she and Ez met almost outside the front door. It was Ez who knocked.

Sally answered, her face tightening when she saw Crista. 'You've heard about the accident then?'

'That's why we're here.'

Sally hesitated, clearly in a quandary. 'You'd better come in.'

Crista knew the hesitation had been because of her and wondered if she would have been refused

398

entry if she'd been on her own. She couldn't believe Sally would have done that.

'How bad is he?' Ez queried as soon as they were inside.

'Shocked more than anything. Lucky for him he had his leathers on or he could have done himself some real damage.'

Both Ez and Crista heaved sighs of relief. 'Has the doctor been?' Crista asked.

'There are only a few scrapes and bruises, which I can deal with myself. There's no need for the doctor.'

Sally took them through to the living room where Daniel was sitting in a chair looking, to Crista's amazement, pretty pleased with himself. He was wearing a dressing gown with the leg bearing the scrapes and bruises poking through.

'I was just about to clean his leg and then bandage it,' Sally said.

'Hello, Nan. Hello, Aunt Ez,' Daniel greeted them in a rather off-hand manner.

'So what happened?' Crista demanded.

Daniel shrugged. 'Misjudged a turn, that's all. It's no big deal.'

'You could have killed yourself, you silly sod.'

Sally instantly bridled. 'There's no need for that, Mother. It was an accident, pure and simple. Could have happened to anyone.'

Ez shot Crista a warning glance, which Crista ignored.

'Nonsense,' she snorted. 'I've seen him driving round the village, going like the clappers, far too fast, showing off. It was only a matter of time before something happened.'

Sally bit back her fury.

'That's a load of crap.' Daniel laughed. 'You must be mixing me up with someone else, Nan.'

'It is not crap, as you so delicately put it. And I know my own grandson when I see him. And recognise his bike.'

'That's enough, Mother,' Sally snapped. 'You're only out to cause trouble.'

'I am nothing of the sort.'

'He does drive rather fast at times,' Ez said quietly. 'I've witnessed it myself.'

'Are you ganging up on him as well?' Sally hissed.

'You know I'm not, Sis. I'm only telling you what I've seen.'

'I've had enough of this!' Daniel exclaimed, coming to his feet. 'I'm off to my room.'

'But I haven't done your leg yet,' Sally protested.

'It'll keep until these two have gone.'

Crista was outraged. 'You should learn some manners when talking to your elders,' she snapped. 'Most definitely.'

'Bullshit.' And with that he strode from the room, slamming the door behind him.

'Now look what you've done, you interfering old cow!' Sally screeched.

'Enough of that, Sis!' Ez retorted, eyes sparking fire. 'I think you should apologise.'

'I'll do nothing of the sort. I'm not having anyone, my mother or otherwise, coming into my home and insulting my family.'

'I wasn't insulting him, merely telling him a few home truths,' Crista insisted.

'To put it bluntly,' Sally barked, 'it's none of your

damned business. Now I think you'd better both leave before even more gets said.'

'Come on, Mum,' Ez urged quietly, knowing Sally to be right about more being said.

Crista knew it too, inwardly berating herself for jumping right in as she had. But the thought of Daniel's being involved in an accident had given her a tremendous fright. Not trusting herself to utter further, she turned on her heel and headed for the outside door where she was joined by Ez.

'It wasn't your fault, Mum,' Ez said as they walked off down the street. 'You were concerned, that's all.'

'The cheek of that young man,' Crista fumed. 'The trouble is he's always been spoilt by Sally. Ever since he was a baby.'

'Modern youth.' Ez sighed, shaking her head. 'They're unbelievable at times.'

'Not your two.' Crista smiled at her, momentarily conveniently forgetting Nick's recent foray into dope.

'That's because Pete and I have been far more strict than Sally and Ben. I blame Ben myself. He should have stood up to Sally more. Not let her rule the roost the way she does.'

Weak, Crista thought. She'd always considered Sally's husband that, from the first day she'd met him. Weak as the proverbial dishwater. 'Oh well,' she sighed. 'Daniel is all right and I suppose that's the main thing. Though it could easily have been otherwise.'

Ez wholeheartedly agreed.

'What are you doing?' a curious Dickie asked Maggs.

'Marking off the calender. What does it look like?'

The penny dropped. 'Are you counting the days

401

till we go on holiday, is that what this is in aid of?'

Maggs nodded.

Dickie found it funny, and yet touching at the same time. 'You really are dying to get away, aren't you?'

'Damn right I am. Aren't you?'

Dickie thought about that. 'Well yes, of course. But obviously not as much as you.'

'A whole fortnight away from this pub and Ford,' Maggs breathed. 'It'll be heaven. Not that I have anything against either the pub or the village; it'll just be wonderful to get away for a while. A change of scenery, change of faces. Not having to serve behind the bar.'

'Hey, you're not doing so much of that since I took on Gemma. You've got far more time to yourself.'

'True enough. And thank you.'

Dickie sat at the table, about to busy himself with the paperwork that running a pub entailed, paperwork that seemed to get more and more voluminous with every passing year. Bureaucracy running riot in his opinion.

He paused before getting down to it, smiling to think that at least he'd been spared the shorts as far as the holiday was concerned.

At least he'd been spared those.

Max and Crista watched as the digger's arm descended to tear into the ground. The laying of the bungalow's foundations had begun.

'How long will it all take?' Crista asked quietly.

'You mean the entire construction? A few months if all goes well. Possibly a little longer. I'm assured it's difficult to be precise about these things.'

402

'Excited?'

He turned to smile at her. 'What do you think?'

'I think you are.'

'And you'd be right. It's a big day for me. A very big day.'

They continued watching as a grabful of red earth was dumped on to the back of a waiting lorry and the digger clanked back into position for another scoop.

'Well, now you've seen that how about we go home and have some coffee?' Crista suggested. 'I know I could certainly use a cup.'

Max roused himself. 'Good idea. But can we stay for just a few minutes longer before we leave? This is an occasion to remember.'

Crista laughed. 'Of course we can.'

Which is precisely what they did.

'Now don't you worry, Ez and I will take good care of the pub. And if there are any problems I'll sort them out. You have my word on that,' Gemma assured Dickie.

'And it's a beautiful day to be travelling,' Maggs enthused, glancing through a nearby window up at the sky where the sun was shining brightly.

'Want some help with those cases, chap?' the taxi driver asked, appearing in the doorway.

'If you could take one I'll bring along the other.' Dickie replied.

The driver glanced to where Dickie's missing arm should have been, but tactfully didn't patronise Dickie. He heaved up the case nearest him and left.

Dickie gave the bar a last look over, hating leaving

the pub for even a single day. Next to Maggs, it was his life.

'Ready?' Maggs smiled, guessing what was going through his mind.

Dickie took a deep breath. 'As I'll ever be.'

Gemma came out to the taxi and waved them off, bustling back inside once they were gone as there was bottling up to do and one of the beer lines to be cleaned before opening time.

'There you are,' declared Crista, handing Gemma a cup of coffee.

'Where's your lodger?' Gemma queried, having noted Max's apparent absence.

'He's gone over to watch the builders, which he does on a daily basis. I should imagine they must be sick to death of him being there.'

Gemma laughed. Crista had told her about the bungalow Max was having built during their initial get-together.

'Had a phone call from Dickie yet?' Crista asked, tongue in cheek.

'They only left this morning!' Gemma exclaimed in surprise.

'You don't know Dickie like I do. He's a born worrier, especially where that pub's concerned. He's one of those people who thinks he's utterly indispensable. You wait and see, he'll be on the phone night and day if Maggs lets him.' Crista sat down facing Gemma. 'It really is good having you back in the village.'

'And it's good to be here. Though as I said to you the other night, I'm amazed at all the changes. I've even heard that the Swain house and mill are up for sale.'

'So I believe.'

'Who'd have ever thought it,' Gemma mused, having a sip of her coffee. 'I liked Max, by the way. He's nice.'

'Very.'

Gemma regarded Crista shrewdly. 'I couldn't help noticing how friendly the pair of you are.'

Crista was caught unawares. 'Well, yes. We get on. I shall be sorry when he moves out.'

'Oh?'

Crista stared at her friend. 'Just what are you insinuating, Gemma?'

'Nothing at all. I swear. I only wondered, that's all.'

'Wondered what?'

'If there was anything between you.'

'Don't be silly,' Crista said quickly. 'Of course there isn't. What on earth gave you that idea?'

'If I hadn't known differently I'd have thought you were married. You seemed so together, so much of a couple.'

'Is that the impression we gave?' Crista frowned.

'To me you did. There again, I'd never met the two of you together before so perhaps I was seeing things with fresh eyes.'

Crista didn't reply. She was feeling quite stunned. She'd had no idea she and Max might appear that way.

'Have you ever thought about getting married again?' Gemma went on.

'Have you?'

Gemma smiled. 'Not yet. It is only eight months, and I did love Tony. But I do know I don't want to spend the rest of my life alone. I'd hate that. So the answer is, not yet, but I'm not against the idea of eventually remarrying either. If the right chap comes along, that is.'

'It's never entered my mind,' Crista said slowly. 'Jamie and I had such a perfect marriage that the thought of someone else simply doesn't seem possible.'

'Well I'd consider it if I were you,' Gemma advised. 'Before it gets too late.'

'I doubt Max thinks of me like that at all,' Crista protested.

'I wouldn't be so sure about that. At the very least he's extremely fond of you, that was blindingly obvious. His wife's also dead, isn't she?'

Crista nodded.

'Then he's free as well. I know if I was in your shoes I'd certainly snap him up. Darned tootin' I would.'

Crista suddenly shook her head. 'This is nonsense, all of it. Max and I are good friends, nothing more. That's all there is to it.'

'Lovely coffee,' Gemma commented, and changed the subject. She could see from Crista's face she'd certainly given her something to think about.

Chapter 25

Maggs and Dickie stood at the ship's rail watching the proceedings dockside as they got under way. Already holding his hand, she squeezed it when the final hawser was cast off and they began to move, her expression one of sheer exultation.

'Next stop Jersey.' Dickie smiled at her.

'I can't believe we're actually, finally, on our way.'

'Well, we are.'

'Oh, Dickie,' she breathed. 'I've been looking forward to this so much. I've felt like a kid waiting for Santa to come.'

He laughed, thinking that was exactly how she'd been. 'Well we're off now, sweetheart. And won't be back for a fortnight.'

Maggs momentarily closed her eyes. 'Sheer bliss.'

Dickie had never loved her more than he did at that moment. Leaning forward he kissed her tenderly on the mouth.

'Why you sexy old thing.' She beamed.

'Is that a complaint?' he teased.

'Not at all. Quite the contrary. I liked it.'

He kissed her again.

Maggs sighed deeply with satisfaction, telling herself this was going to be the most wonderful holiday of all time.

They both looked up when seagulls suddenly began screeching overhead. One of the gulls went into a steep dive to snatch something from the water in its beak before wheeling away again.

'Shit!' Maggs muttered when a large plop of rain hit her squarely on the nose.

'What is it?'

'It's starting to bloody rain.'

Within moments the drops were rat-tat-tatting off the deck.

'We'd better get out of this,' Dickie said. 'Otherwise we'll be wet through.'

Maggs had intended to stand on the deck watching England until it was lost to view, but neither she nor Dickie was wearing a mac or carrying an umbrella. 'I suppose so,' she reluctantly agreed.

'Tell you what, why don't we find the bar and have a couple to pass the time?'

That immediately cheered her up. 'Sounds good to me.'

Still hand in hand, they hurried towards the nearest hatch and companionway that would take them below.

Maggs stared in dismay round their hotel room. The Royale might indeed have once been a place of splendour and opulence, but that was clearly long ago. The carpet underfoot was close to being threadbare, the wallpaper faded and tatty. To crown it all she was certain she could smell mothballs.

'What do you think?' Dickie asked hopefully.

'It's a dump.'

His heart sank to hear that. What was more, he totally agreed with her. 'It's not much cop, is it?'

Maggs shook her head. 'It looked fine in the brochure. But now I actually see it . . .' She trailed off in disappointment.

'We could ask for another room, I suppose.'

'I somehow doubt that would make any difference. They're probably all like this.'

Dickie didn't remind Maggs it was she who'd chosen the hotel, mainly because of its central position. 'So what shall we do?'

She shrugged. 'Make the best of it. What else can we do?'

'Change hotels?'

'And lose our deposit? Not likely. Anyway, who's to say the other hotels are any better?'

'I'm sorry, Maggs. Truly I am,' he whispered.

'Not your fault, Dickie.' Crossing to the window she stared out over Liberation Square and the harbour beyond. 'At least it's a good view. I can't fault that.'

'You're right,' he agreed, joining her at the window. Out to sea a grey, dank mist was rapidly rolling landwards, promising more rain.

'I'm sure tomorrow will be heaps better.' She smiled, trying to put a brave face on things. 'In the meantime I'll get unpacked and then we can go downstairs for something to eat. How about that?'

'Suits me. I'm starving.'

Maggs realised she was as well. It had been a long day with only a snack on board, and certainly too much alcohol, which had left her slightly muzzy-headed. But when they eventually went down to the restaurant it was to discover they were too late to be served, which annoyed them both as it really wasn't that late. Their only option was to go back upstairs again to fetch their coats, and face the rain that was now lashing down.

Crista paused in her ironing to stare at Max fast asleep in a chair. How comfortable he looked, she thought. How very much at home. She smiled in memory, for Jamie had used to do the same thing, especially if he'd been called out the night before, and sometimes when he hadn't, simply exhausted after a long and tiring day.

Time and again the conversation with Gemma had popped into her mind. It had made her view Max in an entirely different light. There was no doubt that for his age he was still a remarkably handsome man, even if he did have a typically large Jewish nose. How old was he? she wondered. Certainly older than her, though she didn't think by a lot. She enjoyed his company, very much so, because he was just so easy to be with. And funny too on occasion. He had a good sense of humour. He was articulate, clever, very knowledgeable about all manner of things, and a perfect gentleman. What else could a woman ask for? Oh, and he was rich, which meant he didn't have any ulterior motives regarding her money.

What was it Gemma had said? They looked so together, so much of a couple. It had been with a shock afterwards that she'd realised Gemma was right. Not only looked like one, but had come to act like one since Max had first appeared on her doorstep.

She could only speculate on what Max actually thought about her. Did he view their relationship as more than friendship? Had the idea of marriage crossed his mind?

Crista laid the iron aside, having decided to make a cup of coffee. When it was ready she'd rouse Max and offer him one. He'd been asleep long enough; any more and he'd be wide awake in the middle of the night.

Would it be a betrayal of Jamie? she asked herself as she filled the kettle. Part of her said yes, another part no. After all, the hard and bitter fact was that Jamie was dead, and life went on. Her life. If there was a little more happiness to be had before she too passed on, then surely it would be foolish not to grab it with both hands.

If only she could ask Jamie for his opinion, and advice. Discover what he thought she should do. Find out if he would consider it a betrayal. But Jamie had loved her just as she'd loved him, and surely that meant having the best interests of the other person at heart? In which case, logically, Jamie would have told her to go ahead, grab the happiness that might be so unexpectedly on offer in her twilight years. Of course he would. Just as, if the position had been reversed, she'd have told him to do the same.

Crista hung her head for a moment. The truth was, she desperately wanted to be cuddled again, with love and tenderness, the way Jamie used to cuddle her.

How on earth could there possibly be anything wrong with that?

Maggs woke up and briefly wondered where she was. Then she remembered: the Royale hotel in Jersey, on holiday. Their third day there.

Dickie was still fast asleep beside her, his mouth open, as it usually was, catching flies as she'd so often teased him. A glance at the closed curtains told her it was light outside, another at their travelling clock on the bedside table that it was time to get up and go down for breakfast.

She slid from the bed, full of high hopes about what they would do that morning, shrugged into her dressing gown and padded over to the window.

The smile of anticipation vanished from her face when she drew back one of the curtains. It was raining, still bloody raining, just as it had been more or less since their arrival. She swallowed her disappointment. There would be no sunbathing that afternoon, no long leisurely walk along the seafront, no paddling in the sea.

She heaved a great sigh, one that came from the very depths of her being. This rain couldn't last, she told herself. Of course it wouldn't. They were simply having a bad start to their holiday, that was all.

'Maggs?'

She turned to smile at him. 'You're awake then.'

'What's the weather like?'

'Pissing down, if you'll pardon my French.'

Dickie swore, which for some reason made Maggs smile again.

'Why don't you come back to bed?' he proposed suggestively.

'What, and miss breakfast? No fears. It's paid for and I want it. Damn right I do.'

He could tell from her expression that there was no point in either arguing or pleading. Her mind was made up: breakfast it was going to be.

412

Marching to the bathroom Maggs put the stopper in the bath and turned the water on. At least there was no shortage of hot water, she consoled herself. That was something.

Crista heard the click of the receiver being replaced in its cradle and Max reappeared, rubbing his hands. 'That's it,' he announced breezily. 'I've had an offer on my house in Golders Green which I've accepted. We should be able to exchange and complete in a relatively short time as there isn't a chain. How about that then?'

'Did you get a good price?'

'An excellent one. I'm more than pleased.'

Crista thought about it. 'Does that mean you'll have sold before the bungalow is finished?'

'I should imagine so.'

'Then what about your furniture?'

'Well, I had considered putting it in storage,' he replied slowly. 'Then I decided to get rid of most of it and start completely over with brand-new stuff. My furniture wouldn't suit the bungalow anyway. Far too cumbersome.'

'Get rid of it?' Crista repeated, frowning. 'But surely you'd want to keep it for sentimental reasons if nothing else?'

'Because it belonged to Rebekah and myself?'

Crista nodded.

'I thought about that as well and it seems to me that a completely fresh start would be best. Oh, there are a few items I'll keep. A lamp I'm particularly fond of which we bought together in the Caledonian Market one Sunday morning. Some solid silver cutlery,

King's pattern, which is extremely valuable and pleasant to use. And of course all the tools and other bits
and pieces in my workshop. But . . .' He hesitated.
'The past is the past, and that's in my head. I don't
need pieces of furniture, or anything else, to remind
me of it. A new home and new furniture for a new
life, Crista. At least, that's how I see it.'

Crista wasn't sure she agreed with that, or that she
could bear to part with many of the things she and
Jamie had shared during their years of marriage. But
maybe Max was right.

'Why don't we celebrate my selling the house?' he
suggested with a broad smile.

'What are you proposing?'

'There's a new restaurant opened up recently in
Exeter. Why don't we give it a try?'

'Go out for a meal?'

'That's it.'

Her immediate reaction was what would the village
say if they were spotted? Tongues would go into overdrive and her reputation might well end in tatters.
She'd passed on the London trip for that reason, but
this was hardly in the same league. Max had been
lodging with her for quite some time now; surely the
pair of them going out for a meal together was reasonable. Particularly as they were celebrating something.

'Well?' Max prompted.

'I'd love to go.'

'Good!' He beamed. 'I'll telephone ahead and make
a reservation. Seven thirty for eight suit?'

'Fine.'

'I'll see if I can get through right now,' he declared,
and left the room again.

What could she wear? Crista wondered. She'd have bought something for the occasion if she'd known about it in advance. No time for that now, though.

She hurried upstairs to her bedroom and began rummaging amongst her dresses.

Maggs stopped outside Jersey's one department store. 'I want to go in here,' she declared.

'What for?'

'A cardigan, that's what for. I never thought to bring one with me and I'm absolutely freezing.'

Dickie had to agree it was cold. 'Can we get a couple of vests for me?' he queried. 'I could use them in this weather.'

Maggs hadn't thought to pack those either, it never having entered her head that a cardigan or vests would be needed. 'I'll tell you what,' she said, knowing Dickie's loathing of shopping. 'Go to that pub across the street and wait for me there.'

Dickie's relief was obvious. 'OK then.'

'And while I'm inside I'll look round for a few presents to take back with us. Something for Gemma and Ez, and maybe Crista if I see anything suitable.'

'Good idea.' He nodded.

'Off with you then.'

She'd be joining him as soon as she could, Maggs thought as she went through the store's main doors. A brandy or two wouldn't go amiss.

'This is more like it,' Maggs declared, gazing round the candlelit restaurant they'd found in one of the city's back streets.

Dickie topped up her wine glass, and then his own. 'How's your fish?'

'Mmm,' she murmured. 'Absolutely delicious. I'm enjoying every mouthful.'

'Me too.'

'If I have one complaint it's that the sauce is slightly too rich for my taste. But apart from that the turbot is perfect.'

Dickie felt relaxed for the first time since their arrival in Jersey, and made a mental note to come to this restaurant again before their holiday was over.

Maggs watched as he cut and speared a piece of sea bass with his fork. He was an expert at eating solely with that implement. At home it was rare for her to dish up anything where a knife was necessary. Stews and casseroles were great favourites.

'The weather forecast is better for tomorrow,' he commented. 'Perhaps we'll be able to get down to the beach at last.'

Maggs fervently hoped so, but doubted it. The forecast wasn't that good. But at least they might be able to have a decent walk along the seafront without being rained on and blown to bits.

The waiter who'd served them came over and asked if everything was all right, and Dickie assured him it was. The waiter gave a small bow and left them to it.

'The wine's nice too,' Maggs said, having just had another sip.

'Not bad.'

She smiled. Neither of them was really a wine drinker as there wasn't much call for it in Ford, where the tipples of choice were still mainly beer, cider and spirits.

'I suppose you'd rather have a pint with the meal?' she teased.

Dickie shrugged. 'It's what I'm used to.'

'Then it's good to have a change. Broaden your horizons. Experience new things.'

'I've drunk wine before,' he protested.

'But not often.'

'A few times. Here and there.'

'And nothing of this quality.' She had another sip, marvelling at the rich, warm smoothness of it. The wine they had at home was rubbish compared to this.

Dickie paused to stare at Maggs, delighted to see how happy she was. And if she was happy, so too was he. Maybe the holiday wasn't going to be such a disaster after all.

Maggs woke to hear Dickie groaning horribly. She sat up in bed to find he was doing the same. 'What's wrong?' she demanded anxiously.

'Stomach. Terrible cramps.'

She leant across and switched on the bedside light. It startled her to see the colour of Dickie's face, a pale shade of green.

'Got to get to the toilet,' he suddenly announced, and literally shot out of bed. When he reached the bathroom he slammed the door shut behind him.

Maggs also got out of bed and put on her dressing gown. She was beginning to have a suspicion of what might be wrong. 'Are you all right?' she asked from outside the bathroom door.

'Oh my God, Maggs!' he wailed. 'The world is falling out of my arse.'

'And your stomach?'

'What do you bloody think!' he snapped back.

Dickie's tone told her, knowing him as she did, that he really was bad. 'Is there anything I can do?'

'Not for the moment. Go back to bed and leave me here. I'm going to be a while.'

Maggs's face screwed up in distaste when the smell hit her. Quickly she retreated from the door and, minutes later, was opening their window to try to deal with the matter.

Dickie didn't emerge again for hours. When he finally did, he looked gaunt, haggard – and still green.

'No doubt about it in my opinion,' Doctor le Noa pronounced later that morning. 'It's food poisoning.'

Just as Maggs had thought. 'So, what's to be done?' she queried.

'Well, nothing to eat or drink apart from water and a dry biscuit or plain bread, without butter and the like, for the next twenty-four hours. I'll also leave you a prescription for some tablets which should help. Just follow the instructions on the label. Apart from that there's little else I can suggest.'

'Sodding fish,' Dickie muttered. It had to have been that. Had to have been.

'Did you also have fish last night, Mrs Trippett?' le Noa inquired.

'Yes.'

'No after-effects?'

She shook her head. 'None. I feel just fine.'

'Trust my luck,' Dickie groaned, feeling extremely lightheaded as he had done for hours now.

'I suggest you get back into bed, Mr Trippett. And stay there.'

418

Maggs couldn't help glancing at the window, through which she could see blue sky. For once it wasn't grey or raining.

Le Noa produced a pad and wrote out the prescription. 'Get this filled as soon as you can,' he advised Maggs. 'And make sure your husband takes the entire course.'

'I'll do that.'

Le Noa regarded Dickie sympathetically. 'Rotten thing to have. Had it myself once from some dodgy prawns. An experience I've no wish to repeat.'

'Me neither,' Dickie attempted to joke.

'Right then, that's that,' le Noa declared.

'Thank you for coming, doctor. We do appreciate it.' Maggs smiled.

'That's my job.'

Dickie crawled back beneath the sheets while Maggs saw the doctor out.

'I wonder how Aunt Maggs and Uncle Dickie are getting on?' Ez said to Gemma just before midday opening.

'Having a wonderful time, I should imagine.' She grinned. 'Maggs must have him well under control. He hasn't phoned once yet.'

They both laughed.

'Jammy beggars,' Ez said enviously. 'I wish it was me having a holiday somewhere nice and sunny instead of stuck in dreary old Ford.'

Maggs's face was stony as they finally emerged from the interminable tunnels that formed the German Underground Hospital, one of the 'must see' sights on Jersey and a leftover from the occupation. Dummies dressed in German uniforms, male and female, wireless sets, medical facilities, flags, sleeping accommodation . . . all boring as hell as far as she was concerned.

'Jesus Christ, I don't believe it,' Dickie muttered beside her. 'It's not raining for a change, it's sleeting!'

It was too, Maggs noted grimly, filled, yet again, with despair.

'We'd better make a run for the bus,' Dickie declared. By the time they got inside they were soaked through.

Maggs didn't think things could get any worse, but they did. Two days later, having just returned to the hotel after wandering round St Helier for the umpteenth time, Maggs sat on the bed and buried her head in her hands.

'What is it, pet?' Dickie demanded when he emerged from the bathroom.

'I've lost my purse. I've been through my bag and coat pockets thoroughly and I've somehow lost it.' And with that she broke down in tears.

Dickie was instantly sitting alongside holding her with his arm. 'Don't be so upset. We'll get you another tomorrow.'

'All my money was in there, Dickie. All of it!'

Christ, he thought. She'd been carrying, he now remembered, most of their holiday cash.

'What are we to do?' she wailed, quite beside herself.

'I'll report the loss to the police and then go to the bank and make some sort of arrangement. They're bound to help us out.'

'I've had enough, Dickie. I can't take any more. I want to go home as soon as possible.'

'But we've paid . . .'

'Forget about that,' she interrupted, staring at him through red-rimmed eyes. 'I just want to go home.'

'All right, darling. All right,' he crooned. 'That's exactly what we'll do. Just as soon as I can arrange it.'

How could she have been so stupid as to lose her purse! Maggs berated herself. How could she!

Her tears continued to flow.

'I feel as if I'm going to die,' Dickie groaned.

Poor man, Maggs thought. First food poisoning, now sea sickness. Luckily the heavy seas weren't having any adverse effect on her. From all around the large saloon they were sitting in came sounds of equal distress. It was proving a horrendous passage.

The boat yawed, then crashed violently back into the sea and began rolling again. There was the distinct smell of sick in the air.

'Why don't you try and get some sleep?' Maggs suggested. 'Even a half hour or so would help.'

Dickie saw the sense in that. 'Do you think they'd mind if I stretched out on this bench?'

'Not in the least.'

She stood as he did so, closing his eyes. 'I'm just going to the toilet,' she lied. 'Will you be OK?'

'I'll be fine, Maggs. On you go.'

She left him to make her way unsteadily up the length of the saloon.

'Another brandy, please.'

The young barman regarded her with concern. This would be her sixth large one in a relatively short space of time. Still, she didn't appear drunk, and certainly wasn't being loud or causing any kind of disturbance, so he served her.

Maggs was sitting staring straight ahead, a peculiar, lopsided smile on her face. She was far from being drunk. In fact she'd have said she'd never been more sober in her life.

For several moments she focused on the barman, thinking how handsome he was. He reminded her of someone, but she couldn't think who. The someone was too far back in time.

'Rough weather, eh?' The barman smiled.

Maggs nodded, but didn't utter.

Obviously didn't want to have a conversation, the barman thought, and moved away, suddenly clutching at the bar when the boat seemed to corkscrew under him. He glanced at Maggs who remained as she'd been, apparently unaffected by the boat's movement.

When he glanced again in her direction shortly after that she'd gone.

Chapter 26

Crista was walking home from the shops when she bumped into Abigail Nicholls that was, who'd married Tom Woolocombe the butcher. 'Hello.' She smiled. 'Haven't seen you in a long time.'

'It has been a while,' Abigail agreed. 'How are you?'

'In the pink. Yourself?'

'Not too bad. My eyesight is playing me up a bit these days and Tom's forever nagging me to go to an optician, which I suppose I'll get round to sometime.'

'Age.' Crista nodded. 'It's catching up with all of us. With me it's arthritis. Though I have to say I'm pretty free of it at the moment.'

'From all accounts that doesn't seem to have stopped you having a right old time of it,' Abigail teased.

Crista frowned. What on earth was she talking about? 'What right old time is this?'

'The whole village is talking. You were seen out one night wining and dining with that lodger of yours. Mr Rubin, isn't it?'

Crista's heart sank. So they had been spotted after all. Damn! 'No reason why I shouldn't go out with him,' she replied defiantly. 'He was celebrating the sale of his house in London and asked if I'd join him. I couldn't see why not.'

'I've heard about the bungalow he's building on Sarah's Portion. It's costing him a fortune, they say.'

'Hardly that! It isn't costing more than any other bungalow of that size.' She changed her tone. 'You shouldn't listen to so much gossip, Abigail. Most of it's either wrong or made up anyway.'

Abigail didn't take kindly to the rebuke. 'But you did go out with him?'

'I've just said so, haven't I? To celebrate the sale of his London house. And a lovely meal it was too. I thoroughly enjoyed both it and the evening.'

'He's a Jew, isn't he?'

Crista stared hard at her friend. 'He is. But not practising, I understand.'

'He's still a Jew though. Not many of those here-abouts.'

'No, I suppose there aren't. He's certainly the first I've become friendly with.'

'Friendly, eh?' Abigail smiled thinly, a glint in her eye.

'Is there something wrong with that?' Crista queried, beginning to get annoyed.

'No.'

'Then why do you make it sound as if there is?'

'I'm not implying anything, honestly!' Abigail protested.

'Well don't. For your information I'll have you know Max Rubin is one of the kindest, gentlest, best-mannered men you could meet. He's certainly the best paying guest I've ever had.'

'You do seem to hold him in high regard,' Abigail commented, the glint still in her eye.

'I do. And the fact that he's Jewish has absolutely nothing to do with anything, as far as I'm concerned. If he's typical of the race then we could do with a lot more of them round here. Now, if you don't mind I have to get on.'

'Of course, Crista. We must meet up soon and have a natter. A proper one, that is.'

To see what more you can find out? Crista thought cynically. Well bugger that. 'We must,' she agreed, having no intention of doing so.

She was angry as she continued on her way. So the village was talking about her and Max having a meal together. She could only wonder what else they were saying because of it. No doubt putting two and two together and coming up with five.

She'd lived in a village all her life. But sometimes, on occasions like this one, she hated village life.

Positively hated it.

There was a police car parked outside her house. Crista stopped in puzzlement. What on earth was going on?

'Is that you, Crista?'

'Yes, it's me, Max. I'm back,' she called out in reply as she hung up her coat.

'We have a visitor.'

She entered the room to find a policewoman standing beside a troubled-looking Max.

'This is WPC Nolan,' Max declared. 'She's got some bad news, I'm afraid.'

Fear stabbed through Crista. 'I see.'

'Mrs Cristabel Murray?'

'That's correct.' Crista nodded.

'As Mr Rubin informed you I'm WPC Nolan. Would you care to sit down?'

'What's happened?' Crista demanded in a tremulous voice. She could only think it had something to do with Daniel and that damned motorbike of his.

'There's been an accident. Your sister Margaret has vanished from the cross-Channel Jersey ferry, presumably washed overboard during gale-force winds. The coastguards are out trying to find her.'

'Dear God!' Crista whispered, numb from shock.

'Do you have any spirits in the house, Mr Rubin?' the police woman asked. 'Mrs Murray might want a drop.'

'I'll only be a moment,' Max replied, and hurried off.

Crista swallowed hard, and then swallowed again. 'How?' she managed to say at last.

'We've no idea as of yet. Simply that she appears to have vanished overboard, presumably washed off the deck.'

'And Dickie?'

'He's taken it very badly, as you can imagine, and has been sedated. It was he who requested you be notified as soon as possible.'

Max returned with a bottle of whisky and quickly poured Crista a measure. 'Try and swallow some of this,' he said. 'It'll help.'

'Water, Max.'

'Oh, of course.' He hurried off again.

Crista shook her head in bewilderment. How could such a thing have happened to Maggs? It was simply unbelievable.

'As we understand it,' WPC Nolan went on,

'Mr Trippett was seasick and lay down on a bench where he fell asleep. Before he nodded off his wife informed him she was going to the lavatory. The last person to see her was a barman on board who poured her several brandies. According to his testimony she was there one moment, gone the next. It was shortly before the ferry docked that Mr Trippett finally raised the alarm, having been asleep some of that time, and searching high and low for his wife the remainder. The ferry itself was thoroughly searched after it docked and the passengers had disembarked. There was absolutely no sign of Mrs Trippett anywhere.'

Max returned again and Crista took a sip from the glass he handed her.

'I'm terribly sorry,' WPC Nolan said sympathetically. 'This must be awful for you.'

Tears welled in Crista's eyes. 'More awful for Dickie. He idolised Maggs. Positively worshipped her. Has done all the years of their marriage. And before.'

The policewoman produced a pad and jotted down some figures. 'If you ring this number you'll get through to the Plymouth police who are dealing with the matter. I'm sure they'll be most helpful.'

Max accepted the small piece of paper on Crista's behalf.

'You said the coastguards are out looking for her. Does that mean she may still be alive?' Crista asked, her voice shaking.

WPC Nolan glanced at Max, then back at Crista. 'I wouldn't hold out much hope, Mrs Murray. Not in those seas and considering the amount of time she must have been in the water. The coastguards feel it their duty to go out as a matter of course. Miracles do happen, after all.'

Crista drank a little more of the whisky, then put the glass aside. Far from helping, it was just making her feel sick.

'Is there anything else you want to know that I might be able to assist with?' WPC Nolan asked quietly.

Crista shook her head. 'No.'

'Then I'll take my leave of you.'

'I'll see you out,' Max offered, and escorted the policewoman from the room. When he came back a few minutes later Crista had dissolved into floods of tears, her entire body convulsed with grief.

'Hold me, Max. Please just hold me,' she begged.

Max swiftly crossed over, knelt down and put his arms round her.

'Oh, Max,' Crista keened. 'Oh, Max!'

There were tears in his eyes also as he started to rock her gently back and forth.

It took a while but finally Crista regained something of her composure. 'Thanks, Max,' she whispered, wiping her nose with a tissue he'd fetched.

'That's what friends are for, Crista.'

She glanced up at him and smiled, grateful for his presence and the comfort he'd given her. 'I think I'd like a nice cup of tea,' she said. 'And then I'm going to ring that number the WPC wrote down to see if I can speak to Dickie. He might want me there, in which case I'll pack a bag and catch the first available train to Plymouth.' She shook her head. 'Poor Dickie. Poor poor Dickie. He must be in a terrible state. Quite demented.'

'You won't have to catch any train,' Max replied. 'I'll drive you. And willingly so.'

Appreciation glistened in her eyes. 'Thank you, Max.'

'Anything for you, Crista. But let's wait till you speak to Dickie before we make any plans. I suggest you deal with the tea and I'll ring Plymouth police and find out what's what. Is that all right?'

She nodded. 'Fine.'

On impulse he went over and kissed her on the cheek. Then he turned and headed for the telephone, leaving her staring after him.

'I finally got through after several attempts,' Max informed her twenty minutes later. 'Dickie is at the coastguard station waiting for the search boat to return. The police will get in touch with him as soon as they can and ask him to ring here.'

'Did they say how he was?'

'Not too good, according to the person I spoke to. But holding up.'

Crista sighed. 'I suppose all we can do now is wait.'

'Do you think we should let Ez and Gemma at the pub know?'

Crista considered that. 'Let's hang on for a bit until we're absolutely certain. As the WPC said, miracles can happen.'

A woman in the Channel with a gale blowing? Max doubted there would be any miracle. Doubted it very much.

They both started when, at long last, the phone rang. It was almost nine o'clock in the evening.

429

'That should be Dickie,' Crista declared, coming quickly to her feet. Max thought it best he stay where he was as she rushed from the room. Albeit it was getting late he was still prepared to set off for Plymouth that night if it was required.

'Dickie?'

'Crista?'

'Oh, Dickie. Is there any news?'

He sobbed before answering. 'The boat came back half an hour ago. They'd had to give up due to lack of light. They didn't find her. Not even her body.'

Crista closed her eyes for the briefest of seconds. 'How are you?'

'I just . . . I just . . .' He broke down and started to cry.

'Would you like me to come down and be with you? Max has offered to drive me there.'

Dickie took a deep breath. 'No need for that, Crista. I'll be all right.'

'Are you sure?'

'The coastguards have been ever so kind. I'm staying the night with one of them not too far from here. The doctor gave me a sedative earlier because I was so distraught, which made me sleep for a while. I kipped at the same chap's house then, with his wife looking after me.'

That eased Crista's mind a little. 'So when will you come home?'

'Not for a few days. There are things to do here, forms to be filled and all sorts. Also the police want to interview me again. Go over what I've already told them.'

'Have you any idea what happened, Dickie?'

'None at all.'

'We had a policewoman here who said you'd fallen asleep on a bench while Maggs went to the toilet. And that was the last you saw of her.'

'Apparently she had a few drinks in one of the bars and then must have gone out on deck. God knows why. Maybe she wanted some air as it was rather stuffy inside. There was also the smell of sick everywhere as so many people had thrown up due to the weather. It truly was horrendous.' Dickie stopped talking and began to cry again. 'It's a nightmare, Crista,' he choked at last. 'That's what it is, a nightmare. I keep praying I'll wake up and everything will be as it was, that I'm dreaming all this. Only it's real.'

Crista wiped away her own tears. 'Is there anything at all we can do?'

'Nothing. But thank you for asking.'

'She was my sister, Dickie, as well as your wife.'

'I know that.'

'Shall I tell Ez and Gemma what's happened?'

'Please.'

'Max and I will go down shortly.'

'Thanks, Crista.'

'And you're absolutely certain you don't want me there?'

'I can cope. Somehow anyway. Now I'd better go.'

'Bye for now, Dickie.'

'Bye, Crista. Say a prayer for Maggs tonight.'

'I will. That's a promise.'

And then he hung up.

Ez and Gemma were stunned when Crista broke the news to them after the last customer had gone.

'Washed overboard?' Ez repeated, eyes wide with shock.

'That's what they think. Apparently a terrible gale was blowing at the time.'

'But why would she go out on deck in that weather?' Gemma queried with a frown.

'According to Dickie it was stuffy in the saloon with a smell of sick everywhere. He thinks she merely stepped outside to get a breath of fresh air. And that was that.'

'No witnesses, I take it?' Ez asked.

Crista shook her head.

Gemma slid from her stool. 'I need a drink. And I mean a stiff one. Anyone else?'

Ez said she'd have one, Max also. Crista declined with a wave of her hand. .

'And Uncle Dickie's staying in Plymouth for a couple of days?' Ez queried.

'So he told me. Forms to be filled out, and so on.'

'How is he?'

'As you'd imagine. That was a real love match as far as Dickie was concerned. I doubt he'll ever be the same again.'

'I'll get these,' Max declared, sliding a fiver on to the bar.

Gemma hesitated for a moment, then accepted the money and rang up the till.

'What a horrible way to die,' Ez reflected morosely. 'All on your own, drowning in the middle of the Channel.'

'It doesn't bear thinking about,' Crista croaked. 'I can only hope and pray she went quickly.'

Gemma sat again, having poured herself a large gin

and tonic. 'Maggs and I were great pals at school. Abigail Woolocombe too. You wouldn't believe some of the things we got up to. Talk about being naughty! Tame by modern standards, I suppose, but outrageous way back then.'

An entire hour was spent in reminiscing before Crista and Max broke up the gathering, saying they had to head home.

As they walked up the road, for once not giving a damn who saw, Crista slipped an arm round Max's.

Crista came groggily awake when there was a knock on her bedroom door. 'Max?'

'Are you decent? Can I come in?'

'Wait a moment,' she called out in confusion. Sitting up in bed she drew a little shawl, which she normally wore when reading, over her shoulders. 'It's all right now.'

The door swung open to reveal Max carrying a tray. 'I thought you might like breakfast in bed for a change. It was a late night after all. Here you are.' He placed the tray carefully on the bed.

Crista stared in astonishment at the boiled egg, toast, jam and honey before her. 'No tea?' she teased.

'Now, Crista, I know you never drink until after you've eaten. I've sat and watched you do it many times. So I'll bring the tea through when you've finished that lot.'

Crista was deeply touched. 'You shouldn't be doing this, Max,' she chided. 'You're the PG. If anyone gets breakfast in bed it should be me bringing it to you.'

He laughed. 'Stop complaining, woman. As the saying goes, never look a gift horse in the mouth. Or, in this instance, breakfast. Now you tuck in and give me a shout when you're ready for that tea.' He was at the door when he briefly halted, a twinkle in his eye. 'Nice nightdress, Crista. Very pretty. It suits you.'

She couldn't help colouring. 'Get away with you, Max Rubin.' Then, hesitantly, 'But thanks for the compliment.'

She glanced down at the nightie after he'd gone. Yes, it was a rather pretty one, she decided. Smiling, she picked up her knife and sliced open the egg. It was done exactly as she liked.

There again, she'd have expected nothing less from Max. He was that sort of man.

For some reason most customers in a pub fail to realise that everything said at the bar can be heard behind it. And customers at the bar seem to forget the presence of those serving, only remembering about them again when they wish to order. Those were two facts that Whispering Smith was suddenly confronted with several days after Maggs had disappeared and word of her demise had got round.

Whispering broke off his conversation with Percy Matford when he was confronted by a blazing-eyed Ez.

'How dare you!' she exploded. 'How fucking dare you!'

Whispering blinked nervously. 'Dare what?'

'I heard what you just said.'

The colour drained from Whispering's beer-flushed face.

'Oh shit,' Percy Matford muttered, wondering if he too was going to cop it.

Other customers had stopped to turn their attention to what was happening at the end of the bar.

A finger stabbed almost into Whispering's face. 'You just said that Aunty Maggs probably wasn't washed overboard but fell over while pissed as a rat. Your exact words. Pissed as a rat.'

'It was only a joke, Ez,' Whispering gulped.

'What's going on here?' Gemma demanded, bustling up.

Ez explained.

Gemma was incredulous at Whispering's lack of sensitivity, and downright nastiness, in making such a public accusation. In Maggs's own pub too!

'It was only a joke, Gemma,' Whispering repeated, cravenness in his voice.

'In ultimate bad taste.'

He pulled a face indicating his agreement.

'I think you'd better go. The pair of you,' Gemma ordered. Then, after a look at Ez, 'And not come back, *ever*. The pair of you are banned for life.'

'You can't mean that, Gemma,' Whispering protested.

'I bloody well do.'

'You're not in a position to ban anyone for life anyway.'

'Oh no?'

'I shouldn't think so,' Percy chipped in ineffectually.

'Then I shall tell Dickie what you said when he gets back and you can take the matter up with him if you wish.'

'Oh, don't do that, Gemma! Please?' Whispering begged. 'Dickie would go berserk.'

'Damn right he would.'

'Can't we apologise?' Percy asked hopefully. 'Besides, it wasn't me said that. It was him.'

'Thank you, *friend*,' Whispering snarled at his drinking chum.

'Well I don't want to be sodding banned for life. I like this pub. You were the one with the big gob.'

'And you agreed with him,' Ez declared. 'I heard you.'

Percy dropped his head in shame. 'It was only pub talk,' he said. 'You know what it's like when you get a few drinks inside you. You can go a bit over the top.'

'Exactly.' Whispering nodded.

'A woman is dead,' Gemma reminded him. 'And you think that's funny? And what if what you said got round the village as being true? What then? How do you think Dickie would feel?'

'I never thought,' Whispering mumbled.

'Tough. Now get out the pair of you. And don't ever come back.'

'Please?' Percy begged.

'Out!'

Gemma and Ez watched the unhappy duo trail disconsolately from the pub, Percy stopping at the door for one last glance round. Then he too was gone.

The trouble was, Ez reflected, they might well have been right. Who was to know what state Maggs was in at the time, except perhaps Uncle Dickie? And if she was drunk then a pound to a penny he'd never admit to the fact.

No, the mistake Whispering and Percy had made was uttering the possibility in public, giving it potential credence.

436

Hell mend them, as Maggs herself would have said. Hell mend the pair of them.

Max manoeuvred his way through the crowd to where Crista was standing alone. It was the first chance he'd had to speak to her privately since leaving the church.

He smiled. 'How are you?'

'Oh, there you are, Max. I was looking round for you.'

'I've been about. Chatting here and there, getting to know people I didn't.'

Crista nodded to the far end of the pub where an accordionist was belting out all the old favourites: 'The White Cliffs Of Dover', 'Roll Out The Barrel', and so on. 'What do you think of the entertainment? For a wake, that is.'

'I approve. Dickie is right in saying we should be celebrating Maggs's life with fun and laughter. He's convinced that's exactly what she'd have wanted. Everyone to have a good time and go home well oiled, as he put it.'

Crista grinned. 'Well, he knew Maggs better than anyone. So I agree, he probably is right.'

'What did you make of the service?'

Crista thought about that. 'The vicar spoke well, and there was an excellent turn-out. Nice things were said about Maggs. It was as good, if that's the right word, as these things can be.' Her mood darkened a little. 'If anything upset me it was the fact there was no body to mourn, no body to bury or cremate afterwards. It did seem odd. Strange.'

'I can understand that,' Max said sympathetically.

'Death by misadventure, according to the inquest.

437

No one's fault. Maggs just happened to be in the wrong place at the wrong time, that's all.'

'She got a lovely day for it,' Max mused. 'The sun was shining and there wasn't a cloud in the sky.'

'Yes, that was a bonus, I have to admit.'

'And Dickie held up well. Far better than I thought he would.'

'Me too. I expected him to go to pieces, but he surprised me. And now look at him!'

They both glanced over to where Dickie was busily serving drinks behind the bar, chatting away to customers.

'I don't think we should be fooled, though,' Crista said quietly. 'It's just an act to get through the day. It'll be different when everyone's gone and he's alone in bed.'

That statement brought back painful memories for Max, remembering the day he'd buried his beloved Rebekah, and the following night.

Crista suddenly stared him straight in the eyes. 'You've been a brick over all this, Max. An absolute brick. To be honest, I don't know what I'd have done without you.'

He smiled and, reaching out, took her hand in his and squeezed it. Nor did he let her go for quite some time.

A fact that didn't go unnoticed by the ever-watchful Sally.

Chapter 27

'Honestly, I don't know how you manage to keep your house so neat and tidy,' Sally declared. 'It's a mystery to me. There again, I prefer things a little more homely.'

Ez glanced at her sister, highly amused. 'It's quite simple, Sally. The answer is called daily housework. You must have heard of it?'

Sally scowled. 'Are you having a go at me?'

'Not in the least. You asked a question, I answered it. That's all.'

Sally settled further back into her chair. 'So what did you make of the wake?'

'Was all right I suppose.'

'I thought having an accordionist there was in very poor taste. He made it more like a party than a wake.'

'That's what Uncle Dickie insisted on. He was convinced it's what Aunt Maggs would have wished.'

Sally sniffed. 'Well I wasn't impressed. Not one bit.'

'You seemed to rather enjoy yourself as I recall.'

'I'd hardly say that!' Sally snapped back. 'I was simply entering into the spirit of the thing.'

Ez didn't reply, just smiled.

'And what about Mum and that Jew boy? All lovey dovey they were. I couldn't help but notice them holding hands. At their age too!'

Ah, Ez thought. Now they were getting down to the reason for Sally's visit. It was to bitch about Crista.

'Well?' Sally demanded.

'I consider Max to be an extremely nice man. Very pleasant. As for being Jewish, so what? This isn't Nazi Germany, you know. We don't gas them here.'

Sally flushed bright red. 'I didn't mean it like that.'

'Then how did you mean it?'

'Oh, come on, Ez, holding hands at their age. How embarrassing can you get?'

'I don't see that's embarrassing. And why should age have anything to do with it? Just because Mum's relatively old, or getting on as I prefer to call it, doesn't mean she can't have feelings like other people. Besides, it was her sister's wake and Max was probably just being supportive. Bucking her up.'

Sally frowned. 'Do you really think that's all it was?'

Ez shrugged. 'And what if it wasn't? Would that be so awful?'

Sally was visibly shocked. 'What about Dad's memory? Our father.'

'Listen,' Ez said patiently. 'She's been rattling around that big house all by herself for years. Now she's got company there, someone to look after and care for. I haven't seen her so happy or carefree since Dad died. You should be pleased for her, not upset.'

'But I am upset. What do we know about this Max Rubin? Absolutely nothing.'

'That's not true,' Ez pointed out. 'He's retired, moving down here from London, and was a jeweller

440

by trade. I'd say that was fairly comprehensive myself. What do you want for God's sake, his birth certificate along with letters of recommendation?'

'They say he's well off,' Sally declared, changing tack.

'So I believe. He had his own jeweller's shop which he sold. And a house. So he can't be short of a bob or two, can he?'

'It hardly puts him in Mum's financial league.'

Ez's eyes narrowed. 'What are you driving at?'

'Do you think he might be some sort of gold-digger? Latching on to Mum because he thinks she's a good thing?'

Ez couldn't help laughing. 'I simply can't believe that.'

'But it could be true?'

'You mean he came all the way down to Devon simply to get hold of a rich widow? I'd imagine he'd have far better pickings in London if that was his aim.'

'Perhaps it wasn't his intention. But lodging with Mum, and realising her situation, might have given him the idea.'

'I doubt it very much. He just isn't like that.'

'Well I'm not so sure. The whole thing stinks as far as I'm concerned. Very much so.'

'You're letting your imagination run away with you, Sally. Anyway, you forget Mum in this equation. She's more than capable of looking after herself. You should know that.'

Sally shifted uncomfortably in her chair. 'She is getting on, don't forget. Perhaps she's lost her judgement.'

'Mum lost her judgement!' Ez was incredulous.

441

'Her mind is as sharp as it's always been. If there was anything iffy about Max Rubin she'd have cottoned on long before now. You're worrying about nothing, believe me.'

Sally's expression indicated she remained unconvinced. 'Say what you like, it still worries me.'

It suddenly dawned on Ez what this was really all about. 'It's not Mum you're worried about, it's your inheritance. Isn't it?'

'Don't be ridiculous,' Sally retorted sharply. 'That never even crossed my mind.'

'No?'

'No it did not.'

But Ez knew her sister only too well. It wasn't like Sally to show concern for others, even her own mother, without an ulterior motive. She was anxious about what would be coming to her when Crista finally passed on.

Disgust welled up in Ez. That and contempt. 'I don't know why you're so bothered anyway,' she lied. 'You're not even speaking to Mum.'

'That's to teach her a lesson. She shouldn't go poking her nose into my affairs.'

'She didn't poke her nose into your affairs, Sally. You asked her for money and for once she refused. And rightly so in my humble opinion. It's high time you stopped squandering money and learnt to make ends meet like the rest of us.'

Sally came abruptly to her feet. 'I'm not staying here to be insulted. I'm off.'

'Suit yourself. But what I just said is the truth.'

Sally didn't reply, merely flounced out of the room. The front door banged shut behind her.

Ez sighed. There were times when she could quite cheerfully have wrung her sister's neck.

Selfish to the core, Ez thought. That was Sally.

It was Nick himself who answered their knock. 'Nan!' he exclaimed when he saw who was standing there.

'Well, I did warn you I'd call in from time to time. And here I am.'

Nick's face was a picture, such was his surprise. 'How are you?' he stammered.

'Very well thank you. Aren't you going to ask us in?'

Nick's eyes flicked to Max, and then back to Crista. 'The place is a mess,' he whispered. 'A complete tip.'

'I wasn't expecting anything else where six young lads are living together. I'd still like to come in.'

'Of course, Nan. You'll just have to take us as you find us.'

He reluctantly escorted Crista and Max through to the living room where he introduced them to Malcolm and Tristram, the only two of his housemates who were presently at home.

Crista inwardly shuddered at the state of the place. It would have been the understatement of the year to describe it as untidy, on top of which it was absolutely filthy, with dirt everywhere. The room positively reeked of old sweat and cigarette smoke.

'How about a cup of coffee, Nan?'

'No thank you,' she replied hastily.

'Mr Rubin?'

'Please, Nick. I believe I could use one.' He was braver than Crista.

Nick vanished, leaving Crista and Max to make

small talk with the housemates. At the same time, Crista was surreptitiously looking around, searching for anything which might indicate drugs were being used. She failed to spot a single item that might be incriminating.

'Can I use your toilet?' she asked Nick when he returned with the coffee.

Was that panic she saw in his eyes? She wasn't sure. It might have been.

'Surely. This way, Nan.'

When they reached the bathroom door he smiled apologetically. 'There isn't a lock, I'm afraid. It got broken. But don't worry, I'll make sure no one disturbs you.'

'Thanks, Nick.'

She slipped inside and closed the door firmly behind her. The bath was half filled with water in which various bits of clothing were floating, the preponderance appearing to be socks and underpants. Her eyebrows arced in surprise when she saw a bra lying to one side.

She searched thoroughly and quickly, but to her relief found nothing apart from a packet of unopened johnnies, which she considered entirely reasonable. She remembered to flush the toilet, as if she'd used it, before rejoining the others.

'I've just told Nick that we were hoping to take him out for a meal, and he's said he'd love to come,' Max informed her.

'Good.'

Malcolm and Tristram appeared crestfallen that they hadn't been invited too. For a moment Crista was tempted to do so, but resisted. She wanted it to be just the three of them.

'Can you recommend anywhere, Nick?' Max inquired when they were outside.

'There's an Indian just a few minutes away. We like it and go there when we can.'

'Crista?' Max queried.

She hesitated. 'I've never eaten Indian food,' she confessed. 'Is it awfully hot?'

'Then you must try it,' Max declared with a smile. 'And it doesn't have to be hot. Nick and I will guide you through the menu.'

Crista wondered what she'd let herself in for as they made their way up the street, but as it turned out she thoroughly enjoyed the meal, and Max promised to take her to an Indian in Exeter he'd heard good things about.

Max placed the port and lemon in front of Crista and sat facing her, his own a large malt whisky. They were in the bar of the hotel where they were staying, having decided beforehand that a trip to Bristol and back again in the same day was a little too much for Max, especially as they'd be returning at night. Max had therefore booked them into two double rooms, something they'd intentionally not mentioned to Nick who believed they were heading back to Ford when they'd left him.

'Well?' Max queried. 'What's the verdict?'

'I think the way he wolfed down that meal told me everything I wanted to know,' Crista replied. 'They don't have that sort of appetite when on drugs.'

Max nodded his agreement.

'Nor was there anything incriminating in the house that I could see. Of course I didn't get to look in his bedroom. It just didn't seem necessary somehow.'

'The other two lads didn't worry me either,' Max declared. 'No tell-tale signs that I could spot. Their skins were healthy enough, for students that is, and their eyes were clear. So I think Nick has kept his word and you've nothing to be concerned about. Don't you?'

'That was my judgement as well, I'm happy to say.' Crista picked up her port and drank some. 'Mmm!' she murmured appreciatively. 'This is lovely.'

'Glad you like it. The bottle had a particularly good label I was pleased to note.'

'I can't tell you how relieved I am about Nick,' Crista declared. 'I was certain he'd keep his word to me. But there again, you never know.'

'Especially where drugs are involved.' Max nodded.

'Exactly.'

Crista suddenly started in her chair when there was an enormous crack of thunder. 'Dear God, listen to that!' she exclaimed.

'Sounds like we might be in for a bit of a storm.' As if to confirm Max's words rain began hammering against a nearby window.

'Thank goodness we decided to stay overnight,' Crista commented. 'It would have been awful you driving home in this.'

Max couldn't have agreed more.

They remained in the bar for another half an hour before going upstairs, where they agreed on a time to meet for breakfast.

'Thank you again for everything, Max,' Crista said earnestly at the door of her room, which was next to his.

'My pleasure that I was able to help.'

'You are a sweetie.' And Crista vanished inside.

As the hours ticked slowly by the storm became even more violent, crack after crack tearing the night sky. Occasionally the cracks and booms were interspersed with jagged flashes of lightning.

Crista tried her best to sleep, but couldn't. Ever since childhood she'd been terrified of thunder and lightning, and this was, by far, the worst she'd ever experienced.

By three in the morning she was a gibbering wreck, her nerves completely shot. And still the storm showed no signs of abating.

Max was woken by an urgent knocking. Getting out of bed, he first flicked on the bedside light, then shrugged into his dressing gown.

'Who is it?'

'It's me, Crista. Will you let me in?'

He unlocked the door and opened it, and she instantly hurried past him into the room.

'What's wrong, Crista?'

Her entire body was shaking as she explained in a tremulous voice.

'Oh, Crista,' he said, taking her into his arms and holding her tight.

After a few moments, with the comfort of his arms about her, she began to calm down. 'Can I stay here for the rest of the night, Max? I won't bother you.'

'Of course you can, Crista.'

'I'll try and sleep in the chair. And I might be able

447

to knowing you're here in the room with me. That I'm not alone.'

'I'm not having that,' he replied. 'You'll sleep in the bed and I'll have the chair.'

'I can't do that, Max.'

'You will,' he declared in a no-nonsense voice. 'And I'll hear no more on the subject.'

A hint of moisture crept into her eyes. 'You're ever so kind to me.'

Max fought back the urge to stroke her hair. 'Enough of that. Into bed now.'

'Take a couple of the blankets, Max. You must keep warm.'

'There's a spare in the cupboard. That'll do me. Once I'm wrapped in that I'll be warm as toast.'

'Sure?'

'Absolutely.'

'Oh!' Crista exclaimed when there was yet another deafening crack of thunder.

'Into bed now. And snuggle down.'

He watched her pad across the room and slip under the covers. 'OK?'

'OK.'

He found the spare blanket, which wasn't a particularly thick one, and arranged himself in the chair, after which Crista clicked out the bedside light.

'Night, Max.'

'Night, Crista.'

Crista had dozed off, but woke to hear Max shifting restlessly in the chair. It must be ever so uncomfortable, she thought. He'd be stiff and sore in the morning. And all because of her.

'Max?'

'Yes, Crista?'

'Listen, this is silly. We're both grown-ups, after all. Why don't you get into bed with me and we can both be comfortable?'

He didn't reply.

'Max?'

'What about your reputation? I know how high a regard you have for that and the last thing I want to do is compromise it.'

She had to smile. He truly was a sweetie. 'Who'll ever know? I certainly won't be telling anyone. Will you?'

'Of course not.'

'Then where's the harm? I'll feel an awful lot better if you do.'

'Are you absolutely certain about this?'

'Absolutely. Now come on.'

He loomed out of the darkness and next moment was in bed alongside her.

'I thought I'd be warm with the blanket round me, but I wasn't. I was freezing.'

'Then we've done the right thing.'

'Goodnight again, Crista.'

'Goodnight again, Max.'

It was the first time she'd been in bed with anyone since Jamie died. It was odd, she thought. Especially after all these years. Odd, but comforting at the same time.

She liked it.

'I'll tell you one thing,' Max declared at breakfast next morning.

'What's that?'

'This egg is nice, but not a patch on those you serve up at home. Doesn't even begin to come close.'

That domesticity pleased her. A lot.

'How's your fish?' he asked.

'Very enjoyable.'

'Good.'

They sounded just like an old married couple, she thought, and smiled.

'Penny for them?'

Crista shook her head. 'Personal.'

'Oh, sorry.'

She abruptly changed her mind. She would tell him. 'I was just thinking we sound just like an old married couple the way we sometimes talk.'

He regarded her with amusement. 'The thought has crossed my mind also. Not this morning, but other times.'

'And?'

'And what?' He frowned.

'What do you feel about that?'

'How do *you* feel?'

Crista laughed. 'Play fair. I asked first.'

His expression became contemplative. 'I'm not sure I should say in case you misinterpret my meaning.'

'Oh?'

He picked a slice of toast from the rack and began slowly buttering it.

'Max?'

'It makes me feel very good inside.'

'And?'

'Happy.'

That surprised her, for being with him made her feel that way too. 'I see,' she murmured.

'It doesn't seem right when I'm not with you, when we aren't together. As if something is missing.'

Crista reached for the coffee pot. 'Top up?'

'Please.' He studied her intently as she poured. 'And what about you?'

'What about me?'

'How do you feel? It's your turn now.'

Crista topped up her own cup. 'I think we get along terribly well,' she replied at last.

Max nodded his agreement.

'And . . .' She trailed off, wondering if it was wise to articulate the next bit.

Max ate his toast and waited in silence.

'I never realised how lonely I was until you arrived at my house. Not right at that moment, of course, but as our relationship developed. As we became friends.'

'My sentiments precisely.'

'Were you lonely too?'

'Very.'

'I suppose that's what happens when you've been in an extremely close marriage,' she said quietly.

'I suppose.'

'As I was.'

'As we both were.'

Crista suddenly didn't want any more breakfast and pushed her plate away.

Max didn't know how it had happened, but the mood between them was suddenly broken.

'We can hit the road as soon as you wish?' He smiled.

Crista didn't reply to that. Just nodded.

★ ★ ★

Gemma found Dickie sitting at the kitchen table staring into space. She noted he hadn't yet shaved.

'How are you this morning?' she asked in a cheery voice.

'Fine, thanks,' he replied in what was almost a whisper. He didn't glance in her direction but continued to stare into space.

'It's almost time to open up. Do you want me to do it?'

'Please, Ez.'

'It's Gemma, Dickie. Not Ez.'

'Sorry. My mind's elsewhere.'

She could see that. 'Would you like some tea or anything?'

He shook his head.

'Nothing at all?'

'No thanks. I'll get myself something when I want it. You open up and I'll be with you shortly.'

'You don't have to. Have you forgotten Ez is on with me?'

'Oh, so she is,' he replied in a faraway voice. 'Good. No need for me to hurry then.'

Or get dressed, Gemma thought, for he was still in his pyjamas and dressing gown.

When Gemma left him a few minutes later he was still staring blankly into space.

'I'm really worried about Dickie, you know,' Gemma confided to Ez shortly afterwards.

'He's been worrying me too. He's become all withdrawn, and . . . well, peculiar.'

Gemma gave a final wipe to a glass and put it away. They'd had customers in on opening, but it had now

452

gone quiet, giving them a chance to chat. 'I was wondering,' she mused darkly. 'Do you think he might be having a nervous breakdown? It is possible, after all, having lost his wife.'

Ez thought about that. 'I'm not sure.' She frowned. 'But if we think he is should we speak to the doctor?'

Gemma swore when she dropped another glass she'd just picked up, though luckily it didn't break. 'I'm all fingers and thumbs this morning,' she muttered.

'Unlike you.'

Gemma retrieved the glass and began to rewash it. 'My mind's just not on the job, that's all. It's thinking and worrying about him upstairs that's doing it. I've known Dickie a long time, don't forget. Always liked him. Always had something of a soft spot for him really.'

That was news to Ez.

'I just hate to see him as he is,' Gemma went on. 'If only there was something I could do to make him snap out of it.'

'It would help if he came down and worked. But he's hardly been behind the bar since the service.'

'True on both counts,' Gemma acknowledged. 'He's up there now, unshaven and unbathed, sitting staring into space. Thinking about Maggs no doubt.'

'No doubt,' Ez agreed. 'What about if I got my Mum round? She might be able to get through to him.'

'That's a possibility.' Gemma nodded. 'But let's leave that idea for a bit yet. Same with speaking to the doctor. Let's hope he can come out of this off his own bat.'

Further conversation was halted when a customer appeared and Ez moved down the bar to serve him.

A dull-eyed Dickie opened the tallboy drawer and took out one of Maggs's nightdresses. Crossing to the bed he sat cradling it in his lap.

After a few minutes he raised the nightie to his nose and smelt the scent of her which still clung to it. Faint now after washing, but still there none the less.

'Oh, Maggs,' he whispered. 'My darling Maggs.'

Dropping his head he began to weep silently.

Chapter 28

'So, how are you getting on, Pete?' Max asked. He hadn't visited the bungalow for a while.

'Fine, as you can see. We'll be done in another couple of weeks and then the decorators can move in and do their stuff.'

Move in, Max thought. At this rate it wouldn't be long before he was doing the same. Part of him was looking forward to that, another part was not. For moving into the bungalow meant leaving Crista's, and what a wrench that was going to be.

He decided it was time to ask her the favour he had in mind.

'Another glass of wine?' Max inquired halfway through the evening meal.

'Yes please.'

Max rose from his chair and poured, then topped up his own glass as well.

'I was a bit wary to begin with, but I'm beginning to enjoy having wine when eating.' Crista smiled at him.

'Only beginning?' he teased.

'You know what I mean,' she retorted lightly.

How easy it was to be with her, Max reflected. How easy and . . . satisfying. Yes, that was the word. Satisfying. Relaxing too. He'd certainly come to think of Crista's home as his own.

'I had a letter from Nick this morning,' she went on.

'And how is he?'

'He swears still on the straight and narrow. Don't ask how, but I somehow know he's telling the truth.'

Max nodded his approval. 'Nice young man. Let's hope it stays that way.'

'Amen.'

Max had a sip of wine, regarding Crista over the rim of his glass. 'I have a favour to ask,' he announced.

'Oh? What's that?'

'I was at the bungalow earlier and, according to Pete, the building work is almost complete. It's time for me to start thinking about what I'm going to put inside. As I've mentioned in the past, apart from a few bits and pieces, mainly from my workshop, I'm going to buy all new.'

Crista nodded. She recalled his saying so.

'And I was wondering if you'd help me choose those things?'

Crista had suspected this was in the wind from several hints he'd recently dropped. 'I see,' she murmured.

'You know, furniture, carpets and the like. What do you say?'

'I'm not sure.'

'Why not? You'd be helping me a lot, Crista. I doubt I'd be very good at that sort of business anyway.

456

What will be needed is a woman's hand. Most definitely.'

It amused her to witness the puppyish look that had come across his face. Amused, and thrilled her at the same time. 'What if my taste isn't the same as yours?'

'I don't see any problem there. I'm sure it will be.'

'And what if it isn't?'

'Then we'll compromise. Just like that "old married couple" you were on about a while ago.'

Crista considered his request. It was a tall order, and could take some time to accomplish. Time she had plenty of, she reminded herself. None the less, this wasn't a decision to be taken lightly.

'I must admit I'm extremely flattered,' she prevaricated.

'Then you'll do it?'

'Hold on, Max. Not so fast.'

His face dropped. 'I'm sort of counting on you, Crista. Truly I am. I'd be terrible at picking anything. I'm certain of it.'

Crista smiled. 'You're trying to blackmail me into feeling sorry for you, Max Rubin.'

'I'm nothing of the sort,' he protested.

'Oh yes you are. Coming the little boy lost act, as if you were ever that.'

He took a deep breath. 'All right. But it would be lovely to have you there by my side. Adding that woman's hand I spoke of. And to be honest, and this is no exaggeration, I have awful colour sense. Matching this and that, contrasting one colour with another. If I'm left to my own devices the inside of the bungalow will probably end up looking like a bordello.'

Crista arced an eyebrow. 'And how would you know what the inside of a bordello looks like?'

'I don't,' he replied hastily. 'But what I imagine one must look like.'

She came to a decision, thinking it would be an exciting project to be involved with. 'Would money be an object?'

'None at all. Within reason, that is. But I would want everything to be of the very best quality.'

That excited her even further. Money no object! What woman wouldn't jump at this sort of chance? Not many she could think of. If, indeed, any.

'Well?' Max pleaded.

'When shall we start?'

His face lit up with pleasure. 'Thanks, Crista. I knew I could rely on you.'

'So when shall we start?'

'How about first thing Monday morning?'

'Suits me.'

'Then it's agreed.'

She nodded. 'It's agreed.'

Picking up their glasses they both drank to it.

Dickie suddenly blinked out of his reverie and focused on Gemma, who was doing his ironing. 'It's very kind of you to do that for me,' he acknowledged.

'Well we can't have you going down to the bar looking as though you'd slept in your clothes, can we?'

Dickie gave her a soft smile. 'Many women would. It's hardly part of your job, after all.'

'Well I'm not many women, Dickie Trippett. Besides, we've been friends a long time. Right?'

'A long time,' he echoed.

Gemma placed the iron on its end and held up the shirt she'd just finished. 'How's that then?'

'Looks perfect to me.'

'Good. You can wear it when you go downstairs.'

An introspective glint came into his eyes. 'Maggs wasn't much of an ironer. In fact she hated doing it.'

'I don't exactly love ironing myself. It's simply one of those things that has to be done.'

'Maggs,' Dickie murmured, and shook his head.

Gemma stared hard at him. 'She's gone, Dickie, and that's something you've simply got to come to terms with. Meanwhile, and I'm sure she'd agree, you've got the rest of your life to be getting on with, and making the most of.'

Gemma knew she was playing with fire, and risking alienating him with what she was going to say next. 'I don't think Maggs would be all that impressed to see what you've become. Sitting around, day after day, moping and crying. I rather imagine she'd despise you for that. I can just hear her telling you to get off your lazy arse and stop bloody skiving. You've had your time of grief, plenty of it in my opinion, so now get on with it.'

'Those are harsh words, Gemma,' he croaked.

'That's as may be. But they're true ones, and in your heart of hearts you know it.'

Dickie hung his head and for a few moments Gemma thought he was going to burst into tears. But he didn't.

'She was my life, Gemma,' he choked. 'My life.'

'*Was*, Dickie. Past tense. Hard as it may be to accept, that's the case.'

459

'You're being cruel.'

'Am I? Perhaps. But sometimes you have to be cruel to be kind. And this is one of those occasions. Besides, Maggs was never your entire life. The pub here is a huge part of it. Come on, try and deny that?'

He looked up and stared at her, his brow slowly furrowing. 'The pub?'

'Yes, Dickie, the sodding pub. Your other great commitment. This place that you've cherished as if it was a human being instead of cob and thatch. This place you've nurtured down the years as if it was your own flesh and blood. Your child even.'

Dickie nodded. 'You're right, Gemms. Absolutely right.'

'And now that child needs you more than ever. So what are you going to do about it?'

An expression of determination crept over Dickie's face. 'Look after it, of course.'

'Then get off your backside and do so. Get back to work properly.'

He took a deep breath. 'A shave and bath first, I think. Then downstairs.'

'The reordering needs doing. Plus other paperwork that's been stacking up because it needs your personal attention. And last, but hardly least, the customers have been missing you. A landlord's place is behind the bar during opening hours, as you well know.'

Dickie suddenly smiled. Going to Gemma he kissed her on the cheek. 'Thanks, Gemms.'

'Thanks yourself. Now hop to it. I want to see the old Dickie Trippett in action before the hour's out or I'll want to know why.'

'He'll be there, Gemma. I promise you,' Dickie declared, and strode resolutely from the room.

Gemma let out a great sigh of relief. Her tongue-lashing had worked, or seemed to. For the time being at least.

It was a start. Hopefully, a new beginning.

'Gold-coloured curtains.' Max beamed at the assistant, who immediately replied she'd fetch some materials right away.

Crista groaned inwardly, waiting for the girl to move off before she spoke.

'Max, if I hadn't known you were Jewish I certainly would by now.'

He stared at her in puzzlement. 'How so?'

'Gold this, gold that. You want everything gold-coloured. It would be like living in the middle of Fort Knox.'

'You don't approve, then. But why does it show I'm Jewish?'

'I have it on good authority that Jews love gold, gold, gold. That the insides of their houses scream it at you. Far be it from me to criticise, but it is a bit over the top wouldn't you say?'

'I hadn't thought of it that way, Crista.' He frowned.

'It's desperately trying to impress, Max. Look at me. See how successful I am. I'm worth a fortune! Tasteless, Max, that and vulgar in my humble opinion.'

He blushed. 'Sorry.'

'I think you should try and be a little more subtle in your colour schemes. Have more variety.'

'So what do you suggest?'

She touched him lightly on the hand. 'You're not upset, are you? I'd hate to give offence.'

Max smiled. 'You haven't upset me, Crista. I don't think you could. And remember, that's why I asked you along. To keep me right.'

'Good. At least I won't have to wear sunglasses every time I come and visit you now.'

Max threw back his head and laughed, thinking that very funny.

When the assistant returned with rolls of various gold materials Crista told her they'd changed their minds.

It was the talk of the pub. The landlord was back to his old self again, always on parade during opening hours, laughing, joking with the customers; in other words business had resumed as normal.

Ez shook her head in amazement as she watched Dickie in action, the wreck he'd become after Maggs's demise apparently no more.

'I can't imagine what happened to change him so quickly,' she said to Gemma.

'I had a word.'

Ez turned to her. 'You?'

'That's right. I simply told him a few home truths, that's all.'

'Well, whatever you said seems to have done the job.'

Gemma smiled. 'It does, doesn't it.'

'You're to be congratulated.'

'Thank you.'

'Would you care to tell me what you said? I'm fascinated.'

Gemma thought about that. 'I think it should remain between Dickie and me. It was rather personal, after all.'

Ez heard something in Gemma's voice that made her wonder, especially since Gemma had already confessed to always having had a soft spot for her uncle. If she was right it would be a turn-up for the book. And one she certainly wouldn't disapprove of. But it was early days yet. Far too soon after Maggs's death. Far too soon.

But who knew what the future held?

'Am I interrupting, Mum?' Ez asked.

'Not at all. I was just sketching.'

That took Ez aback. 'Sketching! Since when did you take up art, Mum?'

'Would you like a coffee?'

Ez shook her head. 'I've not long had one.'

Crista considered having one herself, then thought better of it. She was trying to lose weight and couldn't drink tea or coffee unless it had sugar in it.

'It's not art, dear,' she explained. 'I'm trying to design a garden for Max. A small garden, which is all he wants. And deciding where to position bushes and trees to provide something of a windbreak for the bungalow. Sarah's Portion can catch a lot of wind during the autumn and winter so I'm trying to shield the house from the worst of it.'

'I see.'

'Max has asked me to help with furnishing and generally doing out the house, a woman's hand as he calls it. Including the garden seems a natural extension of that to me.'

'I'm sure you'll make a good job of all of it, Mum. You always do when you put your mind to something.'

The compliment pleased Crista. 'I wouldn't go that far, but I try my best.'

Ez pulled out a packet of cigarettes and lit up.

'There's an ashtray on the mantelpiece,' Crista pointed out.

Ez rose to get it.

'So how's Sally,' Crista casually inquired. 'Have you seen her?'

'Back along. She's fine.'

'And Daniel?'

'Still careering round on his motorbike. He'll get himself killed one of these days if he's not careful.'

Crista's expression became grim. She desperately hoped that would never happen. 'Did Sally mention me when you spoke?'

'She did, in fact.'

'And?'

'She's worried about you and Max becoming so close, if you want to know the truth.'

'Is she now. And why's that?'

Ez fidgeted before replying. 'I don't want to tell tales out of school, Mum.'

'Then don't.'

'It's just . . .'

Crista waited patiently for Ez to go on.

'It's the money thing. Her inheritance. She's scared stiff Max is some sort of con man.'

Crista stared at Ez, her eyes glinting with amusement. 'Is she indeed.'

'Well that's what she said.'

'Worried on her own account in other words. But that was always Sally's way. And I doubt she'll ever change.'

There was silence between them for a few seconds, then Ez said, 'Can I ask you a question you might tell me is none of my business?'

'You can ask. But I don't promise to reply.'

Ez fidgeted some more. '*Is* there anything between you and Max?'

'We're very good friends, Ez.'

'I know that. What I mean is . . . is there anything else?'

Crista glanced away, wondering how to answer that. The last thing she wanted was to get egg on her face. 'How would you feel about it if there was?' she asked, evading the question for the moment.

'I'm not sure, Mum.'

Crista nodded that she understood.

'I like Max. I think he's a terrific man. But no one will ever replace Dad.'

'Oh, I quite agree. Your dad was your dad and always will be. That will never change.'

'And you loved him.'

'Very much so. I would have thought that was evident.'

'It was, Mum. And he loved you just as much as you loved him.'

'Yes, he did.'

Ez took a deep breath. 'But he's dead, nearly eleven years now. And you're on your own.'

Crista didn't reply to that.

'I've said for a long time that you must be lonely rattling round this place on your own, which is why

I wanted you to sell up and move into a smaller house. One that's more compact and manageable.'

'On occasion you were quite insistent,' Crista acknowledged with a wry smile.

'Only you're not lonely now with Max here to look after and keep you company.'

'True. To be honest, I was lonely. I just never realised it until Max arrived on the scene to highlight the fact.'

'And now?'

'Now what?'

'He'll be leaving soon.'

Crista bit her lower lip. 'Yes he will. Sadly. Sadly for me that is. I've become used to having him around.'

Ez squashed out the remains of her cigarette and immediately lit another, which earned her a disapproving glance from her mother.

'I think what I'm trying to say,' Ez went on slowly, 'is there wouldn't be any objections from me if you and Max were to take up together. In fact I'd be happy for the pair of you.'

'Would you?'

'Yes, Mum. I would. If it made you happy then it would make me the same.'

'Thank you,' Crista whispered, deeply moved.

'So what is the situation, Mum?'

Crista considered her reply. 'Nothing has actually been said. Although, I believe, it's in both our minds. However, I could be wrong about Max's future intentions. That's always a possibility. So now you know what's what.'

Ez nodded her understanding. 'I hope you don't mind me bringing this up?'

'Not really. At least I now know where you stand on the matter. Should it transpire.' Crista laid her sketch pad aside. 'I do believe I'll have that cup of coffee now. And a slice of chocolate cake I made yesterday.'

Ez's eyes widened. 'You never mentioned chocolate cake when you offered me coffee.'

'Well it's there. Want some?'

'Yes please.'

'And a coffee now?'

'You've twisted my arm.'

'I won't be long,' Crista declared, coming to her feet. 'How's the arthritis, by the way?'

'Not too bad this time of year.' Crista stopped to stare at Ez. 'That's one of the many things Max and I have in common. He suffers from it as well.' She started to chuckle as she continued on her way.

'How about the house drink then,' Dickie said to Gemma as he locked the door behind the last of the night's customers.

'I'll pour. What would you like?'

'A pint of that local crap to check it's as bad as always.' He shook his head. 'I swear to God I don't know why people drink the damn stuff, but they do. All I can put it down to is local loyalty.'

'It sells and makes you a profit so don't knock it,' Gemma admonished.

'Fair enough. I can't complain about that. I just wish it tasted better, that's all.'

'Then why have any?'

'Perversity I suppose. Sheer perversity.'

Gemma laughed. 'What are you like, Dickie Trippett? I don't know.'

He joined her at the bar. 'I've got a special job for you tomorrow morning when you come on shift.'

'Oh?'

'You'll find some large cardboard boxes upstairs. I want you to pack everything that belonged to Maggs into them so I can chuck the lot.'

Gemma placed his pint in front of him. 'Are you sure about that, Dickie?'

'I've never been more sure of anything in my life.'

Gemma poured herself a vodka and tonic, then came round the bar to sit beside him. How much better he looked of late, she thought. Fit and healthy again, in complete contrast to what he'd been like directly after Maggs's death. 'Does that include shoes, make-up, all that sort of thing?'

Dickie nodded.

'Then that's what I'll do.'

'The bin men come the day after tomorrow. I'll have the boxes there waiting for them.'

Gemma placed a hand over his. 'I'm certain you're doing the right thing.'

'I can't go on with Maggs's bits and pieces there to forever remind me. Best a clean sweep, that's what I say.'

He had a pull of his pint, and grimaced. 'This beer is still crap.'

Gemma laughed again. 'But you knew that.'

'Just checking, that's all.'

Gemma lit a cigarette, and they began to chat about this and that. It was over an hour later before she left and during that time not another word had been said about Maggs.

Gemma was delighted.

★ ★ ★

'You know, it's going to be a terrible wrench leaving here,' Max said suddenly. Dinner was over and the pair of them were sitting enjoying the rest of the evening. Max paused, then added quietly, 'And you.'

Crista didn't reply, but she was trembling inside.

'Perhaps I shouldn't have said that,' Max muttered, suddenly feeling foolish.

'I shall miss you too,' Crista declared, forcing a smile on to her face. 'Of course I shall.'

'You won't forget you've promised to get me fresh eggs, same as you get yourself?'

'I won't forget,' Crista replied, still smiling.

'And you will visit often?'

'You have my word.'

'And I'll visit you.'

'I'll be cross if you don't.'

'There then. That's all right.'

'You'll soon settle in, Max. You'll see. After a few months it'll be as if you'd been living there for ever.'

That wasn't what he was on about, as she well knew. 'Only another week and that's it, eh?'

'A week today,' she agreed, her heart sinking.

'At least everything will be in place by then. Curtains, carpets, washing machine, beds.' On mentioning the latter a gleam came into his eyes which told Crista he was remembering Bristol. Feeling a blush starting she glanced away. 'I can never thank you enough for all your help.'

'That's what friends are for. To help each other out. Besides, I enjoyed spending all that money. Almost as much as if I was spending it on myself.'

Max grinned. 'I enjoyed it too.' What he didn't add was because it had been time together.

'And I won't have to wear sunglasses when I come visiting,' Crista remarked slyly.

'I know, Jews love to be surrounded by gold. Tasteless, vulgar. Tacky.'

Unlike him as a person, she reflected. Max himself could never be called any of those things. He was quite the opposite. She sighed, then came to her feet. 'I think I'll put the kettle on. Fancy a cuppa?'

'Love one.'

A week, he mused bitterly as she left the room. No time at all. None whatsoever.

Gemma's face lit up with astonishment when she entered Dickie's bedroom – her intention being to change the sheets – and saw what he was doing.

Dickie went bright red from embarrassment as he hastily covered himself with his dressing gown. 'Sorry, Gemma,' he stammered. 'I thought you were busy downstairs.'

'It's OK, Dickie. It's perfectly normal for a man to do that. Especially one who no longer has a wife to cater for his needs.'

Dickie hung his head in shame.

A small smile twisted Gemma's lips upwards. 'Perhaps I can be of assistance,' she said huskily.

And firmly closed the door behind her.

Chapter 29

Max lay in the darkness staring up at the ceiling, having been awake for over an hour according to the luminous travelling clock on his bedside table. His thoughts were in turmoil, a lump that felt the size of a tennis ball lurking somewhere at the back of his throat.

The dreaded day had finally arrived. Not yet dawned, but shortly would. In a few hours he'd be having his final breakfast with Crista, after which he'd be packing the last of his personal things to move into the bungalow later that morning.

All he could think of, over and over again, was how much he'd enjoyed living here with Crista, being with her, sharing with her. And now it was all over. Finished.

There would be no more breakfasts together, no more so many things.

He felt sick to the pit of his stomach.

'Well, that's that!' Crista announced breezily, having accompanied Max to the bungalow to help him settle in for his first day. 'There's nothing else I can do now.'

'Another cup of tea before you go?'

Crista laughed. 'Good God no. I'm awash as it is.'

So too was he, but he'd have had another cup, a dozen of them, if it had meant her staying on a moment longer.

'It's going to be ever so strange,' he mumbled.

'You'll soon get used to it, I promise you. Besides, you've lived on your own before.'

He forced himself to brighten a little. 'You're right. Of course I will.'

'Now I'd better be off. I've got some shopping to do and I want to call in and see Ez about something.'

'I'll walk you to the door.'

'Ta ra then,' Crista declared when they'd reached it.

'Bye for now, Crista.'

'You take care now, Max Rubin.'

'And you, Crista.'

For a split second it was as if they might kiss, then the moment was gone and Crista was striding jauntily down the path towards the street.

The lump from early that morning was back in Max's throat when he eventually closed the door again.

Crista was sitting at the table with her evening meal in front of her. She was staring at the chair where Max would normally have been, now empty.

So, it was back to this, she reflected. Being on her own, eating on her own. No one to talk to, laugh with, share a bottle of wine with. No one to wake up in the morning and make breakfast for. No one to think about, care about, worry about.

No one.

Picking up her knife and fork she began to eat, the food like ashes in her mouth.

'Uncle Dickie, I've been thinking. Now you're back to your old self again you don't really need me here any more, do you?'

Dickie thought about that. 'I suppose not,' he conceded.

'I only ever came in as a temporary measure anyway, to help out. With Gemma here full time the pair of you can easily manage by yourselves the way you and Aunt Maggs used to.'

'Gemma?'

'She's absolutely right, Dickie. We can cope easily enough. We're a good team together, you and I.'

Again Ez heard something in Gemma's voice which made her wonder. A good team together? Surely a strange expression in the circumstances. There again, maybe she was just imagining things.

'So when would you like to finish?' Dickie queried.

'Friday or Saturday night, whatever.'

'Make it Saturday then. I know Pete isn't much of a drinking man, but have him call in for you towards closing time and we'll have a small celebration afterwards. Just the four of us. A little thank you from me to you.'

'That would be lovely.'

'And there'll be a bonus in your wage packet as an additional thank you.'

'There's no need for that, Uncle Dickie,' Ez protested. 'We're family after all.'

'Family or not you were there when I needed you. Be a good maid and don't complain about me showing my appreciation.' He winked at Ez. 'Despite rumours to the contrary, I'm not really mean, you know.'

Ez laughed, for Dickie had always been known as such. Maybe it simply had never been the case, or else he'd changed.

As she got on with the job it crossed her mind that maybe Gemma had something to do with the latter, if that was so.

Crista moved restlessly in her sleep, dimly aware of the rain battering against the bedroom window. If there had been thunder and lightning she'd have been instantly awake. But without those she continued to sleep on.

Dickie was raising a pint to his mouth when he suddenly froze. It was past midnight and he and Gemma were entertaining Ez and Pete as they'd promised. Gemma had laid on a few savoury nibbles.

'Jesus Christ!' he exclaimed softly.

'What is it?' Gemma demanded, suddenly frightened by the expression on his face.

'Look at the door.'

They did, to see water creeping in underneath the bottom of it. Outside the rain was still hammering down as it had been for hours.

'We're going to be flooded,' Dickie said tightly.

'The papers reported a lot of rain on Exmoor yesterday,' Pete reminded them.

All of them, being locals, knew that heavy rain on Exmoor one day could affect their local rivers the next. If it was still raining on Exmoor as heavily as it was in Ford then they could well be in for a flood.

Dickie switched on the outside light and opened the door, swearing when he saw the road in front of the pub awash, the water obviously rising.

'Looks like we're in for it,' Pete muttered, having come to stand beside him.

Ez was instantly on her feet. 'I'll get the coats,' she announced to Pete. 'We must get back and see to our own place.'

Dickie didn't even try to argue. They were entirely right: their first obligation was to try to safeguard their own house.

Pete, surveying the road, thought they'd be lucky to make it with the water that high. None the less, they had to try. A few minutes later, after hurried goodbyes, he and Ez, arm in arm, were battling their way through the ever-rising torrent.

'I'd better get the sandbags out,' Dickie declared grimly to Gemma, trying to remember through a slightly alcohol-befuddled mind where they were.

The following morning Crista was still unaware of what had happened until she came downstairs and found the entire ground floor flooded to a depth of about three feet.

'Dear God,' she groaned. What a mess this was going to leave.

She retreated upstairs again to think about what to do. The electricity was still working, and there had been hot water when she'd gone for a bath so the gas had not been cut off. The only telephone in the house was downstairs so if she was going to use that she'd have to wade.

She'd been sitting on her bed for about twenty minutes when she suddenly heard Max shouting below.

'Crista!'

Relief washed through her. 'Max?'

'Where are you?'

'In my bedroom.'

'I'm coming up.'

When he appeared she rushed into his arms, deliriously happy to see him.

'Most of the village is under water,' he informed her. 'There are some exceptions, my bungalow being one of them because it's on high ground.'

Crista thought of Ez and Sally, hoping they were all right.

'It did stop raining for a bit but it's started again,' Max went on. 'Though not as heavily as before.'

'The rivers must have burst their banks,' Crista mused. 'It could be days before the water recedes and we can do anything about the house.'

'Don't worry about that for the moment. Pack a case, you're coming with me to the bungalow. You'll be safe there.'

'Oh, Max. Thank you.'

'I nearly had a heart attack when I looked out of a window earlier and saw the state of things. I simply couldn't believe my eyes.'

'Welcome to Devon,' Crista said sarcastically. 'We have a history of flooding in the county. Don't we just!'

'I did know about that, but the reality is a little mind-boggling to say the least.'

Crista nodded her agreement. 'I'll start packing that case.'

'Right. And I'll see what's in the kitchen we can take with us. Just to be on the safe side. Who knows how long this could last?'

Max found a plastic carrier bag into which he put all manner of edibles, including a number of tins he came across in the larder. He had just finished when Crista appeared with a canvas holdall.

'I can carry that if you want to bring more,' Max suggested.

'There's enough in here, Max. I'll get by.'

'OK then. I came in through the rear where there's less water than out front, your house being on a small incline. If we go out through the back and up the lane there's dry ground before too long.'

Sure enough, that was so. From there on it was relatively easy going, as the road to Max's bungalow was all uphill.

Crista cradled Max's telephone. 'Ez and family are fine. They were in the pub apparently when the flooding started and were able to get home and start sandbagging against the worst of it. Pete alerted the neighbours to what was happening and they were able to do the same. Ez has said she'll ring Sally and then report back here, if that's all right?'

'Of course it's all right, Crista. Don't be silly. Now how about a nice cup of tea?'

'Wonderful.'

Max went through to his kitchen, filled the kettle and switched it on. Less than a minute later the light on the kettle went out, as did all the other lights in the house.

'Bugger,' Max muttered. He rejoined Crista in

the sitting room. 'The electricity's gone,' he informed her.

'How about the gas?'

'Still working as far as I know.'

'Then we'll boil a saucepan of water and use that.'

Max smiled. 'Clever girl.'

Crista was more than flattered to be called 'girl'. 'In the meantime you fill the bath with cold water. We'll need that in case the supply gets fouled, as can happen.'

'On my way.'

Crista smiled as she watched his retreating back. Imagine him coming to rescue her and offering alternative accommodation during the present crisis. He really was a terrific man.

There again, she reminded herself, she would have done exactly the same for him.

Surely that told her something?

'Thank God I had these candles in,' Max said to Crista that night, the pair of them sitting by flickering candlelight. 'I only bought them as ornaments. But they've certainly come in handy.'

The gas had continued to work so Crista had been able to make them a meal earlier. Afterwards, she had boiled up saucepans of water with which to do the dishes.

'I have to confess,' Max declared, 'I'm rather enjoying this. For some reason it makes me feel like a kid again.'

'I know what you mean.'

'A bit scary though, eh?'

'Don't be silly, Max. There's nothing scary about

478

it. When I was young only a few houses had electricity. The rest got by with candles and lamps. It was the norm then.'

Max sat further back into his chair. 'I can't imagine having a rural upbringing. It must be so totally different from the one I had.'

'I suppose so.'

'Though mine was happy enough. What about yours?'

'Hard at times, not much money coming in. But we got by. Lavender, my mother, could make a penny stretch an awfully long way. Yes, we were happy enough. At least so I seem to recollect.'

'My family would have been very comfortably off compared to yours. But it's the love in a family that counts above all else, wouldn't you say?'

'I totally agree. And there was lots of that in ours. Except between Maggs and myself, perhaps. We were always at odds with one another, but I'm sure that underneath the love was there. At least it was on my part. Do you have any brothers and sisters?'

Max shook his head. 'Only child. And spoiled rotten according to some people. Though I would disagree with that.'

'No doubt,' Crista laughed.

'Well I would!' he retorted. 'And I'm sure I'm right.'

Crista decided to drop that subject. 'I appreciate it's still fairly early but I'd like to go to bed if you don't mind. It's been a strenuous day and I'm feeling wrung out.'

'Of course, Crista. You must do as you wish. I think I'll stay down here a little longer and treat myself to a Scotch or two.'

Just as Jamie used to sometimes, Crista reflected. The two men were alike in many ways, quite different in others. She came to her feet. 'Goodnight then, Max.'

'Night, Crista. Sleep tight, don't let the bugs bite.'

'I'll try not to,' she replied, mock-seriously.

She was about to leave the room when, on a sudden impulse, she went to Max and kissed him on the cheek. 'Thanks again for being my knight in shining armour,' she whispered.

'My pleasure, I assure you.'

He smiled when she was gone. Knight in shining armour? *Oy veh* already!

'I'm going to have to stay here the night, Dickie,' Gemma declared. 'I'm simply never going to get home through that lot outside.'

'You're welcome to. But there's only one snag.'

'What's that?'

'One bed. That's all I have.'

Gemma stared him straight in the eye. 'So? Not shy are you?'

Dickie decided he wasn't.

'Are you awake, Gemma?'

'Sort of,' came the muffled reply.

'I've been lying here thinking.'

'You're supposed to be asleep, not thinking.'

'I'm aware of that.'

There was silence between them for a few seconds.

'Thinking about what?' Gemma found herself forced to ask.

'Maggs and me.'

480

Gemma was instantly all ears. 'What about you and Maggs?'

'I went to pieces when she died. Absolute pieces. The world had come to an end, my world that is, and yet here I am now in bed with you. It doesn't make sense.'

Gemma sat up, switched on her bedside light and lit a cigarette. 'Can I be honest with you?'

'If you wish.'

Gemma took her time before speaking again. 'Could it be, and I don't wish to insult you, that your idea of Maggs was more a long-standing fantasy, or vision, in your head than the real thing? Is that possible?'

Dickie was frowning. 'A fantasy?'

'You saw a Maggs that didn't really exist in real life. Somewhere along the line, before you were married, she somehow became your ideal woman. A woman you put on a pedestal and never let off again. Whereas Maggs as she was, the real Maggs, was nothing like the one in your mind.'

Dickie was intrigued. 'Go on.'

'She wasn't very nice to you at times, was she?'

'No,' he finally managed to admit.

'In fact she took you for granted. Walked all over you. Treated you, on occasion, like dirt.'

Dickie was horrified to realise the veracity of that.

'But now she's dead the fantasy is disappearing very damned fast, blown away like chaff in the wind.' Gemma paused for a draw on her cigarette, then continued. 'Now, let me ask you one simple question.'

'Which is?'

'Was Maggs ever as good in bed as I was tonight?

Or did she ever do for you what I did that day I discovered you in here?'

Dickie swallowed, then swallowed again. 'No, on both counts,' he croaked.

'So perhaps, and I appreciate this is going to sound cruel, she didn't care for you nearly as much as you did for her. Think about that.'

Tears welled in his eyes. Tears of self-pity and a sudden revulsion for the fat woman he'd worshipped all those years.

Gemma stubbed out her cigarette and switched off the light. As she settled back down again she smiled when Dickie's arm came round her.

'Who the hell is that!' Dickie exclaimed next morning when there was an urgent knocking on the pub door.

Gemma was standing beside him when he opened it to discover four of his regulars bobbing about in a rowing boat.

'Are you opening or what?' Billy May demanded. 'You've got thirsty customers waiting here.'

Dickie slowly shook his head in amazement, while Gemma, hand over mouth, was giggling. 'It's wet in here and the pumps aren't working,' he eventually replied.

'You've got bottles, haven't you?'

Dickie nodded.

'And a top shelf?'

Dickie nodded again.

'Then are you open or what? Because if you're not we'll row on up to the Salmon and Pig and see if they are.'

'No need for that, lads. The only reason I wasn't open was because I didn't think I'd have any customers. But as you're here, come on in and state your poison.'

A few minutes later, up to the ankles in floodwater – the bar being considerably higher than street level – and the rowing boat securely tied to a railing, Dickie was busily serving.

Max was standing at his sitting room window staring out over the village. 'I do believe the water's going down at last,' he declared.

Crista went over to join him. 'I think you're right.'

'When it's gone down enough we'll go back to your house and see what damage has been done.'

Crista blanched. 'A lot, I'm afraid. And when the water finally has gone it'll take ages for the damp areas to dry out. But there'll be a great deal to do before then.'

'I'm hoping you'll stay on here in the meantime,' Max said casually. 'Makes sense when you think about it. I mean, down there you're going to be limited to upstairs only, whereas here you've got the run of the bungalow.'

'In that case, Max, I could be here for quite a while.'

He tried not to show his exultation. 'That's not a problem. You're simply staying with me instead of the other way round.'

Crista was delighted he'd made the suggestion and had been hoping he would. 'Then I'll accept your kind offer. Thank you very much.'

Max was about to utter further when the lights suddenly came back on again.

'Well, there's a relief.' Crista sighed. 'Back to normal again. At least here.'

'Yes.' Max smiled. 'Back to normal.'

But it wasn't the restoration of electricity he was referring to.

Crista stared in horror at the devastation which was the downstairs of her house. The only articles salvageable were those like ornaments and pictures above the water line, a water line clearly marked on the walls.

'It's . . .' She shook her head in disbelief. 'Just awful.'

'You knew what it was going to be like, Crista.'

'Knowing's one thing, Max, actually seeing quite another.'

Max squelched across to her, the carpet underfoot sodden. 'Are you OK?'

She looked at him, and suddenly burst into tears.

'There there, girl,' he murmured, taking her into his arms.

'I'm sorry, Max. I'm sorry,' she wailed.

'Don't worry. It's a perfectly normal reaction. You go ahead and cry for as long as you like.'

Her body shook, while tears rolled down her cheeks. 'This was my home for so many years, Max. Where we lived and brought up children. Now look at it.'

He grimaced on glancing round. The room was a wreck, as were all on the ground floor. 'Not very pretty, I have to admit.'

'I feel . . . as if part of my life has been taken from me. As if I've had an arm and a leg cut off.'

'They're only material things, Crista. They can all be replaced,' he said, trying to console her.

'No they can't!' she cried. 'All these things have been in the family for years. They're irreplaceable. Oh yes, I can buy another carpet, a new one. But I don't want that. I want the one that's already there.'

She was being unreasonable, he thought, but didn't blame her as she was obviously in a state of shock. 'Are you insured?' he asked.

'Yes.'

'Where's the policy?'

'Upstairs somewhere. In my bedroom probably.'

There were other questions he wanted to ask, but this wasn't the moment. Perhaps later when she'd calmed down a little. Meanwhile he was wondering what was the best thing to do.

He held Crista till the crying and shaking stopped, then gently released her.

'I'd better make a start on trying to clear up some of this mess,' she sniffed.

'I don't think you should do that. I believe the correct procedure is to get in touch with the insurance company so they can send out an assessor to see matters for himself. When he's done so I'll hire a skip we can load everything in to be taken away. After that it'll be a case, as you've already mentioned, of leaving the place for a time to completely dry out.'

Crista saw the sense of his proposals. 'OK, Max.'

'Are you sure you're fine with that?'

Crista nodded. 'I'll just have to be, I suppose.'

He gave her another cuddle. 'I know it's hard, but it has to be done. There's simply no way this can be put right again.'

'I know.'

'So shall we go upstairs and try to find that policy?'

She shrugged. 'All right.'

'And when we do I'll give it the once-over before ringing the company to initiate your claim.'

How masterful he was, she thought. Thank God he was here to take charge. If he hadn't been she'd probably have fallen apart and been in a right dither.

'Shall we go then?'

He took her hand as they proceeded upstairs and it seemed the most natural thing in the world.

The events of the day were keeping Crista awake, preying on her mind. Every time she closed her eyes she was back in the house surveying the terrible damage that had been done, her entire being appalled by the loss of so many precious bits and pieces.

'Oh God!' she whispered, wishing Max was beside her to give her comfort and reassurance. To hold and cuddle her. To stop her feeling so very lost and alone.

No, she couldn't, most certainly not, she thought when the idea came to her. It would be the most outrageous thing she'd ever done in her life. There again, they had already shared a bed in Bristol, though for different reasons. Or were they so very different?

'Max?' Crista whispered, shaking his shoulder.

He roused himself. 'What's wrong?'

'Can I get in beside you? I need . . . I need to be with you.'

Her heart sank and she began to feel horribly embarrassed when there was no immediate reply. 'Max?'

'Come into bed by all means, Crista. But only if you agree to marry me.'

486

That stunned her. 'M . . . marry you?'

'That's what I said. Marry.'

'I . . . I . . .' She trailed off.

'Well?'

'All right,' she stuttered.

'Then get in.'

Chapter 30

Crista watched as Max sliced the top off his boiled egg, then tasted the contents. Why didn't he say something, she fumed inwardly. They'd been up half an hour now and not a single reference to last night's proposal.

'Ah!' He beamed at her. 'Excellent as always.'

Crista toyed with a piece of toast, becoming more and more upset with every passing moment.

'Did you mean it, Max?' she finally blurted out.

He regarded her steadily. 'Are you referring to our getting married?'

Crista nodded. Max came to his feet, placed his napkin on the table, and left the room. Now what did that mean? Crista wondered. She was still wondering when Max returned a few minutes later to lay a small leather pouch by her plate.

'Tell me what you think of what's inside,' he said, taking his seat again.

Crista was well aware that his eyes never left her as she opened the mouth of the pouch and shook its contents on to the palm of her hand. She gasped when she saw the ring that landed there. It was exquisite.

'Well?' He smiled lazily.

'Is this real?'

'Oh, yes.' He laughed softly. 'It's real all right.'

The stone was a square-cut diamond about half an inch in length on every side. The setting was filigreed gold, the band plain.

'And don't ask, because if I told you its worth you'd probably never wear it in case you lost the damned thing.'

Crista swallowed hard. 'This must be . . . its value . . .' She trailed off, lost for words.

'A considerable amount, yes.'

'Where did you get it from?'

He knew what was in her mind. 'It wasn't Rebekah's, if that's what you're thinking. I made it for someone else.'

'You made it!' she exclaimed.

'Well don't look so astonished. I have told you I made jewellery. That's one of my efforts.'

'It's beautiful, Max,' she whispered. 'It truly is.'

That pleased him enormously. 'Thank you. Now why don't you try it on? It's an engagement ring, by the way.'

Crista glanced sharply at him, noting the twinkle in his eyes, then back at the ring again.

'Does it fit?' he asked when she'd slipped it on her finger.

'It's a little loose.'

'Easily fixed. I'll do it this afternoon in my new workshop.'

She wasn't sure. 'Is this for me, Max?'

'You wanted to know if I meant my proposal. Well, I most certainly did. And that engagement ring is proof of it.'

How did she feel? Lightheaded, her heart thumping, and an enormous sense of joy welling inside her. 'Thank you. I don't know what else to say,' she choked.

'Thank you is enough.' He paused, then said, 'The ring has a history. Would you like to hear it?'

Crista nodded.

Max sat back in his chair, breakfast temporarily forgotten. 'Some years ago I had a well-known East End gangster call at my shop. He wanted me to make him a ring for his ladyfriend and wife to be, he hoped. We discussed and agreed a design, price too of course. He left a down payment and off he went. And that was the last I ever saw of him.'

'Gracious,' Crista muttered. 'What happened?'

'I didn't find out until after the ring was finished and I tried to contact him. He'd simply disappeared off the face of the earth. Utterly and completely.'

Crista's eyes widened. 'Killed?'

'Presumably, and the body disposed of. Unless he decided to disappear off his own bat, for whatever reasons. As for myself, I believe he was murdered. So there you have it.'

Crista gazed at her ring, thinking it a romantic, if chilling, story. 'So you kept the ring?'

'I don't know why. Maybe I was safeguarding myself in case he suddenly turned up out of the blue demanding it. Whatever, I kept it in my possession. And now it's yours. If you still want it, that is.'

'Oh, I do, Max.' She stared at the ring again, then shook her head. 'I've never before owned anything so beautiful, or so valuable.'

'Well, there's always a first time.'

'Then thank you again.'

He took a deep breath. 'There is one question I have to ask.'

'What's that?'

'You have remembered I'm Jewish?'

'Does being Jewish make a difference?'

'It would to some.'

'Not me, Max. It doesn't make any difference in the least, I promise you.'

'That's out of the way then. We don't need to discuss it any further, unless you wish to bring it up at any time.'

'It's an irrelevance, Max, so I doubt I ever will. Both religions acknowledge the same God, after all. And that's good enough for me.'

They stared at one another, each delighting in the other's company and, hopefully, the years together that lay ahead.

'I've come to love you, Crista. I want you to know that.'

'And I you, Max. I want you to know that too.'

Rising from her chair she went round the table and kissed him firmly on the mouth. 'You'd better finish that egg before it goes cold,' she murmured.

Which made him laugh.

'Oh, Max,' she whispered that night when they were in bed. 'It's been so long.'

'And for me.'

There was silence between them for a few moments. 'We don't have to go on,' he said at last.

'It's just . . . I don't want to disappoint you.'

'You won't, Crista. You couldn't.'

She melted inside to hear that. And suddenly what

491

they were about to do was all right. There were no ghosts present. Just the two of them. And they were in love, promised to be wed.

Crista was returning from doing some shopping when she spotted Sally coming towards her. Sally, according to Ez, had been lucky when the flood struck. Her house, thanks to its position, suffered only minimal damage.

'Hello, Sally.' Crista smiled when they met up, having been wondering if Sally would stop and talk or just go sweeping by, something she was quite capable of.

Sally's eyes flashed fire. 'What's this I hear on the grapevine about you and the old Jew boy getting engaged? Surely it can't be true?'

'As a matter of fact it is.'

Sally's face twisted into a mask of hatred. 'He's only after your money. Can't you see that?'

Crista held up her hand. 'If Max was after my money do you think he'd be giving me a ring like this? Don't be daft.'

Sally glared at the ring. 'Diamond, eh? I'll bet it's no such thing. Costume jewellery more like. Zircon at best.'

'It's real, Sally, I assure you.'

'Real my arse! He's conning you, Mum. Conning you rigid. And you're falling for it every inch of the way.'

Crista was beginning to get angry now. 'I am not falling for anything, Sally. I keep trying to tell you Max has far too much money of his own to worry about what I've got. Don't forget he built that bungalow. What do you think he used to pay for that, bottle tops?'

'I still say he's after your money. Money that's rightfully mine in time.'

Crista stared at her daughter, now too angry to reply.

'Besides,' Sally went on. 'It's disgusting getting married again at your age. Quite obscene if you ask me.'

Crista snapped. Her hand flew through the air to crack against Sally's cheek, sending her daughter staggering.

'How dare you,' Crista hissed. 'How dare you!'

'You hit me,' Sally said in disbelief.

'You're darned tootin' I did. And I hope it hurt. Now get out of my way. I've got a meal to cook.'

'You'll find out I'm right one day!' Sally yelled after her as Crista continued on up the street.

A hint of tears crept into Crista's eyes. Sally couldn't be right. Could she?

The jeweller in Exeter removed his eyepiece and placed it on the counter.

'Well?' Crista demanded.

'It's genuine all right. Beautiful square-cut diamond. Flawless, actually.'

Crista sighed with relief, despising herself for coming here in the first place. But she'd had to be sure. Absolutely certain that Sally's accusations were what she'd thought them all along. Rubbish.

'Thank you,' she said to the jeweller. 'I'm obliged. What's the damage?'

He smiled, and shook his head. 'There's no charge. All I did was look at the ring. That's all.'

'Then thank you again.'

'Don't you want a valuation? I'd have that ring insured if I were you.'

'No valuation, it's not required. For the moment anyway. And I'll bear in mind what you say about insurance.'

Crista slipped the ring back on to her finger, gathered up her bag and headed for the door.

She was meeting Max in twenty minutes, her excuse for temporarily going her separate way being that she wanted to do some 'lady's' shopping which would bore him senseless.

She'd known all along the ring was genuine, as Max had said it was. But she'd wanted it confirmed, though she was rather ashamed of that now.

Damn Sally for making her doubt Max. Even for a moment.

'You're still upset about that conversation you had with Sally last week, aren't you?' Max said to her a few evenings later.

Crista glanced at him. 'How do you know that?'

'It's obvious, that's why.'

Crista nodded, but didn't reply. She might never have told him about her run-in with Sally if she hadn't arrived home in tears, after which it had all spilled out. She'd even told him about Sally's referring to him as an old Jew boy, which she'd probably never have done if she hadn't been in such a state. The insult hadn't bothered him one little bit, though he suspected it had upset Crista, coming from her own daughter.

'I think I may have a solution to the problem, if

you're agreeable that is,' Max remarked casually.

Crista frowned. 'And what's that?'

Max explained it to her.

Sally entered the room, nodded to her sister, then gazed suspiciously around.

'It's all right, Sally. Max isn't here. He's gone out so the three of us can be alone.'

Sally rounded on her mother. 'I'm only here because you told me on the phone that it affected my inheritance. Otherwise I wouldn't have stepped over the door.'

Ez thought her sister a right bitch for saying that. She could at least have tried to be pleasant.

'Why don't you sit down?' Crista suggested, forcing a smile on to her face.

Sally sniffed. 'I don't think . . .'

'Sit down!' Crista repeated in her most maternal voice.

Sally caught her breath, then chose a chair and sat.

'Ez and I are having coffee. Would you care for a cup?'

Sally shook her head.

'Or wine if you wish?'

'No thank you,' Sally replied tartly. 'Now can we get on with this?'

Crista's lips thinned in disapproval. 'Right. We'll do that.'

Ez lit a cigarette, curious as to what her mother had in mind. She was really quite intrigued.

'The first thing is the house,' Crista declared. 'Once it's put right again I'm going to sell it, as I'll be Max's wife by then and living here.'

Sally leant forward a fraction, her eyes boring into Crista's.

'What money is realised will be split equally in two, one half to each of you.'

Breath hissed from Sally's mouth and what might have been something of a smile flitted across her face.

'Are you sure you want to do this, Mum?' Ez asked.

'Absolutely certain.' She paused for a moment, then went on. 'At the same time I will settle an amount of money, equal again, on the pair of you. Not all my equity, but a substantial part of it.'

There was now a definite smile on Sally's face.

'But what about you?' Ez asked. 'You'll be leaving yourself short.'

'Not a bit of it, Ez. You forget that by then I'll be Mrs Rubin and I can assure you Max has enough to take care of us for the rest of our days. More than enough and then some. I've seen with my own eyes what's deposited in his bank.'

Sally had the grace to look away.

'Now, there are certain conditions attached. And they all apply to you, Sally.'

Sally sighed. 'I might have known there'd be a catch.'

'No catch, at least I don't see it that way. Number one, I don't want to hear you talk about money, and by that I mean whingeing, ever again. Agreed?'

Sally nodded.

'I prefer to hear you say so.'

'Agreed, Mum.'

'Right, condition number two. You will come to our wedding and conduct yourself in an appropriate manner. I will not have the village gossiping about the fact my daughter stayed away. Agreed?'

'Agreed, Mum,' Sally repeated.

'That's it then.' Crista waited for a moment, then added, 'Oh, just one more thing, Sally.'

'What's that?'

'Next time you see the old Jew boy you might thank him. This was his idea.'

Sally blushed bright red.

'Hello, Crista. Haven't seen you for a while,' Abigail Woolocombe greeted her. 'How are you?'

'Fine.'

'I hear that you've got engaged and are shacked up with the prospective husband.'

And she'd always considered Abigail a friend. What a thing to say! 'I am engaged, Abigail, and here's the ring to prove it.'

Abigail gasped when she saw the size of the diamond. 'Bloody Norah!' she exclaimed.

'And before you ask, it is real. OK?'

Abigail didn't answer, just shook her head in amazement, eyes never leaving the ring.

'As for being shacked up, as you so delicately put it, I'm simply staying at Max's bungalow because my own house was flooded, like many others in the village. I'm using his spare room so we are not, I repeat *not*, sharing a bed,' she glibly lied. 'That won't happen until the wedding night. Understand?'

'Of course, Crista. I was only teasing.'

And I'm the Queen of Sheba, Crista thought cynically.

'Anyway, I shall be looking forward to receiving my invitation.' Abigail beamed.

'Sorry to disappoint you, but we're keeping the

497

numbers down. Only family and close friends,' Crista retorted, enjoying watching the beam vanish from Abigail's face. She had considered inviting Abigail, but not now. Not after what she'd said. The cow.

'Then all I can say is I hope all goes well on the day.'

'We'll do our best to ensure that happens.'

'Bye then.'

'Bye for now.'

Crista continued on her way feeling she'd won that little encounter. Shacking up with Max! What a vulgar way of putting it.

Even if it was true.

'Are you ready for this?'

Crista nodded.

'Then here we go.'

Max opened the pub door and they both went inside. It was their first time out in the village together since their engagement and it would be an indicator as to how the village was reacting to the proposed marriage, and to Crista's marrying a Jew.

Crista was horribly aware of many eyes flicking in their direction, followed almost immediately by hushed conversations where there hadn't been any before. She glanced at Max who, bless him, looked as if he didn't have a care in the world.

Gemma came straight to them at the bar and took their order, having a couple of words and a laugh before moving off to fill it.

Crista needn't have worried. One by one the villagers came over to congratulate them, the men shaking Max by the hand.

'We're accepted as a couple,' Crista whispered to Max during a spell when they were alone.

His reply to that was the warmest smile imaginable.

'Where would you like to go for our honeymoon?' Max queried, straight out of the blue.

Crista blinked. This was the first she'd heard of any honeymoon. 'I didn't know we were going on one.'

'We don't have to. But it would be nice, don't you think?'

Crista sat further back in her chair. Trust Max to pull a surprise like this. 'Have you anywhere in mind?'

'I do. What about Majorca? A very good London pal of mine has been there several times and raves about it. He stayed at a hotel called the Illa D'or in a place by the name of Puerto Pollença. Said the hotel was excellent, Puerto Pollença not yet ruined by the tourist trade.'

'I've never been abroad,' Crista confessed. 'And where exactly is Majorca?'

'It's part of the Balearic Islands, belonging to Spain, situated in the Mediterranean. There should be lots of sun.'

Go abroad? It was an exciting prospect, if somewhat daunting. 'How would we get there?'

'You leave all that to me. I can easily arrange everything.'

'Would it be terribly hot?'

'Is that a problem, Crista?'

'I don't know. It might be,' she prevaricated, not at all sure.

'Don't you like heat?'

'Normally I do, but the Mediterranean? I'll have to think about that.'

'Well don't take too long. I'll have to book it if we're going.'

Abroad. Majorca. This Poll something or other. It all sounded exotic and terribly daring.

Oh, why not! she told herself. Why not live a little? Get adventurous for a change. And it was to be their honeymoon, after all.

'Just one thing,' she said firmly.

'What's that, love?'

'I'm not getting into a swimsuit. Not for all the tea in China.'

Max threw back his head and roared, thinking that hilarious. He had no intention of disporting himself in a pair of bathing trunks either. Not with his skinny legs and pot belly.

'So Majorca it is?' he asked when he'd stopped laughing.

'Majorca it is.'

Somehow, they both just knew they were going to thoroughly enjoy themselves.

'What do you think, Ez?'

'It's perfect, Mum. I can't see you finding anything nicer. Not unless you want to go to Bristol or London, that is.'

Crista studied herself critically in the full length mirror. She was wearing a navy costume comprising a box jacket and below-the-knee skirt, the jacket sporting brass buttons. In her mind she was matching it with a cream silk blouse, preferably with small tie collar.

'Hmm,' she murmured.

'It really does look good on you, madam,' the female assistant gushed. 'And it fits perfectly, no alteration required.'

'For shoes I'd have navy leather court,' Ez suggested. 'Plus a bag of the same colour.'

'What about a hat?'

'Navy straw full brim and – it would be my preference anyway – cream ribbon.'

'Cream gloves?'

'I'd say so.'

Crista took a deep breath, and made up her mind. She prayed she'd find the accessories they'd just discussed. 'I'll take it,' she declared to the assistant.

'Excellent choice, madam.'

'I hope so. It's for my wedding day.'

On hearing that the assistant couldn't do enough for them.

Crista's mind was filled with memories as she gazed around what had been her kitchen for so many happy years. She could hear the children laughing, and arguing, just as she and Maggs had once done. She could also hear Jamie's voice as if he was right there with her.

Dear Jamie. Dear lovely Jamie. Good husband and wonderful father. Sweet, sweet man. She couldn't have said how, but she knew he approved of her and Max. That their forthcoming wedding had received his consent and blessing. That he understood it was simply time to move on. He might be dead, but she was still alive and life was for living, the past being exactly that, the past.

501

Crista was smiling when she eventually left the house, locking its door behind her.

She would never return there, no matter what. Her peace had been made with it, and now it too belonged to the past.

The future was Max.

'I thought I told you to act in an appropriate manner,' Crista scolded Sally. 'You're supposed to look happy for us, not downright miserable.'

The wedding had taken place earlier, and now the reception had started in the village hall, still smelling vaguely of floodwater. The four-piece band they'd hired was getting ready to provide music for the dancing that was to take place.

'If I'm miserable it's nothing to do with you,' Sally replied. 'Daniel dropped a bombshell this morning.'

Crista frowned. 'What sort of bombshell?'

'The stupid sod has gone and joined the army. Can you imagine, joined the army!'

'But why?'

'Said he fancied it. And that was the only reason he'd give me.'

Crista thought about that, and was suddenly relieved. If Daniel was in the army then he wouldn't be careering round on that motorbike of his any more, in danger of life and limb every time he drove the damn thing. Frankly, she couldn't be more pleased. Daniel might be an obnoxious young man, but he was her grandson when all was said and done.

On reflection, Crista decided not to tell Sally what she thought as it would only cause fresh trouble between them. Sally was obviously completely opposed to his joining up.

'I don't know what to say,' Crista lied. 'Except he is supposedly old enough to know his own mind.'

'Hmmh!' Sally snorted.

'Anyway, try not to let it spoil things here for you. OK?'

'I'll try, Mum.'

'Good.'

The conversation was interrupted when Max appeared at Crista's side.

'We've been instructed, by popular demand I believe, to lead off the first dance. Are you up to it?'

'Try and stop me.'

'That's my girl.'

To general and enthusiastic applause they took to the centre of the floor. Max nodded to the band that they were ready, and the band struck up.

'You dance beautifully, Mrs Rubin,' Max said a few moments later.

'As do you, Mr Rubin.'

And Max pulled her even closer, the pair of them in seventh heaven.